Stoney Ridge SEASONS

Books by Suzanne Woods Fisher

Amish Peace: Simple Wisdom for a Complicated World
Amish Proverbs: Words of Wisdom from the Simple Life
Amish Values for Your Family: What We Can Learn from the Simple Life
A Lancaster County Christmas
Christmas at Rose Hill Farm

LANCASTER COUNTY SECRETS

The Choice
The Waiting
The Search

STONEY RIDGE SEASONS

The Keeper
The Haven
The Lesson

THE INN AT EAGLE HILL

The Letters
The Calling
The Revealing

THE ADVENTURES OF LILY LAPP (with Mary Ann Kinsinger)

Life with Lily
A New Home for Lily
A Big Year for Lily
A Surprise for Lily

Stoney Ridge SEASONS

3-IN-1 COLLECTION

THE KEEPER
THE HAVEN
THE LESSON

Suzanne Woods Fisher

Revell
a division of Baker Publishing Group
Grand Rapids, Michigan

Published by Revell
a division of Baker Publishing Group
P.O. Box 6287, Grand Rapids, MI 49516-6287
www.revellbooks.com

Combined edition published 2015
ISBN 978-0-8007-2679-9

Previously published in three separate volumes:
The Keeper © 2012
The Haven © 2012
The Lesson © 2013

Printed in the United States of America

Scripture used in this book, whether quoted or paraphrased by the characters, is taken from:

King James Version of the Bible

Holy Bible, New International Version®. NIV®. Copyright © 1973, 1978, 1984, 2011 by Biblica, Inc.™ Used by permission of Zondervan. All rights reserved worldwide. www.zondervan.com

Published in association with Joyce Hart of the Hartline Literary Agency, LLC.

The John Vivian quote in *The Keeper* is taken from John Vivian, *Keeping Bees* (Charlotte, VT: Williamson Publishers, 1986), 82.

15 16 17 18 19 20 21 7 6 5 4 3 2 1

The
KEEPER

To the world's best sister, Wendy,
who is just the right blend of Julia's and Sadie's best qualities.

Guess who inspired M.K.?

1

Spring came in a hurry. The wind had softened, bare branches were budding, and soon there would be the heavy green shade of the trees. Julia Lapp had already picked peas and spinach out of her garden, and set them, along with baskets of carrots and bunches of asparagus, on the produce table in front of the roadside stand.

When school let out for the year, Julia would get her youngest sister to watch over Windmill Farm's stand, but it wasn't necessary in late April. There weren't too many customers around, not the way it would be later in summer, once the corn started to sweeten up and the tomatoes ripened.

The day was overcast, but gardening was hot work and Julia had been up since five. She glanced in the mirror that she kept hidden against the back wall of the stand. It was a bad, vain habit, catching glances of herself in mirrors and windows, but she couldn't keep from looking. What did she see? A twenty-one-year-old face, with shiny mahogany hair and hazel eyes rimmed with black lashes, and nearly flawless white skin. She pulled herself away from the mirror, silently scolding herself for her vanity. But pleased, all the same.

She should get back to her chores before dinnertime. She placed the honor jar, along with the small chalkboard listing the prices, in the middle of the produce, then hesitated. A few minutes of rest wouldn't hurt.

Julia collapsed into a chair under the shade of an apple tree and sighed in appreciation as a light breeze swirled around her, lifting the strings of her prayer cap. She looked down at her hands and frowned at the dirt under her nails. She and her siblings had been trying to fill in for her father since his heart trouble had started, and she was already weary of plowing, dirt and dust, and the tangy smell of manure that she couldn't get out of her hair despite daily shampooings.

She glanced at the farmhouse and felt a wave of weariness. She hadn't even realized how rundown it was looking, not until Paul's mother pointed it out last month when it was the Lapps' turn to host church. How had it escaped her notice? An upstairs window was broken—a recent victim of her brother's poor aim with a softball. Black buggies awaiting repair littered the driveway in front of her uncle's buggy shop. The entire house was overdue for a fresh coat of paint. Edith Fisher was right—the house was in terrible shape. The whole farm was in terrible shape. There was so much to do before her wedding to Paul in November.

Her thoughts drifted to Paul. Soon, she would be known as Paul's Julia. She said it out loud, savoring each word and its delicious associations—wife-to-be of Paul Fisher. The words were ripe with a sense of promise.

The sound of a horse's footsteps made her look up. It was Paul's sorrel mare. She didn't expect to see Paul today! Her hand flew to her cap. Was it straight? She brushed the back of her hand across her forehead. Was she perspiring? She needed a shower. Did she stink from the day's work? She hoped not.

Paul climbed down from the buggy, tied the horse's reins to a fence post, then approached the roadside stand. He stood, hands clasped behind his back, examining the produce.

"Paul, what a nice surprise!" Julia said, moving to the produce table.

"I was on my way home from work," he said.

She was beaming at him, positively beaming—she couldn't help it! She still pinched herself every morning when she first woke up and counted the days until their wedding on the first of November. Tall, slender, and elegant, Paul had honey-brown hair, shining azure eyes, milk-white teeth.

Today, his blue shirt matched his eyes. He was staggeringly handsome, Julia thought, but it was his smile that she loved best of all. It had a touch of sweet whimsicality about it that made her feel warm inside, as though they shared something private and precious.

Paul took off his hat and picked up a bundle of asparagus. "Most everyone else in April is still weeks from getting much of anything out of their garden. But yours is already producing."

"Helps to get a few things started in the greenhouse." But Paul knew that.

He sniffed a sprig of rosemary. "Sure will be glad when Amos's butter-and-sugar corn comes in. No better corn in the county."

She wondered where the conversation was going. It was not unusual for Paul to approach her like this, circumspectly, indirectly. "Looking for anything in particular?" She smiled. "Or did you just come by to talk wedding plans?"

Paul put his hat on the table. "Jules, we have to talk."

Well, hallelujah! she thought. Paul usually took time to circle up to his point. She often wondered when he was going to say he loved her. It was probably numbered among the rules that so carefully governed their lives—that moment when he could first say the words. There was a Stoney Ridge way of doing everything, Julia knew, and that included love. "So let's talk," she said.

Something was wrong. Paul's blue eyes were avoiding her. He straightened his shoulders and almost looked at her face again before he let his eyes slide down to the ground at their feet.

She sidled around the table and tilted her head. "Paul?"

He rubbed his forehead. "Jules, I have to tell you something and I don't want you to get upset. Just hear me out."

"What is it?"

Paul cleared his throat. "It's about the wedding. I've given this a lot of thought—quite a lot—and I've prayed about this and . . . well, we need . . . I think we ought to just put things on hold for a while." He swallowed hard, then whispered, "I need more time."

Oh no. Please no. Not again. This was some strange, cruel joke. Julia felt as if she was going to be sick. She gathered her breath to speak, but when she tried to find the words, there were none to be found.

"Please, Jules," Paul said. "Try to understand." He reached over to her, but she backed away. "Hold on. I know you're upset. Let me try to explain."

Outrage swooped in to displace her initial shock. "What is there to explain? Why do we need to postpone the wedding? Give me one good reason!"

He studied the ground and kicked a dirt clod away. "There's a number of good reasons."

"Name one."

He rubbed his temples, stretching his hand across his eyes. Hiding his eyes is what Julia was thinking. "There's that incident at church."

"That happened weeks ago! And besides, it was Uncle Hank's doing—it had nothing to do with me!"

"Sure, but you know as well as I do that a person marries an entire family. And you can't deny that your uncle lives up to his reputation as the town character."

Julia crossed her arms. She kept her voice low and measured. She was trying not to sound hysterical. "Sounds as if your mother's been influencing your way of thinking, Paul." She closed her eyes. "It's all because of that auction last summer."

He frowned. "I don't deny my mother has always worried about appearances. And I admit she's fretted quite a bit about us. But this isn't about the price your quilt fetched at the auction."

"I couldn't help that price. Your mother thinks I've gone proud over it, but I'm not. Not one bit!" She hadn't created another quilt top since Edith's criticism. She helped her friends with their quilts, but she had lost her desire to piece another one herself. To be accused of being proud—what could cut her more deeply?

Paul nodded. "I know that, Jules. But then your Uncle Hank pulls a stunt like he did last month, and it only added to Mom's perception that your family is a little . . ."

She glared at him. "A little what?" But she knew what he was struggling to say. She loved her family dearly, but she wasn't blind to their quirky ways. She waffled between feeling fiercely protective of them and feeling . . . a little embarrassed. Still, she was a Lapp. This was the family God had given to her.

Paul risked a direct look at her. "My mother's concerns aren't the only reason I want to hold off, Jules. It's . . . we're so young. We're both barely twenty-one. What's the rush?"

"That's what you said last year, Paul. So we waited, just like you wanted to." She took a deep breath. "So now you want to wait until . . . when? December? January? It can't be past February because there's too much to do in the fields." When Paul didn't say anything, she felt a chill run down her spine. "Are you trying to tell me that you're not ready to get married? Or you're not ready to get married to me?"

"I . . . don't know."

She was hysterical now, her breathing ragged, her tears hot and salty; her eyes stung. "You don't know? You don't know?"

Paul took a deep breath. "No. I don't."

She couldn't believe how angry, how upset she was. Not only was she humiliated, but bitterly disappointed. "This is the second time you have postponed our wedding, Paul! The second time!"

Paul reached for her and she surrendered. She buried her face against his chest and started to cry. His shirt, his smell, her Paul, she loved him so much. He was all she wanted, the one she had always wanted. But she waited one minute, two minutes, and he said nothing. He was shushing into her ear, but he wasn't telling her it was all a mistake, that he was sorry he upset her. It was true, the unthinkable was true! A promise had been broken and it lay shattered at her feet.

She pulled back from him. "You have to go. Leave. I don't want you here."

"Jules, you don't mean that."

"Don't call me that. Don't ever call me Jules again." Her own voice sounded strange to her. She turned from him and ran up the long drive that led to the farmhouse. If she had any pride at all, she thought, when she reached the top she would not look back to see if he was watching her.

She had no pride.

She whirled, but his horse and buggy were gone.

On the way home from school, eleven-year-old Mary Kate Lapp took a shortcut through the Smuckers' pasture. She didn't use this shortcut every day, only when she was playing hide-and-seek on the way home from school with Ethan and Ruthie. Before she jumped into the pasture, she shielded her eyes with her hand and scanned the woods behind her to see if her friends had caught up with her. No sign of them. That didn't surprise her. They had no detective skills whatsoever.

Running through the pasture cut the trip in half and it added a little danger to the day. To M.K.'s way of thinking, the time saved was worth the risk of getting charged at by Ira Smucker's mean and ugly goat. The goat was dirty yellow, with intimidating horns, and a long beard that dangled impressively from his chin. M.K. thought that beard was longer than the bishop's, just as straggly too.

She tiptoed quietly. On a normal day, as soon as she reached the fence, she would yell and yell at the goat so it would see her—she liked having it know she had crept through its pasture without permission—then jump the fence and take off for home. Today, she didn't have time to aggravate the goat. She had much on her mind, as she often did.

Sadie Lapp was idly scrubbing potatoes at the sink, gazing out the kitchen window to the end of the yard where her brother Menno's two bird feeders stood, their platforms heaped with sunflower seeds and cracked corn. The cardinal couple was there, the vivid red male perched on the peak of the roof, keeping watch, as his dull-colored wife was eating. Sadie let out a big sigh.

Even in the natural world, love was a wonderful thing.

Sadie glanced up when Julia came inside. "I saw you talking to Paul down by the stand," she said. "Did you remember to ask him what flavor wedding cake he wants?" She poured cooked and drained noodles into her Ham 'n' Noodle casserole. "I'm thinking that vanilla is safest. Everybody likes vanilla. Of course, it isn't my wedding. It's yours. Yours and Paul's. And you should pick the flavor *you* want." When Julia didn't answer, Sadie turned around. "Jules? Did you hear me?"

Julia had come into the kitchen and slid into a chair at the long harvest table. Her elbows were propped on the table, chin in her hands. "We don't have to decide for a while."

"Well, I just wanted time for plenty of practice. I want it to be perfect." She glanced at her sister. Julia's face was white and pinched. "Is something wrong?"

Julia didn't answer.

Sadie put down the wooden spoon she had been using to stir the casserole and sat next to Julia at the table. "There is something wrong, isn't there?"

Julia shook her head—vigorously; so vigorously, in fact, that Sadie's suspicions were immediately confirmed. Sadie laid her hand on her shoulder, gently. "Julia, you can tell me. What happened?"

Tears filled Julia's eyes. "Paul wants to postpone the wedding."

"Again? Not again!"

Slowly, Julia gave a slight nod of her head.

Sadie covered her face with her hands. "Oh Julia. Why?"

A tear leaked down Julia's cheek and she quickly wiped it away. "He said he didn't really know why, that he just needed more time. When I pressed him for a reason, he gave a vague excuse about the Incident."

"Uncle Hank and the root beer bottles? But that was a month ago!"

"I know, but you remember how upset Paul's mother was." The sound of popping corks in the basement had panicked the horses and caused a small stampede. Quite a bit of damage was done to buggies. What made things worse was that Uncle Hank had a buggy shop. It wasn't long before rumors started to fly that Hank Lapp might have done it on purpose, to drum up business for himself.

"But Paul's a reasonable fellow. He must realize that Uncle Hank is just being . . . Uncle Hank. That his . . . unfortunate incidents have nothing to do with you. With any of us. Surely he knows!"

Julia sighed. "Paul thinks that a family is a family. No one makes decisions alone. His mother thinks Dad could have done something to prevent the . . . the Incident." She smoothed out her skirt and pulled in her lips. "Maybe he's right. Dad lets Uncle Hank do whatever he wants."

"Uncle Hank may be a little eccentric, but he's the closest thing Dad has to a parent."

"Paul said he wasn't being influenced by his mother, but I find that hard to believe . . . why else would he have changed his mind?" Julia's voice broke on the words. A single tear fell and dropped onto her apron, followed by another and another.

Sadie got up from her chair and put her arms around her. Over Julia's shoulder she saw the cardinal husband lift his wings and swoop away, leaving his dull little wife behind. Maybe happiness, Sadie thought, was like a bird, fixing to take wing. Maybe it was never meant to stay.

Julia heard the little bell ring from her father's room. Amos Lapp rang it insistently.

"Dad's tea! I forgot to take it to him." Sadie jumped up from the chair to pick up a mug left on the counter.

"I'll take it up to him," Julia said, wiping her eyes with the back of her hand. The bell continued to ring as she hurried up the stairs with the mug of tea, trying to pull herself together. "You're supposed to be patient," she said as she walked into her father's room and found him sitting in a chair, engrossed in a game of checkers with his youngest daughter. "Where do you think the word comes from?" She set the tea on the table next to his chair. "How are you feeling this afternoon?"

"I'd be better if my children didn't keep me jailed up like a common thief," Amos grumbled.

"Doctor's orders." Julia leaned her back against the windowsill and crossed her arms. "Dad, you've got to do something about Uncle Hank."

Unruffled, Amos picked up a red checker piece and leaped over Mary Kate's black one. He collected the black checker and stacked it on the side of the board. "Uncle Hank is a fine old fellow." He looked over at her. "And he's kin. We take care of each other."

"I know, I know." This conversation wasn't a new one between Julia and her father.

"Jules, Hank is a man who has never worried about what others think of him. Few men can say that."

"That's just it! He doesn't even care that he makes us the laughingstock of Stoney Ridge! What happened last month at church was . . . outrageous!"

"Plenty of folks brew root beer," Amos said. He gave a mock scowl as M.K. double-jumped his checkers.

"But look at the aftermath . . ." Julia stopped short as she noticed that M.K. was listening. Listening hard.

"What aftermath?" Amos asked.

Julia looked away.

"Paul Fisher canceled the wedding," M.K. whispered to him.

Amos looked at Julia, shocked. "What?! When?"

"Postponed!" Julia hurried to amend. "Paul *postponed* the wedding. There's a difference." She glared at her sister. "You were eavesdropping on Sadie and me in the kitchen just now, weren't you?"

M.K. studied the checkerboard with great interest.

Amos frowned at M.K. "Why don't you go downstairs and help Sadie with dinner?"

"I happen to have some real interesting news I might be willing to share and instead I get sent away, like a dog," M.K. said glumly.

"What's your big news?" Julia said, eyes narrowed to dangerous slits.

Amos looked over at Julia. "Is it true about the wedding? Does Paul really want to postpone it?"

Julia tucked her chin to her chest. She gave a brief nod.

"And you think the reason is because of Uncle Hank and the exploding bottles?" Amos asked finally, sounding pensive. "Paul's no stranger to Uncle Hank's ways."

"What else could it be?" Julia said. She turned to M.K. "What news did you hear at school today?"

M.K. shrugged. "I might have heard a few things. Got me to thinking . . . maybe . . ."

"Maybe . . . what?" Julia asked.

M.K. lit up like a firefly. "Jacob Glick called off his wedding to Katie Yoder. And Henry Stoltzfus broke off courtin' with Sarah Miller."

Julia tilted her head. "What? All of them? But . . . why?" She paused. "Oh . . . you don't mean . . . don't tell me!" She covered her cheeks with her hands. "He's back, isn't he?"

M.K. nodded, pleased to deliver the news. "He's back. The Bee Man is back."

"Ah," Amos said, leaning back in his chair. "That explains quite a bit."

"It's happening all over again," Julia said. "Just like last year." Her sadness over the postponed wedding dissipated. In its place was anger. Hot, furious, steaming-like-a-teakettle anger. Directed at the Bee Man.

Amos brightened. "Maybe it wasn't your Uncle Hank's fault at all that Paul wants to postpone the wedding!"

"He certainly didn't help matters," Julia said crossly. "And then along comes the Bee Man this week to really seal the deal."

"Or not," M.K. added helpfully.

2

If asked, folks would say that Sadie Lapp was solid and practical, on the quiet side, and that she was a fine example to today's youth. Or if they were feeling less generous, they said that Sadie was a girl no one ever had to worry about.

What they didn't know about Sadie was that she had a deeply romantic side that she tried to keep well hidden. She felt nearly as bad as Julia about Paul's perpetual cold feet. How could he do such a thing to her sister? Twice, now. After all, getting married was the biggest thing that could ever happen in a girl's life. A dream come true. To marry the man you loved. Sadie could hardly imagine how it would feel to be a bride—though she did try. She had such dreams for her own wedding. She'd already planned the menu, chosen her material for her wedding dress, added special treasures to her hope chest. She had everything ready and waiting.

Everything but the groom, M.K. frequently pointed out.

It was never too soon to plan for such a big event, Sadie would say in her defense. Weddings took a great deal of planning.

Sadie wondered how she would feel if she were in Julia's situation. She thought it would be like an arrow had been shot through her from front to back, leaving her with pain, longing, regret. Julia had looked so sad during dinner and excused herself after eating only a few bites of casserole.

Sadie put her fork down and leaned back in her chair. She glanced at Uncle Hank, seated across the table, scraping crumbs of gingerbread off his plate with the back of his fork. He managed to put away a lot of dinner, despite the day's tragedy. He wanted seconds on everything except the Ham 'n' Noodle casserole. He had always reminded Sadie of a character from the Bible, a prophet, or maybe a shepherd, with his longish hair and untrimmed beard. She could see Uncle Hank was completely unconcerned about Julia's change of circumstances. So was Menno, Sadie's brother, who was preoccupied with helping himself to a second piece of cake. Uncle Hank held out his plate to Menno to be served.

Surprisingly, M.K. seemed to understand the gravity of the situation. She looked up the stairs and back at Sadie. "I could take Julia some cake. She likes your gingerbread."

Sadie brushed M.K.'s cheek with the back of her hand. "I think she just wants to be alone."

"Our Jules is better off without Paul," Uncle Hank said as he reached across Menno to grab the bowl of whipped cream. "Them Fishers always think they're something." He dropped spoonfuls of whipped cream on his fresh slice of gingerbread.

"Amen to that," M.K. muttered under her breath. "Especially Jimmy."

Sadie elbowed her to hush.

"Well, it's true," M.K. said. "In school today, Jimmy Fisher put a black racer snake in the girls' outhouse."

"That is pretty low," Menno said in his slow, deliberate way.

"You can say that again," M.K. said.

"That is pretty low," Menno repeated, ever literal. "That must have scared the snake."

M.K. stared at him. "The *snake*? It scared the living daylights out of me." She coughed. "I mean, out of the *girls*!"

Sadie cut the last piece of gingerbread cake—after all, why save it?—and slipped it on her plate.

Julia couldn't sleep. She was assaulted by an avalanche of thoughts, rolling, tumbling. How could life change so fast? This very morning she had woken earlier than usual, so filled with joy she could have burst. A taste of something unspeakably sweet—a wedding—and then, this afternoon, she had lost it. Paul took her dream and broke it like a fistful of spaghetti over a pot of boiling water. Snap, in half. Gone.

All thanks to the Bee Man.

Out of the blue, the Bee Man arrived in town and filled Paul's head with doubts. Paul had never been particularly confident. She knew that he had difficulty making even the smallest decision, let alone a firm decision about a wedding date. The Bee Man had a way of bringing doubts into Paul's mind—just enough doubts to convince Paul to postpone the wedding . . . again.

The bishop's sermon two Sundays ago was about the necessity of loving one's fellowman. Not only did Julia not love the Bee Man, she thought she might hate him. Wholeheartedly hate him! She knew it was wrong to hate anyone, but how could she love someone so despicable? How was it even possible? She knew that with God all things were possible . . . but this?

She couldn't get that exasperating man out of her head. After two years, the mental ledger of her grievances against the Bee Man had grown thick with entries. Finally, she decided to commit this big mess to prayer. She believed in prayer. Prayer worked.

She bowed her head and asked God to help her love the loathsome Bee Man and to give her the strength she lacked. "Amen," she said and snapped her head back, smacking the back of her head on the headboard of her bed. "Ouch!" She rubbed her head where it hurt. Really, wasn't this also the Bee Man's fault? Everything about that man created trouble—even thinking about him inflicted pain. Who was he, anyway? Where did he come from? She had always noticed how the Bee Man skillfully deflected questions about himself. Even her father—who knew him better than anyone in Stoney Ridge—was reluctant to ask the Bee Man anything of a personal nature.

Julia had known Roman Troyer—the Bee Man—for six summers. He seemed to be particularly fond of Windmill Farm and spent time with the Lapp family each year, and still she didn't know a single thing about him other than he went from town to town with his bees. And he was Amish.

What pleasure did Roman Troyer take in breaking up her engagement to Paul? Twice! What did he hope to gain from it?

The sounds of Sadie and M.K., as they changed into nightgowns and brushed their teeth in the hallway bathroom, drifted through the transom above her door. She heard Sadie remind M.K. to scrub her face because no boy would look at her twice with that milk mustache. M.K. answered back by saying she didn't *want* a boy to look at her, not even once.

Julia's eyes flew open. Suddenly, it dawned on her. Of course. Of course! How could she not have realized? It was all so simple—as plain as day. Roman Troyer was in love with Julia himself.

Too bad, Bee Man. I'm not interested. I never will be! She wasn't going to let Roman Troyer stand in her way with Paul Fisher.

Her thoughts drifted back to Paul, feebly telling her he wanted to postpone the wedding. What would Paul tell others? Her mind was racing—she felt deeply humiliated. But on the heels of her humiliation was an overwhelming sorrow. She loved Paul. Would he ever be ready to get married? Or would he always just like the idea of getting married?

She sighed. A more courageous woman would have told Paul to forget it. A tougher woman would have told him in no uncertain terms what he could do with this halfhearted plan to postpone. But Julia was neither brave nor tough. She just wanted Paul back. She wanted things back the way they were, yesterday, or last week. Before the Bee Man arrived.

Oh Paul. What was he doing tonight? Was he at home with his family, or out with his friends? He had to be missing her. He had to be thinking about her. He was in love with her! She was sure of it. Tomorrow, Julia decided, he would come to Windmill Farm and tell her it was all a big mistake.

Prayer worked, she reminded herself. And so she prayed. *Please please please please please please please please please.*

The last chore of the evening was to move the three cows out to the pasture with the creek flowing through it. It was usually Menno's job, but he told M.K. that he had something he needed to do first, and then he disappeared with a trowel in his hand.

M.K. opened the gate and pushed the rump of the first cow, Pizza. If she could get Pizza moving along, chances were good that Pepperoni and Linguica would follow behind her. They used to have thirty cows, a herd, and it was M.K.'s job to name each new calf. Her father had given her that task the year her mother had passed, and M.K. felt very important whenever a cow was due to calve. After her father's heart started to act up last year, he sold the dairy cows and sheep at an auction. It broke M.K.'s heart to part with the animals. "Just for a little while, M.K.," her father had promised. "Just until I'm back in the saddle, fit as a fiddle." He let her keep a few—her favorites—as long as she promised to care for them. And she did, most of the time, unless she forgot and then Menno would remember. Caring for the animals was the main thing on his mind.

Where was Menno, anyway? She hitched the lock on the gate behind Linguica and ran up the hill. Menno met her as she reached the barn, near Julia's garden. M.K. gasped. In his hands were Julia's prized pink Parrot tulips, dug up, with bulbs attached. Julia loved those tulips! This very morning, she had made the whole family come to the garden to admire them. They were in their glory. At their peak!

"Menno, *what* were you thinking?"

He looked pleased with himself. "Julia is so sad. These will cheer her up."

"Oh, they'll be sure to get a reaction out of Julia! If I were you, I'd hide out in the hills for a few days."

Menno looked confused and M.K. was just about to explain when she heard Sadie call out to them from the kitchen window. Menno spun around on one heel and headed toward the house, and M.K. shook off her shock and followed him. Let Sadie untangle this. Sadie made things clear to Menno. He walked into the kitchen, dropping clumps of dirt from the tulip bulbs wherever he went. M.K. came in behind him, stepping around the clots. Boys. So messy!

Sadie was at the kitchen sink, soaking the last few dishes from dinner. She caught sight of what was in Menno's hands and froze. She threw a questioning look—filled with horror—at M.K., who shrugged her shoulders.

"They're for Julia," Menno said. "To make her happy again."

Sadie put the dish towel down on the counter and exhaled a deep sigh. "Let's get those into a pitcher of water, Menno."

He walked over to the counter and placed the tulips down. "You fix 'em and I'll take them up to Julia."

Sadie found a glass pitcher and started to fill it with water. "She's sound asleep, Menno. Let's wait to show her the pretty flowers until the morning."

He tossed M.K. a smug look. "Mary Kate thinks I should hide in the hills."

"No, you shouldn't hide." Sadie cut the bulb off of each tulip stem. "Once Julia recovers from the . . . surprise . . . I'm sure she will think they're a lovely gesture."

And then she added, so softly that M.K. thought she might have imagined it, "I hope."

Gray light streaked the windows. Julia showered, turned off the water, stepped out, dried off, and ran a comb through her chestnut-colored hair. She'd always been secretly proud of her hair, thick and sleek and luxurious. She took a washrag and wiped the steam off the mirror. She didn't look too bad, did she? Tired, a bit frayed on the edges, but nothing that would frighten the birds off the trees, as her father used to say about people who didn't feel up to snuff.

Fooling yourself, her reflection said. Sore head, sore heart.

In the kitchen, Julia threw herself into a chair, bone-weary after a sleepless night.

"You look lovely, Jules," Sadie said, coming in from the other room with a basket of laundry in her arms. "You're the prettiest girl in our church. Paul will come to his senses soon." Sadie quietly folded the stiff, dry towels and piled them on the table.

Julia made herself smile at her sister. That was an interesting thing about Sadie, she observed. Sadie spoke with a quiet certainty as if she knew what she was talking about.

"I was just going to bring breakfast up for you. In case you'd rather not see anyone . . ." Sadie's voice drizzled to a stop as she fastened her eyes on Julia's face. "I only meant, you can take a day off, Jules."

Julia didn't want to talk, and Sadie—despite the subject of Paul Fisher hovering over the table like a hummingbird—wouldn't make her. Sadie knew that you didn't need to talk all the time. She had a great sense of stillness, making it very restful to be near her.

"I'm fine. Really."

Julia picked up a towel and started to fold it as Sadie poured a cup of coffee and handed it to her. Then she put bacon in the fry pan. The hot bacon sputtered and popped, so Sadie cracked the window open to fan out the smoke. Julia took a sip of the coffee and spit it out. Grounds were floating on top. This time Julia had no trouble smiling. No sisters could be more different, Julia thought as she spooned out the grounds. Sadie had always been most like their father, a peacemaker. She was quite lovely in a round, soft sort of way, with curly light brown hair, a round face covered with freckles, and a shy, friendly smile, mild-mannered and dreamy. A listening person. She was of a fearful nature, but she knew that about herself and said it wasn't such a bad way to be because it led to so many nice surprises when frightening things didn't happen.

Julia glanced out the window. M.K. was having trouble coaxing the cows out of the barn into the paddock. The silly animals milled in a stubborn bunch, jamming the opening and squeezing her against the doorjamb.

M.K. would be twelve come winter. Too soon to tell what kind of woman she would grow into, but Julia thought M.K. took after their mother, at least in personality. Maggie Zook Lapp had been known as a woman who had a curious way of thinking.

Menno appeared at the barn door and pushed the cows through, rescuing M.K. Julia's heart ached sweetly as she watched Menno's gentle ways. Nearly seventeen, Menno had the body of a man, but his mind hadn't developed quite as far.

To an outsider, Menno seemed like any other healthy, handsome young man. But when he spoke, it was obvious that he was different. You'd know from watching or even talking with him briefly that something was unusual. The wheels of his mind turned slowly, cautiously. The doctors never could decide what exactly was wrong with Menno. The consensus was a lack of oxygen caused brain injury during birth.

Unless it was something he felt passionate about, Menno wasn't much of a talker, but he hummed. He was always humming from memory, and off-key, every tune that he ever heard. Uncle Hank had taught Menno to be a first-rate birdhouse builder. He sold the birdhouses at Julia's farm stand and also at the hardware store in town. Menno loved birds. His favorite book was *Bird, Birds, Birds!* and he spent far too much time at the telephone shanty by the schoolhouse listening in to the Audubon Rare Bird Count. He loved all animals, dogs and birds best of all.

The one thing that defined Menno's life more than any other was his relationship with animals. He held them, raised them, loved them, cared for them, healed them.

Julia smiled as she saw Menno and M.K. race up to the house, like they always did, eager for breakfast.

As M.K. and Menno reached the kitchen porch and pulled off their shoes, the front door banged open.

"ANYBODY TO HOME?" boomed Uncle Hank, who always spoke as though he were addressing the deaf.

"Oh no . . . not this early." Julia sighed and rubbed her forehead. Uncle Hank had always been a sore trial to Julia, but the exploding bottle incident put him on very thin ice. Not that he was aware of it.

"Come on in, Uncle Hank!" Sadie said.

Uncle Hank stood in the doorway, grinning like he just tagged everyone in a game of hide-and-seek. In his hand was the lit stub of a cigar.

"No smoking in the house, Uncle Hank," Julia said. "You know the doctors outlawed it for Dad's sake." She put her hand out, palm up, until Uncle Hank forfeited the stub. Julia opened the kitchen door to throw it out. She turned and frowned at him, but he didn't seem at all offended.

"Still settin' to your breakfast!" he bellowed. "I had mine at 4:30!"

The entire town of Stoney Ridge was awake now. Julia filled a coffee mug and handed it to him.

"Say, Mary Kate, if I'd a knowed I'd see you, I'd a put my choppers in." Uncle Hank fumbled around in his pocket and pulled out a full set of fake dentures. They grinned out of his fist. Menno whooped out a big laugh. M.K. and Sadie started to giggle.

Julia shaded her eyes with her hand. It really was too early for this.

"Well, Uncle Hank, how are you today?" Amos asked, standing at the bottom of the stairwell. He was still in his pajamas, Julia noted. More and more often, there were days when he never changed out of them.

"Better'n you, Amos. You're gettin' to look more and more like a plucked chicken ever' time I lay eyes on you." He spied Julia and pointed at her. "That Fisher boy come to his senses yet?"

Julia thought, *Move on. New topic.* "Uncle Hank, was there some reason you came over so especially early this morning?"

His bushy eyebrows lifted on Julia in surprise. "Why, so I did!" He pulled an envelope out of his pocket and unfolded it. He hooked his spectacles over his ears and gave the envelope a close look.

"I've got news. I found somebody to help out while Amos is ailing." He glanced at the return address. "A lady named Fern Graber from Millersburg, Ohio."

"Is she Amish?" asked M.K.

Uncle Hank turned his spectacles on M.K. "Of course she's Amish!" he roared.

"What's this Fern lady like?" Menno asked in his slow way. "Can she cook five meals like Sadie?"

"No one can cook like Sadie Lapp!" Uncle Hank pounded his fist on the table for added emphasis and Sadie blushed.

M.K. had a sudden coughing fit and Julia elbowed her to hush up. Sadie was just starting to learn to cook when their mother passed. She had learned how to make five recipes and that's as far as she got. She didn't waver off those same five recipes: A big ham on Saturday night which gave them leftovers for Sunday, Ham 'n' Noodle casserole on Monday to finish off the ham, Haystacks on Tuesday, Tater Tot Casserole on Wednesday, Cheesy Chicken and Rice Casserole on Thursday, pizza delivered from a local shop on Friday if the budget allowed. If not, grilled cheese sandwiches. The family knew what day it was by what was being served for dinner. Julia, who never had much interest in learning to cook, wouldn't let M.K. or Menno complain about the lack of variety in their meals. She knew how much mastering those five recipes meant to Sadie. They were a link to their mother, just like quilting was for Julia. A reminder of life like it had been.

"How did you happen to find this woman?" Julia asked. She knew from experience that if she didn't immediately steer Uncle Hank back on course, she would be obligated to ride the path he started down, filled with infinite, unrelated details.

Uncle Hank drummed his fingers on the tabletop. "She must be reading my letters in the *Budget*. So she wrote and asked if we needed help." Uncle Hank was a *Budget* scribe and took his weekly letter writing seriously, filling it with all kinds of news—much of which Julia considered to be the family's private business. And then there was plenty of community news, adding his unique "Uncle Hank" spin on events, often irking many of the ladies in the church.

Amos walked over to the kitchen to fill a mug with coffee. He gave Uncle Hank a suspicious glance. "Just what did her letter say?"

"That it sounded like we needed help and she would be just the ticket!" He scowled at Amos. "The right price too, considering you ain't exactly rolling in greenbacks lately."

Amos ignored that observation and took a long sip of coffee.

"What's she like?" Menno asked, buttering his toast to the very edges.

Uncle Hank rattled the letter. His glasses slipped down his nose. "Says here she isn't fond of rules she hasn't made herself. She brooks no nonsense. She has strong opinions and she's not the kind who enjoys surprises. She expects brown-caked shoes to be left at the back door and for the family to don clean socks in the house. And she'll tolerate no muddy-bellied dogs in the house."

M.K. dropped her head on the table with a loud clunk.

Uncle Hank turned one eye in her direction. His eyes had a tendency to wander. "And she has a mustache, fangs, and eats ten-year-olds for lunch."

"Thank goodness I'm eleven," M.K. mumbled glumly.

"Out of the goodness of her heart, she is dropping everything and coming to this family's aid." He leaned over toward Amos. "I'd be a watchin' yourself." His face broke into a big toothy grin. "I smell a trap brewing!"

"We don't *need* help," Julia said crisply.

Peering over his spectacles, Uncle Hank looked around the room. Clutter was everywhere. The kitchen was the worst. Countertops were buried underneath a motley assortment of newspapers and mail. Last night's food-encrusted dinner dishes were still piled in the sink. Even the pattern on the linoleum floor was hard to make out, littered with grass clippings that Menno had tracked into the kitchen and somehow managed to spread through the house. Furniture was shrouded under a white film of dust. They had worked so hard to get it all cleaned up before they hosted church, barely a month ago—that infamous morning when the bottles exploded. But since then, they had been working fourteen hours a day to get the fields ready to plant.

"We've been pruning the orchards and planting the crops and taking care of the animals and trying to get the roadside stand up and going . . . ," Julia started, but even she couldn't deny any longer that they were in over their heads. Her time passed in a blur of trying to get the farm ready for another growing season, caring for her sisters and brother, and tending to her father. It didn't help that Amos was an awful patient, ornery at being so confined, short-tempered and demanding. She fell into bed exhausted each night, woke in the morning, and started all over again.

"Maybe it wouldn't be such a bad thing to have a little help, Julia," Sadie said quietly. "Just until Dad is better."

"That's right, Sadie girl!" Uncle Hank boomed, right into Sadie's ear, and she cringed. "I'm sure Fern Graber is a fine housekeeper and a real good cook. And I'll do alls I can to help out in them fields too, when I get a little more caught up out in the buggy shop."

Julia had to bite her lower lip not to spit out the words that wanted to roll off her tongue: Uncle Hank could be counted on for one thing—he couldn't be counted on.

Uncle Hank circled behind Menno's chair and put a large hand on his shoulder. "But as for this beautiful spring morning, Menno and I have work cut out for us. We're gonna head to town and meet this Fern Graber at the iron horse!"

Menno looked at his father. "What's an iron horse?"

"It's an old-fashioned word for a train," Amos said.

Menno thought that over for a long moment, then threw back his head and barked out that single, joyous "Haw!" that distinguished his laugh from everyone else's.

"Let's be off, Menno!" Uncle Hank shouted. "But first things first. We'll swing by Blue Lake Pond to see if the croppy is bitin'. After all, spring is upon us!"

Menno jumped out of his chair and grabbed his straw hat off the bench. Uncle Hank tipped his hat to everyone as he held the kitchen door open for Menno. Amos looked longingly after them, watching the two men—one old, one young—head down the path with their fishing poles in their hands and a bucket of bait.

3

As M.K. drew close to the house on her way home from school that afternoon, the smell of something savory drifted her way from the open kitchen window. It was Tuesday, Haystack Day, but the smell coming out of the kitchen wasn't anything like Sadie's Haystacks. She eased into the kitchen, as quiet as a person could possibly be. A pot of beef stew simmered on the stovetop, filling the room with a savory aroma.

Her eyes landed on the most glorious sight in the world: On the counter next to the oven were thick chocolate chip cookies, cooling on a rack. M.K. grabbed a cookie and took a bite. Bliss! Which could only be improved upon with a glass of cold milk. M.K. reached into the refrigerator to get the milk pitcher.

"Get your hands out of that refrigerator!" a no-nonsense voice called out without so much as a *how are you today*. M.K. nearly jumped out of her skin. She spun around and came face-to-face with a tall, thin woman, with wiry hair the color of nickels and dimes, staring down at M.K.

"I'm Mary Kate," M.K. said timidly. "But you could call me M.K. If you like. That's what my family calls me . . ." Her voice drizzled to a stop. "You must be . . . Fern."

"I am," the woman said. She stood surveying the room. She was all business. Her eyes were a pair of pale-blue flints striking cold sparks, and she had a look on her face like she was sizing M.K. up and filing her under Trouble—a look M.K. was rather accustomed to from her schoolteacher. "New rule. No one is allowed in the refrigerator."

"But—"

"I spent the afternoon cleaning and organizing it. It was a disaster." Fern frowned. "And now the milk isn't in the right place. And the eggs. Why would anybody move the eggs?" She straightened everything and wiped the shelf with a dish towel. "They don't belong on that shelf!" A storm cloud seemed to form over Fern's head, threatening to shed cold sleet all over the room.

Talking around a mouthful of cookie, M.K. mumbled, "The eggs were in front of the milk."

Fern eyed the second cookie beside M.K.'s glass of milk. "One snack after school. Then nothing until dinner."

M.K. slid the extra cookie back on the cooling rack.

"And there's a smudge on the door handle!" Fern rubbed the handle of the refrigerator with her dish towel as if polishing fine silver.

The large kitchen suddenly began to feel small and confining as Fern's opinions began to take up residence. M.K. quietly backed toward the door while Fern's attention was focused on the smudge. She sat on the kitchen porch steps and finished up her cookie and milk. She dipped the cookie into the milk and took the last bite, savoring it because she knew she wouldn't be able to help herself to another. Fern was guarding them like a raccoon with her kits.

M.K. pondered Fern's no-one-in-the-refrigerator rule and wondered if there would be more rules to follow. No one in the refrigerator? She would starve! She would grow weaker and weaker, languishing away, until she died from malnutrition. Tragic possibilities always lurked near the front of M.K.'s mind, just behind her common sense. "This is outrageous!" she hissed to nobody in particular.

M.K. didn't like change. In her eleven years, she had already discovered that when things changed, they always changed for the worst. Life as she knew it was over.

Sadie finished filling the water bucket for the buggy horse, turned off the hose spigot, and went to find Menno. She followed the tuneless humming that led to him, sitting in an empty horse stall that doubled as a maternity ward for his dog, Lulu. Menno's back was against the wall, and two yellow puppies were nestled in his arms.

Sadie leaned against the bars of the stall. "I'm amazed Lulu will let you hold them. M.K. said she won't let her near them."

"That's because M.K. moves too fast, Sadie," Menno said in his slow, deliberate way. "She's always in a hurry. She makes Lulu nervous. Lulu likes things calm."

"Are you going to put up a 'puppies for sale' sign down by Julia's stand?"

"No."

"Dad said you can't keep them, Menno."

"I know. But I need to find the right home for each one. And then I need to make sure the puppies are happy. Dogs pick their master, you know." He shifted a little against the wall. "Come, look at this, Sadie." He pointed his jaw at the puppy tucked in his elbow. "Does that eye look . . . ," he searched for the word, ". . . gummy?"

Sadie examined the puppy's eye. "Might just be a little sleep in its eye. I'll check it again later today." She didn't see anything wrong with the puppy's eyes, but there wasn't anything she would deny Menno. She adored him.

Sadie looked at her brother. Menno resembled Julia far more than Sadie—he was tall and slender, with thick, shiny, curly hair. He had Julia's hazel eyes rimmed with lashes so thick they looked like a brush. Not fair! Not fair that Julia and Menno took after their mother, while Sadie took after her father's side of the family. Short, round, bordering on plump, large-chested, and her honey-colored hair frizzed up on humid days like a Brillo pad. M.K. seemed to have features from both parents—small like her mother, snapping brown eyes like her father, hair that was colored lighter than Sadie's, but thick and satin-smooth, like Julia's. So not fair. And then she felt a pin jab of conscience.

The barn door slid open and M.K. flew in, feathers ruffled like an offended parakeet. True M.K. style. "Family meeting!" she shouted. "We need to have a family meeting! Right now! It's a dire emergency! Where is everybody?"

Sadie popped up so M.K. could see where she was. She held a finger in silence against her lips. "The puppies just fell asleep."

Menno was watching M.K. with an alarmed look on his face. "Is it Dad? Is he okay?"

"Menno, you know that M.K.'s dire emergencies are never real emergencies," Sadie said quietly, in a voice of one long accustomed to her little sister's fire alarms.

M.K. overheard her. "But it is! We are facing a *terrible* problem!"

"Calm down, M.K.," Sadie said. "Sit next to Menno and look at the puppies."

M.K. came into the stall and crouched down. As she reached out to touch a puppy, Lulu growled at her, so she drew back. She gave Sadie a pleading look. "Even the dog won't listen to me!"

Sadie's heart went out to her little sister. Her daily emergencies were casually dismissed by the family. Crying wolf, they said. Yet Sadie indulged her—she knew that M.K.'s enthusiasms were always genuine and passionate but seldom long-lasting.

Sadie put an arm around her. "You've got my full attention now, M.K. What's the emergency? Why do we need a family meeting?"

"Fern! Haven't you met her?"

Sadie and Menno nodded. "She made me a big lunch," Menno said. "It was amazing!" He cast a sheepish glance in Sadie's direction. "No offense, Sadie."

"None taken," Sadie said. "Why are you upset, M.K.?"

"She said no one is allowed in the refrigerator. Pretty soon, we won't even be allowed into the kitchen."

Menno scrunched up his face. "But how would we eat?"

"My point exactly, Menno!" M.K. folded her arms against her chest, satisfied that she had conveyed the critical urgency of her message. She pointed to the puppies sleeping in Menno's lap. "Dibs on the big one."

Menno shook his head. "You can't just say dibs, M.K. These puppies belong to me."

M.K. waved him off. "Menno, come with me. There's a pot of beef stew simmering on the stove and it is tempting me something fierce. Let's go see if we can sample a bowlful. Maybe Fern won't yell at you. Nobody ever yells at you."

Menno nodded solemnly at Sadie. "It's true. Everybody likes me." He gently placed the sleeping puppies next to Lulu and scrambled to his feet to follow M.K. to the house.

Julia was having an awful day. Awful! She already felt fragile from yesterday's conversation with Paul, and now, Uncle Hank had invited a stranger to become their housekeeper. They didn't *need* a housekeeper. Well, maybe they did, but Julia should have been the one to choose her. *Not* Uncle Hank!

The woman who had arrived at their doorstep earlier in the day couldn't be any more of a mismatch for the Lapps. When Julia first met her, Fern Graber had a look on her face as if she had a kernel of popcorn stuck in a back molar. That was before Fern walked into the kitchen and actually gasped in horror. Within one minute of arriving, she was sweeping the floor and clucking her tongue.

And not only that—Fern Graber had ears on her like a librarian. She was already listening in to their conversations and offering up her opinion on serious matters. Unsolicited. Unwanted.

Just moments ago, as Sadie and Julia hung wet laundry on the clothesline, Sadie asked, "If you had three wishes, Julia, what would you wish for?"

Without thinking, Julia said at once, "I want Paul Fisher to marry me."

"If wishes were fishes," Fern said as she walked up to them with another basket of wet laundry, "we'd all have a fry."

What really irked Julia was that Fern was right. She had hoped for so much and ended up with so little. It seemed to Julia as if her future had been floating above her like a brightly colored kite, waiting to lift her away . . . and Paul had just ripped the kite string from her hand. She could only watch helplessly as her hopes and dreams to be Paul's wife slipped out of her hands, drifting up and out of sight as if carried off by the wind.

Julia sat down on the picnic bench near the clothesline. As she buried her head in her hands, she felt despair grip her. Her chest felt as if it were being squeezed by a giant fist, but she wouldn't let herself cry. If she did, she would never be able to stop.

"Juuu-Leee-Aaaa!!!!"

Julia swiveled around on the bench to see M.K. running toward her, her face in a panic.

"Fern says she's not making our dinner! She says she's here to help Dad and we're old enough to be on our own!" M.K. stopped as she reached Julia, planted her fists on her thin hips and stared at her, defying her to act. Sadie and Menno walked up to join them.

M.K.'s timing was impeccable. Julia needed something to think about other than her own miserable love life. And Fern nettled her. It wasn't unusual to have friends and relatives help out, even to move in, but no one knew Fern. And what was Uncle Hank getting at . . . that Fern was setting a trap for Amos? Was Fern after Julia's father?

Julia shook that thought off. Uncle Hank said all kinds of ridiculous things, all the time. More likely, he had misled Fern into what she was getting herself into. Well, Julia would clear things up. She hopped off the bench and headed to the kitchen to find Fern peeling potatoes at the sink. Sadie and M.K. trotted behind her. Menno sat down at the kitchen table, wide-eyed.

"Fern," Julia said in her most authoritative voice. "While our father is recovering from his heart trouble, the rest of us are working long hours to get the farm ready for planting and harvesting. I'm very grateful you offered to help us, but Uncle Hank led us to believe that you would be helping all of us—not just Amos."

Fern's lips formed a thin, unhappy line, but she kept peeling potatoes. "I can't cook for the entire tribe of you. There's limits on what a person can do." She turned her head and looked at Julia, a long look. "How much is one woman supposed to do?"

Amen! Julia thought. Amen to that.

"If you don't want me to quit, you'll have to take care of yourself," Fern said.

Quit? She might quit? Maybe this was the exit door they were looking for. Julia grabbed a dishcloth and rubbed a spot on the counter. "If you need to quit and return to your home, we certainly understand." She turned to M.K. "Go get your piggy bank, M.K., and we'll pay Fern her wages."

M.K. lifted her hands, palms to the sky. "Why is everybody always asking me for money?"

"Because you're the only who has any," Menno whispered.

Fern's face flushed. Julia had called her bluff. Julia felt a tiny twinge of pity as she pulled six spoons, knives, and forks from the drawer. Just a twinge. "Of course, Sadie could always cook for the four of us while you tend to Dad. You don't mind sharing the kitchen, do you?"

Fern's thin eyebrows rose in alarm.

Julia gave the silverware to M.K. to set the table. "You have three choices, Fern. One . . . you certainly aren't obligated to stay. Two . . . you can let Sadie back into the kitchen." She took the napkins out of the drawer and started to fold them. "Or, three, cook for all of us." She handed the folded napkins to M.K. "Just let me know what you decide."

A pregnant silence filled the room. Fern blew out a stream of air. "All righty, then. But you all will have to eat what I serve." She pointed to Sadie. "Even the overfed one."

Throughout the discussion, Sadie had been feeding steadily from a pan of brownies. She had taken a paring knife from the drawer and cut out a small piece, then evened out the cut by slicing another bite, then another and another. When she realized Fern was referring to her, she froze, midbite, and looked up, horrified.

"Fine. We'll eat whatever you make for us," Julia said. "No complaining allowed." She gave M.K. a look of warning.

M.K. raised her small shoulders as if to ask, "What?"

Fern scowled, but Julia's amiability took the fight out of her. "I don't want people messing up my kitchen."

Julia motioned to everyone to leave the kitchen. Sadie dropped the paring knife in the brownie pan in a huff.

Outside, Menno and M.K. ran to the barn to check on Lulu and the puppies. Sadie and Julia lingered behind, watching the sun slip behind the row of pine trees that framed Windmill Farm in the west, making for early sunsets.

Sadie turned to Julia. "Do I look fat?"

Julia put an arm around Sadie. "No. Not at all. Not in the least bit. Absolutely not." She pinched her thumb and index finger together. "Well, maybe just a little."

"I am! I'm fat!"

"It's just baby fat, Sadie. You'll grow soon and it will disappear."

"I stopped growing a year ago and I kept eating." She let out a soft sough. "I am. I am a fat girl. Fat, fat, fat."

"Sadie, don't let Fern Graber get to you. Fern is just . . . Fern."

Sadie took a few steps down the porch and turned back. "You're sure I don't look fat?"

"I wouldn't want you any other way than how you are right now, Sadie," Julia said truthfully.

Sadie smiled and crossed to the barn.

Julia walked over to the garden and examined the flowers along the front row. She loved her flower garden, small though it was. It had been her mother's garden, her special joy. And now the garden gave Julia constant pleasure. Julia had always felt a special kind of peace whenever she gazed around the garden. The crocuses, narcissus, daffodils, each blooming briefly, sometimes only for a day, then withering. She snapped off the dead blossoms every morning, though she hadn't that morning, so she did it now. When she finished, her hands were stained with yellow and orange from the crocus stamen. As the peaceful scents of the garden stole over her, she felt a peculiar excitement.

It felt good, being so direct and assertive with Fern. Really, really good. And yet to Julia's surprise, she felt relieved when Fern decided not to quit. Her father's heart trouble was taking a terrible toll on Windmill Farm. On all of them. Julia kept expecting her father to make a full recovery. Surely, any day now, his heart would regain its strength. The Lord knew they needed him.

And how Menno needed guidance. He was a strong boy and could work hard at times, but he needed to be told what to do and how to do it. He needed someone working alongside of him. Instead of providing daily instruction, Amos had been retreating from life. He stayed in his robe and slippers, staring out the window of his bedroom. The neighbors pitched in as often as they could, but they had farms to run too. Even with Sadie and Menno's help, Julia couldn't keep up with both the house and the fields. As March had turned to April—spring planting time—Julia often found herself fighting waves of panic. She was drowning in responsibilities.

But now, at the end of this day, Julia didn't feel quite as sad as she had a little earlier. Her spirits had lightened. She reached up to smooth out the furrows of a frown forming between her eyes. She didn't want to mar her complexion with needless worry lines. It was bad enough that she had a too-generous sprinkling of freckles across her nose that even a bucket of lemon juice couldn't fade.

Maybe . . . if she could handle Fern, she could manage anything. Maybe things weren't as bleak as they appeared. Maybe when life became difficult, it only meant one was facing a challenge, an obstacle to be overcome. She was only twenty-one years old, young enough to make changes. She was going to become the kind of person who took no nonsense from anyone. She could do it. After all, even Fern backed down!

She straightened her back and lifted her chin, a matter decided. How could she overcome Paul's reluctance to marry? How could she point him in the proper direction? Sometimes, a man like Paul only needed to be convinced of what he truly wanted. She was going to marry him, as planned. This very November. She would simply have to be more forthright.

Fern opened the one-hinged kitchen door and peered at the rusty hinge, as if wondering how it still remained. She shook her head and called to Julia. "Your Uncle Hank told me to tell you that the Bee Man is due in. Tomorrow or the next day."

Julia's new confidence popped like a balloon. She dropped her chin to her chest, defeated, wondering how an awful stretch of days could turn even worse. It seemed like at some point you'd just run out of awful.

On her way to school the following day M.K. had much on her mind, as she often did. She made a mental list of Fern's new house rules. This morning, as she was lightly hopping down the stairs, Fern told her it sounded like a herd of mustangs were galloping on a concrete floor and that there would be no more running in the house. That, M.K. counted, would be Rule Number 436, right behind Rule Number 435: Do not sneeze indoors. She sighed, deeply aggrieved.

Every school morning, M.K. waited at the crossroads to meet up with her friends, Ethan and Ruthie. Ethan was only nine, but he was brilliant—nearly as smart as M.K. but not quite—so she was willing to overlook his youth. Ruthie was already twelve, kind and loyal, though she had a squeamish digestion that didn't tolerate anything too far out of the ordinary. Still, Ruthie was willing to hold a grudge against Jimmy Fisher for throwing a black racer snake into the girls' outhouse while M.K. was attending to business. Acts of such devotion had earned her a spot in M.K.'s heart.

Jimmy Fisher was a thirteen-year-old blight on humanity, a boy born with his nose in the air. Unfortunately, Jimmy wasn't bad looking. He was a tall blond, the tallest in seventh grade. Every girl kept one eye peeled on him. They looked at him all day long. It made M.K. disgusted and was added to her growing list: Why Jimmy Fisher Should Be Stuffed into a Rocket Ship and Sent to the Moon.

That particular list was started when M.K. was only five. Jimmy Fisher, then seven, played a trick on her. He tucked a walkie-talkie under his dog's collar and told M.K. that he had a talking dog. M.K. believed him and carried on long conversations with the dog during lunch until Sadie found out and blew the whistle on Jimmy. Too late! Jimmy and his friends called M.K. Little Gullie—short for little gullible—from that point on. M.K. wasn't a girl prone to letting go of her grudges. And Jimmy Fisher topped the list of permanent grudges.

M.K. sat on the split rail of the fence, swinging her legs, when she spotted a horse and buggy coming toward her. She shaded her eyes from the morning sun and recognized the horse as belonging to the Smuckers. With any luck, Gideon Smucker would be driving the buggy to town. M.K. jumped off the fence and smoothed her skirts, then waved at Gideon. He pulled over to the side of the road.

"Hey there, M.K.! Need a ride to school?"

Drat! There was nothing she would rather do than arrive at school in Gideon's buggy. She'd love to see the look on Jimmy's face then! But she couldn't disappoint Ethan and Ruthie. "Thanks, but I'm waiting for some friends."

"How's everyone at Windmill Farm?" Gideon asked.

M.K. looked up into his face. He was sixteen or seventeen, tops, with freckled cheeks and a shock of red hair that flopped down on his forehead. Propped on his nose were spectacles that gave him, M.K. thought, a very learned look. Julia said he looked like he was peering at life through the bottom of two Coke bottles. Sadie, more kindly, thought he wore the look of an owlish scholar.

Sadie was the one he was really asking after, in Gideon's roundabout, acutely girl-shy way. He was frightened to death of girls his own age. M.K. thought it was a serious flaw in an otherwise perfect young man. Gideon adjusted his spectacles, acting nonchalant as he waited for M.K.'s answers.

"Everyone's fine. Just fine." She was being mean, but she enjoyed watching his ears turn bright red.

Gideon looked up at a crow cawing in a tree. "How's your father's heart? Improving?"

"Oh . . . about the same."

"And Menno? How's he doing?"

"You know Menno. He's always fine."

Gideon scratched his forehead. "And Julia?"

"She's . . . well . . ." What could she say? She was worried about her sister. Julia didn't complain or speak ill of Paul; she seemed distracted, preoccupied, sad. How could Paul treat her sister like that? Julia might be a little pushy and demanding, a tad overbearing, maybe a little vain . . . but she was also loving and kind and beautiful. She'd practically raised M.K. "Fair to middlin'."

"Edith Fisher paid us a visit yesterday. She told my mother that Paul canceled the wedding. Any idea why?"

"Paul's a dummy. That's why." All of those Fishers were dummies. With all that went on this morning, it nearly slipped her mind that she had a score to settle with Jimmy Fisher. The usual slimy slugs in the lunch pail never fazed him. She cast about for something that would.

Gideon grinned. His smile was dazzling. How could Sadie resist it? "Seems like Julia needs to shake Paul up a little. He doesn't know a good thing once he's got it."

M.K. rolled that remark around in her mind for a moment. Interesting!

"Mary Kate? I asked how Sadie is doing." Gideon was staring at her.

Lost in her thoughts, she hadn't caught what he was saying. She couldn't help but notice his ears had turned fire-engine red. "Oh! Sorry, Gideon. My mind got to wandering. Sadie's fine. Just fine."

"Well, if you don't need a ride, I'll be off then." Gideon made a clucking sound and his horse started off down the road.

M.K. hardly noticed he had left. Without meaning to, he had given her a whopper of an idea. She just might be able to fix two problems at once.

Yesterday, Jimmy had whispered to her that Paul finally came to his senses once he realized that M.K. would be his sister-in-law. When Paul made that discovery, Jimmy said, the wedding to Julia was off. "It would take wild horses to drag a vow out of Paul now."

M.K. thought that feeble remark deserved a response. She didn't know why Julia ever wanted to marry into that Fisher family. And to have Fisher babies! M.K. shuddered.

But Julia loved Paul, and love was a mysterious thing, sickening though it was. M.K. felt any Fisher would make a sorrowful choice for a husband, but she was willing to cook up a plan to help make that happen for her sister. She had a talent for involving herself in other people's business.

An idea took form in M.K.'s mind and a mischievous grin lit her face. At last she had a plan of attack pretty well worked out. Off she darted with wings on her heels to meet Ethan and Ruthie as they rounded the bend on the road. The whole day had brightened.

One thing Julia couldn't deny about Fern—quietly dubbed Stern Fern by M.K.—she was a get-it-done machine. Since her arrival, every closet, cupboard, and corner of Windmill Farm had been scrubbed and polished. Julia wasn't complaining. It was rather pleasant to have a well-run home, even if it did require effort to stay out of Fern's cleaning frenzies. And her cooking! It was *amazing*. This morning, she woke early to find Fern in the kitchen, flipping a tower of blueberry buttermilk pancakes for Menno and M.K.

Late in the morning, Julia came in from the garden to get something to drink. As she poured herself a glass from a container of iced tea, Fern walked into the kitchen and dropped a pile of mail on the counter. "I'd appreciate it if you'd stay out of the refrigerator. Everything's organized the way I like it."

Julia resisted rolling her eyes. "I won't move anything I don't eat." Fern was a monumental pain, but Julia was going to try to be more understanding. Sadie had scolded them all last night after she caught M.K. trying to slip a bullfrog into the refrigerator when Fern was upstairs. "Maybe if we weren't so snippy to her all the time," Sadie had said, "she wouldn't be so snippy herself."

Sadie had a point. They *were* snippy to Fern. Not Menno, but the rest of them were definitely snippy to her, even Uncle Hank. Yesterday, Uncle Hank wandered into the kitchen and Fern told him he smelled a little ripe. And when had he last bathed? Uncle Hank stomped away to his Grossdaadi Haus. Later, though, Julia noticed he had showered and shaved. Fern had moved in and had taken over, with plans to improve them all.

Julia wasn't sure why Fern had come to help them, but she was confident there was some tragic story behind it. For a woman her age—was she fifty? Sixty?—she was quite handsome in a plain way. But she never mentioned a family of her own, no children or husband. Most likely, Julia pondered, her heart had been broken. Remembering the pain of that particular ailment, Julia felt a small wave of empathy for Fern. She took a fresh tack. "Did you grow up in Ohio?"

"Yes." Fern pulled a mixing bowl from the cupboard.

Julia tried again. "Have you always worked as a housekeeper?"

Fern slapped the cupboard door closed. "I don't have time for idle chit-chat. So much to do. Meals to prepare, beds to make, towels to wash. Then I need to get a head start on dinner."

"Someone took my bell," Amos said crossly.

Julia and Fern spun around to face Amos standing by the stairwell. "I took it," Fern said. "Got tired of hearing it ring every five minutes."

"Doesn't that defeat the purpose of a patient having a bell?" He pouted like a child.

Fern put her hands on her hips. "What do you want?"

"I'm hungry. I came down to make myself some lunch."

"I told you I'd make lunch."

"I'm not falling for that again. Yesterday I got a bowl of thin broth."

"And crackers and an apple. Stop being such a baby."

Amos scowled at Fern and turned to go upstairs, muttering halfway up the stairs until his breathing became labored and his coughing started up. Fern followed him.

As Fern's footsteps faded, Julia pondered the changes since she had arrived, just a few days ago. Fern had made herself thoroughly at home in Windmill Farm, rearranging furniture, dusting and sweeping and scrubbing the house as if it was as dirty as a pigsty. But as irritating as Fern was, she was exactly what her father needed. He had been so discouraged by his slow progress that he had stopped doing exercises. Fern would tolerate none of that self-pity. She had made him do his exercises every day since she arrived and ignored his steady complaining. And she was just as bossy with the rest of them—especially so with Uncle Hank and M.K. All but Menno. Him . . . she spoiled. Julia smiled as she heard Fern order Amos to get dressed and take a walk to the road and back.

Fern was a tyrant, a dictator, but not quite the bully she liked to think she was.

4

At the age of fifty, Amos Lapp felt as if he had just acquired a middle-aged mother in the size and shape of Fern Graber and he didn't like it. But then he didn't like much of anything or anyone these days, especially himself. He wanted all of this heart nonsense to go away.

Fern had just brought him a cup of coffee and it was decaf! He wanted real coffee. He waited until he heard the door shut to Fern's bedroom, then tiptoed downstairs. By the time Amos made it to the bottom step, he was wheezing. A year ago at this time, he was plowing fields and planting corn, sunup to sundown. Virtually overnight, because of his weak heart, he had turned into an old man.

Last summer, Amos was out in the barn on a warm afternoon, when he suddenly had trouble with shortness of breath and funny palpitations in his heart, as if his heart were a bubble ready to burst. At first he thought it was just indigestion from Sadie's dinner. The next thing he knew he was lying on his side on the barn floor. Menno came in, found him, and an ambulance was called.

His next memory was being in the Coronary Care Unit with oxygen lines in his nose, an IV in his arm, and hooked up to beeping monitors. Dr. Highland—a man who looked younger than Menno—came to visit him on rounds. He was the same cardiologist who had taken care of him in the emergency room.

"I guess this was serious?" Amos asked.

"Pretty darn serious," the doctor replied. He explained that Amos had suffered a major heart attack—something called idiopathic cardiomyopathy, a disease of the heart muscle.

Dr. Highland couldn't explain why it had happened. Amos wasn't in the high-risk category. He had never smoked, never used nonprescription drugs, was trim and fit from a lifetime of vigorous farming work.

After a series of tests, the cardiologist ended up implanting a mechanical device to assist Amos's heart, and put him on so many pills that he needed a chart to keep track of them all. Over the next few months, Amos's rebellious heart settled down, but during winter, his heart had weakened to the point of being in heart failure. He would become short of breath and fatigued when walking up stairs, taking a shower, or performing the simplest of chores. And always coughing. He couldn't take a full breath without coughing.

The doctor recommended retirement—the thought of which horrified Amos. He always wanted to drop in the harness. Then the doctor brought up the notion of a heart transplant. That stunned him too. His response was immediate and strong—no heart transplant for him. He wasn't afraid to die.

Funny, now that he looked back on that time, he had never felt any fear. His faith had stead him well, and he knew, with as much certainty as anyone this side of heaven can know, that this life was but a hint of things to come.

No, he had no fear of death. It was the thought of leaving his children behind that grieved him.

Amos listened carefully for a moment before tiptoeing into the kitchen. He didn't want to alert Fern that he was on the prowl for coffee. That would be cause for panic. First, Fern's. Then, his, when she started scolding him like he was a five-year-old.

The doctor told him panic was bad for his heart; stress of any kind could take a toll on him.

Amos felt as if he couldn't trust his heart—that it had become as fragile as spun sugar. And he was so tired. Most days, he stayed inside, in his bedroom or at his desk, bored to tears but too weary to do much about it. Some days, he didn't even get dressed.

When Amos reached the kitchen, he went straight to the coffeepot where he knew the real thing was brewing. He could smell it. The real stuff had a strong, genuine aroma—not like that pale liquid Fern tried to foist on him. He grabbed a coffee mug and frowned at the sight of his hands. Thin wrist bones protruded out of his pajama sleeves like knobs on the kitchen cupboards. And his fingers were trembling in a way that reminded him of his grandfather.

As Amos poured the coffee into the mug, he heard the plod of hooves and wheels of a wagon pull into the long drive. He peered out the kitchen window and the tightness in his chest alleviated a bit. The Bee Man was here. Amos was so happy that he wanted to shout to everyone, *Wake up! The Bee Man is here!* On the dawn of this spring morning. Instead, he remained quiet. It wasn't good to get too excited, the doctor had said. He closed his eyes and recited Psalm 23. It was amazing the way the words came to him. After the episode with his heart, Amos had found solace in memorizing Scripture. The ancient words were like a balm, a salve. They eased Amos's weary soul.

The Bee Man looked exactly the same as he led his mule and wagon slowly up the drive and came to rest at the top of the hill. Amos would know him anywhere: that bushy head of salt and pepper hair on a young, smiling face. In the wagon were beehives, carefully protected inside of solid wooden boxes. The hum of the bees sang in the wind through the open kitchen window. Amos set the coffee down and went out to greet the young man.

"So," Amos said, pleased. "So, Roman Troyer, you and your bees, you're back. A sure sign that spring is here." He pumped the Bee Man's hand. "Good thing too. Overnight, the cherry trees blossomed out."

"Good morning to you, Amos Lapp," Rome said. "We're a little behind schedule this spring. Everyone wants my bees in their bloomin' orchards, all at once. We're plumb wrung out."

An amused look came into Amos's eyes. "I suspect the bees are a little more overworked than you might be."

"I think they would agree," Rome said, not at all offended. Rome was impossible to offend. Not that Amos would even try. He was fond of Rome, mystery man that he was. Everyone loved Roman Troyer and nobody really knew him. He was vague about where he had been, even more vague about where he was going. He and his bees traveled the country farm roads, somehow appearing right when the farmers needed him, on the dawn of a new day. He traveled at night when the bees were quiet. And he carted his bees away when the job of pollination was done. Rome wasn't typical for the Amish, who were connected to each other through intricate byways of cousinage that linked just about everyone with everyone else. But Amish Roman Troyer was, through and through.

"I happened to see Menno a few days ago. He's gotten tall. If I'm not mistaken, he's got some whiskers on his upper lip. Have you noticed?"

"I've been ignoring it." Amos clasped his hands behind his back. "So, my friend, how have your travels been this winter? Seen many changes?"

"Too many. Villages have become towns. Towns have become cities. The roads are squirming with traffic." Rome grinned. "Not easy to navigate a mule and wagon loaded with bees." He leaned against the wagon. "And you, Amos? How was your winter?"

"It was fine," Amos said. A pale, unenthusiastic answer, but it was all he could muster.

"Looks like your spring planting is a little behind."

Amos stiffened. "Got a late start."

Rome tilted his head in genuine concern. "I might have heard a thing or two about your ol' ticker giving you some trouble."

Amos waved his worries away. "You know the saying, 'Treat a rumor like a check. Never endorse it until you're sure it's genuine.' Don't listen to idle gossip. I'm just fine."

Amos saw Rome's eyes flicker over his clothing. He was in his pajamas. And if that weren't humiliating enough, Fern stepped out on the back porch and lifted an arm in the air. "Who left this on my clean counter?" In her hand was a coffee mug. She spied Amos and stared him down.

"Blast!" Amos muttered. "If my heart doesn't kill me . . . that woman surely will." He blew out a stream of air. "She's our new housekeeper."

Rome laughed. "Just point me toward the orchard where you want these bees, Amos."

Amos put a hand to his forehead. "The thing is, Rome, money is a little tight this summer."

Rome gazed around the farm. "Whenever you can pay is good enough for me."

"It's just that . . . ," Amos started, "with this drought going into its third year, I'm counting on those orchards. We need as much fruit as we can get out of them."

"I understand, Amos."

"I was thinking that maybe this next winter, you could leave your bees at Windmill Farm and we'll look after them. While you're off adventuring."

Rome thrust his hand out toward Amos. "Sounds like a deal."

Amos shook Rome's hand and stood a little taller, relieved. "Well then . . . cherries are in full bloom. And apricot and peach buds are swelling." He pointed to the north, beyond the cornfields with their small shoots of green. Amos sighed. The corn planting was over a month late. And what could he do about that? Julia, Sadie, and Menno had done what they could and finally, a few neighbors pitched in to help finish it up. *If only Menno were able—*

He stopped himself, midsentence, and shook that thought off. *What kind of thinking is that, Amos Lapp?* The Lord God knew what he was doing when he made Menno. A wave of deep weariness rolled over Amos. A nap sounded pretty good about now. He gave Rome a pat on the shoulder and slowly walked toward the house.

"Amos, before you go . . ."

Amos turned around.

"Have you heard about this brown bear?"

"The one with the cub? I've heard she's been poking around, looking for food."

"The carcass of Ira Smucker's old dog was found last night. Looked like it was mauled by something."

"Old Pete?" Amos looked disturbed. "Something got old Pete? Aw, that's a shame. He was a fine dog."

"You haven't seen any sign of bears in your orchards?"

"No, but . . . I haven't been out there too much this spring." He turned to head to the house.

"Uh, Amos?"

Amos stopped and swiveled around again.

"Amos . . . you might have heard a thing or two about me . . ."

Ah, so that's why the Bee Man seemed to be stalling. He walked back to Rome. "In fact, I did."

"Is Julia mad at me?"

"Frying like bacon."

"I didn't really mean to talk Paul into canceling the wedding. We just got to talking and one thing led to another—"

"I know, I know. You never do mean it, Rome, but you're starting to get a reputation. Some folks are calling you 'The Unmatchmaker.'"

Rome paled. "Paul and a few other fellows asked me what I liked about being unattached. On the move. About visiting places. That's all." He looked miserable. "And then I said that I sure did admire those fellas for knowing, at such young ages, that they had found the one woman they were going to spend the rest of their lives with. The one woman they would grow old with. Day in and day out, year after year, decade after decade. I told them I admired their commitment and resolve."

"Did you happen to stress the 'day in and day out' part?"

"I might have." Rome blew out a puff of air. "You must admit, Amos, that it is impressive. These boys are only twenty or twenty-one."

Amos felt his spirits lighten, talking to this young man. "Rome, I'm a man who believes that things have a way of working out the way they're meant to be." He patted Rome on his shoulder. "But I daresay you've always had a knack for getting Julia's dander up."

"Who's that with you, Amos?" Fern's voice shot through the air like a cannon from the window above the kitchen sink. "What's he got on that cart?"

Amos looked up at her. "It's the Bee Man. Those are beehives."

Out of the window came, "Beekeepers make a lot of money for doing nothing."

"Pretty much," Rome said agreeably.

"And just where does he think he's putting those hives?"

"Out in the orchards, Fern," Amos said in a longsuffering voice.

"Looks like he hasn't eaten a good meal in a fortnight."

Amos looked at Rome and raised his eyebrows, pleased. "I think that qualifies as an invitation." He turned back to Fern at the kitchen window. "Set another place at the table for supper tonight."

Rome waved off the invitation. "I don't want to cause you any trouble."

"I'm plenty accustomed to trouble around this place." She closed the window.

Amos turned back to Rome. "Don't pay Fern any mind," he whispered.

She opened the window. "I heard that, Amos Lapp!"

Amos ignored her. *That woman could hear a feather fall to the floor!* "You come on up to the house when you hear the dinner bell clang. I might not be up to our usual game of chess after dinner, but at least you'll see the family."

Rome wasn't listening. His eyes were fixed on the kitchen window. "What did you say your housekeeper's name was?"

"Fern Graber. From Ohio. Hank found her. She's only been with us a few days." Amos let out a deep sigh. "Feels like months."

Rome stilled, and an odd look came over his face. Amos noticed, and wondered what he had said to make the Bee Man look uncomfortable, but he had used up all his energy for now. He had to go lie down. "See you tonight, Rome."

Rome climbed back on the wagon and picked up the reins. When he looked up, Fern Graber was standing in front of his mule. "I'm not going near the back end with all those bees."

He glanced at the hives in the wagon. "They won't hurt you. Still too cold this morning. They won't be active for another hour, when the sun is on the hives."

She looked as if she didn't quite believe him, so he stepped down from the wagon and walked over to her. He crossed his arms against his chest. "So, Fern. How did you find me?"

"Wasn't easy."

"Maybe because I wasn't asking to be found."

"Gehscht weit fatt, hoscht weit heem." *Go far from home and you will have a long way back.*

He exchanged a long look with her. "Es is graad so weit hie wie her." *It's just as far going as coming.* He climbed back up on the wagon. "I'd better get those bees out to the orchards." He slapped the rein on the mule's rump and gave a curt nod to Fern as he passed. He tried to look dispassionate as he drove on, but the truth was, seeing her disturbed him. This was why he left Ohio in the first place. He didn't want any tethers to his past. Why couldn't she have just let him be?

Then his attention turned to Amos. The appearance of his friend added to his troubles. Amos's skin was the color of frostbite, tainted gray, even though it was nearly May. He looked positively wrung out. Yet, still, when he peered into his friend's weary face, Rome saw echoes of the lighthearted, carefree, and generous man he had once been. Rome wanted Amos to look the way he used to look, when he first met him, brimming with confidence, eager for another year of farming.

For the last six springs, Rome would wind his way to Windmill Farm to find Amos out in the fields, hanging on to a plow behind a gentle draft horse, or examining his green corn shoots for any signs of pests. Or playing games with his children—Amos was famous for his sense of fun. But maybe this winter had taken a toll on Amos. Maybe his heart was worse off than Rome had heard. Amos looked hopelessly burdened.

As Rome's wagon traveled along the path that led to the cherry orchard, he surveyed the weed-choked fields. It stunned him to see how quickly the farm had fallen into disarray. Chickens scratched in the dirt beneath an old maple in the front yard. Next to the barn, Amos's red windmill turned listlessly in the early morning breeze. Rome shielded his eyes and saw that a blade had broken. It seemed that nature was trying to reclaim the land. As he drove along the road, he passed Amos's north orchards. Some parts looked so jungly that you needed a machete to chop your way through. Only the well-fed horses and sheep in the pasture looked prosperous.

Every spring, Rome looked forward to his visits to Windmill Farm. It had always been one of the prettiest farms he'd come across in his travels. The house sat at the top of a gently sloping bit of lawn shaded here and there with maple trees. The house itself was a graceful rambling structure built of creamy white siding and a fieldstone foundation. Twin chimneys rose from the roof, and a galloping-horse weather vane turned lazily in the breeze. Bird feeders and birdhouses were everywhere. And he meant everywhere! From sophisticated purple martin houses on long poles to hollowed-out gourds and pinecones smeared with peanut butter, hanging off trees. It was all Menno's doings.

Off to one side, a windmill—red!—an expansive barn, and a white fence surrounding a pasture where livestock grazed. Since he had first arrived in Stoney Ridge with his bees, years ago, that red windmill spinning its wheels at the top of the ridge was like a beacon to him. And a metaphor. What kind of a Plain farmer—other than Amos Lapp—had a red windmill? But

Amos was like that—he had a love of life that was infectious. And Rome had grown fond of the entire family—irascible M.K., kindhearted Sadie, prim Julia, earnest Menno.

As he passed the vegetable garden, he smiled. Now *this* was the Windmill Farm he remembered. The garden was neatly tended; flowers bookending tidy rows of young vegetables. There was a sense of peace here, of order and tranquility. It looked the way Windmill Farm should look—could look—if Amos were well. This garden . . . it had always been Julia's domain, her pride and joy. It looked like a quilt top.

And then he saw her, bent over, at the far end. Up so early! She didn't seem to hear the thud of hooves and the jangle of the mule's harness. He could have just hurried the mule along and vanished into the orchards, but he had to face Julia, sooner or later. This seemed to be the chosen morning for facing hard things; now was as good a time as any other. He stopped the mule and tied it to a hitch post. He watched her for a few moments, bracing himself for . . . for what? He doubted Julia would outright yell at him. More likely, she would be frosty. Well, he could handle frosty.

He put his straw hat back on, fitting it snugly. Then he hopped over a few rows of spring onions to catch up with her. "Hello, Julia."

She popped up from leaning over a row of asparagus, slicing spears at ground level and laying them gently into a basket. She looked at him for a moment, deciding something. "I suppose it wouldn't be spring without the Bee Man." She put the basket down and crossed a few rows until she reached him. She came up so close to him that he could see little sweat beads on her upper lip. She wiped the sweat away with the back of her hand. "Hello, Rome. Looks as if life is agreeing with you."

He felt more than a little surprised at Julia's calm demeanor. He wasn't quite sure what to expect, but he didn't expect calm. He wouldn't have blamed her if she threw some asparagus spears at him. It was a rotten thing he had done, even if it was accidental. "No complaints. Did you win any prizes for your quilts this winter?"

She stiffened and looked very uncomfortable. "I don't have time to do much quilting anymore."

Rome was puzzled. Why was that such a bad thing to ask? Last summer, Julia's quilt had been auctioned away in a fundraiser for a clinic benefit. That one quilt raised three times as much money as any other quilt auctioned off that day. Folks talked about it for weeks afterward. He had figured quilting was a safe topic, but her face had a tight look on it, like she had just tasted something bitter. Rome decided to try a fresh tack. "I just saw your father."

"Really? Was he outside?"

Rome nodded. Julia's face brightened with that piece of news, which told Rome that Amos must not be getting outside much. That explained the neglected condition of the farm. "That's good. He has been a little . . . under the weather this winter."

"So I heard."

Julia lifted her palms. "But of course. The Bee Man knows all."

The silence between them lengthened. Rome braced himself. Here it was . . . he was in the eye of the storm and he hadn't even realized it. "Julia, I didn't set out to talk Paul out of the wedding."

She took her time answering. "Again. You forgot to add the word 'again.' You didn't mean to try to talk Paul out of the wedding *again*."

"It just happened. One minute we were talking about how well his hens were laying eggs this spring, the next minute we were talking about—"

"About thinking of marriage as a ball and chain. About a man taking time to enjoy his freedom. About seeing the ocean. And traveling. "

Rome winced and rubbed his chin. "That's . . . about right."

"Well, once again, you have influenced Paul to postpone the wedding."

"Julia," he started tentatively, "it wasn't like that—"

She put up a hand to stop him. "Rome, I think I understand something about this situation. Something about you. It suddenly became so clear. Two springtimes in a row, you arrive in Stoney Ridge, you hear whispers about my engagement to Paul—and you convince him to postpone the wedding."

"That's what I'm trying to explain." He pushed his hat off of his forehead, uncovering a hank of thick salt and pepper hair. "I didn't set out to change his mind—"

"I realized why you're so intent on making sure I don't marry Paul." She looked away, a faint blush on her cheeks. "I hope you don't mind if I speak plain."

Rome nodded, curious. "Please do."

She glanced down at her hands and paused for several long moments, as if collecting her thoughts or her wits or both. When she finally looked up, her eyes were simmering with emotion, but he could not tell if she was deeply embarrassed by what she was about to say or if she simply found it uncomfortable to share it. What could be so hard to say?

Her dark-fringed eyes were cast down modestly. "I realized that you might be . . . sweet . . . on me yourself."

Rome choked on the piece of peppermint gum that had been lurking in the corner of his mouth. Julia ended up pounding him on the back. Unfortunately, she pounded like she was hammering a stubborn nail, and he was sure he felt a rib crack. Maybe two. When he got his breath back, he coughed out a weak, "Pardon?"

Emboldened, she looked him straight in the eyes. "It makes perfect sense. After all, I'm the only girl in this town who is immune to your charms. Maybe the only girl in Pennsylvania. I certainly understand why that would be . . . a . . . challenge . . . to you." Her cheeks flamed a deeper pink, reminding him of the blush on the yellow apples just before harvesting.

"But—" He felt dizzy. Part of it might have been his busted ribs, but most of it was trying to get his mind to make the connection between Julia Lapp—Amos's eldest girl—and this bold young woman who stood before him.

"I should have realized it sooner. I mean . . . I'm aware that you've always been attracted to me."

"Wait. What?"

"But my heart is set on Paul. I suppose if I were in your shoes, I'd be feeling a little . . . threatened myself."

"Attraction?" Was that his voice? It sounded squeaky. He cleared his throat. "Threatened?"

"Thank you, Rome, for letting me clear the air on this sticky situation."

Rome was speechless. "Julia, there might be some kind of misunderstanding . . ."

She gave him a pitiful smile. "Trust me, I know it can hurt to be rebuffed. But I felt I had to be truthful with you." She patted him on the arm like a child. "You'll be fine. Really." She brushed past him, cap strings dancing as she jumped a row to reach the spiky asparagus.

Rome stood there for a moment, thoroughly flummoxed. What just happened? Although the words coming out of her mouth seemed ridiculously . . . naïve. Absurd! He was shocked by her forwardness. So bold! So audacious. After all, Julia was four or five years his junior. A child, really. Still, there was a willful tilt to her chin that surprised Rome. She was a woman and a girl at the same time. He looked at her in a new way, as if he had seen her for the first time. His mouth lifted with the beginnings of a new smile.

How had he never noticed? She was darling.

5

Sadie had been working indoors most of the day, ironing for Fern. Before dinner, she wanted to sneak off to see the cherry orchards in bloom. She walked between the long rows of cherry trees and finally sat down in the middle, under her favorite tree, and lay on her back to look up at the sky through the pale pink blossoms. If she squinted her eyes, it seemed as if the blossoms were like a lace tablecloth that covered the cerulean sky. She drew in a long breath, inhaling the woody scent laced with a subtle fragrance of sweet cherry flowers.

For just a moment, she could pretend that everything was fine, that her father was getting better, that Fern would return to Ohio, that life could go back to the way it was. And that Sadie would find something she was good at. Was everybody born knowing what they were good at? She wasn't good at anything, not really. Julia could do everything well. Menno had a way with animals. M.K. was smart as a whip. Sadie was . . . what? Polite? Even-tempered? A friend to all? *Boring.*

She saw Julia cross from the garden to the house. Julia had chestnut-brown hair, smooth and shiny as a satin curtain, and a twinkly smile. Her body was tall and slim and perfect. Best of all, most important, Julia could talk to anybody, parents or boys, and everything that came out of her mouth—the words and the sound of the words—was always just right. It was hard to believe that she and Julia were related. She was flat where Julia was curvy, large where Julia was small. Usually when Sadie got upset about her appearance—which even her own sisters described only as "nice"—she reminded herself to be grateful for her good features: a pair of very nice blue eyes, thick lashes, and a peaches-and-cream complexion—give or take a few zillion freckles.

She knew she shouldn't feel jealous of her sister. Her mind drifted to a proverb Julia would tell her when she was in a funk: "Compare and despair." Or had she said, "Despair and compare?" It was difficult to remember these things when there were so many proverbs jostling in her head, eager to spout advice. Was meh as zwee wisse, is ken Geheimnis. *Three are too many to keep a secret.* Wammer Dags es Licht brennt, muss mer nachts im Dunkle hocke. *Burn the candle by day and you'll sit in the dark at night.* . . . so on and so on and so on. All of these sayings were undoubtedly true and just as easy to dismiss—until the moment you found yourself doing the very thing that the proverb warned you against.

She heard someone call her name and she popped up. *The Bee Man!* She didn't know that he had arrived in Stoney Ridge. Her heartbeat kicked to double time. He'd still had the same effect on her that he'd had since she was nine. And now Roman Troyer was less than eight feet away from her. *Eight feet!*

"How are you, Sadie?"

Roman Troyer walked right up to her and offered her his hand to help her stand. The Bee Man was talking to her! She scrambled to her feet. She wheezed for air, choked, and started to cough. He waited patiently. Her eyes began to tear. She pressed her fingers to her throat, trying to clear the air passage. No words came out of her mouth. Seconds ticked by. Sadie had to say something. Anything! But she couldn't adjust to having the man she'd had a crush on since she was nine years old stand in front of her.

Finally, somehow, Sadie managed to squeeze out a wheezy, "H-hello."

"I've brought my bees," Rome said. He pointed to a towering stack of wooden beehives, humming with life, situated in the center of the orchards. "Found just the right spot for them. There's a water trough nearby, and they'll get full sunlight in the morning. The sooner the hives warm up in the morning sun, the sooner they'll get to work." He wiped the sweat off his forehead. "What are you doing out here?"

Her eyes went wide. Her mind reviewed several witty responses, but in the end she could only seem to spit out, "I . . . I don't know."

"You don't know?" Rome looked at her as if she might be somewhat addle brained.

She took a deep breath. "I'd better go." She ran down the long corridor of blossoming cherry trees that led to the barn, mortified.

Although Julia considered herself a mild-tempered person, quick to make allowances and slow to anger, she felt indignation rise within her when she heard that her father had invited the Bee Man to stay for dinner.

Earlier this morning, it had taken every ounce of grit and determination Julia could muster to try to act nonchalant when the Bee Man found her among the asparagus spears. The *nerve* of that man. How dare he act as if he was apologetic about Paul's decision to postpone the wedding. Everything seemed to be progressing so nicely, right on schedule—and then along came Roman Troyer, with his buzzing bees and his silver tongue and that way he had of convincing a fellow that his life of freedom and independence was the best possible life. He may not have meant to instigate the breaking of her heart, but intention was irrelevant. Once a heart was broken, the words "I didn't mean to" afforded little relief.

And now she had to see Rome again for dinner, thanks to her father. Amos had a fondness for the wandering Bee Man, as did so many girls in their church. Julia had never understood what made people go to such great lengths to befriend Rome. Mothers washed and mended his clothing like he was a long-lost son. Fathers invited him home for dinners to meet their eligible daughters. Julia was always amused at how eagerly her friends gazed at Rome, making fools of themselves. Young boys followed him around and picked up his swagger, imitating the way he wore his hat slightly tilted over his forehead. Close to looking like a cowboy hat but not enough to draw the attention of the ministers.

That was the way with Rome. He stayed safely within the Amish framework but lived a solitary life. And rather than raise controversy, folks tried to think of ways to please him, to entice him to stay. Julia saw that on the first day, six years ago, when Amos found Rome camped out at Blue Lake Pond.

As Rome was with her in the garden this morning, she had tried to study him objectively. His was a handsome face, with its thin blade of a nose and strong cheekbones, and a wide mouth that held a certain wild charm. And his eyes—the color of a cup of Fern's rich coffee. His hair was the same hue as a winter storm, and it curled a little over the back of his collar. But none of that mattered to Julia. What bothered her about Rome—what had always bothered her about him—was how he kept himself detached from others, uninvolved, unencumbered. Julia thought the only things Roman Troyer might truly love were his bees.

Last summer, when Rome first influenced Paul to postpone the wedding, Julia's feelings about Rome turned from mild disdain to downright dislike. To her way of thinking, Rome Troyer was a blight on the landscape, a pox on their district. And still, people welcomed him with open arms.

Well, she was not going to let Roman Troyer get to her. Nor would she let him distract her from her objective—convincing Paul to keep the wedding date. She was sure that once she and Paul married, all of those silly doubts of his would disappear. She wasn't quite sure how to make that happen, but one thing her father had always said, "First the vision, then the plan."

When Julia heard Fern clang the dinner bell that hung by the kitchen door, she closed the roadside stand for the evening. She walked up to the kitchen, carrying the vegetables and early cherries that hadn't sold, plus the honor jar, in a woven basket. Rome was coming in from the orchards and met her halfway along the drive. He took the basket out of her hands. "Looks like you didn't have too many customers."

She shrugged. "It's early in the season." She picked up her pace.

Rome kept her pace. "What would you think if I sold some honey at the stand while I'm here? I've started making beeswax candles too."

She didn't respond.

"I was thinking, maybe I'd give you ten percent. You know, for the trouble of selling them."

If anyone else had offered her this, she would have readily agreed, just to be kind. But there was something about Rome's manner that made her act as stiff as Fern. As starchy and prickly as a boiled shirt. "60/40," she said curtly.

He stared at her for a long moment, then opened his mouth to speak. Shut it. Opened it again. She watched the muscles in his throat work as he swallowed. He was obviously surprised. She could almost read his thoughts: He thought she would be grateful to receive a ten percent cut. He thought he was doing her a favor. "Once folks hear you're selling my sweet honey, they'll come from miles around. Why, they'll be lined up, all the way to town!"

"Excellent point." She started up the hill. "50/50. That's my final offer." Why, she was even sounding like Stern Fern.

"Highway robbery," he muttered. "Fine." Rome hurried to catch up. "Julia, I am sorry. About Paul. Maybe I could talk to him. Get him to change his mind."

She stopped abruptly. "Roman, you give startlingly bad advice. Why would I ever want *you* to try and convince Paul to keep our wedding date?"

He seemed a little puzzled. "Maybe I could talk to Edith Fisher. You know, sweet-talk her a little. So she isn't quite as standoffish toward you."

Julia looked at him as if a cat had spoken. "No. I do not want you to talk to anyone about me." She spoke in a tone as if she were addressing a very young, very dense child.

M.K. came flying down the drive with Menno right behind her. She ran behind Julia as Menno tried to grab her. "M.K., what did you do to Menno?" Julia asked.

"I didn't do anything!" M.K. said.

Menno pointed at her. "She threw a water balloon at me!" His shirt was soaked.

"No, I didn't!" M.K. peered into the basket in Rome's arms. "Dibs on the leftover cherries."

"You can't just call dibs, Mary Kate," Menno scolded. He looked woefully at Rome. "She puts dibs on everything."

Something at the house caught Rome's eye. "Look up there, Menno. There's your water balloon culprit."

Their gaze turned to the Grossdaadi Haus, an apartment-style house above the buggy shop. Uncle Hank was leaning over the windowsill with a red water balloon in his hand, the size of a softball, aiming directly for Fern as she hung some dish towels on the clothesline.

"Uncle Hank! No!" Julia shouted. "Don't do it!"

Too late. The small red water balloon hurled through the air, splattering on the lawn after barely missing Fern's head. She didn't miss a beat. She finished clipping the wet dish towel to the line and crossed the line to head to the house.

"Well, well," Rome said. "Good to see Hank is still the same."

Julia sighed. "He's the biggest child in the neighborhood."

And then, because Uncle Hank wouldn't be satisfied with just one balloon, he wound up his arm to toss another at Fern. Again, it missed and splattered at her feet. She stopped, looked at his window, and calmly said, "You, Hank Lapp, have terrible aim." She walked up the porch stairs to the kitchen, cucumber calm.

Julia thought Uncle Hank seemed a little disappointed that he didn't get a more flustered reaction out of Fern.

Menno cupped his hands around his mouth. "Uncle Hank, you shouldn't do things like that to Fern. She's not used to us yet. And she's trying to help us."

Fern spun around on the porch and pointed to Menno. "No wonder that boy is the pick of the litter. He's the only Lapp male with a lick of sense."

"She's right," Menno said earnestly. "Uncle Hank gets in as much trouble as M.K."

"Hey!" M.K. said, arms on her hips, a little general.

"I heard that, young Menno! Try and catch this!" Uncle Hank tossed a balloon in Menno's direction, but at the last second, Rome pushed Menno out of the way. Unfortunately, Julia was behind Menno. The balloon hit Julia right in her midsection and burst, showering her with cold water. After the initial shock wore off, she seared Rome with her gaze.

A cackling sound like dry leaves floated down from the porch. It was Fern, laughing.

The family went ahead with supper as Julia went upstairs to change into dry clothes. She hadn't said a word after getting hit by the balloon; she just glared at Rome as if he had engineered the entire incident.

Rome had been thinking about Julia a lot today, maybe because he felt more than a twinge of responsibility for Paul Fisher's decision to back out of the wedding. But he was also thinking about Julia because it baffled him that she didn't seem at all interested in impressing him. It was odd being with a woman who wasn't interested in him. Odd and appealing. Oddly appealing.

When she came into the kitchen, she avoided any eye contact with Rome;

he was invisible to her. The only time she even acknowledged his presence was when M.K. mentioned that she had heard at school today that two more courtships had been broken and that the bishop considered there to be an epidemic of broken promises among the young people.

"Bet my last dollar we're going to be getting a sermon on it next week," M.K. said glumly.

Rome squirmed uncomfortably at M.K.'s remark—those same two fellows had been standing with Paul Fisher the other day when he had that infamous conversation about getting married.

"In Ohio, young people keep their courting business to themselves," Fern said.

"It's supposed to be that way here too," M.K. said, "but everybody knows, anyway."

"What has happened to courtships?" Fern asked, shaking her head.

"Ask Roman Troyer, why don't you?" Julia said in a rather schoolmarmish way as she joined them at the table.

All eyes turned to Rome. He occupied himself with buttering his bread.

"Maybe there's a good reason for a man to change his mind," Amos said quietly.

"Dad!" Julia looked horrified. "You're defending him?" She meant Rome.

This evening wasn't going well. Rome suddenly wished he were anywhere but at the Lapps' dinner table.

"I'm only saying . . . ," Amos started, "that sometimes a man just has to do what he thinks is right. Even if he might be wishing things were different." He looked at Rome. "Isn't that true?"

Rome had no idea what Amos was getting at. Did Amos think Rome was sweet on Julia too? He hoped not. Julia Lapp was an intriguing girl, and she was pretty great to look at, but he wasn't the settling down type. Not by a long shot.

Fern had served Amos a special plate of food—low sodium, she said, and jumped up if he needed anything, as if she was afraid he might keel over. Just how sick was Amos? Rome would have to find out more, though since Julia wasn't exactly talking to him, he wasn't sure whom he could squeeze that information out of. He glanced at Sadie, sitting across from him, wondering if she might know more, but he doubted it. Sadie was looking down at her plate, a little stunned. She had filled her plate to overflowing, a double helping of mashed potatoes and four pieces of chicken. Fern snatched it away from her and set in its place a plate with one skinless, boiled chicken breast, and two sprigs of broccoli—even less substantial than Amos's plate.

Menno noticed too. "Why isn't Sadie eating what we're eating? Does she have a bum heart too?'

"No," Fern said. "She's got an overfed problem."

Sadie's head jerked up.

Julia straightened, stiff as a poker. "Fern, Sadie is fourteen years old. She should be allowed to make her own decisions."

"Almost fifteen," Sadie said, casting a sideways glance at Rome.

"She already has a substantial figure," Fern said flatly.

"She's big-boned, is all!" Julia said.

"Bones don't jiggle," Fern said.

"Now, Fern," Amos said, poking at his plate and frowning. "This isn't exactly a meal to get excited over." He looked longingly at Menno's plate, loaded with fried chicken next to a cloud of mashed potatoes with a pat of butter melting in the center. "I thought I smelled fried chicken. I only came downstairs because I thought I smelled fried chicken."

"You did," Fern said. "Just not for you. You're on a low-to-no-sodium diet. And you're supposed to lose weight so that your heart doesn't have to work as hard. I've been reading up."

"I haven't had a good fried chicken in years," Amos said, releasing a martyred sigh.

"That's not the point, Dad," Julia said. "Sadie shouldn't be told what she can and can't eat."

Rome glanced at Sadie to see how she liked being talked about in the third person. Sadie's mouth was a tight little pucker, and her freckled nose twitched like a rabbit.

"That was our agreement," Fern said firmly. "If I cook for all of you, you eat what I give you. Especially that one." She pointed at Sadie. "She's as plump in the middle as a Christmas turkey."

"She has a friendly softness!" Julia said.

"I am right here," Sadie reminded them.

"Actually," Rome said, "I need to shed a few pounds myself. I'll join you in eating light, Sadie." He picked up the broccoli bowl and helped himself to a few sprigs. Sadie looked at him adoringly.

Julia's gaze shifted from Sadie to Rome. He couldn't quite tell what she was thinking. "Fine. I'll join Sadie too." She put back a roll into the breadbasket.

"Not me," M.K. said, reaching out to grab the roll. "Dibs on the rest of the mashed potatoes."

"You can't just call dibs on everything, Mary Kate," Menno scolded. "Can she, Dad?"

Everyone looked to Amos for an answer, but he didn't have one. He looked suddenly spent, as if he had used up all of his energy.

Fern hopped up. "Maybe that's enough excitement for one day."

As she helped him upstairs, Rome heard Amos mutter, "You treat me like I'm an invalid."

Fern snorted. "You're not exactly plowing up fields by moonlight."

"You're no spring chicken yourself."

Their voices, engaged in gentle sparring, drifted into silence. Something about it felt strangely familiar, comforting to Rome. As they walked away, a wisp of memory tugged at him . . . His mother bringing his father soup in bed one day when he was sick with laryngitis, and his father trying to squeak out a thank-you in such a way that they all laughed and laughed.

Had it really happened, or was it something he'd dreamed?

As soon as Fern was out of sight, Julia jumped up from the table and disappeared without offering up an excuse. As Rome was dumping milk into his coffee, he saw Julia drive off in a buggy as if she was heading to a fire. Rome thought it might not be a bad idea to say his goodbyes before Fern came back downstairs. He wasn't particularly worried that Fern would press him with questions while they were in the midst of the Lapp family, but he had no interest in finding himself alone with her. He gulped down the last swig of coffee and stood to leave. As he whirled around to pluck his hat off the wall peg, Fern beat him to it. She stood there, holding his hat out to him. How had she appeared so suddenly? This day was getting stranger and stranger.

"Seems like you and Amos know each other pretty well," she said.

"I'd say so," Rome said.

She folded her arms across her chest. "Where are you holing up while your bees are doing their business?"

"Oh, here and there," he said.

"He's very mysterious," M.K. whispered to Fern. "That's why Julia calls him Roamin' Roman."

Fern rolled her eyes. "Mystery, schmystery. A man who roams is looking for something."

"I do all right," Rome said, a little peeved. He wondered what Fern had up her sleeves. She seemed to have settled quickly into her place in the Lapp household, wanted or not. Good. As long as she was preoccupied with them, maybe she would leave him alone.

Fern rubbed her chin, thinking for a long while. Then she jumped into action. "You three," pointing to Menno, M.K., and Sadie. "We've got work to do." She turned to Rome and pointed a long finger at him. "You. Meet us back here in two hours. Before sundown. Don't be late."

During dinner, Julia decided that Rome was right about one thing: Someone should talk to Paul. Someone like Julia's best friend Lizzie. Lizzie knew Paul pretty well; she might be able to help sort things out between them. As she drove the buggy down the drive, she saw a stranger standing by the roadside stand, a young lady. She looked up at Julia. It was Annie—the granddaughter of a neighboring Swartzentruber farmer M.K. had dubbed "gnudle Woola," *curly wool*, making fun of his long hair and untrimmed beard. Julia hadn't seen Annie since last summer. Then, she was a gangly girl, as slender as a willow reed, as dainty as china. Now, she was a young woman, with generous curves. Pretty too.

Julia pulled the wagon to a stop. "Can I help you, Annie?"

"Menno told me about Lulu's puppies. He told me to come and see them sometime, so that's why I'm here."

"When did you see Menno?"

Annie's face turned crimson red. She shrugged. "He might have stopped by once or twice." She spoke in a small, breathy voice. "Menno's been very nice to me."

Menno? When would he have stopped by Annie's farm? "You might be able to find him up at the house. The puppies are in the barn, in an empty horse stall. I'm sure Menno wouldn't mind if you wanted to look at them."

Annie started walking up to the house.

A spike of concern rose in Julia. She had to force herself to speak calmly, naturally. "Annie . . . you know that Menno is a special child, don't you?"

Annie tucked a loose curl behind her ear. "I know he's special." She spun around and kept walking, hips curving as she walked.

Julia felt time slowing down a bit, all her senses growing more alert. Menno wouldn't be sweet on a girl, would he? The thought of Menno getting involved with someone never even occurred to Julia. He'd always been so childlike to her; she thought he always would. Things were so different these days she could hardly understand them.

She wished she could have a conversation with her father about this, let him do the worrying, but then she thought twice about it. The last thing she wanted to give him was something else to fret over.

The horse nickered and Julia turned her thoughts back to her errand. She flicked the reins and the horse lurched the buggy forward before settling into a smooth rhythm. She was eager to talk to Lizzie. She was sure Lizzie would agree with Julia that the blame for Paul's reluctance could be pinned directly on Roman Troyer. It took everything she had to be polite at dinner. She tried to remember if Lizzie had been one of Rome's adoring fans. So many girls were. Even her own sister. Sadie stared at Rome during dinner as if he held the moon in his hands. Julia wanted to scold Sadie, to kick her in the shins, to warn her it was the same smile he gave everyone. Rome Troyer might not be hideous looking, but he was effortlessly charming, far too confident—he thought he was something. At least she was glad that would be the last dinner she'd have to share with Rome Troyer this year.

As she turned onto Rose Hill Farm, she saw that Lizzie already had a visitor. A familiar horse and buggy rested at the top of the drive. It was Paul's buggy and sorrel mare.

She stopped the horse, heart pounding, then turned the buggy around and left.

Sadie and M.K. hurried to gather a list of things Fern wrote down: buckets, brooms, mops, Clorox, ammonia, and rags. Fern told Menno to harness his pony to the cart, and the girls piled everything on the cart. Then Fern added more things: towels, sheets and pillows, a blanket or two, and rag rugs.

"What do you have on your mind, Fern?" Sadie asked, but Fern wouldn't answer.

She led them out to a small cottage on the far edge of the property. It had been the original house. Amos's great-grandfather had been born in it. Later, his grandfather built the large farmhouse closer to the hilltop because he liked the view. Amos added the red windmill.

Fern took an old key from her apron and jimmied the door open. She walked in, swatting cobwebs. The others tentatively followed. Fern walked around, examining the cottage.

Fern told Menno to get the supplies out of the pony cart and bring them in. The four of them spent the next two hours sweeping out dirt and more than a few dead mice, dusting, scrubbing, washing windows. She sent Menno back up to the house for more supplies, including a bed frame and mattress from the attic.

When they were done, Fern looked it all over, gave a satisfied nod of her head. "It'll do just fine."

"I'm just not sure Roman Troyer is going to want to live here," Sadie said. "He likes being known as the wandering type. What's this going to do to his reputation?"

"His reputation will just have to survive," Fern said decidedly.

At seven o'clock, Rome walked in from the orchards, washed up at the hose spigot, and was suddenly interrupted by Fern.

"Come with us," she said. Ordered was a better word. And how did she always seem to appear out of thin air?

M.K. ran out the kitchen door and leaped off the porch, landing by Rome's feet. She was nearly beside herself with excitement.

"Don't you tell, Mary Kate," Menno warned as he joined them.

"I won't!" M.K. shook her head, dimples flashing.

M.K. grabbed Rome's hand and pulled him along, down past the fields and through a wooded area. She chattered like a magpie the entire way, pointing out bats and lightning bugs and owls. Sadie was on his other side, quiet, looking so pleased she might burst with happiness. Fern and Menno brought up the end.

When they reached the top of a hill, M.K. couldn't contain herself any longer. "Look, Rome." Then, more impatiently, "Look!" She pointed down the path. He almost missed it. A small, weathered cottage, made out of clapboard.

Pine needles dusted the shingled roof and four spindly candlestick posts held up the rickety porch. The once-white paint had grayed and the shutters had faded to a dull green. It was really old-fashioned, with firewood stacked on the porch. The fireplace was the house's best feature; it was made of stacked fieldstone. The windows glowed with yellow lantern light.

M.K. ran to the porch and stood by the door. Rome saw that there was no knob on the door, just a string latch arrangement.

"Hurry, hurry, hurry," she said. "Open it!"

He eased up the latch, and the door swung open. They walked into the living area, which had bare wooden floors and two windows. The main room had little furniture: an overstuffed sofa topped with a quilt, a painted three-drawer chest, and a table holding a kerosene lamp. A potbellied stove sat in a corner. Rome peeked into the bedroom. There was a charming bed with a curlicue iron headboard covered in chipped white paint.

"Fern thought the kitchen could be the room for your honey equipment, since it's got a door to the outside," M.K. said. "There's good sunlight and the linoleum floor can be easily washed."

"In case it gets sticky, Fern told us," Menno said.

Rome looked around the kitchen. A table and two chairs. A shelf with some cans of food. Pegs on the wall, and a blue coffeepot on the stove. He walked from room to room, first once, then twice.

Finally, M.K. couldn't stand it any longer. "Will you stay? Oh Rome, will you stay?" Her small face was shining with excitement.

He gave a nod; he didn't trust his voice.

"Fine, then," Fern said. "Everyone, clear out and let the man have some peace and quiet." Before she left, she added in her dictatorial way, "You'll take your evening meals with us."

Rome stood out on the front porch, watching the four of them head up the path until they reached the top and disappeared down the other side. It was so quiet.

His heart hammered.

This was home. "Dibs," he said softly.

6

Six years ago, Roman Troyer was almost twenty, a typical Amish farm boy. Born and raised in Holmes County, Ohio, where his father owned a sixty-acre dairy. The farm had originally belonged to Rome's grandfather, then his father, and Rome grew up understanding it would one day be his. He was his father's only son, the eldest, with four younger sisters. Rome's mother was the beekeeper in the family. She had several hives of brown bees that she nurtured and protected. Folks drove long distances to stock up on her sweet clover honey. It was the best, the very best.

Two months before Rome turned twenty, his family hired a van and driver to attend the wedding of Rome's uncle, his father's eldest brother, who was finally marrying at the age of fifty-one. His bride was marrying for the first time too, late in life. The two had exchanged letters for over two years before meeting face-to-face and then waited another six months to marry. They were cautious types, his uncle had said. The wedding was a distance, at the bride's house, so Rome volunteered to stay home and take care of the dairy cows. His family and his uncle were on their way to the wedding when a recreational vehicle had skidded on ice and sideswiped the van. They crashed into the guardrail. It wasn't anyone's fault, the highway patrolman explained when he came to tell Rome what had happened. It was wintertime, and the roads were icy. It was just one of those things, he told Rome.

But it wasn't fair how things happened without warning. Rome had woken up that morning to life as usual. Someone's vehicle skidded on ice, a family was wiped out, and his whole reality was changed forever. Rome had lost everyone. He was left orphaned, although that wasn't really a word he wanted to attach to himself. He was, after all, nearly twenty. An adult.

After the funerals, Rome sold off the dairy cows and other livestock at an auction—even his favorite buggy horse. No attachments, not even to a horse. The only things he kept were his mother's beehives. He built a specially designed wagon to hold the beehives, leased the fields to a neighbor, bought a mule to pull the bee wagon, locked the house up tight, and left it all. He ended up in Lancaster County, though it wasn't by design. All that he knew about Lancaster County was that there were plenty of crops needing bees and plenty of Amish, and that no one knew him.

Amos Lapp found him one April day. Rome was camping out by Blue Lake Pond, after an early fishing trip. He had made a small campfire to cook his breakfast. The morning fog hugged the lake's surface. The trees weren't leafed out yet, but blossoms were starting to swell. Out of nowhere, Amos tapped on his shoulder. "You lost?"

Rome jumped up, spilling his coffee into the campfire. "No. No, I'm not."

But the words rang uncertain and Amos cocked his head to one side, taking a step closer, his fishing pole and line dangling at his side. "Those are your beehives?"

"Yes. They are."

Amos sat down beside the campfire.

He watched Rome with a deepening frown, then his eyes rounded upward in a wise, tender curve. "That hair of yours could fool a fellow. You're awfully young."

"I'm not so young," Rome answered, and Amos leaned closer, smiling slightly, as if he were trying to figure him out.

Amos looked at him, looked at the beehives, and said, "Are you and your bees looking for work?"

Rome didn't even think about it. "Yes, we are. I mean, I am."

Amos wrinkled his forehead. "You wouldn't happen to know how to play chess, would you?"

"I do. My father taught me."

Amos nodded. "None of my children have any interest in the game. It's a sore trial to me." He yanked his hat off and ran a hand through his dark hair. "When was your last home-cooked meal?"

Rome looked away. "Awhile back."

And those were the only personal questions Amos had ever asked of Rome. He fit his black felt hat snugly on his head. "Well, come on then." He seemed to trust Rome, intuitively.

Rome followed Amos to Windmill Farm and met his family: fifteen-year-old Julia, eleven-year-old Menno, nine-year-old Sadie, and five-year-old Mary Kate. It was the first time he'd had a chance to look at a mirror too. During those winter months of wandering, his nearly black hair was now peppered with white. It shocked him at first, and then, it suited him. He had been marked. A sign of grieving.

Amos gave Rome his first job in the orchards and quietly spread the word to others about his fine bees. Rome soon found himself booked out for months, traveling from county to county with his bees. Whenever he moved the hives, he had to travel more than five miles away or the bees would get confused and swarm, not returning to the hives. He worked from early March until November, taking his bees from orchards to fields, selling honey from his wagon. In the winter months, for the first few years, he would do construction work or find a temporary job. But the last two years, he asked himself why he was saving so much money when he really had few needs. Instead, he found an Amish farmer who would let him leave his hives on a remote corner of his farm—sheltered from wind—in exchange for honey. A fair exchange!

Rome would wrap the hives with tarpaper to keep them dry. The bees stayed in their hives in the winter months, forming clusters to keep the hives at a steady 99 degrees. As long as they had enough honey and pollen to eat, the bees could overwinter by themselves. Even heavy snowfalls weren't a concern—the snow acted as insulation. As soon as Rome sold off the mule each year, he was free to travel during those coldest months, via Greyhound bus. Once to Florida, to see the ocean. Another time to Washington D.C. to walk through the Smithsonian museums—each day a different one. Another time to Kentucky to the Creation Museum. It was a good life and he was content. He owed much of it to Amos Lapp.

May could be a changeable month in southeastern Pennsylvania. Though it was warm and sunny today, two days ago the temperature flirted in the low forties. Julia crossed from the greenhouse to her garden, carrying a flat of lettuce seedlings. *The Farmer's Almanac* called for rain—even though the sky was bright blue—and she hoped to get these seedlings in the ground, just in case. After two years of drought, she treasured the rain as God's good gift from above and didn't want to waste a single drop.

Suddenly, Roman Troyer was at her side. "Just how sick is your father?"

She stopped abruptly. "Where did you come from?"

Rome pointed vaguely in the direction of the orchards. "What exactly is going on with his heart? I've noticed everyone just talks around it, like a coupla bears dancing 'round a beehive. Last night, Amos moved as slow as I'd ever seen him. He limped out of the kitchen and up the hall. That's not like your father. I'm asking you straight, Julia. How bad is it?"

As she considered how much to tell him, she gazed at the cheery May sunshine and thought what a contrast it provided to this sad topic. "It's not good." She set the flat on the ground, picked up her trowel, bent down on her knees, and started to make holes in the dirt for the seedlings. "He has a condition called idiopathic cardiomyopathy. His heart is damaged. The doctors have tried to see if the condition might reverse itself with some treatments. Sometimes, that can happen."

"Is he getting any better?"

She shook her head and stabbed at the ground. "As the problem gets worse, his heart is growing weaker. His heart has to keep working harder to pump blood through the body, so it tries to make up for this extra work by becoming enlarged. In time, the heart works so hard to pump blood that it simply wears out."

"What then?"

She paused, holding the trowel in midair. "I don't know."

"There's got to be something they can do. He's only fifty!"

"The only cure would be a heart transplant. But Dad won't even consider that."

"Well, what about a transplant list? He should be on it, at least. Maybe he would change his mind."

She shook her head. "Dad won't even consider it."

"Julia, you can do something about this. You need to persuade him to consider a heart transplant."

What Rome didn't know was that she had tried to persuade Amos to at least get his name on the National Transplant List. The doctors had tried. The bishop, ministers, and deacon had tried. He refused. "I can't do that."

"Why not?"

"A number of reasons. First of all, he believes his ailing heart means it's his time to die."

Rome blew out a puff of air. "What else is stopping him?"

She shrugged. "The money."

"You can't be serious. He'd let money stand in the way? The church would help. I know they would."

"They already have. His hospital bills have been astronomical. But it's more than that. He just can't accept the idea that someone would have to die for him to live. He thinks the cost—the sacrifice—is too high."

Rome shook his head. "That isn't right. He must know that person's time was up, anyway. He had nothing to do with that—that's in God's hands."

"That's how he feels about his own illness. It must be his time. He said that it's not such a bad thing, to know and recognize what you're up against."

Rome was quiet for a long moment. "Have you thought about what you're going to do? You'll be left alone to run this farm, raising your sisters and brother. To manage your Uncle Hank. You can forget about marrying someone like Paul Fisher and starting a life of your own."

Julia sat back on her knees and looked around the farm, at the weeds that were overtaking the orchards, at the cockeyed rows of corn that Menno had planted. Before her father became ill, she had thought she knew just what her life would look like: she would marry Paul and they would buy a farm of their own. She would be known as Paul's Julia, rather than crazy Hank's grandniece—and she couldn't deny there was a part of her that longed to be a Fisher, no longer a Lapp. She would move on and start a life of her own.

With her father's illness, that scenario seemed unlikely, if not impossible. It was going to be just like Rome said. She had pondered the notion of talking Paul into moving to Windmill Farm to finish raising M.K. and Sadie. As for Menno, she had no idea what the future would hold. Maybe working with Uncle Hank at the buggy shop? No, that would be a disaster. They would spend all day, every day, fishing or hunting. She would have to find someone else he could work side by side with, someone who could keep him directed on a task. She knew he would never be able to live by himself.

Rome cleared his throat and she realized her thoughts had drifted away from the topic of the heart transplant. He looked at her, expecting an answer to his questions. Had she thought about what she was going to do? Had she realized she would be left alone? Her dad worried her mind the whole day. Did Rome really think she hadn't thought all these things through?

She stood and walked a ways out into the side yard. The house and fields were set on a clearing at a high point; below it were other farms. She pointed to a white farmhouse, tucked against a hill, with a willow-lined stream that wove in front of it like a ribbon. "There's Beacon Hollow. My mother grew up there. Now her brother lives there." She pointed to another house, far in the distance. "That's Rose Hill Farm. My friend Lizzie lives there with her parents. Last winter, we had a work frolic and finished off the Grossdaadi Haus for Lizzie's grandparents, Jonah and Lainey, to move into because Jonah needed to live in a one-story house—he has a bad back." She pointed in the other direction. "If you look hard, you can see the glare of the sun off of a big pond. My cousin Mattie and her husband Sol live on that farm. You couldn't get better neighbors than Mattie and Sol." She turned back to him. "That's the difference between you and me, Rome. I'm not alone. My future may not be what I thought it was going to be, but I'm not alone." She tucked a loose strand of hair inside of her bandanna. "Besides, maybe Dad will get better. Maybe this new treatment will work." She looked at Rome and read his mind. She knew he didn't think that was very likely. Her father was weaker each week.

"The children don't know how serious this is, do they?"

"No. There's no need. Not now." She looked at him. "And I'd appreciate it if you wouldn't say anything."

"I won't. You can count on it. But I hope you won't mind if I try to talk Amos into considering a transplant. I've known a few folks—Plain folks—who have had kidney transplants. One with a heart transplant."

"Feel free. But I thought you were moving on soon."

He lifted his dark eyebrows. "Oh—didn't you hear? Fern set me up in the cottage."

Julia had returned home to an empty house last night and went straight to bed. "Here? That spooky old cottage near that stand of pine? But it's . . . so run down."

"Fern and Menno and Sadie and M.K.—they spiffed it up after dinner."

"So you aren't . . . moving on?"

"I'll be sticking around," he said, smiling broadly. "Just for the summer. In exchange for some work around the farm."

Julia felt as if she'd swallowed a chicken bone.

On an overcast Saturday morning, M.K. tagged along with Fern on an errand in town. Fern took her time at the hardware store, looking for a list of supplies Amos had given her. M.K. wandered off with a promise to return in thirty minutes. She walked down to the farmer's market that set up in front of the Sweet Tooth bakery for a few hours every Saturday morning. She heard someone yell her name loudly, and turned to see Paul Fisher waving to her. He was selling fresh eggs at his family's booth and motioned to her to come over.

"Want to earn some spending money, Mary Kate?"

"I'm always open to making money," she said.

"I need someone to man the booth for a spell while I run home and get more eggs. It's busier this morning than I thought it would be."

Mary Kate was just about to say "Sure!" when Jimmy returned to the booth, chomping on a green apple. He glared at her as he chewed and she squinted her eyes back at him.

"I'll go back to the house for the eggs, Paul," Jimmy said between bites. "We wouldn't want Little Gullie to miss her afternoon nap."

Jimmy! So obnoxious! M.K. fought the urge to throw an egg right at his belly. Instead, she spun around and stalked off. She made her way through the stalls, looking at the fruits and vegetables that sat on the vendor's tables. Carrots, spinach, lettuce, peas, cherries, a few peaches. None looked as good as what came out of Julia's garden.

She stopped to watch a small dog performing tricks for dog biscuits. A man wearing a panama hat stood next to her for a while, laughing along with her at the dog's somersaults. M.K. noticed the hat because Ruthie's older brother was old enough to run around, and he wore a panama hat every Saturday night when he went into town. It made his mother crazy. After the performance, the owner picked up the dog's leash and walked around the crowd with him. "Shake hands with the puppy for a dollar." In his hand was a jar to hold the money. The owner brought the dog to M.K. The dog sat in front of her and held out his paw for a shake.

M.K.'s felt her cheeks flush. "I'm sorry. I don't have any money."

The man in the panama hat handed her a dollar. "Go ahead. That pup wants to shake your hand."

She looked up at the man. He had a kind face and warm brown eyes that reminded her of her father. She stuffed the dollar in the jar and bent down to shake the dog's paw.

When she stood up to thank him, the man in the panama hat was gone.

While Fern was in town with M.K., Sadie was at work in the kitchen, hot and airless as it was on that May afternoon. She missed cooking. No, that wasn't true. She liked Fern's food and was happy not to have to clean up the kitchen afterward. But she did miss feeling needed. And she missed the feeling of being connected to her mother that she felt whenever she was working with her mother's recipes. If Sadie closed her eyes, she could still see her mother cooking in the kitchen, bustling around, humming slightly off-key. Maggie Lapp was always humming.

Fern Graber didn't hum.

A few days ago, Sadie had watched Fern make snickerdoodles to take over to a comfort knotting and she decided to try to make a batch. She found the recipe in Fern's recipe box and set to work, mixing butter and sugar, eggs and flour. She dusted the mounds of dough with cinnamon, just the way Fern had done, and put them in the oven. As she waited for the cookies to bake, she planned to clean the dishes and dry them, putting them away so Fern wouldn't suspect anything. But then she got distracted with the contents of Fern's recipe box.

Just as she pulled the last cookie sheet out of the oven, Menno came into the kitchen. He hopped up to sit on the counter, just like he used to, before Fern had arrived, to keep company with Sadie as she cooked. And to sample the offerings.

"These are good, Sadie," he said after his third cookie.

"Menno, do you think about Mom very much?"

He grabbed another cookie. "I think about her every day." He swallowed a bite. "Before I get out of bed in the morning, I ask God to tell Mom hello for me if he happens to see her walking by in heaven that day."

Sadie smiled at her brother. His simple faith was so pure, so complete. Sometimes, she thought he lived with one foot on Earth and the other in heaven.

But thoughts of eternity were forgotten in the next moment. A buggy came to a stop by the kitchen door, and Sadie saw Fern hop out, sniff the air, and clutch her purchases to her chest. "Someone's been cooking in my kitchen!"

Sadie gasped. She hadn't expected Fern back for a while longer. Every workspace in the kitchen lay covered with cookie sheets and cooking utensils. Egg yolk ran down the front of a cabinet door. The sink was stacked with a motley assortment of bowls and dirty dishes. Fern's recipes were spread out all over the kitchen table. Two hours ago, this room was spotless. How had it become such a mess? She had tried to be so careful!

"Uh-oh," Menno said. He pocketed three more cookies and dashed up-stairs.

Whenever M.K. could slip away from Fern's watchful eyes, she would find Rome and pester him to let her help him with the bees. Beekeeping fascinated her. She wanted to learn everything she could about bees. Rome wouldn't let her out near the stacked supers—the portion of the hives where the honey was stored—in the orchards, despite her begging. She promised to bundle up in protective clothing, like he did, but he refused. "I know my bees," he told her. "I know when they're angry or feeling threatened. I know when they smell a predator in the orchard. I know when they're calm and getting ready to swarm. I don't want you getting stung."

"Have you ever been stung?"

Rome laughed. "More times than I can count. The truth is, beekeepers want to get stung a few times each year. We build up antibodies so the stinging isn't serious."

"Well, then, I think you should let me go out to the supers with you and bring back the frames. I can handle a few stings."

But he was adamant. She was to stay away from those hives—at least twenty feet away. He did finally relent to teach her how to extract honey from the frames back in the cottage kitchen. He showed her how to warm up the uncapping knife in a dish of steaming hot water, then slice the caps open by running the knife down along the honeycombs. Then the frame would be put into the extractor, hand cranked, to spin out the honey. First one direction, then the other, to empty each side of the comb. M.K. loved watching the honey sling out at the sides of the extractor and drip down to the bottom, ooze out the honey gate, into a waiting bucket. Then Rome would filter the honey with cheesecloth before pouring it into clean jars.

"What makes bees want to swarm?" she asked Rome.

"Lots of reasons," Rome said. "In springtime, beekeepers keep a close eye on their colonies. They watch for the appearance of queen cells. That's usually the sign that the colony is determined to swarm. It's not a bad thing to swarm. It can be healthy for the colony to split the hives. And before leaving the old hive, the worker bees fill their stomachs with honey in preparation for the creation of new honeycombs in a new home. That's one of the ways I can tell that they're ready to swarm. They're so gentle that I don't even need gloves or a veil. All that's on their mind is a new shelter."

She opened her mouth to say that maybe she should help him get the frames out of the hives while the bees are ready to swarm, when they were gentle and quiet, but he read her mind and gave her a warning. "You are not to go near those hives. Understand?"

She sighed. "But how do the bees know it's time to swarm?"

"Nature's pretty smart. The bees might be feeling like the hive is getting too crowded. Time for a change. Time to move on."

M.K.'s head bolted up so fast that her capstrings danced. "That's like you, Rome. Maybe you're a beekeeper because you think like a bee."

He grinned. "You might have something there. Though there is such a thing as a solitary bee. It lives on its own, not in a colony."

"So you're a solitary bee." She rolled that over for a moment. "Fern says you can't just go taking your bees from place to place forever."

"She does, does she? Well, you can tell her I've got lots of time left."

"Not really. You're practically elderly. After all, you've got gray hair."

He laughed out loud at that.

Why was that so funny? M.K. would never understand boys.

7

The next week slipped by quickly. One afternoon Sadie sat on the back porch step by the kitchen door with a large bowl of green beans. She was snapping the ends off of them as Rome came up the steps. "Hello there, Sadie."

She froze.

"What are you up to?"

"I'm napping sbeans. Beaning snaps." She shook her head. "I'm snapping beans." She felt her face flush beet red.

An awkward moment of silence followed, before Rome said, "If you don't mind moving just a little, I was planning to go inside to ask your father a question about the orchards."

Mortified, Sadie jumped up to get out of his way. The bowl went flying, spilling beans everywhere. Julia stepped out of the kitchen as Rome tried to help Sadie pick up the beans. "Go on in, Rome. Dad's inside at his desk. I'll help Sadie with the beans."

Sadie waited until Rome disappeared, then slumped down on the top step. "Did you hear that brilliant conversation?"

"Some of it."

"I'm an idiot."

Julia sat down next to her. "Don't worry. He's used to it. He's handsome and he knows it."

"You've pegged him all wrong, Julia. He's not just handsome. Why, he's . . . he's fundamentally good. I just know it." She thumped her fist on her chest. "Deep down."

"Sadie, Rome is more than a dozen years older than you!"

"True love knows no age." She snapped the ends off of a bean and tossed it in the bowl. "I just wish I could say two words that actually make sense when I'm near him."

M.K. came outside and sat on a step, leaning against the porch railing to face her sisters. "Most girls get tongue-tied around Rome Troyer. Not me, of course, but then again I'm not prone to getting the vapors like most girls do when they get around good-looking men."

Sadie threw a snap bean at M.K., and she grabbed it midair and put it between her lips, pretending it was a cigarette.

"Mary Kate, were you ever a child?" Julia said in an exasperated tone, yanking the snap bean from her mouth.

"Just for a year or so," M.K. said. "So . . . our Roman Troyer is really only twenty-five? I figured him to be Dad's age, with that gray head of hair."

"Fifty?" Julia laughed. "Hardly! His hair just turned gray prematurely."

"I love his hair," Sadie said dreamily. "So thick and crisp. And those bold, dark eyebrows."

"He needs a haircut. His hair is curling over his collar," Julia said, clearly annoyed. "And he's not *our* Roman Troyer. He's not *anybody's* Roman Troyer. I never knew anyone so determined to hold himself apart from other people. He uses his charm to isolate himself. It's like he's afraid if he starts caring too much about anybody, he'll lose something."

"But knowing how old he is does change the picture a little," M.K. said thoughtfully. "He sure has nice features. And I like that cleft in his chin."

"He has wonderful features!" Sadie said. "That straight, confident nose. And don't you wonder why he has that small scar in his eyebrow? Even his teeth are beautiful—so strong and square and white."

Julia rolled her eyes. "Listen to the two of you. Mooning over the Bee Man."

"You can't deny he is unbearably handsome, Julia," Sadie said.

"It's a fact, Jules." M.K. reached for another snap bean out of Sadie's bowl. "Why are you so hard on him?"

"Julia has taken a strong dislike to Rome," Sadie explained to M.K. "On account of his influence over Paul and the other boys."

"That's not the only reason!" Julia said. "Rome represents everything

I don't like in a man—he swoops into town and goes through girls like potato chips. Why, look at how he's encouraged our Sadie to fall in love with him—"

"He hasn't needed to encourage me, Jules," Sadie said solemnly. "He's been a perfect gentleman to me."

"—and then he swoops out of town . . . heading to who-knows-where and leaving all of those broken hearts to mend. Roman Troyer is as slippery as a fish. Impossible to grasp. He is living a thoroughly self-indulgent life." Julia crossed her arms against her chest.

Uh-oh, Julia's climbing up on her high horse. Here comes the lecture. Sadie exchanged a brace-yourself look with M.K. Julia had a tendency to think she knew everything, even if she didn't.

"He has no responsibilities to anyone. He never mentions any family, he avoids any and all attachments to others . . . why, he doesn't even have a dog! Just that mule and those bees—they work for him and they don't have any opinions. They're the perfect partners for Rome."

"Bees can have strong opinions," M.K. said. "I know that from personal experience."

"Besides, Paul Fisher manages to avoid attachments too," Sadie said quietly.

"That's not true!" Julia said. "Paul is very loyal to his family."

"Especially his mother's feelings about not wanting to be related to Uncle Hank, you mean," Sadie said.

"Can you blame her?" Julia said.

"I like Uncle Hank," M.K. said. "He keeps life around here interesting."

"You can say that again," Julia muttered.

"It's a mystery to me why you'd want to marry into that Fisher tribe, anyway," M.K. said. "They're standoffish and have their nose in the air. They think they're too good for us Lapps. Edith Fisher isn't just against Uncle Hank, Jules. She's against you too. She says you're not up to scratch as a daughter-in-law. Jimmy told me so."

Julia looked as if she had just been slapped. Sadie's heart went out to her. How could M.K. have repeated such a thing?

Julia straightened her back. "I'm going out to the greenhouse."

Sadie and M.K. watched her go. Sadie gave M.K. a look.

M.K. raised her palms. "What? I'm just speaking the truth! Dad's always telling us to speak the truth."

Rome opened up the squeaky kitchen door. "It might depend, M.K., on whose truth it belongs to." He tapped her gently on the top of her bandanna and went back into the house.

Sadie scrambled mentally backward, wondering how much Rome had heard. She turned to M.K. "Think he heard everything? Even the part where Julia was saying why she didn't like him?"

"I think so."

"And the part where we were talking about how handsome he was?"

"Probably."

"Even about his white and straight teeth?"

M.K. nodded. Then she brightened. "We were just speaking the truth!"

Sadie handed M.K. the snap beans to finish. *Mortified.* She was positively mortified.

Rome went back inside and found Amos at his desk in the living room. "The cherries are in full bloom, just like you said. The peaches are going to be blossoming out in a week or two, and plum and apricot buds are starting to swell. I'm concerned about the weeds in the orchards, though. Too many dandelions blooming. The bees will forage the pollen from the dandelions instead of those trees. It's the pears I'm most worried about. You know that pears need more bees than other fruit flowers."

"Why's that?" Fern said. She brought in two cups of coffee and handed one to Rome.

"Thank you, Fern." Rome looked her right in the eyes. He still wasn't sure how she ended up at Windmill Farm, but she wasn't pestering him with questions or demands to return to Ohio the way he thought she might. He felt a grudging respect grow for her. Maybe it was true—that she just wanted to check up on him. If so, check away! He had nothing to hide, because he had nothing. "Pear flowers produce only a small amount of nectar, which is low in sugar."

Amos looked troubled. "I thought I told Menno to keep the orchards mowed."

"He needs directing," Fern said. "He can't think of those things on his own, especially when he's distracted by those pups." She turned to Rome. "I'll be sure he gets out there today."

It was strange and yet comforting to Rome to see how Fern fussed over each member of the Lapp family. In a short period, she seemed to have a sense of each person's strengths and weaknesses. How had she done it so quickly? "The hives are out there, so Menno needs to wear light-colored clothing," Rome told her. "Both shirt and pants. If he doesn't have light-colored pants, he can borrow a pair of mine. Bees are soothed by lighter colors." He turned back to Amos. "I don't want Sadie or M.K. out in those orchards for a while. While bees are getting accustomed to a new area, that's when they're most dangerous."

"Fern tells me you're staying out at the old cottage. That's good news. Until I'm back on my feet, I'm grateful for every pair of extra hands."

"I'm staying at the cottage for that very reason, Amos. To see if I could help. Can I help?"

Amos nodded. "I won't refuse you."

"Better not," Fern added. "Alle Bissel helft, wie die alt Fraa gsaat hot, wie sie in der See gschpaut hot." *Every little helps, as the old woman said when she spat in the sea.*

Amos heaved a ponderous sigh. "Geblauder fillt der Bauch net." *Talking won't fill the belly.*

"Oh no! My muffins are in the oven!" Fern sailed to the kitchen.

Rome waited until Fern was out of earshot. "Amos, I thought I saw some bear scat in one of the orchards." When he saw the alarmed look on Amos's face, he waved it off. "Never mind. I might have been mistaken. Don't worry yourself about it."

Rome wasn't mistaken, though. He had seen quite a bit of evidence that a bear and her cub had passed through Windmill Farm. Broken branches, scat, the remains of a small animal. The bees weren't the only reason he wanted the girls to stay out of the orchards. Brown bears were common in Pennsylvania, and under normal conditions, they didn't engage with humans. But these weren't normal conditions. After two years of a severe drought, he knew wild life grew even wilder. Especially when a mother bear was trying to forage for food for her hungry cub. He was worried enough that he decided to use a solar-powered electric bear fence—three strands of wire fenced around the hive, connected to insulated posts. A curious bear would get a shock on its nose and that would be enough to send it packing.

Bears were a beehive's biggest natural enemy. They could devastate a hive—tip it over, tear it apart, chew the comb, carry off parts. It wasn't just the honey they were after—they needed a high protein diet and bee larvae fit the bill.

He heard the creak of Fern's bedroom door and thought he'd slip out while Fern wasn't in the kitchen. As he left Amos and walked to the kitchen door, Fern cut him off at the door. She handed him a manila envelope, fat with letters. "Here. You've got a decision to make. It's time."

Julia had an idea. If Rome offered to help out this summer, why not take him up on that offer? Regardless of his shortcomings, and there were many, he was an able-bodied male and the price was right: free. She actually felt a small tweak of gratitude for Fern for finding a way to keep Rome beholden to them for the summer by setting him up in the old cottage.

In the greenhouse, she grabbed a pad of paper and a pencil and started writing. She had to hurry. She kept one eye on the house, waiting to catch Rome after he finished talking to her father. When she heard the squeak of the kitchen door, she rushed out of the greenhouse and across the lawn. "Rome!"

He stopped when he saw her running toward him. Lulu, who had been roaming around the yard sniffing for squirrels, bounded over to him, her red ball in her mouth. Rome took the slimy thing and tossed it across the lawn.

When Julia reached him, she drew herself up to her fullest height. Roman Troyer was a tall man and could be intimidating, but she wouldn't let him have the upper hand. "I always think it's better to clear up things right from the beginning, don't you agree?"

He looked amused. "We're clear enough for now."

"I have a list." She thrust the list out in front of him. It was three pages long, filled with undone work to do around Windmill Farm. Fences to mend, hay to be cut, leaky barn roof to be patched, a window to be replaced. She hadn't even finished the list, but it was a start.

Rome studied the list intently, page after page. "Fine. I'll have to squeeze the tasks around my bees, but I'll get to them."

She eyed him suspiciously. "There's more. I didn't finish."

"Fine." He waited patiently.

"I'd like all of those jobs done before you disappear . . . wherever it is you disappear."

"Fine."

That was it? Just . . . fine? She felt a little disappointed. She expected him to be taken aback, to start making noises about the need to move on. "Well, then, you'd better get started." She brushed past him to return to the greenhouse. She wanted to add more things to the list. *This list will never end!* she decided with a catlike smile. One way or another, the Bee Man would move on.

Rome watched Julia march back to the greenhouse. Despite her order-giving, he found himself intrigued by her. As she pushed the list—three pages long!—into his face, her little chin shot up, her shoulder levered back, and those full lips set in a stubborn line. He pretended to study the list just so he wouldn't laugh at her feigned boldness. Then she pushed past him, nearly knocking him over as she swept by, and his amusement changed to fascination.

At that moment, Rome's enthrallment with Julia Lapp was official. *Boom!* A blow to the heart. She had a way about her that riled him right down to his toes.

This bee season might just turn out to be more fun than he'd had in a long time.

At his cottage, Rome sat at the kitchen table with the manila envelope. He tore the first postmarked envelope open, dated over a year ago, and read the letter.

Dear Mr. Troyer,

We haven't met, but I would like to make you an offer to buy your farm in Fredericksburg, Ohio. I'm prepared to offer you $5,000 per acre—as is. No improvements necessary. A simple, clean transaction.

Roman (may I call you Roman?), I hope you'll accept my offer. I think you'll agree it's a pretty good deal. You can contact me at P.O. Box 489 in Fredericksburg.

Waiting to hear,
R.W.

Then Rome read the next letter, and the next. They were all the same. The only change was that the purchase price kept going up. An offer to buy the farm out from under Rome's feet? For twice the going price for land? From a mystery man named R.W. Outrageous! Insulting.

Intriguing.

It was a few weeks later and Julia's first tomatoes—grown in the greenhouse—were ready for picking. She had a way with tomatoes, which she trained way up high on stakes. They were big monster beefsteaks, big as a softball. You could make a meal out of them.

One night Fern said, "Mary Kate, skin up the road to Annie's house and give her this box of tomatoes."

"I'd rather not," M.K. said. "Annie's grandfather is mean. And it's getting dark. Too scary. I'll get lost and eaten by that bear that's prowling around."

"You could scare off any bear," Fern said, holding out the box to M.K.

"That's not true. Edith Fisher said she's sure she's heard that brown bear and her cub prowling around her hatchery, helping itself to a hen or two. More than twice! She said she doesn't go anywhere without a shotgun. It's true too. I've seen it with my own eyes. She walks around everywhere with it in the crook of her arm."

"That is ridiculous," Fern said.

"I'll keep an eye on her," Menno said, grinning ear to ear.

M.K. found a Kerr quart jar and punched holes in the lid. "For lightning bugs," she told Menno. "In case we need to see our way home." She waved the jar in front of her. "I call it an Amish flashlight."

Menno rolled that over a few times before letting out a "Haw!"

M.K. had only been to Annie's house once or twice before. It was the sorriest excuse for a farmhouse that she had ever seen. Paint peeling off the tired-looking clapboards. The porch roof sagged on one side. One puff of wind might blow it over. There were no flowers bordering the house. Only the barn looked slightly cared for—painted a dark red color. A dim light shone from one downstairs window. Nobody seemed to be around when they went up on the porch to leave the tomatoes.

"HEY, BOY! WHAT BUSINESS HAVE YOU GOT HERE?" A voice sailed out of a downstairs window.

Every hair on M.K.'s head stood up.

"I SAY WHAT BUSINESS HAVE YOU GOT ON MY PORCH?"

M.K. walked a few feet to see a wispy-haired man with a long scraggly beard peering at her through a grimy windowpane. Annie's grandfather.

"Tomatoes. I mean, TOMATOES!" She held one up for proof and set the box on the floor. "THEY'RE FOR YOU AND ANNIE."

The man turned his glare toward Menno. "I RECOGNIZE YOU. ARE YOU THE SAME BOY WHO THREW EGGS AT MY BUGGY WINDSHIELD?"

"NO. I'M MENNO LAPP. ANNIE'S FRIEND."

M.K. stepped out of the shadows. "The boy who threw eggs at your buggy windshield was Jimmy Fisher. JIMMY FISHER." She assumed her most docile expression, the one that had never fooled Fern but seemed to do the trick with Annie's grandfather.

"M.K.," Menno scolded. "You're telling tales again."

"It's true! Jimmy bragged about it at school."

"Daadi?" Another voice floated out from another window. "Who are you talking to?" It was Annie. When she saw Menno, her face broke out in a big smile, matched only by his own.

Annie invited them in for some peach pie, but M.K. wanted to get home. She couldn't stand another moment of yelling at Annie's grandfather so he could hear. And why did he yell back? She wasn't deaf! Menno wanted to stay, so M.K. ran home as fast as she could. Those bear stories gave her vivid imagination too much fodder to chew on. She was sure she was hearing bears at every turn.

She burst into the farmhouse at Windmill Farm, face flushed and breathing hard, and pounded up the stairs two at a time to reach her father's room. As soon as she could catch her breath, she asked him, "Is Annie's grandfather poor?"

"Poor in worldly goods but rich in faith," Amos said.

"But you said they're Amish."

"They're Swartzentruber Amish. Low people."

"What does that mean?"

"Humble. Humble to a fault, some might say. Ultra-conservative."

"They have outdoor plumbing. And Annie's grandfather was smoking. And Menno said they practice bundling."

Julia walked in the room at that. "He said *that*?"

M.K. nodded. "What's bundling?"

Julia paled. Amos frowned.

8

The most puzzling thing had just happened. Rome had just mailed off a package to a beekeeper in western Pennsylvania who had heard about his strain of brown bees. In the package was a screened box of sweetly humming bees, including a new queen. It was a lengthy process to ship a living thing like a bee, and the postmaster had been very patient with him. She picked up the package and peered at it with a curious look. "Bet this will move along quickly and get where it needs to be." Rome turned to leave, but she called him back. "I'm guessing you're the Bee Man. I got something here that looks like it was sent by pony express." She took the bee package into the back and returned with a letter.

She slid the letter across the counter to him. It was addressed with a now-familiar spidery handwriting to: *The Bee Man, Windmill Farm, Stoney Ridge.*

Dear Roman,

Just imagine—with the money I'm offering you, you could move to Sarasota, Florida. No more cold winters. No more lugging bees from one county to another. My offer stands.

Sincerely,
R.W.

P.S. You can now write to me at the post office in Stoney Ridge, P.O. Box 202.

Who was this R.W.? How did he know Rome was in Stoney Ridge? Rome folded the letter and looked around him. Was R.W. here? Was he watching him, right this minute? Just in case, Rome balled up the letter and tossed it in the garbage can out in front of the post office with a large thud.

Rome pondered the mysterious letters as he drove down Stoneleaf Road, passing by the Fisher farm on his way home. He saw Paul struggling with an overturned wagon filled with hay and pulled the buggy to the side. "Could you use an extra pair of hands?"

Paul gave Rome a sheepish grin. "Got myself into a jam here while I was taking some hay out to feed the cows." He gave a gentle swat to the mule, who was now tied to a fence post. "This gal decided to take too sharp a turn and the wagon didn't seem to agree with her way of thinking."

"I'll help," Rome offered. He tied his own horse to the tree. He picked up one side of the wagon and Paul picked up the other. On the count of three, they heaved and uprighted it. Paul tossed Rome a hayfork and they both started to rake hay back into the wagon.

It didn't take long. When they were finished, Paul placed both hayforks on top of the hay and leaned his back against the wagon. "That's the Lapp buggy, isn't it?" He took a jug of water from the front of the wagon and offered it to Rome.

Rome took a swig of water and wiped his mouth with the back of his hand. He handed the jug back to Paul. "It is. I'm staying in an old cottage on the Lapp farm this summer. Trying to help out when I can. Amos isn't doing too well."

Paul nodded. "So I heard."

Rome took out a handkerchief and wiped sweat off his forehead and neck. "Paul, when I first got here, and we had that talk about getting married, I surely didn't mean to imply you should call off your wedding to Julia."

A look of shame covered Paul's face. "You didn't. I mean—I was already waffling, and you sort of drove the point home."

"What point?"

"About how young we were to make a lifetime decision."

"But Paul—that's not necessarily a bad thing. I was just saying I admired how you could make a choice about one woman at your age."

"See—that's the thing. I haven't really decided on Julia. Not entirely.

In fact, I don't even remember proposing to her. One time the subject of marriage came up—one time—and suddenly, she was talking about a wedding. The whole thing just got carried away!" He blew a puff of air from his mouth. "I was able to slow it down last year, but then she started up again this spring. Talking again about setting a date in November. I kept waking up in the night in a cold sweat. That was when you rolled into town and convinced me to call it off."

Rome rolled his eyes. He didn't try to convince *anybody* to do *anything*. Would he ever live that down? "Are you saying you don't love her?"

Paul rubbed his face. "There's the rub. I do. I do love her. But . . . I'm just not settled that Julia is the one and only for me. Julia . . . she just . . . she's so sure we're meant for each other. She's been that way since we were ten. Don't get me wrong—Julia's a wonderful girl. But she's headstrong and opinionated and bossy . . ."

Odd. Those were the very qualities Rome had been admiring in Julia lately. A person knew where he stood with her. He shrugged. "I guess you know her better than I do."

". . . well, suddenly I feel as if I'm no longer in charge of my life."

Now *that* made Rome want to laugh out loud. With a mother like Edith Fisher, when had Paul *ever* been in charge of his life?

"Here's an example: Julia brings me samples of wedding invitations—she's kept all of her friends' invitations. Doesn't that seem like a crazy thing to do? To save those pieces of paper? Anyway, she asks me which one I like best. I told her they all look alike. *What?* she says. How could I even say such a thing? It was like we weren't looking at the same things!" He shook his head. "Women tend to confuse me."

"How much of this doubting has to do with Lizzie?" Rome had heard a rumor or two about Lizzie and Paul.

Paul's eyes went wide. "But how did you—? When would you have . . ." He sighed, and a look of abject misery covered his face. "Plenty. I think I love Lizzie. I love them both."

Rome was relieved. Julia's fizzled engagement wasn't his fault, after all. "Call me crazy, but I don't think you love either one."

"Of course I do," Paul said. "I definitely love Julia. And with Lizzie—well, Lizzie is special. I love Lizzie. There's no other word for it, although I feel differently about Julia than I do about Lizzie. But they both feel like love." He was obviously torn between the two—marrying one meant giving up the other. "The reason it's a problem is that I don't know what to do."

"If you were going to marry Julia, you would have done it already. But you haven't. And if you were that taken with Lizzie, you would have ended things clean with Julia so you could start courting Lizzie. I stand by my word. You don't love either one."

Paul ran a hand through his hair. "Maybe you're right. Maybe I don't love either of them."

But Rome knew Paul was only agreeing with him to be agreeable. That was the thing about Paul. He was a very likable guy. He didn't make waves. He didn't offend anyone. Sometimes, Rome thought Paul was like . . . that strange block of tofu that Fern served for dinner last night. Flavorless. Instead, he assumed the flavors of the people closest to him.

Paul Fisher just didn't know his own mind.

Amos opened one eye and stared out the window. The sun was just rising above the ridge that surrounded the town like an embrace. Shards of pink light pierced the predawn darkness. It was going to be a glorious day, he thought, sliding out from under a quilt his Maggie had made when they were first married. When had he last noticed a sunrise? Why did it take the threat of dying to truly notice how exquisite a sunrise or sunset could be?

No place on earth was as dear to him as Stoney Ridge. He couldn't imagine living anywhere else. Unlike others—Roman Troyer came to mind—who felt the need to travel, Amos felt no such need. Everything he wanted was already here in this small town he so dearly loved—good friends, caring neighbors, and a land filled with soft rolling hills, gentle streams, and rich soil. Living in Stoney Ridge was one of the many blessings he made sure to thank God for each morning upon rising.

His stomach rumbled again and he glanced at the clock. Breakfast wouldn't be ready for a while, so he decided to risk venturing downstairs, taking care not to alert Fern. Hers was the only downstairs bedroom and she had ears on her like a bat. He stopped for a moment, winded, trying to suppress that blasted cough. As he moved soundlessly past her door—quiet as a church mouse—into the kitchen, the early-morning sunlight flooded the room, infusing the room with a sense of warmth and serenity. He felt his heart leap with praise and thanksgiving. And there was the coffeepot on the stove top, filled, ready to go. *Thank you, Lord, for favors big and small.*

He opened the refrigerator, looking for something delicious to snack on before the family woke up. He spotted a Tupperware bowl, carefully lifted a corner of the lid, and took a sniff. Horrors! It smelled like the compost pile on a hot day. Not much of a chance of his stealing a bite of that or anything else. He hastily patted the lid in place and pushed it aside while yearning for the good old days—chicken potpie, meat loaf, potato salad, cheesecake covered with whipped cream—all of which Fern referred to as "Off Limits to Amos Lapp" food.

That woman had turned into the resident nutritionist.

A few days ago, he had his head in the refrigerator, searching for something worth eating, when Fern caught him red-handed. He thought she was safely off to town on an errand, but no! She had already returned. Her arms were filled with an assortment of cookbooks bearing such titles as *Heart Healthy Food, Eating Your Way to Health,* and *No-Fat Recipes That Taste Great.* Fern dumped them onto the counter with a thud. One slid off and crashed onto the floor on the opposite side, near Amos's feet. *Fat-free Delights.* That one, Amos thought, was an oxymoron.

He found something that looked more like a loaf of birdseed than a loaf of bread, but it was all he could find. He cut two slices and popped them in the toaster. Then he found butter—real butter!—hidden behind a large bottle of V-8 juice. He hoped Fern didn't plan to spring that on him today. Last week it had been prune juice. His digestive tract was still off kilter.

He slathered his toast with enough butter to clog several main arteries, filled his coffee mug, and looked around the kitchen to cover his tracks. All clear. Not even a crumb. He picked up his well-worn Bible from his desk and tiptoed slowly upstairs to his room.

Fern was in a hurry to get some new cookbooks at the library one afternoon and didn't notice as M.K. slipped off toward the magazine and newspaper section. M.K. plopped in a chair and picked up a magazine that boasted a headline: *10 Ways to Get Rich Quick*. She sat down and turned to the article. Someone eased into the chair next to her and she shut the magazine tight and braced herself for a lecture from Stern Fern about the evils of wealth. When the lecture didn't begin, she opened one eye, then the other. It wasn't Fern who had sat down. It was the man in the panama hat!

"Hello," the man said to M.K., smiling broadly. "Have you shook any puppy's paws lately?"

"Not hardly. I still don't have a dollar to spare."

He pointed to the magazine cover. "Are you in need of money?"

"I've got a plan to help someone in my family, but I need to figure out a way to pay for it."

The man in the panama hat rubbed his chin. "I might have an idea for you."

Three days later, the Lapp family was sitting in the kitchen having dinner when Annie stopped by. Julia invited her to join them, so Sadie made a place for her at the table and Fern filled a plate for her. Annie sat in her chair, prettily. Her laugh tinkled like wind chimes. She moved more food around her plate than she ate. The sparkle of her gaze played back and forth over everyone, always ending to linger on Menno.

Julia kept a close eye on Menno's behavior. She noticed that he often rubbed his chin—probably to make the point that he shaved. Normally, he stood quietly at the edge of a conversation. Tonight, when M.K. asked him a question, he pitched his voice way down below his bootlaces. He was too bashful to chance a look at Annie, but he drank in her every word. He was wide-eyed with wonder.

At one point, Annie reached out and touched Menno's wrist. Julia didn't draw a breath until Annie's hand slipped back in her lap. Menno stared at his wrist where her fingers had been. Julia saw it and didn't like it. She noticed how red his cheeks had become. As red as a ripe tomato! Who could miss them? They were on fire.

It was lunchtime at the schoolhouse, and the sun was high in the sky overhead. M.K. waited until the big boys were involved with a softball game and motioned to the girls to follow her behind the girls' outhouse. Mary Kate explained she had a new game to teach them. A secret game.

M.K. placed three small seashells on the top of a sawed-off tree trunk.

Alice Esh, a timid thirteen-year-old who spoke in a whisper, was first in line.

"Cross my palm with silver," M.K. told Alice, holding her hand up.

"What?" Alice whispered.

"Gimme a nickel, Alice," M.K. said.

She put Alice's nickel next to one of her own, and then placed a dried-up pea under one of the shells. "Watch the shell that's got the pea, Alice."

Alice nodded, wide-eyed. M.K. moved the shells around and around until Alice looked cross-eyed. Then M.K. stopped. "Okay. Pick the one with the pea."

Alice pointed to the one in the center. M.K. pulled it off with a flourish. Nothing! Alice, who was naturally pale, went even paler. M.K. covered Alice's nickel with her palm and slipped it into her shoe. "Next!"

Later that same day, M.K. and Menno were in the barn, watching Lulu and her puppies. The door slid open, letting in the feeble light of an overcast afternoon, and in walked Rome. Lulu scampered across the floor and flung herself at Rome, knocking him off balance in her exuberance so he nearly lost his hat.

"She doesn't usually take to strangers," Menno said. "You should feel real good about that."

Rome bent down to scratch Lulu behind the ears. "I do. I surely do." He looked up at Menno. "Fern's looking for you. Said you were supposed to be weeding the peach orchard."

Menno nodded. "I started. But then I thought I'd better check on Lulu." He set off toward the orchard at a leisurely pace.

Rome went over to Amos's tool bench and scanned the wall pegboard. "I'm looking for some tools to get that broke window fixed." Lulu followed behind him and sat by his feet.

M.K. sidled up to him. "I have a favor to ask you."

Rome looked at her, amused. "And what would that be?"

"I need some help." She held out a heavy bag of nickels. "And I'm willing to pay you handsomely for your time."

"What kind of help are you talking about?"

"The romance kind. I need you to make Paul Fisher jealous. Over Julia."

Rome folded his arms across his chest. "Call me crazy, but it sounds like you're meddling. Or getting ready to meddle."

"Not at all!"

"M.K., I'm a believer in letting nature take its course."

"I am too. But sometimes nature needs a little help."

He was silent for a while. Then he picked up a hammer and a wedge. "Just what do you have in mind?"

She jumped up on the workbench. "I'm thinking you take her home in your buggy after Sunday church. So word gets around that Julia has a suitor."

"Is this your idea?"

She nodded, pleased with herself.

"Why me? There must be plenty of fellows who'd be delighted to take your sister home in their buggy."

"There are! Plenty. First, I thought you were too old on account of your hair is gray. But then Julia told me that you aren't so very old at all!"

Rome held back a grin. "There are some who find my gray hair to be distinguished looking."

M.K. shrugged, unimpressed. "So once I started giving you some serious consideration, I decided you were the ideal candidate." She held up two fingers. "Reason number one. You and me, we understand each other."

Rome held back a grin. "You mean, trouble knows trouble."

M.K. waved that off. "I meant we both like to fix problems for folks." She picked up a screwdriver. "That's what you're doing, right now. You saw we needed some help around the farm and you're pitching right in."

"What's reason number two?"

"You are just the fellow to make Paul green with envy. You have a history of being admired by the ladies. You've given a buggy ride to just about every pretty girl in the district . . . maybe two or three districts . . . and if Paul thinks you're finally getting serious about his girl, he'll be in a hurry to marry Julia before she changes her mind and falls in love with someone else."

"Now, you bring up a serious concern. What if Julia falls crazy in love with me? That's a very real danger."

Boys! So unobservant! "Not a chance. She's only got eyes for Paul. And besides . . . you deeply annoy her."

Rome rubbed the back of his neck. He stayed silent for a moment, then said, "So what makes you think she'll go with me on this important buggy ride? That could be uphill work."

"You leave that to me." She hopped off the bench. "Do we have a deal?" She stuck out her hand.

But Rome wasn't quite ready to seal the deal. "I was under the impression that you were not a fan of Paul Fisher."

"Aw, Paul's all right. It's his brother Jimmy that I take a serious objection to."

"What's so bad about Jimmy?"

"What's so bad about Jimmy?!" She started to sputter. She felt her face turn a shade of plum, but she couldn't help it. "Why . . . he's horrible, that's what's so bad about him! He's the kind of fellow you should never *ever* let turn a jump rope because he'll trip you sure as anything. He takes the girls' lunches and throws them high in the trees. Why, it's practically a holiday at school when Jimmy's home sick. It just doesn't happen often enough."

"That does sound like a fellow to avoid." He tried to hold back a grin. "But you'd give Paul a chance to turn the jump rope?"

"I suppose." She shrugged. "Julia says she loves Paul. That's all that matters. So . . . deal?" She stuck out her hand again.

Rome looked at her open palm. "I need to think this over before I agree. And I want you to make one thing absolutely clear. I'm not hiding anything from Julia. No deceit."

Uh-oh. M.K.'s eyebrows shot up. She hadn't expected Rome to be a rule abider. Why, he sounded as straight an arrow as Julia! This created a problem. If Julia found out M.K. had cooked this up, she would be facing a year of extra choring on top of her current never-ending round of chores. "But . . . she doesn't have to know that I'm a part of this, does she?"

"You don't think she could figure that out?"

"Julia doesn't know everything. She just thinks she does."

Rome laughed and shook her hand.

M.K. walked to the barn door and turned back to Rome as she pulled it open. She lifted up the nickel bag. "And there will be a bonus in there for you if Paul sets a wedding date and sticks to it."

"M.K., I have to ask. Are you coming by this money honestly?"

It was a scandal how the finger of blame pointed to M.K. on a regular basis. "Absolutely! I'm working myself to the bone for it." She slid the door to a close, but just before it shut, Rome called to her.

"M.K., wait! Why is it so important to you that Julia get back together with Paul?"

She took a deep, dramatic breath. "'Cuz we're sisters," as if that explained everything. "You should be glad you haven't got any sisters. They are a continual worry."

How to explain about Julia? Rome had known her for five or six years; she was a face that belonged at Amos Lapp's farm. If he'd seen her on the street or in a crowd, he probably wouldn't have noticed her. So many women tried to catch his attention, how was he supposed to notice the ones who didn't?

He had never even thought her particularly beautiful. Yet in the last few days he thought she was the most striking woman he had ever known—tall and slender, with thick and shiny chestnut hair that refused to stay tightly pinned. On any other woman, her full bottom lip would have been petulant, but on her, it was . . . well, he had trouble keeping his eyes off of those lips of hers. Rome was finding that he couldn't get Julia Lapp out of his mind.

Surprised by the mere possibility that he might ever find her appealing in any way, he wasn't prepared to pose the question to himself of why he found Julia's opinion of him so important. Why did it matter? He would be moving on in a few months, anyway.

It was just that Julia had taken such a powerful dislike to him, which was more than a little disconcerting, since she was female and he was . . . well, he was Roman Troyer. He wasn't puffed up with himself as she often accused him. It was just a fact, the same kind of fact that he was six feet tall, with dark eyes and gray hair. He seemed to have some kind of effect on women that made them predisposed to him, with very little effort on his part. It had always been so and he never understood it, though it had some distinct advantages. A steady supply of offers for home-cooked meals, clean and mended laundry.

He thought about M.K.'s proposition. He would never take her bag of nickels—the thought of how earnestly she offered it to him made him smile—but maybe she was on to something. Julia had always been single-focused about her devotion to Paul, too single-focused for her own good. And here Paul was seeing Lizzie on the sly. Maybe Paul needed to have a dose of his own medicine—to realize what he might be losing. M.K.'s plan might work. At least he could try to help.

Still, to him, only one course of events made any sense—Julia should forget about Paul Fisher. He wasn't worthy of Julia Lapp. But Rome also knew that people rarely did what made sense, especially when it came to matters of the heart. Wasn't he a prime example of that? Wasn't there a pressing matter in his own life that he couldn't make sense of?

Later that evening, he sat down to write a letter.

Dear R.W.,

If we are going to carry on this curious conversation, I would like to ask you a question. Why do you want my property? You have never mentioned any reason.

Cordially, Roman Troyer

9

Even though the May heat was thick enough to make the brim on M.K.'s bonnet curl and her sweaty legs stick to the buggy seat, she was happy. Happy to not be in school, happy to be headed to Sunday church, happy and excited because she would see her friends today.

A fly buzzed a lazy figure eight in front of M.K. She sat in the place that she always occupied with her sisters, in the middle of the room and at the end of a bench. A good spot from which to observe the congregation. She saw a mouse scamper along the edges of the kitchen. She stole a glance at Jimmy Fisher, who caught her looking at him and stuck out his tongue at her. She wished she had her peashooter with her so she could send a pea flying right into that boy's open mouth. Maybe he would choke to death, she thought wryly, and then immediately took back the uncharitable thought, remembering where she was. People were singing the second hymn, the *Lob Lied*, slow and mournful. She had been thinking, allowing her mind to wander, and had not noticed that the ministers had come in. She bolted to her feet and made an effort to follow the service once it began, but there seemed to be so much to distract her, and after a while she abandoned her attempt.

Fern jabbed her in the ribs and M.K. straightened up, stiff as a rod.

"Hmmm," Fern said, in that way of hers.

Fern. So everpresent. She was putting a crimp into M.K.'s life. Friday noon, Fern had shown up, out of the blue, at the schoolhouse. She found M.K. playing her shell game behind the backstop. Fern had the nerve to put her hands on the two outside shells and held on tight, staring M.K. down.

Somehow she knew that the pea had been dropped in M.K.'s lap. M.K. quietly packed up her game. Fern led her to a big shade tree, far from the schoolhouse. Then Fern told her that gambling was wrong, wrong, wrong.

"I didn't know it was gambling!" M.K. told her. "I just thought it was a game."

Fern sighed. "When money is at stake, it's always gambling." She raised an eyebrow. "It seems to me that somebody as smart as you would have enough sense to figure that out for herself."

It seemed that way to M.K. too.

"Where'd you learn that game, anyway?"

"A man at the library taught me while you were busy looking for cookbooks. He never said anything about it being a gambling game!"

There was a slight twitching at the corner of Fern's lips. Her expression softened a little. After a long pause she spoke. "Don't tell me anything more. I don't even want to know."

Surprisingly, Fern never told Amos that M.K. had been gambling. Of course, she also didn't offer up how she knew about it in the first place, but Fern seemed to have a disturbing knack for knowing things.

The morning sun beat down on her head. Julia was placing produce from the garden out on the shelf at the roadside stand. She put the carrots on a plate, then in a mason jar, then stood back to look at it, frowning. This was the hardest part for her, the presentation. She had no idea how to display the produce so it looked appetizing. She knew it was important to create an eye-catching display to entice those who stopped by, so each day she tried something new. But it never looked the way she wanted it to look. She couldn't get it right and she hated anything that made her feel incompetent. She heard a deep sigh behind her, an exasperated soughing sound that was becoming all too familiar.

Fern.

"What?" Julia said.

"Seems like a girl who spends hours ironing her clothes and prayer cap, and another hour getting her hair pinned just right . . . could figure out how to put together a good-looking produce table."

Julia crossed her arms against her chest, defensive, then dropped them with a sigh. "I know. I can do it with quilt tops, but I just have no imagination for a produce table."

"You don't say." Fern shook her head, then pulled out a roll of twine and scissors. She grabbed a bundle of carrots and tied them gently with the twine, making a neat little bow. Then she placed the bundles in the basket.

She handed the twine and scissors to Julia and turned to leave.

That one little thing looked . . . charming. Absolutely charming. "Wait! Any other ideas?" She waved a hand in front of the shelf. "I'm open to suggestions."

Fern sighed. "I have to do everything around here." She squinted at the table, seeing something Julia couldn't see. "Run to the house and get a checkered tablecloth." By the time Julia returned, the table had been transformed. Mason jars were filled with flowers. One with sweet-smelling roses, another with brightly colored zinnias. A small chalkboard was propped up against the honor jar, left in the center of the table. In colored chalk, the prices for the day's offerings were listed, and a note: *Everything picked fresh today. Please leave the money in the jar. Thanks and blessings from Windmill Farm.* Even the scripted handwriting was neat, elegant.

It looked exactly the way Julia had hoped it would look but could never actually create it. "Fern, you are a wonder!" Julia was truly astounded. "What would we ever do without you?" She reached over and gave Fern a loud buss on her cheek.

Patting her hair back in a satisfied way, Fern said, "You'd do exactly what you were doing, which wasn't much."

Sadie walked up to the stand to see what was going on. In her hand was a half-eaten blueberry muffin. "The table looks amazing!"

"Fern did it," Julia said proudly. "Why, she's got all kinds of talents we're just finding out about."

Fern didn't pay her any mind. Instead, she took the muffin out of Sadie's hand and replaced it with a carrot, top still on, from the produce table. Then she turned and walked to the house.

The weather turned unseasonably hot for the month of May. One afternoon, after Rome had finished a few chores from Julia's endless to-do list, he sat in the shade of a tree near the barn, his arm draped across Lulu, who'd fallen asleep with her nose resting on his thigh. The dog didn't stir as Menno approached.

"Lulu isn't much of a watchdog," Rome said.

Menno chuckled and lowered himself beside him. "No. I guess not. But she's young still. She was only a pup when I found her rootin' around in the alley behind the Sweet Tooth bakery." Menno plucked a blade of grass and began to chew on it. "I've noticed you spend a lot of time with Lulu."

"Lulu spends time with me, not the other way around."

Menno removed the blade of grass from his mouth. "I was thinking that maybe you'd like to have one of Lulu's pups for your very own. They'll be ready for a home pretty soon."

Rome shook his head. "Thank you, Menno, but no."

Menno looked confused. "I won't charge you. It would be a gift. You could have the pick of the litter. Well, Annie got first pick. But you could pick second." There were only two pups.

Again, Rome shook his head, more vehemently than before. "I appreciate the offer, Menno. But I'm not a man who wants a traveling companion."

Menno rose to his feet. "It's just that . . . I think dogs have a way of knowing who they want to be with. Seems like Lulu thinks you'd be a good choice for her pups. She's picked you."

"I'm sorry." He was too. Menno seemed hurt as he left. But Rome wasn't about to waver from his "no attachments" policy. It had stead him well for six years. Why change it now?

Sadie came into the kitchen after working in the garden and saw that Fern had set hot fruit scones on a rack to cool by the window. She noticed one scone was a little larger than the others, so she broke off a corner. Then another corner to even it out, so Fern wouldn't notice.

Her mind drifted off to church yesterday. Julia, Paul, Lizzie, Rome.

Love. It was all so complicated. That was probably why you didn't get to the good kind of love until you were older.

She looked at the scone and realized it now seemed as if it had two bites taken out of it so she nibbled delicately around the edges and soon the fruit scone disappeared. She still felt a little hungry—after all, she had worked long and hard in the garden this morning. So she ate another. She slipped one more in her pocket, in case she got hungry before lunch, and she carefully spread the scones out so that it didn't look as if three—or was it four?—were missing.

Tomorrow, for sure, she would stop eating sweets. That very morning, she had noticed that her apron seemed too small. She struggled briefly to pin it around the small paunch that, since her fourteen birthday, had begun to inflate like a rubber raft around her middle. She retrieved an apron from Julia's laundry hamper, but it was too small around the waist. So she decided to skip an apron altogether yesterday.

She grabbed one more scone, for later, licked her lips, brushed crumbs off of her face, and hurried outside before Fern found her in the kitchen.

Later that afternoon, Sadie waited for M.K. to come home from school and met up with her at the Smuckers' goat pasture. When she saw her, she waved her home so that M.K. would join her. "I need to borrow some money."

M.K. looked at her suspiciously. "Why?"

"I need to get something from town."

"What?"

Sadie frowned. "Why do you need to know?"

"Because you want my money! What makes you think I have extra to spare, anyway?"

"You always have money."

"You tell me what you've got on your mind, first."

Sadie crossed her arms over her chest and lifted her chin. "If you must know, it's to buy a Spanx."

"What's that?"

"It's . . . a body shaper. Something to help me hold my stomach in."

M.K. looked puzzled. "Like a corset?" She made a face. "Does Dad know?"

"Do you need to know everything?"

"Yes. I do."

"Fine. Yes, Dad said that if it was so important to me, go ahead and get one. So I need to borrow forty dollars." She held out her palm. "I'll pay you back in a week or two with an extra dollar thrown in."

M.K. shook her head, but she pulled off her shoe, yanked out the lining, and pulled out two twenties. "Make it two dollars extra."

Sadie snatched the money out of M.K.'s hands and ran to the horse standing hooked to the buggy.

She drove into town and parked at the department store, looked carefully to make sure she didn't recognize anyone, made her purchase, and hurried home. She ran to the bathroom and squeezed into the body shaper. It definitely made her belly flatter. Her bottom too. But it wasn't easy to move around or to sit down. She felt as if she had a yardstick down her back. She blew out a puff of air. This was a small price to pay for a flat belly.

As the afternoon carried on, Sadie felt as if her middle section was in a vise, getting tighter and tighter. She had a hard time getting full breaths of air. And it was itchy. She kept scratching herself and it sounded like a cat scratching a brick wall. She couldn't think, couldn't move, couldn't breathe. She was a sardine in a can! A stuffed sausage! She hated this girdle. Hated, hated, hated it. Finally, right before dinner, she couldn't stand it for another second. She ran upstairs, took off the body shaper, and threw it out the window as far as she could, furious with herself for wasting money.

But ahhh . . . relief! She felt free!

By the time she got back downstairs, everyone was seated at the table. Rome walked in the back door, holding up the girdle. "Does this belong to anyone? I was minding my own business and this came flying at me, out of the sky."

"That's Sadie's new corset," Menno volunteered. "Mary Kate told me about it."

Sadie gasped, mortified, ran upstairs, and threw herself on her bed. She would never eat again.

Why did every encounter with Roman Troyer seem to turn her into an idiot? What must he think of her? Just last night, she was peeling a carrot for the dinner salad when Rome came in to ask her father a question or two. While he was there, just a few feet away from her, talking to Amos, Sadie dropped the carrot peeler for the third time. Rome bent down and picked it up, handed it to her, then nodded toward the carrots she'd just peeled. "Are you expecting a family of rabbits as dinner guests?"

He was standing so close to her that she could smell his shampoo and see dark hairs glinting on his forearms, above the rolled-up sleeves of his shirt. She blinked and looked to see what he was talking about. Instead of peeling just a few carrots for a salad, she'd peeled the entire pile that Julia had brought in from the garden. A small mountain of carrot peels. Enough for a dozen salads. Idiot!

After a while, Fern had come into her room and sat on the bed, patiently waiting while Sadie had finished her weeping. Then, she said quietly, "Sadie girl. We have got to find something for you to do. You need more on your mind."

M.K. and Jimmy Fisher met on the way home from school, not entirely by chance.

Jimmy blocked her path. "You told! You told Old gnudle Woola that I egged his buggy windshield!"

"You did egg his buggy! I heard you bragging about it to Noah."

He scowled at her. "Now I have to wash every window in that crummy old farmhouse. Plus the buggy!"

"Too bad for you." She tried to get around him, but he kept blocking her.

"You'd better watch your step, Little Gullie. I'm going to get even with you."

M.K. stared at Jimmy. Then something came over her and she stomped on his foot so hard that he let out a big "OUCH!" and doubled over to grab his foot. M.K. took off as fast as she could, just in case Jimmy had recovered.

Before crossing the small stream that separated the road from the Smuckers' wheat field, she glanced behind her and didn't see any sign of Jimmy. She bent forward as she scrambled up the steep embankment and headed toward the woods that lay just past the field, another useful shortcut to get to Windmill Farm. She stopped for a moment behind a tree, resting her hands on her knees to catch her breath. It was supposed to be a sin to hate, M.K. knew, but she had trouble not hating Jimmy Fisher. It was probably also a sin to allow her mind to dwell on such thoughts, but M.K. often wondered why God chose to afflict Stoney Ridge with such a vile boy as Jimmy Fisher.

The bushes crackled behind her. Ears straining, she stared hard at the tangled thicket of blackberry bushes.

A breeze came up, stirring the leaves on the bushes and trees above her, rustling, whispering, crackling . . . it sounded like a creature. A bear creature!

She let out a shaky breath. It was only the wind.

But she sure didn't want to meet up with any she-bear and her cub. She wasn't afraid of many things, but so much talk of bears lately gave her the willies. She liked it better when she knew the bears were snoozing away the winter. She ambled on down the trail, relaxing a little. A squirrel scampered ahead of her, disappearing into the trees, tail twitching.

As she neared the edge of the wood, the bushes rustled again. M.K. looked up at the treetops, but this time there wasn't any wind. Could it be Jimmy, playing tricks on her? She wouldn't put it past him, especially as she was about to walk past a small graveyard, tucked in the corner of Beacon Hollow, the Zooks' farm, with gravestones jutting crookedly out of the ground like buckteeth. Is this what Jimmy meant by getting even with her? Out of habit, M.K. hurried past the scary graveyard with just a quick glance. She had to dash through a cornfield to reach Windmill Farm. She tensed as the crackling, rustling noises came again, followed by a low growling sound. Every small sin she'd ever committed in her life passed before her. She broke into a run and made it home in record time.

That night, M.K. slept with three lamps in her bedroom.

10

It was late May. Off-Sundays in spring were some of Julia's favorite days of the year. The weather was usually perfect, like it was today, and neighbors often gathered in a nearby meadow to enjoy fishing in the stream, a softball or volleyball game, and a picnic. On this sunny afternoon, Julia drove Menno, Sadie, and M.K. over to the field and decided to stay when she spotted Paul's mare and buggy. She hadn't had any chance to see him in the last few weeks and hoped he might slip off on a walk with her, like they usually did on lazy afternoons, while the others were involved in a game of softball.

Menno and M.K. hopped out of the buggy to join the game, already in progress, and Julia watched for a moment as she tied the horse to the railing. Ever since her father had taken sick, Julia had a hard time watching these games. Amos Lapp was one of the few men who put himself in the game. He'd ask a little one for some help at bat, then together they'd hit the ball and Amos would swing the child into the crook of his arm, bobbing and weaving around the bases. If he were running the bases alone, he'd always let himself get tagged out. But with his heart ailing, the doctor wouldn't even let him attend church anymore. No crowds, the doctor said. Too high a risk of infection. Julia wasn't sure what crushed her father's spirit more—missing church or missing those softball games. Both, probably.

Out of the corner of her eye, Julia noticed Rome. She didn't know he would be here. He hadn't asked for a ride. Why was he here? She saw him walk up to a picnic table where a young woman, Katie Yoder, was scooping homemade ice cream into cones. Katie laughed at something Rome said, and he gave her an answering smile so charged with effortless charm that Julia could almost see Katie fall in love. Infuriating! Exasperating. It was like watching a predator swoop down on its prey. Why were girls so blinded by charm and good looks?

But then she saw Paul. He was on the other side of the softball field. Julia started to make her way in his direction, moving casually and nonchalantly, as Menno took a turn at bat. She stopped to watch, then cheer when he hit the ball past the outfielders. Unfortunately, he got so excited that he started running in the wrong direction, but M.K. was running from third base to home, grabbed Menno midway there, stepped on the home plate so her run would count, and set Menno off in the right direction. Sadie joined Julia and they cheered for Menno, only stopping when he made it safely to first base.

Suddenly, Julia felt so childish. She felt as if Paul would think she was . . . that she was so pathetically eager to see him again that she was making all this noise so he would know she was here!

And that was true.

Julia gripped Sadie's arm. "Paul's over there, all alone. Walk with me a little so it looks like we just happened to bump into him."

As they turned to go, Paul's mother, Edith Fisher, a large boxy woman, stood ahead of them in their path and fixed her eyes on Julia with a discouraging stare. "Don't let her intimidate you, Julia," Sadie whispered.

Edith gave Julia one of her thin, wintery smiles as they approached her. "Hello, Julia, Sadie."

Julia braced herself. "Hello, Edith. And how are you?"

"I've hardly had a chance to see you since Paul canceled the wedding." There was something triumphant about Edith's expression.

"*Postponed* the wedding, Edith," Julia corrected. "Paul wants to wait a few months. That's all."

Paul was now walking alongside Lizzie over by the creek. Edith noticed too. Julia's heart sank. She could feel her face flush with warmth. She turned to Sadie to leave, but her sister was looking intently at Edith Fisher.

"Paul is young," Sadie said. "But Paul is a good man."

"He's a fine man," Edith Fisher said. "A fine, fine man."

Sadie nodded. "And good men have room in their hearts for more than one person, you know. They can love their mother and their wife." She put a hand on Edith's arm. "Julia would never let Paul forget you."

Julia heard Edith Fisher breathing, a slightly raspy sound, her eyes fixed on Sadie. Then Edith drew herself up tall and turned her attention back to Julia. "Folks are saying that Amos Lapp isn't long for this world. And what will happen to you when he dies? Menno can't take care of the farm. You'll have to sell it."

Sadie's eyes went wide. "What? *What?*" She looked at Julia with panic in her eyes. "Dad is . . . dying?"

Julia put an arm around Sadie. What could she say to that? "Dad is trying some new treatment and it's just going to take a little time to help him get stronger." She pointed to the field. "Menno's up to bat again. Will you make sure he runs toward first base?"

Sadie gave her a wobbly smile, threw a dark look at Edith Fisher, and walked back to the softball game.

After Sadie left, Julia turned to Edith. "Only God knows what lies ahead for my father, Edith. But I do know we are not selling Windmill Farm."

"Well, I hope you don't think you can talk my Paul into managing Windmill Farm! I count on him to manage the hatchery."

Julia looked over at Paul, still deep in a conversation with Lizzie, who gazed at him with adoring eyes. Julia couldn't blame Lizzie for being infatuated with Paul. It wasn't just his dark blond hair, blue eyes, and easy smile that made him irresistible. It was his entire Paul-ness. She turned back to Edith. "I'm not counting on Paul for anything right now."

Suddenly, Rome was at her side. "There you are, Julia! Here's the ice cream cone you wanted." He handed her a cone, dripping with melted ice cream. "Don't forget that you promised to ride home with me today." He grabbed her elbow and steered her to the bee wagon before she could object. He practically pushed her into the buggy. He hopped into the driver's side and flicked the reins to get the horse moving. "You don't have to thank me."

Julia looked at him, baffled. This man's head was full of kinks. "For what?"

"For saving you from Edith Fisher. She's one of those people with whom there simply is no dealing." He pointed out the window past her. "And you don't have to thank me for that, either."

She looked where he was pointing. It was Paul, watching Rome and Julia, with an odd look on his face. A shocked look.

Julia sighed—relief, happiness, elation!

"Paul Fisher is no match for you."

Slowly, she turned to glare at Rome. What did *that* mean? Did he think Paul was too good for her? How rude! Rome was abominable.

And he was oblivious to her indignation. "Julia, when are you going to realize there are other men in this world than Paul Fisher?"

She regarded him primly. "Like you, for example?" She blew out a puff of air. "We discussed this when you first arrived. I am not interested, Roman Troyer."

He wore a strange, bemused look on his face. "Well, I'm terribly flattered, but I'm not exactly the settling-down sort." He gave the reins a small shake as the mule had slowed to a crawl.

Julia snorted. "You mean, the settling-for-anyone sort. You want to have your cake and eat it too."

"I'm a pie man, myself. Cherry pie." Rome gave a sly grin. "I was just trying to help out."

"And why would you go out of your way to help me?"

"Well, excuse me for being a compassionate and caring human being."

Julia rolled her eyes. "As much as I appreciate your misguided help, I have the situation covered."

"So what exactly is your plan to win Paul back?"

She lifted her chin. "I am going to overcome his reluctance. I am going to be more forthright."

His eyes opened wide in surprise, then he started to laugh. "You? You think you need to be *more* forthright?" Laughter overtook him, so much so that tears rolled down his cheeks.

She should have been insulted—she *was* insulted—but at the same time, an urge to laugh had come over her. Rome was so arrogant! And he was also right. Sometimes, she was too bossy. Some of the fire left her. "I really would like to know why you would go out of your way to help me."

He took a few deep breaths to get himself back under control. "All right. You win. The truth? Even though I didn't intend to make your endless engagement to Paul even more endless, I did you a disservice." He glanced over at her. "My folks raised me to believe that every wrong should be made right."

"And where exactly were you raised? Nobody seems to know where you're from, or who your family is or how many brothers and sisters you have." She looked at him expectantly. "And why bees? Of all things, why bees?"

"I'm touched, Julia—to think that you have so many thoughts about me."

She stiffened her spine and looked straight ahead. "It's flattering yourself to think I have any thoughts about you at all."

His face broke into a smile, and she couldn't help smiling in return. The moment seemed to last forever, even as Julia heard the crack of a softball leaving the bat. Then she realized that people were shouting and waving their arms. She looked around and up . . . and saw the ball sailing, a high arc through the air.

"Look at that!" Rome said. "Your brother just hit one that's headed over the fence!" He shouted out to Menno and waved to him. Menno stopped running to see who was calling him, so M.K. ran out on the field and dragged him around the bases.

Rome seemed so genuinely pleased about Menno's accomplishment that something inside Julia melted a little, right along with the ice cream cone in her hand. She quickly licked it before it dripped on her dress.

She wrinkled her nose. So what if Rome was slippery and elusive, not to mention too charming for his own good? He seemed genuinely sincere about helping her win Paul back. Maybe it was time to rise above her dislike.

Rome glanced at her. "You've got ice cream on your nose. Never gonna catch a fella with those kinds of table manners."

Julia gasped and rubbed her nose with her dress sleeve. She promptly yanked back her imaginary olive branch toward Rome. He was incorrigible!

Still, Julia felt curiously elated. She knew it came from the emotion she had felt when she saw the look on Paul's face. That, she felt, could only be a wordless affirmation of the fact that nothing had changed. Paul still loved her, she was sure of it. How strange. How wonderful.

Later on that night, though, doubt returned as Julia was sitting at the kitchen table, glancing through the *Budget*.

Sadie sat down beside her with two cups of herbal tea. "Try this. It's made of a combination of dried herbs from the garden. It's supposed to help digestion. Or maybe it's a cure for a headache." She shrugged. "One or the other. Maybe both."

Julia took a sip and tried not to cringe. It tasted like something made from rancid garbage. "Really . . . tasty, Sadie."

Sadie took a sip and spit it out. "It's awful. Needs more mint to camouflage the taste." She pushed the mug aside. "Paul was watching as you left the game with Rome. He was obviously bothered by the idea of you spending time with Rome. That's encouraging. I really think he's coming around."

Julia propped her chin on her hand. "Then why don't I feel encouraged?"

When Paul first saw Julia drive off from the softball game with Rome, he felt strangely disturbed. But the longer he thought about it, the more it seemed like an opportunity in the making. If Roman Troyer was after Julia, then Julia would let Paul go. He wouldn't have to be known as a heart breaker. It was a free pass! He could start courting Lizzie. He planned to tell her the good news on the buggy ride home.

But as soon as the words came out of his mouth, the smile slid off Lizzie's face. "No," she said. "I can't do that to Julia. She's my friend."

"I already told her that I wanted to postpone things. I thought I'd give her time to get used to that. Next, I'll tell her that you and I are seeing each other."

"Paul," Lizzie said, shaking her head sadly.

"What?"

"Go to Julia and take it all back," she said.

"Are you saying you don't want me?"

"It was just a few kisses, Paul. And now someone's gotten hurt."

In late March, Lizzie had needed a ride from a singing on a Sunday evening. Paul had agreed to drop her off—he passed right by Rose Hill Farm—and they started talking. And talking. Then something happened between them as he helped lift her out of the buggy. It started slowly. One kiss, another kiss, more kissing. He couldn't stop thinking about those kisses with Lizzie. They were nothing like the kisses he shared with Julia. Not even close. He dropped by Lizzie's house every chance he got, hoping there would be a chance for more kisses. So far, no such luck.

"Just go to her," she said. "I'm not coming between you and Julia. You should be with her. I'm just a friend, Paul. That's all I'll ever be." She jumped out of the buggy before he could stop her.

He listened to her footsteps crunch across the loose gravel. What had happened? How could this be? This was too much: to lose them both.

Monday morning arrived and Uncle Hank arrived with it. He was sitting at the kitchen table when Julia came downstairs with a load of sheets in her arms. "JULIA!" he bellowed. "I told you I would help get those weeds in the orchards. I've got a plan all worked out!"

Julia stopped by the kitchen table. "Let's hear it." She slipped into a chair beside Sadie and Menno and braced herself for the news.

"I got to talking to Ira Smucker. He said he would loan us his herd of goats. I just need to set up a wire fence. Something I can move around that could be goat proof."

Rome appeared at the kitchen door while Uncle Hank was explaining his idea. He took a seat at the table. Fern brought both of the men a cup of coffee and sat down herself.

Uncle Hank was delighted to have an audience. He turned to Rome. "What do you think, Bee Man?"

"I've seen a lot of folks using goats to get rid of undergrowth," Rome said. "Only thing is that they'll eat the blossoms right off the trees. They'll eat anything they can get their mouths close to."

"That's the beauty of my plan!" Uncle Hank said. "They're pig goats! Little tiny things!"

"You mean, pygmy goats?" Rome asked.

Uncle Hank banged on the table with his fist. "That's it! That's their name. Why, you've never seen such cute little critters—"

"Hank Lapp, just when were you supposed to get that goat-proof fence up by?" Fern asked, looking out the window. "Because your goats are heading this way."

Uncle Hank bolted out of his chair and stood behind Fern. Ira Smucker and his son, Gideon, were heading up Windmill Farm's driveway with a horse pulling a trailer full of small goats. "Blast! What day is it, anyway?"

"Monday," Rome said, looking out the window.

"Double blast! I didn't think Ira meant this particular Monday morning. I thought he just was talking about some Monday morning in general."

"Some of us live in reality," Fern said. She looked at Uncle Hank with an arched eyebrow. "And others live in their *own* reality."

Uncle Hank huffed, thrust the coffee cup in her hand, and went outside to meet Ira Smucker.

"Hurry with your breakfast, Menno," Julia said. "Our morning just got rearranged."

"I'll help," Rome said. "You don't have to, Julia. Menno and Hank and I can handle the job."

Julia gave him a sharp look. "I thought you had honey to collect today."

Rome gave a half shrug. "Tomorrow is as good a day for honey as today. I'm here to help."

Footsteps came thundering down the stairs as M.K. flew into the kitchen with Amos's breakfast tray. She passed it off to Fern and ran to the door. "Sadie! Gideon Smucker is here! He's so sweet on you he can't put two words together in a sentence." She waved her arm like a windmill. "Come on, Sadie! Let's go see his ears turn red when he tries!"

"Oh, M.K. Schtille," Sadie said. *Quiet.* But she smoothed out her hair and dress and followed behind M.K. Menno hurried to join them.

"Well, well, maybe Sadie might be willing to consider other fellows besides Rome, after all," Fern said.

"Rome doesn't mind sharing one devotee," Julia said, picking up the laundry basket of sheets. "There's plenty of other girls to take Sadie's place."

Rome wasn't paying any attention to them. He was frowning at Amos's breakfast tray. "He hardly ate a thing."

Later that day, M.K. hurried home from school. She had told everyone at school about the pygmy goats and couldn't wait to see them. She ran through the kitchen to drop off her lunch pail and grab a snack. Fern caught her, gave her a large white bucket, and told her to pick some cherries as long as she was lollygagging in the orchards.

Lollygagging? Fern! So bothersome. As if M.K. *ever* lollygagged.

She slipped through the wire fencing that Rome and Menno and Uncle Hank had fixed up and walked among the small goats. There were goats of all colors, and they looked up at M.K. with mild interest before turning back to their weeds. She picked a favorite—a small black-and-white female goat with peaceful eyes—petted her for a while, then took her white bucket to start picking cherries. The bucket was about a quarter of the way full when she heard laughing sounds, like a hyena. Or jackals. Or . . . ! She jumped off the ladder and scanned the orchard for the source of that hideous noise—it came from Jimmy Fisher and his sidekick, Arthur King. They were laughing so hard they had to hold their sides.

She stomped over to them and called over the fence. "What's so funny?"

"That!" Jimmy said, pointing behind her. She turned around to see a large goat that stood out from the rest. He surveyed his new home with an air of disdain and shook his head.

She knew that particular billy goat! "You stole Ira Smucker's goat, Jimmy!"

"Didn't steal him," Jimmy laughed. "Just borrowed him!"

M.K. pointed at him. "Don't you know that the ninth commandment says 'do not lie'?"

Jimmy nudged his friend, Arthur. "Loss dich net verwiche, is es elft Gebot." *"Don't get caught" is the eleventh commandment.*

M.K. heard a bleating sound and her head swiveled in its direction. Ira Smucker's yellow billy had lowered its head and was charging right at her. M.K. darted to the nearest cherry tree and climbed it. The goat bumped his head against the trunk of the cherry tree several times for good measure. Each time, Jimmy and Arthur's laughing fit started up again. M.K.'s outrage nearly choked her, and she could barely hold on to her temper. She was trapped in a tree with a mad billy goat underneath her, and Jimmy and Arthur were enjoying her humiliation at a safe distance.

Boys! So horrible! She broke off branches and threw them down at the billy, but he only chewed up the branches. He gazed at her with his weird yellow eyes as if to thank her for the snack.

Finally, the yellow billy returned to the rest of the herd who had continued eating, unconcerned with the big intruder. M.K. slipped carefully down the tree. She knew she had to get that pail before the billy goat ate up her cherries. She tiptoed over to the pail, bent to get it, heard another bleating sound, and turned to find the billy charging at her with lowered head. She didn't have time to get to a tree, so she took the pail and jammed it on top of the billy goat's head. He shook and shook his head, trying to get that pail off of him. If M.K. weren't so furious with Jimmy and Arthur, she might have even enjoyed the ridiculous sight. As it was, she lost her cherries and her pail. The other goats milled around, curious, and finished off the cherries that scattered on the ground.

Then she picked up a big stick and eyed Jimmy and Arthur, tapping it in her hands a few times. They started backing up and took off running. M.K. ran to the fence, bent over to slip through, when a big arm scooped her up. The arm belonged to Rome, and her legs were dangling in the air like riding a bicycle. "Let me at 'em!"

"They're halfway home by now, M.K." He set her down and took the stick out of her hands. "Using a stick is no way to get even with those two."

She stomped her foot. "They're the scum of the earth! The worst of the worst!" She started to take off after them, but Rome grabbed her shoulders.

"Now you just calm down." He waited until she stopped struggling, then released her. "You stay put while I go get that billy." He pointed his finger at her in a warning way as he jumped over the fence. She saw that he had a rope with him. He looped it around the billy goat's neck and carefully pulled the bucket off the goat's head.

He led the yellow billy out through a makeshift gate into an empty pasture, then returned for her. As they walked back to the house, Rome said, "Jimmy is hoping he'll get you upset, M.K. You'd have the upper hand if you didn't always overreact to him."

M.K. scowled at him.

"Have you thought about just trying to let it go?"

"Let it go? Let it go?" Her voice rose an octave.

"This will just keep getting worse. Jimmy does something mean to you. You do something mean right back to him. Why not try something different? Don't work out a plan to get even with him. Maybe . . . turn the other cheek."

M.K. knew where this was heading. Hadn't she been in church for her whole entire life? Before Rome could start in on a lecture about loving your enemies, she cut him off at the quick. "That might work with some folks. But the problem with Jimmy Fisher is that by the time you've turned the other cheek a couple of times," she patted her face, "you start running out of cheeks."

11

Sadie had borrowed Julia's hand mirror while she was in town. Lately, Sadie studied herself in mirrors as she hadn't before. She wasn't overly encouraged by what she saw.

"You look better today than you did a week ago," Fern said.

Sadie whipped around. Fern was leaning against the doorjamb with some freshly ironed prayer caps in her hands. How long had she been there? Sadie was mortified! Fern came into Sadie's room and opened a bureau drawer to tuck away the prayer caps. While Fern's head was down, preoccupied with the messy condition of the drawer, Sadie held the mirror out to get a better look at herself. Maybe Fern was right. Even though it had only been a week, Sadie's tummy didn't seem to stick out so far, maybe because she didn't have so much time to eat. Fern was forever sending her on errands, and she made Sadie walk, not take the buggy. And every time she wandered into the kitchen for a snack, Fern found something important for her to do right away—take notes from some books about healing herbs, help Menno harvest fruit in the orchard, dig out a new section of Julia's garden to add another section to the herb garden. And this was all on top of her daily chores! There was hardly a moment to rest. To eat.

Fern refolded everything in the drawer and closed it with a satisfied sound. She turned to Sadie and frowned. "Grab that book over there, put it on your head, and walk."

Sadie didn't want to, but she crossed the room toward the table and put the book she found there on top of her head. It slid off right away. She picked it up and tried again with a little more success. Three steps, before it fell and crashed to the floor.

Fern folded her arms across her front. "That was better. I want you to walk like this from now on, got it? Back straight, shoulders straight. The way I do." Fern carried herself as if she had a fire poker strapped to her spine, but there was a poise about her that Sadie longed to emulate. All starch.

Sadie walked across the room with the book carefully perched on her head. She felt taller, more grown-up. And less like a person who was scared of her own shadow.

Rome finished packing up a few things he would need for a trip to the other side of the county. Jacob Glick had made him promise to bring a beehive over right as his pecans started to blossom. Last year, even with the drought, Jacob's pecan crop doubled in production. "The time is now!" Jacob's phone message had said. Rome would move the hive onto the wagon tonight, after sunset, so the bees wouldn't be stressed by the move.

He glanced around the cottage. Had he forgotten anything? His eyes locked on the hand-sewn quilt lying on his bed. His mother called it a memory quilt and that it was. It was one of the few things he brought with him from the farm. His mother wasn't a fine quilter; she used old scraps of fabric to make quilts. A piece of the quilt held his baby clothes. His sisters' dresses. Every time he looked at it, the warm times he and his family had shared before their deaths came flooding back.

Once or twice, he had even thought about giving the quilt away, but he couldn't do it. Instead, he would flip it over to the backside, banishing those images. Usually, it worked, but lately he had trouble keeping memories from popping back up again.

He traced the outline of a lavender patch. His mother's best dress. It reminded him of the day he had deceived his mother for the first and last time. It was a hot August day and Rome was twelve years old. His mother had changed into her lavender dress to go to a quilting frolic. She put Rome in charge of his sisters, but a few friends dropped by with a more interesting plan: swimming in Black Bottom Pond. He paid the next-in-line sister two dollars to take over his babysitting duties, another dollar to each sister to keep quiet, and took off with his friends. One boy brought a rope to loop on a sturdy tree branch that hung over Black Bottom Pond—it was a vine and they were jungle boys. Rome was having the time of his life.

Two things Rome forgot to factor in: the end time for the quilting frolic, and that his mother had to pass right by Black Bottom Pond. He was swinging out over the pond, naked as a jaybird, hollering out ape calls, when he caught sight of his mother standing on the shore, arms akimbo. One thing about his mother: you could always count on her to give you her opinion. And she wasn't shy about implementing that opinion with a willow switch. What he would give to have that August afternoon back again, switch and all.

Rome rubbed his face with the palms of his hands. His mind had traveled so far back in the past, he didn't even realize where he'd gone. He had to stop letting himself wander down those paths. He wanted to leave the past a few hundred miles down the road, shake it off like dust. But that was the problem with the past. It kept finding him.

Sadie went out to the garden to pick strawberries for breakfast. Lulu and her puppy tagged along, doubling the work for Sadie because the puppy kept beating her to the ripe berries. Annie had taken home the one puppy, but Menno still hadn't found the right owner for the remaining pup. When Sadie's bowl was finally full, she walked back to the house and practically bumped into Rome as he came around the corner.

"Mornin', Sadie! I was coming by to let someone at the house know I'm heading out tonight."

Hearing Rome's voice, Lulu and her puppy abandoned Sadie and bounded over to him. Rome reached down to stroke Lulu's fur.

Rome was leaving? Just like that? He wouldn't be here for her fifteenth birthday? When she realized she was staring, she stumbled over nothing and practically spilled the bowl of berries. "Don't leave. I mean, won't you at least come in for breakfast? I'm paking mancakes. Pancakes. I'll make pancakes!" Mortified, she rushed past him and into the kitchen, straight into the pantry, and closed the door behind her.

Sadie heard Julia open the squeaky door for Rome. "What in heaven's name did you say to her?"

"Nothing!" Sadie heard Rome say. "I said good morning. And that I wanted someone to know I'll be gone for a few days."

Just a few days? Hallelujah! Sadie breathed a deep sigh of relief and grabbed the flour bag. She sneaked another glance at him as she came out of the pantry with the flour bag. "Found it! I'll just get to work on those mancakes. Pancakes!" She flushed bright red and whirled around. She hoped Fern wouldn't shoo her out of the kitchen like she usually did.

M.K. burst into the kitchen from the upstairs, Menno trailing behind her.

"Sadie! M.K. wants to throw us a surprise party for our birthday!" Menno called out.

M.K. stopped and looked at him. "Well, *now* it can't be a surprise." She shrugged. "But we'll still have a party!"

"Julia, can Annie come to the party?" Menno asked.

Sadie saw Julia frown. Lately, all Menno talked about was Annie, Annie, Annie.

Rome accepted a mug of coffee from Fern and poured cream into it. "Why, Sadie and Menno, is this your birthday week? So you're both going to be fifteen?" He took a sip, hiding his smile.

"No, Rome," Menno answered seriously. "Sadie and I happen to be born on the same day, but we're not twins. I know it's confusing, but I'm two years older than Sadie. I'm going to be seventeen. We're birthday twins, but we're not really twins."

"You aren't supposed to tease Menno," M.K. whispered loudly. "He doesn't understand teasing. We have to mean what we say when we say it."

"An example to us all," Rome said good-naturedly.

Sadie was grateful that all of the noise in the kitchen diverted attention away from her acute self-consciousness whenever she was within shooting distance of Roman Troyer.

"Well, I can't miss your birthday, Menno. Or Sadie's. I'll just have to be sure I'll be back in time."

M.K. slipped onto a chair next to him. "Friday, Rome. Suppertime. This is one party you don't want to miss."

Fern sighed. "That girl takes everything to extremes."

Sadie poured the batter onto four circles on the hot griddle, waited until they bubbled up, flipped them, and put them on a plate. Then she added pats of butter and ladled them with sticky syrup. She was going to deliver Rome's pancakes without a glitch. Cool as a cucumber. She carefully avoided looking at him so she wouldn't blush, and in doing so, somehow managed to slide the pancakes into his lap. She dropped the plate on the table and ran into the downstairs bathroom.

Sadie stalled as long as she could in the bathroom, brushing her teeth and washing her face, feeling thoroughly foolish. Her feelings for Rome felt like a herd of wild horses, galloping out of control. This had to stop. Finally she managed to creep outside without being detected. When Rome returned from his trip, this idiocy was coming to an end, and she'd behave like a mature woman.

As Fern mopped up Sadie's pancakes from the floor, Julia noticed someone walking up the drive to the farmhouse. She went outside to see who it was.

Rome followed her out. "Julia, I actually stopped by to talk to you for a moment. Privately."

She saw M.K. tip her head in their direction, eavesdropping, so she closed the kitchen door.

"Don't you get nervous wearing those during hunting season?" Rome's dark eyes were dancing as he pointed to Julia's feet.

She had forgotten that she had on a pair of bunny slippers that Menno had given her for Christmas. She knew they were a little fanciful, but she loved them because they were from Menno. She drew herself to her full height, trying to look dignified while wearing bunny slippers. Ignoring him, she waved at the approaching figure. "It's Annie."

"Who's Annie?"

Julia frowned. "A girl Menno seems to be quite taken with."

"No kidding. Little Menno is growing up, Julia."

Julia slowly shut her eyes and pulled in a breath. "Do you think I don't know that?" The irritation in her voice sounded a bit strident even to her ears. She couldn't think about Menno and Annie right now. So much to worry about! "What did you want to talk to me about?"

He shook his head. "I'm heading over near Lancaster tonight. Switching hives from one farm to another. Tomorrow, I want to talk to someone at the hospital about getting Amos on the transplant list."

"At the hospital? You want to march in and put him on the transplant list?"

Rome took his hat off and raked a hand through his hair. "I don't know how I'll do it. I just want to know what needs to happen and how much it will cost and what we could do to persuade him to consider it."

"Dad won't even consider a transplant."

"I know," Rome said with a sigh.

"So you've tried talking to him?"

"A couple of times. He shuts down the conversation."

Rome looked so earnest that Julia found herself softening, just a little. But then she reminded herself that this was the Bee Man, the source of great aggravation. "It really is Dad's decision. No one else's."

"Julia . . . it's just that . . . there aren't many things in life that we can do anything about. Here you have a chance to save him, to keep him around for another couple of decades. You've got to make him see . . . that you all need him to stick around."

She found herself baffled by this man, mildly fascinated by his contradictions. It bothered her when people refused to fit into pigeonholes. It made life murky. The longer he was with them this summer, the more her curiosity about him grew. "You know, Rome, you're starting to break your own rule."

"What rule is that?"

"Not getting involved in people's lives. Isn't it easier just to dole out advice and move on your way?"

For once, Rome had no answer for her.

This was no way to start a day. M.K. gave some serious consideration to canceling the birthday party for Sadie and Menno. If this morning was an indication of how much cleaning Fern thought needed to happen to prepare for the gathering, then the week ahead looked grim. Fern had given her enough extra work to rub the skin off a person's knees.

"I just washed the floor. Now look at it. Just look at the dirt those shoes have left. Do you think I have nothing better to do than to clean up after the likes of you?" Fern must have carried on about those shoes for nearly an hour before diverting her attention to M.K.'s rumpled bed. M.K. had sat on it to tie her shoes. The way Fern set to caterwauling, you would have thought she had committed a murder. It seemed the tiniest mishap could set Fern off.

Personally, M.K. thought Fern's irritable behavior was directly attributable to consuming too much roughage. Fern took everything seriously, especially food, and since Amos and Sadie were on a low-to-no-sodium diet, the entire family was put on it. It was steamed rice and vegetables, broth or tofu, and enough bean sprouts to keep a small barnyard well fed.

At the end of the school day, M.K. burst out of the door to find Fern scowling at her, waiting by the door with arms crossed against her thin chest. M.K.'s mind flipped through the week, trying to narrow down which particular misstep had traveled straight from the schoolhouse to Fern's ears.

Fern pointed to Menno, waiting in the buggy, and told M.K. to wait while she talked to the teacher.

"What did you do now?" Menno asked as she climbed into the backseat.

"Never mind," M.K. grumbled.

Ten minutes later, Fern joined them and told Menno to head home.

From the backseat of the buggy M.K.'s voice welled up. "It was Jimmy Fisher's fault! He said something I took exception to—"

"I got that part of it," Fern said. "You always have your knickers in a twist over something that boy said or did. But I can't be running to that school every whipstitch. And school's just about out for the summer. There's limits on what I can do." She swiveled her head to the backseat and gave M.K. a long look.

"I'll keep a closer eye on her," Menno said.

M.K. glared at him.

At the turnoff to Windmill Farm, Fern pointed to the side of the road. "Menno, you go up to the house and find Sadie. She's got a list of chores for you. I want them finished by suppertime. I want to see that list checked off."

Menno hopped off. "Where are you two going?"

"M.K. and I have an errand," Fern said.

"What kind of an errand?" M.K. waved a sad goodbye to Menno.

Fern slid over to the driver's side and flicked the horse's reins. "Mind telling me why you had a pile of *Seventeen* magazines under your bed?"

M.K. rolled her eyes and rested her chin on her hand, caught red-handed. Of course, she thought. In this house, Fern knew everything. "I got 'em when Julia and I went to town last week to sell cherries and peaches at the farmer's market."

"And just why did you buy them?"

"Someone was selling the whole pile for one dollar."

"So you bought them because they were cheap?"

M.K. shrugged. "I just like to read. And we keep running out of things to read at the house. I've read the *Martyrs' Mirror* a dozen times. I've read *Young Companions* so often I have them memorized."

Fern gave up a rare smile. "And *that* is why we are going to the public library."

They spent time getting a library card set up for M.K. Then Fern walked around the bookshelves like she owned the place, piling up books in her arms. Every time M.K. pointed to a book that looked interesting, Fern gave off a clucking sound. She had titles in mind.

On the way home, Fern pulled the top book off the pile and handed it to M.K. "There's no time like the present. Start with this one."

M.K. picked up the book: *Keeping Bees* by John Vivian.

"Rome said you've been pestering him to harvest honey."

"He won't let me. Nobody takes me seriously!"

"Well, maybe you need to learn something first. Maybe then he might be inclined to take you seriously." Fern tapped the cover of the book. "And I want a one-page summary of the book when you're done with it. Mind your penmanship too."

Fern! So bossy! M.K. silently fumed, but then she opened the book and her eyes caught on this paragraph:

> A hostile colony will warn you in unmistakable terms. The hum becomes loud, shrill and strident, a high-pitched beeeeeeeeeeee sound—possibly where they got their name in the old days; our word is Old English *beo*, or *bia* in Old (High) German. The vibration rate is unpleasant bordering on fearsome to humans, high enough to cause inner ear discomfort in many animals. It is an adrenalin-generating alarm signal that strikes a primordial chord in humans, the same as a rattlesnake's burrrrr or a dog's grrrrr or an

infant's high keening wail. Bees usually will give you enough time to think better, to close up and return another day. But they may not.

Danger! She was hooked.

Rome had just finished checking on his hives. He moved some brood frames in the center—combs nearly filled with honey—to the back so the bees would start filling the empty frames. He closed the lid, picked up the smoker, and turned to leave, startled to see M.K. running toward him, spewing news like a popcorn popper. Menno trailed behind her, like he always did, and caught up with them in his own slow pace.

"Rome! Am I glad to see you! You'll never guess what's happened. I'm going to be a beekeeper!"

"Slow down, M.K. Start from the beginning," he said, pulling her away from the hives before she got too close to them. As they walked back to the cottage, he yanked his beekeeper helmet off and slipped it under his arm.

"Fern got me a book about beekeeping. So I can help you!" She was ecstatic.

Oh no. Rome wished Fern would have asked him first. If it were Menno who were interested in beekeeping, Rome would have been happy to start training him. Menno had the temperament for beekeeping—calm, unflappable. Menno was never in a hurry. But M.K.? She was overly blessed with enthusiasm and energy. Never still, never quiet. Yet how could he refuse her? She was waiting for him to respond, an earnest look on her small face. "So, you want to be an apiarist."

"No," she said. "I want to be a beekeeper."

Rome sighed. "M.K., bees are wild creatures. You're going to have to first develop a respect for them."

"I have a great respect for bees. I love honey!"

He shook his head. "That's not what I mean. There's much more to bees than honey."

"Well, they can sting. I know that for sure."

"Honeybees are engineers. Brilliant ones. They build homes for themselves that are identical in measurements."

"That's like me," Menno said. "I'm an engineer."

"Huh?" M.K. said.

"I build homes for birds. Each one is identical." Menno looked pleased with himself.

"That's true, Menno," Rome said. "You know how important it is to be precise so the birds will return to nest their young. That's what bees do, M.K. They are constantly working to help the next generation." He glanced at her. "M.K., do you know why bees produce honey?"

"For people to eat."

"Not really. Honey is bee's food. A honeycomb is a bee's pantry. They store up food for the winter. Good beekeepers always leave enough honey for the bees. The bees come first." By the look on her face, Rome could tell M.K. hadn't given any thought to bees other than eating honey.

What had Fern gotten him into?

M.K. jumped up to leave and suddenly reached her hand into her apron pocket. "I forgot! Fern said the mailman delivered this to you." She handed him a letter addressed to The Bee Man at Windmill Farm and dashed up the hill.

Dear Roman,

I have no evil intentions in buying the farm; I am only trying to right the wrongs I've done in my life.

Sincerely,

R.W.

As soon as it was dusk, Rome moved four of his hives onto the bee wagon. It would take him most of the night to get to those pecan orchards, so he wanted to get going while there was still some light left. He had one foot hitched up on the wagon when he heard a familiar voice calling to him.

Fern.

Rome stepped back off of the wagon and walked out to meet her. He had only met Fern a handful of times when his uncle Tom had courted her. He didn't know much about her, other than she was a spinster who worked as a housekeeper for families. As he saw the determined look on her face, he knew the moment he had dreaded had arrived.

"Have you made any decision about the farm?" she asked, when they met on the path that led to the farmhouse.

One thing he had to hand to her, Fern Graber didn't beat around the bush. "No, Fern, I haven't." He tried to sound neutral, unaffected.

"You knew this, Rome. You knew the farm couldn't be ignored forever. I told you to do some thinking."

"You did," Rome said. "You surely did."

"But you haven't done the thinking."

"No. Not really."

Fern crossed her arms against her thin chest. "It's time, Roman. It's past time."

"You mean, put it up for sale?"

"Yes."

"I don't think I can do that," Rome said.

"If you're not going to sell it, then you ought to go home and work the farm. You've been gone a long time. Long enough."

"Six years."

"Six years." Fern shook her head in disbelief. For the briefest of moments, sadness flitted through her eyes. Then it was gone. It happened so fast that Rome thought he might have imagined it. "This isn't what your father would have wanted you to do with his land. I think he'd rather see you sell it than let it fall to pieces."

How dare she assume she would know what his father would think, would feel. How audacious! But he kept his face unreadable.

"Give it some serious thought, Roman," Fern said, before spinning around and marching back to the house.

He wanted to shout out: Did she think he hadn't given the farm serious thought over the last six years? Did she think he didn't care about his family? But he stayed silent. Instead, he went to the bee wagon, hopped up on the seat, and slapped the mule's reins to get it moving.

Sell his family's farm?

Rome couldn't imagine selling it. The farm was the last place he'd kissed his mother's cheek, worked side by side with his father, played with his sisters. He was born and raised there. Sell the farm? Or return to it and leave his migratory life? An impossible decision.

12

Julia found it amusing that Fern took M.K.'s grand idea of a birthday for Menno and Sadie and turned it into a way to keep her little sister busy and out of trouble. Fern and M.K. cleaned the house together, made a grocery list together, shopped together, cooked together. Well, Fern did the cooking and M.K. did the dishwashing.

M.K. invited very specific people to come to the party and wouldn't say who. Julia hoped Paul was on the list but didn't want to ask. M.K. didn't know when to say things and when not to, and the last thing Julia wanted was for Paul to hear from his brother Jimmy that Julia was pining for him. She was *not* pining. Well, maybe she was, but Paul didn't need to know.

On the evening of the party, Gideon Smucker volunteered to arrive early to help barbecue chicken on the grill. Sadie looked annoyed with M.K. for inviting Gideon. Julia couldn't understand why Sadie didn't see how wonderful Gideon was. He clearly was sweet on Sadie, yet she was smitten with Roman Troyer . . . who hadn't shown up yet. On the other hand, M.K. seemed to glow like a lightning bug around Gideon. Maybe that's the way things always were. Maybe love was always mixed up.

When Paul arrived, Julia's heart skipped a beat, then two beats. Paul had come! There was still hope.

From the window up above, Amos sat by the windowsill, a look of longing on his face as he watched Gideon at the grill, slathering tangy barbecue sauce on the chickens. "A fellow could starve to death waiting on his meal up here!"

"Then come down and join the party," Fern called up to him. But Julia knew he wouldn't leave his room tonight. He said he would get pecked to death by well-meaning neighbors, asking questions he couldn't answer.

Uncle Hank emerged from the house, eating a cupcake. "Uncle Hank, be on your best behavior," Julia warned, but she knew he was pretty much on the same kind of behavior regardless of the company he was in.

"Men are all alike. Grown-up children," Fern muttered as she went past Julia with a bowl of strawberries. "There's more in the kitchen to bring out."

Julia went back inside and grabbed a bowl of potato salad from the kitchen. She crossed the yard to put the bowl on the picnic table with the rest of the food. Paul was standing by Gideon at the smoky grill. When he saw her, he made his way over to her.

"Is that German potato salad?" he asked her pleasantly, peering into the bowl. "Sure do love potato salad." He scratched his neck and shyly added, "Jules, I was hoping we could have a talk—"

"I'm sure hoping we can get dinner started." Roman Troyer appeared out of nowhere. "It looks like it's going to rain soon." He put a hand on Julia's elbow and steered her over to the picnic table.

"What are you doing?" Julia hissed. "I thought you'd left town."

His mouth curved faintly. "What, and miss all the fun?"

Julia searched in her mind for a snappy retort, but she was never good at those. Out of the corner of her eye, she saw Menno and Annie slip into the barn. "Oh no. That isn't good."

Rome saw it too. "Who's to say whether it's good or not? Menno isn't like us."

"Exactly."

"I don't mean that the way you're thinking. He doesn't worry about the future like you do, he doesn't trouble himself about endless responsibilities like you do. He views the world as a place of wonder."

"He can barely take care of himself."

Rome took the bowl of potato salad from Julia and placed it on the table. "He's seventeen and he's got a crush on a girl. Why do you have to spoil this for him? Maybe you should try to be more like Menno. Maybe we all should."

She stared at him, astounded. What did Roman Troyer know about her

has already qualified him to be placed on the national transplant list. There's no guarantee as to when a heart will turn up—the priority list is based on need, not how long a person has been on the list. They said the list turns over quickly because patients die. But he also said that hearts come in a lot—mostly from motorcycle accidents, and mostly right after holidays like the fourth of July. They call them donorcycles."

The gist of Rome's message was positive, but the word "transplant" hung in the air between them. There was an awful finality about it; a transplant might be treatment, but it had a ring of desperation to it, a sense of last resort.

"But if a heart is a match for Amos—the right blood type and size, and he said that the donor has to be within twenty pounds of Amos's weight—then the transplant could save his life. Amos is the right age for a transplant—he's young and fit and doesn't have any other health problems." Rome stopped. "Julia—you *have* to talk your father into getting on that list. He'll listen to you."

Julia looked up and was surprised she hadn't noticed how the sky had become clotted with clouds that were gray as pewter. When had that happened? One moment, the sky was clear. The next, it was filled with clouds. So like life. She thought she felt a raindrop, then another. More raindrops. Rome didn't seem to notice.

"If money's the problem, well, maybe I could find a way to help with that. I'm not saying it isn't expensive, but even the coordinator said that money shouldn't be the reason a person doesn't go on the list."

She was touched by Rome's concern for her father. Truly touched. "I appreciate what you did, Rome. And that you're trying to help. I really do."

"Just tell me that you'll talk to him. Soon."

"All right. I'll give it another try. Tomorrow. I promise."

He looked so pleased that she couldn't help but smile. And then he smiled, and their eyes held for a beat too long. His eyes traveled down to her mouth, as if he might kiss her. She could see him thinking about it, then he shifted his glance away.

Suddenly, he looped an arm around her shoulders as if drawing her in for a hug. She was so surprised she was speechless.

"That," he whispered in her ear, "is going to drive Paul Fisher right over the edge." He kept his arm tightly around her so she couldn't pull away.

"Don't look now but he's standing about one hundred yards away from us. I can't be positive, but I think there's a scowl on his face."

She looked. Paul stood silhouetted against a tree, his legs braced, arms tensed at his side. He dropped his head, turned, and walked away.

Julia felt a shock run through her. Even though she knew Rome was teasing, she felt a funny quiver down her spine. She was oddly disappointed —for a brief moment, she had wanted him to kiss her. The realization was startlingly powerful. Her attraction to him irritated her, and she pulled herself out of Rome's grasp. "What do you think you're doing?"

"I'm trying to help you get Paul back."

How had so much arrogance gotten packaged in one man? Julia jabbed her finger at his shirt. "I don't need your help. I can take care of myself."

He wrapped his hand around her finger. "Aw, now, that's not fair. You said yourself that you know I only have eyes for you."

She calmly extracted her finger from his hand. "And I told you that I wasn't interested."

As she walked back to the house, she repeated to herself, "I am *not* attracted to Roman Troyer. I am not interested. No, no, no, no, no."

Dear R.W.,

You said you are trying to right your wrongs. Well, there are many farms for sale in Ohio, especially after this drought. Why my farm? What could it possibly mean to you?

Cordially,
Rome Troyer

Rome finished writing the letter and went outside to sit on the porch steps and watch the sunset. The last time he was in town, he had done everything he could to get the Stoney Ridge postmistress to reveal who had rented P.O. Box 22. He flirted, he cajoled, he complimented. She acted as if she was guarding gold at Fort Knox and refused to reveal anything. He must be losing his touch.

The light sprinkling of rain had quickly passed through, just a tease. The sky was clear again for the sunset. The sun reminded him of a shimmering copper globe hanging low over the hills. He saw an owl swoop out for an evening hunt, accompanied by the sawing sound of crickets. As he leaned his back against the porch post—which felt warm against his back—he thought about Julia, something he'd been doing with increasing frequency. So many women believed they had to flirt with him to get him to notice them. But Julia didn't act like that. She was always herself—amusing, bold, gentle and patient with her father's illness, fiercely protective of her family.

If the timing were different . . . if he had a steady job, a place to live . . . if she weren't in love with Paul Fisher . . . if he were the type of fellow who wanted to settle down in one place . . . but none of that was true. With autumn only a few months away, who'd know if he would still be around?

Rome was a realist. He could have started a respectable business in any of the towns where he visited. He never did, though. Sooner or later, he started feeling panicky, itchy, and he knew the time had come to move.

He stood and stretched. Then he poked around in the shed for a shovel and hoe to start attacking the weeds growing near the cottage's foundation. As he breathed in the smell of honeysuckle, he thought about how he loved this land, the way the hills sheltered the farm. What made Windmill Farm feel different to him, like he was part of it? It wasn't really unusual, not by Amish standards. Those orchards—planted long ago by Amos's grandfather—were keeping the family going through Amos's heart trouble, as well as this drought. Rome knew that his bees were a significant help to the Lapps' yearly income. The cherries were redder, the peaches and apricots were plumper. It felt good to be needed. Was that it? Was that why he found himself drawn to this family?

He wondered how Julia was able to stand Amos's illness, how she had stood it all these months, watching her father dying, breath by breath. She must know how sick Amos was. There was no denying that the disease had taken its toll. A year ago, Amos weighed nearly 180 pounds. Now he weighed 150. The man Rome had once seen effortlessly pick up a hundred-pound bale of hay and toss it in the back of a cart could barely lift a hayfork. Even in the weeks Rome had been there, he'd seen Amos decline—gasping for breath after six stair steps, now only four. Always coughing. Thin and weak from lack of physical activity, despite Fern's steady pressure to make him get up and get moving. Julia must see it too, yet she seemed accepting of what was to come.

She was a curiosity to him—why was she fighting so hard to get Paul back, yet not fighting at all about her father's future?

Normally so strong and determined, tonight Julia had appeared almost fragile. He wasn't used to being confused about a woman. Watching her stomp away, indignant and adorable, whole parts of him were suddenly alive with possibility. A well of tenderness had grown inside him, and something had shifted. He wanted her. No—that couldn't be right. He wanted her to want him.

M.K. had read *Keeping Bees* twice and felt she had a firm grasp on the subject. Rome thought otherwise.

Late on a balmy afternoon, M.K. talked Menno into paying a visit to Rome. It wasn't uphill work to talk Menno into going; if he wasn't off visiting Annie, he could be found hanging around Rome. "Why can't I go out with you to gather honey?" she asked Rome when they arrived at the cottage. "I know plenty about bees."

"Oh? Then why are you wearing those?" Rome pointed to her outfit. She was wearing Menno's favorite fishing shirt, his big leather gloves, and his knee-high rubber boots.

"You said to cover up, head to toe."

"You smell like a fish. That smell will make my bees angry."

"But I figured the fish smell covered up the human smell."

"Honey-loving bears have been robbing bees for a lot longer than you and I have. Bees react to any dark, moving object with a strong animal scent." He raised an eyebrow. "Beekeeping lesson number one: Dress to make friends with your bees. Light-colored clothing, freshly laundered, sun-dried."

"If I go change, will you let me go out with you?"

"Not today."

"Why?!" She was indignant.

Rome frowned. "Mary Kate, you move too fast for bees."

"I'm always telling her that," Menno added.

M.K. scowled at him.

"Lesson number two: bees like things slow, gentle, deliberate. Fast movement makes them feel threatened. They know that predators move quickly—darting bee-eating birds, batting bear claws, lapping raccoon tongues. Move slowly and the bees will know you're a friend."

"I can move slow! I'm just usually in a hurry."

"You came crashing down to the cottage just now like your hair was on fire. Until you learn to enter a room quietly and calmly, I will not consider taking you out to gather honey."

M.K. turned and started to run out the door, then stopped herself. She quietly exited, and as soon as she was out of Rome's viewing range, she bolted to the farmhouse, ran upstairs, changed her clothing into a pale pink dress Fern had just ironed, dashed back, then stopped at the crest of the hill to walk slowly to the cottage. Quietly, she entered, sat on a chair in the kitchen, and primly crossed her ankles. Rome looked up from writing labels on honey jars and shook his head.

"Now?" she asked.

Rome looked at her for a long while.

"She did come in quiet," Menno said.

Rome sighed and put down his pen. "The first thing to do is to observe the door to the hives. That's all. Nothing else."

M.K. was thrilled. "Can I go now?"

"We will go together. You don't go near the hives without my permission. Ever." He glanced out the window. "It's about dusk. Their instinct is to head for shelter, so you should see a lot of bees returning to the hive." He handed her a pad of paper and a pencil. "Take notes and write down what you notice. Even the sounds—are the bees hissing? Or humming? They sing, you know. A sweet and low tone is the sound of a contented hive. Music to a beekeeper's ears. Listen well. That's lesson number three. Remember, you are to do everything slow and smooth. You keep your distance. And lesson number four: do nothing until you feel safe."

This was starting to sound like school to M.K.

Rome walked to the door and held it open. "You two coming?"

Observing the bees was a little disappointing to M.K. Or maybe it was the vigilant way Rome watched over her. He wouldn't let her get closer than twenty feet to the hives. Have patience, he kept telling her. Lesson number 542. He was getting to be like Fern! Even Menno got bored and wandered back to the farmhouse.

On the way back to the cottage, Rome asked M.K., "Well, what did you observe?"

Not much, she wanted to say, but instead she looked at her notes. "Bees fly up high and dive down to the hive entrance."

He nodded. "They nest naturally in hollow trees or someplace well above ground. What else?"

"The lower the sun was setting, the more bees returned to the hive."

"Those were forager bees. Their job was to be out gathering nectar and pollen, to bring it back to the hive. Anything else?"

"A couple of bees just stuck around the outside, like they didn't know what to do."

"Every bee has a job to do. Those were guards to the hive."

She snorted. "Guarding from what?"

"From mice. From hornets. From moths. From birds. From skunks and raccoons. From little girls who get too close to the hive—"

"I get it." She blew air out of her mouth. Maybe beekeeping was harder than she thought.

"Did you notice what kinds of bees they were?"

She knew this one, hands down. "Honeybees."

"There are all different strains of bees. My bees are brown bees. Most beekeepers don't like the brown bee. They're a little more work than other bees, but there's no better bee to collect thick, wild honey. My great-great-grandparents brought them from Germany. They've been in my family for five or six generations. I'm the Keeper of the Bees."

Maybe that's why Rome was so fussy about his bees, M.K. thought. It's his tie to his family.

"A good beekeeper learns to gauge much about the bees' condition from outside the hive, and that time is spent quietly observing."

New subject! Enough talk about being quiet. As they reached the fork in the path that led either to the cottage or the farmhouse, M.K. turned to Rome. "There's something I've been meaning to tell you."

"Go ahead."

"You're fired."

"From teaching you to be a beekeeper?" He whistled, one note up, one down. "That was fast."

"No! I still want to be a beekeeper. You're fired from trying to make Paul Fisher jealous. The birthday party provided ample opportunity for you. Ample opportunity! And all you managed to do was to make Julia as mad as a wet hen. Paul took Lizzie home in his courting buggy!"

"I see," he said, stroking his jaw. "The thing is, M.K., that I don't like to leave a job half finished. And we had a bargain. A deal is a deal."

"Well, you can keep the down payment. Besides, I can't pay you the rest anyway. Fern found out—" She clamped her lips shut.

Rome narrowed his eyes. "Found out what?"

"Never mind. Let's just say, my income has been temporarily cut off."

"Seeing as how I'm living rent-free on your father's land, I'm willing to forgive your debt."

"Rome, did you hear me? You have done a terrible job of making Paul jealous."

"I hear just fine. But I disagree. I'm pretty certain that he's coming around. I think I just need to turn up the heat a little."

How much clearer could she be? "Julia is impervious to your charms. I know this must be embarrassing to you."

"Not as much as it should be."

M.K. shook her head. "I'm sorry, Rome. You're good at beekeeping, but you're just no good at making a fellow jealous. I'm moving on to my second inspiration."

"Mary Kate, are you sure you know what you're doing?"

"I'm sure." She wasn't sure at all.

"Give me another chance. I'll do better."

She blew out a puff of air. "Fine. You keep working at it, but I'm going to give my inspiration a try too." She started to run up the path to the farmhouse, then remembered bee etiquette and slowed to a fast walk. It nearly undid her to move so cautiously.

13

The skies had turned an angry steel gray, but Julia ignored the ominous warnings. She wanted to get out to the southeast corner of the cornfields before the rain broke. They counted on that corn to feed the animals through the winter, when there was no grass left to graze. If they didn't get some more soaking rain soon, the corn crop would be even smaller than last year.

The distant rumble of thunder surprised her. She'd almost forgotten what a summer storm system could be like as it blew through. It had been such a long time without any significant rain to saturate the fields. She looked up at the sky. Maybe today.

As she walked along the dirt path that led to the north field, she pondered an idea for a quilt top that was brewing in the back of her mind. She wanted to get home and draw it in her journal before she forgot it. That's what she did with the quilt tops that popped into her mind, unbidden. She filled up her journal with sketches drawn with colored pencils. She wasn't sure what she would ever do with the sketches—she still hadn't recovered from the sting of criticism from last year.

I wasn't being proud, she thought, as she walked through the knee-high corn rows. She had just done the very best she could. She had used an old Lancaster pattern but gave it a fresh twist with explosions of color and design—was that being prideful? If so, she just couldn't help it. It was the way she gave glory to God. To have Edith Fisher accuse her of pride stung her to her core. She'd lost the joy she felt when she created a new quilt top.

As she stood looking out across the land she knew so well, she felt a flutter of panic. It was no surprise to see the furrows Menno had dug weren't straight and narrow the way they were before her father took sick, but it worried her to see brown on the edges of the cornstalks.

The first drops of rain began to fall. With them came that smell of rain, that dusty smell that was like no other. It was synonymous with joy, with renewal, with life itself. After two years of drought, Julia would never again take a drop of rain for granted.

And rain it was, warm and welcome, with fat drops that splashed on the parched ground. A bolt of lightning split the skies, followed by a clap of thunder that made her ears ring. The rain started falling in curtains, fast and furious. She hurried out of the cornfield and back onto the path. She blinked her eyes, wiped her nose on her sleeve. She was so soaked that her dress stuck to her skin, and her woven bandanna felt like a sodden pancake around her head. Another blast of lightning struck. She jumped as something brushed her legs. Lulu stared up at her, her head cocked to the side. Julia sank to her knees and buried her face in Lulu's wet, musty fur. Her arms trembled as she drew Lulu close. The dog scraped Julia's wet cheek with her rough tongue. Another blast of lightning struck. Lulu howled, and Julia jumped to her feet. She needed to find shelter. The cottage where Rome was staying was much closer than the farmhouse. She ran, her bare feet making her sure-footed in the gritty mud.

When she arrived at the cottage, she knocked on the door. "Rome?" She waited, then knocked again, and gave the string latch a gentle pull. She took a step inside and waited until her eyes adjusted to the dark. "Rome, are you here?" No answer. She hadn't been in the cottage since Fern fixed it up. She used to play hide-and-seek here with Sadie and Menno when they were children, but studiously avoided going inside since the day a bat flew down from its rafters and scared her to the other side of Sunday. Today, it looked quite charming. Clearly, Fern's doings. Just like the produce table transformation. The cottage looked warm and inviting, swept clean and left tidy. The kitchen had been turned into a well-organized honey extracting room: clean jars lined the shelves. Labels for the jars were stacked in a neat pile. The extractor and buckets were spotless.

She closed her eyes, taking in the smell of beeswax infused in the cottage walls. She realized now why it seemed familiar. It was a scent she associated with Rome—a fragrance that felt strangely reassuring, that all would soon be right with life.

A crackle of lightning sounded in the distance. Shuddering, Lulu chose that moment to shake herself off. Julia grabbed a towel from a hook near the sink and began rubbing the dog's chest. As she put the towel back, she was startled by what she saw on the kitchen table. Medical books were spread out all over the table. She looked closer and saw they were opened to heart disease. She saw a yellow tablet filled with notes Rome had taken about idiopathic cardiomyopathy. And next to the books was an open Bible, with another yellow tablet half-filled with Scriptures he had found that referred to a man's heart. His handwriting, Julia noticed, was strong and legible, as if he had been well schooled.

Rome must have bought these books when he went into Lancaster last week.

She doubted he would want to know she had seen what he was researching—otherwise he would have mentioned it. Maybe not. Rome didn't volunteer much.

Something caught at her throat, something that hurt and made a curious melting feeling deep in her chest. A mixture of sadness and happiness, and a strange, sweet ache that after a moment she realized was hope.

Yesterday's storm had washed the air, leaving it sweet and fresh. The first solid rain of the summer, Amos thought, and he thanked God for it. At Fern's urging—some might call it steady nagging—he sat in the rocker on the front porch and tilted back his head, letting the warmth of the morning sun pour over him. Lately, he couldn't get warm, even on hot, humid days. The problem was his circulation, the doctor said at his last appointment. His heart had to work harder and harder to get oxygen-rich blood circulating through his body. He rubbed his hands. They felt stiff and clumsy, like he was trying to play a wooden whistle with mittens on a winter day.

Suddenly Menno came flying up the driveway and blew past him into the house, not even acknowledging Amos was there. He heard Menno's heavy footsteps pound up the stairs, then silence. A moment later, a loud "I FOUND IT!" floated out the upstairs windows. Amos leaned forward on his rocking chair, waiting to see *what* had been found.

Menno came thundering down the stairs again, two at a time, out the back door, and thrust his dog-eared *Birds, Birds, Birds!* book into Amos's hands. It was opened to the American pipit, a small sparrow-sized bird. "Look. I found my bird."

"The American pipit?" Amos read its description. *Pipits nest in the Arctic and migrate in spring and fall. Birders sometimes hope (but never expect) to find American pipits. Occasional stragglers appear south of Canada out of season during storms.* He looked up at Menno. "You think you spotted a lone American pipit? At the feeder?"

"No. Not at the feeder, Dad. It eats bugs." He gave Amos a look as if he couldn't believe he didn't know such things. "I found it on the woodpile." He pulled on Amos's sleeve. "Come see!"

He dragged Amos out to the woodpile, with Amos puffing for air, which triggered a coughing fit by the time they got there.

About ten feet from the pile, Menno stopped abruptly and pointed. "There!"

Sure enough, there was a small brown bird, perched on top of the woodpile, staring back at them. It was completely unafraid of humans—probably wasn't accustomed to seeing them, Amos surmised. The bird bobbed and fanned its tail, hopping from one stacked log to another. Its beak disappeared between wood pieces as it nabbed an ant or cricket or spider.

Amos held up the book and compared the markings of the bird to the picture in Menno's book. "Well, I'll be," he whispered. "I wonder if it missed its north-going bus in the spring? Or maybe it's early for going south. Probably got blown off its course in yesterday's storm." He and Menno stood there, in awe at the sight. "Menno, this little bird travels all the way from the Arctic to Mexico, every year. Across thousands of miles. And yet, it stopped on our farm to pay us a visit." He patted Menno on the back. "And you alone had the vision to notice it. That was no small coincidence, son."

Menno shook his head. "There's no such thing, Dad. You always said that what man calls a coincidence, God calls a miracle." Then his eyes opened wide. "I should call the Rare Bird Alert. They need to know about our miracle." He backed away slowly so he wouldn't startle the bird. When he reached the driveway, he bolted to the phone shanty by the schoolhouse.

Amos stayed awhile longer, watching this little brown bird enjoy lunch on the woodpile. "Thank you, God," he prayed. "For blessings large and small. For a little lonely bird that reminds us that not a sparrow can fall from the sky without your notice." Finally, he turned to leave. He felt lighter, happier, than he had in a long while. *Maybe today*, he thought, *my heart is starting to heal. Maybe God is bringing me a miracle too.*

June turned out to be M.K.'s busiest month, thanks largely to the American pipit, which seemed to enjoy its stay at Windmill Farm. It was in no hurry to leave. When word got out about such a rare bird sighting, visitors came from all over southeastern Pennsylvania. M.K. had never seen so many people at Windmill Farm in all her life. Many Amish bird lovers, but mostly English ones. Sadie ran to the house whenever a car pulled up the long drive. She peeked out the kitchen window as they emerged from their cars—she was curious about English folk but far too shy to speak to them. Menno, on the other hand, greeted each guest like a long-lost friend. M.K. had the crackerjack idea of charging folks for seeing the bird, but when Fern caught wind of it, she made M.K. give the money back.

Fern. So meddlesome!

Fern bought Menno a guest book so that the visitors could sign their names. Each evening, Menno counted up the names. Last night, the number had topped three hundred! Menno was thrilled. Sadie said she was hoping that little bird would soon be on its way and life at Windmill Farm could return to normal. It hadn't occurred to Menno that the bird wasn't staying. His face grew red and blotchy as he tried not to cry, so Sadie took it back.

This afternoon, M.K. was directing cars to park alongside the barn so they didn't clog the driveway. To her delight, the man in the panama hat drove up in a truck and waved to her. His truck was pulling a big silver recreation vehicle that reminded M.K. of a giant can of soda pop. M.K. ran up to the truck and waited until the man hopped out of the cab.

"Hello!" she said. "Are you here to see the bird?"

"I am!" he said, looking pleased. "It's the talk of the town that there's a rare bird on an Amish farm. Wasn't hard to find which farm." He pointed to the long line of cars.

"I'll take you out to see it," she said, abandoning her duties as parking director.

As they walked out to the woodpile, the man said, "Let's see. The last time I saw you, you were in the library, looking for ways to make a quick buck. Did you have any luck with the shell game?"

She frowned. "I wouldn't exactly call it luck."

"Were you able to earn enough money to help your family?"

"*That* would take a mountain of money."

"Why is that?" He seemed genuinely interested.

"My father needs surgery and I don't think I could ever make enough nickels off of the shell game to pay for a new heart."

The man stopped in his tracks. "What's wrong with his heart?"

M.K. scratched her head. "His heart is wearing out. But we're praying for a miracle."

The man rubbed his chin, deep in thought. "I don't believe in miracles."

How sad! M.K. counted on miracles. Every day. She watched the man in the panama hat observe the bird until Fern shouted at her to get back to the driveway and direct cars. A traffic jam had formed at the top of the rise.

Later that afternoon, Uncle Hank stormed into the kitchen. "WHEN IS THAT BIRD GONNA HIT THE ROAD?"

Fern was giving a serious beating to egg whites in a metal bowl. Without looking up, she asked, "What's eating you?"

"MENNO SAYS HE'S TOO BUSY TO GO TURKEY HUNTING WITH ME! And I spotted a flock just this morning. RIPE FOR THE PICKING!" Uncle Hank pulled off his straw hat and tossed it on a bench, then pulled out a chair at the kitchen table and plopped into it. "I need his keen vision."

"Maybe Fern would like to go with you," M.K. added, trying to sound helpful. She looked at Uncle Hank with wide and innocent eyes. The truth was, she was still mad at Fern for making her return money to paying bird visitors. It was a substantial amount of money. And folks didn't bat an eye when she pointed out the cardboard sign listing admission prices: $5 per adult, $2 for children under 12. "She's always telling me she's got eyes on the back of her head."

Uncle Hank eyed Fern with his good eye.

"That's not a bad idea," Amos said, sitting in a chair in the far corner of the room with his feet raised. "She doesn't miss a thing."

Fern continued to beat the egg whites.

Uncle Hank gave that some serious thought. Then he slammed his palms on the tabletop. "Fine! We'll leave at dawn." He jumped up from the table and grabbed his hat. He pointed a finger at Fern. "AND DON'T BE LATE!"

Fern examined the egg whites, now stiff and in peaks, and set down the bowl. "Well, then, Mary Kate, I hope you don't mind getting up extra early to fix breakfast, seeing as how I'll be out chasing turkeys in the morning." She arched an eyebrow in M.K.'s direction. "And I'll expect this kitchen to be spotless when I return."

M.K. exchanged a look with her father.

He shrugged his shoulders in a "Don't-look-at-me. You-started-it" way. "Maybe next time you have a brainstorm, you could run it by me first," he said.

Amos was paying bills at his desk when he heard a commotion on the back porch, then the kitchen door squeak open and shut with a bang. He really should oil that hinge. He leaned back in his chair and saw Fern scolding Uncle Hank.

"Hank Lapp, you're mucking up my perfectly good clean floors with those rubber boots of yours! Look at the tracks you're leaving! Now I'll have to get down on my hands and knees with a Brillo pad to get them off the linoleum."

Something seemed odd to Amos. Getting chewed out by Fern was nothing new to any of them, but he could tell her heart wasn't in the scolding today.

Uncle Hank saw Amos and stomped straight into the living room, hands perched on his hips, rubber boots still on. "You and your big ideas! I will never take that woman shooting with me ever again!"

"That bad, eh?" Amos said, smiling.

"Fern did everything wrong, got nothing right! She chattered too much, disturbed the undergrowth, loaded the wrong gauge shot in the gun, used the wrong luring whistles."

Fern came into the room with a glass of water and a handful of pills for Amos. "Tell him," she said primly. "Tell him what happened."

Uncle Hank glared at her. "Worst of all," he bellowed, "SHE SHOT MORE TURKEYS THAN ME!"

A broad grin spread over Fern's face. "The truth is too much for some people and too little for others." Though she didn't gloat, she did look satisfied as she swiveled on her heels and returned to the kitchen.

Friday began as a mild, sunny day. Julia was pleased to see her father downstairs at the kitchen table, reading the newspaper. She knew this was Fern's doing. Every day, Fern insisted that Amos get out of bed, get dressed, join his family, and do something physical to stay active. No excuses.

This morning, she needed to talk to her father privately and waited until the house was empty. As Julia sat in the chair across from him, he patted her hand with his. He had such big hands. Now they looked frail. When had his skin taken on such a grayish tint? Had she grown accustomed to his frailty? "Menno thinks he's fallen in love with Annie. He wants to marry her."

Last evening, as Julia was turning off the lamp in the kitchen, Menno had come downstairs and announced to her, "Me and Annie are getting married."

"Oh, Menno, for heaven's sake," Julia had said, pushed to the limit of her patience. "How can you get married? You don't know the first thing about marriage, either one of you."

"We know," Menno had said. "We know about marriage."

Julia had hardly slept last night, she was so bothered by Menno's news.

Amos studied the coffee mug in his hand as if it could portend the future. "I always had a feeling," he said, thoughtful and far-off. "Like this was bound to happen, one day or another. And now it has."

"That's it? That's all you have to say about the matter?"

He leaned back in the chair. "They're young, Julia. It'll fizzle out."

Julia was not sure, though. She had a funny feeling from the start about Menno's relationship with Annie. "What if it doesn't?" Julia said. "What if it's a huge mistake?"

Amos lifted one bushy eyebrow. "Folks make mistakes all of the time,

Julia. And God has a way of bringing good out of those mistakes." He dropped his chin to his chest. "We need to leave our Menno in God's hands."

Julia rubbed her face with her hands. "I know you're right. I wish I could talk to Rome about this. He might have an idea."

"You can."

"I can't. He hasn't come around in weeks."

Amos pointed a thumb toward the window. "He's right outside."

"Paul?" She hurried to the window, peered out, and turned back to her father. "That's Rome."

"That's who you said. You wanted to talk to Rome about Menno."

"No. I said Paul."

"My heart may be giving me trouble, but my hearing is just fine. You said Rome."

"I *meant* Paul."

"You said Rome and I think you *meant* Rome."

Julia shook her head and left the room, exasperated.

On Sunday evening, Paul went to a singing at Rose Hill Farm, Lizzie's home. He had been looking forward to it all week, until the moment when Rome Troyer pulled up in a buggy with Julia. When Paul saw Rome help Julia down from the buggy, he set his jaw and looked away. But a moment later his gaze had gone back to studying Rome and Julia. He felt something like fear roil up sour in his belly. Why? Paul was the one who kept holding Julia at arm's length. He should be relieved that someone else was courting Julia. And in a way, he was. But what bothered him was that person happened to be Roman Troyer.

It was the way Rome had looked at Julia. Not that snagging a look at Julia—at most of the girls—was unusual for the young men. It was part of every singing. As the girls arrived, the boys gathered in small clumps and watched them. Tonight, as Julia walked from the buggy to the stone farmhouse, every fellow present had stopped talking, stopped moving. Why, even the buggy horses stilled. Paul had heard the fellow next to him, Isaac Yoder, ease his breath out in a slow, slow whistle.

"She's mine," Paul shot back, surprising even himself with the force of his protest, so that of course he flushed.

Isaac turned his head slowly away from watching Julia gracefully climb the steps of the farmhouse. "Oh? Does Rome Troyer know she's yours?"

Paul looked at Isaac sharply, and Isaac nudged him in the ribs to make him smile. Then, as if of one accord, their gazes had been pulled back to Julia, standing on the porch, laughing at something Rome had said.

Paul felt a surge of jealousy. Julia was his.

This evening wasn't going at all the way Julia had planned. She agreed to go to the singing with Rome with hopes that Paul might notice. She had lingered a little extra long out on the porch, laughed a little extra loud at something funny Rome had said. She hoped to be heading home tonight in Paul's courting buggy, but her plans went awry. Paul seemed to have vanished, and just as Julia started to look for him, suddenly she was being ushered to the buggy by Rome.

"Paul Fisher is a fool," Rome whispered to her as he helped her into the buggy. A lump rose in Julia's throat and emotion welled behind her eyes. He couldn't have imagined how much she needed to hear that right now.

"Thanks." She swallowed hard, trying to get herself under control. An emotional moment with Roman Troyer wasn't anywhere in her plans for this evening.

As the horse jerked forward, Julia decided to steer the conversation away from anything too personal and on to something safer. She spilled out her worries about Menno and Annie to Rome. "Menno simply cannot live by himself, not even for a day. If a fire broke out, he would be frightened and wouldn't know what to do."

Rome was quiet for a moment. "He wouldn't be alone. He would be with Annie."

"He could never be responsible for another human being."

"Who are you to say?"

Embarrassment warmed Julia's neck and cheeks. She was the one who usually had the answers, not the one needing advice. Maybe Rome and her father were right. Maybe Menno and Annie would be okay, more or less, together. Menno seemed not to worry very much about things, but rather to accept the world as a fascinating place where anything might happen. Why did she have to spoil his dream, his life, with troubles about the future?

Julia wasn't entirely persuaded, but she felt calmer now. Talking to Rome had that effect, she noticed; his presence felt so normal, so reassuring and right. Such kind thoughts about Rome surprised her. An image in her mind shifted, like a reflection in a pond turning wavy after she tossed in a stone. As the ripples slowed and stilled, a new picture emerged: Rome Troyer—sincere, steady, even wise. Not at all the arrogant oaf she had made him out to be. He turned to her suddenly, as if he could read her thoughts. His gaze met hers and held it. A soft breeze tickled loose hairs on the back of Julia's neck. For just a moment, she imagined herself as Rome's Julia.

Rome leaned closer to her, surprisingly close, and she thought he might be thinking about kissing her. But at the last moment, he nudged her softly with his shoulder, the way a friend might after a joke. "Listen, Julia," he said, his voice kind and empathetic. "You need to take your mind off all these 'what-ifs.' Things like this have a way of working out for the best." Then he turned his attention to the horse, prodding him to hurry along.

The moon slid behind a cloud. In a passing field, a screeching barn owl swooped in and pounced on a squealing mouse. As the buggy turned into Windmill Farm, Julia wished Rome had taken the longer way home, past Blue Lake Pond. The conversation between them felt unfinished, and for reasons she couldn't explain, she felt a little disappointed that the ride was over. She suddenly realized it had completely slipped her mind to notice whether Paul's buggy was still at Rose Hill Farm.

14

Sadie was luxuriating in an hour of uninterrupted time, a rarity at Windmill Farm on any given day. She was sitting on the porch steps, reading through a book about home remedies that Fern had checked out of the library for her. Fern and Julia had taken Amos into town for a doctor's appointment, Uncle Hank was delivering a long overdue and finally repaired buggy, and Menno had slipped off with Lulu and her pup to visit Annie. M.K. had gone to the orchard to observe the beehives. Rome was . . . who knew where? It was one of those perfect July days when temperatures dipped into the low eighties and an occasional puffy cloud sailed across a flawless sky. The air was filled with birdsong and the subtle scents of dianthus and wild violets. How easy it was to lose herself in the beauty of the day.

Suddenly, an ear splitting scream sliced through the quiet. M.K. ran toward the house from the path that led to the peach orchard. "SAA-AADIEEEEE! There's a bear! BEAR!" She flew past Sadie and into the house, galloped up the stairs, and slammed her bedroom door.

Sadie blew out a puff of air. M.K.'s vivid imagination could wear a person out. It was high time for school to start. She went back to reading her book.

A few minutes later, Sadie glanced up and saw a yearling bear lumbering down the dirt path toward the house, as calm and relaxed as if he had been invited to Sunday supper. Sadie threw down her book and ran into the house and locked the door behind her.

"I *told* you so!" M.K. said as she peeked her head around the stairwell. "No one ever believes me!"

"Hush!" Sadie had to think. What to do?

The bear climbed up onto the porch and pressed its nose against the kitchen window. It was looking right at them!

"Don't move a muscle, M.K."

The bear sniffed around the porch, knocked Sadie's book around, then lumbered down the steps and into Julia's garden. Sadie got Amos's double-barreled shotgun off its wall hinges and found some steel shot shells in a drawer. She had never shot anything before, but she had watched her dad load a gun many times. She knew enough to choose light shells. She didn't want to kill the bear, just hurry it on its way. She went into Fern's bedroom, opened the window a few inches, aimed the gun at the bear—which was helping itself to Julia's ripe raspberries—and pulled the trigger. She peppered the bear in the rear. It howled and ran off to the nearest tree.

The bear sat up in the tree, staring down at the house for the longest while. Finally, it climbed down and lumbered off into the woods. No sooner had Sadie put away the gun but M.K. spotted the mamma bear lumbering along, sniffing after the scent of her cub. Eventually it too disappeared into the woods behind their house.

Sadie and M.K. stayed inside the house for the rest of the afternoon, rifle loaded.

Summer had deepened. The days were hot and humid, the nights cooler, the air drifting with evening mist.

M.K. spent half of an afternoon trying to find Paul Fisher. She knew he was in town because she saw his buggy and sorrel mare parked at a hitching post. She had tried the hardware store first, then the bakery, but no luck so far. Her next stop was the Hay & Grain, so she slipped inside and looked around. Bingo! Paul was chatting with the store clerk. M.K. grabbed a bag of birdseed, hoisted it over her shoulder, and went up to the cash register. She slapped the birdseed onto the countertop and tried to look surprised when she saw Paul.

"M.K., what are you doing here?" Paul glanced around to see if she was alone.

"Ran out of birdseed at Windmill Farm." She tried to pretend she was out of breath. "Needed some. An emergency."

Paul smiled. "Why would birdseed be an emergency?"

M.K. busied herself with getting her money out of her shoes. "Oh . . . because it brings such happiness to my sister."

Paul watched her count out five one-dollar bills. "I thought Menno was the bird lover at your farm. Since when has Sadie been such a bird-watcher?"

M.K. shook her head. "Not Sadie. *Julia.* We're trying to make Julia's last few days on earth happy ones."

Paul cocked his head as if he hadn't heard her right.

"Oh, didn't you hear? Julia's dying. She has—" She searched around the store for something. Her eyes landed on a flyer posting a warning about chickens. "Salmonella poisoning."

"What? I passed your farm just this morning and saw her setting up her stand."

M.K. regarded him sadly. "So brave." She handed over the dollars to the clerk and picked up the birdseed. "I'd better get back." She raised her eyebrows. "Not a minute to spare, you know. Salmonella acts like this." She snapped her fingers in the air.

She was down the street when Paul's buggy came up beside her. "Hop in," he said, eyeing her suspiciously.

This was playing out just as she had planned! Paul opened up the buggy door and grabbed the birdseed from her. In the backseat of the buggy was Jimmy, who looked at M.K. as if she were a rattlesnake.

She froze midair. "Maybe I'll just walk home."

"I told you she was lying!" Jimmy jeered.

M.K. scowled.

Paul pulled her in. "Knock it off, Jimmy. M.K., let's go see how bad off Julia is." He yanked the buggy door closed. "She sure didn't look too poorly when she was nuzzling Rome Troyer the other night."

M.K. drew herself up straight. "Lapp women do not nuzzle."

"I'll say!" Jimmy piped up. "They're as mean as black racer snakes."

She turned around and caught the smug look on his face. "Jimmy Fisher! You know you were the one who put that black racer in the girls' bathroom."

Jimmy shrugged. "Prove it."

M.K. stared at him, astounded. How could one boy be so thoroughly obnoxious?

Jimmy stared back and rested his folded arms on the backing of the front seat.

Paul elbowed him back. "Jimmy, you stop bothering Mary Kate."

M.K. looked at Paul appreciatively. He was a mild fellow, inoffensive, a little awkward, but if M.K. worked hard and squinted her eyes, she could see his appeal. Jimmy, though, was another story. She was making a mental list of Jimmy's faults when they arrived at Windmill Farm. There was Julia, at the stand, the very picture of health. Uh-oh! She thought Julia said she was going to a comfort quilt knotting this afternoon. She doubted Julia would understand why she had fibbed to Paul. On the other hand, Julia might be pleased to see that Paul was worried about her dying. This created a wrinkle, but nothing M.K. couldn't handle.

Paul hopped out of the buggy and started toward Julia. M.K. had one leg out the door, hoping to get to Julia before Paul did, but Jimmy grabbed her arm.

"Since Julia's dying and all, we should give her and Paul a moment alone to say their sorrowful goodbyes."

M.K. tried to uncurl Jimmy's hand and ended up biting it as hard as she could.

He yelped. "You little brat! The only one who's dying at Windmill Farm is your father!"

M.K. gasped. "You are going straight to the devil for telling such a lie, Jimmy Fisher!"

He examined his hand. "You broke the skin with your fangs. I'm probably gonna get rabies."

"Serves you right, you big liar."

Jimmy glared at her. "I ain't lying! Your father is dying. His heart's giving out on him. Everybody knows. It's plain as day." He looked closely at his hand, glanced up at her, then took a second look. "M.K., you must know that." He looked down again and added, softer this time, "Don't tell me you didn't know . . ."

M.K. got out of the buggy and started running toward the house. About halfway up the hill, Julia caught up with her and made her stop running.

"Why would you tell Paul such a ridiculous lie?" Then she took in M.K.'s face. "What's happened? What's wrong?"

"Is Dad dying?"

Julia's head shot up like a mother lion sniffing the air for danger to her cub. "What? Who told you that?"

"Jimmy. Is it true?"

Julia bit her lower lip. "He's not getting better like the doctors had hoped he would."

Both of M.K.'s hands flew up to cover her ears. She tried, tried, tried to block out Jimmy's words, but they kept bouncing into her head. She blinked a couple of times, and Julia reached out and wrapped her arms around her and hugged her as tight as she could.

When she let go, she gave M.K. a smile that didn't quite make it to her eyes. "Let's go to the house. Fern baked a peach pie."

A breeze filtered in through a partly open window, leaving in its wake the soft scents of late summer. Amos breathed in as deeply as he could without triggering a coughing fit, allowing the scents to uncap forgotten memories of happy moments. Days spent on his farm with his Maggie, when the children were just babes. The warmth of the sun on his cheeks as he lay on a hay wagon during a lunchtime break; the down of his grandmother's cheeks as she kissed him goodnight; the feel of his father's big hand covering his as they hammered nails at a barn raising. How easy it would be for Amos to just close his eyes and explore the trails of memory, twisting and turning, winding their way toward this moment.

All things considered, Amos felt blessed. He had been steward of a fine piece of land that had been in his family for four generations. He was given a happy, albeit far too brief marriage to Maggie Zook. He had good friends and neighbors. But of all his blessings, he especially gave thanks for his four children.

Aside from the current condition of his heart, he had lived a wonderful life.

After Amos heard about the blowup between M.K. and Jimmy, he told Fern to send the children upstairs to his room. Who was he kidding? He knew he wasn't improving. Julia knew. Uncle Hank knew. Fern knew. The doctors knew. The time had come to prepare the children for what was coming. Was it so bad for a man to know how God was calling him home? His dear Maggie had no such foreknowledge. He had no fear of death; his great hope was to live in the fullness of joy in God's presence. He would be reunited with his wife, his parents, a brother, and two sisters who had gone before him. It was only when he thought of his children that he felt a great despair, a longing to remain with them for a while longer. It was so hard seeing them, all of them, every day and knowing . . . it might be coming to an end.

They filed into his bedroom and stood around his bed like little soldiers, solemn and serious. M.K.'s red, swollen, staring eyes. Julia, stoic. Sadie, head bowed. Menno, his silent self. Amos looked at each one, his children. He loved each one so dearly. What wouldn't he do for his children?

Rome joined Fern at the doorjamb of Amos's room, and he waved them in. "Where's Uncle Hank?" Amos asked.

"He's off trying to track that bear," Fern said. "It was spotted near the Glicks' sheep last night."

"We need to have a talk," Amos started, his voice shaky. He coughed softly, ending with a dry-airy sound like wind blowing through a whistle. That blasted cough! "I had hoped that the new treatment the doctors were trying would help my heart get stronger." He took a deep breath. "But it doesn't seem to be the case. It seems as if the Lord might be calling me home a little sooner than I would have liked. But it's not for us to question God's timing."

M.K. let out a sob and threw herself on top of Amos. He wrapped his arms around her and stroked her back. Tears started blurring his vision, but he fought them back. He needed to be strong for his family. He knew this was a moment that would affect how they perceived God for the rest of their lives. Isn't that what Rome struggled with? Some tragedy, some kind of loss, that altered him forever? He didn't want that for his own children. Loss was part of life, dying part of living. There was a time for all things, King Solomon said. Amos believed those words with all his heart. And he wanted his children to believe them too. To hold tight to the Lord through these seasons. What else did we have, when all was said and done, but the Lord God?

He glanced at Rome, whose eyes were fixed on Julia. She stood at the foot of Amos's bed, hugging her elbows tightly, holding herself in one piece. Her face was tight. This wasn't new information for her. She had spoken to the doctors last week about what the future looked like. That was his Julia—she looked delicate, like the faintest gust of wind might blow her over, but she was strong where it counted most. Inside.

He remembered when he had first noticed her inner strength. It was the day she had seen her mother buried, and she knew she had three little siblings who looked up to her. He knew he could always count on Julia.

His gaze shifted to Sadie. She looked so sad. *Oh Sadie, don't be sad.* Of all of his children, Sadie worried him the most. She always had, even as a little girl. You'd think he would fret over Menno, but his son was blessed with an abundance of simple faith in God. His mind may not run as quickly as others, but his faith never wavered. God was good, and God loved Menno. That was all the information that Menno seemed to need.

But Sadie—she was so gentle, so timid, so fearful, so unsure of herself. Always in the background, trying hard to be invisible.

Mary Kate lifted her tearstained face. She, of all the children, was the most like his Maggie. She would be fine, even if she didn't know it yet. "What does it feel like to die?"

He put his hand on her small head. "Do you remember how we would wake up before Menno and Julia and Sadie? And we'd sit together—you and me and Mom—and Mom would make hot chocolate for you, and I'd have my coffee, and Mom would have her tea, and we'd sit quietly, listening for the rooster to crow? Then Mom would take the lamp that sat on the kitchen table, and she'd blow out the wick. Because she knew morning had come." He lifted her chin. "That's what it's like, M.K. It's like blowing out the wick of a lamp because morning is coming."

Menno crouched down by Amos's bed. "Dad, does a person have two hearts? Like he has two kidneys?"

He put his hand on Menno's soft hair. "No, Menno. Just one heart per person."

"If I had two, I could give you one."

With that comment, Amos's tears flowed freely. Rome dropped his head, and Sadie sniffed loudly. Finally, Fern had enough of this emotion. "That's enough. Everybody out. He's not going anywhere today." She waved everyone downstairs. As they filed out past her, she said, "We don't put a question mark where God has put a period."

Rome waited at Amos's door until they all left. He had one boot against the doorjamb, with his arms crossed. "What Fern just said—those words are true. But Amos, what if God has just put a comma? Not a period?" He reached a hand for the door and quietly closed it as he left.

A comma? Amos knew what Rome was getting at—a heart transplant. He'd been hammering that home the last few weeks. Amos leaned his head against the pillow. He had been against the idea since he first heard the word mentioned at the doctor's office, months ago. It didn't seem right to him. The Bible said a man was appointed to live once and to die once. He closed his eyes. How could he dare hope for a new heart? That would mean a person's life had been taken. How could he even pray such a prayer?

There were seasons in a person's life. A time when one knew heaven couldn't be far away, when a man's life was ebbing away. This was Amos's last season. He needed to search his soul, to confess all sin—what he had done and what he had failed to do—and to seek God's forgiveness.

A comma, Rome had said. *Lord*, Amos prayed, *you will have to tell me clearly if that's what you want me to pursue. I just don't think I could accept such a thing. It's asking too much.*

A few days later, M.K. was playing a game of checkers with her father when Julia and Sadie came into the room, interrupting. They plopped down in the chairs that had been put in Amos's room for visitors.

"Fern said you wanted to see us," Julia said.

Not *now!* M.K. thought. She was winning!

"Where's Menno?" Amos said.

"He and Uncle Hank are out bear hunting," Sadie said. "Uncle Hank thinks he's got the bear's whereabouts figured out. Between the Smuckers' and the Stoltzfuses' farm." She sat back in the chair. "Of course, Uncle Hank has thought that for days now."

"And he's always wrong," M.K. added, jumping two of Amos's checkers.

Amos frowned at her. "He's doing his best." He picked up his checker and jumped one of hers.

Surprised, M.K. studied the board. "It's no secret that Uncle Hank is a terrible hunter. Even Stern Fern has a better shot."

Just as Amos opened his mouth to defend Uncle Hank, Julia interceded. "Speaking of Fern, she said you had something important to talk to us about."

Amos leaned his back against the headboard. "I'm going to sell off the orchards. I can get big money for that acreage. Enough to put a dent in these hospital bills."

Julia slapped her forehead, gave it a real crack. "So that's it. Well, you can just forget it. We'll find a way to pay down that debt, Dad. The church will help us—you know they will."

"Everyone's suffering after this drought. I can't expect them to pay what they don't have. They've already helped us—above and beyond."

"We can get along without selling off the orchards." Julia's chin lifted a notch. "We always have."

"I'll keep the house for all of you, so you'll always have a home, free and clear. I don't want to leave behind any doubts or debts. And I'll keep a few acres surrounding it, for a garden and pastureland for Menno's livestock."

"Just who do you think you'll sell it to?" Julia asked, firing up. "What if one of our neighbors can't afford to buy it and you end up selling to a developer? Why, they'll bulldoze everything right up to the house. And they'll stick in as many houses as they can fit in. You've seen what it looks like. No yards. Just house after house after house."

"I've made up my mind," Amos said, very dignified. "And you know what my mind is like when I've made it up."

Boy, that upset Julia.

It got quiet then, very quick, while M.K. and Sadie waited to see what Julia had to say to that. It was like watching a Ping-Pong game.

Fern walked in with a stack of fresh laundry. She set the stack down on the bureau top before she turned to Amos. "Just because the boat rocks doesn't mean it's time to jump overboard." Then she left.

15

After supper, Julia and Menno went out to check on the animals and lock the barn. She sent Menno back to the house, and tousled his hair when he gave her a puzzled look. "You go in. M.K. is waiting for you to help her with a puzzle. I'll be in soon."

"But . . . the bear," Menno said. "Dad said not to go out at night by ourselves. He won't even let Lulu out."

She smiled. "I won't be out that long. I promise."

She walked down the drive to the roadside stand. The last few hours had been so emotionally churning, she had forgotten to close up the stand for the day. The honor jar was still there, plus the day's produce that hadn't sold. As she walked, she mulled over the conversation her father had with them. She knew that he was settling his accounts, preparing all of them for his passing. He was trying to solve all of the tangible problems his absence would create—but what about those intangible problems? What about M.K. needing a parent in a role that a sister couldn't fulfill? And how would Sadie cope? She was so tenderhearted and sensitive. If her father sold most of the land surrounding the house—and maybe that was the right thing to do, maybe not—what would Menno do without a farm? What would he do without a father to guide him each day? What would any of them do without their father? He was their anchor.

No, that wasn't right. God alone was their anchor, she reminded herself. God's ways were good and just. If he took their father home now, he must have a good reason.

But what?

She had prayed so often for God to heal her father. She believed in prayer. Prayer worked. Lately, she had prayed and prayed and prayed as she had never prayed before. She prayed one large circular prayer beginning with "Lord, thy will be done" and ending with "Please, God, please, please, please, don't let my dad die."

But God seemed to be saying no.

She reached the stand and saw the honor jar was gone. The produce was gone. She had *thought* she had heard a car door slam during dinner. Someone had driven by and taken it all. It wasn't the amount—maybe twenty or thirty dollars—but it was the last straw on a bad day. Self-pity, which had been buzzing around her all afternoon, settled in. She looked up at the sky. "It's not fair!" she said to herself, eyes filling with tears. "It's just not fair!"

"What isn't fair?"

She whirled around to find Rome watching her, a curious look on his face. "What do you mean, sneaking up on me like that?"

"I wasn't sneaking." He took a step closer to her. "So what's not fair?"

"Everything!"

"Like what, exactly?"

"Like . . . my father wants to sell the land to pay off his hospital bills because he's sure his heart is wearing out on him. And he's probably right!"

"That's why I keep encouraging him to get on the heart transplant list."

"He won't do it. I've tried."

"We have to try harder."

"This is between my father and God. A heart transplant is no simple thing. I don't know how I would feel if I were in his shoes." She crossed her arms against her chest. "Do you?"

"I would fight to live, that's what I'd do. I can't understand why Amos won't fight for all of you. He has a chance—but without that transplant, he's going to die."

"Stop it!" Julia lifted her hands and held them over her ears to shut out the words. She stood frozen, her spine rigid, her hands clamped to her ears. Tears coursed down her cheeks.

Rome wrapped her stiff body in his arms and began stroking her back and shushing her. "There, now, it's all right. I'm sorry I made you cry. Last thing I want is to hurt you. There, now, everything's going to be all right."

Gradually the tension ebbed from her body, and for a moment she sagged against him. He was so solid. So safe.

Safe? The thought made her jerk away. She drew back her shoulders and stood back, despite the tears she couldn't quite stop shedding. "I have to go." She turned her back to him and began to walk toward the house.

"Julia, wait!"

She turned back. Rome reached down and picked up a basket. In it was the honor jar, filled with money, and the day's unsold produce. "I saw you hadn't closed up for the night. I was bringing it up to the house when I noticed a fence board had fallen over there, so I stopped to nail it." He handed her the basket. "Everything's going to turn out all right, Julia."

It was a nice thought, but Amos wasn't Rome's father, and Windmill Farm wasn't his home. Still, he was trying to be reassuring and Julia did appreciate the sentiment. Something caught her eye and she looked in the basket to see a handful of fives, tens, and twenties stuffed in the honor jar. So much money for one day! The most she had ever made. And here she thought it had been stolen.

Impulsively, she leaned over and pecked a kiss on Rome's cheek. Her action surprised them both. She felt her breath catch as Rome turned to look at her more fully. In the fading evening light, his dark eyes seemed black and serious and compelling.

"Hi, guys!" M.K. pranced up. "What are you two doing all alone out here?"

M.K. ran ahead of Rome and Julia to the house. It was close to lightning-bug time, and Uncle Hank said he might have a yarn or two to spin. When Uncle Hank was in a storytelling mood, you didn't want to miss a minute of it. She told Rome and Julia to hurry, but they didn't seem as eager to get to the house as she thought they'd be. Uncle Hank and her father were sitting on the front porch, in rockers that Menno had brought out, like two dotty old men. She'd never thought they resembled each other, but the thinner her father became, the more he looked like Uncle Hank. The thought made her sad.

"THERE YOU ARE, MARY KATE!" Uncle Hank thundered. "I can't start my story without you!"

She sat on the steps with her back against the railing. Sadie sat next to her, and Menno jumped up to sit on the porch rail. Rome sprawled out on the grass, below the steps, where Lulu found him and covered his face with licks. Julia found a place next to Sadie, who had Lulu's pup in her lap. Tonight, even Fern was joining them. She brought an upright chair from the kitchen out on the porch and sat in it like she was at church. "Shoulders," she tossed in Sadie's and M.K.'s direction, and Sadie immediately straightened her back.

Uncle Hank leaned back in the chair, feet spread apart, his head tilted up toward the ceiling, an indication that he was ready to begin. "It was the winter of '58," he started. "I was just a lad, not much bigger than our Mary Kate." He looked down at her when he said that and she smiled. He always began his stories in the same way.

"There had been sightings of a large white buck that winter. Ten points on his antlers! It had become something of a legend. Folks weren't entirely sure if that buck had been made up or if it was a real thing. Lots of speculation was going on about the big white buck that winter.

"Sure enough, one day, that buck passed the schoolhouse, and a farmer was on his tail. The farmer opened the schoolhouse door and called out for all hands to join in a grand hunt. We had a man teacher and, knowing his boys and what would happen, he put his back to the door to keep us boys from fleeing. No sooner had he done it than up went three windows and out poured a live stream of boys. There wasn't a boy left to chew gum. Finally, the teacher followed." He winked at M.K. "He was too timid a fellow to stay alone with the girls."

Menno rolled that over in his mind for a moment and let out a loud "Haw!"

Uncle Hank leaned back in his chair and crossed one big boot over the other. "The deer took off across a field and onto the lake, covered with ice. The deer slipped and one of the big boys—Mose Weaver—came very near to overtaking it. But just as he reached out to touch it . . ." Uncle Hank reached a hand out in the air as if he was trying to touch the buck ". . . the deer found its footing and set off again. Quick as a wink, the deer was on the north shore of the lake. We boys kept our sight on the deer and lit out after it.

"After a long hunt I found the deer in some brush, and gave vent to my gentle voice," to which M.K. snorted and Uncle Hank nudged her with his boot, "and out it ran, well rested and as good as ever. By this time two of the boys had run home and returned with guns. As the deer passed within a few feet of them, they just stood in awe of this magnificent beast. Neither took a shot at it until it was well hidden in the thick bushes. Each blamed the other for not shooting the deer."

"Did anyone ever get that deer?" Menno asked.

"Alas, Menno, none of us tasted venison from that hunt."

"What ever happened to the buck?" M.K. asked.

"What became of the deer I never knew, but that winter, we were all seriously afflicted with buck fever, something only time and experience will cure."

Fern gave a guffaw. "Hasn't done much to cure you. You've got yourself a serious case of bear fever. You spend half your time trying to track that bear and cub!"

Uncle Hank looked offended. "That bear is going to hurt somebody soon. She's getting bolder and bolder. Came right up to old Fannie King's kitchen door last week. Scared Fannie so bad she dropped her choppers!"

Sadie gasped. It didn't take much to scare Sadie, but even M.K. felt a tingle down her spine.

"Uncle Hank!" Amos said. A warning passed between the two. They all noticed. Well, maybe not Menno.

That bear and cub were starting to get everyone edgy. It was the top news of every gathering—who had seen them last, what damage they had caused, how crafty that mama bear was, if it was time to call the game warden in. Sadie shivered, though the night was hot.

Uncle Hank eased up out of his chair, stretched, and yawned. "It is a well-known fact that a buck's tail is not very long, but this one will be an exception unless I come to a close."

It had sprinkled a little in the morning, but now the clouds had broken up and the August sun was bearing down. Julia found Rome out in the pasture where Menno kept his small flock of ewes. She called to him and he waited for her at the top of the meadow. Before she reached him, he wiped the perspiration from his cheeks with his sleeve. He was pushing a small cart filled with clover hay. Menno's ewes had crowded around the cart, trying to snatch hay, and made it difficult for him to move. As she walked toward him, the ewes looked up, regarded her with their sweet, blank faces, and then went back to the serious business of eating. She shaded her eyes from the late-afternoon sun.

When she reached him, she held out a napkin with fresh hot doughnuts on it. "Fern made these for you. She thought Dad and Sadie's diet might be wearing thin on you." They had all lost weight this summer, all but M.K. and Menno, for whom Fern relaxed kitchen rules.

He pulled off his gloves and threw them on top of the hay. He took the napkin from her, lifted it, and breathed deeply. "I could smell those doughnuts frying way out here." He took a bite and closed his eyes. "Takes me right back to my boyhood."

"You haven't mentioned your family. Where did you grow up?" She found herself often wondering about Rome and wasn't about to let this opportunity pass.

He broke off a section of his doughnut. "Here and there." He popped the last bite of doughnut in his mouth and reached for his gloves. He broke open a dense clump of hay, releasing a sudden scent of white clover. He scattered the hay over the ground, so the ewes would leave the cart alone.

"Rome, what would you think about staying a few extra months this fall to help us get through the harvest? Menno does well when he has someone working with him. If you could stay through October—work with Menno on the hay cuttings, supervise the threshing frolics, help us get the corn into the silo." She paused. "The truth is, having you here has brought a peace of mind to my father."

"It's about time for a change of scene soon." He grinned at her. "There's roaming in my blood."

Julia couldn't imagine such a thought. She looked out over the fenced fields, the cows clumped together under a shade tree, a creek that wound its way through the pastures to nourish the land. In the sky, high overhead, she could see the arrows of a flock of geese heading toward the lake. "A home like this—it seems to me that you couldn't find a better place to be than right here. The earth here is generous and outgoing, like the people in Stoney Ridge. It's a place that keeps you anchored to life." She turned and found him staring at her. "But maybe you don't want to be anchored." She hadn't posed it as a question, but she waited for an answer all the same. The emotions that played over his face ranged from sadness to coldness, then settled into something that looked like discomfort.

"Would you at least consider staying through October for my father's sake?"

The rascal returned to his eyes. "What about for your sake, Julia?"

"What about me?"

He gave her a sly grin. "Do you want me to stay?"

"I wouldn't be asking if I didn't think you provided a benefit to my family."

He threw the last of the hay onto the ground. Then he pulled off his gloves and turned to her. "So you want me to stay. Just admit it."

She could feel bright red patches burning in her cheeks. "I'm only admitting that your presence provides peace of mind to my father. That's all."

His gaze slipped from her eyes to her lips. "So you don't really care if I stay or leave?"

"No. I'm only asking for my father's sake."

He stepped closer to her and brushed her cheek with his knuckles. "So this doesn't make you feel anything?" His voice was deep and teasing.

She drew up her chin and met his gaze. She thought about stepping back but decided she should hold her ground. Even the smallest retreat would show weakness, and she wouldn't reveal any vulnerability. At the same time, his nearness made her head swim.

"And this?"

Slowly, Rome lifted his thumb and slid it upward along the curve of her jaw. His touch was surprisingly gentle. She knew she should pull back, she wanted to break away, but her legs wouldn't obey.

As she gazed up into that chiseled face, she tried to remember every grievance she held against the Bee Man. But as he lowered his head and his lips found hers, her reasoning was blotted out. One of Rome's arms slipped around her back, then another around her head. She found herself falling into the kiss. Seconds, minutes, hours later, Rome pulled away. His forehead rested on hers.

"Still nothing?" he whispered.

His kiss was gentle and persuading, sweet and tender, nothing at all like Paul's pleasant kisses.

Paul. PAUL. She sprang back. "Not a thing," she said coolly, trying to not appear as shaken as she felt. She pushed past him to leave.

"Julia, where are you going?"

"Back to the house," she called out without turning around.

"Then you're headed in the wrong direction."

Rome chuckled softly. Julia's small figure was strangely dignified as she walked away from him.

Until that moment, Rome had never seen a woman blush on top of a blush, but Julia managed it when he pointed out she was starting out to the house in the wrong direction. He had to bite on his bottom lip to keep from laughing out loud.

It was mean, he supposed, what he had done to her. Kissing her like that, in broad daylight. It's just that she looked so adorable, standing there with confectioner's sugar on her cheek. She was warm in his arms, and she smelled like a doughnut.

What he couldn't get out of his mind was that she kissed him back! Never in his wildest imagination would he have thought that prim and proper Julia Lapp would have kissed him back, with that much passion. And when she couldn't meet his gaze, he knew she was embarrassed.

Just look at me, he thought, *like some moonstruck teenager.* Roman Troyer, the Bee Man, Roamin' Roman, acting like an adolescent. He felt as if he were eighteen again, young and hopeful and naive, believing that anything was possible.

Julia had done him a favor, asking him to stay, making it seem like it was her idea. He'd already decided he was going to stick around a few more months. He felt a burden to help Amos get through this heart business. To help the whole family get through it. But how long would he stay? Would he still be here through Thanksgiving? Through Christmas? He hoped he might, and it was a strange feeling.

He shook his head and let out a long sigh. Where were those thoughts coming from? He hadn't felt this way last year, had he? Or the year before that?

Before Julia interrupted him, his thoughts had been traveling to another Thanksgiving, years ago, when his mother burned the turkey. And then he remembered the year when his youngest sister had tripped over a dog bone as she was bringing the turkey to the table and sent it flying into his father's lap. Oh, the surprised look on his father's face! The memory made him laugh out loud. But, as always, a sharp tug of pain swept in right behind it. He swallowed hard, banishing the images of the past as he tried to concentrate on feeding the sheep.

When memories of those days popped up in his mind, the images were still as crisp as a new dollar bill. Why were those thoughts hitting him so squarely in the jaw this year? Was it part of turning twenty-five? Feeling older?

He drew in a long breath, inhaling the woodsy scent laced with a clover hay fragrance. He leaned against the wagon and pulled out of his pocket an envelope. He reread the letter that he had picked up this morning at the post office.

Dear Roman,

Suffice it to say, I am someone who has made mistakes, and in buying the property, I am trying to remedy them. You may think I intend to raze the farm and build homes, or condominiums, or a strip center of shops, or an industrial park. Although that would be most lucrative, that's not what I will do. You have my promise. I want to keep the farm as it is.

Don't be a fool, Rome. Take the money.

R.W.

16

Julia awoke in the morning thinking of that kiss with Rome. The question she'd been trying to avoid asking felt like a fist in her stomach. How could she have let him kiss her like that? Then she remembered the way it felt—natural and wonderful. Yet what had she been thinking? Maybe there was something wrong with her.

Julia had no illusions about why Rome had kissed her. By acting immune to his charms, she'd turned herself into a challenge—a challenge he'd forget about the instant one of the local beauties caught his eye.

Yes, the kiss was quite . . . memorable. The only other man she had kissed was Paul, and his kisses were rather staid and formal. Avuncular, almost.

Rome's kiss wasn't like a relative's kiss, not at all. That kiss with Rome . . . she couldn't bear to think of it, of what he made her feel.

She could never deny that Rome was an attractive man, because he was. She also could not deny that he could be a caring, giving man—if he ever truly learned to love someone other than his bees.

Besides, her heart belonged to Paul. Was it wrong to let Rome kiss her? A twinge of guilt washed over her, but she decided to dismiss it. And she didn't kiss Rome—he kissed her! She was only indulging him. Just a whim. Flushing it out of her system. She had to forget what had happened and keep her wits about her. It would never happen again. Never. It was a terrific mistake. Never again!

Determined not to spend any more time analyzing that kiss, she jumped out of bed. Today was a new day. No ruthless man with dark eyes, no kiss she couldn't explain.

Amos smelled something delicious waft up the stairs and into his room. Fern's rich coffee, fried eggs, home fries seasoned only as she could do. Amos savored the savory smells. They were downright intoxicating. When had he last felt like he had an appetite? He couldn't remember.

Was that bacon? Better still, could it be scrapple? Menno must have asked her to cook for him. Fern indulged him. Just the thought of a bite of fried scrapple, slathered in ketchup, filled him with a spurt of energy to go downstairs. He slipped his feet onto the floor and pulled himself to a standing position. There. Step one.

Slowly, he tiptoed to the top of the stairs and waited until he heard Fern go out the kitchen door to hang a load of laundry. He was glad he hadn't gotten around to oiling that rusty hinge, after all. He went down the stairs, into the kitchen, and looked for the crispiest piece of scrapple there was, cooling on a paper towel. He slathered it with ketchup and was just about to take a bite when he saw Fern heading in from the yard. He scurried to the stairs and tried to get to his room as fast as he could, which wasn't too swift.

Back in his room, he sat on the bed trying to catch his breath and suddenly felt an enormous pressure on his chest, like it did when he and Menno used to wrestle and Menno would sit on him. He was faintly aware that the muscles in his left arm were beginning to constrict. His hand couldn't hold on to the scrapple and it fell to the floor, ketchup side down. Blast! He had worked hard for that scrapple.

Amos bent down to pick it up. That's when the room started to spin.

Julia laid the table with silverware. Fern was frying scrapple and two eggs apiece for all of them, like it was Christmas morning.

Uncle Hank burst into the kitchen and sat down at the table. "I came for your coffee, Fern!"

Fern raised an eyebrow and brought him a cup.

He took a long sip and smacked his lips. "That coffee is so rich and sturdy it could float a nail!"

Julia sized up Uncle Hank. His hair and beard were trimmed and his clothes looked clean. He was transformed! Menno stood by the kitchen stove with a mug of tea in his hand, giving Fern suggestions about how to make bread toasted just the way he liked it—nearly burnt but not quite. That was the longest speech that Julia ever heard come out of her brother's mouth. What was happening to him? To Uncle Hank? Even M.K. was chirpier than usual this morning. They all seemed changed, overnight. It was Fern's doings.

Fern sent M.K. upstairs to tell her father to stop ringing that bell incessantly because breakfast was on its way. M.K. was no sooner there than she was back again. She shot into the kitchen like a pack of hounds was on her tail. Her mouth was stretched in a wordless scream, and she was gray-faced.

She grabbed the edge of the table, then fetched up a breath and howled out, "Come quick! It's Dad! He's dead!"

On the way to the hospital in the ambulance, Amos heard the medic declare, in a voice that sounded distant, that he could not find a pulse. Why was he saying that? Amos wondered.

In the emergency room he heard a nurse say, "No pulse, no pressure." Twice, she said it. He also remembered being told, by a calm, soothing, yet authoritative voice, that it wasn't time yet for him to die.

Later, when he woke up in the intensive care room, Amos was told what had happened. He had collapsed, right on the bedroom floor, a bell in one hand, a piece of scrapple in the other. Caught red-handed!

All that Amos remembered was feeling pressure in his chest, a squeezing, as though his heart were a balloon about to burst. The E.R. doctor was able to revive him, but just barely, he was sternly told. "Next time, you won't be so lucky," the doctor warned. "Your heart is at war with itself. Your final defense is a transplant . . . or it is a war you will lose, Amos Lapp."

The doctor looked like a boy himself.

Amos asked the doctor if he had been the one who told him in the emergency room that he was not going to die. The doctor looked baffled.

He replied that he hadn't, nor did he recall anyone else in the room saying such a thing.

Then the doctor gave a broad grin. "Aren't you Amish the God-fearing type? Maybe it was an angel with a message from God." He leaned in close to Amos. "Maybe God is trying to tell you: AMOS LAPP! Get. Your. Name. On. The. Transplant. List."

Amos scowled. He knew the doctor was being facetious—but, he decided, strangely enough, he might be on to something. It wasn't a human-sounding voice. It was too deep, too melodious, too beautiful. Suddenly, Amos had no reservations or doubts about its claim. He believed that voice was from God. Maybe an angel, a messenger, but definitely sent from God.

Julia had told Rome once that he had a smile for every occasion, and he reluctantly realized . . . she was right. He was giving the nurse at the Intensive Care Unit his "Aw, shucks. You-don't-mind-doing-a-little-favor-for-me, do-you?" treatment.

"Ordinarily, only family members are allowed in," the nurse said. She batted her eyes at him with such alarming speed that Rome was afraid she'd blind herself. "But seeing as how all of you Amish folk seem to be related to each other, I'll just say you're a cousin if anyone asks." She gave him a wink.

"Well, thank you, Miss . . . ," Rome cast a quick glance at her nameplate, "Miss Chelsea."

The nurse led him to Amos's room. "Just fifteen minutes, though. Okay, honey?"

He smiled again and the nurse smiled back at him, touching the curls on the back of her neck. The smile slipped off his face as the nurse disappeared around the corner, her white rubber shoes making a squeaky sound as she walked down the hall. He felt a twinge of remorse—the first time he could ever remember such a feeling. Julia had him pegged. He was a flirt. A shameless flirt.

Rome pushed the door to Amos's room and gasped when he saw him, lying in the hospital bed with tubes attached to his nose, one to his arm, blinking machines that let out beeps every few seconds. He saw Amos's beloved Bible grasped in his hands and forced a smile. "Have time for a visit?"

Amos looked over at him. "Well, well, the Bee Man. I can't think of anybody I'd rather see right now." His voice was weak and raspy, but he managed a thin smile.

Rome sat down on a chair across from Amos and stretched out his long legs. "Amos, I only have fifteen minutes and there's something I need to tell you."

"Shoot."

"I spoke to the heart transplant coordinator over at Hershey Medical about what needs to happen to get a person on the list."

Amos stilled and looked away.

"Not that I would interfere in any way—"

"What would you call it then?" Amos asked gruffly.

Rome put up a hand. He wished he weren't sitting below Amos on the chair, like a child. "Hear me out. Julia has told me why you won't consider a transplant."

Amos's gaze shifted to the window.

Rome drew in a long breath. "You've always been willing to give someone a chance. Would you at least listen to what I have to say on the subject?"

Amos turned back to Rome. "Speak your piece."

"Julia said you didn't feel you could accept the heart of another person, knowing he had sacrificed his life for you. But Amos, I think you've got it all wrong. There are parallels between the gift of a donor and that of Christ's gift of eternal life. Your new heart will be given unconditionally, with no strings attached, and without compensation. Free, but it comes at a high price. It requires a great loss be inflicted on the donor. Like Christ's sacrifice for us."

Rome reached over and took Amos's Bible out of his hands. He turned it to Ezekiel 36:26 and read aloud: "'A new heart also will I give you, and a new spirit will I put within you: and I will take away the stony heart out of your flesh, and I will give you a heart of flesh.' That verse is for you, Amos. God is in the business of giving out new hearts. New life." He paused to see how Amos was responding, but Amos had closed his eyes. He waited a moment and then, discouraged, decided Amos had fallen asleep. He left the Bible open to Ezekiel and placed it next to Amos on the bed.

Amos opened his eyes. "Rome, you can tell that boy doctor to put me on the list." Then he closed his eyes again.

Rome heard a sniffling sound and looked up. At the door was Julia. He walked over to her, and for an instant they were looking straight at each other, everything between them falling away. He reached up and touched one large hand lightly against her cheek. She pressed it with her own hand, tears in her eyes.

"Thank you," she whispered.

Amos was discharged by the end of that week, sent home with a beeper that had to be with him at all times. "When a compatible heart is harvested, the transplant coordinator will beep you. You get to Hershey Medical immediately!" the doctor had told him. "Whatever you need to do—taxi, racehorse, or call 911. You just get yourself in there, Amos Lapp."

Harvested. The very word made Amos shudder. It wasn't a crop; it was a human being. A heart.

Still, he felt a confidence that proceeding forward to have a heart transplant was the right thing to do, a conviction that God was guiding him in this direction.

For now, though, he would have to wait. For someone to die so that he could live.

"We need to get prepared," Rome told Julia on the evening after Amos was discharged from the hospital. "To think of some ways to raise money for the heart transplant. Maybe get some folks to help us have a fundraising auction."

It amazed Julia to hear Rome use the pronoun "we." She didn't think it was a part of his vocabulary. I, me, myself, mine. But never "we." Was it possible Roman Troyer was starting to grow attached to people? To care about them? "Do you really think it will happen soon?"

"When the multitudes needed to be fed, Jesus gave them food. When the disciples needed to pay their taxes, he provided a coin. When the time is right for Amos to get a heart, God will provide." Rome pulled out a pen and started jotting things down on a sheet of scrap paper. "So let's do our part and get ready, so we're prepared when God brings your father that heart."

"Julia can quilt," Fern said quietly.

Julia stared at Fern.

"You could make another quilt like that one you made last year that went for such a big pile of cash," Fern said.

"Dad loved that quilt best," M.K. volunteered after slipping into the room.

"How did you know about that quilt?" Julia asked Fern.

"Hank wrote about it in the *Budget*," Fern said. "Fetched big bucks, he said. People called it a Julia Lapp original."

Uncle Hank! Julia's mouth set in a firm line. He hadn't mentioned to them that he wrote about the quilt in his weekly letter. Talk about stoking Edith Fisher's fire.

"You can make another one," Fern said. "Just like that one."

Julia shook her head. "I can't."

"Why not?" Rome asked. "I haven't seen you design a quilt all summer. What's made you stop?"

M.K. sidled up next to Rome. "On account of Edith Fisher," she whispered.

"Mary Kate!" Julia said. "That's family business!"

"Rome's practically family," M.K. said. "So is Fern." She turned to Rome. "Edith Fisher told folks that Julia was becoming prideful after her quilt brought in so much money. And then just after that, Paul postponed the engagement for the first time. So Julia stopped making quilt tops."

Fern huffed. "Edith Fisher has an opinion about every subject and gives it unsolicited."

The conversation about raising money started M.K. brainstorming dozens of ways to raise cash—most of them had to do with other people: Fern could whip up doughnuts and sell them at the fork in the road where construction workers gathered to be picked up by their crew each morning. Menno could double his birdhouse output and sell them door-to-door. M.K. even offered to stay home with Amos during church in the morning to think up more ideas, but Fern waved her off like she would a pesky fly.

"You need church more than most," Fern told M.K.

Julia moved toward the open door that led from the kitchen to the side porch. It was dark and quiet outside, and she could smell jasmine in the night breeze. She loved it all so much. The trees and brooks, the sights and smells. Best of all, she loved watching the moon cast its shadow over the farm.

Rome joined her. They stood silently for a long while, listening to the rustle of the wind as it made the dried corn tassles dance in the fields. Even under her father's efficient management, Windmill Farm hadn't looked this good. The fences that stretched around the paddocks had been repaired and whitewashed. The broken arm of the windmill had been fixed. Everything about the farm looked well tended and prosperous. It was because of Rome. There wasn't anything he couldn't do. He had taken Menno alongside him and worked steadily through Julia's expansive to-do list.

"Fern's right," he said. "You shouldn't let someone else steal your joy in making something you're good at."

"Edith Fisher had a point," Julia said. "I was proud, after winning that ribbon and raising so much money. I love quilt making, but it can become an idol to me. It was best to put it aside for a season."

Rome looked at her in surprise. "But the quilt was auctioned away for a good purpose."

She gave a half shrug. "Even something we love to do can become an idol. I was neglecting my friends and family just so I could create a quilt. I was always preoccupied, thinking about designing my next quilt top. When Dad took sick and needed so much of my attention, it made me realize how selfish I had become."

"You could never be selfish," he said softly.

Julia saw in Rome's eyes something new, something of joy, even hope. Just a flicker. And then it was gone.

After Rome left to go to his cottage, Julia turned off the gas lamps in the living room to get ready to go upstairs to bed. She turned in a slow circle, taking in every inch of this oh-so-familiar room until she faced the trunk that butted against the wall, holding her mother's quilts.

She set the lamp on the bookshelf and knelt on the floor to open the trunk. The soothing smell of cedar chips drifted up as she pushed the lid against the wall. The tissue paper that wrapped the quilts crackled as Julia lifted one, then another. There was a small blue-and-white Nine-Patch crib quilt that had covered each of Maggie Lapp's babies. Below it was a Log Cabin pattern, made of cobalt and yellow, one her mother had made for

Menno when he turned ten. Her hand brushed the vibrant colors, neatly stitched with the three-strand thread that her mother had insisted on. She had said the thread reminded her of the Holy Trinity, holding the world together, just the way thread held a quilt together. It was the last quilt her mother had made. Would Menno remember?

Almost every afternoon of Julia's childhood was spent sitting on the floor next to her mother while she sat sewing at her quilt frame or tracing around templates for quilt blocks. When it came to quilt-making, Maggie Lapp's quilts stood out. She said her quilts were designed to wrap a person with the warmth of loving arms, as healing as homemade chicken soup. She had more orders than she could handle and was often weeks behind in her work, but she always had time for her family—to listen to them natter away about school, teachers, friends, animals, crops, anything that might be weighing on their minds. And the thing was, she didn't just pretend to listen while slipping her needle through the fabric, making tiny, even stitches. She truly listened. She made everyone feel important.

Why, that's where Sadie got that quality, Julia realized.

She wrapped Menno's quilt up carefully, wondering when it might be used. Was he serious about Annie? Was she serious about him? What would her mother say about Menno having a girlfriend? Julia used to try to cobble together conversations she would have with her mother, but the older she became, the less she felt she knew her mother. She had known her as a child, but not as a woman. What would Maggie have said about Edith Fisher—accusing Julia of being prideful over her quilts? What would she say about Rome's idea to raise money to help her husband with a heart transplant? Julia really had no idea.

She startled when she heard a sound behind her. There was Fern, standing against the doorjamb in her usual way, arms crossed against her chest. "My father had a saying: 'Burying your talents is a grave mistake.'"

Julia looked down at Menno's quilt in her lap.

Fern walked up to Julia. "In the Bible, Jesus tells a story about a king who gave his servants some talents and told them to use them in his absence. He gave five talents to one servant, three to another, one to the last servant. When he returned, he wanted to know how they had used their talents. The five talent fellow had doubled his talents. So did the three talent fellow.

But one servant—he buried it." Fern put a hand on Julia's head. "God has given you a good gift and you have an opportunity to give God back a gift. But not if you bury it."

"But . . . Edith Fisher—"

"Edith Fisher is not the king returning to ask the servants about their talents." She bent at the waist and cupped Julia's face in her hands. "You are to answer to God for your life." She turned and left Julia alone.

As Julia sat in the dimly lit room, a frightening—almost exhilarating—sense of purpose came over her. She placed Menno's quilt back into the trunk and gently closed it. She opened the bottom drawer of the corner hutch and plunged her hand beneath a pile of seldom-used linens to pluck out her hidden journal. In it were pages and pages of quilt top ideas, waiting. Just waiting. Waiting for the right design, the right fabrics, the right moment. She slipped the journal into her apron pocket, picked up the lamp, and hurried up the stairs to her room. Maybe the right moment was now.

17

Contrary to popular belief, Julia did very few things in her life with extreme self-confidence, but designing a quilt top had always been one of them. Her mother used to tell her she had a gift for design and construction, the ability to create the most beautiful and intricate quilts imaginable. And now that she'd started designing again, she felt ideas pouring out of her. They were flooding her brain so fast she didn't have time to get them down on paper. Something special happened as she put swatches of fabric against each other, something instinctive. She tackled the quilt top with a surety of purpose, led by an inner prompting.

Everyone honored Julia's request to stay out of the dining room and let her work without interruption or well-meaning suggestions. She started a few patches as trial pieces, just to see how the colors interacted. She laid them out on the dining room table. She stood back to observe her work and ended up throwing them away. She had to start over. They were good, but not good enough.

It was hard. Time was growing short. The fundraising auction Rome had organized was only two weeks away. He was working so hard on it. She wiped a bead of sweat from her forehead. She felt hot, nauseated, and more than a little panicked. What if she couldn't create something special? What if she created the quilt top but couldn't get it quilted in time? What if it didn't raise as much money as last year's quilt? So much to worry about! But she wouldn't think about all that now. She had to stay focused.

This quilt was for her father's new heart—it had to be her best work.

Sadie kept nudging Menno to finish up his breakfast. Julia had scheduled the grand unveiling of the quilt top this morning, and Sadie couldn't wait to see what this quilt looked like. She felt more nervous than a long-tailed cat in a room full of rocking chairs. Finally, Menno swallowed his last spoonful of oatmeal and Sadie jumped up from the table.

"Now, Jules?"

Julia took a deep breath. "Now."

Julia had been working on this quilt fourteen hours a day for the last ten days. She'd barely been seen. She had put up sheets to block off the living room so no one could even peek at the work in progress. Now and then she would emerge to send someone off to the fabric store in town for more thread or a certain color of fabric.

Finally, the moment had come. M.K. ran to the room, with Sadie right on her heels, then Fern and Rome and Menno. M.K., barely able to contain herself, grabbed the sheet and looked for a nod from Julia, then pulled the sheet off.

It was the most exquisite thing Sadie had ever seen: the Lone Star—a common Lancaster pattern—set into bright turquoise blue. Julia had sewn such tiny points together that they almost blurred together like a child's kaleidoscope. Bold colors, ones that normally would never be thought to lie next to each other, came together to provide incredible depth. A two-inch border of simple but tiny nine-patch pieces rimmed the star. The tiny squares—made up from the very fabrics that she had sent M.K. and Menno off to the store with crayons and orders to match that specific color—blended into each other. Dark green faded softly into light green, reds into pinks. Only the corner patches—made up of boldly contrasting colors—jolted one's eyes back into focus. The quilt top was fastened into a large quilting frame, ready for quilting.

Sadie wasn't the only one who was speechless. She, Fern, Rome, Menno, even M.K. who was rarely without words, walked silently around the table, absorbing the sight.

Julia stood by the living room door. "Someone, please say something."

Rome looked up at her. "Words fail me, Julia. It's . . . overwhelmingly beautiful."

"It's awesome," Menno said, using a word he had picked up from Annie.

M.K. threw her arms around Julia's middle for a hug.

Fern was eyeing the quilt with a critical squint. Finally, she gave Julia a satisfied nod. From Fern, that was high praise.

Julia's eyes filled with tears. She tried to blink them back, but Sadie could see relief flood her face.

"Now, you all need to leave so I can get busy with the quilting."

"That's one thing we can help with," Fern said. "The ladies are coming to quilt today." She pointed out the window to two buggies, jammed full of women, rolling up the driveway to Windmill Farm.

Julia joined her at the window. "How did they . . . how did you know?"

Fern shrugged. "Figured it was about time." She turned to Sadie and M.K. "They're expecting lunch, so you two . . . hop to it."

Sadie was stunned.

M.K. read her mind. "She's letting us in the kitchen!"

Fern whirled around and pointed to M.K. "Only because I've seen your quilt stitches." She frowned. "You might as well use knitting needles. All you're doing today is preparing the food that I've already made. And cleanup." She wagged a finger at the two. "That's all. Nothing more."

Even Sadie couldn't hold back a grin when she saw a slightly worried look dance through Fern's eyes.

Two days later, on Thursday afternoon, Sadie was self-conscious beyond belief as she sat in the buggy next to Rome. He happened to be driving by as she was walking home from town after helping M.K. and Menno canvas Stoney Ridge with flyers in storefronts that said "Have a Heart for a Heart." She tried to think of something wise, something witty to say to Rome, but her mind was a blank canvas.

Rome pointed to the flyers in her hands. "Did M.K. talk you into working for her?"

"She came up with the idea of talking the *Stoney Ridge Times* into running a story about the fundraiser, so she and Menno went to go find a reporter," Sadie said. "M.K. can talk anybody into just about anything."

They'd all been working hard on getting the fundraising auction organized, especially Rome.

He laughed. "You've got a good heart, Sadie. I knew it the moment I set eyes on you when you were just knee high to a grasshopper."

Her capstrings dipped as she shook her head.

"Can I let you in on a secret?"

A little thrill went through her. "What's that?" She realized her heart was racing, even as her mind spun with new possibilities.

He pointed his thumb toward the backseat. Sadie turned to look and saw a number of stacked boxes of Kerr jars. "Not those. The jars are for my honey. The other box." Then she saw what he meant: a large box, covered with a saddle blanket. "It's a new treadle sewing machine."

"You're learning to sew?"

He smiled. "Not hardly. It's for Julia. I've fixed that one she has for the last time. It's so old that belts are snapping and screws are rusting out. If it weren't for the fact that your dad kept a box of old parts, I wouldn't have been able to patch it together as long as I have." He lifted a shoulder in a careless half shrug, but a slightly embarrassed look flickered through his eyes. "This one was on sale at the hardware store. The paint chipped when it shipped, so they gave it to me for a song. I can touch up the paint and it'll be as good as new."

Sadie was stunned. Did Rome have feelings for Julia? The truth burst over her. Had she been so blinded with love for Rome that she hadn't even noticed? She fussed with the apron in her lap as if it were a chick she was trying to calm.

"It's not a big deal," Rome said hurriedly. "I just got tired of trying to keep that thing running." A flush stained his cheeks.

She looked up, then immediately looked down again. "She'll be thrilled, Rome." She tried to smile, but it came out feeling fake. "Really. It's a wonderful surprise for her."

At supper that evening, Sadie carefully watched Julia and Rome, sitting side by side. They stole little glances at each other, laughed at each other's comments. It was revelatory. It was a moment of clarity, like the sun breaking through the clouds.

Something had passed between them and Sadie had not even seen when it had happened. She felt a sharp, clean slice through her gut. She had held out hope that, some day, Rome would fall in love with her. She knew it was juvenile, but that was how she felt.

Her life was over.

Rome liked his cottage. It was comfortable, with enough furniture to be functional but not enough to crowd him. The bed was large enough to accommodate his tall frame. Next to it was a washstand and across the room were a chest and a bookcase. Once he was at the cottage, his heart started to settle, like a dog by the hearth, like a baby in its crib.

It was strange. He caught a whiff of something—lavender?—that brought Julia to his mind. That woman had gotten under his skin, and it bothered him. It was more than her beauty, there was something sweet and vulnerable about her that unearthed feelings inside him that he hadn't known he possessed. Feelings that made him think differently about his life.

This summer, an unacceptable longing kept piercing his heart. It was for home, an end point. Everyone kept telling him he was not supposed to be constantly in transit. He was supposed to stop somewhere and feel a sense of belonging. Until now, he kept dismissing such unasked-for advice. But pangs of homesickness kept needling him these last few months despite his efforts to push them away.

He leaned his head back. Rome was sometimes struck by images of his Ohio home: opening up the farmhouse, filling it again with family—a wife, four or five or six children, a dog like Lulu. He could practically see this imaginary family of his playing in the yard, bees humming in their hives near the garden just where his mother had kept them.

What if he returned to the farm in Ohio instead of traveling this winter? Was he ready? Was it time?

These were foolish thoughts. What was wrong with him? He pulled off his straw hat and slammed it on the table. Lulu looked up in surprise.

"Don't pay me any never mind, Lulu. I think I'm getting a little touched by too much sun."

The dog stared at him with soulful brown eyes. Idly, he fingered one of her long, silky ears. He trailed his fingers over the dog's back. Rome didn't like admitting it, but he was going to miss Lulu when he left. He was going to miss all of the Lapps.

What was the matter with him lately? Everything in his life had gone off balance, and he didn't know how to straighten it out. He wished he could talk to Julia about his mixed-up feelings, but that would be counterproductive, considering she was the major cause of his confusion. These last few months, Julia had become much more to him than Amos's daughter. She was his friend. She was more than his friend. There was something about Julia that made him feel at home, at rest. She understood him better than anyone else. Also, he didn't want to kiss his friends. And he definitely wanted to kiss her again.

Was it possible? One thought kept hammering at his thick head like a woodpecker, filling him with an odd mixture of excitement and dread. Could it be? Had he let himself get blindsided? *Me? Roamin' Roman? The Bee Man? The solitary bee?* A queer ache settled deep inside and he felt himself start to sweat.

He was falling in love with Julia Lapp.

At first, the realization stunned him, but as he rolled it around in his mind, he found he liked the sound, the thought of it. He liked it very much.

After the auction, he'd tell her. Would she even believe him? He could hardly believe it himself.

He was going to do his best to start over. A new beginning. For the first time in six years, he was going to set aside his refusal to be attached to anyone. He was going to reach out to someone. To a woman. To Julia.

The very idea of it made him feel foolishly happy. For the first time in a long time, Rome felt an excitement about the future.

One by one, Julia sliced the stems of the massive heads of sunflowers that lined the back row of her garden and carefully laid them on a sheet. She would store the flower heads in the greenhouse. Those sunflower seeds would fill Menno's bird feeders this winter.

Julia saw someone out of the corner of her eye, silhouetted by the setting sun. Paul stood there, waiting for her to notice him. "Jules, I need to talk to you."

"Now?"

"Yes," he said.

She studied his face. He was earnest, supplicant, hurting. He was all there, concentrated on her. Tears welled in his beautiful blue eyes.

"This is just awful. This is just, well, it's confusing." He sounded hurt and lost and miserable. "You and me. This wall that's gone up between us."

She closed the pocketknife. "Paul, this is what you wanted. You said you wanted us to take a break."

"I was a fool. I don't want a break any longer." He reached out for her hands and gazed down into her face.

She risked a look at him. His eyes were the clear blue of a cloudless summer day, his hair the pale bronze of sun-steeped tea. He was considered a handsome man by all who knew him. She had known him most of her life, yet she suddenly felt awkward and uncomfortable around him.

"Marry me, Jules. This time for real."

Julia's heart plummeted and skipped at the same time, like a stone skimming the surface of a pond. She had been waiting for months for this moment. This was what she wanted to hear, wasn't it? Why, then, did she feel so stiff, so detached? "What about Lizzie?"

With a gentle tug, Paul pulled Julia closer to him. His gaze swept her face and lingered on her lips. "I've never gotten over you. You know that, don't you? I don't want anybody but you."

But Julia wasn't quite ready. "How do I know you won't want to have another postponement? That you won't find yourself attracted to another girl?"

Paul's voice was urgent. "Because I won't. I promise."

She was surprised at how hope broke open inside her like a radiance, softening her sorrow and anger. She wanted to believe him. She wanted to trust him.

And then she heard him draw in a deep breath, and when he spoke again, his voice was clear and strong. "Jules," he said again, impatient now. "Say yes. Say you'll marry me. It's not too late for things to be made right between us. Remember? How easy it used to be?" He slipped his arms around her waist. "Remember how we would meet up at Blue Lake Pond when our folks sent us on errands into town?"

Julia hadn't been to Blue Lake Pond in a long while. The place had been special to them, it was their spot. It was the place they had always met when they wanted to be alone. The pond lay like a small, glimmering jewel in the center of the world, where it was safely tucked away from the bustle of town life. It had always been her favorite place. Even on the hottest August days, its spring-fed water was clear and cold, and the thick barrier of trees and underbrush acted like a fence around it. The spot was quiet and private, perfect for secret thoughts.

It was where he had first kissed her on her sixteenth birthday. They had first talked about getting married there, and then he had called off the wedding there, claiming he needed more time.

Julia thought back to that day. They met at dusk, like they always did, after their chores on their family farms for that autumn day were done. It was mid-October, just four weeks before the wedding. Paul was waiting for her, leaning against the tree with his hat brim hiding his face. She called to him and he slowly lifted his head, then dropped it again. Julia knew something was wrong the moment she reached him and looked into his eyes. A person's eyes, they could tell you everything. An awful shudder ripped through her. She never imagined anything could hurt that badly.

Six months later, they talked about getting married again, right on that very spot. And then, this April, he called it off again.

Paul's eyes were partially shadowed by the brim of his straw hat, but she could see him looking at her mouth.

She reached up and gently lifted off his hat, noticing as she laid it aside that there was a small red line across the upper part of his forehead from the band. He leaned forward and pressed his mouth to hers. She was glad—she wanted him to kiss her. She needed to prove to herself that Paul could spark those same fires as Rome.

Julia's first thought was that Paul's lips were dry, stiffer than Rome's. This was a pleasant kiss. It was adequate. Her mind got to wandering, and she tried to bring her attention back to what she was doing by raising her arms around Paul's neck. Were his shoulders a little more narrow than she remembered? Were Rome's shoulders a little wider?

Paul pulled back from her, as if he sensed her disappointment. The kiss hadn't proved anything. No sooner had she thought this than she admonished herself: What kind of thinking is that, Julia Lapp? Are you really so shallow as to decide about love based on a kiss? She lifted her eyes to look into his. "So . . . the first of November, then? Just like we had planned?"

There was a speck of silence, a silence so short, so small, so infinitesimal. So profound.

Paul blinked and focused on the fence, his hat brim hiding his face as he slowly shook his head, then squinted up at her again, clearly struggling to say something. A person's eyes—they told you everything.

Paul had finally given her the truth and she recognized it for what it was. Deep down, she had known it all along. Julia knew he would end up calling the wedding off again. Paul didn't want to marry anybody. Not Julia. Not Lizzie. Not anybody.

"I guess I was thinking next year." He licked his lips. "On account of your father and all. I assumed you'd want to wait."

Julia bent her chin to her chest, and Paul—misunderstanding—kissed her forehead. She lifted her head and gave him a long, steady gaze. "I'm sorry," she said softly. "I can't do it. I can't marry you, Paul."

Blinking wide-eyed, Paul looked like an owl caught in a wash of light. "You can't mean that, Jules. I need you."

"Maybe you need someone, but that someone isn't me."

"It is you. You're telling me you don't feel it?"

She felt something. What was it? Delight at seeing him, at hearing him tell her he wanted her. She had a lot of feelings, but she did not mistake any of them for love.

"You're just upset."

She shook her head. "Strangely enough, I'm not upset. For the longest time, I thought the problem between us was me. I thought I just wasn't enough for you, wasn't good enough or pretty enough. Or my family wasn't respectable enough. But the problem wasn't with me, Paul. It's with you. You don't want to grow up. And I do. I deserve something better." She hadn't wanted to humiliate him, but the words were spoken and she wouldn't take them back because they were true.

"I'm sorry," she whispered, backing away. "I'm really sorry." She was filled up with an emotion that was as thick as syrup, an emotion she could only describe as bittersweet. She was so sure she had loved him, so sure he was the only one for her. She had felt such a bright intensity for Paul that it had blinded her. But now, finally, it had burned itself out.

M.K. could hardly believe her eyes! She was running from the barn to the house when something large caught her eye over at the far end of the garden. She stopped in her tracks.

Bear!

Oh, wait! Scratch that. It wasn't a bear. It was two people. She tiptoed behind the greenhouse and squinted her eyes to see who they were. One figure was Julia and the other was a man. Paul! It was Paul. And now . . . Paul was kissing Julia!

M.K. galloped into the house, up the stairs, grabbed her bag of nickels from under her pillow, and ran like the wind down the path that led to Rome's cottage. In record time, she arrived and banged on his front door. When he opened it, she thrust the bag of nickels at him. "Here! You did it, Bee Man! You did what no one else could do. You got Paul and Julia back together!"

Rome looked skeptical. "What are you talking about?"

"I just saw Paul give Julia a serious kissin' in the garden. And she was not objecting!"

The color drained from Rome's face. "What? Are you . . . sure?"

Boys! So dense about matters of the heart! "I saw it with my own two eyes." M.K. was so excited she felt like she might burst apart. "I'm sorry I doubted you!"

He just stood there, a blank look on his face, and she knew Fern would be wondering where she went to, so she grabbed his hand and slapped the nickel bag in it.

"You earned it, Bee Man. Good work!" She turned and skipped away, so pleased with the turn of events. Suddenly, she stopped and spun around. "Best if we don't say anything about this, though. Let's wait until Julia tells us herself."

And then she was off to the house, the strings on her prayer cap dancing in the dark.

Some days, you would've been better off staying in bed. Rome had opened his eyes that morning to a beautiful autumn day, and spent the day working on an elaborate plan of how to reveal his feelings to Julia. After the family returned from the auction tomorrow, he was going to get Julia in the buggy on some ruse—something forgotten back in town—and whisk her off to Blue Lake Pond in time for the sunset. He had spent most of this afternoon at the Pond, putting clues in place for a treasure hunt. A balloon tied on the hitching tree with instructions to look for two oars. The note on the oars said to find an upturned gray rowboat. The note on the rowboat said to take the oars and row out to the floating dock in the center of the lake. Once there, Julia would find a chocolate fudge cake—her favorite—from the Sweet Tooth bakery that he would have already hidden in a basket on the dock. Earlier today he'd gone into town to pick up the cake and practically choked with embarrassment when he told Nora Stroot, the bakery owner's granddaughter, that he wanted piped icing on the cake to read: Bee Mine.

"Really?" Nora Stroot sniffed, disappointment dripping in her voice. "That's the best you can do?"

Yes, it was. He wasn't good at this expressing-your-feelings stuff.

He had spent hours trying to think of something clever, something heartfelt, something with a hint of romance without going over the top. Then he remembered an anniversary card his father had given to his mother with the Bee Mine tagline. She had loved it. But the disgusted look on Nora Stroot's face fizzled Rome's confidence like a sparkler under a firehose. A portent of things to come. Just a few hours later, M.K. came along with eyewitness information that changed the picture entirely.

That night, Rome lay motionless in the dark, one arm crooked behind his head, staring at the ceiling. So Julia would most likely be marrying Paul Fisher in a few short months. What if Rome had told her he loved her? Would it have made any difference? But he'd never chased after a woman in his life, and not even Julia Lapp could make him start.

Maybe this was a blessing in disguise. The lesson Rome had learned from his family's accident had been a hard one, and he'd never forgotten it. He'd learned that to love meant to open yourself up to excruciating pain.

Hard-earned lessons were the best remembered. He gave away books when he finished them, traded mules before he could grow too fond of them, kept on the move before anyone grew dependent on him.

Things could go wrong. So many things could go wrong.

He couldn't sleep, so he got out of bed, grabbed a slice of chocolate fudge cake, and wandered out on the porch. He tried to enjoy the stars, but his heart wasn't in it. This cottage had been a refuge, the place where he could relax. Tonight, it felt too quiet. He gazed out into the darkness with unseeing eyes.

He wasn't used to feeling unsure of himself, so he swallowed the last bite of cake, brushed the crumbs from his hands, went back inside, and headed to bed. As he passed the kitchen table, he noticed the letters Fern had given to him. He picked them up and read through them again. Then he grabbed a sheet of paper and sat down at the table to write.

Dear R.W.,

I accept your offer.

Cordially,
Roman Troyer

He stuck the letter into the envelope and licked it shut. Tomorrow, he would mail it. A pending matter, decided.

Now, maybe, he would feel an inner release of all that had been troubling him this summer. He would be free. Of memories, of obligations.

Gradually, the nighttime rasp of crickets and the soft, wheezy cry of a distant barn owl lulled him into a dreamless sleep.

18

The day of the fundraising auction had arrived. Julia could hardly sleep. When she heard the first rooster crow, she got out of bed and dressed, then went downstairs and into the living room. The Lone Star quilt was folded neatly on the sofa. Word had spread about the auction, especially after M.K. had posted flyers up all over town, with the slogan "Have a Heart for a Heart." Every single family in their church district had donated goods or services for the fundraiser. Rome had talked a professional auctioneer into providing his services for free. Julia overheard Rome tell Fern they hoped to raise $10,000 today. Imagine! That could take a dent out of her father's heart transplant bill . . . whenever it might occur.

The Lapp family had their hopes raised last week when Hershey Medical called and told them to get Amos in, that they might have a heart available. But no sooner had they arrived than they were told to go on home. The heart wasn't a match for Amos. Julia didn't understand all of the necessary requirements for a heart transplant, but she did believe in prayer. Prayer worked. She prayed daily that a heart would arrive for her father. Then she prayed for the person whose heart would be given, because she knew that meant his or her time on earth had come to an end.

It felt like an odd prayer.

Main Street was bustling. Julia never expected to see such a turnout for her father's fundraiser. Folks from neighboring towns poured into Stoney Ridge after the newspaper article ran a story on the fundraiser—with a special emphasis on the Amishness of the event. M.K. said the reporter was eager to run the story once he heard that there would be Amish foods and handicrafts. "He said that folks would flock to buy anything if they thought it all came from the Amish," M.K. explained as she read the article aloud last night. "He called it the Amish brand." She looked up at her father. "What's a brand?"

"Today," Amos had said, "we will call it God's goodness."

The auction was held on a closed-off section of downtown Stoney Ridge, right in front of the Sweet Tooth bakery, on a Saturday morning in late September. There were people everywhere: Nora Stroot agreed to let them set up the produce wagon in the parking lot in exchange for a caseload of Rome's honey. A swarm of people surrounded the wagon, buying the last of Windmill Farm's vine-ripened tomatoes, sweet corn, pumpkins, and early apples.

Rome was polite enough to Julia as he helped Menno load the wagon with produce early today to sell at the auction, but she could sense he had raised a wall around him. He was just about to climb in the buggy when he saw she was in the driver's seat. He paused for a moment, mid-climb, then said he'd keep Menno company pulling up the wagon in the rear. As soon as they reached town, Rome vanished.

They had come so far in their friendship. What had happened? Why was he acting . . . well, to be fair, like he usually did? Detached, pleasantly amused. Had she done something wrong? Had she said something? She reviewed in her mind the last time they were together. Was it only yesterday morning? They had laughed over something M.K. had said—laughed so hard they both had tears running down their faces.

She slumped down in a seat at the wooden picnic table. Only after she was settled did she realize that her position gave her a clear view of Rome standing in the middle of a herd of women. He looked as if he were having the time of his life, laughing and carrying on, obviously enjoying himself. Almost as if he could feel Julia watching, he lifted his head and turned, letting his gaze sweep over her. Their eyes locked, and for a moment neither of them moved. Then he turned his attention back to one of the girls standing at his side.

If Rome wanted to send a message to Julia, loud and clear, he couldn't have found a better way.

Fern joined Julia on the picnic bench and handed her an apple, cut up into slices. Julia took a slice. "You're awful quiet today. Sadie too." Fern took a bite of an apple slice. "Only one who's never quiet is that Mary Kate." It was true that there weren't many quiet moments with M.K. in the vicinity. Julia could hear her voice now, over by the bakery, calling out to Menno to toss her more corn, lickety-split.

They sat in companionable silence until Fern said, "You're not sorry about Paul."

Julia looked at her sharply. How had she known?

"I saw the happy look on his face when he came to the house last night. And I saw how dejected he looked when he left."

So it looked like Fern knew everything anyway, without any need to tell her. Julia gave a nod. "I'm not sorry."

"Because of Rome?" Fern peered at her, sniffing out the truth.

She read Julia's heart situation right. It was one of her talents. "Honestly, I don't know how I feel about Rome," Julia said. "One minute, he acts as if he's in charge of Dad's future. The next minute, he's as skittish as a sheep if you even ask if he's planning to be home for dinner."

Fern's gaze followed Rome as he walked across the lawn. "That's because he doesn't know what he wants out of life."

"He wants what he wants when he wants it. That's what I think about Roman Troyer."

Fern shook her head. "He's struggling. He doesn't know if he should stay or leave."

Julia turned to face Fern. "How do you know so much about Rome?"

Fern's gaze shifted out to Rome as he joined Menno and M.K. and helped lift some bushels of corn to the front of the wagon. Her forehead knitted. "Six years ago, Rome's family was headed to a wedding. Rome's uncle, Tom Troyer, was getting married. They hired a van to take them since the bride lived quite a distance away. Rome stayed home to take care of the farm. Along the way, there was a collision and the entire family was killed."

Julia closed her eyes.

Fern kept talking. "Rome packed up the house, locked it, sold off the livestock—only thing he kept was his mother's bees—and never looked back. No one knew where he went."

Julia looked over at Rome. No wonder he didn't talk about his family, his past. "I'm surprised he told you all that, Fern. He's never said a word about that to me. Not to Dad, either."

Fern closed up the bag that held the apple slices. Then after one of her long silent spells, she said, "He didn't have to tell me. It was my wedding that Rome's family was headed to. I was going to be Tom Troyer's bride."

Fern? A bride? A brokenhearted bride. "So that's why you're here? You came to Windmill Farm to get Rome back to Ohio?"

She shook her head. "That's not up to me or anybody else but Rome. I take care of people. That's what I do." She put the apple slices into her apron pocket. "But Rome does have a decision to make. Last year, the Troyers' neighbor contacted me. Someone wants to buy the Troyer farm since it's just sitting there abandoned, getting run down. They wondered if I knew how to find him. A few months later, I happened to read your Uncle Hank's *Budget* letters where he talked about the Bee Man, a fellow who wandered from place to place. When he mentioned that they were brown bees, I knew those bees belonged to a Troyer. Nobody has that strain of bees anymore. It was Rome's mother who kept that strain going, and it wasn't hard to figure the Bee Man was Rome. I wrote to your uncle and he wrote back. He added something about he was running himself ragged, holding Windmill Farm together because his poor nephew had a bum heart."

Julia rolled her eyes at that.

"So I asked if he'd be in need of a caretaker for his nephew. Seemed like the right time. Thought I'd come and check up on Rome."

M.K. gave a shout out to her, waving her arm like a windmill to come over to the corn wagon, and Fern released a martyred sigh.

"And I ended up with a batch of troublesome children to keep on the straight and narrow way." She didn't seem too bothered.

Julia grew pensive. How strange and interwoven lives could be.

Fern rose to leave. "You know, Julia, boys get their hearts broken too."

At the Sweet Tooth bakery, Sadie stood in front of the counter trying to decide what to get. It all looked so good! Cinnamon rolls drizzled with thick white icing, cupcakes of every flavor topped with a swirl of frosting, gigantic crackled gingersnap cookies (her favorite), small fruit pies. Nora Stroot stood behind the counter, arms crossed tightly against her chest, losing patience with Sadie's indecisiveness. She let out a long-suffering sigh.

Sadie looked up at Nora. "Everything looks so delicious, it's hard to choose just one!" She bit her lip. "So maybe I'll try one cinnamon roll, one red velvet cupcake, and one gingersnap. Oh, and a gooseberry tart."

"Cancel that order," Fern said as she swept into the bakery. "We'll have two cups of tea."

Another grievous sigh escaped from Nora Stroot before she turned to get their tea.

Fern pointed to a table with two chairs. "Sit," she told Sadie.

Sadie looked longingly at the bakery goods as she sipped on her tea.

"So what's got you looking as sad as a gopher hitting hard ground?"

"Nothing. I'm just starving. I wanted a snack, that's all."

Fern snorted. "You had ordered enough for a week's worth." She added a dollop of cream to her tea and stirred it. "So? What's making you so down in the mouth?"

Sadie's eyes filled up with tears. "Rome loves Julia. And I think she loves him too."

"Keeping Rome Troyer in one place is like . . . well, you may as well chase smoke rising from a fire." She sipped her tea. "So you're disappointed that he doesn't love you?"

Sadie nodded. "Why couldn't Rome have chosen me? What's so wrong with me?"

"You mean, except for the fact that you're eleven years younger than him?"

"Age shouldn't matter!" In many important ways she was practically twenty. Maybe thirty.

"Age matters plenty when a girl is barely fifteen and the fellow is on the sunny side of thirty." She frowned and set down her tea. "Sadie, did you ever wonder why you're filling your mind with thoughts of Rome and ignoring all the boys your own age?"

Sadie was confused. "Because . . . he's Rome!"

Fern shook her head. "Because he's safe. He's a dream. A hope. The real thing is much harder work, but at least it's real. As long as you keep feeding that fantasy about Rome, you hold all these fellows at arm's length."

She pointed out the window. Gideon Smucker was talking to Menno at the wagon and kept casting sidelong glances in Sadie's direction. "Fellows like that boy. He hangs around like a summer cold."

With her chin propped on her fist, Sadie pondered that remark. Was Fern right? Was she hiding behind her fears? She looked over at the bakery counter. Was spending most of her time in the kitchen just another way to hide?

Fern reached out and covered Sadie's hand with hers, a rare display of affection. "Sadie girl, don't waste these years. Time is like the Mississippi River. It only flows in one direction. You can never go back." She glanced at the wall clock, swallowed the last sip of tea, and set the cup down. "Let's go. Julia's quilt will be getting auctioned off soon."

The formal auction had started at two and began with the auctioneer selling off farm tools, some livestock, a handful of quarter horses, flowers and plants, other quilts and wall hangings. The crowd was small at first, but the gathering grew as the time came for Julia's quilt to be auctioned off at 4:00 p.m. The last item of the day. Julia wasn't sure if she should stay for it. What if it didn't bring in the money she had hoped? What if no one bid on it? She should leave.

As she spun around, she caught sight of Paul, standing on the fringe. He had been waiting for her to notice him. She walked over to him. For a moment they simply stared at each other, saying nothing. He looked utterly dejected. She wanted to reach out and take his hand, but she could not do that. She wanted to cry for him, but she could not do that either. So she simply said, "I am very sorry, Paul. Truly sorry."

He tried to smile at her, but he couldn't quite manage it. "I hope your quilt brings in more than last year."

"Thank you." She heard the auctioneer sing out something about her quilt, and she thought she should slip through the crowd, fast, make a quick exit. But suddenly Fern, Sadie, Menno, M.K., and Uncle Hank surrounded her. Sadie clasped her hands around Julia's and squeezed.

"NERVOUS?" Uncle Hank bellowed.

She gave a shaky laugh as she watched the auctioneer. "Extremely."

"DON'T BE," he said, with typical Uncle Hank–like assurance.

She glanced in Paul's direction, but he was gone.

The auctioneer motioned to two men to bring the quilt out. It was hung on a rack, but folded up so no one could see the pattern. The auctioneer started talking in that rushed, frenetic way of his: "And here we have an original Julia Lapp quilt!"

Why did he have to say that?! Edith Fisher turned slightly and caught Julia with the corner of her eye, and Julia cringed.

A hush fell over the crowd as the auctioneer unclipped Julia's quilt so that it draped to the floor. It was so quiet you could have heard a barn owl hoot in the next county. *Everybody hates it,* Julia thought. *It's a disaster. The worst quilt ever created.* Her cheeks felt flushed and she thought about bolting. No, she couldn't do that. She was a grown-up. But she felt like an embarrassed five-year-old.

"Let's start the bidding at one thousand dollars. Do I hear one thousand?" A hand bounced up. "I hear one thousand. Do I have one thousand five hundred?" Another hand. "One thousand five hundred. Do I hear two thousand?" Another hand in the crowd popped up. The auctioneer looked pleased. "Do I hear three thousand?" Another hand. "Do I hear four thousand?"

This went on for another moment—an eternity—until the bidding slowed at ten thousand dollars. Ten thousand dollars! Julia was stunned. The auctioneer picked up his gavel. "Ten thousand dollars going once. Going twice!" He held his gavel suspended in the air. The crowd caught its breath.

"Twenty-five thousand dollars!" shouted a voice.

After a moment of stunned silence the crowd started clapping like summer thunder.

"Sold!" the auctioneer said, slamming the gavel with enthusiasm. "Sold to the man in the panama hat!"

On orders from Julia, M.K. darted through the crowd to find the man in the panama hat at the checkout table and escort him to the family. Julia wanted to thank him, but she also wanted to find out why in the world he had bid so much for her quilt. M.K. wove her way through clumps of people who were buzzing in wonder over the amount of the bid. She was having fun! On a mission of top importance. She stopped now and then to jump up and see if she could still locate the top of his hat. And stopped another time to take note of a woman's teetery red high-heeled shoes. How could anyone walk in those? They were practically stilts. Her eyes caught sight of the man, bending over the checkout table as he wrote a check, so she ducked down one more time and zigzagged through the crowd to reach him. When she made it to the table, she looked around triumphantly.

NO! She was too late! The man in the panama hat had paid for the quilt and left.

A week after the auction, Rome was out among the pippin apples in the orchards, the last variety to be harvested, checking on a row of trees that were twisted and bent, heavy with fruit. When these apples made it safely into the baskets and to the farmer's market to sell, he wouldn't be needed at Windmill Farm any longer. Autumn had come.

He climbed a ladder to reach the crown of one tree, and nearly fell off when he was startled by a voice. He moved a branch out of the way to find Julia peering up at him.

"You're planning to leave, aren't you?"

"These are the last of the crops to harvest. Menno and I finished up three cuttings of hay. It's stacked and in the barn. The corn is in the silo. Your father is on the waiting list for a new heart. And with the money from the fundraiser, you're in good shape to pay for the transplant, at least enough to persuade Amos to go through with it." He gentled the branch back into place. "Seems like the right time to move on."

"Paul wants to marry me."

Rome stilled. "Well, congratulations."

When she didn't answer, he moved the branch again. "Isn't it?"

"What do you think I should tell him?"

He looked through the branches at her, then climbed slowly down the ladder, protecting the apples he had stored in the canvas pouch secured about his neck and lying against his chest. "You should tell him yes. That's always what you've wanted. For as long as I've known you, that's what you've wanted."

When he had both feet on solid ground, she asked him, "Why are you leaving?"

Rome removed the white cotton gloves he wore while harvesting. "This was our deal. You asked me to stay through harvest."

"Fern told me about your family and the car accident."

Rome felt his chest tighten. There it was again—that feeling that his shirt collar was too tight. Like he couldn't breathe. He took a step back. The memories surfaced, one by one, until he shoved them to the back of his mind again.

"I'm so sorry," she whispered, meeting his gaze when he finally looked at her. "I had no idea how difficult the last six years must have been for you."

He wanted to shout out that he didn't need anybody's sympathy. He brushed past her to empty the bag of apples into the basket. "Fern had no business telling you."

"I wish you could have told me yourself." She took a step closer to him. "I thought we were friends. I thought we had something . . . special. Was I wrong?"

He kept his head down, gently letting the apples pour into the basket. "You're mistaken. I've told you over and over that I'm not that kind of man."

"What kind? Are you trying to tell me you're not a good man? Or a caring man?"

He tossed the empty canvas bag on top of the apples in the basket. He faced her, hands on his hips. "I meant . . . the settling-down kind. The marrying kind. The kind of man a girl can count on, for keeps. I'm a drifter. No ties, not to anyone or anything." He was sure that hearing this hurt worse than anything else he could have said, but what could he do? It was the truth.

"Maybe you're the one who's got it wrong, Rome. I think you're the kind of man a girl can count on. You just can't let go of losing your family. You can't let yourself love because you think your heart can't handle it . . . that something bad will happen. But you're wrong. It's true . . . grief is the price for love. But hearts are made to mend. Christ can do wonders with a broken heart, if given all the pieces."

She didn't expect an answer, and she didn't get one. She squared her shoulders, tilted up her chin, but held silent. He thought he saw tears welling in her eyes, but she blinked them away before he could be sure. "So go. Take your bees and head off down the country roads." She took a few steps away, then turned back. "You know what's so sad? Your heart is every bit as damaged as my father's. The difference is that yours is a choice. You think you can avoid pain if you don't let yourself care about anybody. Maybe that's true. But you'll also never feel any love, or any joy."

She walked away, down the dirt path of apple trees. He couldn't let her leave like this. She didn't understand.

"Julia—wait!" He caught up with her. "This summer—it was just a game between us. A game to get Paul back. That's what you said you wanted. That's what you've got." He looked down into her hazel eyes.

For a moment their eyes met with all the hurt and pride and pretense stripped away.

"You, Roman Troyer, are a coward." She turned and left the apple orchard.

Rome stared at Julia's retreating back. How dare she! No one had ever had the audacity to talk to him like this. No other woman had ever challenged him the way she had over the past few months. No other woman had ever been as confident of herself, either.

Was it true? Was he a coward? Things were backward. Things should have been the other way around: he should be wanting to go, she should be begging him to stay. Maybe he had a warped sense of what love should be, but he thought that in love everything would be clear—instead of the muddy, confused, back-and-forths he'd had with Julia.

He threw the gloves on the ground. It didn't matter! He was leaving soon.

19

The door of the cottage squeaked open one afternoon as Rome was packing up his equipment.

Fern.

"I'll be sure to scrub the floor," he told her. "I don't want ants taking over the place." He went back to dismantling the extractor. "Just so you know, I sold the family property. Sent off a letter accepting the offer a few weeks ago. I should be getting the paperwork any day. As soon as the cashier's check arrives, I'm going to give it to you. I want the money from the property to be available for Amos's heart transplant. I'm hoping you'll use it when Amos gets his new heart. But no one, and I mean no one, should know where the money came from."

She walked around the kitchen with her arms folded against her. "So, I guess that means you're not planning to return to Ohio."

He shook his head. "No, I'm not." He took the extractor out to the wagon and placed it carefully in a wooden box. She followed him out. "Fern, if there's something you want to say to me, why don't you just come right out and say it?"

She lifted her chin a notch. "God doesn't make mistakes."

He recoiled at the words. In a way, he'd been expecting a conversation like this with Fern since the day he arrived and found her at Windmill Farm. *Well, fine, let's get this out in the open.* He glanced up at her. "I assume you're talking about the car accident."

"That accident passed through the hand of God."

If Fern had blamed the devil or the fallen world, Rome would agree. He could accept an explanation that involved imperfection, mankind's fallen state, or even his own lack of faith. What he couldn't accept was that God might have allowed the death of Rome's family when he could have prevented it. "Fern, I'm sorry you lost my uncle Tom that day. You lost a man who was going to be your husband. But you didn't lose your entire family in one fell swoop. You lost a new life, I suppose. I lost my old life. My whole life."

"The problem isn't in God—" she glanced toward the sky—"but in us. We can't see things from an eternal perspective."

"I know that." He threw the words like stones. "But why them? Four little girls, each one as precious to me as Sadie and M.K. Two parents—fine, loving people. My uncle, who was like another father to me. Why *every* single one? And why did I survive it?" He frowned. "It's hard to accept the idea that God didn't make a mistake on that day."

Fern stopped him with an uplifted finger. "None of us know the mind of God. The minute we think God needs to answer to us, we are teetering toward pride. God's ways are perfect and ours are not." Her voice softened. "Rome, you're going to have to let go, so your life can move on. Over time, new memories, new people, fill up that emptiness and your life will be complete again. If you don't let go of your grieving, you'll just stay in one spot, suspended in time."

Rome kept his head down and focused entirely on packing empty honey jars into a cardboard box. He didn't know how to respond to Fern. What could he say? That she didn't understand? But she did.

Fern turned to leave but stopped after a few steps. "I'll be sure the money goes to Amos's new heart. And I won't tell anyone where it came from."

"Fern."

She turned back to face him.

"Thank you, for everything. You uprooted your life for me this summer."

She tilted her head. "You were the reason I came. But you're not the reason I'm staying. God never takes without giving. He gave me a new family to look after. I needed them as much as they needed me. Maybe more."

Floating down on the wind from the house came a loud whooping sound. Fern and Rome looked up and saw M.K. running down the path toward the cottage with an empty pail in her hand. Menno was closing in on her, an outraged look on his face. His clothes and his hair were drenched with water.

Fern sighed. "And heaven only knows this family needs some serious looking after."

That night, after the sunset, the Lapp family gathered outside to say goodbye to Rome. The mules were harnessed to the bee wagon, the bees were safely settled into their hives, Rome had packed his few belongings.

He went first to M.K. "You keep studying bees, M.K. Next lesson is to observe how bees wind their way back to their hive. Beekeepers call it a beeline."

"Easy," she said.

"It's not a straight line."

Her little face squinted in confusion. She was about to object, then she burst into tears.

Rome wrapped M.K. in his arms.

"We're all going to miss you, Rome," Sadie said.

That nearly undid him. Somewhere in the passing week, Sadie had lost her shyness in Rome's presence. He pulled her into the hug.

He released the two girls and moved down the line to Menno. With a lightning-quick motion, Rome hit the tip of the hat and flipped it off the boy's head. Menno flinched and stepped back; his hair was matted as though he hadn't even run a comb through it that morning. "Keep your eye on Uncle Hank, Menno. Since he won't act his age, you'll have to be grown-up enough for two."

Menno thought that over for a long moment, then let out a honk of laughter. He shook Rome's hand solemnly.

"Slander!" Uncle Hank roared as he walked over to them from the Grossdaadi Haus. "If I leave for a second, my good name gets slandered!" He grabbed Rome for a handshake, pumping his hand up and down.

Rome moved to Amos, who held out a fistful of long fire matches to him. "Hold these sticks together," Amos said. "See if you can break them." Rome looked puzzled but did as Amos asked. The sticks wouldn't snap. Amos reached out and took one long match. He snapped it in half like it was a dried leaf. "By itself, one can be broken. Each one of us can be broken. But together, we're strong." He put his hand on Rome's head, a prayer, a blessing. "Never forget you have a place in our family circle, Bee Man."

And now Rome felt a well of emotion. He should be the one offering the blessing to Amos, but he found that words failed him. Would he see Amos again on this side of eternity? All he could do was to grip Amos's hand with both of his and hope that it conveyed all the gratitude he felt toward this kind man. He moved to Fern and found the emotional relief he needed.

"Would you at least send a card now and then?" she said. "Just let us know you're still among the living?"

He smiled and gave her a stiff hug.

Then he reached Julia. She looked at him and he looked at her and he felt himself waffling. What could he say? He had dreaded this moment, even more than saying goodbye to Amos. "Take care of yourself," he told her awkwardly.

Lulu jumped up on Rome's cart and sat down, facing forward. Rome reached up to get her down, but Menno stopped him. "No, Rome. Lulu has picked you. She wants to go with you."

For a split second, Rome thought he might crack. He looked at Lulu's dark brown eyes and could feel her pleading with him. *Take me! Let me go with you!* He inhaled sharply. "I can't, Menno. She belongs here, at Windmill Farm." He ordered Lulu down and she hopped off, tail between her legs, and sat down next to her puppy—the one Menno had still to find the right master for.

Rome turned away and jumped onto the wagon without looking back. He picked up the reins and the mule started to move along, slowly and steadily, into the darkness.

The old patterns of Rome's life were repeating themselves. He was drifting.

A silvery mist hugged the ground like a blanket, and the slanting rays of the sun brushed the leaves still lingering on the trees, painting them yellow, red, and brown. Fall had always been Julia's favorite time of the year.

As she walked along the apple trees, trying to decide if there was enough fruit to justify another picking before a deep frost hit, she wondered if she would forevermore associate autumn with saying goodbye. First to Paul, then to Rome. Maybe, soon, to her father. Amos was weaker with every passing day.

Julia tried not to wonder where Rome was. Where did he go? What had he been doing? It didn't matter, it was none of her business, he owed her nothing, they had taken no vows and made no promises.

The odd thing was that after Fern had told her about Rome's family, she began to understand his strange inner workings. The accident had made him fiercely, desperately independent. No wonder he couldn't tolerate growing attached to her. She knew Rome cared for her, she saw it in his eyes and his actions. But she also knew he wasn't capable of anything more. He wouldn't even take Lulu with him, and that dog had meant something to him.

As she walked among the apple trees, she prayed. She prayed about the mixed-up feelings, the uncertainty she felt about Rome. Prayer worked. She believed in prayer. The word *trust* kept circling through her mind. Trust. She turned the word over and over in her mind. Trust went hand in hand with faith. *That's what I need*, Julia thought. *To trust God's ways.*

Maybe that was her problem with Paul. She was so busy telling God how to fix things between her and Paul that she hadn't given God a chance to chime in. Maybe she could have saved everybody a lot of trouble had she ever asked God if Paul was the right person for her. *No!* God would have said. *I've got something better in mind for you, if you'd just have a little patience.* She could practically hear God's voice. Not out loud, but in her mind. In her heart.

So, Lord, this time, I am asking you to take over. Rome is yours, and you know his heart. You know what's best for him. And you know what's best for me. Please watch over him now, wherever he is. Help him find what he's looking for. Give him joy, Lord. Give him peace.

Overhead, a fluff of a cloud was framed with pure golden light from the sun that was hidden behind it. Awed by the sight, she studied the outline of the cloud within the frame, light splaying around its edges.

As she gazed at the cloud, she was filled with feelings she couldn't explain. Peace, joy, reassurance—all swirling together. It seemed as if the heavens parted and she caught a glimpse of God's connectedness to this earthly existence. She'd never had such an awareness of the presence of God.

The sun was starting to set now, and it was getting cold, but in her heart there was radiant light. She remained where she was until M.K. called to her to come in. She wanted to savor this new peace. She knew she would never, ever forget this moment in the apple orchards. It was meant to stay with her.

The air was bright and pure; the leaves on the trees glistened and the Blue Lake Pond flowed softly, lapping against the shore with a gentle rhythm. Rome closed his eyes as though to contain the landscape and the deep sense of peace it evoked. He had been camping by the lake with his bees the last few days, waiting for a certified letter to arrive from Ohio, bearing a cashier's check for his family's farm. Waiting, waiting, waiting. What was taking it so long? He wanted to get that check to Fern for safekeeping. To leave Stoney Ridge with clean accounts. No regrets. No second thoughts.

And yet, he did have second thoughts. He leaned his head against a tree and closed his eyes. Suddenly he was overcome with a sense of homesickness, a dull ache that had settled around his heart. He missed Windmill Farm. He missed the cottage. He missed the Lapps. He missed Julia. He hated knowing he'd hurt Julia. "Take care of yourself," he had said, as if he were talking to a pal. How inadequate. How childish!

The only reason he'd acted so cool and detached was so he didn't leave her with any mixed messages, any confusion.

This was better for her, for him. She would marry Paul. He would have an unencumbered life. It was better for both of them.

So why did he feel as if he had lost something precious? As if he was losing his home all over again?

What was home, really? Just a place to lay your head.

No. It was so much more than that. It was the place where a person belonged. Where a fellow would be missed. It was a part of a man. Something that couldn't be sold or taken for granted.

He was seized by a moment of panic. Why had he sold the Ohio farm? It was like giving away his right arm. How could he have done such a thing?

His father would be ashamed of him. Was it too late? Could he stop the process?

He hurried to town to get to the post office before it closed at five. He would send a letter—a telegram. He would stop the sale.

When the postmaster saw him come into the post office, she reached below the counter and pulled out a large manila envelope. "It just arrived, Bee Man. Those papers you wanted from Ohio. Now you can be on your way."

It was too late.

The transaction had been completed. He ripped open the envelope and read the enclosed letter. Then reread it, again and again. He had to sit down. He went outside of the post office and found a bench. Was someone playing a joke on him?

The cashier's check was included for the full amount of the property. But also included was the deed to the farm. Paid in full. Returned to Roman Troyer. A gift.

At dusk, Fern sent M.K. and Menno over to the Fishers' with two bushels of apples to make cider. "Edith said her apple tree wasn't delivering the goods this year because we hogged Rome's bees."

"It's cuz those bees have good sense to stay away from Jimmy Fisher," M.K. muttered.

"Go," Fern said. "And don't dawdle. It'll be dark soon."

They got about halfway to the Fishers' when M.K. was struck with inspiration. "Menno, let's cut through the cornfields. It'll save us going way down on the road."

"I don't think so. It's getting dark."

"Come on!" She started into the fields. "I do it all the time. Just watch for snakes." She was deep in the middle of the field when she stopped abruptly. Staring intently through the dried cornstalks, she thought she heard a strange sound. Maybe she heard a snake behind her, maybe not.

Menno caught up with her. "Let me go ahead of you. I'm taller than the corn."

M.K. grinned. Menno was proud of his height, nearly as tall as their father. He worked it into conversations all summer long. "Fine, but just keep going in a line, along that row. Can you see the lights from the house straight ahead?"

A dog began barking and Menno stopped. "That's Jimmy's dog, Menno. He won't hurt you."

"I don't know about this, Mary Kate."

"It's fine!"

"Do you hear that dog yapping?"

"He's always yapping." That dog was crazy, as crazy as Jimmy. It was barking its head off like it had seen a ghost. She gave Menno a gentle push to move forward. "Hey, I heard a good joke we need to remember to tell Uncle Hank. What's got a head and a tail, but doesn't have a body?"

Menno worked on that for a long moment before giving up. "I don't know."

"A coin! Like a dime or a quarter. Get it?" She then explained the joke to Menno until he understood it and gave out a big haw. By the time he stopped laughing, they were nearly through the cornfield to the woven-wire fence that ran alongside the yard to the Fishers' large henhouse.

"Let's cut through the chicken yard to get to the house."

Menno started to object, but before he could get the words out, M.K. found the gate into the chicken yard and led the way across hen grit and worse. "Pinch your nose, Menno, so you don't have to smell the stink. And be careful where you step or Fern will have a fit." Nothing smelled worse than a henhouse on a windless night.

M.K. could hear the chickens flapping their wings in the henhouse. Chickens weren't the brightest of birds, and easily flustered, but something felt eerie to her. It didn't help that Jimmy's dog was having fits. She was glad to see it was on a tie-down.

She heard a strange ripping metal sound, as if the henhouse door was getting wrenched from its hinges, then every hen in the place rose up and screamed. The bucket of apples dropped from Menno's fingers, spilling everywhere. M.K. stopped to help him, when suddenly, something or someone burst out of the henhouse and stood, scanning the yard. The air behind it was white with feathers. M.K.'s breath was cut off, and her heart hollered.

"Bear! Run, Menno!" M.K. screamed. "It's the bear! Run! Get to the farmhouse!"

She flew toward the house and landed on the top step of the porch, banging on the front door. Rapid explosions went off from an upstairs window in the house, followed by a burned-powder haze that hung in the air. And an eerie silence. Even the dog went still. Everything was waiting.

"Menno?" M.K. shouted into the night. "Menno? Where are you? Menno?"

As M.K. realized he wasn't answering, she screamed.

20

At seven o'clock that night, Sadie came downstairs and asked Julia where M.K. and Menno were. When Fern told her they hadn't gotten back yet, a strange look came over Sadie's face. She went outside on the back porch to wait for them, restless and anxious. "Something's wrong."

Within minutes, a strange wailing sound drifted up the hill. Julia ran to the kitchen door and saw a small figure running toward the house. "Juuu-Leee-Aaaa!"

Julia flew out the door and ran down the hill to reach M.K. Her little sister flung her arms around her waist. It took awhile to calm M.K. down and get the facts straightened out, but Julia pieced together that Menno had been accidentally shot and was taken to the hospital in Lancaster by ambulance. As they came back up the hill, they found the family—Fern, their father, Uncle Hank, Sadie—waiting on the porch.

"We'll all go," Amos said gravely.

"Dad, are you sure you should go?" Julia asked. "I'll go, find out the extent of Menno's injuries, and call you. Sadie or M.K. could stay in the shanty until I call."

Sadie stood next to her father and held on to his arm. "He needs to be there, Jules. We all do."

It would take forever to get her father dressed and ready to go. He struggled to get enough air for the simplest of acts, how could he hurry for this?

The same thought must have run through Fern's mind. "You and Sadie go on ahead. The rest of us will follow as quickly as we can."

Julia nodded. Fern's voice was calm, reassuring.

"I have to come too," M.K. said. "Please let me come. Please, please, please." Her little face was white and pinched.

Julia and Sadie went down to the phone shanty, called for a taxi driven by a Mennonite fellow who lived nearby, and waited. And waited.

Finally, two headlights appeared on the road. The ride to the hospital felt like an eternity. When they reached the Emergency Room, they tumbled out of the car. Julia told the driver to go back to Windmill Farm to get her father. The hospital door slid open and Sadie, M.K., and Julia stepped into a crowded waiting room. Julia asked a man at the counter about Menno. He looked up Menno's name on the computer, asked if they were family, then pointed toward a hall and said to go talk to a nurse at the station through the doors. They walked down another hall to a door that said NO ADMITTANCE. Julia had to push the button and talk into a speaker box to tell the nurse why they were there and whom they wanted to see.

A nurse was waiting for them as the door opened. "Come with me."

"Where's Menno?" M.K. asked, starting to cry again.

Julia held her close against her. She wanted to cry too. This all felt like a bad dream that she couldn't wake from. How could Menno have been fine, just a few hours ago, and now he was in a hospital? How could life be so fragile?

The nurse handed M.K. a box of tissues. "I need to talk to your older sister about a couple of things first. Then I'll take you to your brother. I promise." She motioned to a quiet space by the nurse's station so Julia followed her. "Were you told what happened?"

"I know there was an accident. Someone was trying to shoot a bear and they ended up shooting Menno."

"Your brother received a bullet wound to his head. He's on a ventilator and IV, oxygen and a catheter."

"Is he in pain?"

"No."

"Good." Oh good! Oh, thank God. A wave of relief washed over Julia. "We'd like to see him."

"Soon. You need to know, he's in a coma. He's unresponsive."

Julia felt as if she might faint. She held on to the counter with both hands.

"Do you need to sit down?" the nurse whispered.

Julia breathed deeply for a moment. Was she going to be sick? She closed her eyes and tried to recite a psalm. Finally, she said, "All that matters is that he is alive."

"Yes, but—" The nurse stopped abruptly. "Let me take you to see him."

Julia followed her through another door and into the room where Menno lay, but the boy who lay on the bed did not look like her brother. Julia glanced around at the monitors. She recognized the jagging line for the heart, the numbers for the blood pressure and oxygen levels—it was the same kind of monitor her father had been hooked up to. Menno's chest rose and fell, his left hand was taped to a board with the IV line in the back of his hand. His head was bandaged down to his eyebrows with a turban of white gauze. It was a horrible dream. Like someone was pummeling her with hard blows. One more and she might crumble.

It was so hard to see Menno like this. She wanted to protect him. She was *supposed* to be able to protect him. She was his older sister! She had always watched out for him. Julia curled her fingers around his right hand on top of the sheet. His hand was so cold. She had heard once that even in a coma, the patient could hear.

"Menno, it's me. It's Jules. Your sister. Can you hear me?"

No response, not even a flicker.

Julia sat down in the chair by the bed, still clinging to Menno's hand. She remembered a time he'd fallen from a horse and his sweet face had been so battered and bruised she hardly recognized him. She stroked his hair that was sticking out under the gauze.

She shot a look through the window at Sadie, who had tears running down her cheeks. M.K. had her face buried in her hands. Julia glanced over to the doorway to see a doctor standing there. Had he said something to her? "Yes?" The word came out in a croak. She tried again. "Yes."

"I'm Dr. Lee." He held his metal clipboard against his chest, a barrier between them. "I admitted your brother."

The doctor studied the monitors, checked Menno's eyes responses with his flashlight, skimmed the bottom of his feet with another instrument, pulled out his stethoscope and listened to his heart and lungs. He turned to her. "Menno's condition remains unchanged." Another blow to Julia's gut. "Are you Menno's guardian?"

From some distant place, Julia could hear herself say, "Of sorts. I'm the eldest in the family. My father will be here soon, but he isn't well. If there's something about Menno you need for us to know, I'd appreciate it if you could tell me first."

The doctor cleared his throat and his shoulders rose and fell in a sigh.

"Will you be taking him in for surgery soon?"

"Surgery?"

"To get the bullet out of his head," Julia said. Just how experienced was this doctor? He didn't seem to know what to do next.

Suddenly she felt herself shaking so hard she had to sit on a chair. She grabbed her elbows and leaned forward, head down. "You think he's going to die, don't you." Julia's voice was a dry rasp.

The doctor crouched down beside her. Then, slowly, in a gentle voice, "Miss Lapp, when your brother came into the hospital, he was already comatose. The brain function is minimal. We've done all we can do for him."

At the window, Julia saw a nurse leading her father, Fern, and Uncle Hank to meet Sadie and M.K. The nurse quietly opened the door and let them file around Menno's bedside. Fern and Uncle Hank stood against the wall. Fern gave M.K. a gentle push to go stand by her brother. Sadie leaned over and whispered something in Menno's ear. Julia heard only the sounds, not the words. It reminded Julia of when they were young. Menno's language was slow to develop, and Sadie, though two years younger, spoke sooner than he did. Her mother used to say that Sadie was God's gift to help Menno along. Sadie seemed to understand what Menno wanted to say before he had words of his own to use. She would whisper something to him, like she was doing now, lean close to him, hearing something from him that only she could hear.

Amos picked up Menno's hand in his and stroked it gently. The doctor quietly explained the situation to everyone.

"But he is breathing," Amos said, "and his heart is beating."

"Yes, because he is on the ventilator," the doctor said gently. "If we turn that off, he won't last long."

Julia stared at the monitors. The steady *beep beep beep*, the snaking lines of tubing, the sucking sound as Menno's chest lifted and fell. Was it true? She studied her brother's face and his arms and hands. Beautiful Menno, special Menno. He had taught them all so much—patience, loving unconditionally, daily reminders to slow down and notice things—to *really* notice. She took his hand in hers, this calloused hand that had gently nursed so many animals back to health, this hand that had built so many birdhouses to shelter birds.

"Stay with us, Menno," she whispered, clutching his hand even harder. "Don't leave us."

Julia saw Sadie lean close to Menno, matching her breathing to his shallow breathing on the monitor. "What is it?"

Sadie shook her head, a minuscule movement. She turned her head slightly, then her shoulders dropped. With tear-filled eyes, she turned to Julia. "He's gone. He was here a moment ago, but now he's gone. He waited until we were all together. He's left us."

The doctor seemed puzzled and examined the monitors. "Nothing's changed."

Julia and her father exchanged a look. Sadie knew.

Julia had to get some fresh air. She told Fern she would be back soon, and went out into the hallway. There was a small garden area for families and patients to sit in, so she followed the arrows leading to it and went out into the dark night air. She lifted her face toward the stars.

So many thoughts in an instant, overlapping, colliding thoughts, thoughts without words.

She sat quietly for several minutes. She was too stunned to cry. She had lost more than her brother, she had lost part of herself. She couldn't remember a time when Menno wasn't there. She rubbed her temples. *What are we to do, Lord?* She didn't even know how to pray for Menno, for all of them. Words seemed inadequate for the pain that seared through her. A deep groan poured out of her soul, a wordless prayer. Was this what the Bible meant when it said that the Holy Spirit prayed for us?

She didn't know how long she had been out there, looking at the stars, praying for Menno, when she heard a familiar voice gently call her name. She looked up and blinked. Was she dreaming?

"Rome!" She flew out of the chair and across the small space. "Thank God! Thank God you're here."

He hauled her up against his chest and held her so tight she couldn't breathe. Her fists gripped the cloth of his jacket and she burrowed into him, rubbing her face against his chest. With that, the tears broke loose and she sobbed into his chest. She tried to tell him what had happened to Menno, but he shushed her.

"I've already been to the room. I heard all about the accident."

"How did you know? Who told you?"

"I was heading out to Windmill Farm tonight to ask Fern . . . never mind . . . long story . . . I'll explain later. When I passed by the Fishers', Jimmy told me what had happened. I came as soon as I could."

Julia wiped her tears off of her face. "The doctor said we need to take Menno off the ventilator. He said Menno's brain is . . . he said that there's no sign of brain activity."

Rome led her to the garden bench where she was sitting when he came in. He sat down beside her. "Julia, there's something you need to consider. As awful a situation as this is, something good might come out of it."

"What are you talking about?"

He took her hands in his. "Menno's heart. It's meant for your father."

Julia felt a brutal slap out of nowhere. She pulled her hands away, but he wouldn't let them go. "You're saying . . . that Menno's heart be given to my father?" Her voice shook.

"Yes." He waited a moment before continuing, letting her absorb that thought. "Think about it, Julia. If Menno were here, he would want you to consider this. I know he would. But he's not here, and I need to do this for him. The heart may not even be a match. I'm not even sure what the protocol is about organ donation, but we need to try. You need to convince your father to try."

Her face scrunched up again and the tears resumed.

More urgently, he said, "We should do what Menno wanted."

She was squeezing his hands now, hard, so hard, but she couldn't help it. She was a bundle of nerves. "I can't make that kind of decision for him. I don't know what he would want."

"Yes, you do. Do you remember, a few weeks ago, when we were in your father's room and he told Menno and Sadie and M.K. that he was dying? Do you remember what Menno asked? He asked him if a person had two hearts, like two kidneys. He said he would give Amos his heart if he could. He said those very words."

Her grip relaxed. "I remember. He did say that." Her hands slipped into her lap.

Rome stood. "I'll be right with you when you talk to Amos. But it needs to come from you. He'll listen to you, Julia." He held his hand out to her.

She looked at his hand for a long moment, then put her hand in his.

Rome watched Amos listen carefully to Julia, and to him, but he could see it was Uncle Hank who made the difference.

Hank put his hand on Amos's shoulder and said, "That boy's life was a gift from start to finish. This is his final gift to you, Amos. You would be wrong not to receive it graciously."

Amos looked at Hank with searching eyes. Hank loved Menno like he was his own. In a way, he knew Menno better than any of them. They spent hours together, hunting and fishing and talking.

"Our Menno would want this, Amos," Hank said. "More than that, he would delight in this coincidence." He held up his finger. "No, he would correct me. He would say that what man calls coincidences, God would call a miracle."

Amos quietly said he needed some time alone with Menno.

Rome saw Julia cross the room and sit next to Uncle Hank. She put her hand over his, and he clasped hers tightly. They remained that way until Amos returned from Menno's room, about ten minutes later. He told Rome to go find that heart doctor, Dr. Highland, the one who looked like he was ten. He didn't need to tell Rome twice.

As Rome hurried through the halls, he felt an awe at God's perfect timing. God was always in the business of redeeming, Fern had told him once, if only we let him. He prayed in the elevators, prayed in the hallways, prayed as he waited for the doctor to be paged. *Lord, let this be a match. And then let them agree to give the heart to Amos. Don't let Menno's death be in vain.*

Dr. Lee took Julia aside to ask if the family would consider allowing other organs for donation. "I realize you have a great deal to cope with right now, but there is a question I need to ask. Would you be willing to let Menno's other organs help save other people?"

They wanted more of Menno? Julia felt a wave of nausea. How could she possibly make such a decision, at this moment in time?

"Julia, your brother can give the gift of life to someone else with his heart, lungs, liver, kidneys. His corneas will help someone see and his skin will heal burns. Medical science has learned of ways to use so much healthy tissue. But, of course, Menno is not of age, so we would need your father's permission. Would you speak to him?"

She didn't answer right away. "Give me some time."

"Of course. But, the longer Menno remains on the machines, the fewer organs we can use."

She got up and slowly walked out of the room, down the hall to Menno's room. She passed the garden where she had talked with Rome, and felt a pull toward it. *Dear Lord*, she prayed, *I can't even imagine life without Menno. And now my father has a chance to live. I don't know what you have planned for my father. I want to believe you will send us a miracle, but if you can't, I know that you will take him home to be with you in heaven . . . the ultimate healing. Whatever you decide, Lord, thy will be done. I only ask that you give me strength to help me through.*

As soon as she finished praying, the word *trust* popped into her mind, the way it had just a few days ago, when she prayed about Rome. Was it just a few days ago? It felt like a lifetime. But maybe that's why God gave her that unique experience. To fortify her for what was coming.

Trust.

A quiet peace stole over her soul, replacing the heavy garment of fear she was wearing. She could feel the tension in her shoulders release and the tightness in her chest from constant worry begin to dissipate. She took a deep breath and looked up at the diamond-studded sky. Was Menno looking down on them now?

She went back down the hall and into Menno's room. Fern and Sadie looked up when she came into the room. M.K. was curled up in a chair, asleep. Amos was stroking Menno's hair. Uncle Hank sat in a chair, head in his hands. Rome was at the window, leaning his back against the sill.

"The doctor wants us to think about donating Menno's other organs," Julia said. "Not just his heart. His lungs, his liver, his kidneys. Even his corneas and skin." She looked down at her clasped hands and swallowed hard. When she spoke, her voice was raw with emotion. "I think we should say yes. I think Menno would have said yes. He's with the Lord. He doesn't need his earthly shell any longer."

Rome's eyes caught hers, his expression tender, sad, amazed.

Sadie went over to her father and put a hand on his shoulder. "I think Julia's right. I know she is. Menno would have wanted to give anything he could to help someone else."

"Dad?" Julia asked. "It's really your decision."

Amos gave a brief nod.

The door opened and Dr. Highland, Amos's cardiologist, walked in. "The team is waiting to check the viability of Menno's heart. It'll take a few hours. The transplant coordinator has asked the Organ Procurement and Transplantation Network to review factors to distribute the heart to Amos. So far, the blood type is a match, your weight and size fit within the parameters. The chance of rejection is greatly reduced when the organ donor is a family member. And your heart is in such bad shape that you're high on the transplant list. This looks good, Amos. This looks like it might be the heart that is meant for you. If the OPTN gives us its blessing, you'll be transferred to Hershey Medical by ambulance." He looked over at Menno. "It's time to say goodbye."

One by one, each family member gave Menno a kiss and told them they loved him. Then it was time. The doctors and nurses surrounded Menno as they prepared to turn off the ventilator. The family stood against the wall. The machine blew out its last wheezing breath, and the doctor looked at the clock to record the time of death. In a deep voice, stronger than it had been in months, Amos prayed aloud the Lord's Prayer.

Menno Joseph Lapp's time of death was officially recorded as Thursday, October 27, 11:52 p.m.

That was what the death certificate would state. But Julia, Sadie, M.K., Fern, Uncle Hank, Amos and Rome knew that Menno had been taken to be with the Lord over an hour ago, when the family first gathered around his hospital bed.

It was long after midnight. Sadie noticed Edith Fisher sitting alone in the waiting room and went over to sit by her.

Edith looked up and said, "You must think I'm a horrible person."

Sadie made a calming gesture. "No, Edith. I don't think you're horrible."

"I was home alone, and heard the dog barking. Then I heard screaming and I knew that bear was out there—she's been helping herself to my hens on a regular basis—and the boys weren't home so I grabbed Paul's rifle off of his bedroom wall and I just started shooting. I couldn't see much because of the dark, Sadie. I didn't know that Menno was there. Or M.K. I thought the bear was attacking the dog. I just panicked and started shooting." Edith's eyes filled with tears. "When I found out a bullet hit Menno, I just . . . I don't know how you'll ever be able to forgive me."

"We already do, Edith. We know it was an accident. Accidents happen."

"I was always so fond of Menno."

"Everybody was. Menno knew you would never mean to hurt him, Edith. It was God's time to call him home, and God doesn't make mistakes."

Edith's head bounced up. "Julia will never forgive me. Never."

"She will. She will forgive you, because she's Julia." Sadie had no doubt of that.

"What will Paul say?" She rocked herself back and forth in abject misery.

"Paul loves you. No one is blaming you for an accident."

Edith started sobbing again.

"Would you like me to get you something? A cup of tea? A glass of water?"

"Would you. . . . just sit with me for a minute?"

"Everything is going to be okay," Sadie said. She felt Edith relax, as if she believed her.

Other than that first meeting in the hospital garden, Rome hadn't had a minute alone with Julia. She was constantly being taken aside by nurses or doctors or hospital workers who needed papers signed. So much paperwork.

The bishop and the deacon arrived at the hospital to offer support and prayers. Menno's funeral needed to be planned in the midst of all of this. Rome was so proud of Julia—she was handling the pressure with calm and poise. Her twenty-one-year-old face looked middle-aged and careworn. This long evening of profound decision making had exhausted her. He didn't know how she was holding up, hurting from the loss of her brother and frightened for her father. An hour ago, they received word that the OPTN agreed to the transplant. They had looked at several factors: blood and tissues were ideal matches to reduce risk of rejection, the weakened condition of Amos's heart and the length of time he had been on the transplant list, as well as the geographical convenience of the donor heart. It was a go, the doctor said. There was no turning back for Amos. This was it. They were all aware of that. Amos's last words to all of them, as he was being wheeled away by the nurse to prepare for the trip to Hershey, were: "I will have joy in the morning." Either way, he meant.

As Rome watched Julia down by the nurse's station, an unexpected wave of longing was triggered. Into his gut came that restless feeling of searching, of wanting. Something unthinkable pulled at the edges of his brain. He tried to push it away, but it only gathered strength. What if Julia had been right? He was letting fear dictate the course of his life. These last few days had given him time to think, to sift through the rubbish in his life that was shackling him.

In that moment, watching Julia, he understood what he needed to do. Maybe it would work, and maybe it wouldn't. Maybe it would take heartbreak to a whole new level.

21

Amos's operation began well before dawn on Friday morning.

Julia had accompanied her father in the ambulance to Hershey Medical. Fern and Edith took M.K. home. Uncle Hank, Sadie, and Rome hired a taxi to go from Lancaster General to Hershey, about thirty minutes away, to keep vigil with Julia in the waiting room . . . waiting.

She glanced at the clock again. Five more minutes and it would be seven hours. Sadie had fallen asleep, curled up on two chairs, with her head in Julia's lap. Uncle Hank paced up and down the halls. Rome sat quietly, across from Julia, hands clasped, head down, his lips silently moving. She knew he was praying and the sight touched her.

At the sound of footsteps, Julia glanced up the hall. When she saw the surgeon who performed the transplant with his face mask hanging around his neck, she rose to her feet and practically dumped Sadie on the floor.

The doctor smiled at her. "I have good news for you. That new heart is beating away like it belonged there." The surgeon's smile looked as tired as she felt. "Amos is in recovery. He'll be heavily sedated for the next day or so, depending on how he responds."

Julia ignored the tears trickling down her cheeks and smiled away. And kept on smiling. She sniffed and nodded. "Thank you." Her father had a new heart. A new life.

Sadie squeezed her hand, sharing the thought. Uncle Hank patted Rome so hard on his back that he almost lost his footing, and they all laughed, a mixture of relief and joy.

"A word of warning," the doctor said as he took Julia aside. "Now we fight the rejection battle."

This warning, sobering though it was, had not succeeded in dampening Julia's pleasure at the operation's success. She had seized upon the positive words the doctor had uttered: there should be no reason why there should be any complications. There was much to be relieved about.

And there was much to grieve about.

The next day, Julia was allowed into her father's hospital room. Already, she could see signs of returning health. The blue tinge was gone from around Amos's mouth and eyes, even his fingernails were a healthy pink. When Julia took his hand, the warmth of it sent spirals of joy dancing up her arm and lodging in her heart. She had seen him for just a moment when he was getting wheeled from recovery to his room and was startled by how cold his hand was. The nurse explained that his body had been chilled down for surgery and it would take several hours to warm up again. Last night, he had been heavily sedated, but today, when she squeezed his hand, she received a squeeze in return. His eyes fluttered open and a slight smile moved the corners of his mouth.

He tried to speak but couldn't because of the tubes running down his throat to allow the ventilator to breathe for him. The surgeon gave him a pad of paper and pen to communicate. Julia hung there, waiting for her father's first words.

Slowly and carefully, with the doctor's help, he scrawled, "When can I go home?"

Julia laughed for pure joy until she wanted to cry. It was a miracle. She could see the vein in her father's neck pulsing. Deep in his chest, Menno's heart was pounding a steady beat.

"All depends on how well you do, Amos," the doctor said. "Minimum stay is usually a week."

Julia was surprised. "That's all?"

"Amazing, isn't it? But he was in fairly good shape when he arrived—a lot of folks waiting for transplants are knocking at death's door, and your father had been trying to stay in shape."

Fern! Julia breathed a prayer of thanks for that bossy, wonderful woman, sweeping into their lives so unexpectedly. So profoundly.

"Besides, we find people heal better at home." The doctor checked Amos's responses, wrote some notes on his pad, and nodded to Julia. "We'll keep him pretty heavily sedated today and see how he's doing by evening. The respiration therapist will be working with him to keep the lungs clear. So far he's handling the anti-rejection meds. There's a catheter inserted in the side of his neck that enables us to take biopsies from the inside of the heart. We'll take samples and test them five times a day. If all goes well, the samples will be tested daily for a while after you return home, then every other day, then every other week." He paused. "For now, though, we wait."

Julia looked at her father, resting there, and couldn't hold back a smile. She was beaming! "And pray. We wait and pray."

On Saturday afternoon, there was a great flurry of coming and going at Windmill Farm as ladies appeared and worked themselves to the bone—helping quietly and without fanfare. The church at Stoney Ridge was like that. The house was cleaned from top to bottom, the pantry and refrigerator were filled with food, the living room was emptied and benches were brought in as scores of friends and neighbors came through to view Menno, laid out in the front room. Fern remained at the house, directing traffic, while Julia stayed at the hospital with their father. Sadie felt almost useless.

She tried to help Fern but couldn't concentrate on her tasks. Fern finally told her to go outside and get some fresh air. Too much had happened, too quickly. She could hardly believe how life had changed, in just a few days.

As she walked down the driveway, she found Annie at the roadside stand, as if she'd been waiting for Sadie. Beside Annie was one of Menno's pups, now about five months old. Sadie bent down and scratched the pup behind the ears.

"It made Menno happy that you have one of his pups," Sadie said.

The puppy wandered off to sniff around the mailbox.

Annie kept her eyes downcast. "Menno was real good to me."

Sadie nodded. She wouldn't cry. She wouldn't cry. Once she started, she didn't think she could stop.

"Sometime, maybe, you could come pay a visit to me. Maybe we could talk." Annie looked as if she wanted to say more but didn't.

"I'd like that, Annie."

"You know, you were special to Menno. You understood him best." Annie whistled for the pup, just like Menno had taught her, and walked away.

Then the tears began for Sadie.

Sunday was, blessedly, an off-Sunday, and the family had a quiet morning before the taxi driver arrived to take them to Hershey. They were able to have a fifteen-minute, one-on-one afternoon visit with Amos. M.K. insisted on staying at home, despite Sadie's urging her to join them, so Fern volunteered to stay at home with her. Sadie couldn't hide her exasperation with her little sister. She knew M.K. was hurting, but she wouldn't talk about it. What more could Sadie do? Sadie was hurting too. They all were hurting.

When they reached the hospital that afternoon, a nurse smiled when she saw them in front of the nurse's central monitoring station. "Thirty-six hours and no signs of rejection, other than a slightly elevated temperature," she volunteered, "which is common after major surgery. The doctor was just here. He said your dad is doing so well, he'll be dangling soon."

"Dangling?" Sadie asked.

"Sitting up, feet over the side of the bed. Precursor to standing on the floor."

Julia and Uncle Hank insisted that Sadie go in first to visit with her dad. She had only seen him briefly, right after surgery. She wore a gown over her dress, a face mask, and paper slippers over her shoes—to reduce the chance of infection for Amos. As Sadie pushed the door open, she felt her stomach twist into a tight knot. Her father was connected to a network of wires and tubes—some attached to the heart monitor, an IV, a blood pressure cuff. Swathed under white sheets, he looked so small. It was a stark contrast to the rugged, deeply tanned figure of her father that was fixed in her mind from childhood. The lights were dimmed in the room, but the bank of machines that pumped and hissed with beeps of their own were still visible, their monitors casting a soft, diffused light. Her eyes filled with tears, but she fought them off. She needed to get used to this, if it was true what Fern had said—if she was a healer.

"Dad?"

Amos looked up, his eyes unfocused. It took him several seconds to focus. "Sadie?" he asked, his voice a mere whisper, then his eyes flew open wide with recognition.

The nurse stole quietly into the room. Slowly, she raised the head of the bed so he was sitting nearly straight up. Amos gasped as she moved his feet toward the edge, but he sat up with his own muscles.

"No rush now, we'll take it easy," the nurse said.

Sadie laid a hand on his shoulder when she saw Amos quivering.

"Okay, now swing your legs over slowly," the nurse instructed.

Amos inched his heels toward the side of the bed, hanging onto the nurse's forearm. Sadie held her breath.

The nurse scooted the IV line out of the way. "Good, you're almost there. Feeling faint? Don't forget to breathe."

With his feet hung straight down from his knees, fairly close to sitting straight up, he let out a whoosh. "Made it."

"Way to go, big guy."

Amos gave her a thumbs-up sign.

"You did it. How's it feel?"

"Wobbly. I don't think I'll be walking quite yet."

"No, but standing by tonight." The nurse put her stethoscope to Amos's back. "Good and clear. Just what we like to hear." She looked into Sadie's eyes. "You want to hear?" When Sadie nodded, she slipped the earpieces into Sadie's ears and held the disc against his back.

The nurse put the stethoscope back in her pocket. "You got a real thumper there. How you feeling?"

"Like I just plowed ten acres with a stubborn mule."

When Amos was lying down again, with the bed propped back up, he puffed out his cheeks and blew out a breath. "You know, tiring as that was, I can tell I'm getting more air than I have for a long time. I've been weaker than this at times at home lying on the couch." He glanced at Sadie and saw tears streaming down her cheeks. "What's this?" He reached out a hand to her cheek.

"Dad, that's Menno's heart beating inside of you." She leaned her forehead against his and held his hand against his bandaged-up chest. "Menno is part of you."

Monday was a very big day. Five hundred and thirty-two people attended Menno's funeral. M.K. counted. It was a way for her to keep her mind away from thinking about the pine box right in front of her that held her brother's body. As soon as the graveside service in the cemetery was over, she waited until Fern's back was turned, and then she ran. She ran as far as she could and didn't stop until she was completely out of breath and had stitches pinching her side. She found the shortcut to Blue Lake Pond and walked down to the shore, holding a fist against her side. She flopped down on the shore and stared at the still water.

The sky was bright blue and the air was crisp, a hint of winter on autumn's heels. The day was beautiful and it was cruel. It was Menno's favorite kind of day.

Out of the blue, Jimmy Fisher sat down next to her on the sandy dirt.

She scowled at him. "What are you doing, sneaking up on me like that? Can't you see I want to be alone?"

"I wasn't sneaking," he said. "I saw you run off. Thought you might need some company."

"I don't."

But he didn't leave and she was glad. They sat there for a while, watching the water lap the shore.

Finally, Jimmy spoke. "The game warden caught the bear and her cub. He took them up to the mountains. They won't be bothering anyone anymore."

M.K. rested her chin on her knees.

"My mother feels awful bad. A police officer came to our house and had her fill out a report about the accident."

"I don't blame her. None of us do. If anyone's to blame, it's me. It was my idea to take a shortcut through your cornfield. That's the reason your mother got scared. If we were coming down the driveway like normal people, we wouldn't have had to go through the chicken yard and make your dog even crazier than it is. Then your mother wouldn't have started shooting at anything that moved." She rubbed her eyes. "I should've stayed with him. I shouldn't have left him. I knew he got confused when too much was happening too fast. I left him alone. He must have been so frightened."

"The bishop said it was Menno's time. Maybe it was, maybe it wasn't. I don't know how to sort all of that out." He turned his head toward her. "Maybe it was just an accident. Sometimes, bad things happen and there's just no explaining them."

She kept her eyes straight ahead. "That's as hard to get my head around as the bishop's way of thinking."

"Maybe because . . . the problem is . . . you can't forgive yourself."

A single tear leaked down her cheek, then another. Soon, tears were rushing down her cheeks. She started to sob. Jimmy patted her on her back, then finally threw an arm around her shoulder as though trying to impart some of his strength.

He waited until her sobs subsided before he said, "If the bishop was right, that it was Menno's time, then I guess God has something else in mind for you to do."

With a gentleness she didn't think was possible of Jimmy, he wiped her tears away. He looked at her with earnest eyes. "I always did figure God had something special in mind for you. You're not exactly . . . an ordinary girl."

If this were any other day, and she weren't so tired and so sad, she might have popped him one. Instead, she decided that she would ignore that remark. They sat companionably for a while longer until Jimmy rose to his feet.

"Let's get back to the house before you're missed." He reached out a hand for her and helped her to his feet.

She hesitated, almost expecting him to let her hand go so she would fall back, the way she had seen him trick plenty of unsuspecting girls on the schoolyard.

But this time, at least for today, he didn't.

The nurse stood right behind Amos, ready to catch him if he did fall. It was time to walk. Something he had done since he was a baby, and right now, it felt like he was climbing Mount Everest without oxygen.

"Okay, one foot at a time. Put them forward. Keep your back straight, let that walker roll forward, nice and slow."

Amos made it to the doorway before he had to stop. "Whew." He braced his arms on the walker and leaned forward. The nurse braced the walker in front of him and helped him to a chair.

"Not sure how I'll get back up." Amos leaned against the chair. "But I'm up and walking, and while I feel weak, I can breathe and not get dizzy." He drew in a breath and let it out. Would he ever grow accustomed to that wonderful feeling of taking a full breath? He had been intubated for two days. How Amos hated that tube down his throat! He didn't even mind the discomfort from the incision that ran from his throat to just below his sternum—metal stitches that looked like the laces of a tennis shoe on an X-ray. He didn't mind the feeling that he had been hit, head-on, by a truck. But that little tube down his throat? It terrified him. He had to breathe with the rhythm that the machine established. It was hard for the mind to tell the body to let the machine breathe for you. It felt like the final stages of drowning.

When the tube was pulled from his throat, he sucked in his first full breath of air. Bliss! It felt cool. It felt sweet. Only a newborn baby, he thought, could understand the joy of filling lungs with air for the first time.

He stood and slowly made it back to his bed. As he inched into the bed, he saw Julia standing at the door.

"You all right?" Julia asked softly.

He caught a yawn and suddenly felt like a deflated balloon. "Just tired. I start to feel good and then I guess I overdo it."

Sadie brought in a cup of ice chips. She sat next to Amos's bed and held the cup out for him. Julia straightened up the room. The early afternoon sunshine was streaming through the blinds, capturing floating dust particles.

Suddenly, Amos's EKG monitor started picking up its pace, faster and faster. A high-pitched alarm went off and a nurse flew into Amos's room. She brushed past Fern, who was standing tentatively at the door with a worried look on her face.

"What happened?" she asked, checking knobs on the monitor and taking Amos's pulse. The beep of the monitor slowed back to a steady pace.

"Nothing!" Amos said. "Fern walked in and the machine went haywire."

"Oh," the nurse said. Then her eyes went wide. "Oh!" She winked at Fern. "Better warn him next time you're coming."

Julia glanced over at Sadie, a question in her eyes.

Sadie sidled over to her and whispered, "Don't tell me you haven't noticed!"

Amos felt his cheeks burning, as obvious as two circles of red felt. This was quite possibly the most mortifying moment of his entire life.

Rome didn't know how Julia was holding up. She must be exhausted, trying to keep everything on an even keel. He kept hoping to find a moment alone with her. The opportunity came late Thursday afternoon, at the hospital.

"Julia." He touched her shoulder as she left her father's room. "Let's go somewhere to talk." He led her out to the hospital garden and pulled out two chairs to sit in. "Today is the third of November."

She nodded. "I know."

"M.K. said you told Paul no."

She nodded again. "I'm a little surprised you're still here, Rome." She sounded tired. "My father is on the mend. I'd have thought you'd have left by now."

"Julia, I'm staying."

She tilted her head, as if she hadn't heard him right. "You're going to stay in Stoney Ridge?"

He swallowed hard. He managed a jerky nod. He had to do this for her. But he had to do it for himself too. He was tired of his wandering, scared of the person he might become if he kept on like this—a man with a life so small it could fit on the back of a bee wagon.

She regarded him stubbornly. "You thrive in new places. It's putting down roots that gives you trouble."

"You told me I needed to grow roots, and you were right. So I'm going to try."

"Try?" Her voice sliced through him. "You'll try? You either have the guts to take a risk or you don't."

"I won't know until I try." He took her hands in his. "I mean it, Julia. We belong together."

She pulled her hands away, stood up, and walked a few paces before spinning around to face him. She planted a hand on her hip. "And then one morning I will wake up, and you and your bees will be gone."

He walked over to her. "You'll wake up one morning, and turn to me in bed and say, 'Good morning, my wonderful husband.'"

Her bluster faded and her lower lip trembled. "Haven't you tried to tell me all summer that you're not the settling-down kind? Do you think I would seriously consider marrying a drifter?"

"How about a reformed drifter?" She still didn't believe him. *Okay, Rome, it's now or never. Say it. Say it, Rome.* "I love you, Julia. And once you get over being mad at me, I think you'll discover that you love me too." There. He said it.

She eyed him suspiciously. "If you leave, I'm not coming after you."

"Fair enough."

"I need time to think about this."

"Take all the time you need. As long as you agree to marry me."

A shy smile started with her lips and ended with her eyes. All her sass and strut was slipping away. He closed the distance between them in two strides, pulled her into his arms, and kissed her exactly as he'd been planning to do for a week now.

She kissed him back too.

On the day that Amos was discharged from the hospital, the weather turned cold, a hint of winter around the corner. Amos would spend the next few months making regular trips back to the hospital for biopsy tests to watch for rejection. He was grateful Windmill Farm was only thirty minutes from Hershey, otherwise he would need to remain near the hospital. He was dressed and ready to leave, with the blasted face mask on to protect him from germs, but was told to wait for someone from the hospital billing department to stop by his room.

This was the moment he had dreaded. He would be presented with a bill for eight hundred thousand dollars, less ten percent if he paid cash. It was a horrifying thought. The money from Julia's quilt would be a start, but there would still be a sickening burden placed on his church family. But . . . it was done. And Menno would never want him to think this way. This heart was God's good gift. It was priceless.

Still. Eight hundred thousand dollars. A staggering sum!

He heard a knock on the door and in walked his daughters—Julia, Sadie, and M.K., followed by Fern and Rome. Uncle Hank was watching over the farm. Amos's heart felt full to the point of overflowing. His family had arrived to accompany him home from the hospital, all wearing paper face masks so only their eyes were visible. On their heels was a small young fellow with thick glasses, wearing a suit that looked two sizes too big for him. Where did the hospital get their employees? From a local elementary school?

"Mr. Lapp, I'm George Henson, from accounting." In his hand was a fat file.

Filled with unpaid bills, no doubt, Amos thought, but he said instead, "We're able to pay a portion of it now, and make monthly installments."

George Henson pushed his glasses back up on the bridge of his nose. "Mr. Lapp, I just wanted to let you know that your hospital bill has been paid in full, and a fund has been established for your yearly pharmaceutical needs. And those will be substantial. About twenty-five thousand dollars a year."

Paid in full? Amos was stunned. "But . . . how?" He looked at each one of his family members. His daughters were dumbfounded. Rome and Fern kept their eyes fixed on the floor. Amos zeroed in on those two. "What do you two know about this?"

Fern and Rome exchanged a look. "I admit that I paid part of that bill, Amos," Rome said. "But nowhere near that amount."

"Where would you get that kind of money?" Amos asked him.

"I sold my family's farm." Rome looked over at Fern. "At least, I thought I did. Then, in the mail, the deed was returned to me. Someone bought it from me, then gifted it back to me."

One of Fern's eyebrows twitched. She eyed the small man in the suit. "When was Amos's bill paid off? And how was it paid?"

The man looked ill at ease. "The remainder was paid off by a cashier's check, just ten minutes ago. But that's all that I'm at liberty to say."

She huffed. "I *thought* I saw him down the hall!" She frowned and pointed a long finger at Amos. "Don't move. I'll be right back."

Amos sighed.

Julia didn't know what she felt more astounded by—that her father's hospital bill had been entirely paid in full, or that Rome had sold his family property to help her family. And to think he hadn't even wanted anyone to know! She was touched beyond words. Life was endlessly perplexing. She looked over at Rome as he played a game of tic-tac-toe with M.K. on the back of a hospital bill as they waited for Fern to return.

Not six months ago, she would never have believed it if someone had told her how life would play itself out. To think she was in love with Roman Troyer, the Bee Man, Roamin' Roman! And he was in love with her. It defied logic. It was strange. It was wonderful. It was strangely wonderful!

Rome glanced up at her and smiled with his eyes. Soon—maybe tomorrow, maybe the next day—she would tell him that yes, she would marry him.

Fern pushed the door open. Behind her came a man wearing a panama hat.

"You!" M.K. said. She jumped up and ran to him. "You're the man who taught me how to play the shell game!"

"You're the one who bought my quilt at the auction," Julia said.

The man stood at the end of Amos's bed, looking sheepish.

"Did you buy my farm?" Rome asked. "Are you R.W.?"

The man gave a slight nod.

Rome was confused. "Why did you turn right around and give it back to me?"

"Why?" Amos asked. "Why would you be spending your money on my family?"

"Go on," Fern urged the man. "Tell them."

The man looked at his feet. "Money is something I happen to have plenty of. I, well, I made a lot of money on building motor homes years ago. Money isn't a problem for me." The man rubbed his hands together. "But a clean conscience—that's something I can't seem to buy."

"What's troubling you?" Amos asked softly.

The man swallowed hard, but couldn't speak. He looked over at Fern. She waited a long moment, then she, too, choked up. The man closed his eyes and tried again.

"My name is Richard Webster." He looked at Rome to see if he recognized the name, but Rome's face was blank. "I'm the cause of your sorrow."

"What are you talking about?" Rome asked.

"I'm the reason they're dead. Your family. Your uncle too—Miss Graber's fiancé. I'm the one who caused the accident. Six years ago. I'm the one." The man pulled out a handkerchief and wiped his face.

This man was hurting, Julia could see that. A strange combination of sorrow and joy spread through her. His pain—she had seen that same raw pain in Rome. She looked at Rome. What was he feeling? What was he thinking? His face was unreadable.

"Have you been watching us?" Amos asked. "Spying on us?"

The man shook his head. "I spend my time traveling around the country in my motor home. I paid a detective to do a little research and found out Fern and Rome were both in Stoney Ridge this summer. So . . . I came here. I just wanted to see . . . if there was something I could do to help out. To make things right."

Rome cleared his throat. "You wrote me a letter after the accident. I read it. I wrote you back. I told you that you were forgiven."

"I did the same," Fern said.

The man shook his head. "You wrote me that one time—but you never answered my other letters. You never let me do anything to make it up to you. You wouldn't accept my offers of money."

"But there was no need," Rome said. "You weren't guilty of anything. It was an accident. I knew that. I forgave you, long ago. So did Fern. There's no need for anything else."

The man took off his hat. "There is a need. I need to know you *truly* forgive me. Words—they're cheap."

Julia could see the shame eating away at the man. Didn't they see what this man wanted from them? It was as plain as day. She walked up to the man and put a hand on his arm. "Would you join us for dinner at Windmill Farm on Sunday? We'd like to have you come to our home. We'd like to get to know you." She swept an arm around the room. "All of us would like to get to know you. To thank you for what you've done. We want you to know that you're truly forgiven."

The man looked at her, surprised and hopeful. "If . . . if it wouldn't be too much trouble." He cast a furtive glance at Fern and Rome.

Rome walked up to the man. He covered Julia's hand, still resting on the man, with his own. "No trouble at all." He looked at Fern. "You don't mind, do you, Fern?"

"I'm used to trouble out at Windmill Farm," Fern said.

A look of abject relief covered the man's face. "Then, yes, if you're sure, well, I'd be honored to come." He put his panama hat back on. "I'll be off then. Until Sunday."

"Twelve noon," Fern said. "Don't be late."

"I won't, Miss Graber," the man said. "I won't be late. You can count on it."

When his hand was on the door handle, M.K. called out to him. "Mr. Webster, do you happen to like dogs?"

"I do. Been looking for a dog to keep me company on my travels. But it has to be the right dog."

M.K. nodded. "The dog has to pick you."

He looked a little puzzled, but then his face filled with a thoughtful smile. "That's when you know it's right. I've always thought it's best to let the dog do the choosing." He tapped his panama hat snugly on his head.

After the door closed, silence filled the room.

Finally, Amos cleared his throat and spoke up. "Well, if someone isn't going to wheel me out of here, I'm going to walk myself out!"

That broke the spell, and they all laughed. Sadie pulled the door open and M.K. skipped out. Fern grabbed the handles of Amos's wheelchair and pushed. "That's all we need—to have you trip and break a leg."

"At least I'd be close to the emergency room," Amos shot back.

Rome and Julia smiled at each other as the voices faded down the hall. He reached down to pick up Amos's suitcase and held the door for her. Julia looked back to make sure they hadn't forgotten anything. But she knew they would be bringing all that had happened in this hospital room along with them. Memories as real as Menno's heart, a part of every breath.

Life was endlessly perplexing.

"Ready to go home?" Rome asked, holding a hand out to her.

She slipped her hand into his. "I am."

Acknowledgments

There are two subject matters in this story that took a great deal of help from others to "get it right": beekeeping and heart transplants. Thank you to Troy and Susan Buuch for sharing their vast knowledge about beekeeping with me—especially helpful was the information about how an Amish person, without electricity or vehicles to transport hives, would keep bees. And a very special thank-you to Ron and Mary Westgate, for telling me the story of Ron's heart transplant. With Ron's editing, I tried to depict Amos's illness and heart transplant as accurately as I could, but this is a work of fiction. Any blunders—or maybe a better way to say it would be "any stretch of circumstances" (such as having the Organ Donation Transplantation Network swiftly agree to allow a recently deceased family member to donate a heart)—belong to me.

And I feel compelled to add a note about the Swartzentruber Amish in this story: According to Erik Wesner of AmishAmerica, there is only one Swartzentruber church district in Pennsylvania and it is in Cambria County, not Lancaster County. Another stretch on my part, but remember . . . this is fiction!

A thank-you to a few other people who answered questions for me: Karla Hanns, my Canadian Facebook friend, for her expertise in quilting, and Sherry Gore, another FB friend, for answering questions about shooting bears.

And the entire Revell team who does so much, start to finish, to help my book be the best it can be: editors Andrea Doering and Barb Barnes, who have the first (Andrea) and last (Barb) look at the manuscript. I hope we are sharing this journey for a very long time! And a special thank-you to the art (Cheryl), marketing and publicity departments (Twila, Michele, Janelle, Deonne, Donna, Sheila, Claudia), and the tireless sales reps! There are others at Revell too who have a hand in making a book come to life and get into the hands of readers. Working with all of you is an honor.

To Joyce Hart, my agent, for your professional support.

To my selfless first readers, Lindsey, Wendrea, and Nyna: how can I ever thank you? Your input and suggestions are invaluable.

My heartfelt gratitude to my husband, Steve, for his loving support and encouragement in this author gig.

And finally, to God. What a blessing you have bestowed on me! I'm incredibly grateful for the opportunity to write books that, I hope and pray, reveals you to readers in a new way.

The HAVEN

To Lindsey, my darling daughter.
My first cookie turned out! She turned out *great*.

1

It never failed to amaze Sadie Lapp how the most ordinary day could be catapulted into the extraordinary in the blink of an eye. She was still a little dazed. She couldn't shake the feeling that it seemed her whole life had been leading to this particular moment. She had a strange sense that this day had come into her life to change her, to change everything.

But that didn't mean she felt calm and relaxed. Just the opposite. She felt like a homemade sweater unraveling inch by inch. As she caught her first glimpse of Windmill Farm, she hoped that, maybe, things could get straightened out, once she reached home.

Sadie had spent the winter in Berlin, Ohio, helping Julia and Roman, her sister and brother-in-law, settle into Rome's childhood home. A part of every day was spent shadowing Deborah Yoder, an elderly Old Order Amish woman who was known as a healer. Knowing of Sadie's interest in healing herbs, Rome arranged a meeting with Deborah that resulted in a part-time job. A part of Sadie wished she could have spent years studying and watching the wise old woman.

But last week, Sadie woke and knew she needed to return home. When Sadie told Julia, her sister's face fell with disappointment. She had expected Sadie to stay through the summer and tried to talk her out of leaving. But Old Deborah understood. "The wisest people I know," she had told Sadie, "learn to listen to those hunches."

The taxi swerved suddenly, jerking Sadie out of her muse. A few more curves in the road and she would be at Windmill Farm. She hoped the family was there for her homecoming. Wouldn't it be sad to try to surprise everyone, only to arrive to an empty house?

Maybe she should have called first, to let her father know she was coming. But he would have asked her why she was changing her plans and she didn't want to say. Maybe she should have at least tipped off Fern, their housekeeper. The one person she knew she couldn't confide in was Mary Kate, her twelve-going-on-thirty-year-old sister. It was well known that M.K. liked to babble and tell. She was the self-appointed bearer of all news—truth or otherwise.

Sadie gazed out the window. Coming home felt harder than she thought it would be. The family was much smaller now. It would be quieter without Rome and Julia. Without her brother, Menno. Even Lulu, Menno's dog, was living with Rome and Julia now. Sadie leaned her head on the back of the seat and closed her eyes for a moment, remembering. They used to be a family with a mom and a dad, three sisters and a brother, and crazy Uncle Hank. Pretty normal.

Until her mom passed and her dad, Amos, developed heart trouble. Then Uncle Hank found a housekeeper in *The Budget*. The sisters secretly called her Stern Fern. She took some time to warm up to, but she was just what the Lapp family needed. Sadie would have to add the Bee Man to the "just what we needed" list too. When Roman Troyer came to live at Windmill Farm last summer, life took a happy upturn. For Julia, especially.

But then Menno died in a terrible accident and his heart was given to his father. Everything changed again.

They weren't a normal family anymore. Julia had married Rome and moved to Ohio. And wasn't that also the way life went? Sadie thought, moving the basket beside her out of the direct sun. One minute you felt like laughing, and the next thing you knew, you were crying. She glanced at the basket. Would she ever feel normal again?

As the taxi passed along the road that paralleled Windmill Farm, Sadie scanned the fields, horrified. Dozens of cars were parked along the road. Near the barn, horses and buggies were stacked side by side. The amount of people up there looked like ants at a picnic. There was even a television van with a large satellite dish on top, like a giant sunflower turning to the sky. She unrolled the car window to get a better look. What on earth was going on?

She told the taxi driver to pull over at the base of the hill rather than go up the drive. After paying the driver, she stood by Julia's roadside stand, a small suitcase flanking her on one side, an oval-shaped basket on the other, a small box in her hand. She wasn't quite sure what to do next. The thought of walking up that hill into a crowd of strangers mortified her. Strangers were on Sadie's avoid-at-all-costs list. She was shy to the point of sickness among strangers. When she was out in town, she almost swooned with fear.

Why had she let the taxi drive off? Why hadn't she called her father first, to let him know she was on her way from Ohio and to find out what was going on at home?

What *was* going on at home?

Suddenly, a familiar voice came floating down the hill, followed by pounding footsteps. "Saaaa—dddieeeee!" Mary Kate was running toward Sadie, full blast, arms raised to the sky, a look of pure joy on her face.

Sadie threw open her arms and hugged her little sister. "Mary Kate, you've gotten so tall!" Fresh and tall and sleek, though starting to fill out her dress. Her little sister was on her way to becoming a woman.

"You didn't let anyone know you were coming!"

"I wouldn't even recognize you if I passed you on the street!" She handed M.K. the small container. "Rome sent along a new queen bee for your hives. I worried through the whole trip that the queen would escape out of that box and sting me."

M.K. peered through the screen top of the box. The brown bee queen was gripping the screen with its tiny fuzzy black legs. "Oh, she's beautiful!" M.K. was enamored with bees. Sadie liked to stay clear of them. "You won't believe what's been going on around here!"

"Take a breath, M.K., and tell me what all these cars are doing here. Is everyone all right? Is Dad doing all right?"

M.K. put the bee box on top of Sadie's suitcase and glanced at the house. "Dad's having a good day today. I've never seen him look so proud and pleased. When the president of the Audubon Society gave him the letter for Menno, I thought Dad was going to bust his britches."

"What letter? What are you talking about?"

"For all those rare birds Menno found! Turns out he spotted more rare birds than anyone else in the state of Pennsylvania. The Audubon lady brought a newspaper reporter with her." She stretched her arms over her head and released a happy giggle. "And right when they were presenting the letter to Dad, the game warden drove up. He sent an intern to stock the creek with trout and he spotted another couple of rare birds. This pair is an endangered species, and it looks like they're settling down to raise a family right on Windmill Farm! So that meant the game warden had to put No Trespassing signs up all over the farm. Of course, that was like sending out a skywriter with the news that Windmill Farm has another rare bird. Suddenly the whole town arrived. Even a telly-vision crew." She pointed to the news truck. "They're trying to film the birds. That's got the Audubon lady all upset. She's worried so much interest will disturb the birds. But the game warden says that the public has a right to observe the birds, as long as they're not trespassing on private property. I don't think there's anyone left in town—they're all up there listening to the game warden and the Bird Lady and the news reporter. It's better than a volleyball game." She spun herself in a little circle and clapped her hands, her grin wide. "And now you're home too! This is the best day, ever!"

"The entire town is up there?" Sadie said. *Oh no.* "Even folks from our church?"

"Everybody! Even on a perfect spring day—folks just dropped their plows in the fields and hurried over. Fern is trying to figure out how many think they're staying for supper." M.K. turned to look up the hill. "There's Dad!" She cupped her hands around her mouth and called out, "Hurry, hurry, hurry! Sadie's home!" She turned back to her sister. "Uncle Hank is trying to get himself on the local news. It's making Edith Fisher mad as a wet hen." She drew herself as tall as she could, hooked her hands on her hips, made a terrible prim face and, in a husky voice that sounded eerily like Edith Fisher, said, "Pride goeth before a fall, Hank Lapp!"

As kerfuffled as Sadie was, she couldn't help but laugh. M.K. was a regular little mimic, as good as a tent show, Uncle Hank said, and he would know. Under normal circumstances, Sadie would have enjoyed M.K.'s imitation of Edith Fisher, but these weren't normal circumstances. She was preoccupied with the mighty flood of news M.K. had dropped on her. The timing for her homecoming could not be any worse. How had this happened? Why, oh why, did she feel she should come home on this day, of all days? Why did she happen to be in the bus station—at that exact moment—earlier today? She had to believe it was meant to be. What other explanation could there be? The circumstances of the day couldn't be accidental.

Nearly down the driveway, Amos Lapp held his arms out wide for Sadie and she ran into them. She breathed in the sweet familiar smells of her father, of rich coffee and pine soap. Maybe . . . everything was going to be all right.

"What a wonderful surprise, Sadie! Today of all days! Why didn't you let us know you were coming?" Amos leaned back to look at her, hands on her shoulders. "I shouldn't be surprised. Not a bit. You always had a way of knowing the right place to be at just the right time." He sounded so pleased. "Did M.K. tell you the news about our Menno? Did you hear that the president of the Audubon Society brought a letter congratulating us on Menno's keen eyes for birding?" He shook his head. "Our Menno. He would've been pleased."

"I think Menno would have wondered what all the fuss was about," Sadie said. "He would have told all these folks that they should be out looking for rare birds themselves."

Amos smiled, a little sad. "You're probably right. You always knew him best."

Sadie looked at her father, really looked. He had gained a little weight and it suited him. But his warm brown eyes had dark circles underneath, as if he wasn't sleeping well. He looked positively careworn.

"Let's get you up to the house, through that clump of people, so you can wash up and get something to eat." He reached down for her suitcase, noticed the bee box, picked it up, and peered into it. Then he handed the bee box to M.K.

"Dad, there's something—"

"Say, does Gideon know you're coming?" Amos lifted his head as he picked up the suitcase. "He'll be anxious to see you. I wish I had a silver dollar for every time he asked me when I thought you'd be coming back."

"Gid's my teacher this spring, Sadie," M.K. said, eyes fixed on the queen bee. "Did you know that? He's the best, the very best! So much more interesting than his crotchety old maid sister—"

"Ahem," Amos interrupted, giving M.K. the look.

"Yes," Sadie said. "Of course I know Gid is your teacher. You've told me hundreds of times. And no, Gid doesn't know I'm coming. I was trying to surprise all of you." She turned to her father. "Dad, before we go up to the house, I need to tell you something—"

A strange little squeaking sound came out of the basket behind Sadie's feet. M.K. peered into it and looked up, shocked. "Sadie, it's . . . you . . . you have a baby!"

Amos crouched down to look. He pulled back a little quilt blanket to reveal a tiny baby. The baby started waving his arms and crying like a weak lamb. Amos looked up at his middle daughter, stunned. "Sadie, what's this?"

Sadie took a deep breath. "Dad, that's what I've been trying to tell you. I need . . . some . . . help."

Will Stoltz pulled out the tape to rope off the area below the ridge where the American peregrine falcon pair had claimed their nest—just a scape, because falcons didn't use nesting material. They were smart, those birds. Very possibly the shrewdest birds of all. Falcons chose the highest point in the area to provide an easy vantage point for hunting.

A week ago, in late March, Will had been stocking streams with trout for the game warden, and lo and behold, he spotted a pair of American peregrine falcons. The male—actually called a tiercel—was about one-third smaller than the female, and the pair seemed to be soaring in the sky in specific flying patterns. When Will saw the male bring food to the female, he knew they were courting. He smiled. Falcons mated for life. The male would select a few sites for a scape and let the female pick the place she wanted to raise her clutch. Very civilized, he thought. He would do the same, if he ever married.

He nailed one end of the yellow Keep Out tape to a tree. There was a line of people standing behind the tape, with telescopes and cameras fitted with enormous zoom lenses. This was a big event to hit Lancaster County. Even for the state of Pennsylvania—an endangered species on its list had chosen a little Amish farm to nest in. Will knew the game warden was determined to squeeze every ounce of publicity he could out of this American peregrine falcon pair—partly for the sake of the falcon pair but mostly to breathe life into his sagging career.

Last year, Game Warden Mahlon Miller had been criticized for not giving enough protection to a bald-headed eagle pair that had built a nest in a tree in an unfortunate location—a popular civic park. One of the eaglets had been killed by a kid messing around with a BB gun and Mahlon Miller had been publicly chastised. Eagles were increasingly common to parts of Pennsylvania, unlike falcons, and Mahlon wasn't going to let anything happen to jeopardize these rare birds.

Will thought Mahlon was taking the right precautions as game warden, but he felt a little sorry for the Amish family who hosted these falcons. He didn't know how the family would be able to stand having a protected nesting site on their farm. Talk about a loss of privacy for utterly private people! Strangers would be crawling all over the farm, eager to see the falcons. And these falcons weren't going to be leaving soon. They looked like they had taken their time finding just the right piece of real estate and were settling in for a long stay. If these raptors liked the location, they would return year after year.

A crow flew into a nearby tree and let out a loud caw. Another answered back, and soon it sounded like a full-fledged heated family discussion was going on.

Will started to walk back to the farmhouse to tell the game warden that he had finished marking off the area for the falcons. At the top of a ridge, next to a red windmill with spinning arms, he paused to look around. It was a beautiful farm. It was talked about in the birding community. There were more species of birds identified on this farm than any other farm in the county, including eight rarities. It made Will curious. Why here? Why this farm? What made this place more bird friendly than another? So many farms around here were Amish—most were very eco-friendly, used minimal pesticides, and welcomed birds. So why were more birds sighted on this farm than the one next to it?

Will had been to Windmill Farm once before, though no one would have recognized him. Last year, he had come to see for himself when he heard about the American pipit on the Rare Bird Alert. He couldn't believe it when he saw it, but there it was. A small, brown, nondescript bird, half the size of a robin, sitting on a woodpile. It ate crickets out of an Amish teenage boy's hand.

Will's interest was piqued. He wanted to know more about this farm and this family. Especially now. Windmill Farm might prove very useful to him, if he went through with this opportunity that had fallen, out of the blue, into his lap and promised him a way to get out of the mess he was in, without having to involve his father . . .

Late in the afternoon, Twin Creeks Schoolhouse was bathed in warm, sleepy sunlight that fell in speckled patterns across the polished wood floor. The old walls and ceiling beams creaked and moaned, sounding every bit like an old man stretching as he rose from his favorite chair. Gideon Smucker had been hearing the sounds for a few months now, and found them oddly comforting.

Gid closed the math book, took off his glasses, and rubbed his eyes. He was barely able to keep one day ahead of his brightest scholar, Mary Kate Lapp. He thought the complicated problems in this book would keep M.K.'s nimble mind busy, but he didn't realize how many mental cobwebs he would need to brush off just to correct her work. He leaned back in his chair and clasped his hands behind his neck. He was glad the other scholars weren't as precocious as Mary Kate. He'd be sunk.

He still couldn't believe he was here, teaching the twenty-one scholars of Twin Creeks School. He loved book learning but never imagined himself a schoolteacher. His sister, Alice, had been teaching at Twin Creeks for seven years. A week before school started up again after Christmas, Alice was injured in an unfortunate sledding accident. She broke both of her legs, requiring a long, slow rehabilitation. Desperate, the school board asked if he would fill in for Alice. How could he refuse the three members of the school board, or Alice? But even more startling was the discovery that Gid loved teaching. He felt he had been born to teach, in a way that he never felt behind a plow. His mind felt so challenged by teaching, so active and alive.

Gid glanced at the clock on the wall: five o'clock. He needed to get home soon and help his dad with evening chores. He wanted to finish the letter to Sadie before he went home. He'd been writing steadily to her over the last few months and was hoping she'd be coming back from Ohio soon. If he mailed it tomorrow, she would receive it on Saturday. Too soon? Did he seem too eager? He didn't want to come across like he was pining for her. He wasn't. He most definitely wasn't. Not much, anyway. Maybe he should hold off mailing it for another day or two.

He went through this every week. He would send her a favorite book or two of his, scribbled with marginalia, along with a brief note at least once a week. He worried constantly that he was going to push Sadie away by being too obviously smitten by her.

To him, Sadie was like a delicate hummingbird, easily frightened off. And why should a girl like her ever be sincerely interested in a fellow like him? He was clumsy, tongue-tied, awkward socially. He hoped that through the books they shared, she might see what was in him that he couldn't seem to express in person. Why was it so much easier to write something to her than to say the same thing to her? If he could describe things with written words, couldn't he do the same aloud? Maybe when Sadie came back, he would be able to say these things to her.

He overheard someone describe him once as a young man without deep feelings. He did feel deeply, he knew he did. But what he felt was so confusing and required so much work to figure out, and then even more to get it to the surface and express it, that it was easier to keep quiet and concentrate on writing, something he could see. He imagined all kinds of sweet things he wanted to tell her: how there were times in church when a beam from the sun caught her hair and glinted and he thought she looked like an angel. How much he loved those pronounced dimples in her cheeks. And those freckles that covered her nose and cheeks. He knew she hated them and tried to get rid of them with lemon juice, but he wished she wouldn't because he liked them. And her laugh . . . it was like the sound of wind chimes. He sorely missed Sadie, as much today as when she left for Ohio four months ago.

Gid was in eighth grade when he first realized he was in love with Sadie Lapp. Not that he let anybody know he was besotted. Especially not Sadie.

He had learned the hard way that just because you felt something didn't mean you had to tell other people. His friends had a way of twisting things around, finding something in the most commonplace remarks to jab at a person and make fun.

He had plenty of reasons to keep his mouth shut on any romantic topics.

First off, nobody would believe he knew what love was at his age. Second, Sadie was even younger than he was. Third, Sadie had never given him the slightest indication that he was anything more than just another boy to ignore at school.

But then, last December, Gid gathered enough courage to ask Sadie if he could take her home from a singing, and she nodded shyly. The night was clear and cold and their breath was frosty on the air as the horse pulled the buggy across the frozen ground. In the soft moonlight it was easier to talk, and both of them seemed reluctant to reach her farm and have the evening end. That one time led to another ride home from a singing, then an ice skating party, and a few other times when they didn't need a gathering as an excuse to see each other. Then came the last time together, just after Christmas, the night before Sadie left for Ohio with her sister and brother-in-law. Gid didn't know when he would see Sadie again.

Gid had stopped the horse near the side of the barn, where M.K. couldn't peek out the farmhouse window and spy on them like she did on a regular basis. He helped Sadie out of the buggy.

Sadie glanced toward the house. "Perhaps we should say goodnight here," she said.

Gid moved in front of her to block the cold wind. He had never kissed a girl, but he'd given it a great deal of thought. Quite a great deal. He lifted her chin so she would look at him. For a moment they stood absolutely still. Then he dropped his head down to softly cover her lips with his. Her hand came up to touch his cheek, and when he lifted his lips from hers, they stood there with their warm breath intermingling for a moment. None of the books or poetry he had read had done kissing justice.

It was the single finest moment in Gid's nineteen years of life.

2

As the sun started to dip into the horizon, the excitement over the falcons slowly petered out. Cars and buggies left the farm. Will had just finished taping off the area near the falcons' scape and was walking back to the farmhouse to let the game warden know he had finished. When he reached Mahlon, he quietly mentioned the concern he had about so many onlookers. The scape was situated in a place on the farm where there weren't any fences. Folks could easily trample through the fields, he explained to the game warden, and climb up that ridge to get a closer look at the scape. It worried him, he said. The female might not lay eggs if she became stressed by the presence of onlookers.

"I know all that," Mahlon said, sounding annoyed that an intern for the game commission would try to tell him basic bird facts. Then his face relaxed. "Imagine if the clutch ended up with four or five viable eyases. Even two or three."

Will whistled. "It would be big."

"Might be the first successful breeding pair in this county."

Will scratched his neck. "We could do a drive-by each day on our way to work and back." Since his internship had started last week, he had been boarding at Mahlon Miller's house.

"Oh, I've got a better plan to protect those falcons than Keep Out tape and a daily drive-by."

"What's that?" Will asked.

Mahlon gave him a smug smile. "You."

Will's eyes went wide. "Uh, but . . ." This wasn't exactly what he had in mind for his internship—not that this internship was his idea in the first place. It wasn't. It was his father's idea. A way to make Will pay for getting suspended from the university for the semester. That was why he was living with the game warden—it was part of the deal his father struck with Mahlon. A few years ago, Will's father, a doctor, had performed a risky operation on Mahlon's mother and saved her life. There wasn't anything Mahlon Miller wouldn't do for Will's father.

Will took off his cowboy hat and spun it in his hands. "Just seems like it's asking too much to stay with an Amish family."

Mahlon dismissed that with a wave of his pudgy hand. "I've already thought that out. I'm going to see if you can stay in that empty cottage over there." He pointed to a small, tidy-looking cottage underneath a stand of pines, not far from the falcons' scape. "That way, you won't interfere with the family at all. You're going to babysit those falcons until the chicks are banded and ready to leave the scape." Mahlon folded his arms across his chest. "I'm friends with Amos Lapp, the Amish farmer. I don't think he would mind having you stay, especially after I offer your help around the farm. He could use the help and you could use the work. Kind of a barter arrangement."

Will felt a little stunned. He had always made it a point to dodge physical labor—academics were more to his liking. Plus . . . he was lazy. He knew that about himself and accepted it happily. And here he was, about to be offered up as a farmhand. He didn't even know what farmers did all day. Watch their crops grow? Muck out horse stalls? Oh, this wasn't good. Not good at all. He opened his mouth to object as Mahlon tossed his truck keys to him.

"I'm going to go clear it with Amos," Mahlon said. "You go pack up your belongings from the house and get back here. Pronto." He spun on his heels to go find the farmer, a wide grin on his face which, Will thought, had something to do with the thought of having his intern move out of his house. Just last night, Mahlon's wife seemed particularly touchy about the three-day-old forgotten meatloaf sandwich left in Will's backpack that had attracted a mouse in his room. Maybe two. Maybe a family.

Will walked down the driveway to the truck, reviewing this turn of events. As he backed the truck to turn it around, he pedaled down a new lane of thinking. Maybe this was a gift in disguise. A beacon in the gray fog that covered his future. He woke up this morning wrestling with his conscience about a recent opportunity that had been presented to him. With this last swift decision, made by Mahlon, Will was going to take it as a sign to stop overthinking the situation. The matter was decided.

At the kitchen table, Mary Kate waited patiently for Sadie to pass the potatoes, but her sister seemed to be deep in thought. Sadie's eyes kept misting over like she was trying to not bust out crying. Something was bothering her.

M.K. wasn't sure why Sadie was suddenly in such a mood, but for now, she was hungry, especially after spending the last hour carefully introducing the new brown bee queen to the hive. Bees were very fussy about newcomers, especially one that would now reign over them. She reached over Sadie and tried to help herself to a large cloud of mashed potatoes, but her sister moved the bowl out of her reach.

Amos lifted his eyebrows. "Sadie, would you mind passing food around the table?"

Sadie made a point to pass the bowl of mashed potatoes to Fern, bypassing M.K. She lifted her chin. "Mary Kate is oblivious to the kind of trouble she created today."

M.K.'s eyes went round as saucers. "What did I do that was so bad?"

Sadie looked at her, astounded. "You told people that I brought a baby home from Ohio."

M.K. raised her palms in wonder. "But you did! That's the truth!"

"That's NOT the way it happened!" Sadie glared at her. "I did not *bring* the baby from Ohio. The baby found me, in the bus station in Lancaster, while I was waiting for a bus to Stoney Ridge." She passed the platter of roast beef to Uncle Hank, seated across from her. Then she picked up her fork and poked at the mashed potatoes on her plate. "Who all did you tell?"

M.K. had her eye on Uncle Hank, who was spearing large slices of roast beef onto his plate. She hoped there would be some left. "Just a few people."

Sadie narrowed her eyes. "Who, exactly?"

M.K. put up her hand and counted off her fingers. "Ruthie. Ethan.

Solomon Riehl and his little boy, Danny." Uncle Hank passed her the platter and she grabbed it eagerly.

Relief covered Sadie's face.

M.K. lowered her head and quietly added, "And maybe Edith Fisher."

"Noooooooooo!" Sadie looked like she'd swallowed a firecracker. "Edith Fisher will spread the news through this entire town by morning."

M.K. took a large mouthful of roast beef and mumbled, "I still don't understand why it's so bad."

Sadie glowered at M.K. "Lower your voice or you'll wake the baby up. I just got him to sleep."

M.K. looked at her father and raised her palms in exasperation. She mouthed the words, "But I'm not talking loud! Sadie is!"

Fern, sitting to the right of M.K., placed her hand on her forearm. "Denk zehe mol, schwetz eemol." *Think ten times, talk once.* "How many times have I told you that?"

Too many to count, M.K. thought. Along with zillions of other bromides about talking too much, moving too fast, acting without thinking, accepting correction, being humble, on and on and on. Fern was famous for her sayings. M.K. thought she must study them so that she could whip one out at just the right moment.

Sadie got up and checked on the baby, sleeping in the little basket in a corner. "M.K., you had no right to tell people anything about the baby. I was barely home for five minutes and you couldn't keep quiet. You just don't *think*. And now you've started all kinds of rumors about me."

Uncle Hank's fist hit the table. "NO SIR! No one would dare say a mean word about our Sadie. I WON'T HAVE IT!" He clamped his jaw, but his emotions passed quickly, like a racing thundercloud. He picked up a few biscuits and generously lathered them with butter.

"Don't be so sure," Fern said. "Folks think that a rumor is truth on the trail."

Uncle Hank took a bite and chewed it thoughtfully. "I did hear someone say something about Sadie's absence being mighty suspicious. But, DAGNABIT!"—that was the only cuss word Fern would allow out of Uncle Hank, so he made plenty of use of it—"I set them straight. I said she was exiled to be with relatives for the winter."

"Exiled?" Sadie said, horrified. "You used the word 'exiled'?"

Uncle Hank stroked his chin. "Exiled? I said excited."

Sadie was mortified. "You *said* exiled!"

Uncle Hank frowned. "I said excited and I meant excited! Your ears must be full of cotton. I said 'Sadie was excited to be with relatives for the winter.'" But he didn't look quite convinced.

Sadie crumpled. "See? I told you! Folks are going to think I *had* this baby! And it's all M.K.'s fault!" Looping her arms to rest on the table, she slid lower and let her forehead rest on her fists.

M.K. was disgusted. It was a scandal how often the finger of blame pointed to her. She thought she was sharing happy news. What could be so bad about having a baby come to stay with them? Her friend Ruthie was thrilled!

"Would you go over everything one more time, Sadie?" Amos said.

Sadie lifted her head and sighed. "I arrived at the Lancaster bus depot and had to wait for the Stoney Ridge connection, so I started to read my book and must have nodded off. When I woke up, there was a basket by my feet." She pointed to the basket. "And in the basket was *that* little baby."

"No note?" Fern said.

Sadie shook her head. "Just a bottle and a can of powdered formula. And some diapers."

M.K. pinched her nose with her fingers. "Not enough of them."

"You didn't remember seeing anyone?" Amos said.

Sadie shook her head. "It was pretty busy when the bus arrived, but then, when I woke up, it had cleared out. I walked all around the station looking for someone, and then I went to ask the stationmaster if he had seen anyone who was holding a basket."

"What did he say?" Fern asked.

"I tried to explain myself a couple of times, but I don't think I did a very good job of it. He finally pointed to the basket and asked if I was feeling okay, and maybe he should call the police or paramedics because they can help with confused people." Sadie frowned. "I didn't want the police or paramedics to take the baby away. Or me, either. And just then the Stoney Ridge bus arrived and I got on it. With the baby." She set her elbows on the table and rested her chin in her palms. "Dad, what are we going to do?"

Amos sat quietly for a long while. Too quiet for M.K.

Finally, she couldn't hold back any longer or she would pop. "We should keep him! Don't you see? He was brought to Sadie by an angel! Ruthie said there are angels all around us. Ruthie knows about these things, now that her dad's a minister." As soon as the words flew out of her mouth, she regretted them. The entire family looked at her as if she had spoken Chinese.

Then Sadie spoke. "Mary Kate might have finally said something today that was worth saying." She looked at her father. "I think she's right. That baby was meant for me. For all of us. I think that's why I felt such a strong pull to get back here today, Dad. I was meant to be in that bus station, at just that moment. On this day, of all days. I'm just sure of it, and I think I felt sure of it in the bus station too. Today was no accident. That baby is meant for us."

Amos fingered a seam on the tabletop. "Sadie, I'm not sure that's for you to decide."

Sadie's eyes went wide. "Well, why ever not? The baby was given to me."

Fern picked up the basket of biscuits and passed it to Amos. "Bringing home a baby isn't the same thing as bringing home a stray kitten or puppy."

As Amos broke a biscuit in half, a puff of white steam was released. His eyes were fixed on the biscuit as he quietly said, "We need to do what's best for the baby. And what's best for the baby is to find his family."

Something awful began to break in M.K.'s mind, and Sadie's too, judging by the stunned look on her face. *This isn't fair! The baby was given to Sadie! To all of us.*

Sadie's eyes started to well with tears. "Dad, we have to keep this baby. We just have to."

Amos looked a little puzzled. "We'll get it all sorted out, Sadie. But we want what's best for that baby."

"We're what's best for that baby," Sadie said, more forcefully. "I know that's what the mother wanted. I'm sure of it."

"What makes you so sure of that, Sadie?" Amos said. "Anyone who would abandon a baby in a bus station must not be thinking too clearly."

"But she left the baby with me." Sadie had stopped crying now. "Not with anyone else but me."

Uncle Hank slammed his palms on the table. "SHE'S ABSOLUTELY

RIGHT!" He was getting excited now, and that meant his raspy voice would get louder and louder. "THAT ANGEL KNEW OUR SADIE WOULD BE A STELLAR CHOICE!"

This was starting to get interesting, M.K. thought, observing the exasperated look on her father's face. She had never seen Sadie so adamant about anything before. She always thought Sadie could sit on a fence and watch herself walk by. She was *that* prone to changing her mind, to seeing a situation from all directions. But as she looked over at her sister, she realized a change had come over Sadie since her visit to Berlin. More than one change. Usually, Sadie was the one to mollify others, a peacekeeper, determined that no one should remain unhappy for long. Tonight, she held her chin up high, a look of determination set in her eyes. She looked trimmer, taller, and even held herself differently. Shoulders back. Why, she was practically perpendicular! A 90 degree angle.

And wouldn't Gideon Smucker be proud of M.K. for finding geometry in something as mundane as a person's posture? Watching Sadie, M.K. straightened her back, hardly aware she was doing it.

Just as Uncle Hank opened his mouth to jump in on the what-to-do-with-the-baby discussion, Fern lifted her hand to ward him off. "It's been a long day. And if I know newborn babies—and that baby can't be much older than a month or so—it's going to be an even longer night."

Sadie looked confused. "Why is it going to be such a long night?"

Uncle Hank burst out with a snorting laugh. "By tomorrow morning, Sadie girl, you might just be changing your tune about keeping that baby!"

In that way Fern had of bringing the whole world up short, she pointed to Uncle Hank and said, "Whether that baby is here for a day or a month, he's going to need some things we don't have. You need to go to the Bent N' Dent tonight to buy more supplies." She pulled a list from her apron pocket and handed it to him. "Lickety-split. Store closes at seven."

Hank shoveled one last biscuit into his mouth. "Better hurry up and pray, Amos, since I seem to be Fern's factotum." He winked at M.K. "See? I'm using them big words you keep trying to jam into my head."

M.K. beamed. She adored her father's uncle. "I'll go with you, Uncle Hank."

Amos bowed his head and the family followed suit. As soon as he lifted his head, M.K. jumped up, grabbed her black bonnet off the wall peg, and slipped out the door before Fern could call her back to help wash dishes.

As Uncle Hank went to get the horse to hitch to the buggy, M.K. stayed on the porch, tying the bonnet ribbons under her chin, listening to the conversation continue at the table through an open window. She heard Sadie ask her father, "What exactly did Fern mean about babies and long nights?"

"Babies need to eat every few hours," Amos said.

"What?" Sadie said. "You can't be serious!"

M.K. saw Sadie turn to Fern for confirmation. Fern was at the kitchen sink, adding dish soap into the basin.

"He's right," Fern said loudly, over the sound of running water. "Around the clock."

Sadie groaned and dropped her forehead on the table with a clunk. Then her head popped up. "Maybe we could all take a shift!"

M.K. saw Sadie look at her father, who was not uttering a peep behind his nest of beard. He was studying the ceiling with great interest. Then she saw Sadie whip her head over at Fern.

"Oh no, don't look to me," Fern said in her crisp way. "This is *your* miracle. Besides, I don't do babies. They're a heap of trouble."

M.K. popped her head in the window and whispered to Sadie, "I know all about babies. It can't be that hard. I'll help." Then she jumped off the porch and ran down to Uncle Hank, waiting for her in the buggy.

3

The next morning Sadie woke up with a start, a jittery mess. The morning sun beamed bright through her front window. How could it be morning already? She had been up with the baby four times, maybe five, no signs or stirrings of M.K. or her father or Uncle Hank, until Fern finally came into the kitchen around 4:00 a.m. and told her to go to bed, that she would take a turn.

That was the way it was with Fern. She complained about having to take care of everybody, but then she took care of everybody.

Sadie was exhausted. How could such a tiny baby eat so much and cry so much? Downstairs, she heard the sounds of morning going on. Familiar, contented noises. The hinge of the kitchen door squeaked as her father went out to the barn. Bacon hissed and sizzled in a frying pan on the stove. She heard M.K. gallop down the stairs, talk to Fern for a moment, then gallop back up. Sadie's bedroom door burst open. "Fern says to get up. She said that baby is starting to make noises about breakfast. She said to tell you she can't be expected to be babysitting while you're sleeping 'til noon."

Sadie yawned. "Can't you take a turn and feed the baby?"

"Me?" M.K.'s eyes went wide. "Oh no. I've never actually fed a newborn baby before. I might break him. Besides, Dad needs me out in the barn."

"What happened to your big promise to help me with the baby last night?"

M.K. shrugged. "Never heard him." She spun around, and then turned back. "Are we just going to call him That Baby or are we going to give him a name?"

Sadie looked at her blankly. The thought hadn't even occurred to her. "I don't know. I guess we should."

M.K. whipped a list out of her apron pocket. "Here are my suggestions: Kayak, Level, Radar, Murdrum—"

"What kind of names are those?"

"They're palindromes. Words that can read backwards or forwards. Gideon Smucker taught us all about them. I've been naming all of the new chickens these names."

Sadie put up a hand like a stop sign. "I'm not naming that baby after one of your chickens."

"Solos. Tenet. Racecar. Rotor. Madam. Dewed—"

Sadie threw a pillow at M.K., but she had seen it coming and was halfway down the stairs by the time the pillow reached the floor.

Sadie stretched and yawned, then rolled her feet onto the cold floor. She dressed quickly, pinned her hair in a tight knot, and covered it with a bandana, pondering baby names. M.K. was probably right—they did need to call that baby something other than That Baby. But naming him seemed so . . . real. So permanent. If only she could have somehow hidden the baby from the eyes of other people in Stoney Ridge, just to have time to think this all through. But nothing stayed hidden in Stoney Ridge for long, and by the end of the first day, everyone in the community would know this baby had been dropped on the Lapps like an unwanted puppy.

When she reached the kitchen, Fern was already giving the baby a bottle of formula. Silently, she handed the baby to Sadie and went outside to hang a load of wash on the clothesline. After Sadie finished feeding the baby, she changed his diaper, placed him in the basket, and carried the basket outside to help Fern. She rubbed her eyes with her right hand, then rested her palm over them against the brilliance of the day. From an oak in the yard, a plump red robin whistled and chattered, and another answered from across the yard.

As soon as Fern saw her, she handed the bag of clothespins to Sadie. "I need to get out to the garden before it gets too warm. You finish up here."

Fern went around the back of the house to reach the garden and Sadie picked up where she had left off, hanging wet towels. The baby had fallen asleep, and the morning sun was warming Sadie's back. As she clipped a towel onto the line, worries swooped down on her like pigeons on bread crumbs. What was she to do about this baby? What if no one ever claimed him? She wasn't ready for this. She looked forward to getting married one day, dreamed about it, planned every detail of her wedding. Someday, she wanted children. But someday wasn't supposed to have arrived yet.

Maybe it would be the best thing for everybody to let the church find a family who could raise him. She was glad that her father didn't know what she knew about the baby—what she *thought* might be true. She considered telling him last night, but there didn't seem to be a quiet moment for such a conversation. And her concerns about her father's health spiked last night. He looked so tired after dinner. She had assumed that the heart transplant would have cured him. Fixed and done, like replacing a new engine in the lawn mower.

Maybe a heart transplant is never really over. She saw the amount of pill vials in the kitchen. The pills, she knew, were to suppress his immune system so that it wouldn't reject the heart. But it also made him susceptible to all kinds of illnesses. He couldn't even plow the fields this year like he used to because of the fungus that was in soil. Too risky. Maybe a heart transplant was a way to prolong a person's life, but the life might never be quite the same.

The baby let out a sound and she bent down to check on him. One eye squinted open, followed by a big yawn, then he drifted back to sleep. He was a cute little thing, with downy dark hair and a rosebud mouth.

It wouldn't be hard for someone to love him. She thought of Mattie and Sol Riehl. Mattie was always taking in foster babies. Maybe Mattie and Sol would want this baby. But then she frowned. If Mattie and Sol took in this baby, the state of Pennsylvania would get involved. The Riehl home was frequented by social workers who checked up on the foster children. She had heard Mattie complain about what a headache it was to work with government agencies. And there had been that time when Mattie and Sol were hoping to adopt a little girl who had lived with them for over a year, only to have the Child Protective Services return the little girl to her mother. It had broken Mattie's heart. No, Sadie did not want the government to catch wind of this parentless baby and make decisions for his welfare.

Last night at dinner, her father had said that they would all need to decide what was best for the baby. What would he say if he knew what she knew? But then, she reminded herself, she didn't know anything for sure. It was just a hunch. That was all. Nothing more than a hunch. She should probably do a little investigating before she said anything to anyone.

She reached a hand into the clothespin bag and came up empty. Since the baby was sleeping peacefully in the basket, she decided to leave him as she scooted back to the house to get another package.

After Sadie found the spare bag of clothespins that Fern kept in a kitchen drawer, she opened the kitchen door and froze. A stranger—a man—was crouching down by the baby's basket. She'd never seen him before. He was wearing a straw cowboy hat and cowboy boots. Her heart started to race when she saw him reach down to pick the baby up. Without thinking, she grabbed her father's rifle off of the wall rack next to the kitchen door and shouted from the porch.

"You there!" She aimed the rifle at the young man.

The man spun around to face Sadie. His eyes went wide when he saw the rifle aimed at him.

"Don't make any quick moves, you . . . you . . . baby thief!" Sadie spoke distinctly and authoritatively. She surprised herself.

The man carefully put the baby back in the basket and stepped away from it, hands held high like he was surrendering.

Sadie felt like a mother tiger protecting her kit. "Who are you and why are you trying to steal that baby?"

"Ma'am, I'm . . . I'm not trying to steal your baby." His eyes were wide and innocent looking, but Sadie wasn't going to be fobbed off that easily. "I was walking by and heard him crying and I was just going to hold him. That's all."

The baby was making noises, little mewing complaints at first, and now was starting to wind up like a siren. How could a tiny baby have such a loud, ear-piercing cry?

The cowboy pointed to the baby. "I've always been pretty good at getting babies to stop crying." He took a step closer to Sadie and she lifted the rifle, so he backed up. "I'd feel a little better if you would stop aiming that rifle between my eyes."

A thick strand of hair whipped loose from her simple bun, effectively shielding her eyes. "I'd feel a whole lot better if you'd identify yourself and try to explain what you're doing on my farm at this time of day."

"Sadie Lapp!" Amos was marching from the barn over to Sadie. "Put down that gun. What on earth are you thinking?"

Sadie lowered the gun. Her father reached her and snatched the rifle out of her hands. "He was trying to kidnap the baby!"

The man visibly relaxed as soon as the rifle left Sadie's hands.

M.K. came skipping out of the barn. "What's going on?"

Silence. Finally, Amos said, "With all of the hoopla yesterday, I forgot to tell you girls about this game warden intern . . ." His face scrunched up as he tried to remember the young man's name.

"Will Stoltz."

"That's right. Will Stoltz is staying in the cottage and babysitting the falcons."

"Not exactly babysitting," Will Stoltz said, holding a finger up in the air. "More like protecting an endangered species from an overly zealous public."

Sadie stared at the man. Now that she wasn't shaking from holding a gun at him, she noticed that he wasn't very old. Twenty, twenty-two, tops.

"I'm not a kidnapper," Will Stoltz said earnestly. "I'm with the game warden."

"You thought he was a kidnapper?" M.K.'s eyes grew as wide as saucers. "Sadie, were you going to *kill* him?"

Amos rolled his eyes. "Not with an empty rifle, she wasn't. And Sadie, what were you thinking? Since when does a Plain person point a gun at another human being?" He shook his head. "Will, the daughter that gave you a scare is Sadie, my middle daughter. And this one here is Mary Kate, my youngest." He raised an eyebrow at M.K. "She needs to be heading off to school." He flipped the rifle up on his shoulder. "Sorry for the cold reception." He turned and walked back to the house with the rifle.

"No problem!" Will called out to him cheerfully. "Easy mistake to make."

Sadie scowled at Will and brushed past him to pick up the baby. The baby was really crying now, howling mad. Louder and louder. Sadie was starting to panic. Maybe something was seriously wrong with the baby. Maybe that's why the baby was abandoned in the bus station. This baby was defective. "M.K., go get Fern."

"Why?" M.K. said.

"Because I can't get the baby to stop crying and I don't know what's wrong with him."

"Let me try," Will said. As Sadie hesitated, he added, "Like I was trying to tell you, I'm pretty good with babies."

Still, she was reluctant to pass the baby to him, so he added, "I won't hurt your baby."

"Oh, that's not her baby," M.K. offered, giving Sadie a look that said "See? I am *not* spreading rumors" look. "Sadie found that baby at the bus station. Just yesterday. We don't even have a name picked out yet. But I'm working on it. My latest suggestion is Otto."

"Hush, M.K.," Sadie whispered.

The baby's face was bright red and a tiny little tear leaked down his cheek.

"No kidding, you're not the baby's mother?" Will said. "The way you were coming at me with that gun, you reminded me of a mama bear, thinking I was a threat to her cub."

Sadie hardly heard him. She was at her wit's end trying to calm the baby. Nothing seemed to work. She gave Will one more head-to-toe look and decided he didn't look terribly threatening, so she handed the baby to him. He swept the baby against his chest and gently patted his back, bouncing gently as he walked around in a circle. M.K. was peering around Sadie, watching the young man. Sadie could tell that M.K. was fascinated. They both were.

The baby's crying slowed, then stopped entirely. Sadie and M.K. exchanged a look.

Sadie looked Will up and down. "How did you do that?"

"It's all in the jiggle," he said in a loud whisper. "And babies like to be pressed up against your shoulder, not held low in your arms like you were doing. Must help with gas pains."

It wasn't long before the baby drifted off to sleep again. Ever so gently, Will bent down and tucked the baby into the basket. He rose and brushed his palms against each other. "Easy, once you get the hang of it."

Standing this close to the intern, Sadie saw that he had blue eyes. Really blue eyes, framed by thick brown lashes and strong straight brows darker than his hair, blond hair that swept into his eyes. He was sunburnt and needed a shave, but he was quite nice looking, sort of rugged. He was wearing jeans, dirty at the knees, and a plain white T-shirt under his short-sleeved khaki shirt. He tipped his cowboy hat to them, smiled, and went on his way. He had the kind of a smile that could have melted a glacier.

Sadie and M.K. watched him stroll over to the barn, thumbs hooked in his jeans' pockets, whistling a tune.

"Good thing you didn't kill him, Sadie," M.K. said. "We might be needing him." She sniffed the air and scrunched up her face, zeroing in on the odor wafting up from the baby in the basket. "Think the cowboy changes diapers?"

Right before Will slid open the door to the barn, he turned and watched the Lapp sisters head to the house. Sadie was taller than M.K. and older, but he could see she wasn't as sure of herself, even with a rifle in her hands. It took everything in him to keep a serious look on his face, to not bust out laughing with the way that gun was shaking like a leaf in the wind. He doubted she could have stopped quivering long enough to pull on the trigger, even if it happened to be loaded, which, thankfully, it wasn't.

Most of the guys he knew probably wouldn't notice Sadie so much at first. She wasn't the blonde bombshell that his fraternity brothers panted after, but she was pretty in a simple, soft way. Sandy blonde hair, a small nose, a stubborn chin. Freckles. She had the prettiest eyes—big and blue, kind of skittish, the way a doe looks when she's deciding whether to bolt for the woods or stand her ground. She wasn't thin but she wasn't fat. Average-sized, maybe a little round and curvy, but it seemed to suit her. Her voice was low, like music. And she walked back to the house, holding that baby's basket, with a gracefulness that seemed surprising for a farm girl. As she opened the kitchen door, she turned and gave a shy look back at him. Cute, like a soft summer day. That's how he would describe her looks. Very, very cute. It was quite possible being here was going to be more tolerable than he had feared only yesterday.

He slid open the barn door and waited until his eyes adjusted to the dark. He heard Amos Lapp rummaging around in a back room. He followed the noises but stopped just before he reached the feed room. High on a shelf was an assortment of empty birds' nests. He pulled out an empty butter tub and found tiny eggs no bigger than the tip of a finger, pecked with a hole. The thieving work of a blue jay, he surmised. Another tub held random feathers. Somebody on this farm loved birds like he did.

Will found Amos in the feed room, pouring out scoopfuls of oats into a bucket. Amos looked surprised at the sight of him.

"Well, hello there," Amos said. "I thought you might be my girls, coming to help."

"I think I might have scared them off," Will said.

Amos stopped scooping. "Sorry about that. Completely slipped my mind to tell them you were staying at the cottage for a few weeks. So much excitement going on last night."

"That was sure a lot of people yesterday. Do you mind all of those visitors?"

"Used to it, I guess." Amos dug the scooper into the barrel of oats. "We've always had a lot of rare bird sightings on this farm."

Will saw that Amos had filled one bucket and grabbed another for him, replacing it so he didn't miss a beat. His nails were clipped short, Will noticed. Large hands, working hands.

Amos nodded. "How are the falcons this fine morning?"

"I saw the male head out to hunt. The female is sticking close to the scape, which might mean she's getting ready to lay a clutch."

Amos finished filling the second bucket. "Well, that's what we want." He stood up carefully, tentatively, as if he wasn't completely confident that his body would obey him. It surprised Will. Amos Lapp seemed healthy and strong, fit and slim. A craggy, chiseled, suntanned face. If he were trying to describe Amos Lapp to his mother, he would compare him to John Wayne—his mother's favorite spaghetti Western actor. She loved old movies. Will bent down and grabbed the buckets. He might as well start making himself useful.

Amos started walking toward the center aisle of the barn, stopping by each horse to scoop oats into their feed buckets.

"I was hoping for a chance to talk to you about the rare bird sightings on your farm," Will said. "I'm an avid birder, myself. It's interesting to me that Windmill Farm has had an unusually large amount of sightings. What makes your farm different from others?"

Amos walked to the next stall and lifted the feed tray. "It's not much of a mystery. A lot of Amish farms attract birds. One of the many benefits of plowing with a horse instead of a tractor. Using aged manure instead of chemical fertilizers. I'm not sure we have more birds on Windmill Farm than any other Amish farm."

"Still, there have been more sightings on this farm than any other in the state of Pennsylvania. Even the staff at the game warden's office talk about this farm."

"Well, we might not have any more birds visiting the farm, but we might have spotted birds more than others." Amos stopped and turned to Will. "My son loved birds. He spent 90 percent of his time outdoors and had a gift of noticing God's creatures. He could identify each and every variety of fowl that migrated through our area."

Will noticed that Amos's cheeks were flushed and he was slightly out of breath. He also noticed that he spoke of his son in the past tense. He wondered if that might be how his own father referred to him lately, as if Will were dead to him.

When Amos finished scooping the last of the oats, he turned to Will. "Menno was his name. He'd be about your age. He kept a list of all the birds he sighted. I'll get it for you, if you want to see it. I think he'd be pleased to share that information with a fellow bird lover."

Will lit up. "I'd like that very much. Does he live far away?"

Amos paused and cast his eyes up. "Menno passed on, six months ago."

"Oh, I'm sorry. I thought maybe . . . he had just left your church." Will didn't know a great deal about the Amish, but he had taken a course in sociology in college. He knew about shunning.

Amos lifted his dark eyebrows in surprise. "No, not Menno. I don't think he would ever have left the church. He died in a shooting accident."

"Oh no," Will said. "He was in the wrong place at the wrong time. I'm so sorry."

"No. Menno was in the right place at the right time. His life was complete. The timing of his passing was in God's hands. But his heart lives on."

"Of course," Will murmured, feeling he should say something. "Of course it does. You'll never forget him."

Amos gave him an odd look, with a sad smile. Then he opened the top of his shirt to reveal a large scar that ran down the center of his chest, starting just below his throat.

"Oh," Will said. "You meant that literally."

Amos heard the wail of a baby as he walked up to the house from the barn. He wasn't sure just what to do about this baby. Should he contact the deacon? But would that mean the baby would be given to a childless couple? Maybe that was for the best. And maybe the sooner, the better. It troubled him to see Sadie's protective, unreasonable attachment to that baby. Imagine—a daughter of his, holding a rifle against another child of God! The sight was almost comical if it weren't such a serious breach of judgment. So unlike his Sadie! He walked into the kitchen and heard footsteps overhead. "Fern?"

"Upstairs."

Just the sound of her voice made him feel better. She'd know what to do about the baby. She'd distract him from worrying about his heart, from his tension over keeping up the farm when he couldn't even plow the fields himself. She had a way of making him forget things—she could make him smile, make him mad. Fern was like a buffer. No, she was more than his buffer. She was his—

He took a deep breath and leaned against the counter. He didn't know what Fern was to him. Not exactly a friend, although she understood him better than other people he'd known for years.

Fern came downstairs and held out her hand to him, palm side up, with pills in it. "I found these on your bedside table, when I was changing your sheets." She placed a hand on her hip. "You forgot to take them last night."

"I meant to. I fell asleep. I'll take them now," he said.

A slight frown creased her brow, but she replied patiently. "No. You're not supposed to double up."

Amos frowned right back at her. "I can manage my own pill taking, Fern."

"Apparently you can't. I called your cardiologist and made an appointment. He wants to see you Monday afternoon." She held up two fingers. "Two o'clock."

Amos glared at her. "You had no right to do that."

"Something's not right lately and you know it. You look as worn out as an old man's slippers. You're not getting enough exercise. You're as limp as a boiled noodle. And I know you aren't sleeping well. I hear you prowling around in the kitchen in the middle of the night. You're—"

He held up his hand like a stop sign. "Fine. I'll go."

Fern's voice softened. "Don't look so woebegone. It might be that your medications need adjusting. Might be as simple as that."

Amos watched her head into the kitchen to put his pills back in the little amber vials. *Or it might be that my body is rejecting this heart, this beautiful, precious heart that once belonged to my son.*

4

M.K. held a glass up to the wall between Fern's downstairs bedroom—where she had been sent to put freshly ironed pillowcases on the bed—and the kitchen. It was a trick she had read in *Case-Solving Tools for the Everyday Detective*, a book she had checked out from the library. She listened for less than a minute before she was overcome with shame at what she was doing. The thought was tantalizing, but oh, how awful if she got caught!

But then she heard voices in the kitchen. She put the glass back up against the wall, listened carefully for a few minutes, then bolted upstairs to find Sadie. She burst into Sadie's bedroom without knocking and found her lying on her bed reading a book about baby care. "Sadie! You won't believe what I just heard."

"Wunnernaase!" *Nosy.* Sadie frowned at her.

M.K. offered her a smug smile. "Wunnernaase un Schneckeschwenz." *Nosy and curious.*

"M.K., how many times have we told you to stop eavesdropping?"

She lifted her chin. "Fine. I'll just keep the news to myself."

"Fine."

M.K. hung around for a few minutes, peeked at the baby sleeping in his basket, and waited until Sadie couldn't stand it any longer.

Sadie sighed and put down her book. "What exactly did you hear?"

M.K. sidled up to the bed and sat down. "Dad's heart is acting up."

Sadie sat straight up, stunned. "What do you mean? Tell me exactly what you heard. No embellishment. No exaggeration. No editing. And who was doing the talking?"

"Fern and Dad. She's making him see the heart doctor on Monday."

Sadie leaned back on the bed, her face ashen.

"The doctor can fix him. I heard Fern say that very thing. She said that maybe he was just tired because his pills needed adjusting." M.K. patted Sadie on the shoulder. "He'll be fine. Fern said so."

"How has Dad been the last few months? Think, M.K."

"I'm *always* thinking." She rose from the bed and tucked one hand under an elbow, then tucked her chin into the palm of her hand, pacing the room as she thought about Sadie's question. Now that Sadie mentioned it, something did seem a little off with their dad lately. "He seemed fine up until a few weeks ago. Then he started acting tired again, like he did when he first got sick." She brightened. "But yesterday, he sure seemed happy after the Bird Lady brought him the fancy letter for Menno. And then, you came home." She peeked into the basket as the baby let out one tiny squeak. "Last night, though, he seemed sort of sad. Maybe the baby's got him worried."

Sadie was quiet for a long time, watching M.K. fuss over the baby. "I think we need to try and reduce Dad's stress."

M.K.'s eyes went wide. "What stress do I possibly cause? You're the one who nearly killed a harmless game warden intern this morning."

Sadie ignored that reminder. "Mind that you don't get into any trouble at school."

M.K. knotted her forehead. "That is a perfectly ridiculous comment. Especially now that I have a teacher who actually makes the day interesting."

Sadie snorted. "Probably helps that you haven't broken his legs in a sledding accident like you did the last teacher."

"That was not entirely my fault!" M.K. was outraged. People were always blaming her. "Why would anyone in their right mind stand at the bottom of a hill when folks are sledding?"

"Especially when one of those folks happened to be Mary Kate Lapp—a girl known for speeding out of control on hills," Sadie said smugly. Then she clapped her hands to her cheeks. "Gid! I haven't even thought about him since I got back. He's probably heard by now that I'm back."

"Not to worry," M.K. said, bouncing back on the bed. "He knows you're busy with the baby."

Sadie jerked her head toward M.K. "You told him too?"

"No! You told me not to." She studied her feet. "But Ethan Yoder might have," she mumbled under her breath.

"What did you say?"

M.K. cleared her throat. "I said . . . Ethan Yoder might have."

Sadie shot to her feet. "And how would Ethan have heard?"

"Maybe . . . Susie Glick."

"How would Susie Glick know?" Sadie was really mad now, steaming like a teakettle.

M.K. was very focused on a shadow of a tree branch, dancing on the wall. "Ruthie might have said something."

Sadie propped her fists on her hips. "And Ruthie only knows because of you! It always circles back to you and the words that tumble out of your mouth."

M.K. scratched her head. "I think that's a bit of an overreaction, Sadie."

Sadie glared at her. "What did Gid say?"

M.K. looked up at the ceiling. "Nothing, actually. He didn't say a word. Not a thing. Just got real quiet. He had everybody read for the rest of the afternoon, which suited me just fine because I'm in the middle of *Taming of the Shrew* and I want to find out what happens between Kate and Petruchio."

The baby started making noises and Fern bustled into their room. "There, there," she cooed, as if he had been hollering for hours.

"I'll get the baby's bathwater ready," Sadie said.

"I'll help," M.K. said.

"The both of you are making that baby spoiled as can be," Fern said, snuggling the baby on her shoulder and patting him gently on the back. She tucked her chin over his head, nuzzling him.

M.K. stood behind Fern and tapped the baby's tiny nose. "Dad tried to change his diaper this morning. You've never seen such a complicated process. We'll have to ask him to do that chore more often, just for fun." Because changing a diaper was one task she was never, ever going to perform. You had to draw the line somewhere.

Late Friday afternoon, Gideon Smucker drove the buggy down the road toward Windmill Farm, following another buggy.

A little girl was watching Gid through the open back window. She'd turned in her seat, climbed onto her knees, her head tilted slightly to the side, as if she were curious about him, or confused by him. Her dark hair floated in wispy, tangled curls around her face, her pale blue eyes regarded him with a concern that seemed out of place in the round orb of a child's face. She couldn't have been more than five, maybe six. He didn't recognize her, but in another way, she reminded him of his own boyhood. He loved sitting in the back of the buggy when he was that girl's age, watching the world unroll around him. Life seemed so simple, so unencumbered.

Unlike now.

When Ethan Yoder told him that Sadie had returned with a baby, he felt as if she had delivered a blow to his gut. He was completely, thoroughly shocked. He couldn't stop thinking about it, wondering about it, hoping Ethan had his facts wrong. But then he returned home after school let out and his sister, Alice, had heard the same story from two friends who had stopped by to visit with her.

He knew he had to see Sadie, to talk to her, face-to-face. Maybe this was all a terrible mistake. He couldn't believe it. Sadie, his Sadie, had a baby. This sting of betrayal was the sharpest emotion he'd ever felt. It was like someone was carving his heart out with a dull kitchen knife.

As he drove up the road that led to Windmill Farm, he saw Sadie up by the farmhouse. "Whoa." Gid pulled back on the reins, drawing the horse to a stop by the side of the road. He reached a hand under the buggy seat and pulled out a pair of binoculars. It felt wrong, like he was a Peeping Tom. He'd never done anything like this before, but he justified his spying on Sadie by telling himself he was just gathering facts.

He saw Sadie walking on the porch, back and forth, with something in her arms. Then he heard a wailing sound carry down on the wind. That was the sound of a crying baby. He focused the lens. Yes, there was definitely a baby in Sadie's arms.

Gid let the binoculars drop. Should he go up to talk to Sadie? To find out more about this baby? He should. He definitely should. He needed to be man enough to get up there and ask her directly. Whose baby is this? What's happened to us since you left? He picked up the reins to get the horse moving, but then his attention was distracted by someone coming out of the open barn, pushing a wheelbarrow filled with hay. A stranger. Or at least a stranger to Gid. A young man with shingled hair, cut differently than Plain men wore theirs, and a confident way of holding his head. When the stranger saw Sadie, he set the wheelbarrow down and crossed over to her. Gid picked up the binoculars again and focused them on Sadie. He saw the man lift the baby out of her arms and press the child against his shoulder. The wailing sound stopped.

Tears prickled Gid's eyes. He couldn't do it. He couldn't see Sadie. What if she told him the very words he didn't want to hear—that there was someone else? He slapped the horse's rump with the reins, startling it to lunge forward. As Gid came to the driveway to Windmill Farm, he drove right past.

Will handed the baby, now quiet, to Sadie and went back to pushing the wheelbarrow filled with hay out to the horses in the pasture. He had to keep his chin to his chest to keep from smiling. He could hardly resist releasing a snort of amusement when he observed the deep shade of red Sadie Lapp's face blazed whenever he spoke to her. She was so painfully shy! It was charming. Refreshing, in a way; so different from the kind of girls he was accustomed to at the university.

When the youngest daughter, Mary Kate, had rushed to find him in the barn, begging him to help Sadie get that baby settled down, Will found himself powerless to turn her down. He was getting a kick out of being the only person who could quiet that baby. Twice in one day! It felt good to solve someone's problem. True—it was pretty much a given that it's easier to sort out other people's issues than your own. If only his problems could be solved so easily. Still, his mother would be proud of him. She always said he had a special knack with children. She wanted him to be a pediatrician.

Then his smile faded. Like an echo in his mind, he could hear his father's voice, riddled with disgust, stamping out his mother's compliment. "Snotty noses and ear infections. That's the main job of pediatrics." If he was really in a snarly mood, he would add, "Women's work."

It was ironic that Will's father didn't have any daughters. He had often wondered what his father would have been like with a daughter, but then, Will would never have wished such a fate on any girl. It was hard enough being Charles William Stoltzes' only son.

A tiny slice of movement snagged Will's attention. Someone was watching him from the kitchen window. Mary Kate. He didn't doubt for a minute that girl knew everybody's comings and goings. He could tell her mind spun faster than the arms of the red windmill on a blustery day.

A woman came out on the porch to fill a bird feeder. She was an older woman, in her forties or fifties, as thin as a broom handle. When he saw her face, he could have sworn he was looking at Katharine Hepburn. A handsome woman, unsmiling, yet with unfathomable depths in those steel flint blue eyes—that's how his mother described Katharine Hepburn's appearance. His mother was a nut for Katharine Hepburn movies. His father indulged her on her birthday and watched a few movies with her. This woman on the porch could have been Katharine Hepburn's double. Wouldn't his mother have enjoyed this coincidence? He would have loved to take a picture of her on his cell phone, but he didn't dare. He had a hunch the Katharine Hepburn look-alike would have boxed his ears.

Two horses trotted over to the fence and leaned their heads over the railing to pick at the hay. Will split up a flake of hay and tossed it over the fence. A mother and colt walked up to the hay on the ground. The mother horse pushed her head against one of the horses that had beat her to it. The gelding gave up and looked at Will to solve the problem, so he tossed another flake at the gelding. Even in nature, Will thought, mothers protected their young.

A buzzing sound startled him. His cell phone! It seemed so out of place on an Amish farm. He reached for the phone and held it against his ear. "Will Stoltz."

"You were supposed to call in yesterday."

Will's heart plummeted. He gulped back panic. "Mr. Petosky, I thought we had an agreement. We left it that I would call you. You don't call me."

"I don't like having to track you down," Mr. Petosky said. "That's not our deal. What's going on?"

"It's too soon to tell. Look, I just got here yesterday."

The voice turned dark. "Please tell me you have some good news for me."

"Mr. Petosky, I've barely unpacked. And the Amish farmer has a long to-do list for me."

"Hey, all I'm asking for are updates. And as soon as the time is right, you complete your task. It's as simple as that."

Simple. Right. That's why Will's stomach was rolling like a tiller in the fields.

The voice softened, as if reading Will's mind. "Remember, Will, this is a win-win. The bird wins and you win."

"And you win," Will said. "Don't forget that, Mr. Petosky."

A husky laugh filled the air. "Right. A three-way win. Everybody wins." Mr. Petosky cleared his throat. "Check in tomorrow."

Will snapped his cell phone off.

Sadie tucked a strand of hair behind an ear, her gaze following the tall cowboy as he strode to the pasture. Earlier today, she hadn't looked directly into his face, too embarrassed by her mistake of assuming he was a baby thief. Now, though, as Will Stoltz helped her quiet the baby again, she had an opportunity to peruse his features without his knowledge. And she liked what she'd seen. His thick, wavy hair, combed straight back, reminded her of her father's hair. Where Amos's was dark brown with streaks of gray, the cowboy's hair was brown with sun-bleached streaks.

When she came into the kitchen and tucked the sleeping baby into his basket, Fern had just put a casserole into the oven. She asked Sadie to finish cleaning up some pots and pans for her while she went to the basement to get a jar of canned peaches. That's all they'd been eating lately—peaches for breakfast, lunch, and dinner. Fern wanted to use them up before the new crop set on the trees.

Sadie picked up a mitt to put a hot skillet in the sink, then ran some water into it and braced herself. She had always felt frightened by the reaction of a hot skillet to cold water, both the quick angry hiss and the clouds of rising steam. Fern said she had to get over all of these silly fears. Skillets and steam didn't scare Fern one bit. But then again, nothing scared Fern.

Sadie looked out the window at the cowboy who, she just learned, wasn't a cowboy at all. He just liked the hat and boots. He was a student at a university in Philadelphia. Taking a semester off to find himself, he had said. Had he been lost? she wanted to ask, but thought twice before saying it aloud.

She saw Will glance up at the farmhouse as he fed hay to the sheep in the pasture. He waved to her and she waved back. He picked up a baby lamb in his arms and pretended it was his dance partner, sweeping it around as if he was waltzing in the pasture. Then he gently set the lamb on the ground, turned to Sadie, and made a grand bow. Alone in the kitchen, Sadie laughed out loud. When Will popped back up, his lips spread into a grin beneath the brim of his felt cowboy hat. For a minute, Sadie caught herself just . . . watching him smile. He had a really nice smile, actually. A little impish. The expression seemed kind of mischievous, as if the two of them shared a private joke and Will was enjoying it.

She would think a fellow like Will Stoltz would have a lot of girls fluttering around him at that fancy college. It wouldn't be hard to fall for a boy like that. She tilted her head, wondering if she could hear his heart beat if she laid her cheek against his chest. She had such foolish thoughts as these. *Sadie Lapp, just where will that line of thinking get you? Into trouble!* she upbraided herself. Another part of her brain answered back: *What's so bad about a little bit of trouble?*

Such questions seemed to constantly buzz in her head like mosquitoes, but she felt far short of answers.

As Gideon Smucker pulled the buggy up to the barn at Goat Roper Hill, his family farm, his father came out to meet him. Gid leaped from the buggy and walked around to release the horse from its tracings. Wordlessly, his father pulled the buggy and leaned it up against the barn. Gid led the horse into the stall and filled a bucket with fresh water. He tossed a forkful of hay into the horse's stall. His father followed him in, standing in the center aisle of the barn.

"Something on your mind?" Gid asked. It wasn't like Ira Smucker to not have his hands busy.

Ira sat down on a hay bale set against a wall, leaning forward, steepling his fingers in front of him.

Gid paused in lifting another pitchfork of hay to look at his father. It was strange. His father couldn't seem to look Gid in the eye, as if it was taking everything in him to try to act calm.

Finally, Ira spoke. "Being a minister, well, it's not easy."

Gid knew that to be true. His father was chosen by lot to be a minister nearly three years ago, just before Gid's mother had passed. Gid often thought that the timing of becoming a minister had been a gift to his father. His father was a quiet man, well respected by others. He would have become even quieter if it weren't for the demands of being a minister. And Gid knew that folks counted on Ira's sound judgment. He didn't say much, but when he did, folks listened. Gid tossed a forkful of hay over the stall's door and moved onto the next stall. He faced his father, hooking his elbow on the rounded end of the pitchfork's handle. "What's happened?"

Ira cleared his throat. "There's some talk brewing about . . . about Sadie Lapp."

He leaned the pitchfork against the wall. "About the baby." Gid closed his eyes. "I just drove past Windmill Farm and saw her walking that baby. I didn't talk to her, though. I just couldn't."

Ira nodded sympathetically. "I know my own son well enough to realize Sadie hadn't told you anything about having a baby." He sighed. "I remember what it's like to be a young man. There are certain temptations. Sometimes, a couple in love gets ahead of their wedding day."

Gid's eyes popped open. It hadn't occurred to him that Sadie had been in love with this other fellow. What had gone so wrong? When had she met him? Was she seeing him while she was going out with Gid last December? He counted back the months and slammed his palm against his forehead. Stupid, stupid, stupid! She must have been seeing this other fellow at the same time she was spending time with him! Who could it have been?

Ira's cheeks turned scarlet. "In a . . . situation . . . like this . . . I think it's best to face things head-on." His father kept his eyes on a piece of hay that he was twisting in his hands, back and forth, back and forth.

A horse shuffled straw with his hoof in his stall. A starling flew from one side of the barn to the other, disappearing into a nest in the rafters. In the silence that followed, it slowly dawned on Gid what his father was getting after, why he was acting so strangely.

Gid wondered what Sadie had told people. Had she led others to believe that Gid was the father of that baby? He wasn't! He most definitely wasn't! Gid bit down on his tongue to hold back words of protest.

If he told the truth, he thought about what that could mean for Sadie. She would be under the bann for six weeks, then confess her wrongdoing before the church. And even though she would be restored in full fellowship, there would always be questions, talk, murmurings. She would be raising this baby alone. The quiet pressure might be so intense that she would want to leave the church. To start fresh somewhere else.

With someone else.

And what would happen to them? There wouldn't be a "them."

It would play out the way it had with his second oldest sister, Martha, called Marty. She had met someone while visiting relatives and came home carrying that someone's child. What made it worse was that someone was a married man. Gid was only thirteen at the time, but he remembered the shame that fell over Goat Roper Hill, as real as a covering of deep snow. Marty sat on the front bench and confessed as their mother sat in the back row and cried. It seemed his mother didn't stop crying that entire summer. His mother claimed that everywhere she went, she heard a hiss of whispers: "*They're* the ones with the adulterous daughter."

His father said she was imagining things and to stop making Marty feel as if her life was over at nineteen. "It isn't," Gid vividly remembered his father telling his mother. "God is in the business of second chances." But his mother said that while God might give second chances, people weren't as generous. Then she told him he just didn't understand the way of the world and she started crying all over again.

Whether the pressure came from outside the home or inside it, Marty had enough. She left home before the baby was even born. She worked as a waitress over in Harrisburg and was living with another someone. Every so often, she called home and asked for money to fend off the bill collectors. Her father would always send a check off to her, no questions asked.

But no requests for her to come home, either.

Gid snatched up the pitchfork and jabbed it into the mound of hay with enough force to bend the tines. If he lied and said he was the father of Sadie's baby, it would mean that he, too, would be put under the bann for six weeks. He might even lose his teaching job. And then he and Sadie would be expected to marry. Immediately.

In a way, it wouldn't entirely be a lie. He could, essentially, become the baby's father. That baby was part of Sadie, and Gid would raise him and love him as his own. He loved Sadie. He didn't doubt that for a moment. And Gid couldn't imagine his life without her. He wanted to spend the rest of his days with her, filling a house with children and serving God.

He would do this for her. He loved her that much.

He gave a little jerk, setting his feet in motion. "Dad," he said, in a voice so steady that it could not be his own. "I want to marry Sadie Lapp. As soon as possible."

A broad smile lit Ira's face. He turned to his son and nodded, satisfied, then ambled toward the barn's wide opening, leaving Gid alone with his thoughts.

5

At first Sadie thought she was woken by the moonlight streaming into her window. Full, orange, the moon seemed to teeter on the windowsill. The light spilled into the bedroom and across the wood floor. Then a broad beam of light swept over her bedroom wall and along the ceiling. She popped up on her elbows. Heart pounding, she climbed out of bed and knelt at the window. At first she could see nothing; then she saw someone below her window. A tall, dark figure silhouetted against the moonlight. He held the flashlight up to his face so she could see him. It was Gideon Smucker, looking up at her, motioning with his free hand for her to come down. She pulled up the window sash.

"Hang on a minute, I'm coming down." Her heart zinged into her throat, and before she could talk herself out of it, she dressed, slipped downstairs, slid her feet into flip-flops, and went silently through the back door.

He was waiting for her. "You've come home," he said, holding out a hand to her as she approached him.

She smiled at him. His eyes were beautiful—a deep, clear blue, as blue as a robin's eggs, with impossibly thick lashes fanning outward. Looking into his eyes ignited something in her and she never quite knew how to describe it. Unsettled was the closest feeling she could claim. He was so sure about her, so certain that she was meant for him. It made her nervous, but pleased too. More pleased than nervous. "No one knew, not even Dad. I wanted to surprise everybody."

"You did just that. You certainly did."

They headed toward the maple tree in the side yard—on the opposite side of the house from M.K.'s bedroom. Sadie plunked down on the swing that hung from the tree's large branch. Gid leaned his back against the tree trunk and stared at the clouds rushing through the night sky. Gid wasn't much of a talker, but those eyes of his—they told her everything he felt. Tonight, there was something in his reserved expression that spilled out sorrow. Something was wrong.

Gid's gaze shifted to a spray of lightning bugs dancing past them. "I remember coming here once and watching M.K. chase lightning bugs."

He stopped and swallowed, then looked up into the trees. It hit her then that he was just as nervous as Sadie was.

"Gid, you might have heard things," Sadie whispered.

He kept his gaze angled toward the night sky. "It's okay, Sadie. I want to make this better for you."

She caught his sleeve and gave it a tug, forcing him to look at her. "Make what better?"

He looked at her for a long moment, dropped his head, then squeezed her hand that was still on his arm. "Your . . . circumstances."

She was confused. "I don't know what you mean. What needs to be made better?"

"You know. The baby."

She blew air out of her cheeks. "M.K. told me that you were told."

His head snapped up. "I didn't know it was a secret."

"It's not. Not exactly." She watched the moon pass behind a cloud. "I mean . . . I would have preferred the news to not have gotten out like it did. So that I could figure out what I needed to do without everybody's opinion."

Gid didn't say anything for a long time. "Folks are quite surprised at this . . . situation."

Okay. Now she was mad. This wasn't a situation! This was an orphaned baby. "Why is it anybody's business?"

Gid looked flustered.

"I'm sorry if I sound testy," she said, still sounding testy, "but I have a hard time understanding people who talk about you behind your back."

"It's just natural, I suppose. I remember a lot of talk when the same thing happened to Marty—"

"Marty? Marty!" She flinched, as if suffering a physical blow, and yanked her hand out of his. "But it's not the same thing. Not the same thing at all!" She searched his eyes. "You believe that, don't you, Gid?"

There was a beat of silence. "I want to," he said quietly. Gid scuffed the dirt with the toe of his boot, eyes down.

"How many others are thinking what you're thinking?"

He rubbed his neck. "Quite a few. Most."

A chill swept through her soul. How far was this rumor traveling? She envisioned the faces of her neighbors—Sol and Mattie to the east, her Zook relatives at Beacon Hollow to the south, Jonah and Lainey of Rose Hill Farm to the north, Carrie and Abel to the west. She couldn't imagine any of them believing such a lie. She lifted her chin. "So our friends and neighbors would just prefer to believe the worst about me."

"You have to admit, it doesn't look good." Gid ducked his head, bright color staining his cheeks. The singing wind shifted the clouds again, flickering shadows and light over Sadie's face. He took a deep breath. "Love covers all wrongs. I forgive you."

Such beautiful words, and yet, from somewhere deep inside, Sadie felt a well rising, filled with fury. She was livid. "If you're going to pull one verse out of the Bible and toss it at me like a preacher"—she stood and faced him—"then how about this one: 'Love believes all things, hopes all things.'"

His eyes sent her a silent plea. "That's exactly what I'm trying to do, Sadie."

"Then why don't you ask me for the truth?"

Gid tipped his forehead against Sadie's. "I'm sorry," he murmured.

She leaned against him, breathing in his familiar scent: sandalwood. She could feel his breath, his words, falling onto her.

"All right then, Sadie. I'll ask you for the truth. Who is the baby's father?"

Gid's question set off a cavalcade of emotions in her. She was on the cusp of bursting into tears right in front of him. "Gideon, do you trust me or not?"

"I trust you," he finally said.

"No. You don't. Not really." She stepped away from him. "If you did, you would never have needed to ask me that question."

She ran to the farmhouse and went inside, bolted up the stairs, and flopped herself on the bed, making the springs squeak.

How could so much have changed, in such little time? Why didn't she just stay in Berlin with Julia and Rome? And Old Deborah? She wouldn't have to deal with a boyfriend who believed lies about her, with a newborn baby who cried like he was getting stuck with a pin, with a father whose second heart was giving him trouble. A week ago, life was so much simpler. How could she stay here? How could she face going to church, knowing what people were thinking about her? What Gid was thinking about her!

Sadie turned toward the window and curled into a ball. She wished her mother were here to ask advice. It seemed the older she got, the more she missed her mother. A shred of a memory, long forgotten, flashed through her mind—a day when Sadie came home from school with hurt feelings because someone had told her she was as dumb as a box of rocks. Book learning came slowly for Sadie. She just couldn't remember details the way M.K. and Julia could. She was forever slowing her class down, causing them to lose spelling bees and math quizzes. On that day, she had missed the word "utter," spelling it "udder." An innocent mistake! But one that brought whoops and howls of belly laughter from the boys. Even the girls. They teased her about it all day long.

Her mother had met her at the door with freshly made gingersnaps. When Sadie told her about the spelling bee, her mother said, "There are two kinds of smarts in this world: book smarts and people smarts. Frankly, I think people smarts is worth much more than book smarts. And you've got more people smarts in your little finger than most folks have in their whole bodies." Then she covered Sadie's small hand with her own and gazed steadily into her eyes. "Someday, Sadie, folks are going to be coming to you for advice to solve their problems. You just mark my words."

Fat chance.

Sadie slipped out of bed and sat by the window, resting her fingertips against the smooth glass. She propped her arm on the windowsill and rested her chin on the back of her wrist. Stars glittered overhead, beautiful against the velvety backdrop of black sky. The round moon hung low in the sky. How often had she sat here and made wishes on the stars? She scrunched her eyes tight and started to cry again, softly at first, until tears were flowing down her cheeks and she could barely hold back a sob.

She felt someone rubbing her back. Sadie's eyes opened wide, blinking out at the soft night scene. Fern had come to comfort her. Sadie turned her head slightly. She took a few deep breaths.

"Was that Gideon's voice I heard out there?"

Fern. She heard everything.

Sadie gave a quick nod of her head. "My little sister did me the great favor of telling a few people that I returned with a baby, and a few people told a few more. I just found out that everyone in the church thinks this baby is mine."

Fern let out a sigh padded with exasperation. "Mary Kate never meant to hurt you."

"I know. But what about everyone else? I can't believe people are spreading lies about me."

"So Gideon believes such nonsense too?"

On a strangled sob, Sadie barked out, "He told me . . . he forgave me!" New tears threatened, but she sniffed hard and brought herself under control. "For what?! I didn't do anything!"

Fern bit on her lip, as if to hold back a smile. "Gid's a man of deep convictions. Responsible. Those are good traits, Sadie. Schtill Wasser laaft gern dief." *Still waters run deep.*

"But his convictions are wrong!" She frowned, fighting back a wave of worry. "Why do people only believe what they want to believe?"

"Easier, I guess. They don't have to think."

"How am I going to be able to face everyone in church, knowing what they are thinking about me?"

"Don't pay any attention to such idle gossip."

"You're the one who always said, 'A lie can travel across the country and back again while the truth is lacing up its boots.'"

Fern sighed.

"And you've also said that gossip is like mud thrown on a clean wall. It may not stick but it leaves a dirty mark. And how many times have you said a rumor is about as easy to unspread as butter."

"I've also said, 'Was yeders duh sott, dutt niemand.'" *Everybody's business is nobody's business.*

Sadie wiped a tear off her cheek. "Maybe I should go back to Berlin. It was easier there. People didn't gossip there."

"Sadie, look at me," Fern said in a gentle but authoritative voice. When Sadie twisted around to face her, she continued. "It's time you got your wits together. After all, you're nearly full grown, aren't you?"

Sensibly, Sadie left that unanswered.

"You want to rein in that line of thinking—lumping everyone in the same pile. So, maybe a few are spreading tales. But more than a few want to help. Mattie Riehl and Carrie Miller stopped by today to see the baby. They brought over a bag of baby clothes and blankets. Mattie said she'd love to babysit, anytime we need help. Bess and Lainey offered to have a baby shower. Never forget—these neighbors are your friends, through thick and thin. Nobody ever said they were perfect. They make mistakes, just like you do. And they make mistakes in Berlin, Ohio, too. You just weren't there long enough to notice."

Over in his basket in the corner, the baby started making noises. Sadie groaned. She was growing familiar with his noises. Those little peeps and squeaks would start getting bigger, and bigger, until that ten-pound bundle was screaming bloody murder.

"I'll take this shift," Fern said. "You get some sleep."

Sadie lifted her head to look at her. "How do you do it, Fern? How do you handle coping with all of the problems my family seems to have?"

Fern brushed Sadie's cheek with her rough fingertips. "I do what I have to do," she said matter-of-factly. "You of all people should understand."

Amos woke with a start. He could have sworn he heard something outside, a door slam or the sound of a horse cantering. He looked outside his window but couldn't see anything on this moonless night. Then he heard the cry of the baby and decided that sound must have been what woke him. He checked his alarm. Two a.m. and he was wide awake. He hoped it wouldn't be another sleepless night. It could be worse, he thought. It could be a night with dreams.

Amos ran a finger along his scar. It still amazed him—his sternum had been buzzed open by a saw and held apart with a metal spreader. His weak, damaged heart was replaced with a vibrant, healthy heart. His beloved son's. He held his hand against his heart, taking comfort in the steady beat: *thump, thump, thump.*

Even though Amos knew there was no scientific evidence to support this theory, he couldn't deny it: he felt as if Menno's heart was altering his psyche. It wasn't like some of the strange stories of cellular memory that people liked to tell him about. The latest story he heard was about a man who gained a miraculous ability to paint after receiving a heart from an artist. When Amos heard that, he wanted to ask: what if the fellow just had extra time on his hands after his surgery? What if he just had a desire to try something new? No—Amos thought the whole notion of cellular memory was a bunch of mumbo jumbo.

But ever since the transplant last fall, he kept having strange dreams that involved Menno. He woke in a cold sweat, unable to remember the dream but left with the same feeling each time—that there was some unfinished business he had to take care of. When he mentioned the dreams to the doctor, he was asked if he believed in the theory that souls on "the other side" tried to contact us.

"Now," Amos said, trying to hold back from obvious scorning of such a ridiculous theory, "why would a soul bother with that if he were in the presence of the almighty Lord?" The doctor had no answer for him.

Amos had no doubt that Menno, enjoying heaven, was untroubled by the worries of this world. His son was wholly restored, from imperfect to perfect, and he was in the company of his mother and others who went before him. Menno knew the end of the story, and it was good. "In your presence is fullness of joy," wrote the psalmist.

But Amos couldn't shake these dreams. It felt as if maybe God was trying to remind him of something he had forgotten, or misplaced, or more likely, to nudge him to pay attention. He prayed about them, asking God to reveal the meaning of the dreams to him, the way he had to Joseph in Egypt. Once, he had even gone through Menno's belongings to see if there might be a clue. Nothing, other than an overdue library book. And it was a book of Charlie Brown and Snoopy cartoons! What unfinished business could there have been of a nineteen-year-old whose mind was that of an eight-year-old boy? He just couldn't figure it out.

It was Friday. It had rained all night, a hard, driving, drenching downpour. As M.K. toyed with her scrambled eggs, she could feel the edge of danger mounting within her. She knew that today would be the day.

"Will you listen to me while I'm talking to you?" Fern said to her.

"Ah . . . what?"

"When I'm talking to you, I want you to listen. You sit there like you've got cotton stuffed in your ears."

Fern always had a thing about M.K. not listening. She scrunched around in her seat, pretending to listen to her, but her mind was a million miles away, working out a plan.

"You'd better be home right after school today," Fern said. "No dilly-dallying."

M.K. lifted her chin. "I don't dilly and I don't dally."

After breakfast, M.K. and Sadie worked in silence as they cleaned up dishes. Finally, she tapped Sadie's shoulder. "Are you going to stay mad at me forever?"

With a sigh, Sadie turned from the sink. M.K. tried to make her face look as contrite as possible. "I'm not angry, M.K., I just don't think you realize the kind of trouble you stirred up when you told people I brought back a baby from Ohio. It's just . . ." But once again, she fell silent.

When Sadie wouldn't talk, M.K. knew it was best to just try to change the subject. "If you're not angry, then let's go find out who might be missing a baby."

Sadie turned to face her.

"I've been doing some thinking by using my crackerjack detective skills. I know the baby was wearing a Onesie—something that any baby might wear. No clue in that. No clue with the brand of diapers. Just regular old Pampers. But the basket the baby was left in . . . I think that basket might hold a clue."

"How's that?"

"I was examining it earlier. It's handmade. And it's pretty new. There's a tag on the bottom. I'm thinking we should take it to a basket shop and see if they might know who made it, or who it was sold to."

Now Sadie looked at her with interest. "You might be on to something, M.K."

M.K. nodded, her eyes sparkling with mischief. "It's called connecting the dots. I'm particularly good at it."

Then Sadie's face clouded over. "Maybe . . . we don't want to know."

"What do you mean? Dad said that the baby should be with his mother."

"What kind of mother would abandon a baby? Maybe the baby is better off with us."

M.K. wrinkled her forehead. "Sadie, maybe you shouldn't be getting too attached to that baby."

"I can't help it. There's something about him. I just feel he is meant for me. For us. I can't explain it. It's like a deep-down knowing. This baby is for us."

M.K. shrugged her small shoulders. "Maybe you're right. Maybe Dad's right. But I'm going to take a trip to that basketmaker as soon as I can slip out this afternoon without Fern catching me. Are you coming with me?"

Sadie hesitated. She looked at the sleeping baby. "We'll go. But I'm driving." She gave M.K. a look as if she was bracing herself for a challenge.

Would M.K. dare to miss a ride with Sadie as pilot? It could be more exciting than sledding down Flying Saucer Hill on an icy day.

6

At five foot three inches, Sadie had to sit on a telephone book to see over the dashboard of the buggy. Her buggy driving skills were not exactly her strongest suit. She had always avoided driving the buggy. One sibling or another usually wanted to be in the driver's seat and she happily acquiesced. But last night Fern had reminded her that she was nearly a grown woman and Sadie hadn't stopped thinking about that comment. If she was going to start her life as an adult, she was going to have to be brave.

Then she couldn't find M.K. Nothing unusual there; M.K. never came when she was called. M.K. said it was because her mind was always on other things. Sadie finally found her up in the hayloft, reading.

"Let's go," Sadie called up to her. "The baby is asleep on Fern's bed and she has a long list of things she wants me to get at the store." She held up the baby's basket. "A golden opportunity!"

M.K. flew down the hayloft ladder and beat Sadie to the buggy, hopping in on the passenger side.

Sadie banged her door shut, and the horse startled and reared a few feet. Sadie screamed and dropped the reins. Her high-pitched scream made the horse startle even more, and then, the mare bolted. The buggy shot forward on the curving front drive, then veered straight off the drive. M.K. was holding on to the door handle with both hands. They were gunning over the grass, shade trees were looming by, fences flickered past, the entire world was a blur. Chickens scattered, feathers flying, as they saw what was headed in their direction. Sadie was pinned against the seat and M.K. seemed to somersault on the front seat.

Think, Sadie, think. You're a grown woman now. Think!

Sadie grabbed the loose reins and yanked as hard as she could. They blasted between two trees, and right over Fern's newly planted flower bed. They sailed over neat rows of impatiens—red, pink, then white—but the front wheels of the buggy dug into the soft flower bed and caused the horse to slow from a canter to a trot, a trot to a walk, and finally, to a stop. Sadie collected her wits, at least those that hadn't been shaken out of her, and turned to check on M.K. Her little sister had both feet braced against the dashboard of the buggy, and her eyes were really big. She never saw M.K. scared, except maybe when Sadie was driving.

M.K. took a few deep, gulpy breaths. "Cayenne? Why in the world did you harness up Cayenne? She's barely buggy broke. She's as skittish a filly as they come."

Sadie wiped perspiration from her forehead. "She was the only horse in the barn."

M.K. peeled out the door on her side, ending up in a pile on the grass. "I hate to say it, Sadie, but being in a buggy with you at the helm could be hazardous to a person's health." She spit a feather out of her mouth. "You kill more chickens driving the buggy than the Fishers on butchering day." She brushed herself off and checked for damages. "Either I drive or I'm staying home."

Ten minutes later, Mary Kate steered Cayenne into the Bent N' Dent, a small Amish corner store without any signage out front. Sadie went into the store to get the items on Fern's list and told M.K. to wait in the buggy. Waiting was never a strength for Mary Kate, and she soon grew bored with watching the horse's tail swat flies.

Another buggy pulled into the Bent N' Dent and she poked her head out of the window to see who it was. She scowled when she saw Jimmy Fisher, her arch nemesis, jump from his buggy. They'd had a running feud since the first day she started school. It was set aside briefly after Menno died, but soon resumed again. It was unfortunate, M.K. always thought, that Jimmy happened to be blessed with good looks and a charming personality, because the spoiled youngest son of Edith Fisher was usually up to mischief. He was the sort of boy who couldn't settle until he'd jerked a girl's bandanna off her head or tripped someone walking down the aisle at church. And he was the only boy Mary Kate knew who smoked on a regular basis: cigars, cigarettes, pipes, or corn silk. He was a scoundrel of the worst kind.

Under ordinary circumstances she wouldn't pay any mind to Jimmy Fisher. But as she watched him stride toward the store, she realized he had grown tall as a stork, seemingly overnight. It must have been coming on him in stages, but she hadn't noticed until today, and she couldn't believe it. Mostly, she saw him from afar, and he was always striding in the other direction.

Jimmy Fisher had begun to leave the skinny boy behind and was cutting the fine figure of a lanky man. His knees were working through his britches, and his wrists had grown out of his sleeves. She noticed how fuzzy sideburns were beginning to grow down the sides of his face. He would turn fifteen this summer.

With a smug look on his handsome and horrible face, Jimmy saw her and sauntered over to her buggy.

"Well, if it isn't Mary Kate Lapp," he said, placing his hands on the open window. "I see you're taking your old nag out for an afternoon stroll. Hope she can get you home by supper."

Blond though he was, you could see a whisper of whisker under his nose. His neck was filling out, and she thought he had a cold he couldn't shake off before she realized his voice was changing. She looked down, and his boots were like boats.

It was amazing. She couldn't get her mind around it. One day Jimmy Fisher was a bratty little boy, and the next he was a bratty young man.

"My filly could beat your bag-of-bones gelding any day of the week," she said, lifting her nose in the air.

He leaned closer to the buggy. "So I hear there's a little scandal happening out at Windmill Farm."

She ignored him.

"A little ten-pound, bald-headed, diaper-bottomed scandal."

She continued to ignore him.

"Funny how life goes, isn't it? Who would have ever thought sweet little

Sadie would have a race with the stork." He tsked-tsked, shaking his head, as if he were scolding a small child for dripping an ice-cream cone.

Now that really got M.K.'s goat. A person could only take so much, especially from the likes of Jimmy Fisher.

Mary Kate pointed a finger at his chest. "You. Me. Your worthless gelding. My sleek filly. From here to Blue Lake Pond and back again." She glanced at the store. She needed to get back in time before Sadie came out.

Jimmy perked up. "Now?"

"Now." She gave him a sweet smile. "Unless, of course, you need some practice."

"Me and my gelding, we don't need any practice," he shot back. "What's at stake?"

"When I win, you will keep your mouth shut about anything that has to do with the Lapp family."

"And when I win?"

M.K. narrowed her eyes. She hadn't thought this through. Then a brilliant thought bubbled to the front and the corners of her mouth curled up in a devilish grin. "I won't tell anyone that you were the one who let Jake Hostetler's bull out."

Jimmy's mouth opened wide in outrage. Clapped shut. "I never did!"

"That's a big lie, Jimmy Fisher, and it'll only get bigger."

The bull breakout had been the talk of the town for a week. Jake Hostetler's bull had broken through two neighbors' fences to get to the Masts' dairy farm. It had taken eight men over two hours to get all of the Masts' cows gathered and contained and Jake's bull back home. The Masts were not entirely unhappy about the outcome as they had a prize sire visit their farm without the usual stud fees, but Jake Hostetler was furious. "The Masts sure would like to know who got their cows all stirred up and crazy with desire." She lifted her voice and carefully enunciated the word *desire*, just to rub it in.

Jimmy's eyes shifted to shifty. She was getting nearer the truth, never a short trip.

"On. The. *Sabbath*."

Jimmy's ears burned like fire, and his broad shoulders slumped. So she was right! She wasn't entirely sure it was Jimmy who had started the mischief, but she had a strong suspicion. She wondered if the pressures of life had unhinged his mind. Even at the best of times, his mind hung by a single, rusty hinge.

He glared at her. "Down to Blue Lake Pond and back again."

She gave a short jerk of her head.

Jimmy ran back to his buggy and hopped in. They lined up the horses, side by side, at the edge of the Bent N' Dent parking lot. "Ready?" he said, watching M.K. from the corner of his eye. She was doing the same.

The horses quickly surmised that something was up. Their ears, cocked forward, were sharpened to a point. They were retired racehorses and knew the drill. Cayenne pawed at the ground with her right front hoof.

M.K. made sure she had the reins tightly held. She looked for traffic and saw no car in sight, either direction. "Go!" she shouted, and her mare hurtled into action. Jimmy slapped his reins on his gelding's rump and his buggy lunged forward.

The race was on and they were off.

Sadie walked out of the store just in time to see the backs of two buggies kick up dust as they thundered down the road. It didn't take a genius to figure out what was going on. Through the window, as she had paid for her groceries, she had seen Jimmy Fisher buzzing around M.K. She sighed and reviewed her options. This might be a blessing in disguise. She wanted to go do a little sleuthing that didn't involve her little sister's nose for news. She put her groceries on a bench, told the clerk that she'd be back soon, and hurried down the road. She cut through one field and came out on a seldom-traveled lane that led to a run-down old farm. At least, it looked run-down to someone from the Old Order Amish, who took pride in the upkeep of their farms even though they weren't supposed to be prideful. This farm belonged to an elderly Swartzentruber man. He lived there with his granddaughter, Annie.

As Sadie approached the house, she saw it looked even worse than a year ago, the last time she had been here to visit Annie. An old house without a speck of paint stood set back from the dirt lane. A few outbuildings had caved in, and the privy stood at an angle. A handful of scrawny chickens pecked dirt. The big shade tree in front of the house had just leafed out and made shadowy patterns. The yard wasn't mowed. Even in full daylight, the place had an eerie feel to it, a little like a graveyard when you're all alone, and you could almost feel ghosts lurking about, even though Sadie didn't believe in ghosts.

A skinny, pathetic-looking yellow dog let out a halfhearted "woof!" as Sadie walked along. The dog cocked its head, then came forward cautiously to sniff her. Sadie went down on one knee.

"Where did you come from, big guy?" Sadie held out her hand, palm up. "It's a wonder you haven't been eaten up by a bear." She ran her hand along the dog's side. "Your ribs are poking through. How long since you've eaten?" The dog sauntered off to lie in the shade.

Sadie hadn't noticed an old man sitting in a chair on the porch, slumped, with his jaw dropped. He could be dead. He could be a dead body somebody left here. But then something made him stir, maybe the dog's gentle woof. His eyes opened, and he looked up under his worn black hat, then yanked it off to have a better look at her. He was as bald as an egg and needed a shave. His neck shrank back from the collar on his shirt. He was looking at Sadie like he thought he knew her. Sadie's mind whirled. She wanted to run away, but she had to see this through.

"THERE YOU ARE. I WANT MY DINNER." The old man's jaw wobbled as he spoke, and Sadie could see there was not a tooth in his head. He had an unusually loud voice for such a withered old man. The old man squinted at her over his glasses. "I WANT MY SUPPER IS WHAT I WANT." He looked around the front yard. "ANNIE, I'M HUNGRY. IT'S PAST SUPPERTIME."

Now Sadie was up on the porch, gripping the post. She was Annie, and he wanted his supper, and she didn't know what to do. "I'm not Annie. I'm Sadie. SADIE LAPP. NOT ANNIE."

The old man's eyes were just watery slits now, and he was getting really excited. A big cane was tucked behind his chair. The old man thrashed around in his chair, looking for his cane, and she wanted to keep out of its range.

The yellow dog gave out another feeble woof. Sadie looked at it again. Something dawned on her—this was the puppy her brother Menno had given to Annie a year or so ago, now full grown. The realization made her sad. Menno took pride in his pups' well-being.

"WHEN IS ANNIE COMING HOME?"

"I'M HUNGRY. I WANT MY DINNER."

"WHEN WILL ANNIE COME HOME TO MAKE YOUR DINNER?"

"YOU'RE ANNIE AND I'M HALF-STARVED."

"I'M NOT ANNIE. I'M SADIE LAPP. HOW LONG HAS SHE BEEN GONE?"

"WHAT?"

"HOW LONG HAS ANNIE BEEN GONE?"

He blinked at her a number of times, like a fog was lifting. "DON'T YOU HAVE SOMEPLACE YOU NEED TO BE?"

He had a point. It was definitely time to get going. Sadie was in new territory here, but she knew where she wanted to go next. She had to try one more time. "I'LL GET YOUR DINNER FOR YOU."

The old man brightened.

Sadie walked up to the porch, expecting the old man to tell her to leave, but he seemed to be delighted to have someone solve his immediate problem. She slipped into the house and found the kitchen. The furnishings were sparse. Bare necessities only. It worried her to see what little food was in the house.

She didn't know much about this tiny Swartzentruber colony. They seldom interacted with Sadie's church, but she would have thought they'd be looking out for this old man. She found some bread, peanut butter, and jam, made a sandwich for him, filled a glass of milk—sniffed it first to make sure it hadn't gone sour—and found a small tray to take it out to him. She peeked out the window and saw he had his eyes closed. She put the tray down and looked around the room. Emboldened, she went down the hallway, opened a door, and poked her head in. It must be the old man's room, because it was dark and smelled musty. Then she looked into another room, tiptoeing in as her eyes adjusted to the dark. Something familiar caught her eye and she bent down to examine it.

So this was it.

The breath she hadn't realized she was holding whooshed out of her.

"WHERE'S MY DINNER?" sailed through the open window from the front porch.

Sadie closed the door to the bedroom and picked up the tray with the sandwich and glass of milk in the kitchen. She hurried outside and handed the plate to the old man before he could rise from the chair. "Perhaps it's time to be running along," she said in a loud and strange voice. "GOING." She waved goodbye to make her point.

The old man was gumming the sandwich and didn't even look up. The yellow dog followed Sadie down the path to the road, despite her efforts to shoo him home. Finally, she turned and tried to drag the dog back to the old man, but the dog sat back on its heels and wouldn't budge.

"TAKE IT!" the old man yelled. "THAT DOG IS A DOOZY. I DON'T WANT IT."

Sadie walked back through the fields to the Bent N' Dent, deep in thought, with the yellow dog trailing behind her. When she arrived at the store, Mary Kate was waiting for her with an odd look on her face and a very lathered-up buggy horse. She waved to Sadie to hurry. "Maybe we'd better skip the basketmaker today and get on home."

Sadie opened the buggy door and let the yellow dog jump in. M.K. seemed so distracted, she didn't even look twice at the dog. Sadie barely shut the door as M.K. slapped the horse's rump with the reins and headed home. Sadie watched her for a while, amused by the tense look on M.K.'s face.

"What happened to Jimmy?" Sadie finally asked.

Eyes straight forward, M.K. said, "Jimmy who?"

"M.K., he's not bleeding to death in a ditch somewhere, is he?"

M.K. flashed her a look of disgust. "No!" But she wouldn't offer another word.

M.K. was always up to something and Sadie wondered what. She had this urge—just a slight one—to grab her little sister by the ankles and dangle her over the side of the buggy until she started talking.

As they pulled up to the barn at Windmill Farm—in record time, Sadie noted—Fern walked out of the house to meet them with a crying baby in her arms. M.K. rushed to get the horse out of its shafts. She waved Fern's questioning glance off. "Got to take care of the horse, Fern," she tossed over her shoulder as she walked the horse down the hill to cool it off before returning it to the barn. Fern turned to Sadie with a question in her eyes.

Sadie shrugged. "I'm not entirely sure what happened, but it had something to do with Jimmy Fisher."

Fern, who had heard all this before, released an effluvial sigh. "It always has something to do with that boy. Those two are like oil and vinegar." She lifted an eyebrow. "What happened to my impatiens?"

Sadie's attention was suddenly riveted to the sky, where the male falcon, the one Will called Adam, soared above them. The baby let out another big wail and Fern passed him off to Sadie. "He's fed, he's dry, and he keeps on crying." She cocked her head. "And where are the groceries?"

Sadie smacked her own forehead. "Oh. Oh no! I left them at the store."

Fern looked at her as if she might have a screw loose.

The yellow dog leaped out of the backseat of the buggy and jumped up on Fern, drenching her face with wet licks. Fern pushed it off and walked back to the house, muttering away about how it was easier just to do things herself.

7

Sunrise would stir Will in just moments, and he could hardly lift his head off the pillow. Every single muscle in his body ached from the farmwork he had been doing. It was backbreaking work, day after day. It was the best time of his life.

On a Saturday morning, he knew there would be plenty of bird-watchers lined up with their scopes to watch his birds. His birds. He was already thinking they belonged to him. He felt oddly protective toward them. It started when he named them Adam and Eve. He stuck his stocking feet in his boots and looked around for his binoculars. He had just moved in a day or so ago, and the cottage was already a mess. Clothes were strewn all over. Some groceries he had bought were still on the kitchen table, next to a banana peel and a half-eaten piece of wheat toast, and a dirty napkin. He frowned, looking around the room. He really was a slob. He drank milk and orange juice from the carton. He dipped his toast in the peanut butter jar. He left the cap off the toothpaste and squeezed it in the middle. He didn't pick up his socks or make his bed. Why bother? He was just getting back into it tonight.

He finally found his binoculars under a newspaper, and grabbed a granola bar out of a box to stave off hunger. He wasn't quite sure how he was going to manage cooking for himself. Not that he had much experience with cooking in the first place, but he sure couldn't figure out the appliances in the kitchen. Where were the wall switches? And he still had to learn how to light the kerosene lamp. He tried again and again last night, went through a box of matches, and finally gave up and went to sleep. But he liked this little cottage. It was simple living at its best. As he lay in the snug bed last night, covered in homemade quilts, he could have sworn he smelled a faint scent of beeswax, infused in the walls. The scent was very homey and appealing.

He jammed his hat on his head and hurried outside to scan the sky. Adam and Eve were already up, soaring over the creek bed that wove through Windmill Farm. He watched Eve—the larger of the two—soar high and key in on something down below. He watched her virtually stop in the air, then dive straight down as if she was heading right into the water, only to make a last-minute turn and soar back up to the sky with a small bird in her talons. Effortless! Will kept his eyes trained on her. Just as he expected, she flew to a nearby place on the ground and tore the bird to pieces, quickly swallowing them. The falcons were vulnerable on the ground and preferred to spend as little time there as possible. They have a special pouch in their throats to hold food. It would be digested later, when Eve was safely in her scape.

Adam flew over a field and caught a small bird in the air. He disappeared into a treetop. Will noticed a group of bird-watchers had just arrived and were setting up their telescopes. He walked over to politely remind them to stay off the property. He wasn't too worried about this crowd—anyone who set an alarm for predawn to watch a bird catch his breakfast was a pretty tame type. It was the feeding at dusk that seemed to bring out a rowdier crowd.

Eve flew back to the scape, which Will thought was indicative of impending motherhood. He followed Adam's flight path and ended up passing the farmhouse. Sadie was out on the porch, filling a bird feeder with sunflower seeds. He'd never seen so many bird feeders or birdhouses at one home. It was a regular feeding station. Tall purple martin houses, stacked like condominiums, lined the far end of the driveway. Hollowed-out gourds hung from the limbs of a large maple tree in the front yard. Small wooden birdhouses sat on tall poles. If a bird were smart enough to get to Windmill Farm, it would find plenty of food and shelter.

"Mornin'," Will called out. "Your birds sure are regular customers. I thought I saw someone filling up that feeder just yesterday."

"Well, it's springtime," she said.

"You must spend a fortune on birdseed."

"Not at all. We grow dozens and dozens of sunflowers along the back side of the vegetable garden." She put the container of seeds on the ground. "Have you ever noticed how much birdsong there is, so early in the morning?"

"The race to reproduction," Will said professorially, as he watched her replace the top on the feeder.

Sadie's face went a shade of crimson.

Will tried hard, without success, not to smile at her modesty.

"I didn't think you'd be awake yet on a Saturday," she said. "You're welcome to join us for breakfast. That is, if you haven't eaten yet." She stammered her request in embarrassed politeness, then finally looked up at him with an almost mortified expression on her face.

How could he refuse?

But he hadn't expected this. He hadn't thought about being invited over so soon. Or so early in the morning. The effects of the granola bar had worn off long ago and his stomach was growling. "Well, sure . . . I guess so. I don't usually eat much breakfast, though, but I wouldn't mind a cup of strong coffee."

A shy smile curled Sadie's lips. "Oh, wait until you try a cup of Fern's coffee. She's known for her good cooking." She took the broom that was resting on the porch rail and swung it at a few curled brown leaves along the stairs. *Swish, swish.* "We figured you might be having some trouble figuring out how to live without electricity. You'll have to be sure to let us know if you need anything."

The broom was still swishing. Will found himself watching her. She reached up to her forehead and tucked a wisp of hair back under her prayer cap, then positioned herself again like a golfer at the driving range. She was a careful sweeper, going all the way to the edges. What a serious, methodical little person she was. He wondered what she did for fun.

She stopped abruptly and straightened up when she noticed he was observing her. "The problem with sunflower seeds is that the hulls make a mess." Then she went down the steps and out in the yard to fill a bluebird feeder. A dinner plate with a hole drilled into it was positioned on the pole under the feeder to deter squirrels. Pretty clever, Will thought, but the feeder itself was a sorry excuse; the roof was rotting and the pole was leaning over precariously as if it would topple right over if a crow or blue jay landed on it. She needed a new one. Maybe he should get her one after his time at Windmill Farm came to an end, a parting gift. But by then she might know what he had been up to, and she might not want a bird feeder or anything else from him.

But he had nothing to worry about, he told himself again. He kept reminding himself of that. What he was doing wasn't wrong. Not wrong at all. In fact, you could say it was very right. A good thing to do. A win-win.

Wonderful aromas greeted his nose as he stepped up on the porch. He was even hungrier than he had thought. The kitchen door began to swing open slowly, with a squeak as if its hinges needed oil. Then he saw a face peering around the edge at him—the woman who looked like a middle-aged version of Katharine Hepburn. His first impression was that she was scowling at him, but when he looked more closely, he saw that she was merely looking him over and sizing him up. She seemed as lovable as a mountain thistle. They stood there looking at each other for a moment, and then he heard Amos's voice from behind her.

"Well, for pity's sake, Fern, let him in." Amos looked at Will over the woman's shoulder and smiled. He pushed the door wide open and motioned for Will to come in.

Amos pointed to a straight-backed chair across from him on the other side of the large kitchen table. The seat sounded like a creaky hinge when Will sat down. The girl who had watched him from the window, Mary Kate, galloped down the stairs like a newborn filly but stopped abruptly when she saw he was sitting at the table. She sidled into a chair, across from Will, eyes glued to him. Fern brought Will a cup of coffee and, nervously, he gulped it down. No one spoke for a few moments and he wondered if he had done something wrong. He had seen *Witness*. He knew they drank coffee. Should he have waited to drink it? Was there a certain tradition to drinking Amish coffee that he should have known?

What was he doing here? he asked himself. Not just the breakfast invitation but the whole business.

It was so hot in here. Was he getting sick? He wondered what made it so hot in the room, but then he realized it was the woodstove. He'd forgotten how much heat radiated from a woodstove. Will glanced quickly around the large family room. Everything was in its place. And plenty of seating—two large sofas, a rocker, a bench with a colorful knitted afghan folded on it. Bookshelves lined the far wall, filled with titles. Large picture windows brought in plenty of natural lighting. What would his mother say about this room and its decor? What would she call it? At times, she could be a snob. He could hear her brittle voice: "This isn't shabby chic—this is just plain shabby."

Sadie finished sweeping the porch and came inside. She peeked at the sleeping baby, tucked into a corner in the room, and sat next to her sister. Fern finished bringing in platters of food and sat down. Will had never seen so much food in all of his life: stacked blueberry pancakes, pitchers of maple syrup, smoked sausages, a bowl of steaming scrambled eggs, grapefruit. It looked like a smorgasbord! Will picked up his fork but stopped when he realized that Amos Lapp had bowed his head and everyone had followed. Except for him. Will wondered what went on during those seconds of silence. Then Amos lifted his head and everyone dug in like it was their last meal.

The kitchen door opened and in blasted an older man with wild and wiry white hair sticking out from under his black felt hat. "WHO HAVE WE HERE?" he hollered as he caught sight of Will. His face practically beamed with happiness.

"Uncle Hank, this is Will Stoltz," Sadie said. "The game warden wants him to babysit the falcons." She passed the stack of pancakes to her father.

Will lifted a finger in the air. "Not really babysitting," he hurried to explain. "More like protecting an endangered species from an overzealous public."

Uncle Hank emitted a noise that was part laugh and part snort. "So you're set on trying to give the love birds a little privacy!"

"Oh, fuss and feathers, Hank. Sit down and eat." Fern clucked at him until he settled down to eat, but he talked and joked and told stories throughout breakfast. Uncle Hank got Mary Kate giggling so hard that milk came out of her nose.

The food was better than any Will had eaten for a long time. The baked oatmeal was wonderful—crisp on the outside and soft and warm and mealy on the inside. Will wasn't fond of scrapple but took some to be polite. It was surprisingly good, heavily doctored with sage to mask the contents of offal.

Sadie refilled his coffee. And when it was over, Amos bowed his head again, then everyone hopped up and got to work. Amos and Hank went to the barn, Mary Kate went off to feed her chickens, Sadie tended to the baby, so he helped Fern gather dishes from the table and take them to the kitchen.

"You can go on out and help Amos," Fern said. "Now that spring is in full gear, he'll need a lot of help."

"Is he healthy?" Will handed a big platter to her. "I mean, I saw this . . . long scar." He pointed to his neck.

Fern started filling up the sink with hot water and added liquid soap to it. "Don't ask Amos about the scar on his neck," she said. "He doesn't like to speak of it."

Will brought in the last two platters from the table. "You mean about the heart transplant?"

Her hands splattered the water. In her surprise, she looked right at him. "You mean he told you?"

Will nodded like it was natural. "Seemed like he wanted to tell me." She looked a little disappointed, so he thought it would be best to change the subject. "Have you known Amos for a long time?"

She let out a deep sigh. "Some days, it seems like forever. Other days, it's like I hardly know him." She swished her hand in the sink to get the water sudsy. Then she pointed to a towel for him to dry the dishes. He guessed he wasn't going to make as quick an exit as he thought.

"It plagues me," she said. "I have been taking care of his household for over a year now—"

Will gathered that she meant Amos.

"—through thick and thin. And there's been plenty of both. For days on end that man can hardly string two words together." She scrubbed the spoon she was holding until it shone before she went on. "I always knew he seemed to be drawn to a barn like a magnet, always finding something to tinker with out there. But I never thought there was much talking going on." She handed him the spoon to dry. Dishes and utensils were coming faster and faster now, as she was starting to get herself worked up. Will was having trouble keeping up. Drying a dish wasn't something he had done much of. He thought letting dishes air-dry was more than good enough. Better still, paper plates.

"But the minute my back is turned, Amos starts talking, and freely, to you of all people. A bird sitter!"

Will lifted a finger. "Just to clarify . . . I'm not exactly a bird sitter. I'm trying to keep an endangered species away from an overzealous public." He had the spiel memorized now.

She wasn't listening to him. "To a boy who isn't much more than a stranger! I have half a mind to walk out to that barn and ask him why men are the way they are." She handed him a platter. "I suppose there just isn't an answer."

Will saw the conversation drifting in a no-win direction. For such a tight-lipped woman, she could talk a blue streak once she got started. When Sadie came to the kitchen to ask Fern a question, Will took the opportunity to leave. It was high time he should head out and chase off any bold bird-watchers.

Afterward, walking up the hill to the falcon scape, Will felt slightly stunned from the whole experience. It wasn't exactly the enormous quantity of food he had consumed or the Lapp family or the conversation. It was just everything together. He had never felt quite such a sensory overload.

The aroma of Fern's strong coffee triggered memories for Will of morning at the table with his father and his mother, at their grand home in Wynwood, a small upscale suburb outside of Philadelphia. But the smell of coffee was where the similarity ended. Breakfast was the one time of the day when his father was calm—before the busyness of his work claimed his energies and consumed his thoughts. Silence reigned. In fact, his parents rarely spoke during breakfast beyond an occasional polite inquiry after the other's health, or how they slept. But after the workday claimed his father, he treated everyone differently. Indifferently.

Yes, breakfast in the Stoltzes' home was a quiet affair, interrupted only by the rustle of newspaper pages as his parents exchanged sections. Cold cereal and coffee were the only items on the menu. Sensory underload.

No wonder Will felt stunned.

M.K. hadn't made up her mind yet about the yellow dog that followed Sadie home. He was a crazy dog, with an unpredictable streak running through him. They ended up calling him Doozy. He would bark at the silliest things without warning, like a leaf skittering across the driveway or a shadow moving across a windowpane, or a towel flapping on the clothesline. On the other hand, he was very predictable about other things. Every single time a buggy came to call, for example, Doozy could be found hiding under the porch. The poor thing was half starved and flea-bitten, and though Fern usually didn't have a sympathetic bone in her body, for some reason she took to this pathetic creature. When M.K. pointed out this contradiction to her, Fern raised one eyebrow and replied, "What I like best about dogs is that they wag their tails instead of their tongues."

Fern! So prickly.

M.K. left Fern baking in the kitchen to go see what Sadie was doing with the baby. She curled up on Sadie's bed and watched her sister feed the baby a bottle. He would drink a little, then fall asleep, then jerk awake and start drinking as if he were starved. The baby held one hand up in the air, fingers splayed like a starfish. M.K. loved looking at his little hands. They were so small, so perfect.

Her mind drifted to the unsolved dilemma: to whom did this baby belong?

"Later today, maybe I can take the basket and go ask around town."

"No," Sadie said with an uncharacteristic firmness. "You've already created enough problems. The last thing I want is to have you poking your nose into this."

M.K. looked up at her, serious, and blinked once. How were they going to figure out who the baby's mother was with *that* attitude? This business with Sadie reminded her of doing math problems. Sometimes they worked out. Sometimes you were back where you started.

Sadie put the baby into his basket and covered him with a little blanket. "M.K., I think maybe we have a special job ahead of us. Something important."

Mary Kate was just about to ask what she was talking about as she heard the yellow dog wander up and down the hallway, completely stumped by this new environment. He wasn't the brightest of dogs. He came into Sadie's room and curled up on the small rug by the side of her bed. "Fern is going to have a conniption when she finds you indoors." The dog looked up at her with sad, brown eyes. Then he cocked his head, ran to the window, and let out a low growl.

M.K. jumped off the bed to see what he had noticed. "Oh no," she said. Her mouth was suddenly very dry. Edith Fisher had rolled up the driveway in her buggy. Worse still, Jimmy Fisher was beside her, looking angry and sullen. She looked down at the dog, who was still growling a little. She patted his head. "Maybe you're smarter than you look."

She saw her father walk out of the barn to greet Edith, who was out of the buggy and walking toward the house. Jimmy followed behind, hands in his pockets, scuffing the gravel with his feet.

She knew what this was all about. She had hoped to avoid this, but it figured that Jimmy would try to pin this on her. She saw her father look up at the house and catch sight of her in the window. He motioned to her to come downstairs. She sighed, deeply annoyed with Jimmy, and went out to meet them. Sadie followed behind, far too happily, M.K. noticed.

When they reached Amos, he said, "M.K., I understand you challenged Jimmy to a buggy race, from Bent N' Dent to Blue Lake Pond."

She glared at Jimmy. "Nolo contendere."

Her father paid no mind to her Latin. "And I understand that a police officer pulled Jimmy over after clocking him at thirty-five miles per hour—" He stopped abruptly and turned to look at Jimmy. "Really? You got that old gelding up to thirty-five miles per hour?"

Jimmy brightened. "Sure did."

Amos whistled, one note up, one down, impressed.

"Amos Lapp!" Edith Fisher snapped, trying to remind Amos of the gravity of this matter. She could snap with very little provocation.

Amos turned to M.K. "And when you heard the police siren, you made a fast break into someone's driveway, leaving Jimmy to get caught by the police officer."

M.K. started to smirk, but Jimmy saw it and glowered at her. Her smile faded.

Edith drew herself up tall. "The police officer brought Jimmy home and said he would forget about a ticket if Jimmy would complete thirty-five hours of community service. One for every mile per hour, he said." She touched the back of her bun. "Fortunate for us that policeman happens to be a regular egg customer at our hatchery." Her glance shifted to M.K. "It only seems fair to have Mary Kate do the community service. She's the one who tempted my Jimmy. After all, what boy can turn down a challenge?"

What?! M.K. was outraged. She wondered what would happen if she gave Edith Fisher the shock of her lifetime. *For your information, Edith Fisher, your son Jimmy has a ten-speed bicycle hidden behind your stinky henhouse! He sneaks out late on Saturday nights and goes roaring around Stoney Ridge.* It was a piece of valuable information M.K. had stumbled upon and tucked away, with many other Jimmy Fisher crimes and indignities and grievances, for future use.

"It's high time Jimmy took responsibility for his actions," Fern said. "You coddle that boy, Edith."

Everyone whipped their heads around to face Fern, who had appeared out of nowhere like she usually did. Just as Edith was about to get up on her high horse, Amos held up a hand to stop her.

"Now, Fern," Amos started. "We have no right to tell Edith how to raise her boy."

Let Fern talk, Dad! M.K. started to say but thought better of it. Jimmy Fisher *was* coddled. She tried to hold back from shouting by conjuring up a picture of Jimmy staked out in the desert with vultures plucking at his flesh and flies swarming all over his gorgeous head. Unfortunately, she couldn't make the image gruesome enough. Still, it was a satisfying thought.

"They should both do the community service," Fern said. "It would do them good."

Fern! So intrusive!

Amos nodded. "Now, that does seem only fair, Edith."

"I know of someone who needs help," Sadie said.

M.K. looked aghast into Sadie's steady blue eyes. *Et tu, Brutus?* She would have loved to say it aloud but what was the point? Gid was the only one who understood and enjoyed her references to Shakespeare. Everyone else always looked at her as if she were speaking Polish.

Sadie ignored her silent pleas. "An older man. Someone from the Swartzentruber colony."

"But they all left the area," Amos said. "A few months ago, the colony up and moved to Ohio to join a larger settlement."

"This old man must not have gone with them. He's all alone," Sadie said. "Maybe on Saturdays, Jimmy could do yard work and M.K. could help with the cooking and cleaning."

M.K. envisioned months and months of Saturdays down the drain. Worse still, she would have to spend them with the likes of Jimmy Fisher. She raised a finger in the air. "Before this is a fait accompli, I'd just like to point out that—"

Cutting her off at the quick, Fern said, "Sounds like an ideal solution."

And that was it. M.K.'s fate was sealed. Her Saturdays, for the foreseeable future, were ruined.

Even Edith Fisher looked placated. "I suppose that would suffice. I'll go along with them on Saturday, just to make sure everything is on the up-and-up." She arched an eyebrow in M.K.'s direction. "You've got no more direction than a newborn calf, and even less good judgment. Seems as if there's enough trouble going on here at Windmill Farm. I would think you would give your poor father a break."

"My sentiments exactly," Sadie said, poking a finger at M.K.

Amos raised an eyebrow. "I'll go talk to the old Swartzentruber fellow. Plan on them starting next Saturday."

M.K. sighed and Jimmy blew air out of his mouth. Edith spun on her heels.

"Jimmy! Come along!" His mother's voice sailed from the buggy.

Jimmy leaned close to M.K. and squinted at her. "You're making those big words up."

She squinted back at him. "What big words?"

"No lo contend and feet accomplished. You were throwing them around awhile ago."

"They're in the dictionary," she said sweetly. "Right in front of the word *snitch*."

8

During breakfast the next morning, the baby woke up and started to wail. The entire family covered their ears as Sadie tried to settle him down.

"You know," Amos said, "I hadn't thought about this for years, but Menno used to yell like that."

Sadie's head jerked up. "Really?"

"Yes, just like that. As if someone was pinching him." He smiled wistfully. "He had colic. We tried everything. Even tried all kinds of formulas—just like you're doing."

Fern leaned forward in her chair. "Did anything work?"

"Let's see. It was awhile ago, you know." Amos looked up at the ceiling, as if watching a memory pass overhead. "Goat's milk." He looked pleased. "Worked like magic." He snapped his fingers.

Fern looked at him as if a cat had spoken. "And you're just thinking to offer that up now?" She reached over and scooped the baby out of Sadie's arms. "Go to Ira Smucker's right now and get fresh goat's milk."

Sadie hesitated. "Let M.K. go."

Fern sighed. "Fine." She turned to M.K. "Get a couple of clean jars from under the sink. Lids too. Tell Ira you need the freshest milk he's got. See if he'll even milk a goat for you while you watch. And then bring that milk back here. No lollygagging." She gave M.K. a gentle push in the direction of the kitchen.

M.K. huffed. "I don't lolly and I don't gag."

The baby took a few gulps of air and started to wind up again, like a siren. M.K. grabbed the jars and lids and darted out the door.

Not thirty minutes later, Ira Smucker returned with M.K. in his flatbed wagon, with large containers of sterilized goat's milk, still steaming, and a goat. Fern and Amos went out to meet them.

"It's nothing," Ira told Fern when she thanked him for being so thoughtful. "This goat is a good milker and has a sweet disposition too. Goats can be pretty ornery." He sneezed a loud sneeze, whipped out his handkerchief, and covering his nose, honked once, then twice.

"That's good to hear. I had a very unpleasant experience with a goat once." M.K. nodded in solemn agreement.

Ira put the handkerchief back in his vest pocket. "If the milk agrees with the baby's digestion, I thought it'd be easier to have a goat here, rather than having to keep sending M.K. trotting over the hill for fresh supplies." He led the goat off the wagon and handed the rope to M.K.

"Take her to that far pasture," Amos said. He turned to make sure M.K. was headed to the right pasture and was surprised to see her losing a game of tug of war with the goat. The goat had dug in its heels and wouldn't budge, despite M.K.'s efforts to pull it forward. Amos went over to help her and M.K. thrust the rope in his hands, scowling.

"I never did like goats." Suddenly her attention was riveted to the wagon where Fern and Ira were standing. "Would you look at that? Who would have believed it?"

"What?" Amos looked to where her eyes were fixed.

"Why, Ira Smucker's ears are burning up red. Redder than a beet."

Ira sneezed again and honked into a handkerchief.

"Well, maybe he's sick," Amos said.

"Oh no. It's just like Gid. His ears go as red as a tomato every time he gets around Sadie. Like father, like son."

They locked the goat into the pasture and M.K. went skipping off to the house. Amos turned back and watched Fern and Ira talking. She was laughing at something he said. What could he have said that would be funny? Ira wasn't funny. Not funny at all. Rather serious and somber, especially since his wife passed on. It would appear that Ira was smitten with Amos's housekeeper. The thought nettled him. He walked over to join them.

Ira swallowed, his Adam's apple bobbing up and down. "Would you mind if I saw the baby?"

Amos's mouth dropped open. Snapped shut. Since when was Ira Smucker interested in babies?

Fern lifted her chin to Ira and narrowed her eyes. "Are you catching a cold? You shouldn't be around the baby if you've got a cold." She lowered her voice. "Or Amos, for that matter. He shouldn't be exposed to a cold. With his heart trouble and all."

Amos stiffened. Fern treated him like he was a six-year-old!

"No," Ira said solemnly. "Hay fever. I get it every year about this time."

"A farmer with hay fever?" Fern frowned. "Never heard of such a thing."

"Runs in my family," Ira said sadly.

"Well, since it's allergies, I suppose it would be fine to see the baby." She turned to Amos. "Would you mind bringing in those milk containers while I show Ira to the house?"

And off the two of them went, with Fern chattering away to Ira all about the baby as they walked. Amos was left to haul in the milk containers.

He reached to pick up a container and hoist it to the ground, feeling strangely left out. *And just what is that all about, Amos Lapp?* he asked himself. *Are you feeling like a scorned teenager because you think you might have had a claim on Fern Graber? Do you honestly think you stood a chance with her? Well, think again.*

Amos knew he wouldn't exactly be a woman's dream man. What woman would want to marry a man who took twenty-seven pills a day to keep his body from rejecting his heart. It always, always came back to that.

Sadie was at the end of her rope. The baby seemed to be in agony. He stiffened, his back arched, and let out a whopper of an ear-piercing scream which sent M.K. flying out of the house to find Will Stoltz.

Sadie was a little annoyed that M.K. kept fetching Will from his important bird business whenever the baby started to holler, but he didn't seem to mind. He would arrive at the house with a pleased grin on his face, head straight to Sadie, and take the crying baby out of her arms. And the baby would settle right down, relieved, as if he knew he was in the hands of a professional. Sadie was relieved too. Will had a knack for soothing this baby.

All morning long, Sadie had been walking the baby around the family room, through the kitchen, and back again. A big circle, around and around, trying to lull him to sleep. When she made a pass through the kitchen, she noticed Fern and Ira heading toward the house. As Ira drew closer to the house, Sadie saw his head jerk up in alarm as he caught the first sound of the baby's screech. Ira doubled over and Sadie thought he was going to drop to the ground in horror, but then she saw he was merely overcome by a big sneeze. Then another and another. It was quite a dramatic fit of sneezing. Finally, he wiped his nose with his handkerchief and strode a few steps to catch up with Fern.

Sadie pushed the squeaky kitchen door open with her knee and handed the baby to Fern, completely exasperated. "I can't do a thing with him."

"Ira brought some fresh goat's milk to try," Fern said, talking over the baby's wail.

Ira remained on the porch, gripped by another sneezing fit.

"Hay fever," Fern said, letting the door close. "He'll come in when he's ready."

Sadie watched him for a while. "Gid gets hay fever like that too." She tilted her head. She went into the kitchen and opened a cupboard, took out a container, and opened it. Inside was a chunk of honeycomb from one of M.K.'s hives. Sadie picked up a knife and cut off a section of honeycomb. She put it on a napkin and took it outside to Ira.

"Chew this," she said, handing him the napkin. "Some folks say that chewing honeycomb every once in a while will relieve hay fever and stuffy noses."

He sneezed again, honked his nose again, sneezed, honked, and decided to give the honeycomb remedy a try. Sadie watched him earnestly as he chewed. And chewed. And chewed.

"Do I spit out the wax or swallow it?"

"Chew and chew, then spit out the wax."

Behind him, Amos climbed up the porch with the goat's milk container and handed it to Sadie. She went to the kitchen and took out a clean bottle, filled it with the warm goat's milk, capped the bottle with a rubber nipple, and held it out to Fern. She shook her head and handed the baby to Sadie.

Sadie sat down in the rocking chair and fed the baby. The baby gulped and coughed and spit at the strange taste, but then he settled down to suck. Sadie looked up at Fern.

"Don't get too hopeful," Fern said. "It's not the eating part that troubles him. It's the digestive part." She turned to Ira. "Would you like some coffee? I can brew a fresh pot."

"Thank you, Fern, but I should get home." Ira walked up to Sadie and put his hands on his knees to bend over and peer at the baby. "Well, with that coloring, there's no doubt who he belongs to."

Sadie looked up to ask, "Who?" just as the baby took in too big of a mouthful and started to choke. She held him up against her chest, the way Will had shown her, and jiggled him, patting his back. Dandling, Will called it. When the baby stopped sputtering, she tucked him back in her arms to feed him.

Ira clapped his hands on his knees and straightened up. "Amos, would you mind walking me out? Something I'd like to discuss with you."

Sadie opened her mouth to ask Ira who he thought the baby resembled, when he spun around, his face brightened. "Why, Sadie Lapp! I haven't sneezed once since you gave me that honeycomb!" He scratched his head.

"Chew on a little each day and see if it helps," Sadie said.

"My sister sent me some honeycomb from Indiana," Ira said. "I'll give hers a try."

Sadie shook her head. "It needs to be local honey. It's the pollen that you're allergic to. I'll give you a chunk to take home."

"I'll get it," Fern said, hurrying to the kitchen to wrap up the honeycomb. "I always said Sadie was a born healer." She put the honeycomb in a Tupperware container and handed it to Ira.

In a low voice, Ira said to Fern, "I'll see you on Saturday, then," and she nodded and smiled in return.

Sadie wondered briefly why her father was scowling at Ira, but then the baby started to choke and sputter again. She blew air out of her cheeks. Fern was right. Babies were a heap of trouble.

Amos walked Ira out to his wagon, chatted for a while, waved goodbye to him, and practically bumped right into Fern as he turned around to head to the house. Where had she come from? A gust of wind swept in and knocked his hat off. As he bent to pick it up, he remembered something he hadn't thought of for a long while. As a child, he thought of the wind as a person with many different voices, somebody you never quite got to know very well because it would arrive without warning and then leave just as suddenly. A lot like Fern. "Oh, didn't see you there. Sorry about that."

"What did Ira want to talk to you about?"

Amos frowned. "Fern, if Ira wanted the world to know what was on his mind, he would've just stayed in the kitchen."

She ignored him. "Was he asking about Gid and Sadie?"

Amos lifted his eyebrows. "How did you know that?"

"He's talking about Gid and Sadie getting married, isn't he? And soon."

How did Fern seem to know things without being told? It was unnerving. Nailing shingles to a twister would be simple compared to understanding Fern Graber. "Maybe."

Now it was Fern's turn to frown. "Well, Gideon Smucker better have himself another think." She turned and looked at the house. Will was following M.K. up the porch steps and into the farmhouse.

Amos was annoyed. Fern thought she knew his own daughter better than he did. "Sadie is too young to be thinking about marriage, but Gideon Smucker is a good fellow. He's crazy about Sadie. Always has been. And last fall, Sadie didn't seem to mind having Gid around here."

"That was then and this is now," Fern said enigmatically.

Amos sighed with the old frustration of this conversation. It bothered him when she spoke in puzzles. Why couldn't women just say what they meant? Be clear and to the point. Instead, he often felt like he was chasing a tumbleweed on a windy day.

She turned and looked right at him. "What kinds of things were you going to have the bird boy do around the farm?"

"The bird boy? Oh, you mean Will. Plowing, mostly. Help with chores, I suppose."

"He doesn't have any farm experience."

"What makes you say that?"

"His hands. Too soft. They're not even calloused."

Amos looked down at his own hands. Rough, large, a few small scars.

"You've got to get that bird boy busy."

"He is busy! M.K. keeps dragging him into the house to settle down the crying baby. And he seems to be the only one who can do it."

"That's not the kind of busy I mean. You've got to keep him outside, away from the house."

Amos heaved a stretched-to-the-limits sigh. "Fern, what exactly are you getting at?"

"Have you seen the way he looks at Sadie? He's paying too much attention to her."

No, Amos hadn't noticed that. A more mismatched pair than Sadie and Will would be hard to imagine. He hardly knew Will—he had given his permission to let him stay at Windmill Farm solely because of the game warden's request. But he didn't think Will was untrustworthy, the way Fern assumed all English to be. Maybe a little immature and misguided, according to what Mahlon Miller had told him, but not a bad apple. And as for Sadie having more than a casual interest in Will? Well, Amos had faith in his daughter's judgment. "Sadie has a good head on her shoulders. Surely, she wouldn't be drawn away by this boy."

Fern gave him a look as if he were a very small child. She spoke slowly and carefully. "Have you seen the way she blushes when she's around him?" She shook her head. "Sparks are starting to fly."

"What?"

"Whenever you see a person's face turn red, you know something is up."

Would that also pertain to Ira Smucker's ears? he wanted to ask. *And what did Ira mean about seeing you on Saturday?*

The kitchen door opened, squeaking on its hinge. Their attention turned to see Sadie and Will, laughing over something.

Fern stepped forward, arms akimbo, like a teapot with two handles. "Keep that bird boy busy."

Could Fern be right? She usually was. He worried suddenly that Sadie might have so little experience with men that she would be easy prey for somebody like Will. He would have to keep an eye out. But then again, she might be misreading the situation. He knew Fern was suspicious of all English folk. Maybe she was just overreacting. Amos watched Fern pass Will, talk to him for a brief moment, point to Amos, then head to the house.

Will walked up to him. "Fern said you wanted to talk to me."

Amos blew air out of his mouth. Ah, Fern. She had a way of making things happen. "Will, have you ever plowed? With a horse, I mean. Not with a tractor."

Will's eyebrows shot up in alarm. "Plowed? Uh, no. Not with a horse. Not with a tractor, either." His smile drooped.

Amos put a hand on his shoulder. "Well, Monday morning, first thing, you are going to learn. Meet me at the north pasture at dawn. The soil will be just right after last night's drenching rain. Moist, but not too wet."

"Dawn?" Will scratched his head. "That's actually the time of day that's best for birding. The game warden wants a list made up of all invasive birds on the property."

Amos nodded. "As soon as you're done with your bird list, you come find me and we'll get you started." He patted Will on the back and strode off to the barn, enjoying the startled look on the boy's face. If Will Stoltz thought his Sadie was a girl to pursue, he needed to think again. Then his grin faded as he pondered Fern's comment that Sadie would turn down Gid's interest. And that she might be growing sweet on this English boy. Why were women so complicated?

It was a miracle. As soon as the baby drank his first bottle of goat's milk, he stared at Sadie as if he couldn't quite believe she had taken so long to figure that one out, then he finished the bottle, closed his eyes, and fell into a deep, restful sleep. Sadie gazed at the sleeping infant—the perfection of round cheeks, peach fuzz on his head, minuscule ears. She touched the bottom of a tiny foot, and the toes curled. "Really, he's a beautiful baby when he's not doing all that wailing."

"I made another list of name suggestions, Sadie," M.K. said, coming over to Sadie with two still warm-from-the-oven chocolate chip cookies in her hand.

Sadie broke off half of one cookie and took a bite. "No more palindromes."

M.K. shook her head. "Even better. Onomatopoeia—call him Ono. Allegory—we can call him Al. Hyperbole—shorten it to Hi."

"Joseph," Sadie said decidedly. She reached out to break off another piece of cookie.

M.K. tilted her head. "Menno's middle name?"

Sadie took another bite of cookie. "We can call him Joe."

M.K. put the cookie in her hand on the table and stooped down to peer at the baby in the basket. "Joe sounds too old. Can we call him Baby Joe? Or Joe-Jo?"

Sadie put a hand out to grab the cookie and Fern covered her wrist, holding it there until she released it.

"Joseph it is," Fern said. "And now, Sadie, you need to get back to work. Whenever you start eating nonstop, it's your stomach's way of telling your brain that you are fretting and need more on your mind." She pointed to a stack of books on the counter. "M.K. and I picked those up from the library. You've got to keep up your healing work. You don't want to forget all that you learned from Deborah Yoder."

Ever since Sadie had helped cool down an overheated girl at a barbecue, Fern was convinced that Sadie was a natural healer. Gifted, she said, and Fern didn't hand out compliments like candy. Sadie was less convinced of her talent. She had loved working beside Deborah, helping people with discomfort or ailments. She was fascinated by the use of herbs to help people. It seemed to Sadie that God had planned all along for plants to provide gifts of healing, and he was just waiting for someone to discover those secrets. But there was so much still to learn, and being responsible for others was always a worry.

But she couldn't deny that she needed more on her mind. Since the moment she had returned home, she was forever eating or thinking about eating. It wouldn't be long before she gained all of that weight back. Over the last year, she had worked so hard to keep food in the right place in her life—she knew it was a good thing in the right portions, meant to nourish her body, but her mind needed a different kind of nourishment. Fern had helped her to see the difference. Sadie had made such improvements in her eating habits—eating only when she was hungry—yet here she was, right back to fretful snacking.

Sadie ran a finger along the book titles: *Home Remedies, Common Sense Cures.* She slid into a chair and opened one of the books to a page about kidney stones. "Fern, do you think I'm capable of learning all there is to know?"

Fern leaned toward Sadie, her expression serious. "I know you are. But what's more important, Sadie, is for you to know you are. Nix gewogt, nix gewunne." *Nothing ventured, nothing gained.*

Swallowing, Sadie offered one slow nod.

"Ira Smucker didn't sneeze once after you gave him the honeycomb. Early this morning, Orin Yoder saw me at the phone shanty and asked if I knew what to do with canker sores. He said he suffers from them continually. I told him I'd ask you if you had a cure."

"I do, actually. Old Deborah taught me how to treat them. Just make a paste of alum and put it on the sore."

"Well, Sadie. What are you waiting for? I think you have your first client."

A slow exhalation shivered out of Sadie. Ready or not, her healing work was about to begin.

Will felt as if he had been waylaid, a crosscut blow from the front, a kick from the back. He was minding his own business, walking out of the house, and the housekeeper trapped him into attending church. He had barely recovered from that blow when the farmer commandeered him into plowing fields. The invitations were loaded with obvious intention. Will knew the drill. Hadn't he spent years trying to avoid both? Hard work and church.

He let his mind do a rapid rewind, racing backward. He hadn't meant to get sucked into an invitation to church, but Fern caught him off guard. He had been feeling pleased with himself for being so useful as a baby calmer-downer and, suddenly, *wham!* She asked him what church he planned to attend while he was staying on the property. When he gave her a blank look, *wham!* She told him he could come with them and to be ready at 7:00 a.m. Sharp.

He thought he was smarter than these only-up-to-an-eighth-grade-education Amish. Ha! Pride goeth before a fall. It was one of those proverbs that his father told him, a few thousand times. And boy oh boy, was he ever falling a lot lately.

A month ago, Will had just received an acceptance to University of

Pennsylvania's medical school—the same place where his father was a teaching professor and had a practice at the university hospital. Will was within a few short months of graduating from college. His future looked bright. It was all going according to plan.

Then it all fell apart. *Whoosh!* One fell swoop.

Two weeks ago, Will had been tinkering around on his computer with Sean, one of his fraternity friends, and hacked into the college's registrar site. Sean was delighted—he quickly got into his files and improved his recorded grades. Will didn't touch his own file, but then again, he didn't need to. He was a straight-A student. He was going to graduate at the top of his class.

It didn't take long for someone in the registrar's office to get suspicious when Sean, a C student, normally teetering on academic probation, asked for his transcript to be sent to Harvard to accompany his application for law school. Sean was called in for questioning, cracked immediately, and sent them off in Will's direction.

Will had been suspended for the semester and lost his acceptance to medical school. Something about ethics. Something about making Will an example to others.

Will had tried to explain it all to his father, but he wouldn't listen to any excuses. His father had always felt Will didn't think before he acted and that was hard to deny. But in this particular case, Will didn't do anything wrong. Sean did. But Will had never been able to win any kind of dispute with his father. Dr. Stoltz owned the truth, pure and simple.

Then his father told him that he had already made plans for Will's spring and summer, that Will needed to learn how to work—to work hard, to fully appreciate the opportunity he had blown. His car would be sold, his monthly allowance cut off. Will was going to be an intern for a game warden in Lancaster County. If Will didn't mess up, then his father might consider paying for that final semester of college so that he could at least graduate and get back on track.

Whose track? Will wanted to shout, but he held back. Even he wasn't that big of a fool as to back talk his father. You didn't do that. No one did.

Still, Will was so outraged by his father's controlling demands that he stormed out of the house. He would move away, get a job, and figure out the rest of his life without a penny from his father! He sought out his fraternity friends for consolation. He spent the evening drinking away his woes with them, and ended the night with an unexpected twist: a brake light on his car was out—the very car his father was going to take back to the dealer in the morning— and he was pulled over by a police officer. Just a routine check, the officer said, but then he sniffed the air and asked if Will had been drinking any alcohol that evening. Will spent the next few hours drying out in the bowels of a Philadelphia lockup. By dawn, Will had made two decisions: one, he was not going to let his father know about this DUI, no matter what it would take. And two, he was going to spend the next few months interning for the game warden.

But he never expected *this*. To be plunked in the middle of an Amish farm. No car. No money. No television. No internet access. Not even a radio. He did have his cell phone, but he had to stand in certain high spots on the farm to get reception.

He gazed around the farm. He was sure the game warden had told his father about this latest development by now. Will could just imagine the delight on his father's face. And what would he do if he learned that Will was plowing fields? Even better . . . he was spreading them with manure! His father would break out a bottle of his finest champagne. He would dance a jig.

Will wanted to quit this ridiculous bird-sitting/field-hand job. He could. There was just that sticky little problem with the law that he needed to keep under his father's radar. He had two options: he could quit, but then he would have to face his father. Or he could stay, but he'd have to figure out how to actually do the job. Like, how to plow a field. And go to an Amish church service.

Hard to say which option was more frightening.

9

The hymn ended on a long note, the voices echoing from the rafters. Then, with a wave of his hand, the Vorsinger brought the singing to an end. Sadie drew a deep breath and sat down, hoping Joe-Jo would sleep through the service. She glanced across the large kitchen to catch sight of Will. He was seated next to Amos, about midway among the men's benches. He squirmed on the hard, backless bench. Their eyes met, and he silently mouthed, "How long does this last?"

"Three," she mouthed back.

He couldn't understand her so she held up three fingers.

His eyes widened in alarm. "Three hours?" he mouthed.

She gave a slight nod of her head, just as Fern jabbed her in the side with her pointy elbow.

From her other side, M.K. jabbed her. "Don't look now, but Gid's watching you."

Of course, Sadie's gaze shifted immediately to Gid. He was squinting at her as if he wondered what was going on in her head. Could he tell? She had no idea. Her thoughts and emotions were all over the map, like they didn't know where to land.

He had a look on his face that touched her. It was so sweet and so sad and so filled with love. She melted like butter. Then she stopped herself. *Don't you go soft on him, Sadie Lapp,* she told herself. *He's the one who believes the lies about me.* She turned her head and lifted her chin, a silent signal to him that she was still upset. She knew Gid was sensitive enough that he would feel her emotion, as real as if she had shouted.

Sadie sensed, more than saw, an icy glare aimed in her direction. Out of the corner of her eye, Esther, the deacon's wife, was watching her. With her salt-and-pepper hair and delicate features, Esther could have been pretty, but there was something off about her. Her mouth, Sadie decided. She looked like she'd just spit out something that tasted awful.

The baby let out a yawn. One eye was open in a squint, like a pirate, as if he was halfway in between waking and sleeping. That worried Sadie and she shifted him in her lap, which caused both of his eyes to pop open.

Fern glanced at the baby, then at Sadie. "If he starts his yammering, take him outside."

"Can't you do it?" Sadie whispered.

"No," Fern said, her eyes fixed on Ruthie's father, the new minister, who had just stood up to preach after a long and quiet interchange among the ministers and bishop as to who would begin.

Joe-Jo let out a squeak and Sadie sighed. Ruthie's father took his new responsibilities very seriously, especially preaching. In just a few months, he was getting a reputation of being the most long-winded, dry-boned preacher Stoney Ridge had ever heard.

Sadie turned to M.K. "Will you take a turn with the baby?"

"Not a chance," M.K. whispered. "Babies don't like me."

The baby's face turned red as he started to strain. Oh no. This was worse than Sadie had feared. Sure enough, Joe-Jo's lower regions emitted a horrible gurgling sound, then a sour tangy odor wafted around her. The women in the bench in front of Sadie turned back to look at her as if they had never heard a baby make such noises. M.K. pinched her nose. Worse still, the baby let out a howl. Once, then twice.

Sadie jumped up and scurried out the side door with him, then rushed to the barn, far from the house so the baby wouldn't disturb the service. Inside, she plunked down on a bench against a wall. Sadie searched the barn. A row of cows munched contentedly from hay boxes, and a bird peeked over the edge of a nest snug against the rafters. Other than that, the barn was empty.

As she was rooting through the makeshift diaper bag to find a fresh diaper, she heard a door slam shut. She leaned forward on the bench and looked out through the open barn door. Will strode down the porch steps that led out into the sunshiny yard and straight toward her. A cat trotted ahead of him, tail sticking up as straight as a poker. The cat glanced back now and then as if to make sure he was still following. Sadie couldn't help but smile.

Will came into the barn and blinked rapidly as his eyes adjusted to the cool, dim light. He grinned broadly when he spotted Sadie, snatching off his hat to reveal a thick thatch of sun-streaked hair. "Thought you might need some help quieting the baby," he said cheerfully. "Is the goat's milk helping with his colic?"

"I think so," Sadie said. She felt her cheeks start to pink up and tried to will them to stop. She glanced over at the farmhouse, hoping that no one in the house could look out the window and see them. "He hasn't had a big crying jag since yesterday morning."

He patted the gray mare that stuck her head over the stall for affection. "Is this service really going to last three hours?"

She nodded. "Fern should have warned you."

Will grinned. "I have a feeling she intentionally kept that to herself."

No doubt, Sadie thought. Fern seemed to have taken an instant disliking to Will, and Sadie wasn't sure why.

"And it's all in that language?"

"Two languages, really. The preachers preach in Penn Dutch, but when they quote Scripture, it's in High German."

"So you're fluent in three languages?" He let out a whistle. "I can barely manage English."

She smiled. "All the Amish know three languages." She put a blanket down on the bench and placed the baby on top to start the preparations to change his diaper. She hoped Will would take the hint and go back to the farmhouse before someone noticed them.

He didn't. He sat across from her on a hay bale and stretched one long leg. "Sure is a beautiful day. I'd just as soon pay my respects to the Almighty outside than in a stuffy house." He grinned at her. "Did you see that mouse scurry along the walls? My mother would have screamed to high heaven if she saw that." He started in on a rambling story about going to church as a child, and at some point Sadie stopped listening and just started to change the baby's diaper. If the smell and sight didn't bother him, then she wouldn't let it worry her. She was rattled enough by the presence of Will. She knew she shouldn't pass more time with him, especially here, at Sunday church.

They'd scarcely met, yet she felt . . . tingly. Confused. Undeniably impressed by his strong presence and protective ways. His thoughtfulness. And, she admitted, his deep voice and warm looks disturbed her in a thrilling way. Was this how it started? You fell for someone because of the tilt of his smile, or because he could make you laugh, or in this case, because he made you feel as if the two of you shared a special connection. With a jerk, she stopped herself from that line of thinking. *Oh, Sadie Lapp, this isn't good. This isn't good at all.* She was *not* starting anything with Will Stoltz.

She wrapped the yucky diaper in a plastic bag and stuffed it into the diaper bag. Then she brought out the bottle of goat's milk.

Will, still talking, stopped midsentence. "Want me to feed him? I'm not so good with diapers, but I can feed a baby." He reached out his hands for the baby.

"Will," she started, then hesitated. "You should probably get back into the service."

"Why?" he asked, looking genuinely surprised. "I thought I'd keep you company."

Sadie winced. "It doesn't look right for us to spend time together."

Will scoffed. "That's ridiculous! We're just two friends, talking on a spring morning."

How could Sadie phrase this in a way a non-Amish boy could understand? "It's not just a spring morning. It's a Sunday morning. A churchgoing morning. The best day of the week. A morning of worshiping God, an afternoon of friendship. Heart and soul—Sundays are meant to fill you up. And the young men don't talk to the young women. At least not until later in the day, after lunch."

Will was stunned. "You're pulling my leg."

She shook her head.

"And lunch too? So we're not just heading home after the three hours?"

He looked so woebegone that she nearly laughed out loud. Some of her shyness left her.

"You'll enjoy the lunch."

"Will you sit with me?"

"Oh no! No, no, no. You'll eat with the men. The men eat first. The women and children eat later."

That shocked him even more. "So . . . many . . . rules."

"Oh, you don't know the half of it!"

"Does it bother you? All those rules?" He lifted his knee. "Rules bother me."

Somehow, that didn't surprise her. "When you grow up with these rules, you don't even think twice about them. It's just the way it's always been."

He looked at her. "Maybe that's the problem. Folks don't think enough about the rules. Maybe the rules need to be streamlined a little." He made an axing motion in the air. "You know, simplify things."

A male cardinal whistled from a branch on the tree outside the open barn door, catching Sadie's eye. The little bird was strutting along the branch, hoping to woo a mate. "I suppose our life may seem complicated to an outsider, but to us, the rules are supposed to create simplicity. We don't have to worry about what to wear or what fancy car to buy."

"You don't get many choices, though."

"No, but we don't have as many problems that come with choices, either."

"Like what?"

"Like . . . debt."

He jerked his head toward her, as if she hit a sore spot. "Touché." He stood up to leave. "Well, I'd better get back inside so I don't tarnish your sterling reputation." He winked at her and sauntered back to the house, slow and easy.

Her sterling reputation? She supposed it might seem that way to him, but from the cool reception she received this morning from some of the women, it didn't feel like a sterling reputation. She felt quite tarnished. On an ordinary morning before the church service started, Sadie and her friends clustered to share the latest news. Over by the horses, the young men clumped together, smacking one another on the back, shifting their gaze toward the girls, bragging about the number of calves or lambs or pigs born on their farm since last Sunday's church.

Today, however, Sadie was not welcomed into the circle like she usually was, like she hoped to be after returning home from a long stay in Berlin. A few faithful friends ventured over to get a glimpse of the baby. No sooner did they ooh and aah over the baby but their mothers captured their arms and escorted them straight up to the farmhouse without giving them a chance to say a word. Her throat tightened, recalling the embarrassment of those moments when a few others sent supercilious looks of disapproval her way. She felt the needles of a hundred eyes on her, and every whisper held her name. How could things have changed so quickly? For the first time in her life, she knew of no rule that could tell her how to behave.

A plain brown female cardinal flew close to the red male, clearly intrigued. The male did a little smug hop, drawing closer to the female. That boy got just what he was after, Sadie realized, with his dashing red feathers and bold whistle.

Will returned to the farmhouse and tried to slip back to his seat on the bench next to Amos and Hank without being too obtrusive, but he moved a hymnal to sit down and accidentally dropped it. He was sure that every single person in the room turned to look at him, stunned. Was he the first person to ever drop a hymnal?

The preacher was still preaching, in a language Will couldn't understand, and he didn't know how he was going to be able to sit still for at least two more hours. Maybe he shouldn't have asked Sadie how long this service lasted. Maybe it would be better not to know. He glanced at others around him and wondered who they all were, what their lives were like. Did they act this pure and pious all the time? The woman in the far corner on the left with those two daughters—did they ever fight? Did her husband ever forget her birthday? Did he ever make harsh, sarcastic remarks to their children?

He watched the minister wave his arms expansively as he delivered his sermon. He gazed meditatively at the church members, first the men, then he turned to face the women. Did that minister enjoy a good joke? Had he ever gotten drunk and given anybody a black eye? Cursed? Did he ever have a lustful thought?

Or what about the plain little man sitting in front of Will? He looked pretty timid, but maybe he drank and smoked on Saturday nights. Across the room, next to Fern, was a woman with three young children. The little boy, probably one or two years old, had received numerous pokes from his sisters seated on either side. Now he moved over to sit on his mother's lap.

Will looked at Mary Kate, whose chin was lifted high and eyes were darting around the room. He wondered what went through that busy mind of hers. Sadie told him he had no idea how many rules governed their lives. How could someone like M.K. ever be satisfied with this strict Amish life? It seemed to him that every day looked like the day before, and the day after.

After a while, Sadie came inside and wedged between M.K. and Fern. The baby must have fallen asleep, because Will saw Sadie tuck him into the basket by her feet. He watched her for a while, mesmerized. The more time he spent with her, the more attractive she became to him, with her soft light hair, the long neck, those eyes the color of an azure sky. Will wondered if she knew she was pretty. He doubted it. She seemed terribly naïve. How would someone as pure and innocent as Sadie ever survive in the cruel world?

He almost smiled at the irony of his thoughts. From one family came M.K., who seemed like the type who would want to push every envelope: Draw a line and watch me cross it! And then there was Sadie, who saw the rules of the church as comforting, the way a snug seat belt in a car is meant for your protection. How could two sisters begin at the same spot but end up as such different individuals?

As soon as the church service ended, it was as if someone had fired a warning shot. The young boys in the back rows all leaped into action, crowding into the aisle and bursting out the door to soak up the sunshine. Gideon Smucker stepped into the aisle to let the boys gallop past him. He wanted to try to get a moment alone with Sadie, but Fern stood next to her like a mother bear shielding her cub. Before the service started, Gid had watched a few girls snub Sadie. He thought he had seen tears in Sadie's eyes. His own eyes stung in sympathy. How could he fix this?

When their eyes met, she grew flustered and pivoted away. He tried to draw near to her as she was heading to the kitchen to join the women. He raised his eyes and let himself feast on her for just a few seconds. Strands of loose hair fluttered across her cheek. He could hardly resist touching her cheek and smoothing back a wisp of hair. Twice, he opened his mouth to speak; both times, words failed him. *I love you, Sadie!* he called out silently. *Do you love me? Just a little?* But, of course, she didn't hear him. And after that, Sadie avoided looking at him. Discouraged, he decided he would just make up a feeble excuse about needing to get home and skip lunch altogether.

"Gideon Smucker! You hold up there a minute."

Stifling a groan at the sound of Fern's voice, Gid came to a halt just as he reached the door.

Fern's stern frown sent folks scuttling out of her way. "I need your help with something. There's a young fellow staying at Windmill Farm to babysit the falcons. His name is Will Stoltz and I want you to sit with him for lunch."

Gid looked over at the English fellow. He was standing on the outskirts of a group of Amish men who were milling about, discussing the weather. "He looks like he's got plenty of company."

"That's the truth. He does seem to make friends easily. Sure does buzz around Sadie."

Gid had noticed Will Stoltz had hopped right outside when Sadie had gone out from the service with the baby. What was Fern trying to say—that Will Stoltz was interested in Sadie? Or could Sadie be interested in him? Not possible!

"I'll eat with him," he told Fern. *I'll keep him away from Sadie*, was what he meant. He slammed his hat onto his head and charged out the door.

The lightning bugs were out in full force. Sadie sat on the swing in the backyard and listened to the night sounds. The last few nights, after settling the baby down, she had started coming outside to pray. There was something about being under the open sky, she found, that made it easier to put her thoughts into prayers. She had a lot to pray about these days. She felt an urgent decision bearing down on her. "Lord, this can't all be for nothing," she cried aloud.

"What's for nothing?"

She spun around and saw a flicker of light from the far end of the back porch. The flicker became a glow, accompanied by a ribbon of aromatic smoke. Uncle Hank's deep chuckle resonated in the night. He smoked a pipe every so often, but rarely before witnesses. "Did you think it was the

Lord Almighty answering you back?" Another chuckle. "Well, Sadie, come on over here and join me since you're up."

Sadie made her way to the edge of the porch, where Uncle Hank sat in one of two rickety straight-back chairs. Sadie sank into the second chair, smiling when a barn cat stretched out her paws and meowed in greeting.

A thin band of smoke circled Uncle Hank as gentle puffs rose from the pipe's bowl, flavoring the air. The smoky scent was sweet, earthy, manly. Uncle Hank took a draw on the pipe, creating a soft glow in the bowl, and blew the smoke toward the ceiling. "I'm quitting soon. Real soon. Maybe tomorrow. Maybe next week. But in the meantime, I'd appreciate it if you didn't tell Fern about this. You know how she thinks I'm going to burn the porch off the house one of these times."

"Your secret is safe with me," Sadie said.

"Want to tell me what's keeping you awake?"

Sadie let out a deep sigh. "If you don't mind, I'd rather not." She didn't have to say anything. He knew. People underestimated Uncle Hank, and he liked to keep it that way—he often said it was comforting to have such low expectations placed on him—but Sadie knew he grasped the heart of important matters in a way few others did.

"Don't take a few mean-spirited remarks to heart, Sadie. NOSIR. There will always be folks that behave like a flock of chickens, peckin' on the one they see as the weakest."

Sadie nodded. She had witnessed the hens' ill-treatment of one poor bird in the coop—the one M.K. named Toot. Sadie's heart stirred with pity each time she glimpsed that bedraggled, skinny hen huddling in the corner of the coop. She had tried to rescue it and raise it as a pet in the barn, but Toot kept escaping and heading right back to the coop. In a way, Sadie thought she understood Toot's logic. That poor hen would rather be with her friends, pecked at and heckled, than be without them.

10

Will Stoltz had never worked so hard in all his life. On Monday morning, Amos set him behind two harnessed-up chestnut Belgians with white manes. They carried the odd names of Rosemary and Lavender, the gentlest, biggest beasts known to mankind. When he asked how the horses got their names, Amos said that he always allowed his children the privilege of naming the animals. Julia named the cats, Menno named the dogs, M.K. named the chickens, and Sadie named the horses. All of the horses had names of herbs or spices, he explained, because that was Sadie's main interest. The newest buggy horse was named Cayenne. Now, that was a name that needed no explanation. Will had already noticed Cayenne, pawing away in her stall like she was trying to break free.

Amos promised him that plowing the field would be as easy as dragging a spoon through pudding with the help of these two mighty Belgians. "You'll have it done in no time!" he said, patting Will on the back as he turned to leave him. Rosemary and Lavender dragged the plow back and forth, turning the ground over, exposing rich, dark soil. Thick as it was, only the horses' combined strength made the task bearable. After turning the plow in the opposite direction, Will's arms felt shaky. Like they might rattle right off. He was pretty sure his arms would go completely numb before he finished this field. If, that is, he ever finished. He might expire right here, in the middle of a field, and not be found until the buzzards circled over him.

But there were worse things than having to deal with two gigantic horses and a plow all day—like having to deal with his own problems. He couldn't believe it when he heard his cell phone ring in his pocket. He groaned, recognizing the ringtone he had set for Mr. Petosky—a startling alarm. How was it possible to get extremely sketchy service on this farm, but whenever Mr. Petosky happened to call, he seemed to be in just the right spot for it to come through? He stopped the horses and sat down on the plow to answer the phone. "I thought we had an agreement that you would wait until I called with updates."

"So sue me," Mr. Petosky said. "Any activity with those birds? Are you scouting them out?"

"Yep, morning, noon, and night," Will said. He looked up and saw Adam fly over the cherry orchard, off in the distance. Or was it Eve? It was hard to spot the difference in size without his binoculars. "Look, you're going to have to be patient. You can't rush nature."

"Think it's going to work?" Mr. Petosky asked. "Are they sticking around?"

"I think so. The falcons like this farm. The female is staying close to the scape. Wouldn't surprise me if she lays her clutch this week."

"Good. Good. Keep an eye on those birds."

Will had sensed from the beginning that Mr. Petosky had a lot more interest in these rare birds than he let on. "That's what I've been doing, Mr. Petosky," he said, his voice thin on patience.

"Well, I'm just trying to give you some tips, that's all," Mr. Petosky said. "How do you like living out there in the boonies?"

"It's not the boonies." Will looked around, praying no one would come by.

Mr. Petosky snorted. "Don't tell me you're starting to enjoy living with those kooks."

"They're not kooks, Mr. Petosky. They're a very nice family." Probably the kindest people Will had ever met. "They're not like you think."

That only got Mr. Petosky laughing out loud. "Imagine that! Will Stoltz, trust fund kid, bound for medical school until he gets himself kicked out of college—"

"Suspended. There's a difference."

"—trying to pay off his lawyer to get rid of his DUI before his old man hears about it—imagine a kid like you wanting to be Amish."

"I never said I wished I were Amish. I only said these are nice people."

Will was irritated now. "Look, Mr. Petosky, if there's nothing else you need from me right now, I really need to get back to work."

"That's fine, kid. Just remember that June 16 is right around the corner."

Will heard the click of a hang up.

Rosemary and Lavender looked at him with their big brown eyes and long eyelashes, wondering what he wanted. *What do I want?* he thought as he shook the reins to get the gentle giants moving. *What in the world do I really want?* Life here was nothing like Philadelphia, but he felt just as lost.

When Gid returned to the house after school let out on Monday, he wasn't surprised to find the deacon, Abraham, sitting on the back porch with his father, sipping iced tea. That sight was nothing new. The ministers and bishop and deacon often had church problems that needed discussing. Long conversations, looking at the problem from every angle, trying to find solutions that were fair and just and pleasing to God. So as to not interrupt them, Gid went through the side door and washed up at the kitchen sink. The back door was left open and he heard Abraham say, "This is on shaky ground, Ira. There's no real cut-and-dry answer."

"But you wouldn't ask him to quit, would you? If he married her in six weeks' time?" He heard his father let out an exasperated sigh. "He loves teaching, you see."

Gid grabbed a dishrag and took a step closer to the door.

Abraham took awhile to respond. "I heard of one community that let the fellow continue teaching because the pupils wouldn't have to shun him, seeing as how they aren't baptized." Gid heard Abraham settle back in his chair. "But most would make him stop until he was a member again in good standing."

Gid leaned against the door. He thought something like this might be stirring after receiving a few chilly receptions in church yesterday. Before lunch was served, he had walked up to his friends, deep in conversation, and they suddenly stopped talking, looked uncomfortable, and the circle broke up. If this was how he had been treated, how must Sadie be feeling? His heart went out to her. He wasn't going to let her face this alone. He threw down the dishrag and went out to the porch.

Abraham looked up when he saw Gid and smiled, standing up to welcome him. The deacon was shorter than Gid by several inches. He reached out and gripped his hand firmly. "Have a seat, please," Abraham said, and he waited until Gid had sat down before he took the chair facing him. Gid was reminded of how he felt when he met with the ministers about becoming baptized, and in a sense he supposed that was what this was all about.

Abraham steepled his fingers together, as if praying before he began to speak. "I take it you heard what we're talking about?"

Gid nodded.

"A child is always a good thing. We thank God for bringing this little boy into our lives. But we need to make things right for this child." He glanced at Gid. "Just because a marriage starts off on the wrong foot doesn't mean it can't find its right path." The deacon crossed one leg over the other and set his Bible on top of his thigh, both hands resting on it. "So, your father tells me you are willing to make a confession that you have sinned. Is that true?"

Gid nodded. He could make a confession like that. He definitely could. He knew he was a sinner. Didn't his thoughts often wander down slippery paths?

Abraham clapped his palms together, pleased. "So then, I will ask the bishop if we could let you keep on teaching."

Ira asked Abraham a question and the two went back and forth for a while. Gid was beginning to breathe more easily now that he realized that he probably wouldn't be called on to do much talking.

Abraham turned to Gid. "And after six weeks' proving time, then the bann will be lifted, and you can marry." He clapped his hands together. "And then . . . a fresh start!"

Ira gazed at Gid, waiting for him to respond to Abraham. But what could he say? If he objected to getting put back or marrying Sadie so quickly, he would be betraying her. "What I mean," Gid started, "is that . . ." but then he couldn't think of what to say or how to say it. This was what he hated so much about conversations in which he was forced to participate. He could never end his part right. He was always trailing off lamely and leaving thoughts unfinished. Maybe he should suggest using pencil and paper for a conversation sometime. He was sure he could come across better if he could write his responses. Or better still, if he could find the words in the works of Shakespeare or Wordsworth, and they could speak for him. But that wouldn't really be addressing the heart of this dilemma. He didn't need Shakespearean language for that.

There were a few things Gid knew for certain about himself: He wasn't the life of the party. He didn't enjoy casual conversations, like striking up conversations with people standing next to him in a grocery line or at the hardware store. In fact, he couldn't remember ever doing such a thing. He didn't make friends easily or quickly. He knew those things about himself. But he was loyal to a fault. When he loved someone, he would stick by to the bitter end.

Abraham was waiting for his answer. Fumbling to speak, he blurted out, "I want to make things right for Sadie."

Abraham stood. "Well, then. I guess that's that." As he passed Gid, he placed a hand on his head like he was giving him a blessing.

Gid looked at his father. "That's it?"

Ira leaned back in his chair and sighed, relieved. "That's it."

Will Stoltz felt muscles he never knew he had. After putting the plow upright in the barn with the other tools, Amos told him that now he should spread manure from the compost pile over the field he had just plowed. Shoveling manure atop the field took the rest of the afternoon. Oh, how his father would relish that sight! The way Will's luck was going lately, he was surprised the game warden hadn't dropped by to check on the falcons while Will was knee-deep in manure.

Thinking of the game warden reminded him that he had better hurry to go observe the falcons at dusk. He hadn't spotted any eggs in the scape, but any day now, he was sure one would appear. Hopefully, more than one. A niggling doubt poked at him, but he pushed it away. He *wasn't* doing anything wrong. Not technically.

As he left the barn, he saw a horse and buggy pull up the drive. He shielded his eyes from the western sun and thought he saw Sadie in the driver's side. He smiled. His luck was turning.

Will met Sadie as she pulled the buggy to a stop. He opened the door to help her down. "Where have you been?"

"To the store. I left a few things there." She reached into the backseat to get a couple of packages of cloth diapers. "And Fern says it's time to switch this baby from paper diapers to cloth." She wrinkled her nose. "I was a little disappointed to hear that." Then she got a whiff of Will. "Why, you're as dirty as a peasant in a mud puddle. What have you been doing today?"

"Your dad got me plowing." Will pointed over to the field. He was proud of his work. Palm on his forehead, he heaved a mighty sigh. He opened his palm and looked at it. His hand was filled with blisters. So was the other hand.

"Oh no! Will, didn't you use gloves?"

"Believe it or not, I did."

"You've got some serious blisters there, and more coming."

"They're not all that bad. I was just pouring some water over them when you arrived. They actually feel much better now." More likely, his hands had lost all feeling. His arms hadn't lost that shaky feeling, as if he were still plowing.

She looked at him as if she didn't believe him. "You'd better come up to the house. I'll fix something up for those poor red hands of yours. I have just the thing to speed up their healing." When he hesitated, she added, "You'll be sorry tomorrow if you don't let me help you now."

"I've got to get out to the falcons before the sun sets." He looked down at her. Strands of hair fluttered across her cheek. Automatically, he reached over and used the back of his fingers to tuck them behind her ear. A slight blush stained her cheeks, which charmed him. She was so unlike the girls he had known. "I'll stop by later, after you all have supper, if that's okay."

Side by side, they strolled toward the house. Mouthwatering aromas wafted from the house and Will's stomach rumbled. Sadie glanced up at the house, then back to Will. "Join us for supper."

Will winced. "I'm not so sure your housekeeper would want that. She isn't too fond of me."

"Don't mind Fern. At first, she can be as prickly as a jar of toothpicks. It takes awhile for her to warm up to folks. But she does love to feed people. We eat at six."

His stomach rumbled again, louder this time. Sadie's lips parted and laughter spilled out of her.

Will smiled. "Then I'll be back in an hour."

Amos barely had one leg out the door of the Mennonite taxi as Fern peppered him with questions about his appointment with the cardiologist. This was exactly why he refused to let her accompany him to the doctor, even though it was clear he had ruffled her feathers. She promised she would stay in the waiting room, but he knew she would somehow worm her way into the doctor's office with a laundry list of questions. He was a grown man, for goodness' sake!

"So what did he say? Is there trouble brewing?"

She had such a worried look on her face that he felt himself softening. It was nice, really, to have someone fuss over him. He closed the car door and waved goodbye to the driver. "Everything's fine, Fern. Just fine."

"Fine, as in Fern Graber's version of fine, or in Amos Lapp's version?"

The sweet moment between them fizzled. What was *that* supposed to mean? "Fine as in everybody's version of fine." He started to walk toward the house.

She caught up with him. "Did he give you every test for rejection? Stress tests, biopsies?"

"He gave me every test known to man. I have no blood left. I've been completely drained by those sharp needles. And it took all day long!" That's what annoyed him about being sick, most of all. Losing time for his farm. He glanced over at the field he had put in Will Stoltz's care. He cocked his head and squinted his eyes. The furrows should be straight, like a ruler; Will's furrows wove like a ribbon of rickrack.

"If everything is so fine, then why are you feeling so tired and wrung out?"

Amos glanced at her. Should he tell her? She was peering into his face, concern written in her eyes. She was waiting for him to explain. He looked past her to the setting sun, dropping low behind the pines that framed the house to the west. "The doctor thinks my problem is I haven't grieved for Menno."

She tilted her head.

"He thinks so much happened, so fast, that I just put off my grieving for my boy. And now, it's catching up with me." He missed his son in a way there wasn't words for. He clung to the past so hard it was like leaving an arrow embedded instead of pulling it out and letting the wound bleed clean, then heal.

"I've wondered the very same thing." She nodded solemnly. "He's a good doctor."

He turned his head sharply toward her. "Then why didn't you say something? You could have saved me a doctor's visit."

"You were due in, anyway. Besides, you're not exactly the easiest man to try to tell what to do, you know." She folded her arms against her chest and held her elbows. "So what did the doctor recommend?"

Amos felt a surge of stung pride, recalling the doctor's advice. He had told Amos there were some interesting facts about heart recipients that weren't true for other organ recipients: 75 percent were male, 25 percent were female. In addition, he said, most of the transplant cardiologists and surgeons were men. And yet, the doctor explained, men have a harder time coping with the surgery than women do. More depression, for example.

"Why would that be?" Amos asked him.

"My theory is that men are uncomfortable with the idea of accepting someone else—heart, spirit, or piece of meat, whatever way you want to view your donor heart—into their bodies and their being. Simply put: receptivity is not easy for men."

Amos would never tell Fern *that* particular piece of information. He could hear her response now: "Amen to that. Amen!"

Amos waved a pamphlet in the air. "He wants me to go to a grief support group." He set his jaw. "But I'm not going."

"Now I see where M.K. gets her famous stubborn streak." Fern took the pamphlet from him and skimmed it. "Wouldn't really hurt to talk to somebody about your grieving."

"I'm not talking to a bunch of strangers."

She closed the pamphlet. "Maybe not. But you could talk to somebody. Somebody caring and understanding. Somebody you trust."

"Like who?"

She paused, tilted her head, and Amos watched her expression go from hopeful to saddened to resolute. Then it passed and her brow wrinkled as her eyes traveled over the field with the cockeyed furrows. "Maybe like Deacon Abraham." She pointed to a horse and buggy driving along the road. "He's coming up here, now. Probably to talk about Sadie." She took a few steps toward the house, then stopped and swiveled around. "Ask him to stay for dinner."

"Fern, hold up. Why would Abraham want to talk to Sadie?"

She took a few steps back to him, with a look on her face as if she thought he might be slightly addle brained. That look made him crazy, especially because he often felt addle brained around the females in his household.

She tilted her head to the side and plunked a small fist on her hip. "Have you noticed how quickly rumor becomes fact in this community?"

Her frown grew fierce—a ridiculous expression for someone who could be pretty when she smiled.

"Here they come. Looks like Esther's with him." She took a few steps toward the house, then stopped and swiveled around again. "Send Esther up to the house. You be sure to tell Abraham about what the doctor said. About grieving for Menno."

Did that woman ever stop handing out unasked-for advice? What irked him all the more was that she was usually right. Under his breath he muttered, "Yeder Ros hot ihr Dann." *Every rose has its thorn.*

She spun around. She had heard him. She heard everything. "Ken Rose unne Danne." *There is no rose without a thorn.*

Impossibly weary, Amos sighed and went to meet his friends.

"Abraham," Amos said, shaking the man's hand after he'd tied up his horse to the hitching post.

Esther went up to the house to visit with Fern. The two men walked together, away from the house.

Abraham couldn't keep a grin off his face when he heard Amos tell the story of the visiting bird boy and surveyed the cockeyed furrows. "Well, wheat seeds can grow and flourish and reach for the sky whether the rows are straight or crooked. Maybe there's a lesson in that for us, eh, Amos?" He gripped his hands behind his back. "But I can tell there's something you want to tell me."

Why, Abraham was as prescient as Fern! It baffled Amos that some people seemed to be able to see what wasn't visible. He was a man who relied heavily on his sight and hearing. He looked into his dear friend's kind brown eyes. "I just came from the doctor. I thought that I was having heart trouble again. But the doctor said my heart was fine, that the problem was I hadn't grieved for Menno. I buried it, he said, amidst all the busyness of the heart transplant and trying to get well. Grieving has caught up with me."

A flicker of surprise passed through Abraham's eyes. He stroked his wiry gray beard, deep in thought, and gave a sad half smile. "So, in a way, you are still having heart trouble. The kind that can't be fixed by doctoring."

Out of the corner of his eye, Amos peered up at the male falcon, soaring over the fields, hunting for an evening meal to bring to his mate. He was the size of a crow, with a three-foot wingspan, a dark head with a pale breast cross-barred with dark brown. "What do I do with that information, Abraham? I can't switch feelings on and off like a diesel generator."

"You're not new to grieving, Amos. I remember how it was when you lost your Maggie. You didn't heal from that loss overnight. Grieving takes time. It can't be rushed."

How well Amos remembered what it felt like when Maggie had passed. It was like a limb had been torn from him, with no anesthetic. The pain was so deep then, he wondered if it would ever lessen. Just yesterday, his thoughts had drifted back to a lazy Sunday afternoon, long ago, when the children were playing in a tree fort in the backyard while Maggie and he sat on a wooden swing nearby beneath the canopy of a maple. He thought those days would last forever.

"God's ways are not ours, Amos. As much as we rejoice that our loved ones are in God's holy heaven, we miss them." Abraham looked into the sky to see the falcon swoop down on an unlucky bobolink flying low in the field. "Memory is a strange thing. At times, so sweet. At times, so painful. But it's what separates us from fish and fowl and beast. God wants us to remember his gifts and blessings." He put a hand on Amos's shoulder. "There's a difference between keeping memories alive and using them as an excuse not to start living again." He pulled his hand away and crossed his arms against his chest. "My advice for you is to talk about Menno. Remember his life. Celebrate the gift of a son God gave you, even if it was for a brief time. I think, by remembering, it will allow your grief to surface. And, in time, to heal." He patted Amos's back. "Talk, Amos Lapp. Talk and remember."

Abraham made it sound so simple, but Amos knew it wasn't. Grief was a hard, lonely thing to bear.

Suddenly, he realized that Abraham had something else on his mind.

Abraham's eyes were fixed on the farmhouse. "And now I'd like to talk to Sadie. Alone."

11

Sadie saw her father and Deacon Abraham talking outside her bedroom window, over by the field Will had plowed. If, that is, you could call it plowed. It looked more like a giant hand had scooped down from the sky and raked its fingers haphazardly through the dirt. The sight of the wiggly furrows made her smile. Any eight-year-old boy in her church could have done a better job, but, of course, she would never tell Will that. He had seemed so pleased with his efforts.

She studied herself in the mirror as if seeing herself for the first time. Usually, she only looked to see if the knot she wore on the back of her head caught all the strands, even the one that always seemed to work its way loose. Now she pulled out the pins that held her hair and let it tumble. She shook it free and studied her face like it was the map of some unknown country. Was she pretty? She shook that thought off, as quickly as it came. That was vain, and mirrors don't tell everything.

Her thoughts traveled to the conversation she had with Will, just a short while ago, and to the way he brushed back a swoop of her hair that had come loose.

It still shocked her that she talked to a stranger, a boy stranger, the way she talked to Will just now. But there was something about him that made talking so easy and natural. She'd never felt so comfortable around a boy before, around most people, and certainly not an English boy. It was nice to be able to share her thoughts with someone outside the church, someone who had a different point of view, who saw things more objectively and didn't layer a situation with shoulds and shouldn'ts.

A door banged open and Sadie heard M.K.'s voice yell out, "Saa—ddeeee! Dad wants you to come outside and talk to Deacon Abraham!" followed by Fern hushing M.K., scolding her that she would wake the baby.

Sadie took a deep breath. She had expected this visit. Maybe not today, but soon. This had just turned into a horrible day. The worst day of her life.

Sadie had thought by the time she had reached her late teens, she would be able to speak her mind, but she had yet to figure out a way to quell her constant need for approval.

Fern had told her once that she needed to be bolder, that there was a time for submission, and a time for boldness. But Sadie wasn't a naturally assertive person. Even horses took advantage of her. Just today, the buggy horse—her father's oldest nag—wanted to go right when she wanted it to go left. They ended up going right and she had to go far out of her way to get to the Bent N' Dent. Right turns only.

Enough. She had had enough of getting walked on and pushed around, even by an old horse! Enough! She would face this ridiculous accusation head-on.

Sadie twisted her hair into an orderly arrangement. A half-dozen pins slipped into place, and her hair and prayer cap assumed its normal style. She blew air out of her cheeks. If only she could discipline her mind and her heart as efficiently.

Outside, as Sadie passed her father, he gave her a light squeeze on her shoulder. Did he know what the deacon wanted? She had seen them talking together for quite a long time. But her father didn't say anything to her, didn't give anything away with his eyes. She steeled herself and went out to meet the deacon, patiently waiting by the fence. When she reached him, Sadie had to hide her hands behind her so that he couldn't see how much they were trembling.

Abraham was a kind man, and he looked quite sad. "Sadie, I just came from having a long talk with Gideon Smucker. He admits that he's the father of this baby. He's willing to go before the church in two weeks' time, and confess to all. And then he wants to marry you, after the proving period, in six weeks' time."

"Is that what he said?" she asked in a shaky voice.

The deacon nodded. "He said he wanted to make things right for you. He didn't want you to have to face this alone."

Sadie discovered she was clasping her hands so tightly her knuckles ached. She relaxed her grip, flattening her palms on her thighs.

"So, Sadie Lapp, I'm here to see if you are willing to confess as well, to have a time of proving, then to marry Gid and make things right."

Sadie's lips quivered. Her chest grew tight. How dare Gid let others believe he was the father of that baby! And by doing so, he let others believe it was Sadie's baby. Gid had actually contributed to the spreading rumors . . . not through a lie, but through his omission of the truth. And wasn't that a lie? What you didn't say could be just as damaging as what you did. On top of it all, Gid had the unmitigated gall to look as if he was rescuing Sadie from a troubling fate. Tears clouded her vision, but she kept blinking them away. Once she was out of sight, she could fall apart—but not in front of the deacon. What a fool she had been to care about Gid, to think he was someone she might love one day. She wanted to escape to her room, bury her face in the pillows, and cry this intense hurt away.

Minutes ticked by while the deacon waited for a response.

Sadie was terrified: like the first time she jumped off a diving rock at Blue Lake Pond, like the night she knew Gid was first going to kiss her, like the day when the bear came up to the house and poked its nose at the window. She had trouble getting a full breath, and then she felt a little dizzy.

Off in the distance, Sadie heard M.K. shout, "She's going down!"

Sheer horror shadowed the deacon's face, and then it was like someone pulled the curtains. Everything went dark. The next thing Sadie knew, she was getting scooped up in Will's strong arms and pulled so tight against his warm chest that she could feel his heartbeat.

Will had finished observing the falcons—no sight of eggs yet—and he was heading to the farmhouse when he saw Sadie talking to an older Amish man. Actually, she wasn't talking. He was looking intently at her and she was just standing there, knees locked like a stiff soldier. She noticed Will as he approached. Her eyes looked panicky, like she was a squirrel caught in traffic—too frightened to move. Then he heard M.K. give a shout from the farmhouse porch and Will bolted to catch Sadie, just as her head was about to hit the fence post. He lifted her in his arms like she was a bag of feathers and rushed to the farmhouse with her, the Amish man following close behind. Will laid Sadie gently on the couch as Fern and M.K. fluttered around her.

"What happened?" Fern asked.

"We were having a talk and she just . . . fainted," Abraham said, visibly upset. "Dropped like a stone."

Sadie's eyes fluttered open. She looked bewildered as everyone crowded around her. M.K. brought a cold, wet cloth and slapped it on her forehead.

Fern intervened just as Amos opened his mouth to say something. "Why don't you take Esther and Abraham outside and give Sadie a moment to pull herself together."

It wasn't posed as a question, Will noticed. It was an order. Fern ushered everyone out the door. She held the door open and pointed to M.K. "Your hens require your attention." Her gaze turned to Will next, and he knew he was about to get ordered out, but the baby let out a healthy squall and Fern's attention was riveted to the basket in the kitchen.

"You all right?" he whispered, leaning close to Sadie. "What made you faint?"

Sadie pulled the dripping wet rag off of her face. "The deacon. He was laying a sin on me."

"You could never sin!"

Sadie pulled herself up. "No one is without sin, Will." She put her hand to her forehead. "But I didn't happen to commit this particular sin."

He glanced in the kitchen and saw Fern jiggling the baby, trying to settle it. It was the first time he felt grateful for the baby's loud cry. It provided a moment of privacy. "What particular sin was he trying to lay on you?"

Sadie rubbed her face with her hands. She let out a deep sigh, and then, to Will's surprise, poured out the story of how people assumed the baby was hers—when he wasn't!—that the quiet guy he had lunch with at church yesterday—Gideon Smucker—didn't deny he was the baby's father—which he wasn't!—and that the deacon was expecting Sadie and Gideon to marry and set things right.

Will was outraged. He made sure Fern was out of hearing distance and leaned close to Sadie. "You need to stand up for yourself. I know about these kinds of people—they will wear you down and plan out your entire life. You've got to have a backbone."

She hugged her arms across her middle, as though she were cold. "How can you be so sure of that?"

"Because I've been in your shoes. This type will run roughshod over you if you don't open your mouth and speak up."

"Will Stoltz." Fern eyed him from the kitchen. "Come and make yourself useful. Get this baby to stop his yammering while I tend to Sadie."

Will rose to his feet. "You gotta learn to speak your own mind. Otherwise, you'll get swept along like a twig in a creek. You'll wake up one day and wonder whatever happened to your life. If you have strong feelings, Sadie, now's the time to say so."

Sadie went very still.

M.K. ran to the feed room in the barn, filled up the container with cracked corn, and flew to the chicken coop like she had wings on her feet. The chickens lived penned up in a coop on the far side of the barn. Downwind. After Julia got married and moved to Berlin, charge of the chickens was handed to Sadie, who promptly turned the responsibility over to M.K. Chickens and Sadie didn't get along. If she had to keep them, she said, she'd as soon not eat them. But M.K. had a hand with fowl. She named them too, every chick of them, before they feathered out. Fern said better not name anything you're fixing to eat. But M.K. went right on naming them.

The last hen pecked at M.K.'s bare toes as she tossed cracked corn inside the chicken coop. "Try being mean like that again, Kayak, and I'll have Fern introduce you to the inside of a pot." Holding the corners of her apron, she hurried Kayak into the coop with the other chickens and locked it tight for the night. She didn't want to miss a minute of excitement going on inside the farmhouse. She saw Uncle Hank come out from his buggy shop and waved her arm like a windmill. "Uncle Hank! Hurry! Hurry! Hurry! Sadie's got the vapors!"

They rushed over to the farmhouse and found Sadie, upright and talking, with color back in her cheeks, sitting at the kitchen table with Amos and Abraham. Will was walking the baby and Fern was at the kitchen sink, looking like she had a kernel of popcorn stuck in her back molar. But then, that look on Fern was not unusual. She was scraping carrots like they had done something that made her mad. She wasn't idle. She didn't know how to be idle. Daylight never caught Fern sitting down.

They stopped talking for a moment as Uncle Hank and M.K. came in and sat themselves at the table. "Maybe we could finish up this conversation tomorrow, Sadie," Abraham said.

"No," Sadie said. "We can settle it now, Abraham." She looked around the room at everyone, then her eyes rested on the baby in Will's arms. "I have something to tell you. Something I haven't wanted to say until I knew for sure. But I think the time has come to tell you everything I know about the baby."

In a clear, calm voice, she explained about the baby in the bus station to Abraham. M.K. was amazed, watching her sister talk to the deacon with such confidence.

After she finished, Abraham let out a long breath. "Sadie, why didn't you just tell me that in the first place?"

"But you didn't ask, Abraham. You just told me what I had to do to make things right. You never asked me for the truth."

Nose in the air, Esther huffed. "Such disrespect!"

For a span of a heartbeat, no one said anything. For an instant, Sadie felt free. She'd told the truth. Then she felt dreadful. "I'll agree with you there, Esther."

Esther's tiny mouth was pursed full of triumph as she looked around the room.

"It's disrespectful to assume the worst about someone. It's disrespectful not to hope the best for another." Sadie turned to Abraham. "I'm not trying to be rude to you, Abraham, but no one has ever asked me for the truth. Not you, not Gideon, not my friends and neighbors. Love is supposed to think well of others. Not tell tales and gossip."

Struck dumb by Sadie's lengthy, emphatic speech, M.K. could only stare at her in amazement.

Abraham looked at Esther. "Did you not tell me that you talked with Sadie about the baby at church yesterday?"

"She talked *to* me," Sadie said quietly. "She never talked *with* me."

Esther narrowed her eyes. "You could have offered up the truth. You never said a word."

M.K. exchanged a glance with Uncle Hank. There was so much electricity charging the air, she wondered if she'd be hearing a thunderclap soon. The tension in the air practically sizzled.

Abraham lifted a hand. "You're right, Sadie. I hope you can find it in your heart to forgive me."

Sadie reached out and covered his hand with hers, a silent offering. The baby let out a wail and Abraham glanced at him.

"Well, one problem is taken care of, yet we have another. What shall we do about this little one? Babies just don't appear out of thin air."

"This one did," M.K. offered. "We think an angel brought him to Sadie." Everyone sent startled glances in her direction, as if they'd forgotten she was there.

Abraham smiled. "Even a baby brought by an angel needs a family."

"Two parents," Esther added. "A real family. Children are a blessing and a responsibility. He's not just a doll for you to play with, Mary Kate."

Red heat swept through M.K. She forgot that she was a child and Esther an adult. She forgot it was the deacon who sat before her. She barely felt Fern's fingers digging into her arm. "You can't just take a baby and give him to this or that person like he's no more than a stray dog!" She wasn't exactly yelling, but she was very close.

"You Lapps have your hands more than full already," Esther pointed out, her voice sounding shrill as a pennywhistle. She turned to her husband. "I can think of a few families who would welcome a child."

M.K. was shocked. "But the angel brought him to us!"

Esther frowned at her.

She knew she was pushing it, but she couldn't help herself. It wasn't fair! "How about for the baby? What's fair and reasonable for him? Or for the rest of us?" She was on the brink of bursting into tears. She looked up at Sadie, expecting to see her sobbing right along with her.

But she wasn't. Sadie rose from her chair, standing tall and straight, calm and serene. "This baby does have a family," Sadie said firmly. She bit on her lips, as if bracing herself. "There's something else about this baby, something I haven't wanted to say until I was sure." She went over to the trunk that held her mother's quilts and lifted it open. On top of the pile lay a yellow and blue crib quilt. She picked it up and brought it to her father.

"Your mother made that," Amos said. "All of you babies slept under it."

Sadie took a deep breath. "I think this baby belongs to Annie." She turned to Abraham and Esther. "She's the young Swartzentruber girl who lives with her grandfather." As everyone started murmuring, she held up a hand. "Let me start at the beginning. It was really M.K. who gave me an idea. She suggested we find out who made the baby's basket."

M.K. beamed at that remark. Her detective skills were paying off.

"Until M.K. mentioned that, I had forgotten that Annie was a basketmaker. On a hunch, I went to visit her grandfather last Friday while M.K. was having that buggy race with Jimmy Fisher. He seemed pretty confused—at first he thought I was Annie. It seemed like he was waiting for her, but I could tell he lived there alone. I made some supper for him because he said he was hungry. I could tell that someone had been there pretty recently—there were some casseroles in the freezer with last week's date on them—the day before I found the baby at the bus station. And I found this quilt, folded, in Annie's bedroom. The dog I brought home—that's our Lulu's pup, all grown up." Sadie took a deep breath. "I think it was Annie who saw me sleeping in the bus station and left the baby with me." She lifted her eyes to look at her father. "She must have had the quilt because Menno had given it to her. He must have known about the baby. Do you remember how he told Julia he wanted to marry Annie? But then . . . he died. And Annie was left to have the baby alone. I think Annie left the baby with me because the father of the baby was Menno. Our Menno."

Everything slowed. Fern stopped peeling carrots and froze. M.K. felt frightened by how quiet the room got, and she didn't scare easily. She didn't know how Sadie got through that brave speech without her voice breaking in two.

It was Uncle Hank who broke the ice. He rose to his feet and strode to Will, taking the baby out of his arms. Tears streaming down his face, he gazed lovingly at the baby. "THIS IS WONDERFUL NEWS! I knew there was something grand and glorious about this little one the very first time I laid eyes on him. God has given us a great gift, Amos. Our Menno has left us with a child."

After Abraham and Esther's buggy rolled out of the driveway, Amos stood for a moment looking up at the stars through the treetops. He tried to absorb all that had happened today and it felt mind-boggling. He felt a flood of feelings, at the top was sorrow over his Sadie. How could anyone accuse Sadie of such a sin? His soul told him to forgive, but his heart ached with the unfairness of the situation. And on the heels of those feelings came another, one of awe and wonder. There was this child in the house, one of his own. He lifted his head and saw that more and more stars were now visible in the bruised sky. A chilly breeze blew and a few night birds twittered.

"Heaven's dazzling us with stars, like thousands of angels winking at us," Fern said.

Amos jerked his head down. Where had she come from? She was as stealthy as a cat on the prowl.

"Did Abraham have anything else to say?"

Nosy. Fern was downright nosy. "He said he would write some letters to the Swartzentruber colony and see if he can find out how to locate Annie." He kicked a dirt clod on the ground with his boot. "And he said that if I felt the need, it would be all right to have the baby's blood tested. To make sure he's a Lapp."

"So what did you tell him?"

"I told him it wouldn't matter what the results were. The baby is one of ours."

She smiled at him, and he couldn't help but smile back.

"I suppose you, in your infinite wisdom, knew Abraham stopped by to talk to Sadie about this . . . this ridiculous gossip."

She gave him a sweet look then, as if he were a naïve child. "Did you not notice how a few people treated Sadie at church yesterday? Like she might be contagious."

No, he didn't.

He had been so preoccupied with worry over his heart—convinced his body was starting to reject it—that he was hardly aware of anything yesterday. He couldn't even say what the sermons were about. Or whom he sat next to for lunch. His body might have been at church, but his head was elsewhere. A blanket of guilt covered him. He had been so focused on himself that he hadn't even thought about what might be going on in his daughter's life. What kind of a father was that? "Surely not everyone treated her that way."

"No, but it felt like everyone to Sadie. You know how sensitive she is. She felt as if she had to protect Menno."

"I can't bear the thought that anyone would think ill of Menno." He wiped his face with his hands. "He's not here to explain or defend himself, or even to confess."

"Amos, Menno was God's special child. No one will accuse him of anything."

He sighed. "If some folks were so quick to accuse Sadie of sin, what will they be saying about Menno?" He glanced at her. "I know that's why Sadie didn't want to tell us about the crib quilt. Or who she thought was the baby's father. Menno meant so much to her. She knows folks will talk."

"If folks want to say hurtful things, that's something God will have to deal with." She put a hand on his arm. "There's good in all of this, Amos."

"Like what?"

"Just today, your doctor told you to talk about Menno, to get your grieving out. Maybe this little baby is part of God's healing for you." She looked down at the ground. "He even looks like Menno, with that thatch of unruly hair. Menno never did comb his hair."

Remembering his son's wild hair, a slight smile tugged at Amos's lips. He felt a stone lifting from the pile weighing on his heart, shucking off into the newly plowed field. The tightness in his chest eased a bit.

"And did you see how Sadie stood up for the truth? Maybe God is using all of this gossip nonsense to help her become a strong woman." Fern looked over at the house. "When I first arrived here, she was afraid of her own shadow. Today, I saw a girl become a woman."

Amos mulled that thought over. It was true, what Fern said. Sadie was showing more backbone than he ever thought possible. He was grateful to Fern for those encouraging words, and tried to think of how to tell her that he appreciated it. That he appreciated *her*. That his feelings for her were growing in ways he had never, ever expected, that she filled his thoughts more and more each day. She turned to him and their eyes caught and held. Amos leaned closer, so close that the space between them felt intimate. *Something was happening.* His heart pounded like he was a seventeen-year-old boy again, an odd staccato that echoed in his ears. He cleared his throat.

"Fern, I find that I have grown rather fond of you," Amos had intended to say, but for some reason the words came out as, "Fern, dinner was good."

She tilted her head as if she hadn't heard him correctly, then she squinted her eyes as if he might be sun-touched.

Dinner was good? *Dinner was good?* Nice work, Amos Lapp, he chided himself. Just what a woman wanted to hear.

But the moment had passed and Fern turned to leave. Over her shoulder, she tossed, "Amos Lapp, has it occurred to you that you're a grandfather?"

Back at the house, M.K. took care of the baby while Sadie and Will gathered dishes from the table and set them in the sink to soak. Uncle Hank sank into his favorite chair by the woodstove. He was into a sack of pecans Sadie and M.K. had gathered last fall. In a litter of shells he was trying to pick out nutmeats. Sadie seemed to see for the first time how twisted and knobby his hands were. Arthritis had gotten to his joints, and he had pain he never spoke of. Tonight, Sadie thought, she would mix up a special tea to help him with the pain.

As Sadie went back and forth from the table to the kitchen, she was glad to see her legs were holding her up, solid and sure, though she prayed her trembling wasn't still noticeable. She had never been so bold in all her life as she was tonight. She actually said some things she wanted to say. But the thing was, she wasn't sure if it made things better or worse.

Sadie's conversation with Abraham had ended on a sweet note, as he took her small hands in his large, calloused ones. "You've reminded me of an important quality of love today, Sadie Lapp," he said. "Love believes the best in others."

Sadie readily forgave Abraham. How could she not? Yet she couldn't quite keep her hands from shaking. It occurred to Sadie that she had actually confronted Esther—one of the most intimidating women in their church. Some would say the most intimidating woman. Which proved to Sadie that she could confront people when push came to shove! That little epiphany made her day.

But all of those thoughts would need to be sifted through later, when she was alone. As for now, Will Stoltz was waiting for her to bandage his blistered hands. She filled a bowl of water for him to soak his hands, first, and ended up sloshing the bowl of water onto the table hard enough to spill some water on the floor. She wiped it up and fetched another clean towel from the hall closet, then poked her head around the edge of the doorjamb to find Will waiting for her in the kitchen, a patient look on his face. The very first time she saw Will she had the vague thought that he looked sad, but the second time she realized it was mainly the shape of his eyes. Everything else about him looked pleasant enough, handsome, but his eyes, even when he smiled, pulled down a little at the corners. His jawline was square, and his thick hair had just the slightest hint of a wave in it. Not fair! Not fair that a boy had such thick, wavy hair. She would have loved such hair.

She took a deep breath and squared her shoulders. *Watch that line of thinking, Sadie Lapp,* she told herself. *Jealousy will only take you down wicked and twisted paths.* "Come to the table. After your hands soak for a while, I'll put some healing salve on them."

Will smiled, sat at the table, and held his hands out to her. She plunged his hands into the bowl of water. Dirt was caked into the blisters and Will winced as the water hit the open sores. She made a mental note to get to work on expanding her herb garden with a variety of herbs that Old Deborah had taught her about, if only to keep some healing remedies handy. She moistened several diamond-shaped pigweed leaves and placed them, one at a time, on the tender, reddened flesh on Will's palms. "Leave them sit a spell. You'll still blister some more, but not as bad. You'll heal quicker too."

"That feels much better. Thank you. The sting is almost gone."

She glanced at his face. "Your hands looked as dirty as if you'd been digging for worms."

"Now there's an idea. Digging for worms sounds like a lot more fun than plowing. Do you like to go fishing?"

"No. How did you ever manage to plow a field with those blisters?"

He shrugged. "Just kept at it. Will you go fishing with me?"

Sadie glanced over at M.K. on the couch, feeding the baby a bottle. She knew her little sister was straining to hear every word. "Maybe," she whispered.

She pulled the leaves off his hands and had him rinse in the bowl. She took one of his hands and dried it carefully with a towel. Then she gently spread a salve over it.

Will made a face. "That is vile smelling! What's in it? Kitchen waste?"

"Comfrey." Her lips twisted into a reluctant smile. "It might smell bad, but it will speed up the healing." She bandaged his hand carefully with gauze and snipped off some lengths of adhesive tape to wrap around the gauze.

She dried his other hand and applied the comfrey salve. "You'll need to be careful with these wounds."

"I don't know how to thank you for helping me."

"Keep them covered for now. You don't want them to get infected."

Will caught hold of her hand to keep her from concentrating on bandaging his wound. "It wouldn't be the worst thing I could think of to come back and have you take care of them." His fathomless blue eyes gazed into hers in a way that made her pulse skip more beats than was healthy. "Maybe I can use these blisters as an excuse to spend time with you if you won't go fishing with me."

"I like to go fishing," M.K. piped up. "So does Uncle Hank!" She looked at him happily.

"THAT'S A FINE IDEA, MARY KATE!" Uncle Hank boomed, startling the baby. He put a finger to his lips and whispered, "We'll go tomorrow. First thing!" He scratched his head, remembering something. "No, scratch that. I promised Edith Fisher I'd get her broke-down buggy back to her. Saturday, then. Crack of dawn! We'll take Menno's little one too. Can't start him out too early."

"I can't go Saturday," M.K. said glumly. "I've got community service with that horrible—"

Sadie pointed a finger at her to shut off the flow of words. "Don't start on a list of complaints about Jimmy Fisher. We already know everything."

Uncle Hank kissed the top of M.K.'s head. "I'll make you a deal. I'll help you and Jimmy out on Saturday. Then, if there's time, we'll do some sunset fishing."

Will laughed and Sadie felt herself relax even more around him. He rose to his feet to get ready to go and she was surprised by a tweak of disappointment. Except for those brief times when she thought she saw a sadness flit through his eyes, his heart seemed as light as the breeze, with an ability to absorb all that went on around him and take it all in stride.

So unlike Gideon. It wasn't right to compare Will to Gideon. Comparing a Plain man to an English man was like comparing apples to oranges, deserts to oceans, elephants to lions. But everything felt so serious with Gid. So awkward. But then, she was awkward too. Maybe that was the problem. Maybe they were too much alike. In her mind flashed a vision: she and Gid at a table, surrounded by awkward children. An entire awkward family. She shook her head to clear it of that image. Since when had she ever given serious thought to marrying Gideon Smucker? No! Never! But maybe someday.

Will picked up his cowboy hat and fit it on his head. "Well, Sadie, if you need me to rescue you in the future, just give a holler. I'm right over the hill."

Sadie put one hand up close to her face and gave a tiny slow wave like a shy child. His impish grin put a twist in her heart, and her face tingled with warmth.

12

It was funny what Mary Kate Lapp could do for a room. She burst into Twin Creeks Schoolhouse on a gray, misty Tuesday morning and lit it up. The room was actually brighter when she came inside, Gid thought. It sparkled. She sparkled.

She held out a plate of warm doughnuts, drizzled with chocolate. "I wondered if you've already had any breakfast. You haven't, have you?" M.K. looked at him longingly, with the transparent plea written all over her face: Please say you didn't, that you're famished and were just this minute wishing for some homemade doughnuts.

"Well, I did have a little something," Gid said. "But not enough to satisfy my appetite," he hurried to add when her eyes clouded. Her face crinkled with delight, and she held the plate out farther.

"They're still warmish," M.K. said. "They've been setting on top of the stove."

"I'm sure they'll be good . . . thanks."

"I made them myself. I woke up really early this morning and was just waiting around for something to do."

Gid doubted that. Mary Kate kept herself busy. She had more inner resources than any twelve-year-old needed.

"Fern says I need more on my mind so she's trying to turn me into a crackerjack baker. The doughnuts are best with coffee, Uncle Hank said, and he would know because he ate seven this morning—do you have any? Coffee, I mean?" M.K.'s eyes darted to his desk.

"I'm not a coffee drinker. I'm sure the doughnuts will be . . . well, just fine without it . . . the way they are. Thanks."

Gid didn't know what to say, though it didn't seem to matter because Mary Kate was blessed with the gift of conversation. The doughnuts did look good—golden and fried, with just the right amount of chocolate. Though, Gid had to admit, you could never have enough chocolate.

"Go on, taste one," she said, and as he bit into one, her eyebrows scrunched together, and her face tightened.

He nodded his head and smiled. "It's good," he said, talking around the mouthful of chewy, sweet cake. "Very good. It's delicious."

"See? See there? Aren't they good? The best I've ever made." And she clapped her hands together as she laughed.

Then it grew quiet. Gid knew her well enough to know there was something else on her mind. M.K. covered the plate with the foil and set it on his desk. "Well, I might as well just tell you. You'll hear about it soon enough."

This was going to be about Sadie. Gid's stomach twisted. The bite of doughnut in his mouth suddenly tasted flat, gummy, like he would have trouble swallowing it. He set down the uneaten half. "Something's happened."

M.K. told him about last night's revelatory goings-on, blow by blow, not leaving out a single detail. The longer he listened, the worse Gid felt. As he heard about Will scooping Sadie up in his arms when she fainted—and of course, M.K. had to act that part out with a dramatic flair, swaying like a poplar tree—he had an irrational flash of jealousy in which he imagined himself running that bird sitter out of town, or slinging him into outer space with a large wooden catapult. Just thinking about it felt pretty good. Almost as good as doing it.

For a second he felt guilty as he remembered one of the bishop's sermons about sin and how if a person thought about doing something wrong in his heart it was the same as doing it. But wasn't he talking about big things like murder and adultery? And wouldn't it be good for everybody if the bird sitter were to pack up and head off to wherever it was he belonged?

And then came the shocker. He swallowed and stared at M.K. "This baby . . . you're telling me this is . . . *Menno's* baby? Annie and Menno's?"

"Sadie's pretty confident of that fact. And I don't think my sister is the type to jump to conclusions."

M.K. looked at Gid in pure innocence, but the words she spoke cut him to the core. No, Sadie wouldn't jump to conclusions the way he had, the way others had. It hit him like a right cross, then—why Sadie told him that if he really trusted her, he would never have needed to ask her such a question.

Stupid, stupid, stupid! A large splinter of guilt wedged into his heart. Sadie had hurt him; in return, he'd hurt her. He had wounded the very person he had tried to protect.

The doughnut that he ate felt like lead in his stomach. No wonder Sadie wouldn't even look at him at church on Sunday. He was the worst person on earth.

As the baby slept, Sadie went into the kitchen to blend some herbs into a remedy that could be brewed as a kind of tea. It was a mixture to break up colds that Deborah had taught her to make: ground ginger and cayenne pepper. A pinch of that, added to a mug of hot water, apple cider vinegar, and honey, sipped throughout the day, could shorten a cold's duration. Sadie sneezed twice as she stirred the mixture. Just sniffing it, she thought, could clear the sinuses. An added benefit to the remedy!

Uncle Hank burst into the kitchen, hopping on one foot. "SADIE! I need your help! I'M DYING! Every move is a misery to me!" He sat on a chair and thrust a bare foot on the table. Sadie went over to see what was causing him such misery and saw a thorn in his leathery heel, imbedded deeply. The area around the thorn was swollen, red, and angry. "How long has this been bothering you?" she asked.

"DAYS! MAYBE WEEKS!"

"Well, why didn't you . . ." She shook her head. "Never mind. I know just how to help." She hurried to the refrigerator, took out some carrots, and grated them into a bowl. She put a towel under Uncle Hank's foot, then applied the grated carrots to the area around the thorn. "You just wait awhile. You'll see. It'll draw the thorn right out." Hopefully, she thought, before Fern came inside and saw Uncle Hank with his foot on the kitchen table. Fern's patience for Uncle Hank always hung by a thread.

Too late. The door squeaked open. Fern's eyes narrowed. "Hank Lapp. You get that dirty foot of yours off my clean table!"

"NOSIR! IT IS AN EMERGENCY!" Uncle Hank roared. "Sadie's doctoring me. We're considering amputation."

While Hank was sputtering away with Fern, Sadie found the tweezers in the medicine box. She brought a warm, wet rag to the table and wiped the carrots away from the thorn. The carrots drew the thorn out and Sadie was easily able to pull it out with the tweezers. She held up the tweezers. "Voilà!"

Uncle Hank turned away from complaining to Fern and looked at Sadie, wide-eyed. He wiggled his toes. "SHE'S A MIRACLE WORKER! First, she cures Ira Smucker of hay fever—"

"Actually," Sadie said, "the rain we had last week cleared out the pollen in the air."

"—and next, she has saved my foot from gangrene! SHE'S GOT THE TOUCH!"

"Not hardly," Sadie said, cleaning up the mess of the carrots. "It was just a thorn in your foot."

"Could've saved yourself a heap of trouble in the first place by wearing shoes," Fern pointed out.

Uncle Hank paid them both no mind. He prided himself on his ability to share news of marvels and curiosities and other odd bits of news that might be of interest to folks. Word of Sadie's healing abilities spread rapidly throughout Stoney Ridge. People came to think Sadie could cure anything and she didn't know how to tell them different.

Uncle Hank said she should hang out a shingle to advertise her healing work, but she didn't. She wouldn't even take any money for helping. That way folks couldn't get mad at her if the remedies didn't work or made them even sicker. That happened once, last fall, when she gave Edith Fisher the wrong remedy. Edith had sent a note to Sadie via Jimmy via M.K., asking for a laxative. At least, that's what it looked like, in Edith's spidery handwriting. So Sadie sent over some slippery elm. It turned out Edith wanted something for insomnia. Edith had to miss church the next day, for obvious reasons, and wouldn't let Sadie forget it.

Gid loped into the kitchen on Saturday morning, freshly showered. His sister, Alice, was taking a batch of corn muffins out of the oven—a complicated thing to do when a person relied on crutches. But at least she was out of the wheelchair and her broken legs were healing and she wasn't grumbling about Mary Kate Lapp quite as regularly as she had been. Amos Lapp had offered to send M.K. over to Goat Roper Hill on Saturdays while Alice recovered from her injuries—a kind of penance—but Alice wouldn't hear of it. After teaching school for seven years with Mary Kate Lapp as a student, Alice was convinced that any interaction with her translated to steady trouble. She was convinced she would end up in a body cast. "She's about as bad as a boy for devilment, with a spark in her eye for warning," she had told Gid more than once. Dozens of times.

Gid thought Alice was slightly paranoid. Personally, he liked the spark in M.K.'s eyes. She was his favorite scholar, and not just because she was Sadie's sister. She was as bright as they come and had the best of intentions, though she rarely thought before she acted. His sister had no appreciation for M.K.'s zest for life. In fact, she was suspicious of it.

Alice had an acute sense of doom and disaster. She even kept a shoe box filled with newspaper clippings of house fires and buggy accidents. Just in case, she always said, if anyone asked why she kept them. And that's when his father would quietly mutter, "And we wonder why she's still unmarried."

Gid took a corn muffin, broke it open, and breathed in the steam. "Mmmm, good," he said, mumbling, and grabbed another. He hopped on the counter, expecting Alice to swat him away, but she didn't seem to mind his company.

"Any improvement in the Sadie Lapp department?"

Gid practically choked on the muffin. Alice pounded on his back.

"I guess not," she said dryly.

Gid swallowed, coughed again. "She's still pretty mad."

"Well, what would you expect, Gid? You assumed the worst about her. A woman doesn't get over that kind of hurt and humiliation easily."

Gid didn't think that now was the time to point out that it was Alice who had told him the baby was Sadie's in the first place. "She's not even talking to me. How can I get her to listen to my apology?"

Alice sighed. "Are you absolutely sure you want to court Sadie Lapp? You know those Lapps are—"

"Alice." Gid's voice held a warning tone. This conversation wasn't a new one.

"Fine. I do happen to have an idea." As she told him about it, he gave her a skeptical look.

"You're sure that Sadie would like that?"

"You can count on it. Jay Glick asked Susie Hostetler to marry him in that very way. The girls are still talking about it. Girls love that kind of thing."

Gid wasn't as confident as Alice, but he had to try something. Twice this week, he had stopped by Windmill Farm in the night and shined his flashlight on Sadie's window. She had ignored it and he had left, defeated. Alice's plan might just work.

Gid stopped by The Sweet Tooth bakery and picked out pink petit fours—tiny little cakes covered with smooth icing. He asked the owner's granddaughter, Nora Stroot, if she would pipe a letter in icing on each petit four—he described it just the way Alice had told him to. Then Nora Stroot told him that would cost an extra fifty cents per letter and Gid gulped. Resigned, he pulled out his money. "Okay. Here are the words I want:

I ♡ U
MEA CULPA

"That's only eleven cakes," Nora Stroot said. "You're paying for a baker's dozen whether you get them or not. But I'll still charge you for the piping."

Gid bit his lip. "Then make it 'Y-O-U.'"

"What does 'mea culpa' mean?"

"It's Latin for 'my mistake.'"

Nora Stroot raised a pencil-drawn eyebrow. "Sure she'll figure *that* out?"

"Absolutely." Wouldn't she? Mary Kate certainly knew it. Of course, Sadie would know it too.

"You must have done something incredibly idiotic." She waited for Gid to elaborate on his stupidity, but he stood there in stony silence. She sighed, giving up, and turned away to write the letters in white icing on the petit fours, set them in a pink box, wrapped it with a ribbon, and handed it to him. "That will be twenty-five dollars."

Gid swallowed. "Thank you."

He took the bakery box right over to Windmill Farm and knocked on the kitchen door, but no one was at home. The door was unlocked, so Gid thought it would be wise to leave the box of petit fours on the kitchen table so they wouldn't melt in the sun. He saw that someone had left some sandwiches on the table, covered with plastic wrap. He pulled the ribbon off the box and opened it, then grabbed a pen off the kitchen counter and wrote on the top of the box: *To Sadie from Gideon*. Just so there was no mistaking who had brought these little cakes.

He hoped Alice was right about this. He had started to doubt her advice on the ride home from the bakery. What did Alice know about courting, anyway? She had never had a boyfriend. Maybe he should just take the little cakes and go home.

Suddenly, he heard a baby's cry upstairs, then Sadie's voice soothing the baby. She was home! Panic streaked through him. Before he left, he turned the pink box around, lid open, so that she would see it as she came down the steps into the kitchen. He looked at the pink box again, straightened each lettered petit four so it would read just right, took a deep breath, and hurried to leave. Quietly.

This past week, Amos seemed to be feeling more like his old self. He still went about his farm chores slowly and methodically, but he was starting to feel the old bounce in his step. He couldn't even remember when he had last felt a bounce in his step. Why, it had been years!

Amos and Will had spent the last few mornings out in the fruit orchards, trimming dead branches, and moving M.K.'s hives from one orchard to another so the bees could work their magic. Amos's muscles ached from the hard work—a wonderful ache. Will didn't know much about farming, but he was an able and willing worker. He liked to talk too. He asked all kinds of questions about the birds on Windmill Farm and that always seemed to lead to Menno and his birding. Will had a keen interest in birds, all kinds, and Amos was happy to oblige him. Talking about Menno like this, in this way, felt like a healing balm to his soul. Each time they talked, Amos felt the knot in his chest release a little more.

It was past noon and they were famished. At breakfast this morning,

Sadie had said she would run lunch out to them after the baby woke up from his nap since Fern was at a quilting frolic, but Amos didn't think they could wait much longer. "Will, if you wouldn't mind running back to the house, Fern left lunch for us on the table. And some iced tea in the fridge."

Happily, Will dropped his gloves and started up the hill. "Bring something sweet too!" Amos called out. As long as Fern wasn't there to monitor his low-fat, heart-healthy diet, he might as well go for broke.

Will stomped off his dirty shoes and walked into the kitchen. The house was quiet except for the sound of water splashing upstairs. Fern was gone, so maybe Sadie was giving the baby a bath. He was a little surprised to find himself hoping to see Sadie for a minute. Or two.

"Your dad sent me to get lunch," he called up the stairs. "He wants to eat now."

"It's on the table," came Sadie's muffled reply. "You can take everything."

He washed his hands at the kitchen sink and filled the cups on a tray with iced tea from the fridge. On the table were a plate full of sandwiches, a bowl of fruit, and a pink bakery box. He put the plate and a couple apples on the tray, then reached across the table to grab the pink box. On top he saw words scrawled: "To Sadie from Gideon." He rolled his eyes. If Sadie didn't want the pink box, then it was clear to Will she had no interest in that hapless schoolteacher.

Will piled the box on the tray, but it slipped and fell to the floor. Will set the tray down. He knelt to open the box and found little cakes, all topsy turvy. Girly cakes! His mother used to serve those petit fours when she had friends over to play bridge. To Will, it was one more piece of evidence that there was something *wrong* with that schoolteacher. He popped a cake into his mouth, then another. Delicious! Will tucked as many cakes as he could on the sandwich plate. He set the pink box on the table. "Thanks for the sweets," he called up the stairs to Sadie. "I took as many as I could and left the rest."

He strained to listen, hoping Sadie might come down to say hello. But he could still hear water splashing upstairs, so he flipped the lid onto the box, picked up the tray, and headed out the door. Amos would get a kick out of those little girly cakes for dessert.

Sadie couldn't believe that a baby could make so much work out of such a little task. She had started to change Joe-Jo's diaper and reached down to get a new one as he released a spray that covered Sadie, her dress, her hair and prayer cap, his own undershirt, the floor, the bureau top. What hadn't been sprayed? She gave the baby a bath, diapered and dressed him—was it the fourth time this morning?—set him in the basket, and stuck her own head under the sink faucet to wash her hair as she heard Will's voice calling from the kitchen. He had come to the house to pick up lunch.

Fern had fixed sandwiches before she left for the frolic. It was good timing to have Will stop in so he could carry everything out, because she didn't know how she would manage juggling the baby and the sandwich tray and the iced tea. She tried to hurry as she rinsed shampoo out of her hair so she could join Will downstairs, but the next thing she knew, he called to say he was leaving, and something about how sweet it was to have things ready on the table.

Wasn't he wonderful to notice?

Five minutes later, Sadie's hair was towel-dried, a fresh cap pinned on, and she was in a clean dress. She took one more look in the mirror that hung on the bathroom wall. She wished so much to be tall and slim that she almost hoped to see a tall, slim girl. But in the glass she saw a small, round girl in a blue dress. Even the face in the mirror was round. Her chin had a soft curve, and her nose was almost right, but her eyes were too far apart, and they didn't sparkle. They didn't sparkle at all. At least her hair wasn't such a bad color. Once, after church, Gideon had told her that the sunlight beamed on her hair and it looked golden. She tipped her head to see if the sun from the window bounced off it. Was it golden-y? Suddenly Sadie realized that if anyone saw her preening in the mirror right now, they would think she was vain! She picked up the baby and went downstairs, stopping abruptly when she saw a pink bakery box. On top it said "To Sadie from Gideon." Inside the box were four little cockeyed tiny cakes. U-L-I-E. Huh? What did Ulie mean? What was Gid trying to say? Then she gasped. You lie.

Tears filled Sadie's eyes. How cruel! How insensitive. How downright *mean*. What was wrong with Gideon Smucker? How dare he accuse her of lying! Then anger swooped in and displaced her hurt feelings. She picked up the box to throw it in the garbage, but thought twice. She might as well eat the little cakes. They did look delicious, even if the message was unspeakably rude. *Then* she would throw the box away.

And she would never, ever speak to Gideon Smucker again.

Will had lied to Mr. Petosky. On Sunday, Eve had laid one egg. He had observed her standing in or near the nest, guarding the egg. Will knew she would lay another egg or two before incubation would begin. On Monday morning, when Mr. Petosky called, there were two more eggs. And this morning, there were four eggs in the dug-out scape.

He had climbed a tree to see the eggs. The eggs were slightly smaller than a chicken egg, mottled with a dark, reddish-brown pigment. Eve would begin incubation now for the next thirty-three days. Once it began, Eve would sit on the nest and rarely leave the eggs unattended. Adam would give her brief reprieves so she could fly off and hunt for food.

And then the eyases would only stay in the nest another four to six weeks before they tried to fledge.

He was going to have to tell Mr. Petosky the news soon. There looked to be four viable eggs in the scape. He just wasn't quite ready to have Mr. Petosky breathing down his neck. He needed time to think. He was pretty sure Mr. Petosky would find a way to confirm Will's findings.

All kinds of things could happen to these eggs. Often, there could be "egg failure." The female would push an egg that has failed to the side of the scape. If an entire clutch was lost, the female may attempt to re-nest several weeks later, often in a different location.

"Nice view up there?"

Will looked down the tree to find Sadie peering up at him. He shimmied down the trunk and hopped off as he neared the end.

She tilted her head when he smiled at her. "Are you all right?"

"Most of the redness is gone." Will wriggled his fingers at Sadie. "The skin isn't as taut as it was before, and the blisters don't appear to be anything that will last more than a day or two."

"I didn't mean your hands, but I'm glad they're doing better." She crossed her arms behind her and leaned her back against the tree. "You had a strange look on your face."

"Me?" Will said, looking straight at Sadie. "Strange? Stranger than normal?"

Sadie smiled, then shook her head slowly. "Don't mind me. Every now and then, I just get this odd feeling that you're carrying around something heavy. But then, the feeling passes and you seem right as rain. Better than rain." She paused. "I might be wrong. Maybe you're not sad or confused about something at all. Maybe I'm imagining things. I've been known to do that."

She wasn't wrong. In fact, she couldn't be any more right. He was sure she had all manners of herbs and remedies for everything else, but what could you do about what was bothering him? He doubted she had herbs for a guilty conscience. Or a concoction for soul sickness.

What was wrong with him—what made him do the things he knew he shouldn't do and what kept him from doing the things he should? Maybe his father was right. Maybe he did have a demon inside him. "My father would say I am suffering from acute laziness."

"What does your father do for a living?"

"He's a neurosurgeon."

She looked puzzled. "What's that?"

"He operates on people's brains."

"So he drills holes in people's skulls?"

"Well, not really. He specializes in endovascular work—the vessels that bring blood to the brain. A lot of problems in the brain occur in those arteries and veins, but there's all kinds of technology that allows him to treat them without drilling open the skull. Much less invasive. No cutting bones or opening someone's head. But endovascular neurosurgery is the most dangerous of all the specialties of neurosurgery. Most of the people he sees have run out of options. They're either going to die, or my dad will operate and save them."

"He must be a smart man. It's hard to imagine having the courage to operate on a brain."

"Dad says the brain is like a melon, with a thick, leathery covering inside the skull—the dura mater—that gets pulled back and the glistening surface of the brain is exposed. He says it's like putting on a diving mask and looking beneath the surface of the water at a coral reef: a whole new world opens up."

Sadie shuddered. "He has such a responsibility. What if he made a mistake?"

"I don't think my father makes mistakes." Will scratched his head. "Ever. He's pretty confident that he's the best neurosurgeon in the country."

"What makes him so sure of that?"

"Everybody tells him so. Other doctors send their toughest cases to him. From all over the country."

She gave him a shy smile. "I can't imagine having that kind of confidence."

"Sadie," Will said, "if you had the kind of self-confidence my father has, you wouldn't be you." He shifted his gaze to a flock of ducks coming in for a landing near the creek. "You wouldn't even be someone you'd like."

Sadie rose and walked down the bank to the creek. He watched her from afar. He noticed a curious stillness about her. She was, at her center, as tranquil as Blue Lake Pond on a windless night. Just being near her had a calming effect. He discovered he was in no hurry to be elsewhere, that his normally impatient, easily bored nature somehow found the patience to stand back and just be.

You're good for me, Sadie Lapp.

For the briefest of moments, Will entertained a fantasy—that he and Sadie were together like this, really together. Caring for a small farm, raising a family.

He chased the fantasy away, swatting it as if it were a mosquito about to bite. He and Sadie Lapp belonged in different worlds. She wasn't his type, much as he wanted her to be.

As he noticed how absorbed she was by the nature around her, it seemed as if she were no mere observer of the world but right in the middle of it. He'd wondered if she knew there was something special about her. Probably not.

Will walked down to join her. There were six ducks, honking and rustling about in the creek. Sounding remarkably similar to last Sunday's long-winded

Amish preacher, she called out, "Troubles are often the tools by which God fashions us for better things!"

Blank stares from every last one of those ducks. She sighed. "I'm practicing my newly acquired boldness on them. It doesn't seem to be working."

"Don't take it to heart," Will said with a grin. "My guess is they just haven't been to church lately."

13

For the first time in her life, M.K. could not imagine life without school and books. She had only one more year of formal schooling ahead of her. After that, it would just be one endless day of chores after another. She was already worried that crotchety Alice Smucker would come back next year and Gid would return to full-time farming with his father. She thought he preferred teaching to farming, though he would never say so. Gid was private about his feelings. He was a first-rate teacher, the best. The very best.

M.K. had always annoyed Alice when she finished her work early and grew bored. Alice would tell her to redo her work for the practice. By contrast, Gid stayed late in the day so that he could give her new assignments the next morning. He always had something new for her to puzzle out and she loved the challenges. Shakespeare for studying the beauty of language, Galileo to read the mystery in the night sky. She had learned the names of all the stars and constellations. She was struggling a little with geometry—she preferred algebra. But today, Gid corrected her paper and handed it back to her with a smile. "You're getting there."

When Gid smiled, his dimples deepened and his eyes shimmered with satisfaction. M.K. had trouble concentrating after getting one of his smiles.

Sometimes, she would stay after class and help him clean up, chattering away about a piece of poetry she had read or an essay, and he would listen carefully. He commented now and then on her thoughts, offered her some suggestions of different poets, and even brought in a book of beginning

Latin for her—to help understand the roots of words, he said. He never patronized her, not once.

She watched him work with the second-grade class. He was so handsome! It was a tragedy that Sadie refused to fall madly in love with him. It would be sheer heaven to have Gid as a brother-in-law. She would get to see him every day for the rest of her life. Maybe she could live with them! She planned to never marry because she thought all boys—except for Gid and her father and Uncle Hank—were short on brains and long on foolishness. She had no patience for them.

Gid was playing a game with the second graders—at least, they thought it was a game. It was a clever way to encourage reading comprehension. The three second graders had all read a short story and Gid was quizzing them on details in the story. Each time they answered correctly, they took a giant step closer to the blackboard.

That was what made Gid so remarkable—he was always thinking up ways to make learning interesting. Not too long ago, he had a "100 Days of School" celebration. Everyone brought a collection of one hundred items. Most of the kids brought in pennies or marbles—pretty dull stuff. M.K. brought in one hundred two-week-old chicks. It was great fun until the chicks pecked through the boxes and escaped, scattering around the room. Then Ruthie sat on one and that got her all bug-eyed and tearful. After Davy Mast called her a chicken killer, she couldn't stop crying. She sniffed and sobbed all afternoon until finally Gid sent her home, along with M.K. and her boxes of ninety-nine chicks. M.K. sighed, thinking back on that day. Like many of her plans, this one went awry.

She noticed that Gid dismissed the second graders and brought up the third graders. Now, why couldn't Alice Smucker have ever thought of ways to make school fun? Except for the occasional mischief of Jimmy Fisher and his cohorts, every day with Alice Smucker was identical to the day before. Last fall, as the new school year started, it was almost—though not quite—a letdown that Jimmy had finally graduated eighth grade and was no longer in school.

Almost. But not quite.

Stoney Ridge was as different from Will's life in Philadelphia as anything could be. He thought of how, at the end of a day, he would get back to his fraternity house after his last class, watch TV or play a video game, or head over to Chelsea Van Dyke's apartment and have a beer, maybe neck with Chelsea on the sofa if she was in the mood for necking. She usually was.

Here, on this Amish farm, he was working himself to the bone. Each night, he trudged back to the cottage and flopped on the bed, exhausted. The next thing he knew, birdsong was welcoming the new dawn. When he heard the sweet music of the birds, a smile creased his face.

Will considered himself to be a closet birder. He never let anyone in his college fraternity, or any girlfriend for that matter, know how he loved birds and spent vacations on bird-watching expeditions. If he were to hunt birds, his friends would admire him. But observe them? Study them? It would be laughingstock, fodder for ridicule.

Bird-watching was the one activity he and his father enjoyed together. Dr. Charles William Stoltz could identify each and every type of the enormous variety of fowl that migrated through southeast Pennsylvania. He was a truly dedicated birder. The birds were proof in some way that Will's father did have a tender side. Most of their good moments together were spent taking long walks through the woods with binoculars hanging around their necks, thumbing through field manuals. Beyond that, Will's study of them gave them something to talk about. His father preferred taking him along on birding expeditions rather than any of his brainy bird-watching doctor friends. Will was quieter, he said.

It was the only compliment his father had ever given him. And Will wasn't really sure it was a compliment. He was quiet around his father because he was thoroughly intimidated by him.

Briefly, he thought about wanting to tell his father what Amos had said to him this morning. Amos had pointed out the field he wanted Will to plow under but instructed him to leave the far corner alone because the bobolinks were nesting. "They earn their rent by giving us pleasure," Amos had told him. His father would enjoy that kind of thinking.

Even though the spring morning was raw and bleak, awash in gray, Will was hot. He wiped the sweat from his brow and sat back on the plow, admiring the morning's work. He thought his plowing skills were improving.

The furrows in this field weren't quite as wobbly looking as yesterday's, and much better than the day before. He was faster too, which suited him, because he was pretty sure he had felt some rain sprinkles. From the looks of those clouds, he wouldn't be surprised if a drizzle turned into a steady rain.

For now, he needed food. He thought about what he could scrounge up in the cottage when he saw Sadie wave to him from the fence, near the water trough. He led the horses over to the water trough and let them drink their fill. Doozy was chasing imaginary birds on the other side of the fence. He worried about that dog.

Sadie gave him a shy smile and lifted a basket. "I brought lunch."

"Ah! You're an angel."

"Better eat it first, then decide. Dad and Fern took the baby with them to go visit Annie's grandfather—to let him know to expect some help on Saturday. So I made lunch."

Will splashed his hands in the horse trough and hopped over the fence. Sadie was already setting up a picnic under a shade tree. He sprawled on the ground and let out a deep sigh.

She handed him a sandwich. "When will your falcons become parents?"

Will unwrapped the sandwich and took a lusty bite. How was it possible that food tasted better here? This sandwich he was eating, for example. The bread was homemade, the smoked turkey was real turkey, the lettuce was crisp, the tomato ripe. Delicious! "In about a month. Hopefully, they will be good parents too." He glanced at her. "That's not always the case." Not with animals, not with people. Certainly Sadie couldn't understand that, for she'd come from a family where warmth and belonging and love were like flour and sugar, staples in the pantry.

She threw a crust of bread over to Doozy, who pounced on it like a cat. "God seems to give most animals a basic instinct of how to care for their young. I've always thought it's another way he shows us how he loves us."

"Parents—" He stopped, and felt his stomach twist. "I hope God loves us more than parents do. If he doesn't, I'm doomed."

"Your parents weren't loving?" she asked tentatively.

He emitted a bark, humorless mirth. "Not exactly." Love, in Will's family, had always come with strings. It was a reward for perfect behavior. It wasn't handed out for free.

"Some people have a hard time showing love to the ones they care the most about."

He gave her an odd stare. "Do you always see the world this way?"

Sadie reached in the basket and handed him a bright green apple. "What way is that?"

"Always looking for the good in a situation." He took a bite of the apple and chewed. "I can't think of too many girls who would be happy to have a baby dropped in their laps."

"This wasn't just any baby. But this baby—this one is a gift to us. It connects us to Menno." She looked up at the sky. "I think God knew my family needed this baby."

"Life isn't always that way, you know. Some things just don't work out for the best." He took a few more bites of his apple and tossed the core away. Then he tilted the thermos to his mouth and drained it. He felt better now, much better. "The way I see it, I think it's better not to expect too much out of life. That way, you don't get beaten down or disappointed by people. It's better to meet life head-on, eyes wide open, so you're not blindsided in the end. Cut off. Left to drift in a canoe without paddles." The last sentence tumbled with a ridiculous amount of emotion. He pressed his fingertips to his forehead and closed his eyes, embarrassed. They had drifted way too far into personal issues, and he thought he might be making an idiot of himself.

"The Bible says that for those who love God, things will work out for the best. Like the way the baby worked out to be the best." She glanced at him. "Don't you believe in God's goodness?"

They locked eyes.

"I believe in you, Sadie Lapp, and your goodness." He'd only known her for a week now, but he could tell she was a genuinely kind, genuinely good person.

"But I'm not, Will. No one is truly good. We're all on the same level in God's sight. We're all sinners in need of his mercy. But the amazing thing is that God loves us anyway. And he can straighten us out and smooth out all the wrinkles and put us to use again."

Will opened his mouth but nothing came out. He was seized with a sudden curiosity about Sadie. What would she have been like as a child?

What did she want her life to look like in five years? In ten or twenty? There was so much about her that he didn't know. He raised her hand and impulsively pressed a soft kiss on the back of it. "Thank you for lunch." He jumped up and hopped over the fence to get back to work. Before he climbed back on the plow, he tipped his cowboy hat to her and grinned.

The week dragged by interminably—but finally it was Saturday. M.K. charged into the kitchen, her very being radiating sparks of excitement. She had a plan all worked out for today. The most brilliant plan she had ever come up with! She knew Fern wondered why she was so especially cheerful, but she would have to wait to find out.

Edith Fisher and her son Jimmy pulled up to the house at eight o'clock sharp, as expected. Uncle Hank and M.K. were waiting for them, arms filled with tools and gloves and hampers filled with groceries. From the backseat of the buggy, M.K. directed Jimmy to drive to a tired-looking house on a tired-looking lane. She hadn't been there since before Menno had passed, and it had looked bad then. Knee-high weeds filled the front yard. Spiderwebs hung from every corner. The old man was sitting in his rocker on the front porch, like he had been expecting them. Then she remembered that he might be, since her father and Fern had dropped by earlier in the week to let him know they were coming today. Fern had taken him a casserole and come home clucking with disapproval that an elderly Amish man was living alone. "What is the world coming to if the Amish aren't caring for their own?" she muttered all afternoon.

M.K. would never say it aloud, but sometimes she thought that Fern sounded downright prideful about being Amish, as if they could do no wrong, unlike the English, who could do no right. Such thoughts were best left unsaid, she decided, and felt that it was a sign she was growing up. She was starting to have a filter—just like Fern always said she needed—and it amused M.K. that the filter was being used for Fern!

When the Swartzentruber colony decided to up and move to Ohio, Annie and her grandfather stayed behind. Amos thought it might have had something to do with the baby's arrival, though Fern chimed in that she was pretty sure Annie had taken pains to hide her pregnancy. There weren't many signs of a baby in that house, she pointed out. "Certainly no signs that a baby was going to be staying."

Amos said he had tried to encourage Annie's grandfather to join up with the Ohio colony, but he refused to leave. He was just waiting and waiting for Annie to return.

Annie's grandfather was really old. So old that the skin on his neck moved up and down like a turkey wattle as he swallowed hard. So old that the veins on his hands stood out like large, blue hoses. When he noticed M.K., he squinted so hard that his forehead knotted up. "ANNIE?"

"No, I'm Mary Kate. MARY KATE LAPP."

The old man crumpled. She nearly fibbed and said she was Annie after the old man looked so disappointed. But Uncle Hank read her mind and elbowed her, nodding his head toward Edith and Jimmy to fob her off. It wouldn't be right to lie, not with Edith Fisher standing right next to her with her can-and-string telephone line, direct to heaven. M.K. didn't think God would mind a little white lie to make an old man happy, but Edith Fisher would think otherwise.

They walked inside the house and found it was worse than the outside. The kitchen was a wreck—crusty pans in the sink, a sticky floor that needed a good scrub. Smelled bad too, an acrid smell that was worse than Joe-Jo's diapers. They went out to the backyard and couldn't even see the path to the barn, the weeds were so tall. Leaning against the barn was an old buggy—a black top without the reflective triangle on the back—belonging to a Swartzentruber.

"Where do we even begin?" Jimmy said under his breath.

M.K. had no idea.

Off in the distance, M.K. heard the sound of an arriving horse and buggy. Then another, and another. She rushed to the front. It had worked! Yesterday, she had quietly invited all of her friends and neighbors to come to help.

"What is—" Jimmy started to say as he came up behind her and saw the lane crowded with buggies.

"What is going on?" was what he was going to say, M.K. thought, oozing smugness. During Friday lunch, she had one of her brainstorms. It was a bolt from the blue, and not a minute too soon. She felt very proud of herself for coming up with the idea, even though she was a little disappointed that it had taken her so long to think of it. "I invited them. Thirty-three of them." She turned to him. "I figured that if we have to give up thirty-five hours, it would be more efficient if thirty-five people gave up one hour. Then we'd be done with this community service nonsense and I can have my Saturdays back for fishing with Uncle Hank."

Even Jimmy Fisher couldn't hold back a grin of admiration on his handsome face. "Bischt net so dumm wie du guckscht." *You're not as dumb as you look.* "Think it'll work?"

M.K. looked up at him. "Absolutely!"

"Graeh net zu gschwind," said a familiar voice from behind her. *Don't crow too soon.*

The wind went out of Mary Kate.

Fern! So meddlesome!

Jimmy started laughing so hard at M.K. that he had to double over.

Combining double bossy powers between Fern and Edith Fisher, folks were organized in groups of two or three and given tasks to complete. M.K.'s plans for the day fizzled as she finished a task and was given another one, again and again. And again.

By midafternoon, the work crew had made a serious dent in the transformation of Annie's grandfather's house, inside and out. There was food in the cleaned-out refrigerator, fresh linens were put on his bed, rugs were beaten, floors swept and wiped down, windows washed. Outside, the weeds had been mowed. Fern had even brought some potted flowers for his porch. "To cheer him up," she said, "while he waits for Annie."

"She's never coming back," M.K. said. "She gave us that baby because she's never coming back."

"You can't be so sure of that," Fern told her. "A mother has mighty strong feelings for her baby."

"Not so strong that they stopped her from abandoning the baby," M.K. said.

"She didn't really abandon him," Fern said. "She put him in Sadie's care for safekeeping. She must have been awfully scared and overwhelmed."

"Then she should have just married someone."

"Marriage isn't always a solution to a problem." Fern smoothed some stray hairs off of M.K.'s forehead. "Things in this world aren't always so white and black." She picked up a broom and a pail filled with dirty rags and headed out to the porch.

"Well, at least we have Annie's grandfather set up so he'll be all right by himself," M.K. said hopefully.

Fern eyed her over her shoulder. "We have him set up so that you and Jimmy can come each Saturday and keep up with the housework and bring him fresh food." Out loud, she subtracted seven from thirty-five. "Let's see. Just four more Saturdays."

"That many?" M.K. asked in a puny voice.

Fern wasn't listening. "Don't you agree, Hank?"

Uncle Hank was helping Annie's grandfather into his chair on the porch where he liked to sit and watch the world go by—not that much of the world was going by this little dirt lane. He lifted up the old man's feet and placed them on a pillow. "You betcha! I might even come with you two next Saturday. I'll bring my checkers."

Annie's grandfather brightened at that thought. But it worried M.K. Since when did Uncle Hank volunteer for work? Ordinarily, he woke early and tinkered with a few buggies that were sitting in his buggy shop, since he was up at that hour anyway. But then he figured he'd done his day's chores and off he'd go to fish at Blue Lake Pond.

"What would you say to that, Edith? You coming too?" Uncle Hank looked over at Edith and winked, which flustered her. Edith Fisher never flustered.

Edith looked away, and her hand crept up to the knot of hair on her neck. "We'll see." A rosy blush crept over her face.

Their eyes met.

M.K. and Jimmy exchanged a dark glance, a rare moment when they saw life from the same vantage point.

What was happening to the world? Everything was upside down.

14

Weeks passed, and life at Windmill Farm fell into a routine. With the weather growing hotter and more humid, the family tried to rise early in the morning and do chores before the worst of the day. The baby slept for longer stretches now and was putting on weight. Now and then, he would have a colicky day, but the goat's milk had helped considerably.

Sadie loved the baby's soft, round cheeks best of all. She couldn't stop kissing those fat cheeks. She wondered how long it took for a baby to become yours, for love and familiarity to set like mortar in bricks. Maybe that was the process described as bonding: knowing a child so well you knew him as well as you knew yourself.

As she cradled Joe-Jo in her arms, she thought about her neighbor Mattie Riehl, who had been a foster mother for a baby girl and had hoped to adopt her, but then the birth mother changed her mind and refused to relinquish parental rights. Afterward, she remembered Mattie saying that life felt overturned, like freshly plowed earth. Life had to start over.

At least every other day, someone stopped by Windmill Farm to seek Sadie out for a remedy or advice. She felt encouraged to keep going, to continue learning about healing herbs and offer remedies to people for minor ailments, aches, and pains. She loved helping others, but she assumed that she was making little difference in the day-to-day lives of most people. She rested in the knowledge that she had given them all she could to make their lives a little better.

Deacon Abraham stopped by one sunny morning to ask Sadie if she would pay a call on his wife, Esther, who suffered from persistent headaches. "She's been to every doctor and chiropractor she can find, had every treatment and test and scan imaginable, and they can't find anything that's wrong."

This was just the kind of ailment that worried Sadie. The very reason she didn't charge people for her remedies. If the best medical minds of Lancaster County couldn't help Esther, what could she possibly do? And on top of that worry bounced another one: Esther frightened her. Sadie had never seen a smile rise all the way to her eyes.

Abraham sensed her hesitation. "Just . . . go talk to her, Sadie. For my sake."

So Sadie went to Abraham and Esther's farm. The brick house lay nestled amidst a sea of carefully tended greenery and neat outbuildings. Chickens clucked in a fenced yard, and a cow lowed from a small pasture. Esther's mare stood within the buggy shafts, her head low, apparently dozing. Sadie drew her buggy alongside Esther's and the mare stirred, nosing the visiting gelding. He nickered in reply.

Leaving the horses to get acquainted, Sadie walked stiffly across the yard to the house.

Esther met her at the door. "Now's not a good time for a visit, Sadie. I've got a frightful headache today."

"Abraham asked me to come by." She held up a little bag. "I brought some special tea that might help."

Esther looked suspiciously at her. "I suppose it couldn't hurt."

She opened the door and led Sadie to the kitchen. As Sadie brewed the tea, Esther told her all about the headaches. When they started, how often she had them, how they made her head pound as if a woodpecker were hammering away at her. How incompetent doctors couldn't find any reason for them. She left nothing out, filling the air with blame for others, as if they had given her the headaches. Did Esther always look for the dark side of things and judge?

Before Esther could start on another grievance, Sadie handed her a cup of tea, and she sipped it, then made a face. "It tastes like tree bark."

"It is. It's made with the bark of a willow tree." Sadie sat down beside her. "So you say the headaches started a few years ago?"

Esther nodded.

Sadie felt a strange stirring in her heart. "And the doctors can't find anything wrong?"

"No. But that doesn't stop them from taking my money." That thought inspired her to launch into another tirade against modern medicine.

Sadie wasn't really listening to her. She had traveled back to a time when a woman arrived at Old Deborah's door. The woman's face was tight and pale, riddled with anxiety. Old Deborah listened to her ailment—Sadie couldn't exactly remember what it was but thought it was something like neck pain. Similar to Esther, this woman had spent a fortune on doctors and treatments and tests and scans—without any relief. Old Deborah listened carefully in that wise, knowing way she had. Then she took the woman's hands in hers and told her what she thought the problem was. At first, the woman was shocked, angry even. Then she cried. But when she left, she was a different person. Calm, at peace, and as far as Sadie knew, her neck never bothered her again.

Sadie had the strangest feeling that the cause of Esther's headaches was the same as that woman with the neck pain. As Esther kept talking, Sadie was praying, and waiting for an answer, listening for God's voice to speak to her heart. She had learned that the most important part of her prayers was the waiting and listening. *Go ahead*, she heard God whisper. *It's okay to speak the truth in love.*

Sadie's lips quivered. Her chest grew tight. She was clasping her hands so tightly her knuckles ached. She forced herself to relax her grip, flattening her palms on her thighs. She knew one thing—she had to be willing to speak up, regardless of the response she might get. *Please, Lord God, give me boldness.*

"Esther, there is something I'd like you to think about. Emotions can affect the health of our bodies, for good or for bad. Stress, anger, and resentment can have powerful negative effects. Those bitter feelings are like an acid that eats away at its container."

Esther looked at Sadie as if her barn was short a rafter.

Sadie's heart was thumping so loudly, she was sure Esther could hear it. Why did she have to say anything like this? She could have just given Esther the willow bark tea and left it at that. That's all Abraham had asked of her.

For a brief second, Sadie thought about running. Just dropping everything and bolting. No explanation. But what would that serve other than to confirm to Esther that Sadie Lapp was crazy? This made no sense! Still, she felt that strange inner stirring to keep going. *Oh Lord God, please help!* "Is there anyone in your life whom you have not been able to forgive?"

Esther's face frosted over. Minutes ticked by while Sadie waited for Esther's response. She opened her lips, but no sound came out.

Sadie was scared. Deborah had always said that some health problems were spiritual and emotional in nature, but she didn't tell Sadie which ones. What right did Sadie have to ask someone such a personal question? Especially someone like Esther!

Sadie studied Esther carefully. A vision popped in her mind of watching a cobra puff up, fangs glittering, preparing to strike. Sadie scooted her chair back a little, just in case. But after a few more long, painful seconds, Esther suddenly deflated like a balloon in her chair, dropping her head to her chest. She uttered a name that Sadie would never have expected to hear from her.

"Emma."

For a moment Sadie thought she had misunderstood Esther.

"Excuse me?"

"Emma. My daughter. For leaving the church, like she did. With that man. Steelhead."

Sadie had forgotten that Esther's daughter had left the church. It had happened years ago, when Sadie was just a little girl. "Do you want to tell me about it?"

Without hesitation, Esther began to talk, describing how Emma had eloped with an English man—a former convict, she hastened to say, wrinkling her nose. "Emma works in a quilt shop in town. Right in Stoney Ridge! And never comes by to see me, not ever. Not once."

"Have you ever invited her to come for a visit?"

"Of course not! Emma is shunned. I'm married to a deacon. I'm held up as an example to others. Emma is the one who chose to leave. There are consequences to that decision. There are reasons for shunning. Sin endangers us all."

"I understand your feelings," Sadie said. "It's clear that you feel stress over Emma."

Esther held her hands tightly in her lap, so tight that her knuckles had turned white. But she wasn't ushering Sadie to the door, as Sadie had thought she would.

"You feel as if you've lost a daughter."

"I *have* lost a daughter."

Sadie nodded. "Maybe you even feel that she's rejected you, as well as our church. But, Esther, this bitterness toward Emma might be hurting your health and stealing joy from your life."

She paused for a few moments to see how Esther was responding. Her eyes were downcast, fixed to the tabletop, but her hands were tight fists in her lap.

"Jesus said that if we forgive others, he will forgive us. But if we don't forgive others, God will not forgive us." She reached out and covered Esther's hands. "I think you need to forgive Emma."

Esther looked genuinely surprised. "I don't know . . . how I can do that."

As soon as the words left her mouth, she began to weep. Sadie got up and scrambled to find a box of tissues.

This was new territory for Sadie, but she had an idea of what needed to come next. "If you're willing, we can pray, right now, for your heart to be changed."

Esther was crying so loud that Sadie handed her the whole box of tissues. "I'm going to pray now."

Esther gave a brief nod.

"Lord God, Esther chooses to forgive Emma for the things she did that hurt her. Now you continue, Esther. What do you want to forgive Emma for?"

Esther took a deep, shuddering breath before she spoke. "I forgive Emma for making poor choices. I forgive her for thinking only of herself. I forgive her for breaking her vows to you."

"Is there anything else you need to forgive Emma for?"

"I forgive Emma for . . . for . . . choosing Steelhead over her own mother." The words whooshed out of Esther, as if she had been waiting to say them for years. That confession started Esther on another round of weeping, but Sadie didn't mind so much. She had the most wonderful feeling that God was doing some housecleaning in Esther's heart.

"Esther, we all need to be forgiven. Each one of us. Would you like to ask

God to forgive you for holding these feelings of resentment and bitterness against your daughter?"

Esther was so ready that she didn't wait for Sadie's words but offered her own. "God, please forgive me for holding this bitterness toward Emma. And . . . Steelhead, for taking her away." It was as though a long silence between Esther and God had been broken. A sense of relief came over the room as Esther wiped her eyes and nose.

As Sadie got ready to leave, she thought that Esther hardly looked like the same person. Sadie had actually observed a calm wash over her, like an ocean wave. Her countenance had gone from austerity to softness.

Two weeks later, Sadie saw Esther at church. Esther lowered her voice and whispered, "I stopped by the quilt shop and saw Emma." She squeezed Sadie's shoulder. "Of course, we'll just keep that between ourselves."

Abraham found Sadie, after lunch, and thanked her for the herbal tea she had left for Esther. "Her headaches are so much better that she hasn't needed any of her pain medication. Sadie Lapp, that tea of yours really worked."

"It's always God who does the work," Sadie said.

Sadie had never seen anything have such a transforming power. Asking God's help to forgive had turned a harsh woman like Esther into a kinder, gentler person. The result was amazing. Forgiveness, Sadie decided, was the best medicine of all.

Amos had been filling the lawn mower with gasoline and spilled it on his shirt. He went to the house, gave a wave to Fern in the kitchen, and bolted up the stairs to get a fresh shirt before she smelled the gasoline on him and chewed him out for ruining a good piece of clothing. At the top of the stairs, he stopped suddenly. It was a miracle, one he hadn't even been thinking of lately. He had walked up the stairs—upstairs!—without having to stop halfway, without gasping for air. Why, he had practically taken the steps two at a time, like a young colt!

He changed his shirt and passed by Sadie's room, where the baby was starting to stir in the basket. Joe-Jo was nearly outgrowing it, and they should be thinking about getting a crib soon. Amos listened to the even rhythm of the baby's breathing. He picked him up and held him close, as close as he could. He put the baby's tiny hand over his heart. "Do you feel that, little one? That's your father's heart, beating away."

When he turned, he saw Fern standing at the doorjamb with a soft look on her face.

He felt a little sheepish. "At my last appointment, the doctor said that I should stop referring to it as Menno's heart and call it mine. He said it would be better for me to think of it as mine as I take all the drugs to fool my body so it doesn't reject it." He kissed the baby's downy head. "But I can't seem to think of this heart as belonging to me."

"Doctors don't know everything. He didn't know that Menno had the biggest heart in the world." Fern walked toward him and put a hand on the baby's back. "I can't think of anyone's heart I'd rather have than Menno's."

Amos watched her for a moment as she stroked the baby's back and he thought it was a shame that Fern wasn't a mother. Though, he quickly corrected himself, in a way, she was everybody's mother. Someday, maybe soon, he would have to tell her how much he appreciated her. How much they all counted on her. What a difference she had made in their lives.

Of course, she had no way of knowing what was running through his head. She turned to go. At the door, she stopped and quickly reverted to her starchy self. "Where did you hide that shirt with gasoline? It's going to take all afternoon to get that stain out."

Caught red-handed! "Under the bed."

As he heard her hunting for the shirt in his room, he leaned his chin on the top of the baby's head and nuzzled him close. What was it about Fern that made a person feel like he was out on a snowy night and had just turned the horse and buggy down the lane that led to home?

Blessed. He was a blessed man.

One morning in the middle of May, Sadie was in the kitchen getting a bottle of goat's milk ready for the baby as Will knocked softly on the kitchen door and waved through the window. He had started a habit of popping in for a cup of coffee after he did a dawn check on the falcon couple.

Fern opened the door for him and said, "No secret what you're after." She tried to sound gruff.

Will gave Fern a kiss on her cheek. "Can you blame a man? There's no better coffee on this green earth."

Fern huffed, pleased. She handed Will a mug of hot, steaming coffee with two spoonfuls of sugar already mixed in, just the way he liked it. Little by little, day by day, Sadie had watched Will win Fern over with his easy charm and smooth compliments.

"No eyases to report yet," Will said. "But it wouldn't surprise me to find a chick or two has hatched any day now." He walked over to where Sadie was sitting with the baby.

The baby opened his eyes and blew a spit bubble. "Isn't he wonderful?" Sadie's voice held awe. "He hardly ever cries anymore, and I think he knows me more than anyone else."

"I'm counting on the first smile," Will said, watching the baby over Sadie's shoulder. He finished off the last sip of coffee and put the mug on the kitchen table. "I'd better get back to Adam and Eve. Since it's Saturday, the bird-watchers will be out in full force."

"Don't forget about the gathering tonight!" Sadie called.

Will grinned and waved to her through the open window.

"Sadie, don't tell me you asked Will to the gathering." Fern frowned.

"Why not? You invited him to church and he's come twice now. Same thing." To be fair, Sadie knew it wasn't the same thing. She knew Fern wanted Will at church to see how very different a world he was entering.

"It's not the same thing. Not at all." She wagged a finger at Sadie. "I've warned you to not get sweet on him. A boy like that—he thinks he can talk any girl around to his side with a smile and flicker of his eyelashes."

Isn't that exactly how he got you in his corner? Sadie wanted to ask but knew enough not to.

Sadie couldn't begin to explain how she felt about Will Stoltz. She couldn't truthfully deny Fern's assumption. A tiny piece of her was, as Fern had put it, sweet on him. How could she resist? Will had openly sought snatches of time with her, moseying by the garden when she was picking vegetables or appearing in the barn when she was preparing the horse for the buggy. She had recognized his ploys and managed to remain kind but cool in the face of his attentiveness, accepting his assistance without encouraging him to pamper her.

Will *was* charming. He was also handsome and funny and unpredictable and . . . oh how he made her laugh! Of course, there was always that other complication . . . he was English.

But if he weren't—if there wasn't a caution, an invisible boundary about the English that had been drilled into her as a child—Sadie would be falling head over heels in love with Will Stoltz.

Then there was Gid. Many times now, he had come over late at night and flashed his beam up at her window, but she ignored it and didn't go down to meet him. Compared to Will's silver tongue, Gid was . . . solemn as an owl. Lacking passion. He had little to say, and when he did say something, it seemed to come out all wrong.

Life was so complicated. A few months ago, everyone would have assumed that she and Gid would end up together one day. But Sadie had never felt absolutely convinced of that. She wasn't sure what held her back from wholeheartedly returning his affection until she had started spending time with Will. In just a month, she felt as if she knew so much about Will—little things, like the fact that he hated tuna fish but loved sardines, or the reason he wore a cowboy hat was because he thought his head had a funny shape. It didn't. His head was beautifully shaped.

And she knew big things about him too—there was pain in his eyes when he spoke about his father. He felt as if he couldn't do enough to make his father proud of him. When Sadie held up her gentle and good father next to Will's, she knew that her childhood was one long sunny spring picnic in the country compared to his.

Her thoughts traveled to Gideon. What could she say about Gid? She cataloged everything she knew about him:

He was almost twenty years old.

He had red hair.

He had a passel of older sisters who were married and raising families of their own. All but Alice. Oh, and Marty too.

He had a widowed father.

He was a schoolteacher.

He suffered from hay fever every spring.

He wore glasses.

He liked to read.

These were facts that everyone knew about him. Although they had grown up together, she was realizing that she hardly knew him, not really.

Gideon Smucker spent most of Saturday afternoon washing and polishing his buggy, thinking up what he would say when he stopped by the Lapps' to see if Sadie wanted a ride to the gathering. It had to be executed very carefully so that it would seem like a casual thing and not so he would appear to be desperate or cloying. No, never that. He didn't want Sadie to feel smothered. Girls didn't like to be smothered, he had heard one of his sisters say.

More than a few times, he had gone over to Windmill Farm late at night to try to talk to Sadie. He flashed the beam of light against her window, but there was no response. Either she was sound asleep, not in her room, or most likely, she was ignoring his signal.

She was mad at him. Steaming mad. By now, he would have thought she might have forgiven him for assuming—like many others had—that she had a child out of wedlock. Yet she seemed far more angry with him now than she had weeks ago. Was that typical of females? For anger to multiply, like yeast in dough?

It was certainly true of Alice. She hadn't lost a bit of her anger toward Mary Kate for the sledding accident. If anything, she did her best to try to convince Gid that Sadie's indifference to him was a gift. A heaven-sent opportunity to avoid being permanently connected to the crazy Lapp family. "Take it and run!" Alice told him at least twice a week. But he would never do that.

Mary Kate had given him an idea at school last week. She mentioned that the baby was growing out of his basket. He would make the baby a cradle! Sadie couldn't stay mad at him if he gave the baby such a gift—something the baby could use every day. It would be a way to show Sadie how he felt. It was always easier for Gid to show love than to say it. Trying to put what he felt for Sadie into words was impossible. To even say it out loud—those three little words—diminished it somehow, the way a firefly lost its spark in a jar. Simple syllables couldn't contain something as rare as what Gid felt for Sadie.

He had spent the next few evenings in his dad's workshop, cutting and sanding and staining, then placing pieces in a tight metal vise to let them dry, before coming back to stain and sand some more. He rubbed his hand along the narrow rails. They were like butter! When it was completed, he stood back, pleased with his work. Not a single nail was used. Every joint fit together like a glove on a hand. Ideally, he would have liked to wait one more day, for the glue to cure in the joints, but he really wanted to give the cradle to Sadie tonight.

At four o'clock, he set the cradle carefully in the backseat of the buggy, covered it with a blanket, and went off to Windmill Farm, reviewing again what he would say and do when he saw Sadie.

First, he would surprise her with the cradle. Then, he would offer to drive Sadie to the Kings' for the singing. They would have time alone and he could finally explain and apologize for deeply offending her. She would forgive him and things could go back to the way they were, before she left for Berlin.

That was the plan. Ironclad! Foolproof.

As he drove up to Windmill Farm, M.K. flew out of the house, baby in her arms, to greet him before the buggy even reached the top of the drive. He barely hopped out of the buggy as she handed him the baby.

"Isn't he precious?" she asked.

Gid looked down at the little face peering up at him. He had held his nieces and nephews and felt fairly comfortable with babies. This little one was cute, with round dark eyes and a headful of wispy hair. He held out a finger for the baby to grab. "They start out so sweet and innocent and trusting," he said. "So full of awe at anything new, which is almost everything." The baby was smiling at him now, really smiling. A big gummy grin.

Mary Kate leaned over and softly said, "You got the first smile! Wait until Sadie hears this. She's been hoping for that first smile."

Gid looked up at her. "Let's not tell her, okay? Let's wait for her to get the first smile."

Mary Kate was lost in admiration. She gazed at him in such a way that he blushed. He actually blushed. It wasn't like he was a hero or anything, but that was the way she was staring at him. As if he saved someone from getting hurt by a felled tree, or as if he stopped a runaway buggy. It embarrassed him.

"Is Sadie here?" he asked, handing the baby to M.K. He reached into the back of the buggy for the cradle.

"She left over an hour ago with Will. She wanted to show him Blue Lake Pond."

He spun around. "The bird sitter? Blue Lake Pond?" All of his wonderful plans drifted away like smoke from a chimney.

She was staring at the cradle. "Gid, did you make that?" She bent down to rub her finger against the satin finish. "It's beautiful. It's the most beautiful cradle I've ever seen."

He put it carefully on the ground. "Don't use the cradle until tomorrow. Everything needs to set."

She looked at him as if he hung the moon. "This will definitely butter Sadie up. To think *you* made a cradle for our baby."

Gid was mortified. Was he that transparent? Now without a doubt Sadie would be convinced that he was desperate . . . Which he wasn't! He definitely wasn't. "Not a big deal. I was in the middle of making a cradle for my sister's baby. When you said the baby was growing out of his basket—I just thought I'd give you this one. I can always whip up another one for my sister's baby." And now he was a liar. He hardly ever lied! Whenever he did, even a small one, he imagined the devil himself dancing with delight.

She gazed at him with clear, blue-gray eyes, their directness telling him precisely what he did not want to hear—she was probably thinking the same thing. He was a liar of the worst sort.

She sighed. "If this doesn't convince Sadie to start talking to you again, well, then, I don't know what will."

15

Could it have been only a little more than a few weeks since Will had first met Sadie? It seemed that he had known her for years.

He was sitting on the bank of Blue Lake Pond with Sadie, watching the water lap onto the sandy shore. The lake was quiet, still, the surface so glassy—so smooth the sun shined off it like a mirror. The water rolled out in a reflection of the sky, uneven at the edges where it touched the shores, weaving into cliffs and crevices, hiding pitch-black under the shadows of overhanging trees. At times like this, with a beautiful lake looking so calm, without another human in sight, it was hard to believe there could be anything wrong in the world.

A whip-poor-will called in the distance, and from the tangle of branches, its mate trilled out a reply.

Afterward Will couldn't say how it had happened, but as they sat there in the peace of that moment, he started to tell Sadie things about his family that he had never told another living soul. Ordinarily, Will deflected any discussion about his family. He'd always made a point to keep his issues to himself. He wasn't sure if it was Sadie's low musical voice or easy, nonjudgmental manner, but it all worked together to loosen his tongue. Will was astonished to hear himself describe the last time he had seen his father—when he had told Will to pack his bags and leave the house.

Sadie's knees were bent and her elbows rested on top of them. "Do you think he really meant it?"

"He meant it. In the next breath, he told me where I was expected to go—to report to the game warden in Lancaster County. It's like . . . my dad is a barbed-wire fence—the same kind that I put up around the falcons' scape. That's what our relationship feels like. The only thing that holds us together is rusted, sharp, twisted."

Sadie drew a line in the sand with her finger. "And those barbs keep catching you?"

"Yes. Exactly! That's what he did with Mahlon and this internship—it's like he caught me."

"Maybe his barbs are meant to hold you close, not to let you go. Maybe he just doesn't know how to be close to you. Maybe he's afraid he'll lose you. Maybe barbs are all he knows. Fear makes people hold a little tighter than they should."

Will thought about that for a while. He couldn't imagine that fear of losing Will could be his dad's problem. But what if it was? He never knew anything about his father's family. Charles Stoltz had a habit of brushing aside any questions about his childhood. His mother didn't have much to add to the story, and she looked uncomfortable when Will pressed for more details. "I met your father when he was a resident at the hospital," she said. "He was estranged from his parents and put himself through medical school."

Sometimes, he wondered how well his parents really knew each other. Even now, they lived side by side, amicably. They gave each other a lot of space. But they never laughed with each other, or sat around the dinner table, lingering the way the Lapps did, playing board games or working on jigsaw puzzles by the flickering firelight. He thought of the talks he and Amos had in the barn, how much Amos had told him about Menno, his son with special needs. Whenever Amos spoke about Menno, it was always about something he had learned from him. Patience, kindness, or how Menno helped Amos's faith grow.

The world outside Windmill Farm would have looked at Menno Lapp as a problem to be dealt with, a burden to be endured.

Windmill Farm considered him to be a gift from God.

Will looked up at the sky. He had thought more about God in the last few weeks than he had in his entire life. Just last night, Amos pointed to Adam, soaring on thermals, and quoted a Scripture. Something from the book of Isaiah, about how a "youth can grow tired and weary, can stumble and fall, but those who hope in the Lord will renew their strength. They will soar on wings like eagles." It spoke to Will, deep down, in a way he couldn't explain. It felt so right, so appropriate. This spring, he had felt weary. Not physically, but mentally. Weary of his father's endless pressure, of never succeeding or pleasing him. And Will had stumbled and fallen.

Something was changing inside of Will this spring, something was softening. What a fluke! To end up on a quiet Amish farm and find himself reenergized, renewed, inside out.

But it didn't feel like a fluke. It seemed that this place, Stoney Ridge and the people here, had been prepared for him, designed ahead of time as a nurturing nest, a soft place from which to grow new wings.

He looked over at Sadie. "Your parents loved each other very much, didn't they?"

The corners of her eyes crinkled. "Yes, they did. They built a life together. It was a good life, and they were happy."

He slapped his hands on his thighs. "Sadie . . . I'm going to follow your example. I've decided no more resentment."

Her smile faded. "It's really not something you can do without God's help, Will. Only God is the true healer of hurts."

Only God is the true healer. That was a phrase Sadie often said, especially when people came to her for remedies, which they were doing more and more. Hardly a day went by when someone wasn't seeking her out for help. Will worried they were taking advantage of her because she didn't charge them, but she said it brought her pleasure to help others. And then she would always say, "After all, only God is the true healer."

What would his father, the brilliant neurosurgeon, say to that? He would probably be outraged. He believed that a good surgeon shouldn't go into surgery unless he believed he was the sole instrument of healing. But then, his father would scoff at Sadie's remedies too, saying that they were merely anecdotal and that she used unproven, unscientific methods. "My dad wants me to follow in his path and go into medicine." He wasn't sure why he admitted that to her.

"Have you considered it?" Sadie said.

Will lifted a shoulder in a careless shrug. "I considered nothing else. I even got accepted to medical school—assuming that I would be graduating this spring." He took in a deep breath. "So what did I do? Nine weeks shy of graduating with honors, I get myself suspended by doing something stupid."

That was only half the story. He then did something even more stupid, but he just couldn't tell her about the DUI. There were only three people aware of that little problem—Will, the police officer, and his lawyer, Mr. Arnie Petosky, found at four in the morning through the yellow pages at the city jail. This particular lawyer was the only one who answered calls in the middle of the night and took credit cards for payment of criminal defense. "It's your first offense, Will. Sure, you came up a little high on the blood alcohol concentration—and that can usually mean a little jail time—"

Will's eyes went wide.

"—plus a $5,000 fine—"

Will's eyes went wider.

"—plus your license could get suspended. But this was a routine traffic stop. No doubt your constitutional rights were violated—"

Will scratched his head. The police officer had actually been pretty nice to him.

"—we might even end up with a claim. Money back."

Will doubted that. He really just wanted it all to go away. Will was trapped. Up a creek without a paddle.

As the calming water lapped against the shore, Will found himself telling Sadie about hacking into the registrar's office, about losing his acceptance into medical school. He wondered what she thought of him. He was telling her things that shamed him. She didn't say anything for a long while. Sadie was one of those people who knew the virtue of quiet patience.

"So you thought it would be easier to just walk away from your future, from your father, than to try, didn't you?" Sadie spoke quietly, and when he lifted his head, he marveled again at the piercing depth in her blue eyes.

She tucked in her shoulders, like she was embarrassed to have brought up something painful. "I'm sorry. I didn't mean to—"

"It's okay," he said, and he felt her hand slip into his, small and warm. Her face turned upward, her eyes dark like liquid. Slipping a thumb under her chin, he tilted it upward, looked into her in a way he never had looked at a girl—all of the girls he'd dated but never got too attached to. With Sadie, things were different in some way he didn't even understand yet.

He leaned over and kissed her, because they'd talked long enough.

Gid wondered what was wrong with him as he turned right onto the dirt road that led to Blue Lake Pond, through a thick canopy of pine trees. He shouldn't be spying on Sadie like this! This was wrong, wrong, wrong. Unspeakably wrong. But still, his hands didn't seem to get the message from his brain to pull back on the horse's reins. Not until he saw Sadie and the cowboy sitting on the shore. Then, he stopped the horse abruptly.

He watched them for a moment or two, trying to decide if he could interrupt without looking like a fool.

Though the distance was enough that they didn't hear his horse and buggy approach, Gid tried to make sense out of Sadie's expression when she looked up at the cowboy. Was it gladness or dismay? Shyness? Or maybe just plain amusement?

The cowboy said something to make Sadie laugh. Gid heard laughter floating on the breeze, the cowboy's deep and husky, Sadie's light and young.

Suddenly something clicked in Gid's mind. He couldn't believe he hadn't figured it out sooner. No wonder she had been ignoring him. A dark thought suddenly began to take form in Gid's mind—he had always felt a tweak of concern that the cowboy was sweet on Sadie, but now he realized that she was growing fond of the cowboy! Gid saw Will's head dip toward Sadie. Quickly. Briefly. Not so briefly he couldn't have kissed her in that time. And Sadie made no move to shove him away from her.

Pain streaked through Gideon. He turned and left.

As soon as Sadie and Will arrived at the Kings' for the gathering, they were called over to join in a volleyball game, already in progress. Gideon was taking a turn as server in the back row, so Sadie intentionally joined the opposing team and Will was sent to Gid's team. She was feeling far too mixed up tonight to spend any time near Gideon. She was still reeling from Will's unexpected kiss. She wished she had been prepared for it—she might have participated. Instead, she responded like a block of wood. A clay brick. A stone wall. And then, cheeks on fire, she jumped up and said they should be going.

But she was not going to let her nerves get the better of her. She was an adult now. Fern had said so. Tonight, she was going to act like she was kissed by handsome cowboys all the time. Practically every day of the week except for Sundays! The truth was, it was only the second kiss from a boy she had ever received. The first one was from Gid and it had made her knees go weak. Today's kiss from Will felt sweet and gentle. Nice. Maybe it would have made her knees go weak if she had been ready for it.

She cast a furtive glance at Gid, but he wasn't looking at her. He was talking to Will, tapping the ball delicately into the air, to show him how the game was played. Will waved Gid off, telling him he had played plenty of volleyball in his day. He threw his cowboy hat off to the side and winked at Sadie. She looked away, embarrassed.

Gid went back to the service line. He cracked his neck on each side, like the prizefighters did at the county fair as they prepared to head into the ring. He was staring at the back of Will's head like he was boring a hole through it. He tossed the ball in the air to serve, and instead of the ball arcing through the air, sailing over the net, it was launched like a rocket, straight at Will's head. Will fell to the ground, face-first.

Every place on a farm had its own sound, if you stopped and listened. Will liked to identify those sounds as he walked through the fields each morning before dawn to check on the falcons. The streams that crisscrossed through Windmill Farm had a soft, gurgling sound. The crops in the fields had a rustling sound, like they were whispering. The trees had a sound—pine needles dropping as the branches waved in the wind. The rocky ridge on the northern edge of the farm had a sound—pinging sounds that echoed.

Will climbed a tree to watch the falcons with a telescope just as the sky began to brighten. Adam flew off the edge of the scape and circled overhead. Will watched him glide on the warming air currents, stretching his wings in the mist. Eve remained in the scape, as he expected, incubating her brood.

Sure enough, a whitish down head with a disproportionately large beak poked around Eve's body. The first eyase to hatch! He expected the next one to hatch today or tomorrow, with the other ones to follow. He watched the small chick until the sun had emerged on the horizon, filled with wonder and awe. It was times like this that he thought Amos Lapp might be right, that God had a plan. It was a phrase Amos repeated often, especially when he told Will stories about Menno as a boy. It seemed as if he always wrapped up a memory of Menno with that phrase, "God has a plan," like it was a benediction. An "Amen."

Will rubbed the back of his head, feeling the goose-egged lump from yesterday's surprising encounter with a volleyball. When he had come to, twenty Amish teens were staring down at him with deeply concerned looks on their faces. Sadie fussed over him the entire evening, bringing fresh ice for him to hold against his head and checking the pupils of his eyes for signs of a concussion.

"I'm fine," he kept reassuring her. She wanted to take him home but he insisted on staying. To be honest, he enjoyed the attention he was getting from everyone. It felt like he had finally broken through that invisible wall that separated him from these Amish people, the wall he felt whenever he was at their church service. All but with that Gideon guy, the one who whacked him with the ball. Sadie was furious with Gideon. He offered up a weak apology to Will, something lame about how a bee landed on him just as he was serving up the ball. "There was no bee," Sadie whispered loudly, after Gideon sauntered off. She glared at his back with a look he wasn't accustomed to seeing on her sweet face. Like she was about to go after him with a shovel as if she was killing vermin.

He wouldn't have missed the barbecue for anything. The food was the best grilled food he had ever eaten, bar none—chicken and steak, smothered in thick sauce, spicy baked beans, coleslaw that was nothing like the soggy mess his mother served, three kinds of pie for dessert. And still, everyone kept fussing over him like he had suffered a mortal blow! Hardly that. His head was harder than a pileated woodpecker's, his father often told him.

Now, if Sadie had insisted that they leave before the singing, it wouldn't have been hard to be persuaded to go. He hadn't realized there was singing involved—she had just called it a youth gathering. But after his third helping of pie, she seemed confident that he was fine and didn't ask him again if he wanted to leave.

Afterward, he was glad they stayed. The singing was different from those long, lugubrious hymns sung during the lengthy Amish church service. For one thing, the host asked others to call out requests to sing. Like eager bidders at an auction, several shouted out song titles. Unlike Sunday church, they sang only one stanza of each, and it was easy to tell these were favorites. Also, unlike church, these tunes were quick, with a beat. The boys took a turn alone, bellowing the melody like they were a marching band made up of tubas and trombones, trying to impress the girls with their deep, honking voices. Then the girls took a turn at it. It had struck Will that the sound of women's voices had a tinny sound—nothing that came anywhere close to raising the roof like the boys did. The girls sounded like a little choir of flutes and piccolos. Except for Sadie's. Her voice rang the truest.

He had a surprisingly enjoyable evening, sore head and all.

The ringing of his cell phone cut off Will's wandering thoughts and pulled him back to the present. He set the scope in a nook on the tree and looked at who would be calling him at 5:34 a.m. Mahlon Miller, the game warden. Will sagged.

"Morning, Mahlon," he said as he answered.

"Have any hatched?"

Not even a hello. Or, how are you, Will? Need anything? Like, food, money, clean laundry, transportation? "First one. I'm watching it now. Looks like a viable eyase."

"Good. As soon as the clutch is hatched, I want you to think about how you're going to band them."

Will was silent for a moment.

"You've banded before. Your father told me you had. He said you had volunteered at a raptor rescue center and banded hundreds of birds."

Aha! Will's father was behind this. "Well, yeah, I've had a little bit of experience with banding. But not out in the wild. Not when the parents were hovering nearby." At the raptor rescue center, Will had become so good at banding that he was dubbed the Band-Aid. Banding birds provided important information on the birds' movements and habitat needs year-round. These metal bands on the birds' legs were uniquely lettered and numbered by the government so that if the birds were observed later, or found injured or dead, they could be identified. "Don't you have an expert bander in the office?"

"Nope. Well, we do have a guy who usually does banding, but he's out on paternity leave. He said you just gotta act quick so it reduces stress on the birds."

What about the stress on the unpaid intern? Act quick so that he didn't get his eyes pecked out by Adam and Eve. Quick so that they didn't try to strike him with their powerful feet. Quick so that they didn't carry him away with their razor-sharp talons and drop him, like a stone, into the field.

Banding a falcon chick was serious work. Adam and Eve would turn into threatened predators if anyone—or anything—messed with their clutch. Just a moment ago, he watched Adam capture, in midflight, a menacing crow that flew too close to the scape. Eve was provided with fresh crow for breakfast. "I thought that fell under game warden duties."

"Nope. It's part of your internship duties."

Will doubted that. "Do you have suggestions?"

"Well, I'd recommend you wait until the parents are away from the scape." He snorted a few times, as if he had made a funny joke.

Will rolled his eyes.

"Timing is critical. Besides watching out for falcons, that's another reason I put you out there on that farm. There's really only one day that is the ideal point to band—the foot is small enough for the band to go over the toes, but not too small that the band falls off. They can start fledging at three weeks—especially the males, and they'll begin to leave the scape for short times." Mahlon took a long slurp of coffee. "As soon as you tell me how many eyases are in the clutch and what sex they are, I'll put in a request for the bands and drop them off next time I see you. You'd better start figuring out how you're going to do it." And he hung up.

Will stared at the phone in his hand. Broken connections—wasn't that the story of his life?

Passing over him, Adam cried out a complaint, letting Will know he was horning in on his territory. As a serious birder, Will knew it was ridiculous to attribute human characteristics to birds, to any animals. Anthropomorphism, such foolishness was called. But still, he talked to wild things like he expected them to answer. He cupped his mouth and shouted at Adam, "I'm not doing anything to hurt your babies. If anything, I'm helping them." Adam circled near him again, uncomfortably close, as if he knew exactly what Will was talking about. He let out a *cack cack cack cack*—one of a wide range of sounds he made. As if he wanted to taunt Will by saying, "Who do you think you're fooling?"

16

Off-Sundays had their own feel. On Sundays without church, everyone was allowed to sleep in and start the day slowly. M.K.'s father was the only one who would rise early, feed the stock, but then he would head back to the couch in the family room and lie down. "Just resting my eyes," he would tell M.K., if she tried to stir him. The only part of the day M.K. didn't like was that Fern didn't make a hot breakfast like she normally did—today's offerings were cold cereal or toast. She said it was her off-Sunday too.

On this morning, M.K. felt as jumpy as popcorn in a skillet, waiting to hear the first sound of Sadie stirring upstairs. She had the cradle hidden in a corner of the family room, covered by a blanket. She knew Sadie would be home late from the gathering last night, and she didn't want to miss seeing the look on her sister's face. She knew better than to wake Sadie up. Even she wasn't that big of a fool.

Finally, M.K. heard Sadie's door open and her light steps come down the stairs. Fern was in the family room, feeding the baby a bottle. Her dad was in his chair. reading the Bible and sipping coffee. Sadie went to the kitchen and poured cereal into a bowl.

Perfect. The moment was perfect.

M.K. cleared her throat to get everyone's attention. "I have here a lovely gift to present to you, made by Gideon Smucker himself, to show Sadie how deep are his affections."

When M.K. was satisfied that everyone's attention was on her, she whipped off the blanket to reveal the cradle. Sadie gasped, and Amos jumped up out of his seat to see it.

Holding her cereal bowl in one hand, Sadie came over to look at it. "Gid made it? Why, it's beautiful!"

M.K. pushed one side of the cradle, to show Sadie how it could rock, but didn't realize how close Sadie was standing to the cradle. When it knocked Sadie's knee, her cereal bowl dropped into the cradle. The bottom of the cradle fell out, clattering to the ground. M.K. grabbed the side of the cradle to hold it in place, but the top rail came apart in her hands. One by one, the dowels popped out like springs. They watched, amazed, as the entire cradle began to collapse, side by side, piece by piece.

Amos bent down and examined a joint. "He must have forgotten to glue the joints."

"Glue?" M.K. said in a small, squeaky voice. "It needed glue?"

"*Forgot* to glue them?" Sadie shook her head. "I doubt it. Oh Gideon. You have sunk to a new low."

Fern blew air out of her cheeks. "That boy. He needs to shake the snowflakes out of his head."

Two days later, all four eggs in the clutch had hatched. Will called Mr. Petosky to give him an update.

"That's good. That's very good news. Have you told the game warden there are four?"

"Not yet."

"Good. Don't tell him."

"I don't have to. There are ten avid bird-watchers staked out who've already spotted them."

Mr. Petosky sighed. "Look, I'm going to need two of them."

"What?! But you only said one. One is reasonable. It won't raise any red flags. We always talked about one."

"That was before we knew there were four viable eyases. It's not a big deal. The game warden will never get suspicious. I'll get you the bands this week so you can just switch them out with the warden's bands. You know as well as I do that the chance of all four eyases making it to the fledgling stage is very unlikely."

"Yeah, but—"

"Stuff happens in nature. All the time. He knows that."

Will didn't respond. He couldn't deny that truth.

"That's what happened to me. Nature took a swipe—just like it took on you with that nasty DUI. I'm just trying to recoup." The hard edge of Mr. Petosky's voice softened as he added, "Look at it this way, Will. This is good for the falcons. A very good thing. To take a falcon chick or two from the wild and allow it to breed in captivity—it strengthens the entire species. This is a good thing for the falcon, it's good for my breeding stock, and it's good for you."

Will heard the click of Mr. Petosky's phone as he hung up. What was it he had learned in an ethics class last fall? Opportunity + pressure + rationalization create a fraud triangle.

Of all the lawyers Will could have found, he had happened upon a falconer. That fact had come up when the lawyer had called Will to tell him his credit card payment had been declined—the very day he had started his internship and discovered the falcon pair. Mr. Petosky had called Will as he was out stocking trout in the creek near Windmill Farm and recognized the shrieking sound of the falcons in the background. They had a very nice conversation about falcons and that was when Mr. Petosky told him not to worry about the legal fees. They could work something out.

And so he did.

The next day, Mr. Petosky showed up at the game warden's office. Will walked him to his car, away from Mahlon Miller's listening ears. Mr. Petosky told Will that he had thought of a way to help Will. He had a little side business of falcon breeding. This spring, a virus had run through his hatchery and wiped out his stock. He just needed a little bit of help to rebuild. A fledgling here, one there, and he would be able to supply his customers and stay in business. Will knew how ethical falconers were—it was a cardinal virtue. And the offer from Mr. Petosky came at a moment when Will was desperate. Mr. Petosky offered to take care of all of his legal bills associated with the DUI. Down to the penny, he said. "The entire unpleasant business will go away, like it never happened." He snapped his fingers to illustrate his point. "You'll be back on track. I'll be back on track. Everything can get back on track." By June 16, the day Will was due in court.

Gid loved this time of day. It was after four and the last scholar had finished up and gone home. A satisfying day of teaching, followed by the gentle slant of the sun as it reached the westward facing windows. The last thing he needed to do was to erase the blackboard. He picked up his glasses and rubbed the bridge of his nose, stood, stretched, and started to wipe the board clean.

"Gid?"

Sadie Lapp was standing three feet away from him.

The tips of Gid's ears started to burn. "Sadie, what a nice surprise." Could she hear his heart? Because it sounded like a bongo drum was in his chest. *Bah-bum . . . bah-bum . . . bah-bum . . .*

Sadie had a way of holding her hands at waist level, close to her body, fingers tightly interlaced. She stood that way, just a short distance from Gid's desk, and took a quick breath as if to say something, but stopped. She shook her head and frowned.

Something was on her mind to say and he thought he might as well help her out. He had to lick his lips because they were so dry. "Did you know that penguins don't have ears?" Oh smooth, very smooth, he told himself. Rule number one, whenever you can't think of the right thing to say, just start spouting pointless trivia. That should warm the heart of any woman.

Sadie looked confused. "I didn't know that."

"Oh. Mary Kate did a book report on that very thing today. About penguins not having ears. She wondered if they realized that they have wings but they can't fly. That they were birds . . . but not really. That got an interesting discussion going in class . . ." His voice trailed off as he caught the baffled look on Sadie's face. *Let's try this again.* "Did you like those little cakes?"

She looked up at him in surprise. "Like them?"

"Was it . . . too hard to understand?" Maybe Mrs. Stroot was right—maybe Sadie didn't know what "mea culpa" meant. He shouldn't have used Latin. Stupid, stupid, stupid! Why did he have to make things so complicated?

"Oh no. You were very clear."

This wasn't going well. Sadie was looking at him as if he were an ax murderer. What had he done wrong? Let's try this again. "Did the baby fit in the cradle?"

"How could he?" She put her hands on her hips and looked—well, an awful lot like her housekeeper, Stern Fern. "Have you completely lost your mind? Why would you try to hurt a baby? An innocent little child?"

"What?!"

"The cradle fell apart. Like dominoes."

Gid was stunned. He thought he had tested every piece of that cradle. He should have held off another day, just to make absolutely sure all of the glue in the joints had dried. He had been so eager to take it to Sadie on the night of the gathering that he didn't want to wait. He never would have given Sadie a cradle that wasn't sound. Stupid, stupid, stupid!

She frowned at him. "The other night, you aimed that volleyball right at Will's head. Don't tell me you didn't. You're much too athletic to not have controlled that serve."

How could he defend himself against that? It was true. Sports had always come naturally to him, and generally, he always held back a little, even as a child on the school playground. But he had never considered himself very competitive. Until now.

She folded her arms against her chest. "And besides, I saw that evil look in your eyes just before you served it."

That was also true. When Gid saw the cowboy kiss Sadie, he was surprised at how suddenly and violently his anger was aroused. When the opportunity presented itself to wallop Will Stoltz in the head with the volleyball, Gid took it.

It was a warm afternoon, thick with humidity, and Gid suddenly felt so closed in that he wasn't sure he could even frame a complete sentence.

"Why would you do such a thing? Then . . . you left those horrible little cakes!"

He blinked twice. "But I thought—" He had tried so hard to get it right! Why were they horrible little cakes?

"What kind of a message is *that*: 'You lie.'"

What?! But that wasn't the message he had left for her! How could this have happened? Confusion swirled through his head like gray fog.

Sadie's controlled calm was gone as her voice snapped like a twig. "How dare you say something like that? Why would you do such a thing?"

A protest sprang to his lips. "But that's not . . . ! Someone must have rearranged the—"

"Oh sure . . . blame others."

His mind, so nimble in front of a classroom of twenty-five scholars, was absolutely paralyzed. He needed to let his mind stop racing long enough to relax, so that he sounded like a normal person, but there was no time! He couldn't seem to string two words together. All that ran through his head was how hurt Sadie must have felt when she saw the little cakes. They *were* horrible! *No wonder she's been avoiding me.*

She was mad now, really steaming. "I thought . . . I thought I knew you, Gid." Sadie's blue eyes were boring into his, glowing with anger, waiting for a reply. "Don't you have *anything* to say for yourself?"

He had plenty to say for himself, but it was hard to get the words organized when she was staring at him as if he was the scholar and she was the teacher. *I'm so sorry, Sadie. For not trusting you. For misunderstanding. For being a clumsy oaf. For everything.* The words were in his mouth, smooth and round like marbles, but what came out was this: "You let him kiss you."

She didn't move. She didn't speak. A slow flush creeping up her throat to her cheeks was the only indication that she might have heard him at all. "I didn't let—"

"I saw it, Sadie. You were at Blue Lake Pond, and he kissed you."

"I . . . he . . ." She sighed. "Yes, he kissed me. I didn't expect it."

"You didn't seem to dislike it."

Between collar and hairline, her neck turned rosy pink. "I was . . . surprised by it."

As fast as a comet streaking across the heavens, Gid's holy outrage passed. She was so lovely; of course another man would court her. He couldn't blame Sadie for seeking someone else. He hadn't trusted her.

But he didn't know how to say all of this to Sadie, and she was growing impatient with him.

"It's none of your business who I kissed or who I didn't. You and I might have kept company in December, but that's all it was. Just a few rides home from youth gatherings now and then."

That's all he was to her? A ride home now and then? That was the sum of what he meant to her? Gid felt as if he was suddenly smaller, deflated. "Not any of my business? None of my business?" For some reason Gid couldn't stop there. Words kept pouring out. "Sadie, ever since you got back from Ohio . . . it seems like you're slipping away."

She didn't answer. Instead, she went to the door and brought back a bag of books. She set it on a desk. "These are all the poetry books you sent me while I was in Ohio. I know you wanted me to read them. I'm sorry to tell you this, but I didn't read any of them."

"Not one?" All of those little notes he had placed so carefully in the margins?

She shook her head. "The truth is, Gid, I don't like to read. Not unless I have to. I know that's a disappointment to you. I know you've wanted me to be a person who liked stories and poetry and enjoyed long discussions about them. But that's not me." She gave Gid a long look. "I'm just not sure where what you want for me ends and what I want for me begins."

Those words hung between them, suspended, waiting for Gid to respond. Struck dumb by her lengthy, emphatic speech, he could only gaze at her in wonder. She'd always been pretty to him. Now, with the sun pouring through the window, gilding her skin and reflecting off her hair, her looks held something more, something deeper than beauty—strength. He read it in her broad cheekbones and determined chin, the firmness of her mouth and set of her shoulders.

A bead of sweat rolled down his back, awakening him from his stupor. As Sadie turned toward the door, his mind struggled frantically for the right words, the ones that would free his speech.

"Sadie, I didn't send you these books because I wanted you to be a different person. I wouldn't change anything about you. Not a thing. You're yourself, and that's what I love. What I've always loved. I wish I had learned long ago how to put into words the feelings that I have for you. Instead, I've only known how to use what others have written. I sent those books to you so that they could tell you what I couldn't—to tell you how much I care for you. That I love you. Just the way you are."

But by the time he got the words out, it was too late. Sadie was already halfway down the road to Windmill Farm.

The thing about a rainy day that Amos liked was that it gave a man a chance to catch up on indoor chores. Amos had been hammering new boards in Cayenne's stall after the horse had kicked holes through the wall. He wondered if he should consider selling that hot-blooded mare. Fern and Sadie wouldn't get near her. He and M.K. handled her well, but it didn't seem right to have a buggy horse that took such serious managing.

"Amos?"

Amos spun around to find Ira Smucker standing behind him. "Ira? What brings you here?"

"My love for Fern. It brings me here."

Such a revelation didn't surprise Amos. It was clear that Ira Smucker was very interested in Fern. Amos still felt the shock of it, though, that Fern, whom he thought was a mature, intelligent person, seemed to be responding quite warmly to Ira's poky and cautious method of courtship. Here was just more proof of the great mystery—how could you ever figure women out? He was fifty-one years old and he still didn't understand women.

Then Amos chastised himself for thinking uncharitable thoughts about his friend. A minister, to boot! It's just that Ira was so deliberate in pace, so measured and careful—identical to Fern's nature—that Amos was certain nothing so seemingly passionless could qualify as real love.

Amos looked at his friend. "You love Fern."

"Yes. I do. I would be a happy man to have her as my wife."

Amos's stomach tightened. "Have you asked her?"

"No." Ira's chin lifted. "I thought I should be asking you." His eyes turned to a barn swallow, flitting from rafter to rafter. "There was a time when I thought you might be fond of Fern, yourself. I would never take her from you, Amos. I'm asking you plain, are you wanting Fern for yourself?" Ira searched his face.

Amos looked away. What could he say? If Fern wanted to marry Ira, he would never stand in her way. He couldn't answer Ira's question. "So, you're asking me for Fern's hand?"

"No." Ira shook his head. "I'm telling you I'm marrying her. I'm seeking your blessing, though."

Will couldn't sleep. He threw the covers back and went outside to look at the moon. It was full tonight, pocked with craters. He listened for a while to the sounds of the night: the howl of a coyote, the hoot of an owl.

He couldn't wait to tell Sadie about the hatched chicks. Imagining her catching a breath and looking so pleased when he told her there were four eyases now, all hatched out and healthy. It crossed Will's mind that he was thinking about Sadie again. He shut down the conversation in his head as soon as he realized what he was doing. It wasn't like him to have his mind linger so long and so often on a girl.

Unsettled. That's how he felt after he spent time with Sadie. He remembered what he thought when he first met her—that if he walked into a room, she wasn't the one he would have noticed. But oddly enough, long after he left the room, she was the one he kept thinking about. She was quiet, more of a mystery; her strengths sneaked up on him instead of smacking him front and center.

It amazed Will to see the knowledge Sadie had of healing herbs. Her education was, for the most part, limited to the four walls of a one-room country schoolhouse. And yet, she seemed to have an intuitive sense of what ailed a person.

Earlier today, he had found her out in the enormous vegetable garden, tending to her herbs. "I envy you," Will had told her when she stood to greet him, brushing dirt off her hands.

She looked at him, surprised. "Whatever for?"

"Your healing work."

"But you're the one who is going to be a doctor."

He shook his head. "Not anymore. Besides, even if I were able to talk my way back into medical school, it would only be a vocation. For you, it's a *calling*." He stood up straighter. "I guess that's how I would describe my father's passion for medicine."

Somehow, Will realized, conversations with Sadie wound their way back to his father, even though he didn't intend them to. "He was always at the hospital, never present for any of the events in a kid's life where you'd want a father to be. Not for school plays or birthday parties. We couldn't even count on his appearance on Christmas morning."

"Is he that important of a doctor?"

"Sadly, yes. How can a kid complain about that, either? The guy was out saving lives."

"But a family is important too."

Will shook his head. "I'm only important to him as long as I do everything he wants me to do and wants me to be. The minute I step outside of that line, I'm cut off."

Sadie was quiet for a moment, and then she said, "You need to forgive him."

That was the last thing he wanted to hear. Shouldn't his father be apologizing to him and asking for his forgiveness?

Softly, she added, "Will, I'm sure you've hurt people too. We all have. You need to be forgiven by others. Why shouldn't you extend forgiveness to your father?"

Sadie's words stuck with him all day, like a burr under the saddle. Maybe she was right. Maybe he was having trouble moving on because he wouldn't let his father off the hook. Leaning against the porch post, he said out loud, perhaps to God, perhaps to himself, "Okay. I forgive my dad. I am responsible for my own life. I will stop blaming him." Nothing dramatic happened. No lightning, no thunder, no warm feeling that he had done the right thing. A little disappointed, Will went back inside to try to sleep.

Every dawn and every dusk, Amos spent time with binoculars around his neck, watching the falcons. They were magnificent—with their golden brown dappled coloring, black streaks on their heads. Will had told him scientists had documented that falcons ate a variety of over four hundred and fifty types of birds. He said that they have been observed killing birds as large as a sandhill crane, as tiny as a hummingbird, and as elusive as a white-throated swift, but a favorite treat was bats. The only bird Amos was happy to hear was on that list was starlings. He had no love in his heart for starlings.

He was up on the hillside tonight, watching Adam in a hunting stoop, when suddenly Fern appeared at his side. You'd think he'd have grown accustomed to her out-of-the-blue appearances, but he was always flustered.

He watched her as she gazed at Adam. He wondered what she might have been like when she was Sadie or Julia's age. She must have been beautiful. But there was something added to her face that was better than youthful beauty.

She had character.

"I can't help but think how Menno would have loved these falcons," he said, handing her the binoculars. "He would have every fact known to man listed on index cards and read them out to us at supper."

"Better is one day in God's court than a thousand days elsewhere." She held the binoculars up to her eyes. "Menno has a better view of God's magnificent creation than we do, Amos. And he doesn't need index cards to remember anymore." She twisted the knobs for a moment, peered through the binoculars again, then handed them back to Amos and went back down the hill.

He held them to his eyes and discovered he now had a much clearer view of Adam. He watched Fern's receding figure for a moment, then smiled. Fern was always doing that—fixing things that were slightly out of focus.

It was the strangest thing. A few days after Will had looked up at the moon and said he forgave his father, he noticed that he could think about his father without a default response of bitterness and defensiveness.

That moment in the night on the cottage porch—something had happened to begin to affect his feelings about his father. He knew it wasn't just a situation of mind over matter. Something—some One—was changing him, inside out.

Questions started buzzing around his mind like pesky mosquitoes: *If this is God's doing, just who is he? What is he like?* When he went into town with Amos that week, he slipped into a bookstore. He told Amos that he was going to get his phone battery charged up and that was true. But he also wanted to purchase a Bible. He ended up buying an easy-to-read translation, small in size so he could keep it in his backpack.

As a freshman in college, he had taken an Ancient Literature class that included some readings from the Bible. The professor had ridiculed the Bible to the class, pointing out all of its inconsistencies. She had been much kinder with *The Odyssey*, he remembered. But that class had shaped his views about the Bible—as an irrelevant, flawed collection of fables and myths. He tried to set that assumption aside and read the Bible with fresh eyes. There was only one question he asked himself: What is God like? That was all.

Over the next few weeks, he alternated between reading the Old Testament—skipping over the genealogies and lengthy scoldings aimed at the Israelites—and stories about Jesus in the New Testament. He found himself continually surprised by what he had assumed about the Bible and what it actually contained. His appetite for Scripture was growing, and he started to seek out moments when he could read a passage and ponder it. It startled him how often those ancient words seemed uniquely customized to his life.

One afternoon, Amos asked Will to take the sheep to another fenced-in pasture to graze. Sheep were loud with their complaints, day and night, and Will grew frustrated trying to get all of them into the pasture. He chased down one black lamb and carried it over to its mother, bawling at him rudely from behind the pasture fence. A verse he had read that very morning popped into his head: "All we, like sheep, have gone astray." Will settled the lamb next to its mother and looked up at the sky. "Okay, okay. You made your point. The Bible is still relevant. I got that."

He heard a familiar *klak klak klak* sound and shielded his eyes to look for Adam. The tiercel was stooping—diving down to capture its lunch. While stooping, his body hyper-streamlined to achieve high speed, in complete control of the kill. Falcons have been clocked at over two hundred miles per hour. They're the fastest animals on earth; three times faster than a cheetah. As soon as Adam caught his prey, midair, he would pull out of the dive. Karate in the air! The sight never failed to fill Will with awe and reverence—though lately he found that awe didn't end at admiration for the bird but for its creator.

And on the heels of that thought came another out of the blue. Something inside Will cracked open. He suddenly had trouble breathing. In that moment, all the anger and resentment and frustration he felt melted into one emotion—regret.

He wished he could share the sight of Adam's stoop with his dad. Will missed his dad.

Amos jerked the buggy shafts off of Cayenne so abruptly that the jumpy horse reared up on her hind feet. "Settle down!"

M.K. stroked Cayenne's neck, watching her nostrils flare. "What's got you in such a mood?"

Amos sighed. "Never you mind me." He finished unbuckling the harness's tracings and handed the reins to M.K. to lead the mare to a stall.

If the situation weren't so serious, it might even be comical. Ira Smucker had quietly told Amos that he was going to ask Fern to marry him tonight. And what did Amos do about it? Nothing. Coward! How many times had he had an opportunity to speak to Fern, to express his feelings to her? Hundreds. And yet he said nothing, did nothing. He just watched another man swoop in and make off with the woman he desired, like Adam pursuing prey. Tonight, as Ira had picked Fern up to head to town for dinner, Amos simply stood there, smoldering like a pine log in a forgotten fire pit.

M.K. brought in a basket brimming with fresh eggs and put them in the kitchen sink. She had to scrub the chicken manure off the eggs, never a task she liked.

"Dad's getting crankier than the handle on an ice cream churn," M.K. said to Sadie. "I don't know what's gotten into him lately. He snaps at me for the smallest thing."

"Fern's gone to town with Ira Smucker tonight, hasn't she?" Sadie said. She had been cooking down a large pot full of plump wild strawberries to make jam. She was ladling the jam into clean jars, then setting them in a boiling hot water bath to seal the lids.

"Yes. They just left a few minutes ago." A light dawned slowly in M.K.'s mind. "Do you . . . are you saying . . . you can't be serious! Dad? Sweet on Fern? Our Fern? Stern Fern?" The thought was too much for her.

Sadie wheeled around from the pot and wagged a finger at her. "You stay out of it. They need to figure this out on their own. There are times to be curious and times to let things be."

Suddenly the thin wail of a baby could be heard, and Sadie stopped the lecture, handed M.K. the wooden spoon, and ran upstairs.

M.K. stirred the jam, watching dark red splatters hit the pot wall. Fern? Fern and Ira Smucker? Fern and her dad? She couldn't get her head around it.

17

Will was walking along the street that acted as a property line for Windmill Farm, replacing No Trespassing signs that had gotten knocked down in the thunderstorm last night. The wind was the worst part of the storm—branches were down all over the farm. He hammered a nail on a cockeyed sign and stepped back to straighten it.

"Hey!"

Will turned to see that schoolteacher approaching him from down the street. Will raised a hand in greeting. Gideon Smucker stopped, his spine stiffening enough to be noticeable from a hundred feet away. A smile curled Will's lips. This should be interesting. It didn't take a rocket scientist to know how this blustering, tongue-tied man felt about Will—suspicious, jealous, threatened. All because Will was spending time with Sadie Lapp. A great deal of time with her. Probably more time than this schoolteacher had a clue about!

Sadie, the woman Will knew he could never have and yet—

No. He wouldn't think he wanted her. She was a diversion, a spring fling, an excuse to spend a great deal of time at the farmhouse, to eat at the Lapp table and enjoy being a part of a healthy, happy family. After June 16, Sadie could renew her relationship with the schoolteacher, with Will's blessing. Sort of.

Now a yard apart, Gid and Will eyed each other up and down, waiting to see who would speak first. If Will were a cartoonist, he would draw two raptors, one head up, one head down, neither willing to look each other in the eye because that would be considered an out-and-out threat.

Gid was taller than Will, and lankier. With those thick glasses, he reminded Will of Clark Kent, the alter ego of Superman. Bumbling, awkward, ill at ease, but good-hearted. Even Will couldn't deny that. Then his insides tensed at the sight of Gid's large, work-roughened hands. Those calluses would scratch Sadie's smooth skin. Surely she wouldn't let those hands touch her.

"I saw you. Early this morning. Talking to a man in a gray car."

You could have heard a pin drop, a heart beat. A blue jay shrieked overhead, breaking the silence. Another screeched in response.

Will had been careless. The man in the gray car was Mr. Petosky. "I was out this morning, yes. I go out every day to make sure the bird-watchers are respecting the Lapps' property lines."

"He handed you something. I saw it."

Will's mouth went dry, and he couldn't think what he should say. Mr. Petosky had given him the bands for the chicks that he had obtained for his breeding colony—the one that had been wiped out by the virus. But he hadn't bothered to notify the government of that fact. Those bands were treated like gold—all bands were registered with the game commission's office. With a dramatic flair, Mr. Petosky had counted the bands out, one by one, as he handed them over.

Will tried, probably too late, to defuse the situation. "You must be mistaken."

"Something isn't quite right." Gid took a step closer to him and pointed a finger at his chest. "You're up to something." His words emerged roughly, as though each one was formed of grit. "Whatever it is . . . leave Sadie alone. I don't want her to get hurt."

The gloves were off and Will stepped closer. "Seems to me that you've done plenty of that yourself," he snorted.

Gid looked as though he was about to explode. "Leave her be," he ground out between clenched teeth. "She's not a girl to be toyed with."

"Gideon!"

Both Gid and Will spun around to face Sadie, staring at them with a shocked look on her face. They had been so focused on each other that they hadn't noticed she was at the end of the driveway, getting the mail from the mailbox. How much had she heard?

She was indignant, but not at Will. "Gideon, my relationship with Will is none of your concern."

Gid's eyes flashed, hurt. "It's my concern if he's doing something wrong. And dragging you along with him."

Sadie's cheeks turned the color of berries. "Gid, calm down. Will and I are—" She hesitated.

Will held his breath in anticipation of her completed statement as to what he was to her.

"Friends," Sadie finished.

Friends? Just . . . friends? A blast of disappointment shot through Will.

"And he's not dragging me along anywhere."

Gid held his fisted hands at his hips as though ready to strike at any moment. "Then why weren't you at the gathering last weekend?" Gid demanded. "Mary Ruth was counting on your help with the girls' alto section. And yesterday, why weren't you at the workshop frolic at Rose Hill Farm? Bess was looking all over for you when her daughter was stung by a bee."

Will knew the answer to those questions. On Sunday, he talked Sadie into going canoeing on Blue Lake Pond. And yesterday, she was heading out to pick wild strawberries in a secret patch near the woods and he offered to help her. They were having such a good time that they lost track of time and didn't get back until the frolic was nearly over.

Gid glared at her. "What kind of friendship is that, Sadie—when it makes you forget about promises you've made to others?"

Sadie was livid. The way her lips looked at that moment—thin and tight—Will wanted to kiss them again, change their conformation to something much softer.

But Will thought it would be wise to take this opportunity to beat a hasty retreat. "I'll just be on my way." He took off up the driveway before either Sadie or Gid could say another word.

As Will loped toward the cottage, he weighed his options. Maybe he should try to forget about Sadie and concentrate on getting his problem solved by June 16. After all, Sadie had no place in his life outside of this farm, nor he in hers, and he needed to get a grip. Pursuing her the way he had been could bring trouble—he had already created animosity with Clark Kent. And Fern was definitely onto him. That woman scared Will. She watched him like a hawk whenever he was near Sadie, which was often. More and more often.

This was a great example of why he didn't like to complicate his life with relationships. It was like walking on thin ice. You never knew when the ice was going to crack and you were going to fall in a hole. Trouble was brewing, and that was the last thing Will needed this spring.

Still, there was just *something* about Sadie. Maybe . . . he would worry about life after June 16 some other day. For now, he had found a girl who was worth the trouble.

Gid was outside chopping wood when the air began to fill with the smell of rain. Daylight was fading away and the wind was picking up, so he put the ax down and stacked the wood. Before he went inside, he sat on the fence, his head in his hands, berating himself. He was such a fool. Stupid, stupid, stupid! He whacked his hands on his knees so hard that he tipped forward, barely catching himself before he landed, face-first, in the freshly plowed soil. It would serve him right.

Sadie, his Sadie, was involved with another man. An English cowboy. He could see it in her eyes as he confronted her on the road—the way she became so flustered, so defensive.

It was his own fault.

He had bungled things so badly—flown off the handle when he never flew off the handle. He accused her of not keeping promises to her friends. He made her feel guilty because Bess couldn't find her for her daughter's bee sting. It might have been true, but it wasn't as if Bess couldn't manage a simple bee sting. Stupid, stupid, stupid!

He hadn't trusted in the Lord to bring her back to him and had tried to compete for her attentions, her affections. And all he had done was push Sadie closer to the man who was winning her heart.

No wonder Sadie considered him to be untrustworthy. He was.

"God, how can I make things right?" he murmured. "How can I get Sadie to forgive me and trust me again if I behave this way?"

Crows screamed overhead, seeming to mock him with their harsh cawing.

Somewhere, in the deep creases of his mind—the folds where hopes and dreams were caught—he had believed that whatever was wrong between him and Sadie was reparable. When you loved someone, it didn't seem possible to suddenly lose that bond.

"Anything wrong, son?" His father's voice was gentle. "You look like you're not feeling well."

Gid snapped his head up. His father was standing a few feet from him with a worried look on his kind face. "I'm all right." Another lie. He wasn't all right. His head ached. His stomach ached. His heart ached.

"Sadie will come around. Give her time." His father leaned on the top rail of the fence beside him.

"Not as long as Will Stoltz sticks around." Gideon straightened up and looked his father in the eyes. People told him that they had the same blue eyes. His father's were older, though, and crinkled at the edges.

"You know it goes back further than that, Gid." His father's mouth set in a stern line. "You jumped to an assumption about her that was wrong. I'm ashamed to say that I did too."

"No, but I've—" He stopped before he said he'd learned his lesson. He had just proved again to Sadie that he didn't trust her, that he didn't think she had good judgment. Stupid, stupid, stupid! Gid pounded his fist on the rough planks of the fence. "Dad, what can I do? How do I win her back?"

Ira's bushy eyebrows shot up. "You don't. You just keep being the man you are."

Gid stared at his father.

"If Sadie is as smart as I think she is, she'll figure it out."

"What if she doesn't?"

"Well, Gid, the way I see it, there are plenty of other fish in the lake."

Maybe. But none like Sadie Lapp.

The sun was rising over the corn rows as Will brewed a pot of coffee and cleared a stack of papers off a chair to sit down at the kitchen table. He had to push a few things out of his way to set the coffee cup down too. He really should take time today to clean up after himself, he thought, looking around at the growing collection of dirty dishes in the sink. He had started to eat most of his meals right from the pan. It crossed his mind that cleaning up was a new thought. He was proud of himself!

Suddenly, the door to the cottage burst open. "HELLO!"

Will jumped slightly and spilled some of his coffee onto the table. Hank Lapp stepped into the cottage, carrying his rod-and-reel fishing pole. It looked like he'd been on the lake, or else was headed that way. He strode across the room and handed his rod to Will. Will had patiently untangled the mess of Hank's line one afternoon, and ever since, Hank considered him the finest untangler east of the Mississippi. He was forever hunting Will out on the farm, handing him his rod to repair.

"Well, Hank, you've got a real bird's nest here," Will observed. "I'll try, but I'm not sure I can fix this one."

"DAGNABIT. I was afraid of that." Hank sauntered over to the kitchen table, pulled things off a chair, sat right down across from Will, and eyed his cup of coffee.

"Here, take this. I haven't had a sip." Will pushed the cup on the table in front of him.

"Oh, no thanks. No, no. I didn't come over here meaning for you to offer me food and drink." Hank picked up the coffee cup and took a sip with a loud slurp.

It always amazed Will to see how much space Hank Lapp took up. It wasn't just his Christopher Lloyd–like appearance: ragged white hair, leathery skin, one eye that looked at you and the other that didn't. It was his presence. He had an outgoing, fun-loving nature and a window-rattling laugh. Whenever Hank found him on the farm, Will felt as if he needed to protect himself from the blinding brightness, the piercing loudness. He wanted to shout out: "Warning! Warning! Protect yourself! Get your sunglasses on! Put on your earplugs!"

Hank picked up a cereal box and looked at the cover. "I'm not stopping you from breakfast, am I?"

"No. Would you like some cereal? I don't have milk." Will didn't have a refrigerator in the cottage, which considerably limited his meal choices—just one of the many reasons he happened upon the farmhouse at mealtimes.

"No milk? Ah well." He reached in the box to grab a handful, as he started talking about a recent fishing trip with Edith Fisher. "I told you about it, didn't I?"

Will was always a little uncertain of how to respond to that question. He couldn't begin to keep straight all the tall tales Hank wove into his fishing stories. Fishermen, in Will's point of view, were pretty much the same everywhere—they talked, they fished, and they talked about fish. It's one of those universal rules.

But there wasn't time to answer. Hank had taken a sip of coffee and started in again. "Now, what was I saying? Oh yes! Edith! It might surprise you to hear that Edith likes to fish. Some of the ladies think fishing isn't ladylike, but Edith isn't one of them. She even makes up her own bait and she's a little secretive about it, which I happen to find appealing in a woman. A little mystery is a good thing, I always say."

With a sinking feeling, Will realized that this didn't have the makings of a short visit. Hank was so easily diverted that Will was afraid he'd never get back to the original point if he didn't stay on task. What was the point of the story, anyway? Maybe there wasn't a point. That was often the case with Hank.

"So the fishing was a little slow the other day. I rigged up a jiggin' hole to trick her. When she wasn't looking, I made a slipknot on her lure and let it go. Looked to Edith like she got herself a fish! She started hootin' and hollerin' 'cause she was sure she had a whopper fish on the end of her lure. Telling me how she was bringing home dinner! When she reeled it in, she sure was bringing in a nicely prepared meal!" Then he threw his head back and laughed with gusto, stopping with a choking snort. "She reeled in a can of Spam! And here's the best part—she stood up in the boat to scold me—" he wagged a finger at Will to illustrate—"and she fell right overboard!" He laughed so hard that tears ran down his cheeks. "Then, she was so mad that she spent the entire way home drenching me in the mighty flood of her words." That started him on another laughing jag. "She's still mad. Says I should have my fishing license taken away." Finally, he pulled himself together and wiped his face. "If a man can't fish, he might as well pull up the sod blanket, if you ask me."

The story went on, but Will lost the thread of it. He emptied the rest of the coffeepot into Hank's cup.

"Anyhoo . . . Edith won't go fishing with me anymore." Hank ran his knuckles over his bristled cheeks. They'd probably get a shave sometime in the next day or two—for sure before Sunday church. "So I came to see if you might like to go fishing with me. Menno used to be my fishing partner, you see, and M.K. is eager to go but she never stops talking long enough for the fish to get a word in. Sadie's plenty quiet, but she's too tenderhearted for fishing and hunting. She refuses to hook a worm. She carries spiders outside instead of smushing them like the rest of us." He looked Will directly in the eye. "I just thought you might like to give it a try."

Will felt honored. He felt like he had crossed over a bridge and was considered a member of the family. "I would. I'd like that. I know I could never take the place of Menno, but I'd like to go with you sometime."

"No one could take the place of Menno. No one should be asked to. But I can't deny you've been a blessing to all of us, Will. Especially Amos. He's finally got his vim and vigor back. It's been good to have you." Hank looked over at Will swiftly, then stood and looked for a place to put the empty coffee cup. The sink was filled with dirty dishes, as was the counter. He finally put it back on the table. He paused at the door and turned around. "Life's full of turnarounds."

"Yes, I suppose it is," Will said, walking over to see him out.

"But it sure is a blessing to know that the good Lord knows about every single thing that happens to us and has a divine, almighty reason for it all, the good and the bad too."

Will closed the door behind Hank and looked at the kitchen counters and sink. What a mess. It would take half the morning to clean it all up—to get hot dishwater, he had to heat up the water on the woodstove. No wonder he hated to wash dishes. But it wasn't just the mess that troubled him. It was everything, his whole life. That would take much more than half a morning to clean up.

What if these Amish people in this little church district were right? What if every detail meant something? What if the ups and downs and stupid mistakes he had made in the last few months had some kind of specific purpose? What if everything that happened to him ultimately fit together into a plan?

The thought was overwhelming. Terrifying and wonderful.

M.K. had been looking forward to this particular morning for five weeks. It was the last Saturday to serve her sentence with Jimmy Fisher at Annie's grandfather's house. When he arrived in his buggy to pick up M.K. and Uncle Hank, he was alone. His mother, he said, was still miffed at Hank for playing a practical joke on her and said she wouldn't be coming today to help.

"You mean, help *supervise*," M.K. said under her breath, and Uncle Hank jabbed her with the pointy part of his elbow.

Uncle Hank begged off. "I better go do some fence-mending with Edith."

M.K. squinted at him. He squinted back. He opened the buggy door and practically shoved M.K. inside. "Now you two work hard and see that old feller gets plenty of loving care." He put Fern's hamper, filled with prepared food for the week, in the backseat.

Jimmy and M.K. didn't speak to each other for the entire fifteen-minute ride to Annie's grandfather. When they arrived, the old man was in his chair on the porch, looking dead, as usual, and M.K. carefully tiptoed up to him to see if he was still breathing.

"GIRL, WHERE YOU BEEN?"

M.K. flinched. He got her every time.

"He forgets," Jimmy said, lugging the hamper past M.K. to take to the kitchen.

"SPEAK UP, BOY! YOU MUMBLE. I'VE SPOKEN TO YOU ABOUT THAT BEFORE."

"I SAID GOOD MORNING," Jimmy said. He lifted the hamper. "BROUGHT YOU GROCERIES."

"COYOTES?" He smacked his lips together. "I AIN'T HAD COYOTE MEAT IN YEARS. GUESS IT BEATS STARVING," he snapped, in his wrinkly voice. "HOP TO IT. STIR YOUR STUMPS."

Jimmy and M.K. exchanged a glance. Jimmy was going to try to fix the sagging porch corner today, so he went back to the buggy to get his tools as M.K. started to unload the hamper. She added some wood to the smoldering fire in the stove so that she could warm up some oatmeal Fern had made for the old man's breakfast. The stove started to smoke and seep soot. "You'd better clean out the stovepipe," she told Jimmy as he passed through, swiping a cookie from the hamper of groceries.

"Me?" He mumbled around a cookie in his mouth. "That'll take all morning. I wanted to get that porch done. I can't do everything, you know."

M.K. held back from giving him a snappy retort. "We can't leave him with a clogged stovepipe. It'll start a fire." M.K. pulled a chair over to the stove. "I'll help."

Jimmy exhaled, a slow whistle. The pipe rose out of the stove and angled at the ceiling. He climbed up on the chair to try to pull apart the lengths but couldn't work them loose. "Botheration! This could take all morning."

M.K. pointed out to him that botheration wasn't a word, but he ignored her. "Sometimes I think you are getting as deaf as Annie's grandfather."

"I hear you," Jimmy grumbled, "but it goes in one ear and out the other."

"Nothing to stop it," M.K. said.

"It's too bad you don't think about things that the average person might actually have to face."

"Like what?"

"Like how to tolerate working alongside one of the most aggravating girls on earth."

It never took long on these Saturday mornings for Jimmy Fisher's manners to go right out the window, which wasn't a long toss. She thought about pushing his chair back so he would fall, but she supposed that might be mean. "And that, Jimmy Fisher, is just one of the many reasons why you don't have a girlfriend."

"Who would want one?" He looked down at her. "Nothing but a nuisance. But if I wanted girlfriends—" he snapped his fingers—"they'd come running."

Sadly, that was true. It was a never-ending mystery to M.K. that so many girls swooned over the likes of Jimmy Fisher.

He hopped off the chair. "I've got a brilliant idea." He reached into a pocket and drew out a metal tin. He opened it and showed M.K. what was inside. "Firecrackers."

It was a well-known fact, to everyone but his mother, that Jimmy Fisher was never without firecrackers. He took three out of the tin. "Just takes a pinch of gunpowder to clear the stove, pipes, and chimney." He snapped his fingers again. "Easy as pie."

For once, M.K. was the one to think twice. "Jimmy . . . I'm not sure . . ."

He waved her off. "Prepare to be swept up in a whirlwind of superior force." He unlatched the stove door, then looked at her and squinted. "Uh, maybe you should stand back."

M.K. went into the other room and watched from behind the doorjamb. Jimmy struck a match to the kindling inside and threw in the firecrackers.

Then quite a lot happened. With an explosion that left M.K.'s ears ringing into the new year, the whole stove danced on its legs. The stovepipe came clattering down from the ceiling, belching a bushel of black soot all over them and the entire kitchen. The windows were covered with coal dust, darkening the kitchen. M.K. thought Jimmy would have been killed outright by the explosion, but he seemed to be still standing. She saw his eyes blinking rapidly in the midst of his coal-blasted face. His eyebrows were missing.

"Maybe one firecracker might have been enough." He spit soot out of his mouth. A burnt-powder haze hung in the room.

It took M.K. a few minutes to get over the shock of it. Then, she roared! "Jimmy Fisher! Er batt so viel as es finft Raad im Wagge!" *That did as much good as a fifth wheel on a wagon!* She stamped her foot and shook a fist at him. Her ears were still ringing. "I won't be hearing right for a week or two!"

"As if you didn't bring this all on yourself."

M.K. and Jimmy whipped around to locate the source of that familiar voice.

Fern! So ubiquitous!

"At this rate, you two are going to be working off your Saturdays for the rest of your lives." Fern said she happened to be leaving the Bent N' Dent when she heard the firecrackers and knew Jimmy Fisher was behind it. So, she decided to check up on them. "Good thing I did," she said, as she folded up her sleeves to set to work. "The two of you without supervision are an accident waiting to happen." She pointed to Jimmy. "Don't look so surprised. A person could hear that explosion halfway to Harrisburg."

"Oh, he's not surprised," M.K. said. "He just doesn't have any eyebrows left."

It took the three of them the rest of the morning to put the kitchen into the shape Fern expected it to be in. By noon, a miracle had taken place. Jimmy scooped a little soot here and there, not much, but at least he fit the stovepipe back together. M.K., naturally, did the work of ten, scrubbing, sweeping, polishing, dusting. The kitchen was restored to its pre-explosion condition. And the stovepipe was cleaned out.

Annie's grandfather slept through the entire thing. When he woke up, he hollered for his lunch.

As Will dipped the oars into the placid, dark water, a glorious feeling of well-being washed over him. Sure, he was broke and facing serious legal problems, but not at the moment. At the moment, he was rowing on a beautiful lake with a gorgeous girl seated before him, serenaded by the soft hoots of a pair of screech owls.

Often, lately, Will forgot that he had a job to do and that Sadie was an Amish farmer's daughter. All he could think about tonight, as they set out for a fishing trip to Blue Lake Pond so that he would have some practice before Hank took him out, was how much he wanted to kiss her.

He blamed the soft spring air, the colors of the evening sky, and that strand of sandy blonde hair that kept working its way loose. He blamed the tiny scatter of freckles on her nose and cheeks. He blamed those sky-blue eyes and that rosy mouth. He blamed the way her soft laugh chimed like bells. Granted, today wasn't the first time his thoughts toward her had turned in a romantic direction.

He rowed the little boat out to the middle of the lake. "It doesn't get much better than this—fishing on a warm spring evening!" A mockingbird imitated the call of a dove. A dove cooed in reply, and he figured the mockingbird had a laugh over it. Will slid onto Sadie's seat and put a worm on the hook for her as she looked away. She didn't like anything to get hurt, she said. Even a worm.

He was so close to her that all he needed to do was to tilt his face and he was in a perfect position to kiss her. He slipped a hand behind her head and pulled her face toward his. Then he was kissing her deeply, but gently, as if he had all the time in the world.

After a moment, she pulled away. "That was nice, Will. Very, very nice." She put a finger to his lips. "But don't do it again."

He studied her face for a moment in disbelief, trying to judge how he should respond. Were his instincts off that much? She was always giving him mixed signals—something he found mysterious and compelling. Certain he caught a twinkle in her eyes, he said, "My deepest apologies. The moonlight has made me lose my sensibilities."

The corner of her mouth ticked, but whether it was from amusement or annoyance, he couldn't tell. Then she laughed, a sparkling fall of notes in the still of the evening. He didn't look right into her eyes but rather at those adorable freckles that were sprinkled across her nose and cheeks, like someone dusted her with cinnamon.

But she had a point. They came here to fish, not kiss. He was ashamed of himself. Okay, maybe not at this exact instant, but by tomorrow for sure. His only excuse was that he liked her so much. The more he'd witnessed her caring ways, the more she had gotten under his skin. There were times when he thought he might be falling in love. She wouldn't believe him if he told her, so he didn't intend to. He could hardly believe it himself.

He cast his line out into the lake and watched the gentle ripples undulate through the calm surface. "What would you say if we went into Lancaster for dinner soon?"

Sadie practically dropped her pole. "I can't." The answer was quick, like she didn't even have to think about it. She shifted her shoulder away from his and kept her eyes on the surface of the lake. "Someone might see us."

A laugh burst out of Will. "People around here aren't stupid you know. They've figured it out."

She pulled farther away, looked at him. "Who has? What are you talking about?"

He read the shock in her voice even though he couldn't see her face—just the outline of her hair and prayer cap, lit by the moon around its edges like an angel.

"People know about us, Sadie. They're not blind."

She stood up. The boat rocked dangerously. "Who knows? And knows what? There's nothing to know."

He wished Sadie would quit moving around so much. One slight misstep and they could both end up in the lake. Wasn't this just what had happened to Edith Fisher? He reached up and put his hand on her shoulder, pushing her down on the bench. "You're going to capsize this little boat."

She pressed her palms together, tucked her hands between her knees, and bowed her head forward. "I can't do this, Will," she said, and her words hovered above them for a second. "Will . . . I . . ." She didn't have to finish the rest of the sentence for him to know he wasn't going to like what was coming next.

Finally, he said it. "You want to just be friends. Buddies. Pals."

Her shoulders rose, then fell. "Exactly."

It was a speech he had given to many girls, but this was the first time he had been the recipient of it. "Is this because of the bumbling schoolteacher?"

She looked at him sharply. "He's not a bumbling . . ." That single strand of hair, pulled loose from the bun at the back of her head, framed her cheek. She guided the lock behind her ear with trembling fingers before answering. "This doesn't have anything to do with Gid." She stiffened her back, lifted her chin. "It has to do with me. And it has to do with you."

"That's the thing I don't get about the Amish. You should be free to choose your life's path, Sadie."

Long seconds ticked by before she lifted her eyes to meet his. "I am free to choose, and I have made my choice. But you . . . are you so very free, Will? It seems as if your life has a giant shadow over it."

Will looked away. He hadn't expected this. His mind spun around and around. This conversation wasn't going at all the way he had planned. He looked back at Sadie, who was still searching his face. He was trapped. He would have to say something. "A shadow?"

"Yes. A shadow. Your father's shadow. Seeking his approval and never getting it." She gave him one of her direct, clear gazes. "So I am going to ask you again: are you so very free?"

The question hovered in the air, and Sadie was still waiting for his answer, stepping into the role of the Almighty, trying to stir up Will's conscience. "You don't know me well enough to figure that out, do you?" The words came out sharper than he meant them to, but he was irritated. He reeled in his line, took the oars, and swung the boat around, then began rowing swiftly toward the shore.

Wisely, Sadie never said another word. By the time they got the boat tied to the dock and started for home, Will was no longer annoyed with her but furious with himself. He never let himself get defensive. He never lost it. He absolutely never lost it. His fraternity brothers called him the Teflon Guy. Nothing ever bothered him.

Why did he have such a strong reaction to Sadie's question? Because she couldn't have been more right.

Sadie was free to choose, and she had made her choice. He was the one who wasn't free. He wasn't free at all.

18

Amos was often amazed at the overpowering love a father felt for his children. Each one so unique, so distinctive, so special to him. Julia, with her blunt, forthright manner. Menno, who had the biggest heart on earth. Sadie, with her sweet and gentle wisdom. Mary Kate, who was always up to something and he loved her for it.

If you had asked him which of his children most resembled Maggie, his late wife, Amos would have said M.K. Without a doubt. They shared the same sense of mischief and adventure. Life was never dull with Maggie Zook Lapp.

But after Menno's baby arrived, that opinion was changing. It startled him to see how much of Maggie was in Sadie. Even her voice had become like Maggie's. That same rise and dip, the half-amused tone, the way you wanted to keep hearing more, like a favorite melody. Just now, he had passed Sadie's bedroom and glanced in. He felt a tightening in his chest. She was humming to Joe-Jo exactly the way Maggie had always done with each of their babies. Maggie was always humming. Wouldn't she have been pleased to know what a fine young woman Sadie has grown into? A strong woman. A respected woman. Why, hardly a day went by without someone coming to Windmill Farm to ask her advice! He overheard Esther tell someone Sadie was the most respected young woman in the church. Imagine that! His timid little Sadie.

Downstairs, the grandfather clock dinged the hour. One . . . two . . .

So fast, he thought. That was how quickly time could get away from you. One moment your children were babies, and in the next breath, they were grown.

Three . . . four . . . five . . .

You could wake up one morning and find out that suddenly most of your life had passed by.

He heard Fern start dinner in the kitchen. Maggie's kitchen. What would Maggie have thought about Fern? No two women could be any more different. He wasn't sure if they would even be friends. Fern didn't have much patience for daydreamers, and Maggie was a first-rate daydreamer. Maggie might have thought Fern's stern ways were rule bound, legalistic, overbearing. Yet Fern fiercely loved Maggie's children, and for that, Amos had no doubt, Maggie would heartily approve of her.

But what would Maggie think if she knew Amos had grown fond of Fern? Fond wasn't the right word. That was the word used for a favorite horse or dog, not a woman. Dare he say it? Could he be falling in love with Fern Graber?

Such a thought astounded him.

What about Ira Smucker? Fern hadn't said anything after Ira had spoken to her of marriage last weekend, but that wasn't unusual. She was an utterly private person. And he hadn't seen Ira since then. That, too, wasn't unusual. Ira was a busy man.

Wait a minute. It *was* unusual. Ira had been stopping by on Wednesday nights to play a game of cribbage with Fern. After Ira had confessed his love for Fern to him, Amos had made a point to hang around while they played. He knew it wasn't right—he felt as immature as M.K. when he eavesdropped—but he thought Ira's attempts at conversation were mind-numbingly dull.

Wednesday had come and gone this week, and no Ira. Amos knew it was childish, bordering on sinfulness, but he felt rather pleased.

One late May morning, Sadie went outside to fill Menno's bird feeders. As she poured black oiled sunflower seeds into the opening of the feeder, she thought of her brother without the sting his memory usually evoked. The baby was like a healing balm to the entire family. Even Julia, out in Ohio, wanted to hear every new thing Joe-Jo was doing: his first smile, his first laugh. Last night, her father dandled the baby on his lap and Joe-Jo kept bending his knees and springing up, over and over, like a little kangaroo. The whole family gathered to watch, mesmerized. Sadie thought of the joy of having a baby around—for two months now!—and thanked God for him. For Menno.

Doozy, hanging around by Sadie to lick up fallen sunflower seeds, saw something and woofed. He perked his ears, then flew across the driveway and jumped up to greet a small figure, standing in the morning shadow of the barn. The figure bent down and buried her hands in the fur at his neck. Sadie set down the container of sunflower seeds and shielded her eyes from the bright morning sun. Her heart missed a beat. She walked down the steps and crossed the driveway. The girl was dressed in English clothes: jeans and a T-shirt that said *Kowabunga!* She wore dime-store flip-flops, and her hair was cut short. But Sadie would know her anywhere.

"Annie," Sadie said.

Annie took a long, shuddering breath. She was thin, so thin, and pale, with dark circles under her eyes as if she hadn't slept in days.

Sadie wasn't sure what to say or how to say it. Annie had come back! A flood of emotions charged through her: sadness, happiness. And anger too. Annie had done a terrible thing. "You probably want to see the baby."

Annie's eyes filled with tears. "I'm so sorry. I didn't trust him with anyone else." Then the tears began, as if she had been holding them back for months now and couldn't keep them contained one more minute.

Sadie opened her arms and Annie rushed into them.

Amos couldn't have been more surprised to come out of the barn and find Annie, weeping in Sadie's arms. They went into the house and Sadie showed her the baby, asleep in the cradle that Gid had made and Uncle Hank had repaired. Annie knelt by the cradle, tears streaming down her face. She watched Joe-Jo breathe in and out, eyes closed. And that was the moment when any judgment Amos might have felt toward Annie slipped away. He saw her for what she was: a frightened young girl, all alone, caring for a grandfather who hardly knew who he was half the time, while caring for a colicky newborn. It was too much.

Amos went into the kitchen to get a cup of coffee. Fern was whipping egg whites for waffles with her lips set in a straight line. Not that he was especially good at picking up what women thought, but her whipping those egg whites into a frenzy wasn't a subtle hint as to how riled up she felt. He thought he knew where her line of thought was traveling.

"It's good that she's here, Fern," he said quietly so that Annie wouldn't overhear. "God always wants to restore his people."

Fern flashed a stern look in Amos's direction. She poured the frothy egg whites into the batter and carefully folded them in. "But is she staying?" She set down the wooden spoon and turned to him. "We have to think of the baby's welfare."

"One step at a time. For now, I can tell you that she's staying for breakfast." He looked over Fern's shoulder to see Annie and Sadie talking in the other room. Annie hadn't left the cradle's side. Amos noticed that she kept glancing at the baby, as if she thought he might disappear. "That girl looks like she hasn't had a good meal in months."

M.K. burst into the house with a basket full of eggs and stopped abruptly when she saw Annie. Her eyes went wide as she took in Annie's appearance. "Annie! You cut your hair!"

Annie put a hand up to her head, as if she had forgotten about her short hair, her absent prayer cap.

M.K. walked right up to her. "Where have you been? We've been looking everywhere for you."

Amos and Fern exchanged a smile. Leave it to Mary Kate to get the answers they wanted.

"I was working as a waitress over in Lebanon. I have a cousin over there."

"Can you believe how big the baby is? Sadie's gotten really attached to him. We all have. We named him Joe-Jo, after Menno's middle name. We're just crazy about Joe-Jo. Even Dad has learned to be a crackerjack diaper changer."

"Only if absolutely necessary," Amos hastened to add.

A light smile fleeted across Annie's face. "You have no notion how much I've ached to come and get him."

M.K.'s eyes went wide in alarm. "But . . . you're just visiting, right? You're not planning to take him away, are you?" She turned to Amos, a plea in her face.

Annie gave the baby a long, telling look and Amos read everything in that gaze. "We'll have plenty of time to work things out," he said. "For now, let's sit down to breakfast and thank God for bringing Annie back to us."

During breakfast, Annie explained that she had returned to her grandfather's house last night and saw that he had been cared for. "The kitchen was spotless."

"That's because of me," M.K. said proudly. "I've been going over on Saturdays and working myself to the bone, cooking and cleaning."

"Hardly that," Fern added primly. "Jimmy Fisher might like some of that credit too. Hank and Edith too. And don't forget that first morning when you talked your entire schoolhouse of children and their parents into working."

M.K. scowled at her and Amos nearly laughed out loud. Fern was always reminding M.K. of her place. His youngest daughter needed constant reminding.

"I figured you all had something to do with it," Annie said. "I have been so worried about Daadi. I didn't want to move to Ohio with the colony. He should have gone with them when he had the chance. I thought if I left, he would go with the colony. I never dreamed he would wait for me to come back."

"Why did you come back then?" M.K. asked, reaching for the jam jar. She took a spoonful of blackberry jam and spread it on her toast, pushing it to the crust and licking the drips on her fingers.

"The baby. I couldn't stop thinking about him, wondering about him. I wasn't worried—I knew Sadie would take good care of him. But I couldn't stay away any longer. I had to come back." She took in a long breath of air. "So I quit my job. I'm here to stay. I'd like . . . another . . . chance at being a mother." She kept her eyes on her lap. "For Menno's sake. For my sake. For the baby's sake."

Amos felt tears prick his eyes as he saw the pain shuddering through Annie.

Annie wiped her face with her napkin. "I won't take the baby from you. I can't be putting my pride before his well-being. I'll wait until you're ready to let me have him." With another long look at the baby's sweet face, she rose. She turned to Sadie. "I'd like to see the baby now and then."

"Of course," Sadie said. "He's a precious little boy. You're welcome to come by any time you like."

"Hold on, Annie," Amos said. "How do you plan to support yourself? And what about your grandfather? He needs full-time care. Our deacon wrote to someone in the colony and they said they would send someone to come get him, after the harvest is in. That's months from now."

Annie nodded. "I haven't worked everything out yet." She lifted her chin. "But I will."

"I'll help," Sadie said. Then, more confidently, "We'll all help." She looked around the room at her family. Her confidence faltered. "Won't we?"

Fern was quiet for a long while. "I've been needing another good egg basket. The one M.K. uses is falling apart. I should like to order one or two from you."

Annie's face brightened. "I could make you one."

"And Carrie Miller was admiring the baby's basket you made," Fern said. "She's having her fourth baby. I thought it might be nice to get her something new."

The baby started to stir then, and Annie's eyes riveted right to the cradle. Amos noted that her fists clenched tight, as if she was itching to scoop up the baby.

Sadie went over and picked him up, held him close to her heart, then turned and released the baby into Annie's arms. "Have a seat. I'll get a bottle ready. You can feed your son."

Fern hurried M.K. off to school and Amos got himself a second cup of coffee. He leaned back in his chair and studied Annie as she held the baby. He could see that she felt awkward at first, tentative, holding the baby as if he was made of spun sugar. Then Sadie pulled up a chair next to her and showed her how to keep the bottle lifted up high so the milk poured down. Annie's whole being started to relax, and she even giggled at something Sadie told her. For just an instant, she looked like the young girl Amos remembered, the girl who Menno had fluttered around all last summer. It relieved Amos. It gave him hope. He knew she was facing a very long, hard road as an unwed mother.

"I'd forgotten the delicate sound of Annie's laugh," Fern said as she sat next to Amos with a cup of hot tea. "It always reminded me of ice tinkling against glass." She took a sip of tea. "You were right. God wants his people restored." She added a teaspoon of sugar into her tea and stirred it. "The sight of Sadie and Annie and the baby, Menno would be pleased, Amos."

For the second time that morning, Amos's eyes pricked with tears. He looked down to blink them away. To his shock, he discovered that his hand had gripped Fern's, just the way he used to hold Maggie's hand.

The last day of school was right around the corner—just two days away. The scholars had been working hard to prepare a program for the parents. They had learned several new songs to sing. A few students had memorized poems to recite. This was going to be the best program Twin Creeks had ever presented to parents. The children had worked so hard to get everything just right.

Alice Smucker, M.K. thought darkly, had never bothered with doing anything new for the parent programs. Not once. The same five carols were sung for the Christmas program, the same five hymns sung for the end-of-year program. Boring! And poetry, to Alice, was fanciful nonsense. Gideon disagreed. So this year, M.K. volunteered to recite the longest poem she could find: *The Raven* by Edgar Allen Poe. She didn't understand much of it, but it fit in nicely with the falcons living on her farm, and she was determined to memorize it.

Just before Gideon dismissed the class, he mentioned that he hoped they could have a picnic after the program, but a tree limb from the big oak tree had fallen on the playground in last night's rainstorm. "Until we get that limb removed and hauled away, we aren't going to be able to have a picnic like we had planned."

Amidst the scholars' disappointed groans, a crackerjack idea bubbled up inside of M.K. She raised her hand to the ceiling. "We can have it at my house! Windmill Farm is just down the street."

Gideon looked skeptical. "Maybe you should ask your father first."

Ask Sadie, was what he meant. "It's no problem at all! Dad loves having folks over and Fern is a fine cook."

Gid hesitated. "Are you sure, Mary Kate?"

"Absolutely!"

Reluctantly, Gideon agreed. M.K. was thrilled! It would be so much fun to have the entire class, and parents and siblings, to her house for a picnic! Gid dismissed everyone and she rushed out of the classroom, catching up with Ruthie to walk home together. They had plans to go spy on Eve in the falcon scape and see if they could spot her babies.

And M.K. promptly forgot all about the picnic.

Amos felt like his old, pre-heart-trouble self. So good that he wanted to celebrate. At breakfast, he asked M.K., "After the end-of-year program tomorrow, did Gid make plans for a picnic lunch for the scholars?"

M.K.'s eyes went wide. She grabbed a spoonful of yogurt to plop in her granola, stalling for time. "Actually, I might have . . . possibly . . . volunteered our house for lunch." She gave a sideways glance in Fern's direction at the other side of the table.

In the middle of spooning out a segment of grapefruit, Fern froze.

"That's a fine idea!" Amos said, pleased.

Fern gave M.K. a look. "And when were you going to spring that on me?"

M.K. scratched her forehead. "I guess I forgot to tell you." She dug into her bowl of granola. "Families will bring things! It'll be easy."

Amos rubbed his hands together. "Tell Gid we'll handle barbecuing chickens if everyone else can bring the extras. They can come here right after the program. And tell him Fern will make her good baked beans and coleslaw too. We'll cook everything."

"We?" Fern asked, raising an eyebrow. "*We* will cook everything?"

Amos grinned. "And tell Gid that I'm thinking it would be nice to have a softball game too." He loved playing sports with children. When his children were little, he would tear around the bases with one of them tucked under his arm. Even when his own children had outgrown the crook in his arm, he would find a neighbor's toddler to tote. When he became ill, it was one of the things he missed most.

Fern and Sadie spent the rest of the afternoon cooking up baked beans, preparing chickens for the barbecue, cutting cabbage for coleslaw. Amos and Will cleaned out the barbecue pit, swept the volleyball court, and prepared bases for the softball game. Amos couldn't remember when he had last felt so lighthearted.

The next day, midmorning, parents crammed into the back of the schoolhouse to hear the scholars' recitations and hymn singing. Even Alice, Gid's sister, hobbled in on her crutches and the children politely welcomed her. M.K. kept her distance from Alice's crutches. She was convinced that Alice Smucker had it in for her, and Amos had to admit that Alice wore a pained expression on her face whenever she caught sight of M.K. Especially pained as M.K. delivered her long and unusual blackbird poem.

Afterward, children and parents poured over to Windmill Farm for the barbecue. Fern and Sadie had skipped the program so they could start the chickens on the barbecue. Amos smelled that sweet, tangy smell all the way down the road. He smiled. Behind him, he heard a firecracker go off, which meant Jimmy Fisher was nearby. In front of him, he saw Annie walking up the hill, holding the baby in her arms so that Sadie could cook. Today was a wonderful day.

While everyone ate lunch on blankets on the grass, Amos went to mark out the baselines for the softball game in the gravel driveway. Home base was the tall maple tree in the front yard. The bases were old goose-down pillows that Fern donated to the cause. Gid pitched, Will caught, and Amos helped the six-and-under crowd at bat. When they hit the ball, Amos would scoop the toddler under his arm and run around the bases, pumping and wheezing, red-faced and panting. He was having the time of his life.

Little by little, mothers and fathers made noise about heading home and choring, so the scholars started to reluctantly clear out. Gid remained behind, having a casual back-and-forth toss with Will. They didn't have ball gloves, so you could hear the smack of the ball in the heel of the hand. No one paid them any mind, until the sound of the smack got louder. Then louder still. The ball was a blur between them now. Gid was red in the face. Will's upper arm strained and glistened.

Then Gid threw a little wild and caught Will's guard down. The ball popped him in the stomach and Will let out a loud "ooof" sound. He doubled over like a deflated beach ball. Then he fell back and splayed as he hit the ground, grinning. The few stragglers who had remained stood around laughing at Will's exaggerated antics.

Will popped up his head and peered at Gid. "Looks like you throw a pitch the way you put together a cradle."

Gid's face tightened.

Quick as a flock of sparrows, the laughs were gone.

Gid took out after Will, sprinting like a panther across the yard. Dust rose behind him. Will had just enough time to make that come-and-get-me gesture with both hands. Then they were squaring off, but not throwing punches yet. Gid pushed Will's shoulders and he fell on the ground.

"Are you crazy?" Will yelled, scrambling to his feet. "What's that for?"

"That's for wrecking the petit fours," Gid growled.

"The what?" Will growled. "I don't even know what pettyfours are!"

Gid grabbed Will in a headlock. "And that's for ruining the cradle."

But Will had a few tricks of his own. He grabbed onto Gid's arm and bent over, heaving him on the ground. "Why would I ruin your cradle?"

Gid leaped to his feet. "Why?" He worked around to swing again and brought a left hook out of nowhere. Will jumped back to avoid it.

Amos would never admit it out loud, certainly not among this small crowd, but he was impressed with this quiet schoolteacher's tenacity.

Gid narrowed his eyes. "You'll do whatever you can to keep Sadie and me apart."

Will ducked and danced. "Oh yeah? Well, why would she ever want a man like you?"

The world stopped dead to listen.

Gid was up in Will's face, now pointing a finger at his chest. "You don't know the first thing about being a man."

That did it. Will sprang. Down the two went, rolling in the dirt, throwing punches. Dust whipped into a fog. They rolled one way, then another, and knocked over the blue bird feeder. Sadie gasped as the dinner dish shattered when the feeder crashed to the ground. And still, they kept at it.

M.K. edged around to Amos and tugged on his sleeve. "They're just having fun, right?"

"I think so," Amos said, then frowned. "I thought so." It was hard to tell. The boys were a frenzy of flailing elbows and kicking heels. All that could be heard were the sounds of grunts and smacks. More grunts than smacks.

The rest of them stood there, watching. Even the baby, held in Annie's arms, looked stunned. His eyes and mouth were three little round O's. Uncle Hank whistled, long and low, then he and Jimmy Fisher started betting to see who would win until Fern put a stop to that.

M.K. looked worried. "Dad—what's wrong with them?"

Amos stroked his beard, wondering when he should step in. "Those two are butting heads over our Sadie."

"But why?" M.K. couldn't take her eyes off the two, dancing and sparring.

Amos glanced at her. "I believe it's called a love triangle."

"But that would mean . . ." She scrunched up her face. "Could Sadie be in love with two different boys at the same time?" She scratched her head. "Where could you look up a thing like that in the library?"

In the midst of the boys' tussle, Amos turned to M.K. How could he make this clear to her? She was just twelve. She wanted simple definitions of love. Love was many things, but it was never simple. Before he could think of how to answer M.K., Fern interrupted him. "Amos Lapp, would you please stop those two before Gid ends up losing his teaching job!"

"What?" M.K. was horrified. "Does that mean Alice would have to take next year's term?" She covered her face with her hands. "Dad! Please! Stop them!"

"They can't keep this up," Amos said, but they did.

Finally, Sadie had enough. She ran to the hose spigot and filled a bucket with water, then rushed over and tossed it at the two. They stopped fighting, shocked and soaked.

"Gid, stop it!" she yelled. "Go home!"

Gid limped to his feet. "I'm not going anywhere." His shirt front was dripping with water and blood. He held one hand, already swelling, close to his chest. You could tell that he'd broken it. He took a few steps toward Sadie until they were practically nose to nose. She glared at him. Amos had never seen his daughter look so angry.

Gid looked at Sadie through a closing eye and repeated himself. "I'm not going anywhere."

Sadie was furious. Mad at Gid, mad at Will. Will came out of the fight with surprisingly less damage than Gid, but he seemed to sense he should make himself scarce, and after Fern gave him an ice pack for his eye, he quietly slipped off to his cottage. Fern told Gid he needed a splint made for his hand before he headed off to the hospital's emergency room for an X-ray. And Sadie was the only one who knew how.

In the kitchen, Sadie wrapped the gauze around the splint she had made to keep Gid's broken hand immobile. They carefully avoided looking at each other. Amos had gone down to the shanty to call a taxi and offered to go with him to the emergency room, but Gid said no, that he could handle himself just fine.

Mary Kate sidled into the room, watching Sadie clean off Gid's face cuts with cottonballs and alcohol. "It was my fault," she whispered.

"What was?" Sadie said, dabbing Gid's wounds so that he flinched. She could have used something that wouldn't sting quite as badly, but she didn't mind seeing him squirm.

"The cradle. The night Gid brought it over—I was carrying it into the house and I was running . . . and Doozy made me trip. I fell right on top of it, hard, and the whole thing kind of collapsed. Nothing broke—it all fit together like a glove. But I didn't know I should have used glue." She looked down at her bare feet.

Sadie stared at her, dumbfounded. "Why didn't you say so? Mary Kate, why would you let me think Gid did it on purpose?"

M.K. studied a fly buzzing on the windowsill with great interest.

"Mary Kate, look at me. When are you going to ever learn? You create problems for other people—and then you let them pick up the pieces!"

"Geduh is geduh, Sadie," Gid said quietly. *What's done is done.* "Let it go."

Sadie looked at Gid, shocked.

"I don't think you can blame her for the cradle collapse. The fault was mine for bringing the cradle over too soon. I should have waited a few more days until the glue cured." The taxi pulled up outside, so Gid picked up his hat with his unbandaged hand. He walked to the door, turned the knob, and opened the door a crack.

Gid released the doorknob and turned to look at Sadie. An uncomfortable silence settled over them. "You're always preaching about how important forgiveness is. You tell other people they need to forgive. But you . . . you won't forgive me. When God forgives, he does it once and for all. He doesn't keep dragging out reminders the way you do. I've tried every which way I can think of and you still treat me like I'm . . ." His voice trailed off. "Maybe . . . you need to take a dose of your own medicine."

Sadie's jaw dropped. This was by far the longest speech anybody'd ever had out of Gid. His words bit to the quick.

19

Annie stopped by every day to see the baby. She fed him, rocked him, cuddled him, offered him her finger to grasp. She lifted her hand with his fist clamped about her index finger to her mouth and kissed his plump little hand. When she got ready to leave, Annie pressed one last kiss on the baby's cheek. Sadie shifted Joe-Jo to her shoulder and patted him as she watched Annie walk down the hill. Annie was such a lonely little figure, and she was heading home to be with her nutty grandfather. The sight of her tugged at Sadie's heart.

Amos came out of the barn and crossed over to where Sadie stood with the baby. "Annie and I have had a lot of talks these last few weeks—about why she left and why she came back," Sadie said. "Good talks. She seems much stronger now, much better prepared to face her responsibilities."

Amos put his hand on the fence post.

"Dad, I think the time is coming when we need to think about letting Annie have Joe-Jo."

"Fern has mentioned the same thing," Amos said. "But we felt it would be best for you to make that decision."

"Maybe we could start slowly. A day here and there, then maybe an overnight. To help her adjust."

Amos took Joe-Jo out of Sadie's arms. "You know that could very well mean she will move to Ohio to join the colony in the fall."

Sadie gave a slight nod. "I keep trying to think of what Menno might have wanted, if he could understand the situation."

Amos kissed the baby's smooth forehead. "I think he would understand that Annie is the baby's mother. She's trying to do the best she can. And he would be pleased that we are trying to help her."

Sadie couldn't stop thinking about Gid's words: *When God forgives, he does it once and for all. He doesn't keep dragging out reminders the way people do.* The way she did.

She gave her father a sad smile. "Soon, then."

Will hardly slept. He kept going over every precaution he could think of for banding the chicks.

Miner's hard hat with LED lamp. ✓
Red helium balloons to tie on his backpack. ✓
Air horn to scare off Adam and Eve if they flew too close to him. ✓
Protective goggles. ✓
Fingerless leather gloves so he could handle the bands. ✓
Cell phone to call for help if Adam attacked him and left him for dead. ✓

A little before 4:00 a.m., he threw back the covers and got out of bed. Bird-watchers were a little on the obsessive side. A group of them had figured out he would be banding today and told him they would set up their scopes at dawn. They knew that banding was done when the nestlings were about three weeks old because, at this stage, they didn't run out of the scape or attempt to fly off. What Will doubted that these birders would know was that at three weeks of age, the young birds could be sexed by measuring the width of the legs. He had promised Mr. Petosky a male and a female. Last night, Mr. Petosky said he decided he wanted three, not two, and Will put his foot down. Two was his limit. Two left in the wild, two brought in for captivity. It seemed fair.

His plan was to get out there, get up the ridge, wait for Adam and Eve to leave the scape, band the birds, remove the two bigger ones for Mr. Petosky, and be done with it. He would lie and tell Mahlon that only two were found in the scape. Mahlon would wonder what had happened to them from dusk the night before—the time of Will's last call to him. But Will wasn't too concerned—there were all kinds of reasonable explanations as to the disappearance of fledglings. They could have fallen from the scape and ended up as dinner for another animal. Even Mahlon said he didn't expect that fourth chick to survive. They competed with each other in the scape, and the older chicks had the advantage: bigger, bolder, quicker. Once the deed would be done, Will was sure he wouldn't feel needles of guilt anymore. It was that time of indecision, of anticipation, that made this whole business seem sketchy.

Dressed and prepared, Will climbed the steep, uneven ridge to reach the scape, just like he had practiced. He stopped at a level place, behind the scape, where he would band the chicks. He planned to band them one at a time. He would pluck one from the scape and band it down below. He would also check it for overall health and condition. If he could get the birds banded quickly and back into the scape without Eve getting too aggressive, he would try to collect eggshell fragments and prey remains for examination. That would make Mahlon happy and hopefully deflect his attention from the two missing chicks. The eggshells could be analyzed for contaminants and the prey remains could provide additional insight into peregrine falcon feeding habits. The use of DDT in the 1950s and 1960s had practically wiped out the peregrine falcons by causing thinning of the eggshells. Even though they were recovering, it was still important to analyze the eggshells for contaminants. With a little bit of luck, he would be done in ten minutes and his pulse could return to normal.

He did have luck—more than a little. Adam was already out hunting. He heard the quacking, duck-like sound he made as he soared over the fields. Hopefully, Will could coax Eve out of the scape with some quail left on a lower rock. Then he could get in, do the deed, get out.

Everything was going according to plan. It was eerie, how easy it was. The bird-watchers wouldn't arrive for another hour, which made Will feel considerably less anxious. He opened his backpack and pulled out a flashlight, turning it on so he could light the area where he would band the chicks. He set out the tools he would need: bands and pliers. A strange thought burst into his mind . . . this must be what it was like as his father prepared for surgery.

Now was *not* the time to think about his father. He quickly dismissed the thought and got back to work.

Will tossed a quail—Eve's favorite morsel—on a rock way out in front of the scape. He held his breath, watching her carefully to see if she noticed it. The scape was so much smaller than he would have expected—only about nine inches in diameter. The depression was only about two inches deep. After a long moment, Eve hopped to the edge of the scape and took a short flight to reach the quail. Will held his breath, watching her for a moment. He thought she might bring it right back to the scape, but she stayed put. Probably hungry.

Okay. *Go!*

Will scaled the rock where the scape sat, grabbed a chick, and jumped back down. He whipped off a glove and picked up the bands Mr. Petosky had given to him. The downy white chick looked at him with those eyes—dark, penetrating eyes, ringed with gray fuzz. It just stared at Will, unblinking. This—this was why falcons have played a prominent role in human history, he suddenly realized. As he gazed back at the chick, he felt the strangest connection. As if the bird knew what he was up to and was disappointed in him. He could almost hear Sadie's voice, poking his faulty conscience: "Is this the kind of man you've become? After all you've learned about yourself this spring, about thc God who cares for you . . . this is who you want to be? This is the moment of decision, Will. Yours and yours alone."

Panic crashed through his mind like waves at high tide, his emotions a brackish mixture of embarrassment, confusion, self-reproach, guilt, fear. A cord of guilt wrapped around him and squeezed hard. He'd created this moment, built it one conversation at a time, and now he was terrified of it. His hands were trembling.

Will heard Adam's quacking sounds grow closer. He heard Eve answer back in alarm. They had spotted him. He had to finish this task. He had to.

Will stared at the cell phone in his hand. He had been hemming and hawing for the last hour. He was about to make the hardest phone call of his life. His heart was pounding, his hands were clammy. Finally, he pressed the button. One ring, two rings, three rings, then a fourth.

"Will?" His father exhaled, impatient. "I've only got a minute. What is it?"

"Dad . . . I'm in some trouble. I need your help."

A woven-wire fence enclosed the cemetery. Amos, Fern, Sadie, M.K., and Uncle Hank met with their neighbors to help clean up the graveyard after the recent storm. They went in by the gate to join the others. They knew a good many residents of the graveyard, though the oldest part went back to the early 1900s. Uncle Hank stopped to examine a small tombstone. "WHY, LOOKY HERE! If that isn't Lovina Shrock! She was my first customer for my coffin-building business. Howdy, Lovina!" He stopped to pull a few weeds around the stone.

"What ever happened to that particular line of work?" Edith Fisher said, coming up to him with a shovel.

Uncle Hank's face lit up. "My clients never laughed at my jokes!" He took the shovel from her. "But at least I never got any complaints." He roared with laughter and Edith rolled her eyes, until a rusty laugh burst out of her.

So Edith must have finally forgiven Hank for pulling a practical joke over her on a fishing trip. Now that twosome, Amos thought, watching the two of them wander off to weed a row of graves, was one of life's great mysteries. M.K. ran off to join her friends as Sadie set the baby in the shade. Fern started to work with a cluster of women.

Amos wandered down a path to Maggie's grave, under a willow tree, near the fence. Menno's was next to her. A branch had cracked and he pulled out his handsaw to trim it. Then he dropped down on his knees to clear away the brush. He traced his finger over the lettering on the headstone:

Margaret Zook Lapp
Beloved wife and mother

He glanced around, making sure he was alone. Satisfied, he started to talk to Maggie as he knelt down to clear weeds and debris from her stone. He did that, sometimes, when he had important things on his mind. He never told anyone. He knew she wasn't in that grave. He believed she was in Heaven, in the presence of the Almighty. But it made him feel closer to her.

"Maggie, you know how I loved you. No one could ever take your place. Not ever. But I remember a time when you were expecting our second baby, and we wondered how we could ever love a child more than we loved our Julia. Then Menno came, and Sadie, and M.K. And one night you told me that now you understood—love isn't finite. It expands, like the yeast in bread dough, you said. I remember you were punching down bread dough when you told me that very thing." He reached over and pulled the rest of the weeds from the side of the gravestone.

"Maggie, there's room in my heart to love another woman, and I think I've found someone I want to start over with. I want your blessing, dearest." He brushed away the weeds and rose to his feet, standing quietly before the grave for a few minutes. As he turned away, he found Fern, not three feet from him. He looked her straight in her eyes, his heart beat like a drum. "Don't."

"Don't what?" Fern asked.

Amos took a step closer to her. "Don't marry Ira Smucker."

She lifted her chin. "I told him no."

Amos felt a smile start deep down in his heart and rise to his face. He took a step forward, putting only inches between them. He reached for her hands. "Fern Graber, do you think you can stand being part of the Lapp family for the rest of your life?" He felt so raw, so exposed. His inner adolescent had kicked in, because he feared her response but at the same time hungered to know the truth.

Fern pursed her lips for a moment, appearing to be considering this.

Amos held his breath until she lifted her face to his. Her eyes softened as she gazed at him. When she finally spoke, her low, husky voice wavered with emotion. "Well, to tell the truth," she said, "I don't know how I couldn't."

Two hours later, Dr. Charles William Stoltz drove up the driveway to Windmill Farm in his champagne-colored convertible BMW. Will was surprised to see his mother hadn't come too. Then he remembered that his mother had sent him a text message that she was off to New York City this week to see a new Egyptian exhibit at the Metropolitan Museum of Art. He was relieved. This was hard enough.

Will's stomach knotted. He tried to pretend it was from hunger, not regret.

Will waited until his father was out of the car to walk over to him. His mother always said that she was drawn to her father because he reminded her of Gregory Peck—raven hair, now with white wings at the temples, even with that little divot in his chin. He was wearing his customary off-duty uniform: tassled cordovan loafers, light gray slacks, and a powder-blue dress shirt with a pair of Ray-Bans hooked in the breast pocket. He didn't wrinkle. Ever. He looked like he was going to his country club for drinks with his weirdly cerebral doctor friends who made jokes about aneurisms and neuron tangles. It had always amazed Will that his father had friends at all; he thought he had the personality of a prison warden. And he seemed completely out of place on an Amish farm.

Will took a deep breath to galvanize himself as his father took a long look at him. "How in the world does a person stay on an Amish farm and end up with a shiner?"

Unlike Will, Charles Stoltz never got ruffled or confused. He never lost his sense of purpose, which was why he found it so difficult to understand that Will wasn't sure he wanted to go into medicine. Will touched his eye. "Long story."

"Have you packed?"

"Not yet. It won't take long to finish."

"So." Will's father got right down to business, as usual—no *How have you been? We've missed you.* "What have you done now?" he said in his quiet, detached voice.

Will took a deep breath. He might as well tell. Everything.

If anyone were looking at them from a distance, they would have seen a father and son, side by side, leaning their backs against the car, arms folded against their chests, long legs stretched out, one ankle crossing the other. They would have thought the two were very laid-back. Ha! His father was as laid-back as a mountain lion. And they wouldn't have known that Will's heart was beating fast, confessing to his father the many ways he had messed up in the last few months. This confession made getting suspended from school and losing his spot in medical school to be a mere blip on the radar. This was big—it involved the law. The DUI. The shady lawyer. Illegally selling a noncaptive endangered species to a breeder. And now, trying to backpedal and get out of it all.

When he called Mr. Petosky to tell him he couldn't do the switch, that he had banded all four chicks with the game warden's bands, there was dead silence, followed by a stream of cussing like he'd never heard before, even in a fraternity house. Mr. Petosky told him to expect to find out that his DUI blood alcohol limit from the night of his arrest was now at the highest level, thanks to a friend at the police station who didn't mind altering official records. Expect jail time, Mr. Petosky told him. Expect a huge fine. Expect to have your license revoked. Expect to say goodbye to ever getting a decent job. And then he flung a few more swear words at him and hung up.

His father listened carefully, asking a few questions here and there. He was completely unreadable. No fury, or worse, disgust, as Will thought there would be. Nor did he offer any answers or solutions. He simply listened. He could have been taking history on a patient, he was that impassive, that detached. If anything, his father grew more outwardly calm, never a good sign. As Will finished his long tale, he saw the Lapps' buggy pull up the drive. He was grateful they had been away up to this point.

His father noticed the buggy too, and made a dismissive gesture with his hand. "We can . . . finish this later." He glanced at Will with eyes narrowed. "I don't think I've ever been so disappointed in you."

Just like that, Will was eight years old again, and those same cold eyes were judging him for getting a B+ in P.E. on his report card. If only his father could have been like Amos, who only cared about his children's happiness and well-being. Will tried to play it cool, but his guts were in a knot.

M.K. was the first to spill out of the buggy. She hurried over to meet Will's father. Sadie went straight to the house with the baby, which didn't surprise Will. He knew how shy she was around strangers. Amos and Fern walked over to say hello. "You must be Will's father," Amos said, offering his hand to Charles. "You raised a fine young man. We think the world of your boy."

Will winced. How could he face Amos once the truth about him was out? He had been so good to him.

"Oh, I think a lot of my son too," Will's father said dryly, shaking Amos's hand. Zing! Aimed at Will, but one that was lost on the Lapps.

Fern tilted her head in that way she had, sizing up Will's father. Will wondered what she was thinking—did they resemble each other? Did Will fall short? Of course he did.

Then her eyes went wide. "Why, Little Chuckie Stoltzfus. I haven't seen you since you tied an oily rag to my cat's tail and set it on fire."

As Amos heard Fern talk to the fancy doctor like he was a small neighbor boy, he thought that just possibly she had completely lost her mind. Had that intimate moment in the graveyard unhinged her? Fern kept circling back to the cat—how it was her favorite cat in all the world and she still mourned for it. Amos knew, for a fact, that Fern didn't particularly like cats.

The fancy doctor glanced at his watch, tapped his foot, seemed as coiled as a cobra. His face was stone, his eyebrows knitted together. And still, Fern chattered on about that cat. Amos was baffled; Fern wasn't a lengthy talker. Short, pithy remarks that brought a person up short—those were her trademarks. The doctor's cheeks were turning fire red. So rot as en Kasch! *As red as a cherry.*

Amos worried the doctor might explode and how could he blame him? Fern was describing, in infinite detail, how the burnt smell of cat fur lingered on and on. He was just about to step in and muzzle her when the fancy doctor met her gaze, head-on. "Fern Graber, I did not set your cat on fire," he said. His voice was smooth, no friction between the words. "My cousin Marvin did."

You could have heard a pin drop, a heart beat. Will's eyes went wide, his mouth dropped open, noiseless.

So, Fern had been after something! Amos's heart swelled in admiration for her. Somehow, she seemed to know just how to pressure this man into cracking, admitting something he apparently had kept hidden for—well, at least for Will's twenty-one years. It boggled Amos's mind—to think Fern grew up in the same church as Will's father in Millersburg, Ohio! Even more astonishing was the shock registered on Will's face. To think that Charles Stoltz, a.k.a. Little Chuckie Stoltzfus, had never told his son that he had been raised Amish.

Fern insisted he stay for dinner, overruling Charles Stoltz's many objections. Amos suspected there were only a few people who ever told this man what to do—and his Fern was one of them.

Dinner was torture. As they settled in to eat, Will sat there, stunned, wordless. Amos felt sorry for him. Will had shared a few stories about his father with Amos—never in his wildest dreams would he have thought that fancy doctor, with all his degrees, had been raised Plain.

Nothing about Dr. Stoltz seemed Plain now. Certainly not the outside trappings—the clothes, the car. Not a trace of a Deitsch accent. Not a mannerism. Not a single hint of his humble beginnings. Even his surname had been modified. All evidence of his upbringing had been washed away, swept clean.

No one said much at dinner. Except for Fern. She just kept on talking, reminiscing about stories she remembered about Little Chuckie—which seemed to mortify him—updating him about the people in his church as if he had asked. Amos thought she might be trying to squeeze information out of him for Will's sake. "So if I remember right, you were dead set on going to college."

"That's right." It was pretty clear that Charles Stoltz didn't want his past sifted through.

"And your father was dead set against you getting a college education." Fern swallowed a bite of chicken. "He was determined to have you farm alongside of him."

Charles remained unresponsive and helped himself to a spoonful of mashed potatoes. He cut two precise squares of his chicken.

"Broke your parents' hearts when you ran off," Fern said. "I sure do remember that."

Charles cut his meat with such intensity that Amos feared he might go right through the plate.

"That's sort of flip-flopped," M.K. said as she poured a pool of gravy over the potatoes on her plate until Fern stopped her. "Your dad wanted you to be a farmer and you ran off to be a doctor. You want Will to be a doctor and he ran off to be a farmer."

At the exact same moment, as if it had been orchestrated, Charles's and Will's forks clattered against their plates.

No one said much else for the rest of the dinner. Except for Fern.

20

As soon as dinner ended, Will's father leaned over and quietly told him to go get packed up, that they needed to leave as soon as he was ready. Will nodded once and said only, "All right."

As Will crested the small hill that led down to the cottage, he couldn't believe what he had learned about his father tonight. He felt a shock go through him, as real as lightning. Once he had opened a hot oven at eye level to put in a frozen pizza and he was hit by a wave of heat so strong and severe that it temporarily blinded him. The discovery about his father had the same effect.

His father was raised Amish? Dr. Charles William Stoltz had once been Chuckie Stoltzfus, a simple farm boy? Did his mother know? It was too much to take in.

So he wasn't the only one in the family who kept secrets! He grew somber. The revelation about his father—as big as it was—only served as a distraction. The reason his father was here tonight hadn't gone away—Will was facing some serious problems.

Will stopped at the doorway of his cottage. The sun had dropped low on the horizon. He watched, transfixed, as the sky filled with deepening hues of red and orange, then purple. In the morning, the sun would rise; tomorrow evening, about this time, it would set. A regular cycle. He stood there for a long moment, marveling at the earth's precise alignment on its axis when so many other things in life seemed crooked.

Suddenly the fact that he was looking at the last little bit of the sun for this day, knowing that it would rise again in the morning, that it was a solid fact the world could count on—it was a very comforting thought. And the fact that the sun had hung in place since the creation of the world and would be there until the heavens passed away—that God had ordained all of this into being. It struck Will that this same God might have a thought or two for him and his future, as well.

The sun had slipped below the horizon, but the sky was filled with an extraordinary lighting. The world seemed different. The cornfields seemed extra green, the pine trees so vivid they were almost jarring. It was like getting a pair of glasses that were overcorrected. Everything seemed startlingly clear to him.

Fern continued her endless monologue of informing Charles of the people of Millersburg, Ohio, as Sadie and Mary Kate washed the dinner dishes. Amos could tell that Charles was growing increasingly uncomfortable with all these unwanted memories thrust upon him. He finally took pity on the man.

"Let's go outside. I'd like to show you the falcon scape before it gets too dark."

Charles bolted from his chair before Amos finished his sentence. They walked to a high spot that held one of Amos's favorite views—you could see rolling fields in every direction. Will had tilled and planted those very fields, Amos told Charles. Since the corn and wheat were knee-high, you couldn't see the wavy furrows and Amos was glad for that. He had a hunch Charles would find fault with Will's plowing.

"I'm glad Will was able to help you," Charles said.

Amos nodded. "We're sorry to think he will be leaving us tonight."

"He's banded the chicks. He's done what he needed to do here for Mahlon. And Will has . . . some things to figure out. I think it's best if we do it together. At home."

It was late and the sun had already slid down the horizon, turning the wispy clouds in the sky to gold, purple, and red. Charles noticed. "I'd forgotten the sheer beauty of nature. Sunsets on a farm are like no other."

Amos nodded. The sunset was particularly spectacular tonight. Maybe it was God's gift to Will, a blessing and a benediction. "I don't know how anyone could possibly visit this part of the world and not believe in the perfect hand of God."

Above their heads Adam floated across the cornfield and let out a shrill whistle. "That's the tiercel."

"The male falcon, right?"

Amos must have looked surprised that he would know such a fact.

"The first car I ever bought was a Toyota Tercel." Charles Stoltz's cheeks pinked a little. "I've always liked birds." He kicked at a dirt clod with his loafer. "I guess there is a small part of me that is still Plain."

"Oh, I have a hunch there's probably a lot of you that is still Plain."

Charles jerked his head around. "I don't think so. I left at nineteen and never looked back. Never wanted to. Nor was I welcomed back."

Adam dove straight down in a stoop, like he was performing for them. They watched his shape shift into an aerodynamic missile. Dozens of small songbirds scattered like buckshot. There was no love lost between the tiercel and the other birds. "Doctoring always seemed like farming to me," Amos said.

Charles raised an eyebrow.

"You learn to fix things, to make things right again. You do your part—do it well, do it thoroughly, and God provides the rain and sun to do the rest. Just like the work of healing."

Charles's eyes were riveted on Adam, who had snatched a barn swallow midair and swooped up to carry it back to the scape. Adam would be back soon. It was taking more and more hunts to keep his family fed. Amos waited a moment, hoping Charles might say something, but he didn't. So Amos did. "Do you know much about falconry?"

"Its history, mostly, as a sport of game hunting, where they wear those little hoods." He looked up, as if gathering details in his mind. "Let's see . . . the first record of falconry was in China in 2200 BC. The tradition made its way around the world—Africa, Egypt, Persia, Europe." He stroked his chin. "Shakespeare was an avid falconer. Then the sport of falconry declined when firearms came on the scene."

Oh. This Dr. Stoltz knew quite a lot about falconry. If Amos ever needed brain surgery, he decided he would definitely want this man to do it. "Falconry is having a revival of sorts. I've read of a blueberry farmer in eastern Washington who uses trained falcons as bird abatement. Not peregrines like our falcons—he uses alpomado falcons. The falcons keep raiding birds out of his crops. He calls them his falcon patrol. Uses about twenty birds. All of the handlers have to get permits to become trainers. It's supposed to be very successful." Amos grinned. "We've been blessed here on Windmill Farm to have Adam and Eve—that's what Will named our falcons. They've helped keep down aviary damage on our crops this spring. Cut way down on those pesky starlings. We're hoping they'll come back to breed here next year."

"Interesting." And Charles Stoltz did seem interested. Amos had finally hit on the right subject to snag this man's attention. Above them, Adam did a looping figure eight. "They are . . . fast."

Amos nodded. "So much of a falcon's life is spent in the air. The scape is only a place to lay and incubate its eggs, to house its fledglings until it can push them out."

The two men were mesmerized by Adam's aerobatics. The falcon was swooping and diving and darting, as if it was having the time of its life.

"Working the falcons is something of an art. The bond between a falconer and its falcon is interesting. It's a relationship of trust. Every time a falconer lets go, the bird has a choice as to whether it will return or not." Amos shrugged. "It could be in Mexico tomorrow." He looked at Charles. "But it has to choose to come back."

"Why would it? Why doesn't it just fly off?"

"Being a predator—it's a hard life. The falcon has learned that life is easier if it returns to the falconer. It will always get fed, even if it doesn't catch something. Even if it's not successful out there. No matter what." Amos watched Adam circle high above and stoop down to nab a bat, then sail with it back to the scape to feed a chick. "Maybe the falcon just knows a good deal when it sees it." He looked back at the little cottage. "But the falconer gives the falcon the choice to return." He walked a few steps, his hands clasped behind him.

Charles remained behind. Glancing at him out of the corner of his eye, Amos realized Charles knew exactly what he was getting at.

At the bottom of the rise, Amos turned to wait for him and pointed to the cottage. "Will's probably about done packing. I imagine he could use some help carrying things to the car."

Amos jerked his chin toward the farmhouse. "I might head on back. Give you a moment to talk to your son." He strode up the hill.

"Amos Lapp?" Charles called out.

Amos spun around.

The hint of a smile tugged at the corner of his mouth. "Why do I feel as if I've just been counseled by an Amish farmer?"

"No charge!" Amos started up the hill again, grinning.

Will finished packing up his belongings and looked around to make sure he hadn't forgotten anything. The place was still a mess. He shouldn't leave the cottage like this for Fern, though he remembered a remark she had made when he had tried to help her with a cleaning project at the farmhouse: "Unexpected things happen around you, Will, and cleaning is not always one of them." *Well, Fern, today I am going to surprise you.* He would leave the cottage as clean as it was when he arrived. He would try to, anyway.

He started a fire in the stove and set a big pail of water on it to boil. Squeezing some dish soap into the sink, he ran cold water and swished his hand in the sink to get the water sudsy. He hadn't heard his father come in, but suddenly, there he was, stacking dirty dishes on the small counter.

"It won't take long to wash these dishes," Will said, glancing at the water that wasn't even close to boiling. "This is the last thing I need to do."

"There's plenty of time," his father said.

Will almost dropped the dish he was holding. He had never remembered a time in his life when his father wasn't tense, eager to move on to the next thing. But here he was, patiently stacking dirty dishes with dried food crusted on them. Will set the dishes in to soak and waited for the water to boil. He and his father stood there, awkwardly, side by side, waiting to see bubbles rise to the surface. Why was it taking so long? In his mind, he heard Fern's voice: A watched pot never boils. Or was it, a boiling pot is never watched? He should have written down her sayings so he would remember them.

Quietly, his father said, "Why didn't you ever tell me you didn't want to be a doctor?"

Time skipped a beat before Will said, "Why didn't you ever tell me you were raised Amish?"

His father wasn't used to someone crossing him. An eyebrow lifted, but he didn't respond. Nor did he meet Will's eyes. He seemed uncomfortable. In a clipped, controlled voice, he said, "I lived under my father's very large and very heavy thumb. I had to break free."

Will snorted. "*That* . . . I can understand."

Then there was silence. It went on that way for a while, the two of them staring at the pot of water, which seemed to refuse to boil, neither one speaking. A perfect example of how things were between Will and his father—neither one would budge.

Sadie had told him that forgiveness was a process, that it didn't happen overnight. She likened the process to filling a bucket of water at a well. God was the well, forgiveness was the water. Sometimes, she said, the bucket would be leaky and it would require numerous trips to the well. But the important thing, Sadie said, was to keep going to the well to fill the bucket.

She also said that someone had to be willing to take the first step. Will blew air out of his cheeks. This was the hardest thing he had ever had to do . . . but it had to start somewhere. Things had to change.

"Dad, I'm sorry." The words erupted from Will in a sob. He pressed his thumb and forefinger into his watering eyes. "I'm so sorry," he repeated, his voice in shreds. "I've made a mess of . . . everything."

Then his father's arms were around him. Will buried his face in his father's neck. He wept, unashamed of his tears.

"I'm sorry too," his father said. "You made some of those choices because you felt trapped." His father released him and stepped back. "Of all people on this earth, I should have known not to assume you were going to do what I wanted you to do with your life." He blew a puff of air. "I'm my father's son. Same song, different verse." He rested his hands on the counter. "Where do we go from here?"

For the first time that Will could ever remember, his father looked unsure of himself. He never second-guessed himself, and here he was, looking baffled, sad, confused. He had Fern to thank for that. She had completely baffled an unbafflable man. Will felt a twinge of pity for his father. "You haven't met Hank—he's Amos's uncle—but he says life is full of turn-arounds."

His father looked at him sharply. Another awkward silence fell.

"Maybe . . . we could start again. You know . . . this time as father and son. Instead of . . . brilliant brain surgeon and numbskull protégé."

To his surprise, his father's eyes closed in pain. "I . . . wouldn't know where to begin."

His total helplessness touched Will. This wasn't easy for his father. "Maybe you could just give it a try."

The water started to boil then, rolling, gurgling bubbles. "Let me show you how we used to wash dishes on the farm," his father said, rolling up his sleeves.

As Will and his father scrubbed and rinsed and dried dishes together, they started to talk. It was clumsy, uncomfortable, stilted, painfully awkward. It was wonderful.

After Will said goodbye to Amos and Fern and M.K., he jerked his head to the side in a silent bid for a private conversation with Sadie. He turned to his father. "There are a few things I need to discuss with Sadie. Could you give us a moment of privacy?"

His father told him he would wait in the car for him. Once Sadie followed Will outside, he didn't waste time. He knew M.K. was watching them from the family room window, but he didn't care. He took both her hands in his and said, "Let me get the worst of this over straight off. Gideon Smucker is absolutely correct. I came to Windmill Farm with the intention of doing something illegal. I was going to try and sell a falcon chick to a private breeder. Then he wanted two chicks. Then three. I needed the money and I was going to do it, Sadie."

She gasped. Other than the sharp inhalation of breath, she neither spoke nor moved.

"In the end, I couldn't see it through. That's why I called my father today. That's why I'm leaving tonight." He took a step closer to her. "Sadie, I care for you in a way I've never cared for a girl before. I couldn't leave here without telling you. I came here as one kind of man, but I'm leaving as another. I'm a better man because of you." The words slipped out as though his tongue belonged to someone else. He didn't try to snatch them back or pretend he hadn't confessed something so serious aloud. Will opened his mouth to comment on her lack of reaction, then realized this must be what she was like as she listened to her clients spill forth their problems—she seemed calm and still and ready to hear anything. "Have you nothing to say to me, Sadie? No words of goodbye?"

Finally, she looked up, her eyes filled with tears. She looked at him as if she was memorizing his features. Then she brushed his cheek with her lips. It wasn't the kiss he wanted. It was a kiss for a child, with something final in it, something of a farewell. Yet she moved nearer than she probably meant to. He wasn't just looking for a sign; he knew—deep down, he knew—something in her wanted him to take her in his arms. He knew it, and he knew she wouldn't let it happen. Sadie who never wavered might have come near the brink, but she stepped back again.

"We'll meet again, you know," Will said.

"Will we?" she said, sounding as if she didn't believe him. Her eyes became blurry and she turned away, but he put his hand under her chin and made her look at him.

"I need to get some things sorted out . . . like, my whole life. But I promise you that we will meet again." He cupped her face with his hands. "Sadie, you and me, what we have—it wouldn't have been the end of the world if we'd seen it through."

She lifted her eyes and looked at him as if she couldn't believe she'd heard him right. "But Will, it would have been the end of my world."

Sadie followed Dr. Stoltz's car out of the driveway, waving until her arm ached. She wondered if she'd ever set eyes on Will again, wondered if what he had said might someday come true. Would they ever meet again? She'd had a sense from the beginning to hold onto him lightly.

Pity for Will welled inside her, along with sadness for what he'd missed in his life. He didn't seem to know what he had been lacking until he saw it this spring with the Lapps. Yet she could see something had shifted inside of him today. The time he spent at Windmill Farm was no accident. It was a chapter in Will's book, but the ending wasn't written yet. That would be up to Will. "May God go with you," she said aloud, as the car's brake lights went on, preparing to round the bend in the road.

Just as the car turned toward the bend in the road, a buggy appeared on the opposite side. A long pole stuck out of the buggy window, and on it, a blue bird feeder. The car honked loudly and then swerved dramatically to avoid the bird feeder. In the buggy was Gid, heading up to Windmill Farm. He waved to Sadie from down the road, using his left hand, still in a large white cast. Sadie knew he had built the blue bird feeder to replace the one he had ruined in the ridiculous tussle with Will. It was a silly sight, really, to see a bird feeder sticking out of one side of the buggy and a big white cast waving to her from the other side.

Gid pulled over to the side of the road as he reached the end of the driveway. "I brought you a new bird feeder." He picked up a dinner dish with a hole drilled in the center and held it up to her. "The squirrel thingamajig too."

Sadie looked at the bird feeder. "How did you ever manage to build it with a broken hand?"

He shrugged. "Simple."

"Nothing's simple, Gid," she said. She lifted her eyes to gaze at him. "But you know that."

The tips of his ears began to turn pink. "Well, you can test it out when I finish installing it."

She took her time, paying attention to her words as she always did. Tilting her head. Taking him in. His eyes found hers, and she felt her mouth curve, offering him a shy smile. "That's all right," Sadie said. "I think it's going to work."

Acknowledgments

In the writing of this book, I had the pleasure of learning about the art of falconry through Kit Daine, falconer extraordinaire. Kit provided more than just information—she gave me a sense of the rare and wonderful bond of trust between a falcon and its trainer. Thank you, Kit, for your time and for sharing some valuable resources. A heartfelt high five to Mela Brasset, for linking me to Kit. And a grateful shout-out to Cheryl Harner, president of the Greater Mohican Audubon Society and blogger behind the Weedpicker's Journal (http://cherylharner.blogspot.com).

On the publishing end, my gratitude goes to the incredible group at Revell. To Andrea Doering and Barb Barnes, thank you for being everything a writer could hope for in editors. Thanks for your guidance, astute suggestions, and encouragement, and for helping Stoney Ridge come to life.

To the crew in marketing, publicity, and art (Deonne, Twila, Michele, Janelle, Claudia, Donna, Cheryl)—I so admire the awesome job you do in bringing the books to the shelves. To my agent, Joyce Hart, thanks for taking care of business so I can focus on writing.

Gratitude beyond measure goes out to reader friends, far and near. Thank you for sharing the books with friends, recommending them to book clubs, and taking time to send little notes of encouragement my way via email and Facebook. Thank you, all of you, for being a blessing, a joy, and a treasure. I hope you find a few treasures of your own in Stoney Ridge, and that this story returns the joy and the blessings in some small measure.

Last but never least, an over-the-top, words-can't-express thank-you to God for the opportunity to write stories of faithful people.

The Lesson

This story is for my youngest daughter,
Meredith,
who happens to be a full-time teacher
and a part-time detective.

1

The year Mary Kate Lapp turned nineteen started out fine enough. Life seemed full of endless possibilities. But as the year went on, a terrible restlessness began to grow inside of her, like sour yeast in a jar of warm water on a sunny windowsill. There were days when she thought she couldn't stand another moment in this provincial little town, and days when she thought she could never leave.

On a sun-drenched afternoon, M.K. was zooming along on her red scooter past an English farmer's sheep pasture, with a book propped above the handlebars—a habit that her stepmother, Fern, scolded her about relentlessly. She was just about to live happily ever after with the story's handsome hero when a very loud *Bwhoom!* suddenly interrupted her reading.

Most folks would have turned tail and run, but not M.K. She might have considered it, but as usual, curiosity got the best of her. She zoomed back down the street, hopped off her scooter, climbed up on the fence, and there she saw him—an English sheep farmer in overalls, sprawled flat on the ground with a large rifle next to him. The frightened sheep were huddled in the far corner of the pasture. Doozy, M.K.'s big old yellow dog of dubious ancestry, elected to stay behind with the scooter.

M.K. wasn't sure what to do next. Should she see if the sheep farmer was still alive? He didn't look alive. He looked very, very dead. She wouldn't know what to do, anyway—healing bodies was her sister Sadie's department. And what if the murderer were close by? Nosir. She was brave, but you had to draw the line somewhere.

But she could go to the phone shanty by the schoolhouse and make a 911 call for the police. So that's what she did. She waited at the phone shanty until she heard the sirens and saw the revolving lights on top of the sheriff's car. Then she jumped on her scooter and hurried back to the sheep pasture.

The sheriff walked over to ask M.K. if she was the one who had called 911. She had known Sheriff Hoffman all her life. He was a pleasant-looking man with a short haircut, brown going gray around his ears, and a permanent suntan. Tall and impressive in his white uniform shirt and crisp black pants, radio clipped to one hip, gun holster on the other. He questioned M.K. about every detail she could recall—which wasn't much, other than a loud gunshot. She didn't even know the farmer's name. The sheriff took a pen from his back pocket and started taking notes. (What would he write? *Amish witness knows nothing. Absolutely nothing.*) But he did tell her she did the right thing by not disturbing the crime scene. He took her name and address and said he might be contacting her with more questions.

M.K. stuck around, all ears about whatever she could overhear, fascinated by the meager clues the police were trying to piece together. When the county coroner arrived in his big black van, M.K. decided she had gleaned all she could. Besides, the trees were throwing long shadows. The sun would be setting soon and she should get home to let her father and Fern know about the murder. It was alarming news!

She took a shortcut through the town of Stoney Ridge to reach Windmill Farm as fast as she could but was intercepted by her friend Jimmy Fisher. Standing in front of the Sweet Tooth Bakery, he called to her, then ran alongside and grabbed the handlebars of her scooter to stop her. She practically flew headfirst over the handlebars.

Men! So oblivious.

"I need your help with something important," Jimmy said.

"Can't," M.K. said, pushing his hands off her scooter. "I'm in a big hurry." She started pumping her leg on the ground to build up speed. Doozy puffed and panted alongside her.

"It won't take long!" Jimmy sounded wounded. "What's your big hurry?"

"Can't tell you!" she told him, and she meant it. The sheriff had warned her not to say anything to anyone, with the exception of her family, until they had gathered more information. She felt a prick of guilt and looked back at Jimmy, who had stopped abruptly when she brushed him off. She liked that he was a little bit scared of her, especially because he was older and much too handsome for his own good.

She glanced back and saw him cross the road to head into the Sweet Tooth Bakery where her friend Ruthie worked. Good! Let Ruthie solve Jimmy's problem this time. M.K. was always helping him get out of scrapes and tight spots. That boy had a proclivity for trouble. Always had.

Distracted by the dead body and then by Jimmy Fisher, M.K. made a soaring right turn near the Smuckers' goat farm, and possibly—just possibly—forgot to look both ways before she turned. Her scooter ended up bumping into Alice Smucker, the schoolteacher at Twin Creeks where M.K. had spent eight long years, as Alice was herding goats across the road into an empty pasture.

A tiny collision with a scooter and Alice refused to get to her feet. "I AM CONCUSSED!" she called out.

M.K. was convinced that Alice was prejudiced against her. And she was so dramatic. She insisted M.K. call for an ambulance.

Two 911 calls in one day—it was more excitement than M.K. could bear. She hoped the dispatcher didn't recognize her voice and think she was a crank caller. She wasn't! Nosir.

Naturally, M.K. waited until the ambulance arrived to swoop away with Alice, who was hissing with anger. When M.K. offered to accompany Alice to the hospital—she knew it was the right thing to do, though the offer came with gritted teeth—Alice glared at her.

"You stay away from me, Mary Kate Lapp!" she snapped, before she swooned in a faint.

Alice. So dramatic.

After M.K. rounded up the goats and returned them to the Smuckers' pasture, she arrived at Windmill Farm, her home and final destination. She couldn't wait to tell her father and Fern about the news! She was sorry for the sheep farmer—after all, she wasn't heartless. But finally, something interesting had happened in this town. It was big news—there had never been a murder in Stoney Ridge. And she had been the first one on the scene.

Well, to be accurate—and Fern was constantly telling her not to exaggerate—M.K. wasn't *quite* on the scene. But she did hear the gunshot! She absolutely did.

She knew Fern would be irritated with her for being so late for dinner. Fern was a stickler about . . . well, about most everything. But especially about being late for dinner. The unfortunate incident with Alice Smucker had slowed her down even more. The accident did bother M.K.—she would never intentionally run into anyone. Especially not Alice Smucker. Of all people!

M.K. set the scooter against the barn. She heard her mare, Cayenne, whinny for her, so she went into the barn, filled up the horse's bucket with water, and closed the stall door. She latched it tightly, her mind a whirl of details. It wasn't until she had pulled the latch that she noticed her father's horse and buggy were gone. She peered through the dusty barn window and saw that the house was pitch dark, its windows not showing any soft lampshine. Where could her father and Fern have gone? They were always home at this time of day. Always, always, always.

This day just kept getting stranger.

Guilt pinched the edges of Chris Yoder's conscience. Old Deborah had taught him better manners than to ignore a neighbor's greeting, but he wasn't interested in being neighborly. All that interested him was fixing up his grandfather's house. For now, it was a disaster. It looked as if a good puff of wind would be all that was required to bring the house tumbling down.

Jenny turned around to peer out the buggy window. "I think she was hoping you would stop and say hello, Chris. She's seems like such a nice old lady."

"Can't," Chris said. "Gotta get home." Erma Yutzy was a very nice old lady, and he had done some odd jobs for her, but she liked to talk and he could never find a way to break in and excuse himself. But it wasn't just that he wanted to avoid Erma Yutzy today. He was always in a touchy mood after a trip to town. People were everywhere—on the sidewalks, in the stores, riding bikes, eating ice-cream cones, sipping expensive coffees. As if nothing bad could happen. As if nothing could hurt them or threaten their sense of security.

"This isn't going to work," Jenny whispered. "We're going to get caught."

Chris glanced over at his thirteen-year-old sister. The last few months had taken a toll on her. She had always been a worrier. She worried about everything and everybody. "It's been working for over six weeks now, Jenny. If we were going to have a problem, we would have had it by now. I think we're home free." He didn't entirely believe that, but he knew it was best to ease Jenny's concern.

Jenny's chin jutted forward. "Plunking me in school is the worst idea you've ever had."

"No, it's not," Chris said. "You need schooling. And I need you to not be underfoot."

"I'm going to need new shoes for school." She scowled at him. "We can't afford them."

She had him there. He had no cash to spare, but he had been prepared for lean times. And he wasn't going to let a few dollars stop his sister from getting an education. Schooling was something he didn't take for granted.

"Think of school as an adventure. Something new." Chris kept the smile on his face and the worry out of his voice.

Jenny leaned her head against the window and closed her eyes.

For a moment he was lost in another time of his life, another season. Was it only two months ago? It seemed like much longer. That was the week that Old Deborah, as close to a grandmother to him as anyone ever would be, passed to her glory.

Hours before she had died, she had covered his hand with hers. "Every now and then, Chris, life throws you something you'd never have chosen in a million years. I know that's how you feel right now."

He looked into her tired brown eyes. "How am I going to do it?"

She smiled. "The Lord taught us to pray, 'Give us *this* day our daily bread.' We're supposed to live one day at a time, not to borrow another day's troubles."

One day at a time. That's how they had been living ever since they arrived in Stoney Ridge two weeks ago, but he hadn't expected things to be this hard. They were scraping by on a wing and a prayer. But there were good things too. They were settling into a new home. He had picked up some odd jobs, like mowing Erma Yutzy's lawn, that provided ready cash. Just today he had gotten a tip at the hardware store about a man named Amos Lapp who needed a fellow to help with fieldwork because he had some heart trouble. Wasn't that a sign of God's just-in-time providence?

A whinny from his horse made him smile. Chris had a magnificent Thoroughbred horse, Samson, that he had raised since he was a foal. The stallion was a legacy from Old Deborah, along with the knowledge that a little piece of real estate in Stoney Ridge was waiting, intended for him from his grandfather. It was a start.

He exhaled. One day at a time.

After Jimmy Fisher watched Mary Kate Lapp charge up the road, he started to head to the Sweet Tooth Bakery but changed his mind. He wasn't really in the mood to try to talk to Ruthie today—she often burst into a fit of giggles when she was around him. Plus, it was getting late and he knew his mother would be wondering where he was. Chore time on the chicken-and-egg farm.

He had really wanted to talk to M.K. She would have a good idea about how he should proceed. Much better than Ruthie. M.K., for all her short-comings, was very reliable about these kinds of things.

Jimmy was in love. At a horse auction in Leola—his favorite pastime—he had noticed an attractive young Amish woman who was selling a two-year-old brindled mare. He couldn't take his eyes off that girl. Shiny auburn hair, snapping green eyes. And tall! He'd always wanted to marry a tall woman. It was a dire disappointment to Jimmy that he wasn't as tall as his brother, Paul. Jimmy wasn't tall at all, but he held himself very straight as if to make the most of what he had. He planned to rectify that genetic flaw for the next generation. Tall was good. It was number five on his list of critical requirements for his future wife.

The brindled mare had fetched a good price, and the young woman was saying goodbye to the horse, tears streaming down her face. Jimmy was touched. Three heartbeats later, he tracked down the auctioneer to find out to whom the mare had belonged. The auctioneer was taking a break behind the large canvas tent while the horse lot was being changed. A stub of a cigar hung from his mouth as he eyed Jimmy. "Why do you want to know?"

"I had an interest in that brindled mare," Jimmy said. That was true. It wasn't a lie. He was more interested in the mare's owner than the mare, but he wasn't lying. "Just wondered if they might be breeders or not." Jimmy kicked a rock on the ground with the toe of his boot. "Giving some thought to becoming a breeder myself. Just thought I'd talk to her, ah, him." He cleared his throat, tried to act nonchalant.

The auctioneer threw the cigar stub on the ground and rubbed it out with his shoe. "I thought you Amish knew everybody, anyway."

"A common misperception," Jimmy said. *Along with assuming we look alike and think alike and act alike.* He nearly said that part out loud, but held back, given that he had become so mature lately. Still, it rankled him how the non-Amish lumped the Amish into one-size-fits-all.

Take Jimmy and his brother, Paul. They might share a passing resemblance—both blond, with their father's strong nose and high forehead—but no two brothers could be more different. Paul was thirty now, still unmarried, still at home under his mother's very large thumb. It wasn't that Paul didn't want to marry and start a family of his own; he just couldn't quite decide on a wife. He was always juggling a few girls, attracted to each one but not in love with any of them.

Jimmy had no trouble making decisions, or falling in love. He fell in love, he fell out of love—but at least it was love! He had passion, and emotion, and wasn't afraid to make a commitment like Paul was. Or, at least, he wouldn't be afraid to when he fell in love for the last time. He planned to marry within two years. It was all planned out. And he had just found his missus. Done! Checked off.

The auctioneer took a loud slurp of coffee and tossed the paper cup on the ground. "Her name is Emily Esh. Father is Emanuel Esh. They live near Bart. Father's a darn good horse trader." He handed Jimmy a card: *Domenico Guiseppe Rizzo, purveyor of fine horses.* "This is the guy you need to see if you want to get into pony racing."

Jimmy peered at the card. "Wait. Is that Domino Joe?" He knew Domino Joe. Knew him well. "What makes you think I have an interest in pony racing?"

The auctioneer glanced at his watch and strolled back to the auction block. Over his shoulder, he tossed, "If you're already acquainted with Domino Joe, then why would I think you don't?"

Jimmy frowned and stuffed the card in his pocket. Emily Esh. What a beautiful name. It had a musical sound . . . what was it M.K. called that kind of thing? Allit, alliter, alliteration. That was it!

Now . . . how to meet Emily Esh? He remembered that M.K. had talked Ruthie into going to a youth gathering in Bart this summer, hoping to meet a more intelligent crop of boys, she had said. "I've known these Stoney Ridge boys forever," she said airily to Jimmy. "And most of them have no idea how to carry on an intelligent conversation. They just want to talk about the latest prank they pulled or about what the best hunting sports are or all about their dogs."

At the time, Jimmy took offense. M.K. was always showing off her big brain, as if it wasn't obvious to everyone that she had a different way of thinking. He had a hunch that she could go to the ends of the earth and she still wouldn't find what she was looking for, because that fellow didn't exist. But now, the Bart youth gathering sounded very intriguing to Jimmy.

He just needed M.K.'s help. He wanted to meet Emily Esh, his future missus.

M.K. waited restlessly for her father and Fern to return home. She went down to the honey cabin, tucked at the far edge of Windmill Farm's property, and wrote on some labels for honey jars, but her hands felt shaky with excitement. She didn't like the way her handwriting ended up looking—like she was nine, not nineteen. Just yesterday, she had finished spinning her most recent supply of honey from her brown bees' honeycombs into long, thin clean jars. She sold her honey at Fern's roadside stand. She wished she had left some chores to do. She swept the floor and straightened up, then went back to the house.

In her bedroom, she spent some time looking for her old detective notebook. She finally found it, tucked deep under her mattress. She opened it to a clean page and wrote SOLVE SHEEP FARMER'S MURDER!!! in bold letters across the top and underlined it three times, breaking the pencil point in the process. She found another pencil and numbered the page from one to ten.

But how?

She pulled out her detective books from the bottom bookshelf and spread them out on her bed.

#1. Look for overlooked clues that the culprit might have left in his haste.
A. Go back to the pasture.

She spent the next ten minutes drumming the pencil against the page as she searched in vain for ideas to proceed. When her head began to ache from thinking too hard, she put her books away and stuffed the notebook back under the mattress.

She thought the house seemed stuffy, so she opened the windows downstairs in the living room and kitchen. A breeze moved into the room, carrying a faint perfume from Fern's rose garden. M.K. sat down, stood up, walked around, sat down again. Her mind was spinning, like dandelions in the wind. She was so antsy that Doozy gave up following her. He curled up in the living room corner and went to sleep. She jumped up and went into the kitchen, knowing just what to do to keep her mind and hands busy.

After her sister Sadie married Gideon Smucker and left home, M.K. was at loose ends—she had finished formal schooling, she was missing the companionship of Sadie and Julia, her married sisters, and she was driving Fern crazy. A serious case of "ants in her pants," Fern diagnosed. M.K. needed something to do, so Fern taught her how to bake bread.

M.K. went into the kitchen and pulled out the flour canister. On the windowsill was a jar filled with a noxious-looking substance, placed where the late afternoon sun would warm it but not too much. She picked up the jar, remembering the first time Fern had shown it to her.

It was the winter after Sadie and Gid's wedding, two years ago. The lower half was a thick gray pillow, looking like something you'd find on the moon. Fern had shaken it up, then opened it. A strong sour smell exploded into the air.

"Phew!" M.K. pinched her nose like a clothespin. "What is that horrible thing?" She leaned closer to inspect it.

"It's my sourdough bread starter," Fern said. "It's been in my family for generations. It came from a carefully tended mother dough that my great-great-great-grandmother brought over from Germany in 1886."

"How could all those grandmothers have kept it alive all that time?"

"Some mysteries are best not to examine too closely," Fern said in her matter-of-fact way. "Starters are sturdier than they appear. But I guard that starter like gold at Fort Knox." She scooped out a hefty measure of foamy pale-yellow-white starter and put it in a bowl. "I refresh it every week so it stays healthy." She turned on the tap, testing the temperature with her fingers. "I add water that's just barely warmer than your fingers." When she got it right she gestured to M.K. "Try it."

M.K. stuck her fingers under the stream. She hardly felt the water. M.K. filled a glass measuring cup and stirred it into the jar of starter. It foamed up.

M.K. jumped back, then stared at it. "Why, it's alive!"

"Exactly."

Danger! M.K. was hooked.

A noise outside jolted her back to the present. She peered out the window, hoping to see a buggy roll up the driveway. But no—it was only a noisy bluejay, gorging himself on black oiled sunflower seeds that filled the blue bird feeder on the porch. M.K. rapped on the window to shoo the greedy bird away.

She took out a large bowl and measured a cup of flour. She used a sturdy wooden spoon and stirred the flour into the heady sponge, filling the air with a sour scent, unique to yeast. She turned the dough out on a layer of fine white flour that she scattered across the surface of the counter. As she began to knead the bread, back and forth, over and under, pushing and pulling, her restlessness began to slip away. Like it always did. She didn't like to admit it, but Fern was right. Her hands needed to be busy.

Two hours later, the loaves were baked and cooling on the counter. They were far more dense than Fern's would have been. M.K. never had the patience to let dough rest as long as it needed. But the kitchen was clean and shiny for Fern's critical inspection just as she walked in. M.K. met her at the door. Over Fern's shoulder, she saw her father near the barn, untacking the horse from the buggy shafts.

"Where have you been?" M.K. asked. "I've been waiting for hours!"

A wall came up, chilled the air. Fern didn't speak immediately. Doozy let go of a soft, joyous woof and his tail wagged slowly, then stopped.

"Where have *you* been?" Fern replied, sharp as a pinch. "You were due at the schoolhouse at six. There was a work frolic to get the schoolhouse ready for school on Monday."

M.K.'s hands flew up to her cheeks. "I forgot! I forgot all about it."

Fern frowned at her. "If you were a bird, you would be a hummingbird. Flitting from place to place. You can't be still."

"But there's a reason! Something has happened!"

"So we heard," Amos said in a weary voice as he opened the kitchen door and walked into the room. His weather-tanned face, with its work wrinkles running down his cheeks, looked exasperated. "You ran into Alice Smucker. How did you happen to do that?"

Oh. *Oh!* M.K. had forgotten all about the collision with Alice Smucker. Her mind was wholly preoccupied with the shocking murder. "Well, there's rather a lot of Alice."

Amos raised a warning eyebrow at M.K. "Alice Smucker will be unable to start the school year due to a mild concussion."

"Really? She *actually* has a concussion? The doctor really, truly said that? Because—"

Amos sent M.K. a warning frown, but too late.

"—Alice can be a bit of a hypochondri—"

Amos held up his hand to stop her. "Mary Kate, it doesn't matter whether the doctor said so. That's what Alice Smucker believes she has, and it was because you didn't look where you were going on the scooter and you crashed into the poor woman."

"Dad, it wasn't really that big of a crash. More like a tiny bump."

Amos shook his head. "She has a ferocious headache and can't teach for the foreseeable future."

"That's a shame," M.K. said.

Amos and Fern exchanged a look.

The first ripple of concern fluttered down M.K.'s spine. "What?"

"The members of the school board were at the work frolic," Amos said. "They came to a decision about who can fill in for Alice."

"Well, Gideon, of course. He's done it before. He's a fine teacher. Better than Alice." M.K. hoped Sadie wouldn't mind having Gid gone all day. She had little twins, a boy and a girl, who ran her ragged. At least, they ran

M.K. ragged whenever she popped in for a visit. To M.K.'s way of thinking, children ran everybody ragged.

Amos and Fern exchanged another glance, and M.K. sensed something dreadful was coming, like the stillness right before a storm hit. She felt the hair on the back of her neck tingle. "If not Gid, then who? Who?" In the quiet, her question sounded like an owl.

"The school board has decided you will fill in for Alice," Amos said.

"Me? Me?" she said with a squeak. "Teach school? You want me to teach school?" She was outraged! It was just an accident. She hadn't run into Alice on purpose! "No! No, no, no, no, no. I can't do it! Absolutely not!" The very thought terrified her. Stuck in a hot room with twenty-five slow-witted children, all day long? *Boring!* Supremely boring! "Dad, you've got to tell the school board that I just can't do it. Tell them you and Fern need me to help at Windmill Farm." She swept her arms in a wide arc, accidentally knocking over something from the counter onto the floor, where it shattered. She looked down, horrified. It was the jar that held Fern's one-hundred-and-fifty-year-old bread dough starter. She covered her face, then peeked through her fingers to gauge Fern's reaction.

At first, Fern looked stunned. Then her mouth set in a straight line. "Clean up that mess. Then you'd better get ready. The school board wants to meet with you tomorrow, 8 a.m. sharp, at the schoolhouse."

M.K. said nothing. As she scooped shattered glass and tangy-smelling starter into the garbage, she felt that the whole day had taken an unsatisfactory turn. She had encountered a shocking murder, she had been suspected of intentionally running her scooter into Alice Smucker (when all she had been doing was riding her scooter), and now there was this uncomfortable expectation that she would teach school.

Suddenly M.K. was looking ahead, into the terrible future. Her life had been completely rearranged. This was too much. It was all too much!

What a day. The worst of her life.

2

The early morning air was quite sharp, hinting of summer's end. Amos stood by the barn and watched his youngest daughter zip off on her scooter to meet with the school board. Mary Kate had a woebegone look on her face, as if she were heading off to the gallows. He nearly caved, nearly gave her an excuse to tell the school board that she was needed at the farm and couldn't possibly teach school. But then he would have to face his wife with that news and the thought stopped him short.

Besides, he knew Fern was overly blessed with a sixth sense about his children. Last night, she told him that Mary Kate had turned down Ruthie's request for her to go through baptism instructions this fall. For three years now, Ruthie had pleaded with M.K. to join her in the classes and M.K. always said no, that she wasn't ready. This time, Ruthie was going ahead without her.

"That restive spirit has always worried me about M.K.," Fern told Amos. "It's nothing new, though it's getting worse. She slips around rules, she reads books in church, she sticks her nose where it doesn't belong, and now look at this." Out of her apron pocket she pulled a folded piece of paper and thrust it at Amos.

He unfolded the paper. "A passport application?"

"I sent her to the post office to mail a package to Julia and Rome, and look what she came back with."

"Where did you find it?"

"It had slipped under the bench in the buggy."

He folded it and handed it to her. "Put it back where you found it. She'll be looking for it."

Fern slipped it back into her pocket with a sigh. "You're not going to let her know we are aware she is planning to flee the country?"

"She's young," Amos said in M.K.'s defense. His greatest hope in life would be that his children would accept his beliefs and join the church, but he was a believer in free will. He would never insist or put a timetable on that important decision. Time belonged to God. "Younger than most."

"She's nineteen. And I don't think age has anything to do with it."

"Then what do you think her problem is?"

"It's that quick mind of hers. It's got to be kept busy or it gets her into trouble. Teaching school would be challenging for her, Amos. She'll end up learning more than the scholars."

But would the scholars survive her? Amos loved his youngest daughter, but she had a unique way amidst a community that frowned upon uniqueness. How many times had Deacon Abraham taken Amos aside, in his quiet, gentle manner, to suggest ways of redirecting M.K.'s bottomless pit of energy? His daughter always meant well, her intentions were good, but she had a nose for trouble, a knack for being in the wrong place at the wrong time. She thought her real job was to know everyone in Stoney Ridge and everything that was happening. And she was filled with excuses. Nothing was ever her fault. Just like careening into Alice Smucker last night.

Amos wouldn't have said so at the frolic yesterday, with the school board tsk-tsking over Alice's concussion, but he had to agree with M.K. about Alice's hypochondria. Alice was rumored to be absent more days than she was in the schoolhouse teaching. He'd never known Alice not to have an ailment, magnified to serious proportions.

Even Sadie, his middle daughter, who never said an unkind word about anyone, gave Alice a tea remedy each week to help manage her sensitive digestion. Earlier in the summer, Sadie had confessed to Amos that the remedy was just tea and sugar, nothing more. "Alice just wants someone to listen to her," Sadie said. "Since her father remarried, she's just lonely. Once I figured that out, I realized I was wasting time trying to find remedies for her symptoms. I gave her tea and sugar one time, and she said that was the best cure of all." Sadie lowered her voice. "I didn't tell her it was just tea and sugar."

Amos straightened his straw hat. He had a full day ahead—and a young fellow was coming by to see about cutting hay for him.

Maybe Fern was right. Maybe teaching would challenge M.K. and keep her mind out of trouble—like the trouble she could get into by trying to solve the murder of that poor sheep farmer. "Leave that to the police!" Amos had told M.K. last night. But he could see that she was itching to get involved and solve the crime. She gave him six different scenarios last night, accusing every single surrounding neighbor of the terrible deed. As Fern frequently pointed out, once she latched onto an idea, she was like a fox with an egg in its mouth—all the hollering in the world wouldn't make her drop it.

Maybe Fern was right. Maybe teaching school was the answer for M.K. He hoped so.

"Whoa." Chris Yoder pulled back on the reins, drawing the horse to a halt. He leapt from the buggy seat and hopped down to find the owner of this big farm. A soft meow greeted him. He bent over and scooped up a barn cat that wove between his feet. "Who are you?"

"That's Buzz."

Chris looked up to see a tall, muscular, middle-aged Amish man facing him. "Amos Lapp?"

The man nodded. "Are you the fellow sent to me by the manager of the hardware store? Chris Yoder?"

Chris nodded. "How did a cat get a name like Buzz?"

"I always let my children name the animals. My youngest daughter went through a stage when she was naming every animal names that sounded like sounds."

"Onomatopoeia."

"That's it! That's it exactly!" Amos laughed. "I couldn't come up with that word if my life depended on it."

Chris set Buzz on the ground and reached out a hand to shake Amos's. "I was told at the hardware store that you needed some help with fieldwork. The manager, Bud, said you'd had some heart surgery."

"You heard right," Amos said. "I had some serious surgery awhile back and there are limitations as to what I can do in the fields."

"I've had a lot of experience with growing crops." Chris looked over the fields. He could see that the corn tassles were drying out, which meant the corn was about ready to pick. The third cutting of hay needed to get done before the predicted rainstorm at the end of the week. "Should I get to work on the hay? Or the corn?"

"Not so fast!" Amos grinned. "Though I like the way you think. Can you tell me a little about yourself?"

This was the part Chris dreaded. He kept his gaze on the fields. "What would you like to know?"

"What brings you to Stoney Ridge?"

"I need a job." Chris didn't mean to sound rude, but he didn't want to volunteer anything he didn't need to. The less people knew about him and his little sister, the better.

Amos watched him for a while. A long while. Then, to Chris's relief, all that Amos said was, "Let's give it a day's trial, then." He put his straw hat back on his head. "When you hear the dinner bell clang, come up to the house and join my wife and daughter and me for lunch."

"I brought my own lunch. I'll be fine." That was a lie. His first lie. He didn't have a lunch. But he didn't want to get chummy with Amos Lapp and his family. For now, it was better to keep his distance.

Amos Lapp shrugged. "Suit yourself."

Chris chanced a look at him. "Tools for haying in the barn?"

"Yes. Back room."

Chris nodded. "I'll go get started." He hurried to the barn before Amos Lapp thought of anything more to ask him.

A single brown horse grazed under the shade of an oak tree, and a bright flash of blue and orange darted across the road—a bluebird. It was going to be another hot, humid day. Mary Kate's face felt beet red. A bead of sweat dripped down her back. She slowed the scooter as she rounded the bend in the road that led to the schoolhouse. The door of the schoolhouse was wide open. The school board members were already there, waiting for her.

Her stomach twisted into a tight knot. This was a terrible thing. A terrible, terrible thing.

She set her red scooter against the building, told Doozy to stay, took a deep breath, and walked into the schoolhouse. At the sound of her arrival, the men stopped talking and looked up. Orin Stoltzfus, Wayne Zook, Allen King. She knew each of these men—had known them all her life. Yet right now, she felt like she was being judged and came up lacking. Orin Stoltzfus stood up. He had the most experience on the school board. School board members were voted in and served a three-year term. Each year, an old board member finished his term and a new member was voted in.

Orin gave her a warm smile, showing the gap in his front teeth. "Good morning, Mary Kate. So glad you offered to step in for Alice."

Offered? *Offered?!*

Fern! This is all your doing, she thought for the hundredth time. "Just how long do you think Alice will need some relief?" M.K. planned to drop by Alice's later today with a loaf of freshly baked bread. A peace offering. "A few days?"

The men exchanged glances.

"A week?"

Still no response.

The oatmeal M.K. ate for breakfast shifted and rolled, turning into concrete. "Surely, she couldn't have been badly hurt." Meekly, she added, "Could she?"

Orin exhaled. "No, she's not too terribly hurt. But she seems to sense she might be facing imminent demise."

"Oh, is that all? Alice has been predicting her imminent demise for years!" M.K. looked hopefully at the men. "She's had two feet in the grave for as long as I've known her! Everybody knows Alice is as sound as a dollar. Maybe she needs to be working, to keep her mind busy." M.K. put a finger in the air. "Was mer net im Kopp hot, hot mer in de Fiess." *If your brain doesn't work, your feet must.* "Fern is always telling me that."

Orin scratched his neck. "I'm guessing we'll need you to substitute for two weeks. Maybe three, tops."

M.K. blew out a puff of air. "Okay. Three weeks." She could do this for three weeks. "I just want to warn you. I'm not much of a teacher."

Over her head, Orin and Wayne exchanged a look: *Is she always like this?*

"You like to read," Allen King offered. His jowls jiggled through his sparse whiskers as he spoke. "Why, you've got your nose in a book all the time! Just last Sunday, the preacher pointed out that you were reading during his sermon. Remember?"

M.K. remembered. She had tried to leave the book in the buggy, but she just couldn't concentrate on a thing until she found out if Robinson Crusoe was eaten by cannibals. She didn't think so, because it would have made a very strange and abrupt ending to the book. But she had to know for sure. So she slipped it under her apron and sat in the far left corner, against the wall. Ruthie covered for her by leaning forward, keeping her out of range of Fern's eagle eyes. She still wasn't sure how Ruthie's father, preaching at the time—and everybody knew he was a long-winded, dry-bone preacher—happened to notice M.K.'s book. He had paused and pointed a long finger at M.K. "Mary Kate Lapp! Put that book away on the Sabbath."

It was mortifying.

Fern confiscated her book and returned it to the library. She gave M.K. a one-minute lecture about how even good things become idols when they distract us from God. Fern was famous for her one-minute lectures.

"Isn't there anyone else who might like to teach?" M.K. protested weakly.

"Nope," Orin said. "Can't think of any."

"Really? I can think of all kinds of people who would be wonderful teachers: Gideon Smucker, Ruthie Glick, Ethan King, even . . . even . . . Jimmy Fisher!" She nearly choked on the words because, even though she and Jimmy had made their peace over the years, he wasn't the brightest lantern in the barn. But she was desperate! And desperate times called for desperate measures.

"No," Orin repeated, shaking his head. "We are confident you are the one."

All three men looked at her, waiting for her to agree with them. And what could she say? It was her fault that Alice was injured. The families were counting on the start of school. The scholars shouldn't be penalized. She grabbed her elbows. "The thing is, Orin, the thing is, I really don't *want* to be a teacher."

That was putting it mildly. She was absolutely sure she would be bored to death if she were confined to these four walls in this stuffy room. Every day, the same as the day before. Hadn't she put in her time? Eight long years. How much more could she endure from this little schoolhouse?

A general silence met M.K.'s confession. The men exchanged awkward glances. Orin walked up to her and put a hand on her shoulder. "Mary Kate, being Amish means you care less about what's best for you and more about what's best for the church."

Certainly, the inside of M.K.'s head had gone numb. Against her will, she had been strategically cornered. There was no way to respond to Orin's comment without sounding like she was a fence jumper. And she wasn't a fence jumper. She definitely wasn't. Well, maybe a little. Lately, she'd even been thinking of jumping all the way to Hong Kong. Or maybe Madrid. She couldn't quite decide.

This is all your doing, Fern! she thought for the hundred and first time. Inwardly, M.K. sighed, defeated. Outwardly, she agreed with Orin and spent the next half hour getting a tutorial about how to keep the coal heater from acting up on a cold winter morning. She started to explain that she would only be here for three weeks, gone long before winter, so she didn't need to learn how to feed coal into the stove, but she decided to keep her mouth shut. No one listened to a word she said in this town, anyway.

Orin seemed enraptured with this heater, describing each part with loving detail. *Blah, blah, blah.* She stopped listening to Orin when he got distracted with a loose seam holding the stovetop pipe in one piece. She had a bad experience with a stovepipe once—courtesy of Jimmy Fisher—and liked to stay clear of them. Finally, Orin ran out of things to inform M.K. about.

And then M.K. and Doozy slunk home.

As soon as his mother had gone to town, Jimmy Fisher made a beeline to Windmill Farm to talk to Mary Kate. No one answered his knock at the farmhouse. He crossed over to the barn to look for Amos but couldn't find him. Then he saw Fern hanging wet laundry on the clothesline. The soapy scent of fresh laundry perfumed the morning air. Jimmy breathed in deeply—it was one of his favorite smells. But he thought twice about meeting up with Fern and scooted behind a tree. Fern thoroughly intimidated him. Thankfully, he spotted Hank Lapp in his buggy shop. The shop was an old carriage barn, with a small apartment up above where Hank lived. Buggies and parts, in various stages of disarray, littered the shop floor.

"JIMMY FISHER!" Hank boomed, when he caught sight of him. "You're a little late for fishing today, boy. I went out before dawn." Hank Lapp's sun-leathered face exploded into a smile.

Being around Hank always reminded Jimmy of the effects of electricity—instantly, a dark room would be filled with dazzling light and a fellow had to blink rapidly to allow his eyes to adjust to the brightness. Jimmy leaned against the buggy Hank was tinkering on. One side of the buggy was dented, as if it had been broadsided by a car. Buggy and car collisions were a frequent occurrence in Lancaster County, and the buggies always took the brunt of it. But, as Hank often said, it meant he would always have plenty of work.

"I didn't come to go fishing, Hank. Wish I had joined you this morning, though. No, I came by to talk to Mary Kate. Is she working at the honey cabin?"

"Naw. She's down at the schoolhouse. Should be back any minute now." He picked up a long piece of cut fiberboard and held it up against the side of the buggy to see if it would fit as a replacement part. "But she'll be in no mood for yikkity yakking." He motioned to Jimmy to hand him a screw. "BLAST. Cut it too short."

Jimmy's gaze shifted to the hay field. He saw someone out there behind Amos's two draft horses, cutting hay, but he could tell that someone wasn't Amos. "Who's that?"

Hank looked out to the field. "Young fellow Amos hired to cut hay."

Jimmy squinted his eyes. "I can't tell who he is. Someone new? Why didn't Amos hire me?"

"Probably cuz you have a knack for disappearing whenever there's a need for hard work."

Jimmy was deeply offended. "That's not true." Maybe it was partially true.

Hank bore down on Jimmy with his good eye. "I hear you've developed a fondness for pony racing these days."

"I just prefer the front end of the horse to the back end. But I could use some extra cash, seeing as how I have a girlfriend."

Hank strode to the workbench and rummaged around for some tools. "Oh? A new flavor of the month?"

"It's not like that this time, Hank. I think I have found my missus."

Hank frowned at one tool, threw it down, picked up another. "Just how long have you been courting your potential missus?"

"Well, see, that's why I need to talk to M.K. I haven't quite met my missus yet."

Hank jerked his head up. A big "HAW!" burst out of him. "You and Paul are cut out of the same cloth! Immer gucka. Nie net am kaufen." *Always looking, never buying.*

Jimmy frowned. Hank Lapp was hardly one to give marital advice. He was a dedicated bachelor. Hank had been mildly courting Jimmy's mother for years now—if you could call it courting. He showed up regularly for Sunday dinner, followed by a long nap in a recliner chair.

Why Jimmy's mother put up with Hank was a mystery. But then, in a way, the casualness of Hank's courting must appeal to her as well. Edith Fisher could remain in complete charge of her life—and her sons—and didn't have to change anything to suit a man. Jimmy loved his mother, but he wasn't blind to her faults. He remembered how henpecked his own father had been. Ironic for a man who had raised chickens and sold eggs for a living.

"Whose buggy is this?" Jimmy said. He recognized his friends' buggies because they had customized the interiors: fuzzy dice hanging down from the rearview mirror, red shag carpet, a boom box. But this buggy looked pretty plain, stark. Clearly, an adult's.

"Bishop's." Hank turned the fiberboard right side up. "WELL, LOOKY THERE! I had it upside down."

"I thought the bishop's accident happened months ago."

"It did, but it's hunting season, in case you hadn't noticed. I've been needing to spend my time at Blue Lake Pond. Under my watch, many a goose has flapped its last over that lake."

It was always hunting season in Hank Lapp's mind. "Oooo-eee! I'll bet Bishop Elmo's breathing down your neck to get it fixed."

Hank glared at Jimmy, and that wasn't a pretty sight. He had one eye that wandered and when he tried to glare, it gave him a frantic, wild-eyed look. Crazy as a loon. "BOY, DON'T YOU HAVE SOMEPLACE YOU NEED TO BE?"

A flash of red down on the road caught Jimmy's eye. It was M.K., zooming along on her scooter. "I do! There's M.K." He started down the hill. Over his shoulder, he tossed, "Talk to you later, Hank."

Mary Kate saw Jimmy Fisher running down the driveway to meet her, and considered turning the scooter around and zooming away. She didn't know what was on his mind, but when he kept turning up like he had been doing lately, it usually meant he needed advice or money or both. She was in no mood to be generous with either.

She hopped off the scooter as the driveway's incline began, and walked the rest of the way. Doozy ran off to chase a jackrabbit. Poor pup. He tried so often to catch one of those long-eared, long-legged jackrabbits and never could. As M.K. met up with Jimmy, she wiped her forehead with her sleeve. Today was going to be a scorcher.

"What?" she said flatly.

Jimmy gave a look of mock offense. "Is that any way to greet your most devoted friend?"

"I'm in no mood for small talk." She kept walking. "What do you want?"

He kept up with her. "Why is everybody so concerned with your mood today?"

She stopped abruptly. "They're not. That's the *whole* problem. No one is concerned about my mood today or any other day." She blew air out of her cheeks. "Jimmy, do you ever feel like you're a horse in a pasture and all you can think about is getting out of the pasture?"

"No. I feel as if I'm a horse in a race, and I'm in the lead by two stretches. That's how I feel."

She rolled her eyes. The ego of Jimmy Fisher was legendary. "I have just been roped into being the next schoolteacher at Twin Creeks."

"What?" Jimmy tilted his head, as if he hadn't heard her properly. A beat of silence followed. Then another. "You? Of all people, you?"

And then Jimmy started laughing so hard that M.K. thought he might pass out from a lack of oxygen to the brain. Infuriating! She started marching up the hill.

Jimmy rushed to catch up with her, gasping to get his laughing fit under control. "I can't remember a single week going by that Spinster Smucker didn't end up plunking you in the corner, face against the wall, or making you stay in for recess, or keeping you after school. Not one! Not *one* single week!" He was overcome with another laughing fit and had to bend over at his knees to wheeze for air. He patted his knees for effect.

M.K. was disgusted. But what he said was true—she had constantly been in trouble during her years at Twin Creeks School. And it was never her fault! Never. Maybe a few times. She wasn't sure who was happier on her eighth-grade graduation day: she or Alice Smucker.

A straw hat in the distant field caught her attention. She shielded her eyes. "Who's Dad got cutting hay?"

Jimmy inhaled a couple of deep breaths and tried to wipe the amused look off his face. "Some new guy your dad hired." He shifted his gaze out to the field. "I don't know why he didn't hire me."

M.K. watched the new hire. From here, he looked young—twenty, twenty-two-ish. She thought she knew everybody in Stoney Ridge. How did someone slip in without her knowledge? She blamed this teaching job. Too upsetting. "Probably because you're always running off to horse auctions."

Jimmy frowned at her. "I am conducting research."

M.K. snorted and started up the hill again. "Research for pony races, you mean."

Jimmy caught up with her again. "I'll ignore that insult because you're having a bad day. But since we're discussing my future, I'd like to ask for your help in a very delicate matter."

M.K. stopped, intrigued. "What do you need help with?"

"I've found the one."

"The one what? A horse?"

"No! A woman. I'm in love." He covered his heart. "A deep, enduring love."

"Really?" That was a very strange thought for M.K. She often wondered what it felt like to be in love. Being in love, she imagined, would make all the colors in the world more vivid, all the stars shine more brightly, all the moments of her life dance and crackle with excitement like flames leaping in a bonfire.

"I met my future bride. Someone whom I am sure you know. After all, you know everybody."

She smiled. Finally, someone appreciated her. "Who is that?"

"Emily Esh."

"Emily Esh? Oh Jimmy, she's . . ." She paused, trying to find the right words to say. It was easy to see why Emily Esh had attracted Jimmy's attention. She had huge, dinner-plate-sized eyes, an enigmatic, slightly-turned-up-at-the-corners smile, and a figure that curved in all the right places.

"What?"

"She's . . ." How to say this? "She's super brainy."

"So?" His face clouded over. "What's your point?"

"It might be hard to impress a girl like Emily. Not to mention that she has plenty of guys fluttering around her."

Jimmy kicked a dirt clod with his boot. "You think I'm not smart enough for her?"

M.K. looked at Jimmy. "You're enough for any girl, Jimmy." That wasn't the problem. She might be a little hard on Jimmy—he was spoiled and impulsive and insensitive and egotistical—but there was a good heart somewhere under that handsome exterior.

"Will you help me, then? Will you arrange an introduction for me with Emily Esh?"

M.K. let out a puff of air.

"Please? I'll do anything."

"Anything?" She raised an eyebrow.

"Anything." He gave her a sly look. "Besides teach at Twin Creeks School."

She narrowed her eyes. "Help me solve the murder of the sheep farmer."

"What murder?"

M.K. closed her eyes, thoroughly exasperated. Did she have to do everything around here? "Yesterday afternoon, a sheep farmer was shot to death in his field. Orin Stoltzfus told me this morning that the police can't find any clues. That means the culprit is still on the loose."

Jimmy looked at her as if she'd lost her mind.

The sound of a clanging dinner bell floated down the hill. M.K. hadn't eaten much for breakfast and she was starving. "That's the deal. As soon as we solve the crime, I will introduce you to Emily Esh." She hurried up the hill. When she got to the top, she heard Jimmy call her name. She spun around.

"OK!" He grinned. "It's a deal!"

The first thing Chris did when he got home from work was to take a shower. Cutting alfalfa hay all day made his entire body feel scratchy and itchy. But he did a good day's work, Amos Lapp had said, and told him to come back tomorrow. And he paid him generously too before he left for the day. Cash. Enough to buy new shoes for his sister to start school in a few days. And maybe enough to splurge on an ice cream cone afterward.

When he told Jenny that they were heading into town tonight to go school shopping, she balked. "We should go back to Ohio, so Mom knows where we are."

"We've been over this, Jenny. If we stayed in Ohio, Child Protective Services would step in and put you in a foster home. And Mom doesn't need to know where we are. All that matters is we know where she is."

Jenny scowled. But then, she was always scowling. Her face was going to be set in a permanent scowl. "She's going to get out soon. Then things will go back to normal."

Normal? What was normal? Their mother was a part-time house cleaner and a full-time drug addict. Old Deborah had been a godsend to them. She was an older Amish woman who became connected to the Ohio Reformatory for Women by fostering prisoners' children—an informal arrangement, outside of Child Protective Services but blessed by them, that suited everyone. Chris and Jenny had been living with Old Deborah, off and on, since Chris was eight and Jenny was one.

Once a month, year in and year out, Old Deborah took them by bus to Marysville to visit their mother. The program Old Deborah participated in wasn't trying to convert children to become Amish. Its goal was to keep incarcerated mothers involved in the lives of their children. Studies showed that there was less recidivism if mothers felt like they were continuing to parent their children. The Marysville warden had created all kinds of programs to enhance the bond with mothers and children. But Chris and Jenny had stayed with Old Deborah longer than they had lived with their mother. They couldn't help but look Amish, act Amish, talk Amish, and mostly, think Amish. For Chris, for the first time, the whole of his life really began to be transformed into something other than what it had ever been, something leaning toward normal.

It rankled their mother. She made sharply pointed comments about the Amish, but what could she really do about it? Old Deborah was raising her children for her. And doing a wonderful job with it too. She was grandmother, counselor, mentor . . . all wrapped into one warm, loving package. She fed them, washed their clothes, combed out Jenny's tangled hair, took them to the dentist or doctor if they needed medical attention. Old Deborah and her church family were loving toward them. Chris had no doubt they wanted them there. Life was stable at Old Deborah's. No one was on edge—waiting for his mother's dip into addiction. Chris knew what to expect each day at Old Deborah's. It was peaceful and safe and good.

On some level, Chris's mother must have known that her children were better off with Old Deborah than with CPS. Or maybe she just liked having the visits. She never registered any formal complaints about the Amish school or Amish church Chris and Jenny attended, though she gave Old Deborah plenty of informal complaints. But when Chris became baptized in the church last fall, she blew her top. It still chilled Chris to think of his mother's outburst, filled with horrible accusations. He just stood there, taking it, not answering back, just like he always had, but he hadn't been back to see her since.

Jenny didn't remember what it was like before Old Deborah's, but Chris did. And he would do everything in his power to make sure he and Jenny never went back to that. After that scene his mother had made about his baptism, Old Deborah quietly took him aside. She told Chris that his grandfather had sent her some legal papers, right before he died. He was leaving a house in trust for Chris and Jenny, and property taxes were paid out of the trust each year. When Chris turned twenty-one, he would inherit the house and land. When Jenny turned twenty-one, half of the house would belong to her. Old Deborah gave Chris a package with all of the legal paperwork, including a key to the house. "There's just one little hitch. Your mother is the executor of this trust." Old Deborah took a deep breath and closed her eyes, scrunching up her wrinkled face. "I might not have shared that piece of knowledge with her."

"What? Mom doesn't know? Why not?" It wasn't in Old Deborah's nature to deceive anyone.

Old Deborah opened her eyes. "Your grandfather put a condition in the will—as long as your mother wasn't using drugs, wasn't in jail, the house could go to her first. That was the condition until you turned twenty-one. Your grandfather asked me to use my judgment about when your mother should be informed about the will. So I kept waiting for the right moment to share it with her. I wanted to make sure she was truly freed from her drug habit . . ."

"But she never has been."

"No, not for long." She offered up a smile, but it didn't travel to her eyes. "Not yet, anyway."

Not ever, Chris thought. His grandfather must have thought so too. Why else would he create such a will? He knew that Grace Mitchell would spend her life skirting in and out of jail or rehab. Or both.

"I think it's time to go back to Stoney Ridge. This winter, you'll be twenty-one. Your mother is . . . indisposed. The house was meant for you and Jenny."

Chris fingered the cold metal key. A simple little door key that unlocked so many memories. "Stoney Ridge? Go back to my grandfather's house?"

"Yes. This is your chance to start a life of your own." She covered his hand with hers. Her hand was so small and fragile compared to his work-roughened one, but it was powerful in its own way. Like the rudder of a ship. "Chris, one thing I have learned over the years—your mother may not be able to be a good mother, but she does love you and your sister. Her problems get in the way of that love. Lord only knows I wish your upbringing had been different, but maybe you had an extraordinary upbringing, because it has made you an extraordinary young man."

He had trusted Old Deborah in every way, and though she was gone, he trusted her judgment even now. After her funeral, the very next morning, before news of Old Deborah's passing had time to spread outside of the Amish community, he had quietly packed their few belongings, and he and Jenny set off for Stoney Ridge in Lancaster County to claim their inheritance. He felt bad that he hadn't said goodbye to the friends who had been so kind to him and Jenny—the Troyers, especially—but the fewer people who knew where they were headed, the better. He didn't want any news of Stoney Ridge to trickle to his mother. Not now. Not until late January, after his birthday.

What a crazy thing he had done! Traveling the back roads of Ohio and

Pennsylvania with a horse and buggy. It took weeks! Many days, they only covered twenty to thirty miles, and on Sundays, they stayed put. It didn't matter how long it took—Chris wasn't going to jeopardize Samson's well-being. And time was one thing he had plenty of.

Finally, the day came when they arrived in Stoney Ridge. The little town hadn't changed much. The Sweet Tooth Bakery was still on the corner of Main Street, across from the post office and the brick bank. They walked down Main Street and he knew, instinctively, to turn right down Stone Leaf Drive, as if he'd never left. When he came to the lane that led to the house, he stopped and took a deep breath.

Jenny looked up at him. "Did you forget where it is? Has it been too long?"

He shook his head. "I didn't forget." From Ohio—a four-week trip. From his childhood—an eternity.

They walked up the lane and turned into a cracked and crumbling concrete driveway that led to the house. The property wasn't large—it was surrounded by farmland.

"Here it is, Jenny."

"Yuck."

"Hello?" he called out softly.

All was quiet. The house was deserted and looked it. The clapboard frame of the house was just the way he remembered it—brownish gray with chipped, flaking paint, the trim painted white. The porch sagged on one side. A clothesline with bleached-out wooden clothespins was looped between the posts, just under the rafters. A memory wisped like a fast-moving cloud through Chris's head. He remembered his mother hanging her underwear there and his grandfather raging at its impropriety. His grandfather cared about things like that. His mother didn't.

Chris walked up to the front door. He tried the doorknob, expecting nothing, but when it turned in his hand, he let out a surprised gasp.

"What?" Jenny rushed to his side.

He pushed the door open, its hinges screaming a protest.

What he saw made him want to back right up and run. "I guess we're home," he whispered.

3

Mary Kate woke early, after a restless night. Today was the first day of school, and she was the schoolteacher. She had absolutely no idea how to teach school. She slipped out of bed and dressed, then went downstairs. Last night, she had made up a batch of wheat bread dough and put it in the refrigerator. It was a special recipe that required a long kneading time.

She took the bowl out of the refrigerator and turned the dough onto a lightly floured surface. She deflated the dough—gently pressing down to let the air out. By gently squeezing out the excess carbon dioxide, the yeast would be more fully distributed throughout the dough. Then she started the kneading process: turn and fold, turn and fold, turn and fold. She knew she would need the task this morning—kneading bread could dispel a good deal of anxiety from even the most nervous heart.

And it did help. By the time her father woke to head outside and feed the livestock, she was almost calm. Almost. "There's coffee started," she said. Her voice sounded thin and wavery.

Amos poured himself a cup and peered at the bread she was kneading. "Wheat. Hmmm. You must be feeling pretty fidgety."

Panic rose up again inside of M.K. "I can't do it, Dad."

Amos put the coffee cup on the counter. "Of course you can. You've never failed yet at anything you tried to do, have you?"

"Well, no, but I have never tried to teach school."

"You've tackled every job that ever came your way. You never shirked, and you always stuck to it till you did what you set out to do. Success gets to be a habit, like anything else a person keeps on doing."

M.K. felt a little better. It was true; she had always kept on trying, she had always had to. Well, now she had to teach school.

"Remember when Sadie ended up with the job of tending chickens? And she just couldn't bring herself to butcher one. You just picked up that ax and—" he made a cutting motion with his hand—"the lights went out on that poor chicken. You must have only been eight or so."

"Seven."

"And remember when Jimmy Fisher took his pigeons to school and accidentally released them inside the schoolhouse?"

M.K.'s head snapped up. "That was no accident! He let them go on purpose."

"And you helped capture them."

M.K. grinned. "Alice Smucker hid under her desk."

"Now that is not something you would ever do as a teacher. You're too brave."

She put the bread dough into an oiled bowl to rise. Fern would bake it later this morning. She turned to her father. "Do you really think I'm brave?"

He patted her shoulder. "The bravest girl I know."

At ten minutes to seven, M.K. couldn't put it off any longer. She picked up her Igloo lunch box and left for school.

Jenny couldn't believe her ears. "You mean you want me to lie to everyone and say that my last name is Yoder?"

"It's for the best, Jenny," Chris said. The two of them were eating together at the kitchen table. "This is kind of . . . interesting. I don't believe I've ever had Cream of Wheat that looked like soup before." He lifted his spoon and the Cream of Wheat slipped off like a waterfall.

Jenny may have used a little too much liquid.

She had learned a lot from Old Deborah, but mostly about gardens and herbs and remedies. Old Deborah's healing work took up so much of her time that she didn't cook or bake like most Amish women did. As a result, Jenny had never been much of a cook, but now, she realized, things were going to have to change. She had better figure out how to cook if they were going to eat anything that wasn't from a can or a box. "Old Deborah would never agree to a lie. Using her name as ours is wrong, wrong, wrong."

Chris added raw Cream of Wheat into the bowl until it resembled gray wallpaper paste. He took a taste and gagged. Then he put his spoon down, frowning. "Old Deborah raised us like we were her own. She would understand."

Jenny sighed. She knew her brother well enough to know it was useless to try to reason with him. Stubborn. He was just so stubborn about some things. She picked up her brown lunch bag and walked to the door, dreading what lay ahead.

Three hours later, M.K. rang the bell to start her first day of school. Calling the cattle to the trough of knowledge was how she had always thought of it. Doozy took up residence on the front steps—as far as M.K. would let him come—and wouldn't budge.

Before M.K. was a sea of polished wood desks. The children tripped over Doozy as they hurried inside the classroom and stared at M.K. She stood, ramrod straight, and faced all of those scholars.

There were so many! So many beady little eyes.

She racked her brain for what came next. Nothing came to mind.

For the first time in her life, her mind was a complete blank. Empty. She thought she might get sick. She might get sick and die, right on the spot. That, she thought, would serve the school board right.

From the back of the room, Jenny sized up the new teacher. She could see this young teacher nervously knot and unknot her hands. You could tell she didn't know where to begin or which way was up. Her voice wobbled as she said "Good morning" to the students. Wobbled.

"Morning, M.K.," said a few students.

A boy with big glasses raised his hand as high as it could go. "We should probably call you Teacher M.K."

"Yes, of course. Thank you, Danny. Please call me Teacher M.K.," she corrected, but her voice sounded uncertain.

What kind of a name was Emkay?

A big boy leaned over his desk and winked at Jenny. She snapped her head away from him. How rude! Boys were never rude in her old school. But then, there was an abundance of girls in the upper grades. There was only one boy who was her age at her old school, Teddy Beiler, and he was frightened of the girls. Teddy had a permanently startled look on his face.

Then the new teacher tried to take roll and dropped the roll book. Twice. When she dropped it the second time, the big boys in the back of the room quickly changed their seats just to confuse her. And it did. When she straightened up, she looked thoroughly flustered.

"I'll start with the first grade," the teacher said. "Barbara Jean Shrock?"

A little hand shot up. "Here," Barbara Jean said in a thin, piping voice. "But I'm not staying." There was a whistle in Barbara Jean's whisper because she was missing her two front teeth, so *staying* came out as *th-taying*. She sat primly, her purple dress pulled snugly over her small bony knees. The sneakers she wore dangled several inches above the ground. Her tiny hands were neatly folded in her lap.

"Well, let's get through the roll, at least," the teacher said. "Eva Zook?"

Another little girl raised her hand. "Here."

"Now the second grade." This went on for a few more minutes until something happened that interested Jenny. When the teacher reached the sixth grade, she called out, "Danny Riehl?"

"Here," a boy said. It was the same boy who had spoken up earlier. He had a round face and wore big glasses with adhesive tape in the middle. His hair was the color of straw. He was earnest, Jenny thought. An earnest boy.

A tall girl in the back row stood up. "I'm Anna Mae Glick and I need to sit next to Danny Riehl."

The teacher's face shifted to a frown of puzzlement. "Why is that?"

"Because we're going to be married someday," Anna Mae Glick said smugly. "He's already asked me. We're going to get married when I'm twenty and he's eighteen. It's all settled."

Danny, who was sitting a couple of desks in front of Anna Mae, froze. He looked at the teacher in panic. "No, Anna Mae, I didn't say I would marry you," he protested. "I never did."

Anna Mae glared at him. "You did!" she said. "You promised! Don't think you can break your promises like that." She snapped her fingers to demonstrate Danny's broken promises.

"No, I never did," Danny repeated quietly. He looked troubled.

The big boys started snickering. One of them—the one who had winked so rudely at Jenny, said, "Anna Mae, you mean that *nobody* would ever marry you, not in a hundred years."

"You mean that nobody would ever marry you," Anna Mae retorted. "Any girl would take one look at you, Eugene Miller, and be sick."

Yes and no. Eugene Miller did carry with him a strong odor. Pig farmers, Jenny guessed. You didn't want to get downwind of him. And Eugene could be rude, but he wasn't bad looking. He was man-sized and there was a rim of fuzz on his upper lip.

Anna Mae crossed her arms. "M.K., just so you know, Eugene Miller is a nuisance."

Eugene Miller let out a room-shaking guffaw.

"Eugene and I are permanently mad at each other," Anna Mae added. "Just so you know."

"Anna Mae, you are in the eighth grade," the teacher said, consulting her roll book. "You need to sit with your class."

Anna Mae scowled but sat down in her seat, a few rows behind Danny.

Jenny began to wonder if this teacher was going to ever get the class to an actual subject before the end of this first teaching day.

Peering once more into the roll book, the teacher looked relieved at the prospect of getting roll call back on track. She read Jenny's name but seemed puzzled when Jenny was the one who answered. "Shouldn't you be sitting up front with your own grade?"

"I am sitting with my own grade," Jenny said firmly.

Flustered, the teacher glanced at the roll book again. "How old are you?"

"Thirteen."

"I would have thought ten," Anna Mae said loudly.

Jenny glared at Anna Mae. She crossed that girl off her potential friend list. That was unfortunate because there weren't many girls in the upper grades.

"Are you new to Stoney Ridge?" the teacher said.

Chris had warned Jenny to think twice before she said anything. Anything at all. "Yes," Jenny said, slowly and carefully.

The teacher tilted her head at Jenny, as if she was about to ask something else, but one of the big boys sent a paper airplane sailing across the room. It hit the window and fell to the ground. The teacher went to pick it up. Breathing a little hard, she asked, "Whose is this?"

Of course, no one would admit to it. They all kept their eyes facing forward, even the little ones. Teacher M.K. looked up and down the rows at the children, then threw the airplane into the garbage can. A big boy snickered. Eugene Miller. Jenny thought that boy had a saucy way about him. His face held a big grin as he looked right at the blackboard. And the silly teacher didn't do anything. Not a thing.

At that exact moment, Jenny knew that this young woman would never make it as a teacher. She didn't want to be the boss.

M.K.'s armpits were wet and she felt like throwing up. She stared at the children, who were staring back at her.

Six-year-old Barbara Jean Shrock stood by her desk and tugged on M.K.'s dress. "I'm going home."

"Barbara Jean, you can't go home," M.K. said, feeling a rise of panic. "It's only nine in the morning."

Barbara Jean planted her little feet. "You thaid I jutht needed to get through roll call."

M.K. was ready to go home too. This whole experience, the full hour of it, was turning out just like she had thought it would. *Disastrous.* Each time she thought she had the classroom under control, something would happen that was entirely out of her control. The last something was a mouse. She strongly suspected that Eugene Miller had something to do with that mouse in the classroom, but she couldn't prove it. When she told him to catch it, he said, "You're not the boss of me, M.K. Lapp. I remember when you were in eighth grade and you put a black racer snake in Teacher Alice's bottom desk drawer. She practically had a fatal heart attack, right then and there."

And what could M.K. say to that? It was the truth. In fact, it was the essence of the problem. M.K. had been the worst offender of any pupil—by a long shot. Hadn't she just been reprimanded in church for reading a book? How could she possibly try to act like she was in charge when she was known for being the ringleader of mischief? She knew these pupils, and they knew her. It was hopeless. And the thing was—she didn't blame them one bit. She should not be standing here as their teacher.

Eugene Miller was in the third grade when M.K. was in eighth. He was a little too smart-mouthed for his own good, even back then. And he was at that troublesome age now, a renowned prankster. He had dark, shaggy hair that hung in his eyes, and he wore a smirk of superiority on his wide mouth as if laughing at the whole world and everyone in it. Clearly, he was the leader of the big boys, and she knew he could easily influence them to make trouble for her.

And then there was that overly petite new girl—Jenny. She looked at M.K. with unconcealed suspicion. As if she knew M.K. had no business teaching.

It dawned on M.K. that she had probably stared at poor Alice Smucker in the same insolent way as Jenny was staring at her. It was the first time she could recall having a sympathetic feeling for Alice Smucker. Ever. The thought amazed her.

Barbara Jean pulled on M.K.'s sleeve again. "Thee you thometime at church."

M.K. had to think fast. If she allowed Barbara Jean to leave, the entire classroom would think up excuses to leave. Had she been in their position, she would be inventing excuses for each of the students and selling them for a nickel during recess. "Barbara Jean, tell me why you want to go home."

Tears filled Barbara Jean's eyes. "I love my mom tho much. You don't know how hard it ith to be away from thomeone you love *that* much."

M.K. felt tears prick at her eyes. That she understood! She pulled Barbara Jean into a hug and whispered, "I miss my mom like that too." She wiped away Barbara Jean's tears with her handkerchief. Then she wiped away her own tears.

Ridiculous. This was getting ridiculous. Somehow, she had to pick up the pieces of this class and carry on. "How would you like to be the teacher's helper and sit at my desk?"

Barbara Jean gave that some thought.

"If you still want to go home at lunch, then I'll let you go."

Barbara Jean whispered a *yeth*, so M.K. led her right up to her desk.

M.K. felt rather proud of herself. She had actually solved a problem. The feeling quickly dissipated as she heard a high-pitched scream from the back of the classroom. Someone had lit a match and tossed it into the trash can at the back of the room. As M.K. rushed outside with the flaming trash can, she thought she caught a smirk on Eugene Miller's smug face. Why, that boy was another Jimmy Fisher. Worse.

Somehow, she stumbled ahead through the day, one eye on the clock, willing this hour to be over, and then the next and the next.

Chris tried to hold back a smile when he heard Jenny's complaints about the new teacher. He burst out laughing when she described the teacher's looks: bony, wispy haired, wild-eyed, false teeth that wobbled when she talked. His sister had a vivid imagination. "What's her name?" he asked.

"Teacher M.K. That's all I know about her. That and the fact that she has had no teaching experience whatsoever. I'm not even sure she can read. Probably not."

Chris rolled his eyes. "I highly doubt the school board would give the teaching job to a teacher who couldn't read."

"Well, I heard that the real teacher was run over by a crazed lunatic. Just last week. And she's dying as a result. That's a fact. I heard that too."

Chris knew Jenny had impossibly high expectations for teachers and they always fell short. Jenny had yet to find a teacher who challenged her. She was always "bored." But the more he heard about the school day—starting with the fire in the trash can and ending with the disappearance of a little first grade girl, the more he had to agree with Jenny's assessment. This new teacher sounded like she had no ability to control a classroom filled with big boys. No backbone at all. If this was day one, it was going to be a long school year.

He knew what it was like to have good teachers and not-so-good teachers. That was the thing about a one-room schoolhouse. You didn't have much of a choice with your teacher. At least Jenny had a place to be each day, and this hapless teacher was too preoccupied with putting out fires to ask his sister too many questions about her background.

But he did make Jenny promise not to stir up any trouble. The last thing she needed to do was to add to this poor pitiful teacher's problems with the big boys.

Chris had problems of his own on his mind tonight. He stared at the ceiling. The sight of water stains and peeling plaster did little to dispel the cloud of gloom hovering over him.

He was working at Windmill Farm this morning and got caught in an untimely conversation with Hank Lapp, Amos's uncle. Chris had been cutting hay in the north field and noticed the bit for the large Belgian wasn't fitting properly. The big horse kept tossing her head. When Chris examined the bit, he saw that a piece of it had come undone and was causing discomfort for the horse. That wouldn't do. He headed back to the barn to see if he could either fix the bit or find another one.

As he passed by a buggy, a loud voice called out: "DADGUM!"

Chris stopped to locate the source of the voice.

"BLAST! WHERE DID THAT DADGUM THING GO?"

All around the buggy were tools. Chris looked into the shop and thought he had never seen such a mess. Buggy parts and tools littered the floor. Every horizontal surface was filled. A headful of wild white hair popped out from under the buggy and peered up at Chris in surprise. If Chris wasn't mistaken, one of the man's eyes wandered.

"Uh, hello," Chris said to the head. "I'm helping Amos cut hay."

The wild-haired man pulled himself out from under the buggy. "So I heard!" He rose to his feet and thrust an oil-smudged hand at Chris. He pumped Chris's hand up and down. "Hank Lapp. Known far and wide for my buggy repairs."

"Not hardly," came another voice.

Chris whirled around to face another older man with a long white beard.

"When will this buggy be ready, Hank?" the man said. "It's been months now."

"Now, Elmo, what we've got here is a tricky problem," Hank said. "Very hard to fix. Needs just the right part and I can't seem to . . . uh . . . locate the source."

As the two men discussed the buggy, the conversation became more animated, especially on the part of Hank Lapp. Chris decided it would be wise to slip quietly away. On the ground, he noticed a clevis—a little metal pin that held the singletree to the buggy shafts. He bent down and picked it up, then walked to the buggy. He looked up to see if he could interrupt the men, but Hank was waving his arms, talking fast, trying to explain why there was such a delay in fixing this particular buggy. Chris slipped the clevis into place and rose to his feet. Hank abruptly stopped talking. The two men stared at Chris.

"I think I found that part you were looking for." Chris knocked on the singletree that kept the traces from working their way off on their own. "See? It works."

Hank came over to check it out. "LOOK AT THAT! Well, wonders never cease."

Elmo sized up Chris as if he had just noticed he was there. The way he looked at Chris made him nervous. It was like the man was peering into his soul. "And who are you?"

"That's Amos's hired help. New to town." Hank looked over at Chris. "Son, I didn't catch your name."

"Chris Yoder."

"Chris Yoder, this is Bishop Elmo." Hank pulled on the trace holders to make sure they were taut.

The bishop. *The bishop?* Oh, this was not good. Not good at all.

Bishop Elmo, cheerful and bespectacled, took a step closer to Chris. "New to Stoney Ridge?"

"Really new. Just arrived."

"Any relation to Isaac Yoder?"

Chris shook his head.

"Melvin Yoder?"

Chris shook his head more vehemently. He did not want to start down that long road of dissecting family trees. Two thoughts ricocheted through his mind at that moment. One, that Bishop Elmo would ask why he hadn't seen him in church more often once he discovered how long Chris had been here. That could be answered easily—they really just arrived a few weeks ago. A second and far more dangerous question was that the bishop might inquire—no, definitely would inquire, by the way he looked at that moment—as to where Chris had come from. Actually, it was surprising that he'd been able to evade the question so far with Amos Lapp and a few other people he had done odd jobs for, thanks to Bud at the hardware store. Chris quickly searched his brain for something to comment on, hoping it might redirect the conversation.

He held up the bit in his hand. "I left the horses in the field while I fixed this bit. It sure is a hot day. I'd better get back to work." He rushed off to the barn before Bishop Elmo could squeeze in another question.

And still, Elmo managed to call out, "I'll expect to see you in church in two Sundays, Chris Yoder."

Church. A feeling of dread washed over Chris. He would be found out. *Stop it!* he told himself fiercely. They'd come this far, hadn't they?

4

M.K. didn't think it was possible for Day Two as a teacher to be worse than Day One, but it was. The school had never been so noisy, including all of M.K.'s eight years as a student. All over the room there was a clatter of books and feet and a rustle of whispering. Whichever way she turned, unruliness and noise swelled up behind her. She didn't think anything could have been more disruptive to a classroom than yesterday's fire in the trash can, until Eugene Miller left during today's noon recess—taking three other eighth grade boys with him. M.K had a horrible feeling that each day, fewer and fewer students would return after lunch. By Friday afternoon, the schoolhouse would be empty.

Six-year-old Barbara Jean had started the exodus yesterday when she disappeared during lunch.

M.K. gave permission for Barbara Jean to go outside to the girls' room, but then she was gone for so long that M.K. panicked. She raced outside. Where was Barbara Jean? M.K. was hesitant to call out her name. It was unlikely that she'd left the school, wasn't it? But she wasn't in the girls' bathroom, nor the boys'. In just a matter of minutes, she had lost a child. Barbara Jean had gone missing.

Finally, M.K. found Barbara Jean behind the big oak tree, playing with her doll. "Oh, good!" M.K. said, flooded with relief. "I thought I'd lost you!" She was sure Barbara Jean had gone home.

But why should it matter if a few pupils slipped off to go home?

She didn't know why, but it did matter.

Fern had been right about one thing: M.K. was going to have to figure out how to get through this teaching job. For two weeks and three more days.

But how? How?

Amos put the ladder in the wagon. He untied Rosemary's reins from the post and walked her over to Chris, waiting for the horse and wagon by the path that led to the orchards. He had thought Chris would want to head home early this afternoon after he finished cutting hay in that last field, but the boy asked if Amos had something else for him to do. That was easy to answer—work on a farm was never done. Amos had noticed that a variety of early ripening apples were starting to fall from the trees. Another sign of autumn's arrival.

Normally, Amos enjoyed every part and parcel of farming, but picking fruit from trees was one task he was happy to pass off to a younger soul. Up and down that ladder, empty the sack in the wagon, then back up the ladder. Over and over and over. Not easy work for the knees of a fifty-six-year-old man. Yes, he was happy to share that chore.

Amos held the reins out to Chris, but he was preoccupied, staring up at the house. Amos shielded his eyes from the late afternoon sun to see what had caught Chris's attention. M.K. was shelling peas on the porch, and Jimmy Fisher sat sprawled on the steps, his long legs crossed at the ankles, talking to her. Chris startled when he realized that Amos stood behind him and turned abruptly to lead Rosemary up the gentle rise toward the orchards.

Amos walked down the hill and crossed the yard to where Fern was hanging laundry on the clothesline. "Fern, does it seem as if Jimmy Fisher is hanging around an awful lot? More than he used to?"

Fern lifted one of Amos's blue shirts up and hung it upside down so the arms dangled in the wind. "I'll say. That boy is eating me out of house and home."

Amos watched Jimmy throw back his head in laughter at something M.K. said. "I always thought those two would either kill each other or fall in love." He chuckled, pleased. "Guess it's the latter."

Fern gave him a sideways glance. "You think those two would be a good match?"

"Sure. Don't you?" He thought it was a wonderful idea. Being in love with Jimmy might cure M.K. of that restlessness. She wouldn't have time to think about anything else—trying to keep tabs on what Jimmy was up to would keep anybody busy. And M.K. would be good for Jimmy too. He never had a swooning effect on her like he did on all the other girls.

Fern clipped a pair of black trousers to the line. "Was mer net hawwe soll, hett mer's liebscht." *What we are not meant to have, we covet most.* She picked up the empty basket and started toward the house.

Amos puzzled on that for a while. What did that saying have to do with Jimmy and M.K.? Half the time, he had no idea what Fern meant. She spoke in riddles.

Day Three. After M.K. dismissed the students for the afternoon, she put her head on her desk. She was a horrible teacher, just like she had known she would be. And she had an entire two weeks and two days looming ahead of her.

Maybe, if she were thought to be a truly terrible teacher, the school board would fire her. Ah, relief! Followed swiftly by mortification. She would have to move away. Far, far away.

Shanghai. Johannesburg. Reykjavik.

Maybe that wouldn't be such a bad thing. Over the last year, she couldn't stop thinking about what the world outside of Stoney Ridge would look like, what it would sound like. What filled her mind were thoughts of breaking free from this Amish life of careful routine. Every day looked like the day before it. Every day looked like the day in front of it.

There were moments, mostly in church, when she had to sit on her hands to stop herself from jumping up and shouting at the preacher, "You already said that! Over and over again! Every two weeks, the same sermon! The same piece of Scripture! Same, same, same! Let's try something new!" She would love to see the look of surprise and horror on everyone's faces.

Of course, she didn't dare. She would never do such a disrespectful thing. She had been raised to respect her elders.

But, oh, how she would love to do it. Just once!

And then she started to think she might be going crazy. How awful it would be if she really did go berserk one day. She could hear the women clucking about it now . . . "Poor, poor Mary Kate. There was always something a little off-kilter about that girl. One moment, she seemed right as rain. The next moment, a raving madcap."

Deep down, she knew she could never do anything to intentionally hurt her father, or her sisters, or Uncle Hank. Or Fern.

It was a good thing she loved Fern, because that woman was impossible. M.K. knew Fern was behind this teaching job. It had Fern written all over it. Fern had a way of knowing what a person was thinking, without that person ever having to say it aloud. She had no doubt that Fern knew she was toying with the idea of leaving the Amish. Fern always knew.

But teaching a roomful of slow-witted, obstinate children? What a cruel, cruel mantle to place on M.K.

She was pretty sure Fern was savvy to the fact that M.K. had turned Ruthie down about joining this year's baptismal instruction class. She probably knew she had turned Ruthie's pleading down for the third time in a row. Fern knew everything.

Or maybe Ruthie told her. Ruthie just didn't understand. Every year, she begged M.K. to go through baptismal instructions with her, but M.K. just couldn't do it. Not yet.

She knew she would have to decide, at some point. She couldn't walk this line forever—one foot in the church, one foot out. If she left before she was baptized, then she could remain on good terms with her family.

And do what? The practical side of her always took over this internal conversation, and that was saying something because M.K. didn't have a practical bone in her body. She wasn't much of a long-term thinker. It was one of Fern's continual complaints about her. "Act first, think later," Fern said. "That's why you're always in hot water." She was constantly trying to tell M.K. to think "down the road."

So what would it look like, down the road, to leave Stoney Ridge? What would she do? She wasn't prepared to do much of anything outside of the Amish life. Even if she had a car, she didn't have a driver's license. How could she get a job? She didn't have a high school education. And she certainly didn't want to clean houses for English people for the rest of her life. Cleaning houses and waitressing were the only jobs former Amish girls seemed to get. *No thank you.*

She was a crackerjack beekeeper, though, thanks to her brother-in-law Rome. Maybe she could sell her bees' delicious honey in Paris. That sounded like fun. She knew a Plain girl shouldn't flame those desires to see such worldly places, but she did. She just couldn't help herself.

Oh, but there must be something or someplace or maybe even someone out there with enough excitement to satisfy M.K.'s restive nature. She just knew it was out there. Something was calling to her.

She let out a deep sigh. For now, she was stuck. Stuck for two weeks and two more days. She pulled her small Igloo lunch box out from under her desk (there was no way she was going to leave her lunch in the coatroom where Eugene Miller could slip a frog or snake into it—after all, hadn't she endured Jimmy Fisher's mischief for countless years?) and locked up the schoolhouse. She wanted to go investigate the murdered sheep farmer's pasture and look for clues. Solving this crime was the only bright spot of her day.

After school let out, Jenny rushed to the corner mailbox with the letter she had written during the school day. She had to get it in the mail before the day's mail was taken out. She knew Chris was over at Windmill Farm, but she still looked over her shoulder as she read it one more time before putting it in the envelope.

Hi Mom,

Just wanted you to know that Chris and I might not be able to see you for a while. We're together and doing fine. I'm going to school, too.

She chewed on her lip, thinking. Should she have added this last part?

Probably nobody told you, but Old Deborah passed. I thought you should know. Here is four dollars that I saved up. I'll try to send more. Don't worry about us.

Love, Jenny

She had wanted to write more. She had wanted to let her mother know that she and Chris were living in Stoney Ridge, that Chris was fixing up their grandfather's old house and planned to start a horse breeding business. Chris had been adamant that their mother not be told where they were. He would be furious if he knew she was writing to her mom. But she felt like a traitor if she didn't. Her mom may not be much of a mother, but she was the only mother Jenny had.

She licked the envelope, put on a stamp, opened the mailbox, and let the letter slide down its big blue throat.

Men! So frustrating.

M.K. was chased away from the crime scene area by the sheriff before she had time to uncover a single clue. Sheriff Hoffman took his sense of duty to ridiculous limits, she thought. He had a gun in his holster on his belt that he liked to pat, to remind her it was there, at the ready. How was she supposed to know that no trespassing included the first witness on the scene?

Sheriff Hoffman had glared at her. "You stay out of this pasture, Mary Kate Lapp. We got your statement. We'll come to you if we have any more questions. And we won't. You only heard a shot. That's all. That's nothing we don't know. This yellow tape here is meant to keep out riffraff. All riffraff."

Riffraff?! She was *not* riffraff. How insulting. Clearly, the police had no new information. If only they would have let her search the pasture. She was sure she would find a clue to the poor sheep farmer's untimely demise.

M.K. walked over to her red scooter and picked it up. How could she solve this crime when she wasn't even allowed near the crime scene? During school today, when she had the children reading quietly at their desks, she pulled out the most recent issue of her *Crime Solving* magazine. She read about how often a simple footprint could lead a clever sleuth to the perpetrator.

The only footprints she could find, besides those of the dead farmer's, were hoofprints that belonged to sheep. And it was then that Sheriff Hoffman happened to pass by in his patrol car and turned on his noisy siren.

So frustrating!

Maybe she would have to come back after dark, with her father's big flashlight.

She hopped on her scooter and started down the road, deep in thought. She built up speed to crest the hill. Just as she reached the rise, she crouched down on the scooter to improve aerodynamics. She had read about aerodynamics in a book from the library. It had suggested that a rider cut down on any draft by making oneself as sleek and small as possible. She liked to go down this hill with her eyes closed. There weren't many opportunities in the Plain life to let go and go all out. This hill, though, offered a taste of it. Danger *and* risk.

Suddenly, she heard someone yell "Watch out!" then a loud "ooouf" sound as her eyes flew open.

Chris Yoder was heading home from a long day at Windmill Farm. He had ducked through a cornfield filled with drying, green-golden stalks and slipped out to cross the road, when suddenly a flash of a red scooter flew right into him. He yelled, but it was too late. Chris was thrown into the ditch on the side of the road. Headfirst. Into murky, stagnant ditch water.

"I'm so sorry," someone called to him. "Are you hurt? I had my eyes closed and didn't see you."

Even though Chris had landed in water, his head had hit the bottom and he was sure he was seeing stars. He was drenched in smelly ditch water. A big yellow dog peered down at him in the ditch and let out a feeble "Woof." Chris shook himself off and staggered onto solid ground. Life returned to him pretty quick as he sized up his attacker—a young Amish woman with concerned brown eyes. "Why would anybody, anywhere, in their right mind, EVER ride a scooter with their eyes closed?"

The young woman pointed to the hill, flustered. "It's just that it's such a good . . . never mind." She bit her lip. "I said I was sorry."

Chris squeezed murky water out of his sleeve. "You should be."

Now she started getting huffy. "Well, I'm not as sorry as I was a minute ago! Maybe you should look where you're going."

"Maybe you should just LOOK. As in, keep your eyes open."

She started to sputter, as if she was gathering the words to give him a piece of her mind. But then she threw up her hands, muttered something about how this day was a complete disaster, hopped on her scooter, and zoomed away. The big yellow dog trotted placidly behind her.

Chris wiped his face off with his sleeve. Amazing. That girl had the *gall* to be mad at him! The nerve!

But she was cute. Very cute. That he happened to notice.

Stoney Ridge was caught in the grip of an Indian summer. Long, hot days. Long, windless nights.

Late Thursday night, Jimmy Fisher tossed pebbles up at M.K.'s window, but she didn't come down like she usually did. This was their summertime system—he would drop by after being out late with his friends, and she would come down and meet him outside to hear all about it. She thought his friends were hopelessly immature, but she liked hearing about their shenanigans.

Tonight, Jimmy and his friends had climbed the water tank in a neighboring town and dove into the reservoir, forty feet below. Such brave-hearted men. It made him proud to be in the company of these noble fellows. He wondered what M.K. would say about that. He tossed another pebble up at her window. Still nothing. As he looked around in the dark for something more substantial to toss at her window without breaking it and risking Fern's wrath—something he had experienced on occasion and took pains to avoid—a police car pulled up the driveway. Jimmy hid behind the maple tree. His first thought was that Sheriff Hoffman had figured out what he had been doing tonight and had tracked him here. It might have happened once or twice before. But then the car pulled to a stop, the sheriff got out and opened the back door. M.K. bolted out, an angry look on her face.

Wait. What?

Oh, this was too good.

If Jimmy were a more gallant man, he would quietly leave.

But this was too good.

The sheriff banged on the front door. In the quiet of the night, Jimmy could hear a pin drop. He heard M.K. try to convince the sheriff that she could handle things from here, but he didn't pay her any mind. From where Jimmy stood, he could see the front door. He saw a beam of light through the windows as someone made his way to the door. Jimmy heard the click of the door latch opening, and there stood Amos in his pin-striped nightshirt, with Fern in her bathrobe, right behind him. Their eyes went wide as they took in the sheriff standing beside M.K., who looked very small.

"I can explain everything!" M.K. started.

The sheriff interrupted. "Sorry to bother you in the middle of the night, Amos. But I believe this young lady belongs to you."

Amos looked bewildered. Fern looked like she always looked, as if she had expected a moment such as this. "What has she done now?" Fern asked in a weary voice.

"I found her disturbing a crime scene," Sheriff Hoffman said.

"That is not true!" M.K. said.

Fern shook her head. "Was she trying to get in that poor farmer's sheep pasture again?"

The sheriff handed Amos, who still seemed stunned, a large flashlight. "Sure was."

"I wasn't disturbing anything," M.K. said. "I was looking for clues."

"I keep telling you, we don't need any help solving crimes," the sheriff said. He sounded thoroughly exasperated. He turned and headed to his car, then spun around. "You stay out of that pasture, Mary Kate Lapp."

Jimmy slipped behind the tree again. The front door closed and the sheriff drove away. He waited awhile to make sure no one would see him and quietly strolled home.

Oh, *this* was too good.

5

M.K. couldn't stop yawning. She didn't even mind that Eugene Miller and his cronies had left after lunch again. It was easier to get through the afternoon's work without them. She hoped the boys were smart enough to stay out of sight until after half past three, though she doubted it. She almost fell asleep as second grader Timmy King puzzled over subtraction problems at the board. The warm air in the room, the gentle buzz of a bee on the windowsill. "Nicely done, Timmy," she said. She glanced at the clock. Two and a half hours to go. She read out loud for a while, but no one seemed to hear. She thought about dismissing everyone early because it was so hot.

Could she do that? Why not? She was the teacher.

She put down the book. "Let's try again on Monday." Barbara Jean, the youngest of everyone, clapped her hands, making M.K. laugh. Just as M.K. stood and opened her mouth to say, "School's out! Go on home!" the school door opened wide. In walked Eugene Miller, Josiah Zook, Davy Stoltzfus, and his brother Marvin.

And Fern. In walked Fern.

The boys took their seats. "These boys seemed to have gotten lost after lunch," Fern announced, as if she was on a mission to find them. "So I helped them locate the schoolhouse. They won't be getting lost anymore."

A few snickers circled the room. Fern went to a chair in the back and sat down. M.K. knew that look on Fern's face. It was the look that said she was going to be staying for a while. For the next two and a half hours.

M.K.'s heart sank. She turned to the third graders. "Rise, please, and bring your readers."

Tick. Tick. Tick. The clock inched forward, painfully slow. Finally, it was half past three and the class was dismissed. Fern waited.

"Where did you find the boys?" M.K. asked.

"Hank found them fishing at Blue Lake Pond. He's been worried that all the rainbow trout will be gone by the end of September with those four spending their afternoons fishing, so he ran them off and I happened upon them."

M.K. closed up the cloakroom and locked up the front door. "Why do you have the buggy?"

"We're not going home." Fern pointed to the buggy. "Hop in. We've got someplace we need to be."

"Fern, it's Friday! My first free afternoon—"

"Nothing is as important as this."

M.K. knew not to push it. The ride home from the sheriff must have been a shock to her dad and Fern. It was ridiculous, really. All a simple misunderstanding. She had gone out to see if there might be another clue, something the police missed. There was a problem and it needed solving. Hadn't she learned in life to just solve the problem herself?

And suddenly she was under threat of arrest. Again! How was she supposed to know that the police were patrolling the area? Why hadn't they been patrolling when the murder occurred? She would have liked to ask Sheriff Hoffman such a bold question, but of course she didn't dare.

Fern slapped the reins on Cayenne's rear end and the buggy lurched forward. "Is that the way you've been teaching?"

"What do you mean?"

"Was today a typical afternoon? Class by class comes up and reads out loud?"

"That's the way Alice Smucker ran the classroom."

Fern was silent, so silent that finally M.K. couldn't hold back another minute. "I told you that I wouldn't be a good teacher! Dad said I've never failed at anything I've tried to do, but this—"

"Well, see, that's the problem right there."

"What is?"

"Tried. You've never failed at anything you've *tried*."

"I'm failing at this!"

There was a silence, then Fern's voice, sounding soft and hard at the same time. "You haven't *tried* to teach. You're just babysitting. Not even that. The trouble with you, Mary Kate, is you can't see a day ahead."

That was not a new observation.

"You're spending most of your time thinking about solving that sheep farmer's death. You think about it more than the police do."

That was somewhat of an exaggeration, but the sheep farmer murder was taking up a great deal of M.K.'s thoughts. Somebody had to solve the crime before Stoney Ridge was riddled with murders! "I'm teaching the same way Alice Smucker did. Everything's the same. Every single thing."

Fern looked at her as if she might be addlebrained. "You spent eight long years complaining about the time in Twin Creeks School. Seems like a smart girl like you should be able to figure out what's wrong with that logic."

It seemed that way to M.K. too, but she couldn't quite figure out what Fern was getting at. She scrunched up her face as if she was thinking hard, and she was. "How do I know how to teach any different? Alice Smucker was the only teacher I've ever had."

"No, she wasn't."

Fern thought she knew everything, but she didn't. "Oh yes she was!" Then M.K. clapped her hands over her mouth. "Oh, no! She wasn't." M.K. had completely forgotten about Gideon Smucker's brief tenure. He had filled in for his sister, Alice, after there was an unfortunate collision with a runaway sled (a sled that happened to be carrying M.K., but that was beside the point). "But it was easier for Gid. He was a man. The big boys obeyed him. It's always easier for men."

"Why do you think the children obeyed Gid?"

"Probably because Eugene Miller hadn't moved to Stoney Ridge yet."

Fern rolled her eyes.

"Eugene is a bandersnatch, Fern. The very worst of the bandersnatches! He makes Jimmy Fisher seem like any teacher's dream. Eugene makes vulgar noises whenever I turn my back. Yesterday, he put a book up on the doorjamb so that when I walked in, the book fell on my head. And there he was at his desk, with a sweet-as-pie smile pasted on his face. He's just a school yard bully—always making outlandish suggestions and daring his friends to join him. Eugene Miller pushes a person to the limit of politeness. The very limit."

This very morning, she had slipped outside to fill her thermos with water from the pump. When she returned to the classroom, she found that Eugene had drawn a caricature of her on the chalkboard. Never mind that it was actually a rather amusing likeness—he had made a fool of M.K.

"Did the children obey Alice?"

M.K. sighed. "I suppose. She made everything a mind-numbing routine, so the boys used school to catch up on their sleep." Boring. School had been incredibly boring. But M.K. was starting to feel a mild twinge of guilt as she complained about Alice's teaching. It was a new feeling for her. At least the boys didn't disappear during lunch under Alice's tutelage. "Teaching isn't that easy, Fern." She gave herself an A+ for trying.

"No, I'm sure it isn't, if someone were actually trying to teach."

M.K. was insulted. She was trying! Sort of. Now and then.

"Wann epper mol nix meh drumgebt, is es schlimm." *When you don't care, you are in a sorry state.*

M.K. tried not to flinch. Fern's sayings were worse than a beesting, and she knew all about beestings.

"How long do you plan on wallowing in self-pity?"

"Fine." She let out a sigh. "I'm done wallowing. No more wallowing. Really."

"Good."

M.K. waited, sensing from Fern's change in tone something was coming. "Where are we going?"

"To visit Erma Yutzy."

M.K.'s heart sank a notch lower. Any more bad news today and it would be in her stomach. "I don't like talking to old people. They make me uncomfortable."

Fern released a long-suffering sigh. "What a thing to say."

"I'm sorry, but the way they look at me with their watery eyes makes me uneasy. And their skin is like wrinkled crepe paper. Old people can be odd too. Some as odd as a cat with feathers. I never know what to say to them." She could tell by the way Fern was clutching the reins that she was running out of patience. "You can't deny that, Fern. Just last month, Mose Weaver came to church in his pajamas."

"Mose Weaver is having a few forgetfulness problems."

"Well, how old is Erma Yutzy, anyway?"

"She's turning one hundred next month."

One hundred years old?! M.K. was intrigued. What would it be like to have one hundred years of stored memories jammed in your head? It boggled her mind. "Why today? Maybe we should wait for her birthday."

"Can't. Erma's too busy planning her party."

Planning her party? Who would still be alive to attend? Fern stopped the horse in front of Erma's house. M.K. hopped out and waited for Fern to join her.

Fern didn't budge. "I'll be back in an hour or two."

An hour or two? Fern was leaving M.K. alone with this ancient lady for an hour or two? "Fern! What am I supposed to talk about with her?"

Fern simply pursed her lips as if the why of it was too obvious to say.

She slapped the horse's reins and trotted out the driveway. Over her shoulder, she tossed, "Did I happen to mention that Erma was a teacher?"

Oh. *Oh.*

Fern! So overinvolved.

Amos had hired some hardworking hands on his farm, but he had never seen anyone work as diligently as Chris Yoder. It was as if Chris had something to prove—though Amos didn't get the feeling that he was showing off. It was more like the boy had something to prove to himself.

The boy? Really, Chris Yoder was a young man. Amos reviewed what he had come to learn about Chris Yoder: he had a tremendous work ethic, even for an Amish man. He had a kind touch with animals, which Amos admired. Chris hurried off at quitting time, as if he was expected somewhere else. Or maybe someone was expecting him.

That was about all Amos could gather about Chris Yoder. He was as closemouthed as they came, responding to Amos's questions in one- or two-syllable answers. He wouldn't join the family for dinner. Instead, he spent his lunch hour sweeping out the barn or binding hay.

Fern had been too preoccupied with M.K. this week to think twice about Chris, though she did ask about him once. "Who in the world is this hired hand and why doesn't he come to the house and introduce himself, be sociable?" Amos answered by saying he was just the quiet type. That satisfied Fern for now, but he knew that when she did get him in her sights, Chris would sing like a canary, without even realizing he had been questioned by a skilled practitioner. Until then, Amos could wait.

There was something about Chris Yoder that appealed to Amos. He was carrying some kind of a burden, and he was too young or too proud to realize that all he needed to do was to ask for help.

Chris knew that Jenny didn't like going home to an empty house, so he worked through his lunch hour to finish up the day's work. He needed to earn a full day's wage, but he didn't want her to have to be home alone very long. As he walked down the lane from Windmill Farm, he braced himself for a litany of complaints about school: the feebleminded teacher, the tragic shortage of girls in her class, the annoying boys. The fact was, Jenny had always been an intense child. She was all or nothing. She loved you or hated you; there was never any middle ground. He actually felt a little sorry for this new teacher—to be inflicted with Jenny's displeasure.

On the upside for the week, things were working out well with Amos Lapp. Chris had been patching jobs together whenever he could find work on the bulletin board at the hardware store, but he preferred working at one place for a while. Plus, Windmill Farm wasn't too far from his grandfather's house.

Amos paid Chris with cash at the end of each day. He said he didn't like being indebted, but Chris had a hunch that Amos wasn't quite sure if he should expect him again in the morning. He knew Amos was holding himself back from asking questions—he could just sense it. But he didn't ask anything, and for that, among other things, Chris was grateful. Amos Lapp had eyes so kind that they made you look twice just to be certain the kindness in them was real. It sure seemed to be.

It wasn't the meanness in people that surprised him. It was the good in them that he found so unexpected. Would he ever get over that?

Chris did a good day's labor for Amos. He hoped it would continue to work out. Not having to wait for cash until the end of the month meant that he could start buying supplies to fix up his grandfather's old house. Twice now, he and Jenny had driven into town to pick up drywall and tape. He was going to start by repairing the hole in the kitchen wall.

Chris climbed over the fence—the same spot where that cute girl had knocked him over yesterday and sent him flying into the ditch. He looked around for that red scooter, just in case she happened along. Not that he was interested. He wasn't. He had no notion to settle down—not for a very long, long time. He had too much on his plate, too many plans. But there was something about that girl that he couldn't quite get out of his mind. He got a kick out of how flustered she was. And then she was so exasperated with him! As if it was his fault that he was crossing the road like a normal person.

He wiped the back of his neck with his handkerchief. It was humid today. A wisp of a memory tugged at him as he walked down the hill. It had been a warm spring day, one of the first for the year. Chris was seven, and Jenny was an infant. She cried a lot as a baby, especially in the evening. Colic, he remembered a neighbor lady saying when she dropped off a meal to celebrate the new baby. The lady recommended goat's milk. "My son had it too," he remembered her saying as she stayed to rock Jenny to sleep.

It wasn't just colic. His mother had used drugs during Jenny's pregnancy. She and Jenny were both suffering from symptoms of withdrawal—edgy and hypersensitive. His mother had little patience for Jenny's ear-piercing cries.

Later that evening, his mother had become so agitated with Jenny's wails that she threw a frying pan against the wall and it made a gash in the drywall. And then she grabbed her purse and stomped out of the house. She didn't return for hours. Chris didn't know where his grandfather had gone to that evening—probably a gathering of old veterans at the local Grange Hall. He just remembered sitting by the front room window, holding Jenny, afraid to set her down because she might start hollering, watching for his mother to come home. When she did come home, she was high. Even at the age of seven, he knew the signs: slurry talk, bloodshot eyes, clumsy movement.

He remembered how furious his grandfather had been when he saw the condition his mother was in and realized Chris had been left in charge of an infant. He had only allowed his daughter to move back home with two children if she promised to stop using drugs. They had a roof-raising argument that night. His grandfather said he would never fix the hole in the wall—he would leave it there to remind her of what she was turning into. He threatened to turn in his daughter to the authorities. "And don't think you're going to saddle me with them two kids!" his grandfather had hollered. "The cops are going to take 'em and plunk 'em into foster care!" At that point Chris ran to his room and pulled the pillow over his head so he couldn't hear any more.

Chris shuddered involuntarily. He hadn't thought about that night in years. It was strange how memories intruded into a person's mind, uninvited and unwanted.

That was going to be the first thing Chris fixed. That hole.

M.K. found Erma Yutzy out in the vegetable garden, picking the last of the summer beans. Feathery white hair stuck out in tufts around her head, except for that inch-wide strip of bare scalp along the crown of her head like so many other Amish old ladies—a result of years and years of hair pulled and pinned tightly into a bun. She was tiny and frail looking. A good stout wind could carry her off.

M.K. had never paid much attention to Erma Yutzy. She knew her as one of the many elderly ladies in her church, but she had never bothered to stop to talk to her or consider her, other than being careful not to trip her or bump into her at a gathering. She was afraid of old people. They reminded M.K. of a dried-up leaf that would snap in two and crumble if you accidentally bumped into them. Snap. Crumble. Collapse.

"I JUST WANTED TO STOP BY AND SAY HELLO," M.K. called out, loud and clear, as Erma shielded her eyes from the sun when she noticed someone in her garden. "FERN DROPPED ME OFF."

"I'm always delighted to have visitors," Erma said in her thin, wrinkly voice. "Nice to have a reason to stop working." Her face beamed. That was the only word for it. She positively beamed.

M.K. took the basket of beans from her and followed her into the house. Slowly, oh so slowly. It was difficult for M.K. to walk at such a snail-like pace. She never did anything slowly. But imagine—this woman was one hundred years old! M.K. was astounded. Erma had a pair of amazing eyes, brighter than your average blue eyes—maybe a little on the watery side—with a slight tint of something close to turquoise, the color M.K. imagined waters near Fiji to be, although she had never actually seen an ocean. Or maybe the hazy sky right before twilight in the desert of the Sahara, though she'd never seen a desert either.

Erma filled two glasses with lemonade. She added a little twist of mint and handed the glass to M.K.

"Thank you," M.K. said. "THANK YOU," she repeated, enunciating the words.

"You're welcome," Erma said as she settled into a chair. "Now, tell me why you feel the need to shout at me."

M.K. practically choked on her sip of lemonade. "Aren't you nearly deaf?"

"No. I thought maybe you were."

"Well, no. I just thought . . . I mean . . . you're one hundred years old. Uncle Hank roars at us and he's only half as old as you."

Erma smiled. "I've known Hank Lapp for years. He only has three settings on his voicebox. Loud, louder, and loudest." She started to giggle like a schoolgirl, her little shoulders shaking with delight.

Erma Yutzy was not what M.K. had expected. She leaned forward in her chair, intrigued. As the afternoon wore on, M.K. learned all kinds of interesting things about this woman.

When Fern said Erma had been a teacher, M.K. immediately assumed that she would be an old version of Alice Smucker. Erma Yutzy had three things in common with Alice Smucker: they were both maiden ladies and career teachers and they lived alone. Alice lived in a little cottage on her father's goat farm, not by choice. When her father remarried, Alice and her stepmother kept having disagreements about how to organize the kitchen. After Alice had reorganized the kitchen cabinets for the third time—to the way her belated mother had kept them—her stepmother gently suggested Alice might be happier in the little cottage, with a kitchen of her own.

Erma lived alone, by choice. She said she liked her peace and quiet. She had plenty of nearby relatives who kept an eye on her and her home.

But that was where the commonalities of Alice and Erma ended. Erma was winsome in every way and she was nearly one hundred with no plans of dying. Unlike Alice, who had her funeral planned—just in case—at the ripe old age of thirty.

The sound of horse hooves on the driveway caught their attention. Fern had arrived in her buggy. M.K. was shocked to discover that two hours had flown by. They were just scratching the surface! There was so much M.K. wanted to know about her—what was life like for her as a little girl? What changes had she seen in her lifetime?

Erma covered M.K.'s hand with hers. "Mary Kate, I was born into a world of horse-drawn carts on dirty paths, gas streetlights, when you could mail a letter for pennies and a box of Kellogg's Corn Flakes only cost eight cents. Now, I live in an age where there are eight-lane highways and men on the moon and strange little computers that fit in people's pockets."

"Most people call those cell phones."

Erma squeezed her hand. It didn't matter what they were called. She was trying to make a point. "Mary Kate, do you know what keeps me alive?"

M.K. leaned forward in her chair. "What?" She wanted to know.

"I want to see what happens next."

It was suppertime and Amos wasn't sure where Fern or M.K. had gone to. It looked like he was on his own for supper, though he smelled a pot of chili simmering on the stove top and noticed a pan of fresh-baked corn bread. He spooned chili into a bowl and eyed that corn bread again. As long as he was fending for himself, maybe a little bit of butter on that corn bread would be in order. Honey, too.

Just as he was lathering a chunk of corn bread with a thick layer of butter, the kitchen door blew open and in walked Hank carrying a cardboard box, Doozy at his heels.

"AMOS! WE'VE GOT TROUBLE!" Hank set the box on the kitchen floor. In it were four yellow puppies, squirming and wiggling and trying to get out.

"Where in the world did those come from?" Amos asked, swallowing a bite of buttered corn bread as he noticed Fern's buggy coming up the driveway.

"Edith Fisher sent them over with Jimmy. She included this note." Hank pulled his glasses out of his pocket and unfolded the crinkled paper. "'I have given you plenty of notice to find homes for these puppies and yet you continue to ignore me. So I am ignoring you. Until you find homes for these puppies, you are not welcome for Sunday dinners.'" He stuffed the paper back into his pocket. "She is spurning me!" He shook his head solemnly. "Doozy had a moment of reckless abandon, and look at the dire consequences."

Doozy thumped his tail, pleased at his prowess, and Amos set down the bowl of chili. His appetite had just considerably diminished. "Well, I suppose that these things happen."

"What are we going to do with them?" Hank blurted out.

Amos, who was in the middle of putting the butter back into the refrigerator, stopped what he was doing. "We?" he asked. Out the kitchen sink window, he saw the buggy come to a stop by the barn and Fern and M.K. climb out to unhook Cayenne's traces from the buggy shafts. "I always thought of Doozy as your dog."

"He spends most of his time following M.K. around! Why, he's devoted to her."

"I'm not sure about that. He only follows M.K. around when you've gone off to visit Edith."

"He's not wanted at Edith's farm. She turns up her nose at him, you see. Particularly after this moment of indiscretion with her favorite poodle. Edith complains about Doozy an awful lot, mostly about his scent, which I just can't understand. After all, he is a dog. Dogs should smell like dogs." He crouched down to pat Doozy's head. "She refuses to see beyond a few little flaws."

"Think that she'll change her mind about the two of you?" Amos asked. "After all, you've been courting her for seven years now."

Hank sighed, looking wistfully at the ceiling. "I don't think there's much of a chance there. She says Doozy has to go. Said she can't deal with the both of us."

Amos nodded. Hank would be task enough for any woman. Adding Doozy into the equation would put anyone over the edge.

"Maybe you could compromise," Amos said. "Leave Doozy with us."

Hank shook his head. "No deal." A puppy was nearly escaping out of the box so he reached down and tenderly held it against his chest. "They sure are cute little buggers. It'd be a shame not to keep 'em."

Amos rinsed out his bowl of chili in the sink and put it back in the cupboard, dripping wet. He tried to imagine what it would be like to have five dogs in one house, especially in Hank's small apartment above his buggy shop. "Well, I don't know what to say."

The hinge on the kitchen door squeaked as Fern came in. She looked at Hank, at Amos, at Doozy, at the box of squirming puppies, and shook her head in exasperation. "I know exactly what to say. Find homes for your dog's puppies, Hank Lapp."

Hank looked at her, wounded. "We were just discussing the possibility of keeping them."

"Absolutely not." She brushed past him and went into the kitchen to wash her hands at the sink. As she dried her hands on the rag, she noticed the missing piece of corn bread in the pan and eyed Amos, who was trying to skooch the remainder of the buttered corn bread behind his back on the counter. She saw. But before she could start scolding him for not waiting for supper, Hank snagged her attention.

"It is clear to me, Fern Lapp," Hank groused, "that you know nothing about the world of dogs."

"I know plenty about dogs. And even more about men." She took bowls out of the cupboard and frowned when she spotted the water drops in the top bowl. She pulled flatware from the utensil drawer and started to set the table, working around the box of puppies. They were curled into a pile in the corner of the box, sound asleep. "Both need very clear directions and expectations." She resumed setting the table. "The puppies go."

"Well, that answers that," Hank huffed. "I come here for sympathy, and all that I'm getting is heartless advice." He stopped. "Speaking of hearts, who's got a bigger heart than Sadie? Why, she's all heart. She might want one of Doozy's pups. Maybe even two! One for each of her little ones!" His face brightened, like the sun coming out after a rainstorm. He placed the puppy back in the box, picked it up, and opened the kitchen door. "M.K.!" he shouted.

M.K. was leading Cayenne into the barn and stopped short at the sound of Hank's loud voice.

"PUT THAT HORSE BACK IN ITS BUGGY SHAFTS! We've got ourselves an emergency errand!"

Fern came up behind Amos at the window. Together, they watched M.K. ooh and aah over the puppies in the box. "Poor Sadie," Fern said. "She'd better brace herself."

6

Jenny's shoulders ached from painting the kitchen wall after Chris had finished fixing the drywall. For the first time in her life she didn't feel like reading a book before bedtime. The problem with not reading, though, was that she couldn't ignore all kinds of creepy, frightening noises as she lay there in the dark.

This old house was awful, truly horrible. It creaked and groaned like it was in pain. She heard mysterious scratching sounds in the walls and the pattering of feet above her head. She closed her eyes and tried to imagine her happiest day, her tenth birthday, when Old Deborah had taken her to the prison and her mother was in a good mood.

Her mother could be sweet and charming at times, but you never knew what you were getting. You always braced yourself for the first minute, as you sized up the expression on Mom's face.

On this day, though, her mother was in a happy mood. She braided Jenny's hair, taming her long curls into two flat plaits down her back. She taught Jenny a dozen variations on cat-in-the-cradle. It was the happiest birthday Jenny ever had. To top it off, that day happened to be a Friday, a day that Jenny had always enjoyed, although Saturday was her absolute favorite. She had the usual feelings about Monday, a day that she had never heard anybody speak up for, for obvious reasons.

The wind picked up. Somewhere outside, a door banged. A branch tapped at the window. Something whirred past Jenny's face. Her eyes shot open to see a menacing dark shape flutter around her room. A bird? How had a bird gotten into her bedroom? She sat up in bed. It must have come in through the broken window. How many times had she complained to Chris about that broken window? Mosquitoes flew in every night, eager to torment her. It flew past again, swooping and dipping erratically. Wait. That was not a bird. It was a bat! She ran to Chris's room, screaming as she flew down the hallway.

"Who's there?" Chris sat bolt upright in bed. "What's happened?"

"Chris! Th-there's a bat flying around my room! It got in through the broken window pane!"

Chris signed and leaned back, closing his eyes. "It'll probably fly back out the window."

"But—"

"It's more scared of you than you are of it. Get some sleep. I've got a long day tomorrow."

Jenny crept back down the hall with the pillow over her head. She lifted the covers and checked every inch of her bed thoroughly before climbing in. As she lay there trying to sleep, she wasn't sure if it would be better to actually see the bat flying around again and know for sure where it was, or not to see it and wonder.

She hated this house. She hated Stoney Ridge. She hated school. She hated the girls at school who never asked her to eat lunch with them. Not one time. She especially hated the leader of the girls, Anna Mae Glick.

She wanted Old Deborah to be alive. She wanted everything to go back the way it used to be. She knew what to expect while she lived at Old Deborah's. The same friends at school. Meals waiting for her at home. People who cared about her. Nobody cared about them in Stoney Ridge. Nobody.

She didn't want to cry. Tears wouldn't accomplish anything and would only make her pillow soggy. She bit on her lower lip to keep her eyes from filling with tears of self-pity. Once her tears started, they would never stop.

A floorboard creaked. The chimney moaned. Minutes ticked away. Everything went quiet. The bat must have flown out the window. It was okay, Jenny told herself, relieved. Everything was going to be okay.

No sooner were the words formed in her mind than the bat whooshed past her head, making squeaky bat noises, darting and diving and swooping and sailing as if it were putting on an acrobatic show for Jenny.

M.K. had a lot of time to think all that weekend, mostly because Sheriff Hoffman saw her at the post office and told her he would put a restraining order out on her if she got anywhere near that sheep farmer's pasture. He patted the gun as he said it too. So rude! She had merely asked him a few questions about how the case was progressing, and if he had discovered any unusual footprints. "Plenty of hoofprints!" he had told her, cackling in that rusty way of his as he said it. He refused to tell her anything more. He looked annoyed when she expressed the tiniest bit of dismay that it was turning into a cold case and suggested he consider putting more manpower into solving it—because that was when he brought up the restraining order. Outrageous!

At this rate, that poor sheep farmer was never going to have his murder solved. And what about the people of Stoney Ridge? They were all at grave risk with a murderer on the loose. Why wasn't anyone else as concerned about it as she was? It was just one of the many complaints she had about living in a small town. People in Stoney Ridge were more concerned about the price of eggs at the farmer's market than about random, senseless murders.

A plane left a long white trail across the sky, and she wondered where it was going. Maybe someplace like Buenos Aires. Or Tokyo. She wondered what it would be like to go somewhere like Moscow. Most of the people she knew were born and raised and died right in Stoney Ridge.

She was positive that the people who lived in big cities—Istanbul or London—*they* would be worried about random murders. Such a thought made her feel pleased that she had decided to pick up a second passport application at the post office today after losing the first one. She didn't have any specific travel plans, but it seemed like a good idea to have a passport. Just in case. A person never knew when she might need to leave the country in a hurry. Even Canada and Mexico required passports, she reminded herself.

What really irked M.K. was that she needed to go by the sheep farmer's field on her way home. It was her customary shortcut. But she wouldn't give Sheriff Hoffman the satisfaction. So instead, she took the long way home.

Saturday morning, Chris was ready to do battle with the exterior of the house as soon as he and Jenny returned from mowing Erma Yutzy's lawn. Starting at the front door, he swept his way up and down the porch, knocking down spiderwebs, dessicated insect carcasses, a long-abandoned birds' nest, and a forest of dead leaves. Jenny sloshed Pine-Sol all over the porch and attacked it with a mop. The water in the bucket grew grimy with the accumulated grunge. Four changes of water and two hours later, he decided the porch floor was done. He'd scrubbed the old boards so hard that he could see bare wood shining through the faded battleship-gray paint.

The windows were next. The panes were so caked with grime that he didn't even attempt to start with Windex. Instead, he hooked up a garden hose and splashed water all over the old wavy glass, sending a dirty river seeping down over his previously pristine floorboards. Shoot. He'd have to give the porch another rinsing later. But for now, he washed and polished and spritzed the tall windows that ran across the front of the house until they sparkled like crystal in the afternoon sunshine.

Chris had saved the front door for last. He scrubbed away layer after layer of dirt and dust. He spent the next few hours working feverishly. Jenny worked hard too. They scoured and scrubbed until their back and legs ached, and their hands were rubbed raw from all the bleach and disinfectant.

Chris looked over the list of things he needed at the hardware store. He couldn't do anything more until he got more cleaning supplies, so he decided to run into town. Samson needed some exercise—he hadn't taken him out for a few days. Jenny wanted to stay home and read a book in a bat-free room, so he hitched Samson to the buggy.

The hardware store was empty so Chris was able to get his supplies quickly. He loaded the buggy and hopped in, signaling Samson to move forward. The stallion tossed his head and whinnied. He responded to Chris's slightest whistle.

On Stone Leaf Drive, he noticed two small figures in the road up ahead. As Samson gained on them, he saw it was a young Amish woman in a turquoise dress, with an old yellow dog trailing behind her. He recognized that young woman—it was the same one who careened into him the other day. He thought he'd seen her somewhere else, but he couldn't remember.

Chris reined the horse to a stop behind her. "Hey, you. Where's your red scooter?"

She spun around and looked at him. She didn't seem to recognize him, but then, how could she? He had been covered in mud.

Chris saw her puzzled gaze shift from him to Samson. She walked toward Samson and stroked his nose. "Why, this horse is beautiful. Just beautiful. He must be eighteen hands. And pitch-black." She stroked the neck of Samson. "Why, he's a stallion!" She looked at Chris with interest. "Are you going to breed him?"

"Someday. I want to have my own breeding business." He wasn't sure why he admitted that. It wasn't something he told many people.

She ran a hand along Samson's withers. "Well, when that someday arrives, you'll be off to a fine start with him."

"Can I offer you a lift? It's getting awfully warm."

M.K. shook her head. "I'm almost where I need to be." She started walking down the road.

Chris clucked to Samson to get him moving, but he kept him from trotting to keep pace with the young woman and her dog. "I don't even know your name."

She didn't slow down a bit. "That's because we've never met."

"It might not have been a proper introduction, but we have definitely met."

She stopped abruptly and looked at him with a question on her face.

"I'm the one you knocked into the ditch the other day."

She squinted her face as if she was trying to place him. Just how many people did she crash into on that scooter? Clearly, too many to remember.

A frown pinched her face and she threw her arms in the air. "Join the long line of people who blame me for everything that goes wrong around here!" She started marching down the road.

Chris clucked to the horse. "I'm not blaming you. Well, maybe a little. You were heading down a hill, on a scooter, with your eyes shut. Probably going ten miles an hour!"

The young woman turned her face away, her jaw thrust out, and she picked up her pace.

Samson seemed to know to keep up with her. "Look, maybe we can start over. I'm Chris Yoder."

She balled her fists on her hips. "Which way are you headed, Chris Yoder?"

They were nearly at an intersection. Chris pointed straight ahead.

"Then I'm going this way. Come on, Doozy." She turned right at the intersection. As she swung to the right, something slipped out of her pocket. He tried to call out to her—a little awkward when you don't know a person's name: "Hey, you! You there!"—but she wasn't going to pay him any mind.

He jumped down to pick up the paper and unfolded it. A passport application. *What?* What was a Plain girl doing with a passport application? What kind of a girl was she?

He watched her march down the lane, head held high, until she and her dog disappeared around the bend. He couldn't wipe the grin off his face. He still didn't know her name . . . but he was going to find out.

Jenny glanced at the clock on the kitchen counter. Was it already after two? Chris would be back soon. She had been completely absorbed in the book she was reading and simply had to find out if there was a happy ending. She loved happy endings. But now she needed to get this letter written and stick it in the mailbox before the postman came by. And before Chris returned from town. She took out one crumpled five-dollar bill from her pocket and tucked it into an envelope.

Dear Mom,

Chris and I are doing okay. I started school this week. There aren't any girls in my grade, just boys. I feel sorry for the teacher. She's not very bright and the big boys outsmart her. Mostly, she just sits at her desk and sifts through magazines. But at least it gives me a lot of free time to read my books. I miss you. Get better fast, okay? This is all the money I could get since my last letter.

Love you! Jenny

For one long, painful moment, Jenny remembered how her mother looked right before everything fell apart again this last time. She was so skinny that Jenny could see two scapula bones in her back that stuck out like chicken wings. She hardly ate any food. She hardly slept. And she kept getting bloody noses. Old Deborah had pulled Grace into the bathroom to stop the nosebleed.

You'd think her mother would care about what drugs were doing to her body. But all Grace Mitchell wanted, all she wanted, no matter what, was more meth.

That evening, Old Deborah talked and talked with her mom in the kitchen, long after Chris and Jenny had gone to bed. In the morning, when Jenny woke up, her mother was gone. Old Deborah told her that Grace had decided to enter the rehab center. Chris said he was pretty sure Old Deborah hadn't given Grace a choice.

Jenny had faith in her mom, though. This time would be different. Her mom would get better. She had cleaned up twice before. She could do it again. Absolutely. She licked the back of the envelope and ran out to the mailbox. Then she came back in to finish her story in the kitchen—the only guaranteed bat-free room in the house.

The kitchen clock ticked loud in the silence.

M.K. hadn't intended to visit Erma today, but she did not want that flirtatious young man to continue to follow her, and she certainly didn't want to get in his buggy with him. Nosir! She had no idea who he was and had no desire to know, either—though anyone who had a horse like that couldn't be entirely bad. The horse was well cared for, sleek and strong, with intelligent eyes. Where had she seen that horse before? In town, maybe? No. She couldn't quite capture it—but she knew she'd seen him somewhere. She couldn't help but admire such a beautiful creature. But her admiration for its owner ended there. Her curiosity, though, was another story. She happened to notice that the young horse owner turned down the long drive that led to Colonel Mitchell's abandoned house. She hadn't even thought of that house in years and years. It was hidden from the road on a long flag lot, hidden from the road with a long dirt driveway for access.

But back to M.K.'s current situation. The road she turned down went right by Erma Yutzy's, and suddenly, there she was, walking up the driveway. The air was filled with the sweet scent of freshly cut grass—one of M.K.'s favorite smells. Erma was filling her bird feeders with oiled black sunflower seeds when she saw M.K. and her face lit up with delight.

"It won't be long until the skies will be filled with a thick black ribbon of birds as they head south for the winter. Don't you love to put your head back and watch them fly, Mary Kate? Don't you just wonder, 'Where is the end of that long ribbon?'" She sighed happily. "There's so much to wonder about in the natural world."

Imagine that, M.K. thought. Erma had seen one hundred autumns. One hundred years' worth of skies filled with migrating birds. The same skies, every year. And still, she found them fascinating.

The two women sat on the porch in the shade, with a slight breeze wafting around them, and drank iced tea, talking. The conversation began with news about Sadie's redheaded twins and drifted to school, as Erma asked M.K. what she thought about being a teacher.

M.K. groaned. "Awful. Just awful. Part of the problem is that I don't think these children are capable of learning." Maybe Danny Riehl would be the one exception.

"I have learned that most youngsters can do what you ask them to do—even if they don't think so. They just need a little push sometimes to get them moving."

Apparently, Erma never had a scholar like Eugene Miller. He needed a push, all right, right out the window.

"So over the years I learned to give a little push in the right direction when I had to. That's what teachers do."

M.K. leaned forward in her chair. "That's the other part of the problem. I just don't know how to think or act like a teacher."

Erma tilted her head. "What do you think a teacher acts like?"

"Very, very serious. And solemn." Gid was serious. Alice was serious and solemn.

Teaching was serious business. M.K. had a difficult time acting serious and solemn on a full-time basis. It was exhausting.

"And why do you think that would be true?"

"The reason, I think, is because it is an overwhelming task to maintain order. Especially when Eugene Miller is in the room. I'm only five feet three and the older boys tower over me. They ignore me. They run roughshod over all of my attempts to keep the classroom from utter chaos."

"Mary Kate," Erma started. She was one of the few people who called M.K. by her full name and it made her feel rather grown up. "They will see you as a teacher on the day when you start seeing yourself as a teacher."

"But I do! I'm in that stuffy schoolhouse every day, from morning to night. I've been working myself to the bone. I've tried everything! I've tried to teach like Alice. I've tried to teach like Gid. Neither way works. I just can't do it. I can *not* teach."

"Oh, but I think you can," Erma said in that enigmatic way she had. "Mary Kate, there is a remarkable porosity in a one-room schoolhouse. A lesson given to one age group will find its way into others as well. You watch and see. Soon, you will have that entire schoolroom functioning like a well-oiled machine."

She asked about each of the students, and M.K. surprised herself at how much she knew about each one. Much, much more than she had thought she did. "There's a new girl who looks at me as if I'm a stray cat—pitiful and unwanted."

Erma stared at M.K. Then, her little shoulders began to shake, at first only slightly, and then more heavily, until her tiny wrinkled face broke open with a whoop of raspy laughter. She laughed and laughed until tears ran down her face. M.K. felt indignant. She wasn't trying to be funny! She was only trying to describe the way Jenny looked at her—as if she had no idea how M.K. ended up as a teacher. M.K. had the same thought.

An hour later, M.K. walked back to Windmill Farm feeling better about everything. Erma had that effect on her. She was an odd person in a lot of ways, full of contrasts. She was one hundred years old, but thought and acted like a much younger person. She lived alone but loved people.

As M.K. hopped a fence to shortcut through the Smuckers' goat pasture, there was something else about Erma that kept rolling around in her mind. When Erma was with you, she was really, really with you. She was totally focused on you. She fixed her eyes on you and looked at you as if you were saying the most important thing in the world. She would cock her head sympathetically, ask pertinent questions, and offer her opinions tactfully.

Unlike Fern, who never concerned herself with tactfulness.

As M.K. turned up the drive to Windmill Farm, she stopped to get the mail and braced herself to be met with a scolding from Fern. She knew she was running late.

But no! Fern didn't even seem to notice she had gone missing all afternoon. Fern was turning the kitchen inside and out, looking for her coffee can of spare cash. She barely looked up when M.K. came inside.

M.K. tossed the mail on the kitchen table. "What are you looking for?"

"You didn't take my coffee can, did you?"

"No. Of course not."

M.K.'s father came inside and noticed the two women taking things out of cupboards.

"Amos, I can't find my coffee can," Fern said. "You didn't move it, did you?"

"No," Amos said, washing his hands at the sink. "Why would I?"

Fern eyed him. "Well, you were the last one who had it. You've been paying that new hired boy cash from it each night."

Amos grabbed a dishrag. "I always put it back where I found it."

"Wasn't gone yesterday." She opened up another cupboard. "Near on two hundred dollars, if a penny."

M.K. thought for a moment. "Dad, was the new hired hand in the kitchen with you when you paid him?"

Fern stilled a moment as she waited for Amos's answer.

Amos looked from M.K. to Fern. "Now, wait just a minute. You shouldn't be tossing accusations at anyone."

Fern frowned. "I have yet to meet this fellow. He's as skittish as a young colt."

Another mystery! M.K. was intrigued. "Who is this fellow, Dad?"

Amos frowned. "He's the hardest worker I've ever seen."

M.K. hopped up on the kitchen counter, then hopped off again when Fern scowled at her. "Dad, what else do you know about him?"

Amos tossed the dishrag on the counter. "I know that he didn't take money from Fern's coffee can. That's what I know." He noticed the mail on the table and skimmed through it. Then he took his mail to his desk in the living room.

M.K. turned to Fern. "Erma Yutzy said she was looking around for some cash that had gone missing."

"You were at Erma's today?" Fern looked pleased.

"I happened to be walking by her house."

"It's out of the way."

"Not today it wasn't." The more M.K. thought about it, the more she thought there might be a connection. According to the *Adventures of Sherlock Holmes*, a person needed motive and opportunity. She walked to the doorjamb of the living room. "Dad, do you happen to know if that hired hand is working anywhere else?"

"Yes," Amos said, leaning back in his desk chair. "Erma Yutzy's. She's been needing someone to mow her lawn once a week because her great-grandnephew fell out of a tree and broke his arm."

M.K. gave Fern a "See? I told you so!" look, but Fern didn't pay her any mind. She was looking through another cupboard for her coffee can. Clearly, this hired hand had plenty of opportunity. But what would be his motive? "Dad, tell me everything you know about this hired hand."

"I know two things. His name is Chris Yoder. And he's a hard worker." He put on his glasses to read a letter, a signal that he was done talking.

M.K. gave up trying to pry information from him and went back to the kitchen. She reached into the fruit bowl for an apple and took a bite, deep in thought. "I met a fellow named Chris Yoder on the road today. Strange man. Rather accusatory." She chewed and swallowed. "You know what I would do? I would keep a very close eye on that hired hand, that's what I would do. Sounds like this fellow might have a case of sticky fingers."

"You try to make things too simple," Fern said, her head in a cupboard. "You try to make life too simple."

But to M.K., it *was* all so simple. Chris Yoder had been on these very farms and money had gone missing. The two facts seemed to be inextricably linked.

7

M.K. couldn't sleep. Too much on her mind. Too hot a night. Why did they have school in September, anyway? It still felt like summer. If she were on the school board, she would only require pupils to attend school in January, when nothing much else was going on. However, she was happy to remember that she would not be teaching school in January, and not just because she hadn't paid any attention to Orin Stoltzfus's instructions about that coal heater.

Three more days. Just three more days and she could retire from teaching. Ah, bliss!

M.K. had the same feeling she got when she came to the last chapter of a book: a little sorry to see it end but already anticipating the start of a new story. Her time as a teacher for Twin Creeks School was nearly over. The ordeal had been grueling at times, but she had done a good deed by substituting for Alice Smucker. No scholar had died under her care, and two of Eugene's cohorts had started to stay for the entire day. She could leave with a sense of satisfaction. Her teaching career would be over. Done. Finished!

She wondered if she should give the class a formal farewell on Friday afternoon or simply disappear. In the end, she decided that she would make a formal announcement.

She got out of bed and crossed to the window. She sat on the sill and looked at the moon hanging low in the black velvet sky. Thin wispy clouds moved slowly in front of it. The sun would be rising in Athens, Greece, about now.

In her mind, she saw herself climbing up a steep path, walking past white stucco houses with blue shutters, and window boxes filled with red geraniums. She imagined stopping at one point to gaze at the Aegean Sea, far below the Greek village. What words would she use to describe the color of that sea? Turquoise? Azure? Cobalt?

In the quiet of the night, a horse whinnied and another answered back. She leaned her head against the window and set aside her imagined Grecian journey. She reviewed the sheep farmer's murder one more time. She was heading down the street, away from the farmer's pasture. Had she seen anything suspicious as she scooted past the pasture? Nothing came to mind. She didn't even remember seeing the farmer, but there were trees in the pasture. She did remember noticing some sheep along the fence, trying to eat grass outside the fence. She smiled—even animals thought grass was greener on the other side of the fence. Maybe it wasn't, maybe it was. But oh, wouldn't it be wonderful to find out?

When she had reached the far edge of the pasture, she heard the shot and practically fell off her scooter. An eerie stillness followed. One long minute. Then another. And then came a sound.

M.K.'s eyes went wide. Horse hooves! She had heard horse hooves! Somewhere, a horse galloped away. Why didn't she remember it? Was it such a familiar sound to her that she blocked it out? She squeezed her eyes shut—trying, trying, *trying* to remember. Black. Something black. A flash of black. Way down the road, a flash of black. A horse.

She gasped. Her eyes flew open.

It was that which put M.K. on high alert. A Pandora's box of accusations had cracked open in her mind.

She had seen Chris Yoder's black stallion gallop away from the murder scene.

As Chris woke to the sound of rain on the roof, he stretched and yawned. His mind went through a checklist of tasks at Windmill Farm that he and Amos had discussed yesterday: hay cutting, apple picking, pear picking. Amos had said he would teach Chris how to prune the fruit trees, come winter. "Not a single cut is made without a reason," he told Chris.

Chris smiled. He could tell that Amos loved those orchards. He tended them like Old Deborah had tended her herb garden. Amos was a warm, loving man with a keen intellect. He was grateful to God for leading him to work for a man like Amos Lapp. Chris was learning quite a bit from him about how to manage a well-run farm, and he needed to get that experience if he were to have a farm of his own one day.

It was more than that, though. Chris was always drawn to wise, older men as father figures. He guarded his countenance carefully, but he valued those few men in his life who had taken an interest in him. He watched them carefully, studied them. They had taught him how to be a man.

He slipped his feet over the edge of his bed and walked to the window to see how hard the rain was coming down. He might try to get over to Windmill Farm today to talk to Amos about selling the apples and pears at the farmer's market in Stoney Ridge. A few days ago, he had wandered among the vendors. He recognized one person—that fellow who hung around Windmill Farm a lot. Jimmy Fisher, Amos called him. He was selling eggs at a booth to a long line of customers.

An empty booth sat next to Jimmy Fisher and that was when it occurred to Chris that Amos should consider selling apples and pears at the market. He knew Amos had an arrangement to sell most of the varieties to Carrie and Amos Miller so they could make Five Apple Cider, but this year, after a bumper crop, there would still be more apples to sell. More, even, than could be sold at Fern's roadside stand.

Chris sought out the market manager and learned that renting a booth would only cost 10 percent of the day's take. The market manager told him he could have the empty spot next to the Fishers'. That was an added bonus, the market manager said, because there was a local shortage of farm fresh eggs. Egg tended to draw customers to a produce stand. And those good-looking Fisher boys tended to draw customers, he added. Especially female customers.

Then Chris told him he wanted to sell Windmill Farm's apples and pears. The market manager's face fell. "Oh, we have more apples and pears than we can sell. If I let Amos Lapp's orchard fruit in here, it would drive down the prices for my other vendors." He scratched his neck, then his face brightened. "We're short on lettuces. There's big market demand. Ever thought of starting a market garden?"

Chris hadn't, but he did now. He didn't have the space he would need for a garden at his grandfather's house, but Amos had plenty of space. He wondered if he could talk Amos and Fern into letting him work a fallow section of the vegetable garden to sell produce at the market.

Farming was starting to interest him in a way he had never thought about—he had never felt more purposeful, more optimistic about the future. It *was* a good decision to come to Stoney Ridge. Everything, finally, was starting to come together. What he discovered about farming was that a man's worth was judged not by where he started, but where he ended up.

Mary Kate Lapp was no detective, but she was able to put two and two together and draw a conclusion in a matter of seconds—a new neighbor with a mysterious past had moved into Stoney Ridge just a month ago, money started to go missing in the sleepy little town, and a farmer had been shot dead in the middle of his sheep pasture. It was an alarming set of coincidences!

Early in the morning, an hour before school started, M.K. knocked on the sheriff's window.

He beckoned her inside and pointed to a chair facing his desk. "Can I get you some coffee?"

Coffee? Did he think she was here for a friendly chat? She shook her head. "I thought of something! Evidence! Significant evidence. The last piece in the puzzle."

The sheriff took a noticeable breath. "What's the puzzle?"

What puzzle? "The sheep farmer's murder! I've figured out who did it. I'm absolutely convinced. And I think he's also the coffee can thief!"

Clearly, the sheriff did not understand the full import of this discovery. He took a sip of coffee. Maybe he required a lot of caffeine to wake up. "What coffee can thief are you talking about?"

"The one who is stealing coffee cans in Amish kitchens! Everyone's talking about it. He's living at Colonel Mitchell's house. That would be considered squatting. Or maybe breaking and entering."

The sheriff stilled. "Colonel Mitchell's?"

She nodded. "That's what I've been trying to tell you! The murderer is right under our noses!"

"Slow down, M.K. Start at the beginning." He lowered his voice as he spoke, as if he was trying to talk someone out of jumping off the ledge of a tall building. Did he think she was crazy?

She glanced at the clock on the wall. She had to get to the school soon. Sometimes, it seemed as if she needed to do everything in this town.

"Looks like the rain isn't going to let up," Chris said. "Which means no hay cutting over at Windmill Farm." Chris gave Jenny that piece of news as they ate their breakfast of oatmeal and strawberry preserves. It was all she could muster together to eat quickly in the horrible kitchen, and besides, the stove wouldn't stay lit for more than two minutes. "We can get a lot done on the house today."

Jenny didn't respond. She didn't like the way Chris said "we" every time he decided something needed to be done. It meant that Jenny's free reading time after school would disappear. And for what? This old place was a dump. She didn't know why Chris wanted to come here—she thought they could have moved in with some other family back in Old Deborah's church—maybe the Troyers. That's what she loved most about the Amish. It was like having this huge family, with aunts and uncles and a zillion cousins. But Chris was adamant that they needed to go back to Grandfather Mitchell's house and fix it up. He said it was their legacy. Whenever she objected, he only said to trust him.

Chris closed up the small Igloo he had bought for Jenny after she complained about carrying a brown bag, and set it on the tile countertop. "Okay, your lunch is packed," he said. "Don't be late for school." He pointed to the umbrella. "Don't forget that."

"You treat me like I can't remember anything."

"You forgot once."

"That was a long time ago, Chris. I was twelve." She grabbed the Igloo and stomped to the door.

"Jenny!" Chris called. When she spun around, he gently tossed the umbrella at her.

Maybe, she thought, as she opened the umbrella on the front porch, maybe after Chris fixed up the house, he would change his mind about having Mom come live with them. Then Mom could have a place to call home. They could start over, the three of them. Mom would stay off drugs after this last stint in the rehab center. Maybe they could finally be like everybody else, and Jenny wouldn't feel as if she was always on the outside looking in.

She passed by three Amish farms on her way to the schoolhouse. She would look up and see the family working around the yards, moms and daughters hanging laundry on the clothesline, fathers and sons walking to the barn. A deep, inside-out longing always swept through her. The hardest thing of all was when she caught a whiff of dinner cooking at someone's house. Those savory aromas made her eyes fill up with tears, sadness spilling over. She heard someone say once that you can't miss what you've never had. That was one of the dumbest things she had ever heard. She never had a normal family and she missed it every single day.

She saw a car heading toward her on the narrow road so she walked to the very edge and waited until it passed. She sucked in her breath when she saw it was a police car and didn't let the breath out until it passed her by. Police cars always reminded her of her mother.

It wasn't fair, no. None of it was fair.

It didn't bother Chris to have a rainy day today, even if it meant he missed a day's income. He could use a full day to work on the house. He walked around the downstairs rooms, coffee cup in hand, trying to decide where to start the day's work. He made a list of the things he had done and things still to do, which was much longer. Jenny would vehemently disagree, but it was in surprisingly good condition for an old, abandoned house. He wished he had a boatload of cash to do right by the house—new double-paned windows, new countertops in the kitchen to replace the cracked tiles. But all in all, his plan was coming along, right on schedule. Fresh paint was a wonderful resource too. He was doing the things he could afford to do and it was making a difference. It was the best he could do. In the silence that wasn't quite silence—the clock ticking softly, the rain dripping on the roof—his thoughts traveled to his grandfather. He thought the Colonel would be pleased with the repairs to the house.

Replace drywall in the kitchen. ✓

Sand and patch and paint the front door. ✓

Rip out dry rot in bathroom flooring. ✓

Replace flooring in bathroom.

Repaint interior and exterior.

Recaulk windows.

Sand wooden floors and stain. Varnish.

Chris went back downstairs to prepare the caulking gun to recaulk the windows. He had noticed some staining on the drywall under those windows that faced east—the direction most of the storms came from. When he examined where the water was coming from, he could see that the caulking was gone.

Chris started to caulk the windows facing east and, just to be safe, decided he would later seal all the windows. Outside, the storm was starting to ratchet up. The rain was coming down in sheets. He hoped Jenny had made it to the schoolhouse without getting soaked.

Someone knocked on the door, interrupting him. Had Jenny forgotten something? Chris opened the door to a police officer on his porch. He felt as though someone had punched him in the stomach. It was never good news when the police came to his house. The last time he had opened the door to a police officer, he found out that his mother had been arrested again.

"Are you Chris Yoder?"

Chris's heart thumped so violently he could hardly breathe. "I am."

"I'm Sheriff Hoffman. I'd like you to come down to the police station with me and answer a few questions."

"To the police station? Why? For what purpose?"

"I need to ask you a few questions."

"Am I being arrested?"

Sheriff Hoffman tilted his head. "Should you be? Have you broken the law, Mr. Yoder?"

"Of course not. But I have a right to know why you want to take me to the police station."

"I just want to talk to you." The sheriff looked past Chris into the house. "You're new around here, aren't you? Mind if I come in?"

Chris stepped away from the door and the sheriff walked in.

He took a few steps around and whistled. "Lots of work to do."

Chris held up the caulking gun. "That's what I'm trying to do."

"Mind telling me what you're doing here?"

"I'm fixing up my grandfather's house."

"Who was your grandfather?"

"Mitchell. Colonel Mitchell. I called him the Colonel. Everybody did."

The sheriff flipped a light switch but nothing came on. Chris had never called the electric company to turn the electricity on. No need.

The sheriff looked Chris up and down. "Mitchell isn't a Plain name."

"No."

"But you're Plain."

"I was raised Plain. I am Plain. I've been baptized."

The sheriff moved into the kitchen and pushed his booted heel against a worn-out spot in the flooring. "You thinking about ripping up that old linoleum?"

"Maybe."

"Might have hardwoods underneath. My mother's kitchen had indoor/outdoor carpet on top. After she passed, we ripped it up and voilà! Hardwoods." He snapped his fingers, as if it was easy.

Chris knew the sheriff was trying to make him relax. But he had a very bad feeling about this visit.

The sheriff hooked his hands on his hips. "Any chance you happened to be at the farm of Raymond Gould, a sheep farmer, on the afternoon of August 18?"

Chris took a deep breath. "Yes. I was."

M.K. started each morning with roll call. She wasn't really sure why it was necessary—but that was what Alice Smucker had done, and Gid too, so she thought it must be necessary. When she came to the eighth grade, she called out, "Jenny Yoder." Jenny raised her hand.

"Yoder? Jenny Yoder?" Something clicked. "Is Chris Yoder any relation to you?"

Jenny nodded. "He's my brother."

M.K. was a little stunned. She hadn't expected the sheep murderer and coffee can thief to be anybody's brother. She stood quietly, studying Jenny. Granted, Jenny didn't resemble her brother—she had dark auburn hair and he was fair-haired. Except for the color of her blue eyes, they looked nothing alike. He was tall and muscular, she was short and bird-thin. Still, how had she not put the two of them together? M.K. did have a lot on her mind—but she was usually so good at making those kinds of connections.

M.K. heard the rumble of thunder and hurried to shut the schoolhouse windows. Through the window, she noticed the sheriff's car drive slowly past the schoolhouse. In the backseat was Chris Yoder.

As the car passed by, Chris looked over at the schoolhouse. For one brief second, their eyes met.

M.K. spun around to see if Jenny had seen her brother in the police car, but her head was bent over, tucked into the book she was supposed to be reading from. It was a strategy M.K. had used many times herself. A terrible feeling flooded through M.K. When she went to see the sheriff this morning, she hadn't really thought through that Chris Yoder might be arrested and hauled off to jail.

But if he was a thief and a murderer, jail was where he belonged.

Unless, pointed out a small voice in her head that sounded a good deal like Fern, unless . . . he's not guilty. Unless Mary Kate had no right to accuse another person of crimes. Unless he was another Plain person—one of her own. Unless she had no business meddling in police business.

M.K. felt the courage she had started the day with drip away like ice cream on a July afternoon. She interfered with something she should have left alone.

What if Chris Yoder were found guilty? But what if Chris Yoder *was* guilty?

What have I done? M.K. thought. *What have I done?*

As soon as Jimmy heard the news from his brother Paul, who heard it from a girl he was dating, who heard it from her friend who answered the phone part-time at the sheriff's office, he rushed over to tell M.K. He could hardly wait. This was going to be a delicious moment.

The Lapp family was just sitting down to supper as Jimmy rapped on the kitchen door.

Fern opened the door to him. "You have an unusual knack for appearing at mealtimes," she said, as if she wasn't at all surprised—or excited, either—to see him.

Jimmy was in too generous a frame of mind to worry about that. Besides, Fern was already setting another place at the table for him.

Fern's cooking was legendary, so Jimmy was happy to be invited to stay. He took his time, waiting for just the right moment. The moment had to be perfect. M.K. had been cranky lately, with this school teaching and all, so Jimmy thought this would be just the thing to snap her out of her funk.

Finally, in between supper and dessert, Jimmy leaned back in his chair. "So, it turns out that the culprit has been found for the murdered sheep farmer."

"I know," M.K. said quietly.

"You knew? You knew?" Jimmy was astounded. How did she know things faster than he did? She was stuck in a schoolhouse all day! She looked at him strangely, pale and unhappy. "Are you all right? Are you sick?"

"I'm fine," she said, but she didn't sound at all fine.

Come to think of it, she hadn't talked during supper either. Uncle Hank did most of the talking.

"BOY, WE'RE ON THE EDGE OF OUR SEATS!" Uncle Hank roared. "Don't keep us waiting."

All eyes were upon Jimmy—his favorite moment. "As you know, the sheriff has been baffled over this murder."

"Tell us something we don't know," M.K. added mournfully.

Jimmy leaned forward in his chair. He lowered his voice to add suspense. "No one else was around, and no footprints led to or from the scene of the crime. But our trusty investigators sifted through the meager clues surrounding the farmer's death, and they have fingered the culprit." He pointed his finger in the air for a dramatic touch.

Uncle Hank sat straight up in his chair. "WHO? WHO?"

"Turns out the farmer had fallen asleep amidst his sheep without securing his rifle."

"AND?" Uncle Hank yelled. Fern looked at him, annoyed.

Now Jimmy was in his dramatic element. "A moment of neglect, another one of leisure, a wooly hoof on the trigger, and a speeding slug sentenced the sleeping shepherd to his final slumber."

All faces were blank. It was Fern who put it together first. "One of his sheep stepped on the rifle?"

Jimmy grinned. "The coroner's report came back from the autopsy—something to do with the angle of the bullet. It was the only logical conclusion."

"When did they figure it out?" M.K. asked meekly.

"Today," Jimmy said. "I guess they found a witness who saw the whole thing and it all added up to what they had been thinking. You can all sleep easier tonight. The weapon has been confiscated from the flock. The perpetrator has confessed and the judge has handed down the sentence." Jimmy had been waiting to deliver this line all afternoon: "The guilty party has been sentenced to ewe-thanasia."

A moment of silence followed. Then, Uncle Hank and Amos burst into laughter. Jimmy joined in. Tears flowed down their cheeks. Their guffaws were so loud and out of control that Fern and M.K. grew thoroughly disgusted. They gathered up plates and took them to the kitchen, leaving the men to howl like a pack of hyenas, Fern said. But Fern was not the laughing kind.

Jimmy wiped tears from his eyes. "One more thing, M.K. Now there's no reason keeping you from introducing me to Emily Esh!" He turned back to Amos and Uncle Hank and started laughing all over again.

M.K. felt a surge of jangly nerves as she sloshed the dishes with soapy water. The minute Jimmy walked through the door, she knew he had on his I-know-something-you-don't smile. Now she understood why.

She had been so sure, so absolutely, positively sure that Chris Yoder was the culprit. Maybe he had lied to the sheriff. But then, there was that autopsy finding. Forensic science was quite accurate. She knew that to be true because she read it in her *Unsolved Crimes* magazine.

Jimmy sidled into the kitchen. "So, I sure hope your dad and Fern don't have to leave town, thanks to you not setting a good example for the community. All eyes are upon the teacher, I hope you know."

"What are you jabbering about now?"

He grabbed a dish towel and pretended to help her dry the dishes. "Seeing as how you were escorted home by a very important means of transportation the other night." Carefully, he enunciated, "It involved a police car."

M.K. froze. The soapy dish she was washing was suspended in air.

Jimmy whistled two notes. "Did the sheriff cuff you before he took you home?"

She narrowed her eyes. "What do you know about anything?"

"You mean . . . your transportation in a police car?" he reminded. Again, he enunciated the words *police car* with utmost care. He took the dish out of her hands and rinsed it off, calmly drying it.

"I wasn't doing anything wrong," she spat out. "I was trying to help and—" Just then, Fern came into the kitchen with a few condiments to put in the refrigerator and M.K. knew enough to snap her mouth shut. This conversation with Jimmy Fisher would have to wait.

"Why, there it is!" Fern said. "I completely forgot I had put it there while I was cleaning out cupboards."

"What?" M.K. said.

Fern spun around. In her hand was the coffee can that held her spare cash.

M.K. dropped a wet, soapy dish on the floor and it shattered into pieces. *What have I done?* she thought. *What have I done?*

8

Chris tossed the forkful of hay into Samson's makeshift stall, in the garage-turned-barn. Then he clipped a lead rope to Samson's harness and led him outside to brush him down. He stroked the brush across Samson's withers, and the horse nickered, nudging Chris's shoulder with his nose. Normally Chris would laugh at the horse's antics, but not now. Not after a day like today.

Currycombing the horse was Chris's way to calm down and sort things out. Samson was annoyed that dinner was getting delayed, but tonight, it would have to wait. Chris still felt shaky inside after being hauled off to the police station like a common criminal. He was even more shocked by how the conversation with the sheriff had unfolded.

"So, Chris Yoder, tell me why you were at Raymond Gould's farm on the afternoon of August 28th," the sheriff had said as he settled into the chair behind his desk.

"I had been doing odd jobs around Stoney Ridge. I found the jobs on the bulletin board at the hardware store in town. Raymond Gould needed someone to lift hay into his barn loft, so I went over to his farm that morning and he hired me for the rest of the day. Said he has—said he had—a bad back."

The sheriff scribbled down notes as Chris spoke. "Go on."

"I was up in the hayloft, using a pulley to haul bales of hay into the loft. I heard a gunshot go off and looked out the door at the end of the barn.

Down in the pasture was the farmer, Raymond Gould, sprawled flat on his back, and a bunch of frightened sheep."

"No one else?"

"No one. I had a pretty good vantage point from the upper story of the barn."

"Then what?"

"I scrambled down from the hayloft and took off on my horse to call for an ambulance. I remembered that I had passed by a phone shanty near the schoolhouse."

"And then?"

"I went back to the farm, waited until I heard the police sirens, and left."

"You didn't bother to give Gould CPR?"

"I don't have any idea how to give someone CPR." He turned the brim of his straw hat around and around. "Look, Sheriff, I've been around farm animals enough to know when a creature still has life in it. I have to say, Raymond Gould looked pretty dead from the barn." Chris pointed to his head. "The bullet, well, it—"

The sheriff waved that thought off. "Yeah, yeah." He jotted down a few more notes.

Chris was growing impatient. "Am I under arrest? I didn't do anything wrong."

The sheriff leaned back in his chair. "No. Your story checks out. We have two calls coming in, five minutes apart, from the schoolhouse phone. And the coroner's report corroborates your story. Turns out a sheep stepped on the rifle. The safety wasn't on."

"Then, can I go?" Chris started to rise in the chair.

"Not so fast. I've got a few more questions for you." The sheriff tossed down his pen and fixed his gaze on Chris. "If you weren't guilty, then why did you act guilty? Why did you leave the scene?"

Chris stifled a groan. He cleared his throat and tried to answer calmly. "I could see things were taken care of. I had nothing to add. I didn't see the actual shooting. I would have just gotten in the way."

The sheriff raised his eyebrows. "Or maybe you didn't want the authorities to know you were in town."

Maybe. "I haven't done anything wrong. Can I go?"

"Just a few more questions."

"Like what?"

"Like your real name."

"I've told you. Christopher Yoder."

"Your father's name was Yoder?"

"I don't know who my father was."

"Where'd you pick up the name Yoder?"

"My foster mother. She raised me."

"She adopted you?"

"No. Not officially."

"Then why don't you tell me what your legal name is?"

Chris sighed. "Mitchell. Christopher Mitchell."

"Tell me about your mother."

Chris snapped his head up. "What about her?"

"For starters, what is her name?"

"Grace. Grace Mitchell." Chris rubbed his temples. His mother's name always seemed ironic to him. It was as if his grandparents must have known she would require a lot of grace in life.

The sheriff scribbled it down. "Grace Mitchell." He looked up. "Where is she now?"

Chris wanted to tell the sheriff that his mother was none of his business. He hated sharing his personal life with anyone, much less this arrogant officer. But he feared the sheriff would continue to harass him unless he answered his questions. He cleared the lump from his throat again. "I haven't had any contact with her in quite some time." That was the truth.

The sheriff leaned forward in his chair. "Let me be straight with you, Chris . . . Yoder or Mitchell or whoever you are. And maybe, then, you will be straight with me. What I want to know is what happened in your grandfather's house, fourteen years ago."

Whoa. Why was the sheriff ripping the scab off this old wound? *Leave it alone!* Chris pleaded silently. That was such a long time ago. That was the last day he had ever seen his grandfather.

Jimmy Fisher left Windmill Farm after extracting a promise from M.K. to introduce him to Emily Esh. As soon as he disappeared around the bend in the road, M.K. set out for Erma Yutzy's house. This morning's storm clouds had been blown away by a change in the wind, and the evening sky was high and open. She found Erma, as usual, bent over in the garden, weeding.

"Hello, Erma," M.K. called out as she crossed over a row of spinach seedlings.

Erma lifted her head and blinked a few times. "Well, well. My new young friend is here." She leaned on her cane as she straightened up and shielded her eyes from the setting sun. "Can I get you a piece of apple snitz? I just took it out of the oven."

M.K. smiled and shook her head. No one came or went from a Plain home without being fed. "I just finished supper. I was passing by and thought I'd say hello."

But Erma couldn't be fooled. She took a few steps closer to her, pausing for a moment, sizing up M.K.'s mood. "Weeding is good for a heavy heart."

"Really?"

"When you weed, you get rid of the things that distract a plant from growing." Erma watched her for a long moment, then grinned. "It's a metaphor, Mary Kate."

Oh. *Oh!*

"And there are a lot of weeds." Erma pointed to a row of carrots and radishes. "I could sure use some help."

The two women worked their way down the row, carefully tugging weeds without uprooting carrot seedlings. About halfway down the row, M.K. quietly said, "Erma, how do you make something right when you've done something wrong?"

Slowly, Erma straightened up and leaned on her knees. "You ask for forgiveness and try to get things back on track, that's what you do."

"That's it?"

"That's it," Erma said. She pointed to the carrots. "Keep weeding."

Twenty minutes later, Erma's carrots and radishes were safe from the distractions of intruding weeds, and M.K. said goodbye.

As M.K. scooted down the street that led to Colonel Mitchell's house, she wondered what she might find—was Jenny left alone while her brother was thrown in jail today? Was Chris still in jail? M.K. felt terrible. When would she ever learn? This was just the kind of thing Fern was always getting after her for—she acted first and thought second. She had sent someone to jail today! And he wasn't even guilty. Oh, what would her father say if he found out? She hoped he never would.

She zoomed past Colonel Mitchell's driveway the first time, but found it on the second pass. The house was on a flag lot, sitting way back from the road, its long drive edged with overgrown bushes on both sides, hidden from the street. At the end of the long driveway, the house loomed, pale white in the gathering purple dusk. Fireflies flickered in the canopy of the trees, and whip-poor-wills chirped from the high grass. Fat, fuzzy bumblebees hovered in the warm evening air. Under normal conditions, she would stop to identify the variety of bumblebees. Maybe follow them to their hives. Not tonight, though. Tonight wasn't a normal night.

As she neared the house, she slowed, astounded. It was a stately old home, in utter neglect. Something wiggled around in her memory. She suddenly realized that the house backed up to the stand of pine trees on the far edge of Windmill Farm—not far from the honey cabin. If she didn't have the scooter, she could probably get home quicker by slipping through the fields. She set the scooter down, took a deep breath, and started for the porch but stopped when she saw Chris lead a horse out to a hitching post.

Well, at least he wasn't in jail! That was good news.

She smoothed her skirt and took another deep breath before she approached Chris. "Hello."

He looked over the neck of the horse at her, didn't say anything, but calmly continued with his grooming, running the brush down the animal's flank. For a long minute M.K. just watched him. It struck her all of a sudden that he was a very handsome young man, clean-cut and wholesome looking.

She tried again. "We haven't been formally introduced. I'm Mary Kate Lapp. Apparently you have been working for my father, Amos Lapp."

"You look like a Lapp," Chris said.

He didn't seem at all angry. Maybe the sheriff hadn't told him who had turned him in. Maybe that piece of information could remain between her and the sheriff. In her detective books, the witness was always protected. Maybe that's what the sheriff had done. She stood up straighter. Everything was going to be all right! Maybe there was no harm done, other than a minor interruption in Chris Yoder's day. Maybe . . .

"Coming by to see if I got let out of the slammer?"

Oh. She knotted her hands, not knowing what she should say. No, that wasn't true. She knew what to say. She just wasn't accustomed to saying it. Finally, she pushed out the words that needed to be said. "I came over to apologize."

"For knocking me in the ditch? For treating me like I was a leper when I offered to give you a ride home? For turning me in to the sheriff on trumped-up charges?"

Okay. Maybe this wasn't going to be easy. It was obvious she had touched a raw nerve. "Yes. For all those things. I am . . . sorry."

"You should be."

"I am."

Chris walked around her and started brushing the horse's other side. He seemed to have forgotten she was here.

She turned to leave, when suddenly he said, "Any particular reason why you've got a grudge against me?"

She spun around. "No! I don't have a grudge. I just . . . I heard the gunshot that day and remembered your pitch-black horse galloping away and then Fern's coffee can had gone missing—and it all seemed to make sense. Like puzzle pieces that fit together. But I didn't think it all through. I got so excited that I didn't think it through. It's one of my worst faults, Fern says. Acting without thinking."

Chris looked at her, confused, squinting at her as if he couldn't understand her. She knew she was babbling.

"Who's Fern?"

"She's my stepmother."

He nodded. But then he turned his attention back to the horse. "So what's this about the coffee can gone missing?"

"Oh that. Well, that, too, was a misunderstanding. Fern thought it was stolen—" she frowned—"come to think of it, she didn't really think that. She just couldn't remember where she had put it. Turns out she put it in the refrigerator while she was cleaning out cupboards. You see, she takes housecleaning very seriously. Always has. She takes it a little too seriously,

I have often thought." She stopped, realizing she was babbling again. "So it's been found. The coffee can."

She turned to leave again, but then he said, "Since when do Plain people turn on each other?"

She spun around. "Well, you see, that was another thing I hadn't thought through."

He nodded, as if he agreed, and stroked the horse's long back with two soft brushes. One hand over the other, brushing, brushing, brushing, until that pitch-black horse shined like shoe polish.

She decided she'd had enough questions. It was time to ask Chris Yoder a few questions. "You have to admit it's a little unusual to have a young man arrive in this little town out of the blue."

"Something wrong with this town?"

"No, but it's pretty small. Everybody knows everybody's business. Except for your business. And you have a knack for staying out of sight. You haven't shown up at church or any singings. Fern says you won't have lunch with her or Dad. You don't go to church." She tilted her head. "You look Amish, you speak Penn Dutch, but you don't have an accent. It's like you learned it as a second language."

Chris took his time responding. He didn't look away. His gaze was as calm as morning, direct. He stopped brushing the horse and spoke carefully. "Is that what you think I'm doing here? Masquerading as an Amish man?"

Just like that, their fragile truce evaporated. She wasn't born yesterday. He was answering a question with a question. He was just like Sheriff Hoffman—information only traveled down a one-way street. Same thing. Well, she had done what she came to do. Again, she whirled around to leave.

"I've got something of yours. You dropped it on the road the other day. The day when you treated me like I had a contagious disease."

She spun around. He pulled a piece of paper out of his pocket and handed it to her. She knew what it was the moment she saw it: the passport application. She glanced at him, wondering if he had looked at it. Of course he had. He was trying not to smile.

"Any particular reason why you might need to get out of the country quickly?"

She tucked the paper into her apron pocket, trying to look dignified. "One never knows what the future holds."

His face eased a little. "Especially when a person accuses innocent people of murder and burglary. I can definitely see how such a habit might require one to flee the country."

"I wouldn't call it a habit." She frowned.

"What would you call it?"

"A misunderstanding. And since we've cleared this little misunderstanding up—"

This time he did smile, but his smile did not warm the blue of his eyes. "Little misunderstanding? You accuse me of murdering a man? Of stealing from the home of the man who has given me work? You call that a little misunderstanding?"

Here, M.K. nearly faltered. She straightened her shoulders. "I felt it was my duty to protect the citizens of Stoney Ridge." But she knew. She knew. She had made a terrible blunder. Her imagination had always been her biggest problem.

"From a trigger-happy sheep? And a coffee can hidden in the refrigerator?"

A familiar voice behind M.K. gave her a start. "*She's* the one who turned you in to the sheriff? She's the one who's been meddling in our business?" M.K. turned slowly to face the voice.

Jenny Yoder was staring at her with her sharp, birdlike look.

"How do you two know each other?" Chris asked.

"Because *she's* the substitute teacher I've been telling you about," Jenny said in a flat, cold voice. She looked at M.K. with unconcealed suspicion.

Chris looked at M.K., then at Jenny, then back at M.K. "This is the teacher you described as dumb as a box of rocks?" Then he looked back at M.K., shocked.

She was even more shocked! She had been called many things in her nineteen years—impulsive, overzealous, far too curious. But when, in her entire life, had anyone ever thought of her as dumb? Dumb? She was outraged.

M.K. had enough. She marched to her scooter, picked it up, and zoomed down the drive.

The day had started out so nicely, but it was ending as a terrible day for M.K. One of the worst.

But she had discovered something tonight. Chris Yoder carried secrets. And M.K. wanted to find out what they were.

The ante was sky-high. Jimmy Fisher had found just the right horse to race—a two-year-old warm-blooded Thoroughbred, steel-gray, fresh off the racetrack in Kentucky. This deep-chested horse looked like it could run a gazelle to death. He had bought the filly for a song, though he had to weasel an advance from Domino Joe, the promoter of all races, to complete the transaction. This evening's race would wipe clean his growing debt and give him a little nest egg.

Domino Joe's day job was horse trading. He purchased two- or three-year-old Thoroughbreds straight from the track in Kentucky. The horses were retired for various reasons and, with some conditioning, became excellent buggy horses for the Amish. But before Domino Joe trained them for the buggy, he ran a little side business—pony racing on the racetrack.

The racetrack wasn't really a track but a level plowed section of Domino Joe's property, far from any paved roads that Sheriff Hoffman might be moseying past. It was common knowledge but nothing anyone talked about, and Jimmy had seen just about every male he knew, Amish or otherwise, at one time or another down at Domino Joe's track. Just quietly observing.

That's all Jimmy had done too. Just quietly watched. Until a few months ago, when Domino Joe asked Jimmy if he wanted to fill in for a scratched rider. Did he? Oh, yeah. Oh yeah! Jimmy had won that race, and the next one too. Soon, he was racing at least once a week. He won some, he lost some, but then the stakes kept going up and Jimmy couldn't stop himself. He loved competition of any kind. He owed Domino Joe several hundred dollars. Maybe a thousand, if he stopped to think about it, which he preferred not to.

But that debt led him to this particular race on a late evening in September, where the stakes were high. If he won tonight, his debt would be wiped out. He was just ten minutes away from winning. He could just picture Domino Joe's surprised face as he handed him the cash.

Jimmy's heart was beating at what he felt was twice its normal rate, while the last few preparations for the race seemed to take forever. He thought

Domino Joe needed to kill time while the rest of the crowd filtered in to place their bets with a quiet word and a firm handshake. Finally, Domino Joe got things under way.

"Everybody back, give 'em room," Domino Joe directed. "Line your horses up, men!"

Jimmy was racing against three other men on their mounts. As they all led their horses to the starting line, scratched in dirt, Jimmy felt the first taste of terrible doubt. It nearly did him in. These other horses looked as if they could step over him. This felt very different from the other races Domino Joe had arranged for him. Bigger. More serious. Jimmy slipped his feet into the stirrups and settled into the leather basin of the saddle. The reins were wrapped double around his hands.

"One," Domino Joe chanted.

There was not a sound from the entire crowd.

"Two."

Each horse's tensed ears were sharpened to a point now. Jimmy's were, too.

Boom!

The horses hurtled into action. Jimmy managed a perfectly nice, orderly start, but soon, there was a wall of horses in his way, veering rumps that forced Jimmy's filly to fall back. Over the hoofbeats and horse snorts he could hear cheering and shouts of advice from the onlookers, but none of it truly registered. He was aware only that the riders of the other horses shouldered him out of the way, taking turns to rocket back and forth to keep Jimmy safely behind. He tried to collect his wits about him and focus on the turn ahead—that was where he hoped to gain his lead. By now they were thundering toward the last curve and Jimmy leaned as low as he could in the saddle, streamlining matters for the horse.

It worked. His horse seemed to sense that winning was imminent. Her ears pinned back as he stretched out and they edged ahead. They were nearing the lead! Her mane flew in the wind as Jimmy bent low over her neck. Hoof and tooth they flew, as one thought ran through Jimmy's mind: being on the back of a running horse—preferably a winning horse—was the most wonderful place in the world to be. Just one last bend in the track and he had this race won. In the bag.

But the horse didn't make the bend. Instead, she went straight and sailed over the fence. Jimmy lost his stirrups, then the reins, and tumbled off, landing in a farmer's hay shock. Shouts and hoots and whoops of laughter filled the air as men and boys ran down to get a better look at Jimmy's situation. Jimmy's horse raced on, solo, through the alfafa field.

When M.K. reached Windmill Farm, she was surprised to see Orin Stoltzfus's horse and buggy at the hitching post by the barn. Why would the head of the school board come visiting at such a late hour? Maybe he had news about Alice Smucker. Maybe her headache was gone and she was ready to come back to teach. That would mean that M.K. would be finished with teaching two days earlier than expected. Ah, bliss!

M.K. dropped the scooter and bolted up the porch stairs, two at a time, to the kitchen. She slowed before she opened the door—Fern continually pointed out that M.K. entered a room like a gust of wind. At the sight of Orin's face, she broke into a happy smile. "Orin, do you have some good news?"

Orin exchanged a glance with Amos, then Fern. Amos started to study the ceiling with great interest. Fern lowered her eyes and fixed them on her coffee cup.

Something wasn't right. M.K. felt a shiver begin at the top of her head and travel to her toes.

Orin scratched his neck. "Might as well tell you, M.K. Alice quit on us."

M.K. gasped. "But . . . isn't she getting better?"

"Actually, she said now that she's not teaching, she's feeling good. Real good. Sadie—your sister—has been trying to help heal her. Sadie told her that she thought it was the teaching that was giving her so many ailments."

M.K. understood *that*! Teaching could make anyone sick. On the heels of that thought came a terrible premonition—like a dog might feel right before an earthquake. Her eyes went wide. "You can't be thinking that I'm going to fill in for Alice for a full term. Friday is supposed to be my last day!"

Orin took a sip of coffee, as calmly as if M.K. were discussing tomorrow's weather. He avoided her eyes. "To tell the truth, Mary Kate, it's in the best interest of the pupils to have you remain. They're used to you. You're used to them." He chanced a glance at her. "And Fern tells me you're getting some mentoring from Erma Yutzy. Fern said that teaching has been a real good challenge for you."

Fern! So meddlesome.

M.K.'s heart knocked in her chest so fiercely she could scarcely breathe. This was terrible news! She looked to her father for support, but he didn't return her gaze.

She was doomed. She was only nineteen years old and already her life was over.

Later that night, as M.K. tried to sleep, a single, horrifying phrase kept rolling over and over in her mind: *Dumb as a box of rocks. Dumb as a box of rocks. Dumb as a box of rocks.*

There was no doubt in M.K.'s eyes. This was officially the worst day of her life.

9

Chris had just finished removing a broken windowpane in Jenny's bedroom and replacing it, adding a thin line of caulking around it to seal it in place. She was convinced a bat liked to come calling in her room each night to terrorize her. Chris was doubtful that the bat was so single-minded in purpose, but at least the new windowpane would keep the bat—or Jenny's imagination—at bay. He was changing the caulking cartridge when he saw a car pull into the driveway. A man got out of the car and stood in front of the house, looking up at it, before climbing up the steps.

Chris hurried downstairs and opened the door just as the man's hand was poised to knock. "Yes?"

The man looked surprised to find someone at home. Especially an Amish someone. "Well, well, you beat me to the punch." He thrust a business card at Chris. "I'm Rodney S. Graystone. Real estate salesman." He lifted one finger. "Numero uno."

Chris looked at the card.

Rodney flashed Chris a big plastic smile. "You probably recognize my face. I'm on every grocery cart at the Giant."

Chris didn't shop at the Giant supermarket. Too expensive. He and Jenny shopped at the nearby Bent N' Dent where they could buy bulk foods or damaged goods that were marked down.

"I've been interested in listing this house for years but have never been able to locate the owner." Rodney's eager eyes roved behind Chris, trying to peer into the house. "You are the owner, I presume? I, uh, didn't catch your name."

Before Chris could reply, Rodney S. Graystone spotted Jenny in the kitchen and waved boisterously to her in an overly familiar way. Chris stole a glance at the man's face and felt that his eyes were as flashy as the rest of him. His jacket was a brown plaid, and the elbows had been worn to a shine. Slippery, that's what came to Chris's mind.

Jenny disappeared from view, then peeked her head around the corner. "Adorable!" Rodney S. Graystone told Chris. "She's adorable. Same age as my niece. Is she eight? Nine?"

"Thirteen!" Jenny snapped, poking her head around the doorjamb again.

"My next guess." The man turned back to Chris. "Looks like you've been doing a lot of work." He walked up and down the porch, peering in the windows. "I take it you're fixing it up to flip it. Say, I could probably give you some pointers on remodeling—what to do and what's a waste of time."

Rodney S. Graystone was itching to get into the house and have a tour. Chris started to close the door.

"I've got a buyer who's always been interested in this old d—, uh, diamond in the rough. I'm confident I could find you a buyer—" he snapped his fingers—"in the blink of an eye. Cash on the barrel."

"Not interested in selling." Chris closed the door in Rodney S. Graystone's surprised face.

"Keep my card handy, in case you reconsider. I'll stop by now and then, just to keep checking in. In case you change your mind," came a muffled reply.

On the way to the schoolhouse in the morning, Mary Kate noticed a squirrel perched on the limb of a maple tree. It chattered at the sight of a cardinal, darting around the squirrel with a bright splash of red. She watched for a while as the squirrel scolded the cardinal for coming too close to his tree. Then the bird flew off and the squirrel scampered away.

It wouldn't be so bad to be a bird, would it? Summers wouldn't be bad. Winters might get a little challenging. She liked the idea of being able to travel to far-flung places every spring and fall. No passport needed. Birds seemed so . . . carefree.

Unlike a nineteen-year-old Amish woman who had no say-so about her life. None whatsoever. Who was stuck teaching school for an *entire* term.

Fern! *This is all your doing,* M.K. thought for the hundred and thirteenth time.

Fern was always so certain that her opinion was the only one that mattered. Fern had always been so hard on M.K. And to make everything worse, last night her father had sided with Fern. Of all the times! All M.K's life, her dad had stuck right beside her, had been her ally, had been easy to talk into agreeing with her. But when it counted most, Amos turned around and took Fern's side—insisting that M.K. fill in Alice's void.

And why did her sister Sadie have to butt her nose into it? Why did she have to point out that teaching was making Alice sick? Granted, Sadie was a healer and Alice was her husband's sister, but didn't blood sisters count more? She thought so.

M.K. wished her mother were still alive. Maggie Lapp had died when M.K. was only five and she only had wisps of memories of her. If M.K. squeezed her eyes tightly, she could conjure up a memory of her mother in the kitchen, with her black apron pinned around her waist. Under the apron, she was wearing a dark plum dress. She was humming. M.K. did remember that. Her mother was always humming.

Chocolate chip cookies. In this particular memory, that's what her mother was pulling out of the oven. They were M.K.'s favorites. Her mother would scoot them off the baking sheet with a spatula, slipping them onto a clean dish towel so they would cool. But she would always split one down the middle and hand half to M.K. "I think this cookie was hoping we would eat it first," her mother would whisper, as if they were keeping a secret from the other cookies.

Maggie Lapp would never have insisted that she finish out Alice Smucker's teaching term. She would have understood M.K.'s point of view, which was . . .

What was it? Well, that she didn't *want* to teach.

But maybe her mother would say that growing up meant you realized you didn't always get what you wanted. Growing up meant that you start to look for ways to give to others.

Wait. That sounded an awful lot like Fern.

How exasperating! M.K. was getting Fern's voice mixed up with her mother's voice.

As M.K. cut through the corner of a cornfield to reach the schoolhouse, her thoughts drifted to Jenny Yoder. *Imagine anyone calling me dumb!* Yet a little part of it felt true. About teaching . . . she did act dumb. She didn't teach. She just watched the clock.

A feeling of shame burned within her when she thought of how she handled a situation yesterday afternoon. She had caught Jenny Yoder with her nose buried in a book while the class was supposed to be doing arithmetic. M.K. took one look at the book's title, *To Kill a Mockingbird* by Harper Lee, and told Jenny to keep reading. No wonder Jenny thought she was as dumb as a box of rocks.

What is wrong with me that everything I touch turns out a chaotic mess?

She wished she could go home, fling herself across her bed, and put a pillow over her head.

Dry cornstalks started to rustle, like a small animal was following her. The brush crackled behind her and she whirled, ears straining. Suddenly, a boy's round face appeared out of the cornstalks.

M.K. let out her breath. "Danny Riehl! You gave me quite a start."

Danny looked down the dirt path at the school yard where the pupils were starting to gather. "I just thought you should know that the reason Eugene Miller leaves in the afternoon isn't because of your teaching. He slipped out a lot with Teacher Alice too."

"Why does he leave?" M.K. said.

"Because the upper grades read out loud after lunch." Danny poked his spectacles back up the bridge of his nose. "Eugene can't read very well. He doesn't want anyone to know." He squinted up at M.K. "You won't tell him I told you, will you?"

"I won't tell, Danny. Thank you."

Danny slipped back into the cornfield and disappeared. She heard more rustling, then she saw him burst through another section of the field and cross over the fence to meet his friends on the school yard. Danny could be a crackerjack detective, she thought.

Eugene Miller was drawing a picture in the dirt with a stick and stuck his foot out as Danny hurried past. Danny tripped, went flying into the dirt, picked himself up, brushed himself off, and joined his friends by the softball diamond.

So maybe Danny's detective skills needed a little bit of work.

She took a few steps, then stopped. *I am a bad teacher. I am!* M.K. realized. *And while I am not dumb, I have been acting dumb. I have been acting like a bad, dumb teacher.* There was no gainsaying what Jenny Yoder had said. It was just true. Just true.

But that was about to change.

The cramp of panic inside her chest eased a bit. She marched through the cornfield and into the schoolhouse, her sails full of wind, and dropped anchor.

Deep in the barn, Amos could hear Uncle Hank ranting and raving. He finished adding oats to Rosemary and Lavender's buckets—a small thank-you for a good day's work in the fields—and walked over to the buggy shop to see what was eating his uncle.

"I CAN'T FIND MY MONEY!" Hank roared when he saw Amos approach. "I kept it right there." He pointed to an open drawer in the workshop, filled with screwdrivers and hammers and receipts. "That's always where it's been. Until now."

Now, that was an amusing thought. Hank Lapp was many things—inventive, bighearted, a dedicated fisherman—but organized? That would be a quality Uncle Hank would never be accused of possessing. The buggy shop was a disaster. And his Dawdi Haas? Fern refused to step inside.

Come to think of it, Amos hadn't been inside Hank's apartment for over a year. For one, there was no free space to sit down. Everything was covered with newspapers and shoes and dirty laundry. And two, the heavy smell of cigar smoke made Amos hack and cough. And that brought back unpleasant memories of the year leading up to his heart transplant, when he would cough relentlessly, trying to get air.

Hank was pulling everything out of the drawers of his workshop. "Edith Fisher has been missing some cash lately too."

That was interesting. Not about the missing money—it seemed to Amos that Edith Fisher was always sputtering away about not having enough money—but it was interesting that Edith was talking to Hank again. Maybe the spurning over Doozy and the puppies wasn't as final as it first sounded.

That was another thing that puzzled Amos about women—they said things they didn't really mean. Just last night, M.K. said she wanted to move to Oslo, Norway. She thought it would be too cold for children to survive in Norway and that sounded like an ideal climate to her. Certainly, she didn't mean that. He knew she was upset about having to finish Alice's teaching term. He felt a tug of pity for her, but it vanished when he caught a warning glance from his wife. Fern knew best about this kind of thing.

Finally, Hank threw his hands in the air. "AMOS! I have come to the conclusion that there is a thief in Stoney Ridge. Maybe a crime ring. Targeting us older folks."

That, Amos thought, *or more likely, us older folks won't admit we're getting older. And forgetful.*

M.K. rang the school bell and called everyone in, five minutes before school began.

"You're too early, M.K.," Eugene Miller complained as he came inside and saw the clock.

She noticed a fresh bruise on his cheekbone. "Are you all right? How did you get that?" She reached out a hand to touch him, but he flinched and shrugged her off.

"I have some news to share," she said. "Everyone take your seats."

Eugene started to head back outdoors.

M.K. blocked the door. "I don't want any arguing. If I say something is to be done, then it is to be done. And here's another thing. From now on, you call me Teacher M.K. Is that quite clear?"

She gave Eugene a glance of reprimand. He straightened to his full height, towering over her as he glared at her. She glared back. She held his stare. She would not back down. There was too much at stake. Amazingly, he seemed to wither under her fierce glare. He smirked, turned, and plopped in his seat. The rest of the children remained still and silent, all but Barbara Jean. She nodded her small head enthusiastically.

"Teacher Alice is not going to be able to return to teach this year," M.K. said. "So I am going to be her replacement for the term."

Barbara Jean Shrock grinned.

Danny Riehl poked his glasses up the bridge of his nose.

Eugene Miller groaned.

Jenny Yoder clunked her head on her desk.

As Amos crossed the threshold of the farmhouse, he practically tripped over a cardboard box left by the kitchen door. It surprised him to see a box left out, unattended. Fern was a dedicated housekeeper—a bit on the fanatical side, he thought. He often teased her that he didn't dare release his fork during dinner for fear it would be washed and cleaned and put away before he swallowed the bite of food. To see a box left out was unusual, but there it sat, gathering dust, as Fern worked in the kitchen.

She was furiously whisking her new starter—the one she had made after M.K. had knocked over her great-great-great-grandmother's starter, which, Amos suspected, wasn't really as old as she liked to claim. But Fern did this every few days without fail—she called it refreshing her sponge. The tangy smell of yeast filled the air, so powerful that it made Amos sneeze. "A starter is a living organism," Fern often said in its defense, "that needs to be fed and tended. Like a family." He felt a wave of fondness as he watched her give the starter a good stir to bring in fresh oxygen. He sneezed and she glanced up, noticing him for the first time. "Look inside." The box, she meant.

He unfolded the top flaps of the box and crouched down to look. "Why, they're M.K.'s detective books. Is she getting rid of them at last?"

"She came home from school, asked me for a few boxes, and packed them up," Fern said, still whisking.

Amos closed the box up and crossed the room to the kitchen. He folded his arms and leaned his hips against the kitchen counter. "What do you suppose has caused this? Teaching?"

"Maybe."

He grinned. "My little girl is finally growing up. You were right, Fern. This teaching job has been good for her."

Fern didn't seem as convinced. "Seems like something else happened lately, but I'm not sure what. Haven't you noticed how quiet she's been the last few days? Thoughtful and reflective. Very, very unusual."

Amos hadn't noticed. It always irked him that Fern was so observant about his own children, and yet he was grateful too. Irked and grateful. That just about summed up his feelings about his wife. And love. There was love.

They wouldn't even have Windmill Farm today, he was quite sure, if it weren't for Fern. The year his heart was failing, she had become his guiding force, his rudder. She had kept things going. She had kept his family together.

He took the whisk and bowl out of her hands, set them down on the counter, slipped his arms around her waist and kissed her. A kiss that meant serious business too. A down payment for later.

She put her hands against his chest, surprised. "What was that for, Amos Lapp?"

"That was for paying attention to the most important things."

Fern smiled, pushing him away playfully. She picked up the bowl as M.K. bounded down the stairs with another box.

"What are the most important things?" M.K. asked. "I want to know."

Amos looked at her. What were the most important things for his youngest daughter to learn? *Think before you act. Understand the big picture. Put the needs of others above your own wants. Start thinking long-term.*

He glanced at Fern. Or was the most important thing to find the right partner to help M.K. become the person he knew she could be?

Maybe it was all of those things. Serious stuff for a man with an empty stomach. Amos picked up the whisk. "Never miss a chance to refresh the starter!"

One week had passed and Chris hadn't seen any sign of Sheriff Hoffman. He was just starting to relax, to not keep looking over his shoulder when he went into town or tense up when he heard a car drive by. And then one morning, after Jenny had left for school, he walked out of the barn after he finished feeding Samson, and there the sheriff was, leaning against his police car with one ankle crossed over the other.

"Morning, Chris," Sheriff Hoffman said. "Did you give some thought to our conversation?"

Chris put the empty bucket down. "I thought I was clear. I told you everything."

"I need ideas about anything else you can remember."

Chris took a metered breath. "I don't know anything."

"I know. I know you were only seven. I know you had already seen too much for a boy your age. But I'm guessing there might be something else. Something more you might remember if you really tried."

"And how do I do that?"

"Anything that might trigger a memory. Anything that comes to mind."

Two or three small bright-winged birds hopped about on the ground, pecking at the stale bread crumbs Jenny had sprinkled before she left for school.

The sheriff took a few steps closer to Chris. "Look, if you cooperate, I might be able to overlook the fact that you crossed a state line with your sister without the permission of Child Protective Services, and that you're squatting in your grandfather's house."

Chris snapped his head up. "This house will be legally mine as soon as I turn twenty-one. My grandfather wanted me to have it. He wanted me to take care of my sister. I have papers to prove that."

"But you're not twenty-one yet. I checked." The sheriff raised an eyebrow. "So maybe you want to try again to remember. Try real hard." He took his keys out of his pocket and went back to the car.

Chris took a few steps. "That day . . . the day we left . . . I might remember one or two things." There was, he understood, no going back.

The sheriff put his keys back in his pocket and took out his notepad. "I'm listening."

As soon as school let out for the day, M.K. went straight to visit Erma. She found her hanging laundry in the backyard. "Erma, why did you become a teacher?"

Erma continued to hang pillowcases on the line, gathering her thoughts. "I suppose it was because I had such a natural curiosity about people and things. I was always sticking my nose into other people's business. I've always thought of teaching as being a little bit of a detective."

Detective? Had M.K. heard Erma right? Did she say that teaching was like detective work? Her ears perked up.

"A good teacher has to hunt and dig to find the right way to reach each child—to give him a love of learning that will last his entire life."

M.K.'s heart started to pound. "Erma, help me become a good teacher."

Erma sat on the picnic bench and patted the place beside her. "What made Gideon Smucker such a good teacher for you?"

M.K. had to think that over. "He gave me extra math problems. He let me work ahead of my class. He brought me books he thought I would like."

"So he challenged you."

"Not just me. He made things interesting in the classroom. We didn't always know what to expect." She smiled. "Once, he had a handful of us meet at the schoolhouse at five in the morning, to watch the tail of a comet as it raced across the sky." She sighed. "He was a marvelous teacher—the kind that every child remembers fondly for the rest of her life. That's the kind of teacher I need to be, Erma. If I have to be stuck teaching, I want to be that kind of teacher."

Erma nodded. "Teaching has its advantages and disadvantages. But there are golden moments, when you connect with a child."

"But how do I do that?"

"Mary Kate, it begins when you try to see life through other people's eyes."

Erma went back to the business of hanging sheets on the clothesline, so M.K. joined her. She hung one blue-checked dish towel on the line, then another. She thought about each pupil, trying to imagine life through his or her eyes.

Anna Mae, she knew, mostly thought about marrying Danny Riehl. Barbara Jean wanted to be home, helping her mother with the new baby. She played dolls at every recess. What would it be like to see life through Danny Riehl's eyes? He could do math problems in his head and he was the runner-up in yesterday's eighth-grade spelling bee, even though he was only a sixth grader. The word that tripped him up was "Hallelujah." When Danny heard the letter he forgot, he slapped his forehead with the palm of his hand. "Ooh . . . silent *J*! I forgot silent *J*." She smiled at the memory of it. She reached down for another towel and realized she had emptied the basket.

"Which pupil do you worry about the most?" Erma asked.

That was easy for M.K. to answer. "There's a boy, an eighth grader, who is smart as a whip, but I think he is having trouble reading. He tries to hide it, but he's going to be graduating soon. And then what? I feel as if I have just six months to help him."

"What's he like?"

"His name is Eugene Miller. He's a swarthy boy with a wiry build. He wins the sprint races on field day. He has an amazing talent for drawing."

"So he has some things he's good at."

"Yes. He loves drawing and he loves getting attention even more."

"In his own way, Eugene has found a way to get what he needs. I think he'll do all right for himself." Erma was observing a butterfly light on a white sheet, luffing in the wind. "I've found that it's often the people who don't call attention to themselves who have the most to offer."

Jenny. That's who M.K. thought of when Erma said that.

Amos grinned at the sight of watching Uncle Hank try to harness the horse to the buggy with four puppies nipping at his pants legs. He kept hopping around as if he were barefoot on live coals.

A few days ago, Edith had re-reconsidered her spurning of Hank after he came calling with Doozy and four puppies in tow. Now, Edith meant serious business and Hank had been moping around the farm ever since. Yesterday, he tried to find homes for the puppies. No luck, not even from softhearted Sadie, though he tried again last night. She told him that twin babies and four puppies would unhinge her fragile balance. Hank returned home with a forlorn look on his face and four puppies in a cardboard box. Fern saw him coming up the porch steps and headed him off. She pointed toward his Dawdi Haas over the buggy shop.

Insulted, Hank spun around, muttering about women and their lack of understanding.

And then a happy surprise for Hank came late in the day. Edith Fisher had another change of heart. She still didn't want Doozy or his offspring hanging around her chicken farm, but she did pardon Hank. She sent her son Jimmy over to Windmill Farm with a note saying that Hank was invited for supper on Sunday. The spring was back in Hank's step.

It was amazing what a little romance did for a person.

10

M.K. was surprised to see that Chris and Jenny Yoder were at church. They hadn't attended before today, so she figured someone—like Bishop Elmo or Deacon Abraham—had put a little gentle pressure on them.

It had been almost a week since that unfortunate misunderstanding with the sheriff. And nobody blabbed. That was the incredible thing. It was touching—to think Chris and Jenny would protect her from embarrassment. So kind! So unexpected.

By now, if they were going to say anything, they would have. Wouldn't they?

Ruthie's father was the first minister to preach this morning. M.K. had her own rating system for sermons: "boring," "boring boring," and "boring boring boring." Ruthie's father consistently earned three borings. One thing about his sermons: if you were unclear about the point he emphasized, another would be along in a moment. Fern was forever telling her it wasn't the preacher's problem, it was the listener's. "Hald die Ohre uff." *Keep your ears open.*

Fern poked her with her elbow in a warning to sit up and pay attention.

Fern! So ever-present.

M.K. glanced across the room at Chris. He sat next to her father, who had greeted him warmly. Amos Lapp had a knack for tending to fatherless young men. Sometimes, M.K. thought it was a pity he hadn't had more sons. A houseful. Instead, he lived with a covey of women and he often seemed bewildered by them.

Chris's Sunday clothes made him look blonder and taller and grown up. And handsome. He lifted his eyes from the hymnal and looked directly at her, as if he knew exactly what she was thinking. He smiled, and it hit her in the solar plexus. She bowed her head, breaking away from his gaze.

Chris had to bite on his lower lip to stop smiling when he caught Mary Kate Lapp gazing at him in church. She blushed becomingly, he noticed. He still couldn't get over this was the teacher Jenny had been complaining about so bitterly. He was pleased to see Mary Kate had a full set of her own choppers. She didn't wear cloppety shoes. She didn't jiggle when she walked. And she was awfully far from being old.

Mary Kate was sitting next to a young mother with two red-headed twin babies—a boy and a girl. The young mother had a dreamy smile on her face and a faraway look in her eyes, as if she were listening to a pleasant conversation that only she could hear. She didn't seem to notice that her little boy was teething and chewing on his shirt collar.

Speaking of teeth, Chris noticed that Jenny was sitting next to a little girl who was missing most of her front teeth. Jenny had talked about a cute little girl named Barbara Jean at school and he wondered if this might be her. He noticed that Barbara Jean kept sticking her tongue out, as if she was continually surprised to find the teeth had gone missing. He was glad Jenny had someone to sit next to, but he wished she had a friend her own age. The older girls had clumped together before church like clotted cream. Not one included Jenny in the cluster. He had worried it would be a mistake to come this morning. He knew the hearts of these people—they would fuss over the two of them as if they were chicks without a mother hen. They would ask questions about where they came from and want to stop by the house with casseroles and baked goods. As tempting as a good meal sounded—and it really did sound good—it wasn't enough to make him want to come to church and start joining into the community. Not quite yet. The whole notion of it worried him. If they could only lay low until January, when he turned twenty-one. But how could he have said no to the bishop? You just didn't do that.

But then, while the church was singing the *LobLeid*, Chris was filled with a wonderful sense of worship. It felt good, so good, to be back in church. He breathed in the familiar smells of starch and soap and shoe blacking. He had missed it more than he realized. The worship. Reminders that God was sovereign over all. It wasn't good to go too long without church.

The hymn ended and Amos Lapp, seated next to him, took back the hymnal and tucked it under the bench. Someday, in addition to the horse breeding business, Chris would like to have a farm of his own, just like Windmill Farm. Fields, orchards, livestock, bountiful vegetable garden. That was becoming his dream.

Amos had introduced Chris to some of the fellows who were close to his age. He wondered what their dream would be. Jimmy Fisher, he noticed, had an eye for the ponies. By the barn this morning, he had already spotted Samson and asked Chris how fast he had been clocked. "I don't know," Chris said. "I've never raced him."

Jimmy Fisher looked at him as if a cat had spoken. "Never raced him? Never?" He ran a hand down Samson's foreleg. "I could do it for you."

"Why?" Chris asked.

"Don't you want to know how fast he could go?"

Chris shook his head. "No need."

Jimmy Fisher was amazed.

Right then, Chris knew what Jimmy Fisher's dream would be: Thrills.

Jimmy Fisher reached down to pat Doozy's neck. It was warm from the sun. This dog was devoted to Mary Kate and followed her everywhere, even to church. Or maybe he was just trying to get away from those little pups that were constantly pulling his tail and chewing on his ears.

Jimmy had known M.K. just as long as he had known his own brother, essentially his entire life. He treated her like a younger sibling too. He had put a billy goat in the cherry orchard when she was picking cherries. She had let the air out of the tires of his hidden ten-speed bicycle. He had tossed a racer snake into the girls' outhouse at school, knowing full well that she was inside. She had sprinkled water over his entire firecracker collection—just enough to make the gunpowder soft and ineffective. They raced their favorite buggy horses against each other. They were constantly competing, but it never meant a thing. They had a long history together—mostly as enemies, until one day when they put aside their feud and became friends. Good friends.

And now, suddenly, overnight, it had blossomed into love.

How to explain what happened? It was like a switch had flipped and in an instant the world had changed. His mind was racing.

M.K. had taken him along to a volleyball game and barbecue at the Eshes' home last night, so that he could meet Emily, his future missus. At least that's what he had assumed until he was actually introduced to Emily and tried to have a conversation with her. He was at his most charming, warm, and witty, thinking at first that she was just shy. Thirty minutes later, his charm had worn out. She had no sense of humor. None whatsoever. She took everything he said literally and tried to dissect it. "I don't think that could have really happened" or "That sounds like a gross exaggeration." It was like trying to talk to an IRS auditor.

Their lagging conversation was interrupted by gales of laughter. He turned his gaze to M.K., sitting by the fire pit, surrounded by four or five fellows and girls, telling a story about something funny that had happened at her school.

A burst of laughter shook Jimmy back to the present. It would be his turn at bat soon. They were having the after-church-after-lunch softball game and he had talked Chris Yoder into sticking around for it. He noticed how Chris stood at a distance, leaning against the fence, not joining in but not entirely separate either. Chris's gaze often drifted toward left field. That's where M.K. happened to be posted.

Jimmy gave a few practice swings before he stepped up to the plate. His thoughts slipped back to last night at the Eshes' as M.K. was wrapping up the story by the fire pit. The group was hanging on her every word. She was always good at storytelling—which she attributed to years of listening to Uncle Hank—but that was when it hit Jimmy like a two-by-four. He was dazzled by how she had suddenly become a different person. He was out looking for love and it was right in front of him. It had always been right in front of him.

He was in love with M.K. Lapp. He was a hooked fish. A goner.

He stepped up to bat, poised and ready for the pitch, but his mind was fully occupied. The question that faced him: how to convince M.K. that she loved him back? That was going to take some doing.

A week later, on Saturday, the sky was filled with dark clouds. The air felt damp and raw and smelled of coming rain. Chris Yoder was out in the west field of Windmill Farm, cutting the last of the hay. M.K. watched the work progress; it was painfully slow, even though Chris was always working when she looked in that direction—a tiny figure bent over the land.

She had just finished baking a few loaves of honey oat bread and decided to give one to him to take home. They weren't quite as light and airy as Fern's would be—her bread never was—but it would be good as toast. As she wrapped the loaf in a red-striped dish towel, she wondered what Chris thought of her. It was difficult to read him. He was polite, slightly amused, but just that and no more. The logical conclusion she reached was that he did not want to spend time in her company. And why should he? She had accused him of a heinous crime. Two crimes! One big, one small, but crimes nonetheless.

And yet he didn't tell anyone what she had done to him. Nor had Jenny. M.K. felt grateful to them both, but she wondered why. Maybe, Chris just wasn't interested in her.

M.K. wasn't used to having young men lose interest in her. And, the first few times they had met, Chris Yoder had shown a spark of interest in her—she could see it in his eyes. She could tell he thought she was attractive. That wasn't an altogether unusual experience for M.K. Boys had always been attracted to her. But that was just it—they were all boys.

M.K. wasn't the kind of girl who needed attention from boys, and she certainly wasn't the type who fell in and out of love like her friend Ruthie did. But she did like to be taken seriously. She liked that very much.

Chris Yoder did not take M.K. seriously. And Chris Yoder was the first boy M.K. met whom she considered to be a man.

She found herself thinking of Chris a great deal. She tried to stop herself, but couldn't. He was a shy man, she decided, and that was another reason why he seemed reserved. Certainly that would pass, she thought, when they got to know one another better, but she wasn't quite sure how to achieve that. Chris didn't make it easy.

She crossed through the fields with the bread loaf tucked in one hand and a thermos of cool lemonade in the other. When he looked up and saw her, he stopped the horses and waited for her. The odd feeling that she had been experiencing lately came back. She felt her heart thumping. Ridiculous, she thought. Ridiculous.

She handed him the thermos. "Thought you could use something to drink."

He opened the lid and drank it down. "Thank you." He wiped sweat from his brow with a handkerchief.

She held up the bread. "I thought you and Jenny might be able to use a loaf of bread. Honey oat. The honey is from my own hives."

When he hesitated for a moment, she quickly added, "I made too many loaves. We can't eat it all. I'll put it in the barn by your coat."

"Jenny would put honey on everything if she could."

M.K. brightened with that news. Her confidence returned. Honey was an area of expertise for her, thanks to her sister's husband, Rome. He had taught her everything she knew about beekeeping. "I'll give you a bottle of my honey for her to try on this bread. My bees are brown bees—not very common, but they produce a delicious sweet honey."

His eyes crinkled with his smile as he handed the empty thermos to her. "She'd like that."

"Would you and Jenny like to come and have a meal at the house? Tonight?"

M.K. surprised herself. *Oh no.* This hadn't been planned. As he hesitated, she wished the words back. Why in the world had she said that? "My father's been wanting to have you." That was true, actually.

She was afraid to look at him too closely. His eyes, with that unsettling lucent quality, were on her. She looked down at the ground, at the rigging on the horses, at the shoes Chris was wearing, boots that had badly scuffed toes.

"Your father has been kind to me," he said softly.

"He thinks you're a hard worker." She glanced at the sky. "Looks like it's going to rain soon. I should let you get back to work. If you decide you'd like to join us, we eat at six. Nothing fancy, but Fern's a terrific cook. If you're lucky, Uncle Hank might be in a storytelling mood." She started toward the barn.

"What's Fern got planned for tonight?"

M.K. whirled around. "Pot roast. Roasted potatoes. Green beans and bacon."

"Any dessert?"

"Pumpkin pie with homemade vanilla ice cream."

Their eyes met. This time, they held. Chris grinned. "We'll be there."

As M.K. walked through the field, she couldn't stop smiling. Ridiculous, she thought. Ridiculous. But she couldn't wipe the goofy grin off her face.

Chris flicked the reins on the horses' backs, to get them moving. He wasn't sure it was a good idea to accept Mary Kate's dinner invitation, but the mention of a good meal was a powerful temptation. Hardly a day went by that Amos Lapp hadn't extended the invitation to join him for lunch at the house, but Chris always declined. Other invitations had started coming in from other families too—he expected as much after he and Jenny attended church last Sunday. That's the way it was with the Amish—they extended true kindness. It was one of the many things he loved about these people. He was starting to relax a little and think they should go ahead and accept a few dinner invitations. Help out at a few work frolics. Meet people. Get involved.

But then nagging doubts crowded in. Would they start pressing him with questions about his family? Would they want to help him fix up his house? He couldn't risk too much curiosity—look at what happened with Mary Kate Lapp. A few brief interactions, and she had him carted away by the sheriff. Unbelievable! But then again, there weren't too many Amish women who seemed like Mary Kate Lapp.

Still, there was something about her that intrigued him. True, she was easy on the eyes, though he was used to plenty of pretty girls in Ohio. Today, flour streaked Mary Kate's cheek, hiding some of her freckles. He thought about pointing it out to her, but she might feel embarrassed. She was trying to make amends—the loaf of bread, the honey for Jenny, the invitation to dinner. It was sort of sweet to see Mary Kate so ill at ease, so full of humble pie. He had a hunch it was a new feeling for her.

But here's what he hadn't expected about Mary Kate Lapp: she was funny.

She had a way of looking at the world that was just off-kilter enough to surprise him into laughing. She wasn't trying to be funny, but everything about her was amusing.

And here's another thing he hadn't expected about Mary Kate: she was a good teacher after all. Mary Kate was starting to win over his reluctant-to-like-anyone sister. She had given Jenny a word puzzle to figure out and Jenny had spent hours deciphering it: "Beings highly deficient in cranial capacity hastily enter situations which celestial entities regard with great trepidation." A happy scream burst out of her when she figured it out. In common English it meant: "Fools rush in where angels fear to tread." Jenny had raced to school in the morning with the answer.

Encounters with Mary Kate Lapp felt as if someone threw a snowball down the back of his shirt on a blistering hot summer day. Unexpected, startling, shocking. But not unwelcomed.

Jenny was surprised when her brother blew into the house, galloped up the stairs to take a shower, and shouted down that they were expected for dinner at Windmill Farm.

That made no sense to Jenny. No sense at all. Chris was always telling her they needed to keep to themselves and not get too friendly with others. When she called out, "Why?" he opened the bathroom door, stuck his head out, and shouted back, "Pot roast and potatoes!"

Okay. That made sense. The thought of a home-cooked meal made Jenny's mouth water. Just today, she had looked longingly at Anna Mae Glick's lunch: slices of smoked ham between thick homemade bread. A slab of shoofly pie. She nearly threw away her own stupid lunch: stale crackers and rock-hard cheese, and a too-soft apple from the tree in the yard.

Pot roast and potatoes. She could practically taste them now. She was fully supportive of Chris giving in to temptation. In fact, she hurried to get ready!

But then they arrived at Windmill Farm and the family, including four wild puppies, came charging out to meet them. The puppies made a beeline for Jenny, jumping up and nearly knocking her down.

That's when Jenny became steaming mad. Until that moment, she hadn't made the connection that Windmill Farm meant she would be seeing her teacher. It was true that Teacher M.K. was showing a little glimmer of hope as a teacher, but that didn't mean Jenny wanted to be chummy with her. She was still outraged that Teacher M.K. turned her brother in to the sheriff. She was fiercely protective of Chris, and slow to forgive anyone who might cause him harm. She thought about feigning illness, but suddenly caught a whiff of pot roast in the air and decided she would stay. They would eat, and then they would leave. Old Deborah had taught her manners.

Fortunately, the food lived up to its aroma. As the platters were passed around the table, as she listened to the table conversation between Fern and Amos and M.K. and Uncle Hank—who did most of the talking by telling outrageously silly stories!—she felt a wave of missing Old Deborah. Of belonging at someone's table. How she envied these people. She wondered if Chris might be feeling it too. The last two months had been so filled with change that she hadn't allowed herself to think back on their old life. Not much, anyway.

"From your accents," Fern said, passing Jenny a bowl of green beans, "I'd say you didn't grow up in Pennsylvania. Not in Lancaster, anyway."

"Well, we sort of started here—" Jenny began. From the corner of her eye, she caught Chris's infinitesimal shake of his head.

"She's referring to the wave of nineteenth-century immigrants from Europe," Chris hastily filled in. He glanced around, taking in the blank looks on everyone's faces. He picked up the breadbasket and held it out to Amos. "William Penn and all that history."

Fern squinted her eyes at him as if he had completely lost his mind.

"NOW THAT," Uncle Hank interrupted, "reminds me of my great, great aunt Mathilda, who rowed over from the Old Country in a canoe." He helped himself to another serving of potatoes.

"A canoe, you say?" Amos said, calm as a cucumber. He reached out for the butter to spread on his bread roll, but Fern intercepted and moved the butter tray away from him. The man's dark eyebrows sprang up as he gave his wife a look of obvious merriment.

"A canoe and a pet parrot named Oscar," Uncle Hank said, winking at Jenny. "So she had someone to talk to. She liked to talk, that Aunt Mathilda. The problem came when the parrot started talking back to her." He jumped to his feet and shaded his eyes with his hand, as if looking for land. "Paddle faster, Mathilda! Faster! *Sqwuak! Sqwuak!*"

A laugh burst out of Jenny. She laughed in absolute glee, and to her surprise the others joined in, creating a tangible joy that fell upon the room like soft goose feathers. Something bloomed inside of Jenny at that moment, a leaf unfurling in the spring. It felt so good to be a part of a family.

Fern rolled her eyes. "Hank has found a fresh audience for his old tales."

"Uncle Hank's tales are always worth hearing again," Teacher M.K. said. She leaned over to whisper to Jenny, "Unless you happen to be Fern, who says once is all she needs."

"I HEARD THAT," Uncle Hank bellowed. "You, Jenny Yoder, are welcome back every night!" Uncle Hank pinned M.K. with his good eye. "Now that M.K. has gone the ways of crotchety schoolmarms, I've been missing having someone appreciate my fine stories!"

Jenny looked at Teacher M.K. to see if she might be offended, but she was laughing. A warm feeling spread through Jenny. Amos and Fern told her to come back soon, to stop by anytime at all, and the way they said it, she knew they meant it. Fern had even told her to come over for a bread roll making lesson tomorrow afternoon after school, and Jenny thought she just might. She did love those sourdough bread rolls.

Then Jenny turned to Chris. She saw the way Chris was gazing at Teacher M.K. and she thought, *Oh, boy.*

11

When Fern Lapp told Jenny to join her after school and help her make bread rolls, Chris had a hunch that it would end up being more than a onetime occurrence. Jenny had been kind of lost and alone in Stoney Ridge, and he saw the look of longing on her face as they sat down to that pot roast and potato dinner. It wasn't about food—it was about having a place at someone's table. About belonging.

His instincts were right. Two weeks later, it was getting harder to keep Jenny home from Windmill Farm. Chris nearly gave up trying.

Now that Fern had an apprentice, she decided to try selling baked goods at her roadside stand that stood at the bottom of the driveway for Windmill Farm. She was even paying Jenny to work the stand after school let out. Townsfolk were starting to drive out to Windmill Farm to pick up a loaf of bread or cinnamon rolls, because it was cheaper than Sweet Tooth Bakery, fresher and tastier. The bakery owner, Nora Stroot, was livid.

Chris didn't think Nora Stroot should be too worried about it. When winter came, Chris was pretty sure that Fern would close up the stand and think of something else to keep Jenny busy. Because *that*, he knew, was the true motive behind Fern's bread making tutorials. For all her bluster, Fern Lapp was a marshmallow.

It did concern him, though, to see Jenny start looking and acting like Fern. Everything she talked about now was "Fern said this," or "Fern said that." Chris tried to have talks with her, about not getting too attached, and to not become a pest over there at Windmill Farm. In two weeks, she seemed far more attached to Fern than she had ever been to Old Deborah. But then, Old Deborah was . . . really, really . . . old.

"Pshaw," Jenny shot back. "Fern said it's not good to worry too much about what tomorrow holds." Then she would start scrubbing the kitchen sink as if it were a hotbed of germs. And Chris would sigh.

But he knew that every child deserved such moments—times of knowing that someone was looking out for you. He had his own: his grandfather lifting him up out of the backseat of the car after a long drive, carrying him into the house and up the stairs and putting him to bed. The scratchiness of his chin, the smell of his aftershave. Jenny deserved this time with Fern, time to make her own memories.

Jenny was wearing the heart-shaped Lancaster prayer cap now, and Fern showed her how to get her hair to stay pinned in a bun. Jenny was even starting to turn up out of thin air, the same way Fern had of doing. If you asked Chris, Jenny was turning into a cut-down version of Fern Lapp.

Jenny felt a little sorry for Eugene Miller. Today, he showed up at school with a big black eye. She had asked him about his black eye and he told her he was breaking wild colts for the rodeo in his spare time. She didn't think that was true. Maybe, but probably not. Anna Mae raised her hand, probably eager to tell the teacher that she was sure Eugene was lying about the rodeo, but Teacher M.K. never did call on her. She had just acted like it was nothing unusual for Anne Mae to keep her hand aimed for the sky. And in a way, it wasn't.

Jenny had expected Teacher M.K.'s new-and-improved teaching style would mean she would holler at them and hit her desk with the ruler, but now she would just look at the big boys, with her eyebrow up and her mouth a little pushed to one side. It wasn't a mean look—it was a smart look. So the big boys stopped and sat down. It wasn't any fun trying to get the teacher upset because it didn't look like she could be upset.

Teacher M.K. was different somehow. It started on that day when she put Eugene Miller in his place. Then she did something pretty smart, which was good for a teacher who had seemed pretty dumb.

She flip-flopped the day's work, so reading and arithmetic came in the morning. In the afternoon, she introduced a new period: art. Even Eugene didn't slip away for the afternoon when he saw what Teacher M.K. had planned. She brought out paper for everybody, and a wooden box with little metal tubes of paint. She showed everyone how to rule a margin for the picture so there would be a white space all around for a frame. She showed them how to wipe brushes carefully while they were painting. Pretty soon everyone just got quiet, they were so happy making pictures.

Barbara Jean Shrock painted a picture of her baby sister, but she forgot to add eyes and a nose and a mouth. Danny Riehl drew a picture of an airplane. He knew all the different names of airplanes and all about their engines and stuff like that. Anna Mae drew a picture of her and Danny on their wedding day. That made Danny's face go cherry red.

Jenny painted a picture of a rainbow with a pot of gold at the bottom of it. She had always thought it might be nice to find a pot of gold someday. Life would be much easier. Maybe then her mother would be happy.

But it was Eugene Miller's picture that was the best. He painted a falcon that looked so real it wouldn't have surprised Jenny if it had taken flight. He said it was a peregrine falcon and that there was a nesting pair at Windmill Farm that returned year after year. He said he had watched them across the street with his binoculars. Teacher M.K. nodded, and she looked really pleased. Eugene didn't seem nearly as annoying when he was talking about the falcons. Maybe there was hope for him.

Teacher M.K. had hung all the pictures on the wall. The room seemed much more cheerful after that. Everyone couldn't stop looking at them.

That was the day Teacher M.K. put Eugene Miller in his place. That was the day something happened. Something that gave Jenny more to think about than worries about her mom. By the end of that afternoon, the children looked different too. Like something good was going to happen.

On a gray afternoon in October, M.K. went into the Stoney Ridge public library. She sought out the head librarian and asked, "Do you have any books on reading problems?"

The librarian's face turned sad and pitiful. "Are you having a problem with reading, dearie?"

How insulting! "Not me," M.K. huffed. "A student of mine."

The librarian led her to a section of books at the far end of the library. The sunlight from the window was filled with dust particles. It looked like this section of books hadn't been visited very often. She pointed to the bottom row. "Those are the only books we have about reading difficulties."

M.K. pulled out a few books and went over to a table to sift through them. She wasn't exactly sure what she was looking for, but she knew Eugene Miller was a bright boy, imaginative and creative and artistic, but he couldn't read or write at his age level. Not even close. In fact, some of his papers looked like a second grader's. Untidy, mixed-up letters and numbers. He was easily frustrated, became bored, and that's when he would start some mischief in the classroom.

The more she read, the more she thought she was finding what was behind Eugene's reading struggle: something called *dyslexia*. She came across one paragraph that leapt out at her:

"Compared to the average person, a dyslexic generally has very strong visual skills, a vivid imagination, strong practical/manipulative skills—"

Oh . . . that definitely sounded like Eugene Miller.

"—innovation, and an above-average intelligence. Basically the right side of the brain is stronger than the left—and that's what a good artist needs. As a dyslexic you are likely to have a greater appreciation for color, tone, and texture. Your grasp of two-dimensional and three-dimensional form is more acute. You can visualize your art before reaching for the paint brush, and your imagination will allow you to go beyond the norm and create new and innovative expression."

M.K. thought about Eugene's peregrine falcon drawing. It was shockingly beautiful—the minute detail, the haughty gaze in the tercil's eyes, the vicious-looking talons. It was as vivid and realistic as a photograph. That was it! It seemed as if Eugene had a photograph of it in his mind and was somehow able to transfer that image onto paper.

Eugene was always drawing something. A stick in the dirt, pencil sketches around the edges of his math assignment, caricatures on the chalkboard.

She closed the book with a sigh. If it might be true that Eugene had dyslexia, what could she really do for him? She was no expert. She had an eighth-grade education. Most of these words were entirely new to her, and she considered herself a first-rate philologist. Still, she checked a few books out and left the library.

As she walked down the front path of the library, she noticed Chris Yoder coming down the street in his horse and buggy. He saw her and lifted a hand to wave to her. She reached down to pick up her scooter, hoping Chris might offer her a ride home, but when she looked up, he had passed by.

She didn't mind too much about Chris. He was friendly enough, but either he was keeping his distance, or she was keeping hers. She didn't mind too much. Really, not at all, hardly.

Of all people! The very moment Chris was heading to the sheriff's office to have a talk with him, Mary Kate Lapp came strolling out of the library—directly across the street from the office. There was no way he was going to pull into the sheriff's office at that moment. No way at all. He hurried Samson down the street and pulled over at the Sweet Tooth Bakery Shop and waited until he saw Mary Kate zip away, heading in the direction of Windmill Farm. He couldn't hold back a grin from spreading over his face as he saw her zoom away. She was always darting around Stoney Ridge on that little red push-scooter.

He looped the reins around the hitching post and walked into the sheriff's office. Sheriff Hoffman was finishing up a phone call and motioned to the seat across from his desk. Chris sat down and took his black felt hat off, spinning the brim in his hands. Now that it was fall, he had switched from straw hat to felt, along with the other men in his church.

Sheriff Hoffman put the phone back on the receiver. "Chris Yoder. Got something for me?"

Chris shrugged. "I'd like you to tell me exactly what you're looking for."

The sheriff inhaled deeply, then blew the air out of his mouth. He leaned forward in his chair. "Look, Chris. This all happened when you were just a little kid. I've spoken to a child psychologist about this case. He's been clear that it's important to not put any leading thoughts in your head, to just see what you can remember. He said if I try to give you any clues, it might cause you to freeze up. All I can tell you is that every single thing you can remember is helpful to the case."

"So . . . it is a case. An actual criminal case. Something my mother was involved in."

"I don't know for sure. It's just a hunch." The sheriff scratched his neck. "Have you given any more thought to undergoing hypnosis?"

"Absolutely not. I will not. You can't make me. It's against my church, my beliefs—"

The sheriff held up a hand to stop him. "Yeah, yeah. I got it. That's what I figured. So, just keep trying to remember."

Chris rose. "It occurred to me that any information I give you might end up connecting my mother to a crime. Have you thought of that?"

Sheriff Hoffman lifted his eyes and looked directly at Chris. "My job is to find the truth. Somehow, I think that's what you want too. 'The truth shall set you free.' Isn't that in the Good Book?"

"The truth shall set you free." Chris had read those words all his life and never really thought about what they might mean. How would the truth of that day, fourteen years ago, affect him? And Jenny? What would it mean for his mother?

On the way back to the house, Chris pondered the conversation with the sheriff. Old Deborah made Chris read the Bible out loud to her by lantern light nearly every night after the supper meal. She claimed Scripture could be a powerful comfort and help if a person let the Lord's message speak to his heart. Old Deborah's faith was a big sweeping thing and his was faint and faraway.

When he reached his grandfather's house, he hopped out of the buggy and walked around to release Samson from his rigging. He tugged on the bridle, guiding him toward the barn as the new moon slid behind a cloud.

"The truth shall set you free."

But what if the truth meant Chris would lose everything?

It was a sunny, breezy Saturday in mid-October. Working together, Fern and Jenny hung the day's laundry, shooing away those four little puppies that kept trying to snap at the luffing sheets. Fern kept surprising Jenny. She would have thought Fern would have no patience for something as silly as puppies. Instead, Fern stopped trying to hang laundry and gave her full attention to those crazy puppies. She tossed them sticks and tried to teach them tricks, until they finally wore out and curled up in a mound in the sun. Then she went back to hanging towels and sheets.

The comforting aromas of soap and sunshine scented the warm air as the damp sheets made a soft fluttering noise in the breeze. Fern said she liked doing laundry; the act of scrubbing something clean felt good to her. Ten minutes later, they went inside to bake cookies.

Jenny pulled a tray of cookies from the oven and set them out to cool. Fern stuck her thumb in the middle of one cookie. "Do this with each one," she said to Jenny. Then Fern carefully ladled a spoonful of raspberry jam into the indentation. "That's why they're called thumbprint cookies. They're my top seller. Folks love my raspberry jam."

Without thinking, Jenny said, "Old Deborah used to make these, but she liked to use blackberry jam."

Fern glanced up from spooning jam into another cookie. "Sadie got her start in healing from a woman in Ohio named Old Deborah. In Berlin."

Jenny's thumb froze, mid-squish. She didn't dare look at Fern.

"It was when Sadie was living with Julia and Rome for a few months, right after they got married. Julia is Amos's eldest daughter. She married Rome Troyer, the Bee Man."

Jenny swallowed. She didn't know what to say.

Fern put the spoon in the jam jar. "You know Rome and Julia, don't you?"

Slowly, Jenny nodded. "We lived with Old Deborah when our mother was . . . indisposed."

"Ah," Fern said in her knowing way. "I take it that Chris doesn't want anyone to know."

Jenny chanced a look at Fern. "Are you going to let him know I told you?"

Fern tilted her head. "But you didn't tell me. I guessed. And if Chris isn't ready to tell us anything more, we'll just have to wait."

Jenny's eyes filled with tears. "Oh, thank you!" She flung her arms around Fern's middle and burst into tears.

Now it seemed to be Fern's turn to not know what to do. Slowly, she put her arms around Jenny and patted her. "Jenny, you know that you can always count on us to help you and Chris. Rome and Julia, too." She cupped

Jenny's face in her hands, the same way Old Deborah used to. "You just need to let us know if you need help."

Fall's vibrancy was fading. Squash vines and tomatoes had withered to the ground; corn leaves were wispy brown paper flecked with fuzzy mildew, abandoned ears shriveled inside. But in the greenhouse at Windmill Farm, it looked and smelled as warm and humid as if spring had arrived.

When Chris had approached Amos about the market manager's suggestion that lettuce was needed at the farmer's market, Amos's face softened for a moment with pleasure. When he spoke, his voice was quiet and sure. "Good for you. The greenhouse hasn't been used since my eldest daughter married and moved away. Have at it."

He sent Chris directly to Fern, who seemed equally pleased. "The market manager said folks will pay a premium for baby greens," Chris explained, though Fern didn't need any convincing. Together, Fern and Chris plotted out a plan to begin lettuce seeds in shallow wooden boxes in the greenhouse. Chris was discovering that Fern had the intuitive sense of a savvy merchant. She was already figuring out when the baby lettuce would be ready for the market, and how to bag them with a green polka-dotted ribbon. "We'll call ourselves the Salad Stall," she said, already at work on the sign.

Chris doted on those baby greens. Amos helped him with a few valuable tips: he added extra alfalfa meal into the soil to ensure a plentiful nitrogen supply. Lettuce, he said, needed a pH of 6.0 to 7.0. They selected a seed mix that included a variety of lettuces, since Chris would be hand snipping the leaves and not uprooting the plants. He showed Chris how to broadcast the seeds by hand and to tamp down the soil by gently massaging it with his palm. Keep the temperature of the greenhouse at 75 degrees, he told Chris.

None of this Chris knew. He felt as if he was getting a crash course in farming from Amos. He couldn't soak up enough knowledge from him. It embarrassed him how little he knew when he started this venture. Within a week, he had read every book he could find about lettuce. He learned that lettuce was a member of the sunflower family, and it was one of the oldest known vegetables—dating back to Persia, six centuries before Christ walked the earth. He knew now that the word "lettuce" comes from an Old French word, *laities*, meaning milk—probably referring to the milky white sap that came out of mature lettuce stems after the farmer snipped off the leaves.

Chris misted the seedlings three times a day and monitored them daily for any weeds. The greenhouse was the first place he went as he arrived at Windmill Farm in the morning and the last place he left at night. Thirty days after planting, Chris had harvested a small crop of baby lettuce to sell at the farmer's market on Saturday morning. He set up right next to the Fisher boys and their multicolored eggs. Jimmy helped nail Fern's elegant hand-painted "Salad Stall" sign up to the back of the stall. It was a bitterly cold day, with few customers trolling the aisles. Chris noticed there had been a change in the stands at the market. Many local produce stands were gone and crafts had filled their place: handmade wreaths, braids of garlic, shellacked gourds cut into birdhouses.

Maybe this was a mistake. It had seemed like such a good idea, but as the morning wore on and Chris had sold only three bags of lettuce, he felt like a fool. Only a novice would try to grow and sell lettuce in the late fall.

And then something miraculous occurred. First one customer bought a bag, then another, and soon he actually had a small line forming in front of his stand. At the end of the morning, he counted his earnings: forty-five dollars, minus ten percent for his stall fee. On the way back to Windmill Farm, he realized that he owed Amos money for the seed: forty dollars. That left Chris with a fifty-cent profit for a month's work spent sowing, watering, weeding, cutting, and bagging. Fifty cents.

He grinned. He felt like a real farmer.

Teacher M.K. had the scholars practice handwriting every day, right after lunch. She made sure everyone made sharp-nosed *e*'s and perfect *o*'s and straight *i*'s with the dot right smack on top, not floating off into space. Anna Mae liked to make little hearts to serve as the dots on her *i*'s and the teacher did away with those. Barbara Jean was still learning the alphabet. She made Jenny laugh, because she was practicing so hard her tongue stuck out. Jenny wanted to make every letter just so. Perfect.

While they practiced their handwriting, Teacher M.K. read to everyone, walking up and down the aisles. It was a story called *The Jungle Book* by

Rudyard Kipling about a young boy who was raised by wolves in the jungles of India. When Teacher M.K. read to the class, she acted out all the voices, and Jenny forgot right away it was just reading. It got real, like being inside the book. She felt as if she was in that deep, dark jungle with bushes thicker and denser than you could ever imagine, and when the teacher stopped, Jenny felt shocked, as if she had woken from a dream.

Even Eugene Miller liked hearing about the boy raised by wolves. He had stuck around all week.

One afternoon, Teacher M.K. handed the upper grades books she had made with paper stapled down the center. "This is for you to write a story," she told everyone. "Don't worry about the spelling, just write. Anything you want to."

She told the students they could even make things up. The stories didn't have to be true.

Anna Mae and Danny and the other upper grade students were excited about writing a book. But not Eugene. He crossed his arms against his chest and looked mad.

12

Eugene didn't come to school one morning. M.K. felt discouraged. Things had been going so well. She had been trying all kinds of ways to help Eugene: she stopped having him read aloud in class, saving him that painful ordeal. Instead, she had a private time with him when he read aloud.

She had been surprised to discover that he could hardly read at all. He had to read slowly, so very slowly, and the big words gave him fits. She provided reading books for him far below his grade level, to help build his confidence. For the spelling bees on Fridays, she gave him the list of words to practice on Thursday. He needed so much practice. In mathematics, her goal was to teach him to estimate, and to finish a problem by asking himself, "Does this answer make logical sense?" She gave him a box of index cards for key words and formulas. She was doing everything she could to help him.

After school let out for the day, M.K. wiped down the chalkboard. She heard the door open and turned around to see Eugene standing there. He was so tall he was scraping the top of the door, and growing still.

He scowled at her. "I'm quitting school. I already turned fifteen. I don't need it."

M.K. turned back to the chalkboard and calmly finished wiping the last section. She knew this was a critical moment. "You can quit school, Eugene. But you're going to have to keep learning all your life." She put the rag in a drawer. "You can't spend your life quitting things just because they get hard."

He narrowed his eyes. "It wasn't hard with Teacher Alice. I was getting along just fine until you showed up. It's because of your teaching. You couldn't teach a dog to bark. You couldn't teach a fish to swim. Or a bird to sing."

M.K. snapped her head up. She marched up to him and pointed a finger at his chest, which took notable courage because he towered over her. "I am trying to help you. You're a smart boy, Eugene, but your mind works a little differently than other students. That doesn't mean you can't get faster with reading and writing and arithmetic. You can. It's just going to take you a lot longer and you're going to have to practice a lot more to keep up."

He backed up a few steps. "Maybe I don't care."

M.K. stiffened. "Maybe you don't. I can't make you care. I can only offer you a chance." She fixed her eyes on him. "But I think you do care. I think you care very much."

Eugene held her gaze, narrowed his eyes, and called her an unrepeatable name, then whirled around and slammed the door behind him.

Out of habit, Jenny stopped by the mailbox on her way home from school and opened it. She wasn't sure what might be inside, but it was a bright spot of the day. Usually, all that the rusty old mailbox contained was junk mail. Today, there was a thin, gray envelope, addressed to her. Jenny stared at the letter for a long minute. Her heart leapt into her mouth and she felt a little strange, kind of dizzy and a little bit sick to her stomach. Looking over her shoulder, she hurried up to the house, dropped her lunch box, sat on the porch steps, and tore open the letter.

Hey there, Jennygirl! I was so happy to get a letter from you. Doing good here, though I sure am missing our monthly visits. Sorry to hear about Old Deborah. She was a nice old lady but she's been old for as long as I can remember. Write to me soon now honey and tell me about school. And what is Chris doing these days? Has he still gone whole hog over to them kooky Amish? I couldn't imagine why you're in Stoney Ridge until I figured out that my daddy's old house must still be empty. That's where you are, isn't it? Don't you worry. I won't tell. Makes me feel real happy to know where my babies are, safe and sound. Don't never forget that I love you. And don't never forget that I will always be your mama.

XOXOXOXOXOXOXOXOXOXOXOXOXOXOX OXOXOXOXOXO

P.S. Listen, honey, if you can send me some money, it would really help a lot. Cash is king here in the pokey—I need it for cigarettes and stamps and that sort of stuff.

How had her mother figured out where they were living? She had taken such care not to mention anything in her letters and not to supply a return address. She glanced at the envelope. *Stupid me!* The Stoney Ridge postmark would have given it away.

Chris would be furious.

Should she write her mother back?

She looked up at the sky and was surprised to see how thick the gray clouds had become. It would rain soon. She slipped the letter back into the envelope and put it into her apron pocket. Later. She would worry about writing back to her mother later. For now, it was time to start dinner.

You could hear a rumble in the late afternoon sky. Cayenne, the favorite of all the horses, was in her stall. M.K. reached over and touched her nose, and she nickered at her. She could see the horse's breath in the cold air. There was silence, the only sound was Cayenne's steady breathing. Her father had told M.K. once that the barn was the most peaceful place he knew. No voices, only the sound of the animals, their breath and bodies so warm.

M.K. had never felt so thoroughly exhausted in all her life. Physically and mentally. Teaching must be the hardest job in the entire world. And she was never done! Even on the weekends, she found herself thinking up a new way to help Jenny Yoder not shut down when faced with an arithmetic problem or wondering how to keep a mind like Danny Riehl's challenged. Or how to just keep Eugene Miller attending school.

It was too much. It was all too much.

She let her mind drift off to her plan of escape: she would finish the school term, take her passport, and travel to a land without children.

Raindrops started to splatter the metal roof of the barn. A crack of thunder split the sky. The storm would soon pass by. She stroked Cayenne's nose. She should get up to the house before the downpour started.

The barn door slid open and she turned to find Chris Yoder coming in, leading the draft horses, Rosemary and Lavender, by their bridles. He didn't notice M.K. as he led the horses to their stalls and attended to their needs: filling buckets with water and mangers with hay. She saw him rub one of the mares' forehead. The horse nudged closer to him, and though M.K. couldn't hear what he said, his lips moved as though he were singing to the animal. He bent and ran a hand over each of the mare's legs.

Such gentleness.

As he dipped the bridles into water to clean off the bits, he caught sight of M.K. and startled. "I didn't see you there." He looked around the barn. "I thought I might wait out the rain before heading home, but what's the use of weather if you're not out in it anyway? I'll leave—"

"No, wait. Don't go on my account. It should pass soon." Just as she finished that sentence, a loud BOOM blasted overhead and made her jump. She shivered. "When I was little, Uncle Hank would say that thunder meant the angels were moving furniture in heaven."

"Then that would have been the armoire," Chris said. He hooked the bridles on the wall pegs and picked up a broom. He started sweeping down the center aisle of the barn.

It had become so dark in the barn that M.K. lit a lantern and hung it on the wall. She watched Chris for a while. "You don't have to work all the time."

"Yes, I do." He swept the loose straw into a stall. "You work pretty hard yourself. I've seen the glow of lampshine in the schoolhouse early in the morning on my way to work."

Someone had noticed? For some reason, the thought pleased her. "I know why I'm working so hard. I'm trying to prove than I can teach school."

He grinned. "You're making a little progress, from what I hear."

That pleased her too, and she felt her cheeks get warm. "So what about you? What are you trying to prove?"

His grin faded.

She had gone too far. When would she ever learn? Just as Chris started to relax, she scared him back into his shell, like a turtle. "I'm sorry. It's none of my business. My curiosity is one of my worst faults."

The rain was really coming down now. It sounded like a work crew was hammering nails on the roof. Chris put the broom away and leaned his hips against a hay bale, facing M.K. He crossed his arms against his chest and one booted ankle over the other. "I'm trying to prove that I am my own man."

"Was there ever any doubt of that? You seem like a person who knows who he is and where he's going."

He went very still, and for a long minute he frowned at her. She worried that she had said the wrong thing again. "I'm sorry. What do I know?" A cat wove between her feet. She bent over and scooped up Buzz, the long-haired cat who spent most of his day snoozing. Nuzzling the cat's warm fur, she said, "It's just that sometimes I . . . I don't know who I am or what I'm meant to be doing. Fern says I have a terrible restlessness inside of me. She's right. I want to travel and see the world and swim in the Mediterranean Sea—but I love my family and I love my church and I love my bees—and I don't want to disappoint my father or Fern or my sisters. Or Uncle Hank." She ran her hand down Buzz's furry back and he responded with a low purr. "Though, Uncle Hank, of all people, would understand." She set Buzz on the ground and looked at Chris. "But I just can't figure out which way to go sometimes." She was babbling. She had to wrap this monologue up. "Do you ever feel that way? Do you understand what I mean?" *Please, please understand.*

Chris's face grew tight. He shook his head. "No. I don't."

Oh. This wasn't going very well, and the rain wasn't letting up at all. If anything, the thunder and lightning were coming steadily. Even the horses seemed uncomfortable, shuffling their feet restlessly. It was a very dramatic stage for M.K. to bare her soul—to practically a stranger—and she had just made an utter fool of herself.

Chris rose to his feet and crossed the space between them and put his hands on her shoulders. M.K. had never seen eyes so blue, the purest cobalt, like windows to the soul. For a split second, the way he was looking at her, the nearness, she was certain he was going to kiss her. She had never let a boy kiss her before, had never *wanted* to be kissed before. When she had observed Sadie and Gid kissing—which she had done on plenty of occasions—she thought kissing seemed ridiculous, involving odd noises and a lot of awkward nose bumping.

Ruthie had kissed a couple of boys—but only the ones she had fallen in love with. She had described kissing that made her stomach flip-flop and her palms sweat and her head start to spin. M.K. told her she might be confusing kissing with coming down with the flu.

But standing so close to Chris right now, kissing took on a different light. Chris Yoder wasn't a boy. He was a young man. He looked away, then looked back, and gave her shoulders a gentle shake. Something flickered behind his eyes. "I don't feel sorry for you. Not at all. You don't realize what you have here. You have something that most people would give their eyeteeth for in a heartbeat. A family, a place of belonging. A purpose—you're needed in that schoolhouse."

He was practically nose-to-nose to her. Her heart was thumping so loudly she was sure he could hear it. He brushed his fingers over her cheek. She had never felt anything like it: a touch more quiet than a breath.

"You might be the prettiest girl in Stoney Ridge, but if you don't have the smarts to appreciate that—all that—then you don't deserve the life you've been given." He reached behind her and plucked her dad's black slicker, hanging on a wall peg. As he slipped it over his head, he said, "Jenny will be pacing the front room like a circus lion if I don't get back soon. She hates storms. Tell your dad I'll bring this back in the morning." He slid the barn door open, just enough to slip through, then he disappeared.

Through the opening, M.K. watched Chris run down the driveway in the pelting rain. How dare he! How dare he speak to her like she was a child. Why, he was using the very same tone she had used to scold Eugene Miller barely an hour ago. Chris Yoder had a regular way of dousing any momentary warmth she might have felt for him.

Insults. That's all she was getting today. Eugene told her she couldn't teach a dog to bark and Chris told her she didn't have much smarts. Boys! So rude.

Then a small smile crept up on her face. Chris had said she was pretty. The prettiest girl in Stoney Ridge.

No one had ever called her pretty. They had called her nosy and sneaky and overly imaginative. Not pretty.

Jimmy Fisher had just delivered another one of his mother's notes to Hank Lapp. He didn't know what was in this note, but he didn't really need to know. Hank read it and started sputtering away about how insensitive and heartless some females could be. Jimmy's mother, he meant. It wasn't hard to figure that she must have spurned Hank again.

Those dogs of Hank's really irked Jimmy's mother. Granted, Edith Fisher was a woman who was easily irked, but these dogs set her teeth on edge. Hank would promise not to bring them to the Fishers', and that would last a time or two, until he arrived at the door surrounded by yellow fur and black noses. Doozy always smelled like he needed a bath, which he did. Add four little Doozies to the mix. It was too much for any woman to bear! Edith had declared. And Hank was spurned again.

Jimmy listened to Hank's rants and raves for a while, until Hank got distracted by a tool he had just spotted underneath a buggy part. "DAD-GUMIT! I've been looking for that screwdriver for days."

With Hank's head under a buggy, it was a perfect time for Jimmy to slip out undetected. He headed over to the house to find M.K. Wooing her wasn't working out quite the way he had hoped—mainly, because she didn't seem to realize he was wooing her. A few days ago, he brought a bouquet of flowers and she asked if he was heading to a graveyard. He stopped by the schoolhouse and invited her for a hamburger at the new diner, and she said she had just eaten. Jimmy was flummoxed. Never, ever, ever had a girl turned down an opportunity to spend time with him.

Tonight, he had crafted a new plan. He was going to look for an opportune moment—hidden from Fern and Amos's sight—and kiss M.K. One kiss from Jimmy Fisher, and she would be his. He was an expert kisser. Ruthie had said those very words, right before he broke up with her. He always felt a little bad about that timing. Unfortunate.

Fern turned Jimmy away at the door. She said that M.K. was out. Nothing more. Just out. As he walked down the driveway, he wondered if it was just his imagination, or if Fern seemed more prickly toward him than usual. As prickly as a cactus.

He heard a woman's voice and turned to locate the source. Coming down the orchard path was M.K. in her beekeeper's getup, with her big netted hat tucked under her arm. By her side was Chris Yoder. Jimmy raised his hand, getting ready to yell out to them, when he saw M.K. turn toward Chris, her face animated, talking to him intently. Her hands waved in the air, the way they did when she got excited. Chris was loping beside her, hands in his pockets, but he was listening carefully to her. Jimmy could hear M.K.'s voice float all the way down the hill. Then he heard Chris's laughter join with M.K.'s.

What story could M.K. be telling? What could have possibly made Chris Yoder laugh? Whatever it was, why hadn't M.K. told Jimmy that story? Jimmy felt strangely unsettled.

M.K. snapped open a fresh sheet and watched it settle gently over her bed. She smoothed the wrinkles and tucked in the corners. She had always loved the feel of cool clean linen beneath her hands, had always loved to crawl between crisp sheets at night.

Why couldn't these simple pleasures be enough for her? They were more than enough for Ruthie and Sadie and Julia. What was wrong with her? Yesterday, she was helping Fern tackle the basket filled with clothes needing ironing. The sweet smell of steaming cotton filled the room. Treading carefully, M.K. asked Fern if she ever wanted to see parts of the world.

"No." Fern kept ironing. "We should want nothing more than the life God has given us. The problem with you, M.K., is you lack contentment."

Contentment. She didn't have it. Not much of it, anyway. In truth, it sounded boring. Cats and dogs were content, and they slept all day.

Fern acted as if gaining contentment was as easy as taking a vitamin pill and M.K. knew it wasn't.

So M.K. took her scooter out to pay a visit to Erma and ask what she thought about contentment. "Personally, I think everyone should be able to seek their own contentment," M.K. said, as she helped Erma gather ripe grapes from her vineyard.

"The only problem with that thinking," Erma said in her calm way, "is that if one can't find contentment at home, one is unlikely to find it anywhere else."

Oh. *Oh.* Could that be true? Did the fact that M.K. had been discontented living in Stoney Ridge mean she was doomed to a life of discontent?

Then, typical of Erma, she turned the whole thing around. "Mary Kate, I have discovered that I am happiest of all when I have learned to be content at home."

Jenny hated arithmetic. She always just wrote any old numbers down before, so she wouldn't have to think about it. Even if writing stories became fun when Teacher M.K. gave them their handmade books, there was no way she could make arithmetic fun. The teacher had an oven timer on her desk and Jenny kept one eye fixed on it. As soon as it went off, math would be over for the day and they could be excused for recess.

Jenny ran behind the far maple tree and sat on the ground, leaning against the tree. This was where she spent every recess and every lunch. She definitely did not want to spend her precious free time with Anna Mae and her group of giggling girls. Besides, they had never asked her to join them.

Jenny pulled out a paper and pencil from her pocket.

Dear Mom, I miss you a LOT.

She chewed on her lip, thinking. What else could she say to her mother? Chris would be upset with her for tipping their mother off to where they were living. He thought their mother would never be able to stay out of jail for long. The counselor at the rehab center explained that using drugs short-circuited your brain so you weren't the same person anymore. Jenny refused to believe that her mother couldn't change. She believed in her, even if no one else did. When she had asked Old Deborah what she thought about that, a sad look covered her sweet wrinkled face. "I believe God can work miracles, Jenny. But our faith is in God, not in people."

I know you probably don't feel very good, but remember: you can do it! You got clean before and felt really good, remember? Keep getting better and better.

Chris is working really hard to fix up Grandfather's house. He has done so much! It is still awful because no one was in it for a long time, except for a creepy bat. The house looks a lot better than it used to. Chris has big plans for the house because he wants to be a horse breeder. He really likes it in Stoney Ridge. Maybe when you are better, you can come live with us. The Colonel left the house to Chris and to me. Old Deborah said so.

Love, Jenny

P.S. I am trying to save as much money as I can to send to you. Please quit smoking! It's not good for you.

A softball bounced on the ground next to her. As Jenny leaned over to pick it up, Eugene Miller ran up to her. She braced herself. You never knew what was going to pop out of Eugene's mouth, and it usually wasn't very nice, though he hadn't actually been unkind to her. Not yet, anyway. She tossed the ball to him, expecting him to catch it and return to the game.

"Nice throwing arm," he said. "Why don't you come play? We need a good shortstop."

She looked up sharply at him, thinking he was making a crack about her height. She had heard all kinds of smart-aleck comments about her small stature: Thumbelina, Oompa Loompa, Shortcake, Peewee, Itsby Bitsy. If Eugene thought "shortstop" was a new nickname to Jenny, he was sorely mistaken.

But he actually seemed sincere. When she hesitated, puzzled that he was being nice, he put his hand out to help her up. "Come on."

Under Eugene's shaggy bangs were bright blue, smiling eyes. Even though his complexion was marred by acne, he had an attractive smile that made dimples in his cheeks. She was surprised to realize how cute he was, up close like this. She shook her head to erase the absurd idea.

She looked at his hand, waiting for her. She folded the letter to her mother and put it in her pocket. The letter could wait. She took Eugene's hand and jumped to her feet.

It had taken Jimmy Fisher more time than he had expected to figure out where Chris Yoder was living. It was strange that no one seemed to know. He was sure someone at Windmill Farm would know, but Amos was away at a farm equipment auction and Hank didn't have any idea where Chris lived. Even Fern didn't know—and she knew just about everything. He finally tracked down M.K. and she knew. He should have known. M.K. knew all sorts of facts about people in Stoney Ridge that no one else knew.

That afternoon, Jimmy rolled into the long narrow driveway of Colonel Mitchell's old house and found Chris replacing rotted boards in the covered wraparound porch floor. Jimmy couldn't find a hitching post to tie the reins of his horse and buggy and finally decided on a tree branch. He waved to Chris, who had stopped sawing a board when he saw Jimmy drive in. "Looks like you could use a hand."

Chris looked surprised. He hesitated, then said, "I wouldn't refuse it." He handed the saw to Jimmy across the sawhorse.

Jimmy waved away the saw. Instead, he picked up a hammer. "You keep cutting boards and I'll nail them in place. There's an excellent chance I would lose a finger or two by cutting. I'm not known for paying too much attention to details. Too risky." He held up his hands and bent a few fingers down, as if he was already missing a few. "It's killing my career as a classical pianist."

He got a laugh out of Chris at that. That meant a lot to Jimmy, to get a laugh out of a serious guy like Chris Yoder. He had the impression that Chris didn't laugh much. Jimmy would change that, if they were going to be friends.

The two worked side by side for the next hour or so, not speaking unless it pertained to the porch. When all of the rotted boards had been replaced, a small girl brought out a pitcher of water and two glasses. Jimmy had seen her at church and at Windmill Farm once or twice. He had figured out she was Chris's sister, Jenny, but he had a hard time believing she was in eighth grade. She reminded him of an elf. She stared at him as she handed him a glass, as if she had never seen anyone who looked like him before. It was a stare he was accustomed to by women of all ages. He knew he was handsome, had known it all his life. He wasn't being proud. It was just a fact. He gave Jenny his most charming smile and she practically gasped. Her little feet barely made a noise on the steps as she hurried away. She wrenched the door open. It banged shut behind her.

Chris and Jimmy sat on the new porch floor and gulped the water down.

"Did you just happen to be passing by?" Chris asked. "How did you figure out where I live?"

"M.K. Lapp told me."

Chris took a sip of water. "Know her well?"

"I do. Very well. I'm planning to make her my missus."

Chris started coughing, as if he had taken in a sip of water down the wrong pipe. Jimmy whacked his back with enthusiasm. He was always trying to be helpful.

"I owe you a favor," Chris said. "You saved me more than a half day's work."

"Glad to help," Jimmy said. He turned around to look at the old house. "Looks like you've got a lot of work to do. I could try and come over now and then to help."

"I could use the help, but I can't pay you cash. If there's some other way I can return a favor, let me know. I don't like to be beholden."

Jimmy took another swig of water, his mind working. He wiped his mouth with his sleeve. He looked at Samson, grazing in the paddock. He grinned. "Well, now, if that's the case, we might just be able to figure something out."

13

Chris jerked awake from a heavy, dreamless sleep and sat straight up, blinking, trying to gather information as fast as possible. Where was he? Was there any trouble? What had his mother done now?

The soft light of dawn splashed on the slanted walls of his bedroom.

No, he didn't have to worry about his mother. She wasn't here. She was in Marysville, Ohio, in a rehabilitation treatment center. And he was in Stoney Ridge, Pennsylvania.

With a sigh of relief, he fell back on the soft bed and scrunched the pillow under his head like a nest. It was still super-early. Too early to get up.

He didn't want to think about his mother. He didn't want any news about her.

But he did.

When it came right down to it, it just wasn't that easy to give up completely on the family you were born into. As much as he wanted to, he couldn't rid himself entirely of the hope that one day his mother would be well.

Chris wished he'd been born into a regular family, one where everyone was just a normal person. But right from the start something was wrong, because there was no father, and his mother was not equipped for motherhood. She was young, immature, selfish, and loved to party. Chris ended up living with his grandfather, who never did know what to do with his rebellious daughter, even less with a baby. Then his mother moved back home again and life took on a reasonable calm, until his mother and grandfather started fighting all the time and his mother started using drugs for the first time. The thing about methamphetamine was that it was highly addictive. One time, two times, and she was hooked.

The counselor at the rehab center said that meth changed your brain chemistry, so you weren't the same person. There was always hope, Old Deborah would say. Always, always hope.

Hope. He turned that word over in his mind, the way a gold miner might examine a rock for specks of promising glitter. No sooner would he feel the comfort of the word and fear would swoop in from the sidelines to snatch it away. He lifted his head and peered out the window to see what kind of day it was, but his mind was still on Old Deborah.

Old Deborah talked so strangely, so intimately about God, as if the Almighty spoke to her the way he spoke to people in the Bible.

Chris believed in God, of course. He had attended church ever since he started to live with Old Deborah after they moved to Ohio—when he was eight and his mother had been put in jail the first time, for using credit cards from a lady who had asked them to housesit while she visited her sick daughter. His mother was in and out of jail or rehab after that, mostly in. She believed the world owed her something, and she had no problem helping herself to it. Her chief income strategy was to live off the generosity of others, and she always seemed to find kindly people who were willing to give her another chance. Chris didn't believe his mother had the capacity to change. Old Deborah would tell him that nothing was outside of God's capacity to redeem. But it wasn't God whom Chris doubted—it was his mother.

The morning was chilly. Winter was coming. Chris got up, dressed, and went to the living room. He made a fire in the fireplace and it finally began to heat the downstairs. He stayed by the fire for a moment, warming his hands. Samson would be expecting breakfast soon. As he put his boots on, he looked around the room. The walls were repaired and painted. The broken windows were replaced. The stair railing was fastened. The broken latticework around the porch foundation had been fixed. He had ripped out the rotting kitchen flooring and laid new linoleum—he was able to buy linoleum tiles for a bargain because the hardware store had ordered the tiles for a lady and she didn't like the tan color. He didn't really like the color, either, but he liked the price.

He still had a long list of things to do, but the house was getting into shape. He thought his grandfather would be pleased. Memories flashed at random intervals, faster than he could take them in—the way his grandfather ducked his tall frame when passing through a doorway, his uncanny accuracy at reading the night sky and knowing tomorrow's weather, and how his old dog would respond to his slightest whistle. He remembered the way his grandfather would scold him for slamming doors, how mad that used to make him. Chris could never figure out why that was a big deal.

Flashes of his previous life surprised him like this. He sure wouldn't mind hearing his grandfather scold him about those slammed doors now. No, he sure wouldn't.

The sun was hanging low in the sky, casting a mellow autumn glow across the garden. Amos checked the ripening pumpkins. Soon, they would be ready to pick so Fern could can them. He whistled for Doozy and strolled out to the orchards, with the dog trotting behind him.

As he reached the orchard, he feasted his senses, turning his face into the warm breeze. He sampled a still-tart, late-to-ripen variety of apple off the tree and examined the pears, swelling toward perfection. M.K.'s brown bees had worked their magic again.

Ah, Mary Kate.

Amos had stopped in at the schoolhouse this morning to drop off M.K.'s forgotten lunch, and thought he might stay for a few moments, quietly observing in the back. He ended up spending two hours, mesmerized.

Amos glimpsed a side of his youngest daughter he had never seen before. Her quick brown eyes took everything in—she could listen to one scholar's recitation while simultaneously managing the entire wild pack of big boys. It seemed to him that she was a born teacher—patient, creative, dedicated. If a pupil had trouble grasping a concept, he saw her search for a new approach. He observed her trying a different explanation until the light of understanding finally lit a pupil's eyes. He never saw her lose her temper or grow impatient, no matter how thick-skulled or stubborn the pupils could be at times. And Eugene Miller, he noticed, could be both.

Usually, he cut M.K.'s descriptions about people in half. Some truth, heavily embroidered with exaggeration. Not so for Eugene Miller. Watching that boy's sulky behavior, he decided that she was telling the complete and total truth.

"You can do this," she would urge him. "It's not as hard as it seems, take your time." The satisfaction on her face when Eugene finally caught on told Amos that for M.K., the joy of teaching was its own reward. Who could have imagined it? Fern had been right all along—M.K. would rise to the challenge of teaching.

Children. You think you have a sense of who they are, the person they've become . . . and then they surprise you by becoming another person entirely.

He squinted against the sun. His eyes swept over the orchards. These orchards, planted by his grandfather years ago, added to by his own father, had kept Windmill Farm solvent during some lean years when Amos had heart trouble. He stood there for a while, amid the long, even rows of trees, branches weighed down with heavy fruit. A farmer always looked forward, sacrificing long hours in anticipation of a good harvest. A reflection of God's character.

The trees were lovely reminders to him of God's steady reassurance—that goodness and gentleness will someday prevail. He ran his fingertips over a branch and almost marveled, as if he could imagine his grandfather planting the tree as a mere twig. He lifted his head, breathed deeply of the pear-scented air, felt his heart tighten with gratitude.

Herr, he thought, *denki*. Lord God, thank you.

A Saturday came, silent and sun-dazzled. M.K. turned off the burner under the pot of beans. She sprinkled some brown sugar into the pot, then a little ketchup. She stirred in some more of each, then added salt and pepper. She tasted it. *Not bad.* She got the apple cider vinegar out of the cupboard and stirred in a little of that and tasted it again. *Better.*

M.K. moved the pot to the oven, where it could bake peacefully.

She opened the kitchen door and stepped out into her yard.

There, coming up the driveway, was Jenny Yoder. M.K. crossed the yard to reach her.

Jenny was soaked with water. "I'm looking for my brother. Do you know where he is?"

"My uncle Hank talked him into going into town to pick up some buggy parts at the hardware store," M.K. said. "He shouldn't be too long, if you want to wait. What happened to you?"

Jenny looked uncertain. "I was trying to fill a water bucket for the horse and when I turned this, it broke off in my hands." She held up a water spigot. "I can't get the water to stop. It's shooting everywhere, like a geyser!"

Amos was on the far side of the barn, hooking Cayenne's bridle to the buggy shafts.

"Let's ask my dad what to do," M.K. said. She took the water spigot from Jenny and explained the situation to Amos.

He looked at the rusty edges of it. "M.K., get my wrench from my workbench. And see if you can find another spigot in the top right drawer." He looked at Jenny. "Hop in. We'll get that water shut off in the blink of an eye."

"I'll come too," Fern said, appearing out of the barn like magic, startling Amos. He practically jumped.

"Everybody knows Fern has a knack for turning up out of the blue," M.K. whispered to Jenny. "You'd think Dad would be used to it."

The way Jenny looked at her then, almost giggling, filled M.K. with some relief. It was the first time Jenny hadn't peered at her with that suspicious, birdlike glare. Maybe she was finally thawing out.

Chris decided that he wouldn't seek the sheriff out on his trip to town today, but if he happened to see him, he would tell him about the memory—or was it a dream?—that seemed to pop into his head last night.

Maybe. But maybe not.

Of course, just as he pulled into the edge of town, he saw the sheriff's car at the silverstream diner, The Railway Station. Chris thought it was a strange choice for a diner name because Stoney Ridge didn't have a train running through it, but he had heard the burgers were good. If he ever had an extra ten dollars to spend, he should take Jenny out for a burger and shake. If he had an extra twenty dollars, he might consider asking Mary Kate Lapp out for a meal.

Maybe. But maybe not.

After all, she was spoken for by Jimmy Fisher. A pang twisted Chris's gut, and he knew it wasn't hunger. Thinking of M.K. with someone else didn't set well.

Chris had taken pains to avoid Mary Kate after finding out that particular piece of news. This morning, he was even a little rude to her. She brought him coffee in the barn and he refused it, brushing past her as if he was on his way to put out a fire. He wasn't the kind who would ever take another fellow's girl, especially a friend's. And Jimmy Fisher had been a friend to him. He had come over again last Saturday afternoon to help Chris tackle the overgrown yard.

Chris knew Jimmy had an angle—he was itching to borrow Samson for a horse race. That wasn't going to happen, not ever, despite Jimmy's strong hints. Still, Chris couldn't help smiling at the challenge. Jimmy Fisher was the type who made a competition out of everything. How fast you could hammer nails. How quickly you could rip boards off the porch. Everything was an opportunity for a race. Even stupid things, like thinking you could race a hot-blooded stallion at the tracks. Everybody knew you didn't take a stallion to the tracks. Too distracting. Stallions instinctively tried to create a harem. Everybody knew that.

Besides, the thought of gambling repulsed Chris. It reminded him of his mother—always wanting something for nothing.

Jimmy Fisher had an answer for gambling, when Chris asked him why a Plain person was at the tracks. Jimmy said that horse racing was in the best interest of the animal. "These horses are trained day after day to forget the instincts they're born with." Jimmy insisted that racing helped a horse work out its desire to be free, to roam wild, so that it could return to the fieldwork as a happier beast, knowing it had reached its full potential.

There was no point in responding to such a bogus explanation. Jimmy had an answer for everything, Chris had quickly discovered. Still, he found himself enjoying Jimmy's company. Jimmy was hard not to like.

Chris pulled the horse over to the side of the road, trying to decide if he would go in to talk to the sheriff or not. Maybe. Maybe not. Should he? Or shouldn't he?

He'd come so far these last few months, and the slightest misstep could wipe all that out.

"Got something else for me, Yoder?"

Chris practically jumped at the sound of the sheriff's voice right at his buggy window. "Last night," he said, "I woke up from a dead sleep. I had a vision so real that I couldn't remember if I dreamed it or it was real." He took a deep breath. "There was a woman who had come over to help us sometimes. She took pity on our family and used to bring food. She would give me her son's hand-me-down clothes. Stuff like that."

"Go on," Sheriff Hoffman said, leaning his arms against the open buggy window.

"One afternoon, my mother sent me upstairs to check on the baby. Jenny was crying, and I remember hearing my mother's voice get louder and louder. I crept down the stairs, and I saw the neighbor lady holding my mother's arm as if she was trying to stop her."

"Stop her from what?"

This was what was hard to say. "From doing drugs. My mother is—was—is a drug addict. Methamphetamine. Back then, she would buy a lot of Sudafed and make her own meth."

The sheriff didn't miss a beat. He was probably used to this kind of thing, but it still shamed Chris. "Go on. What happened next?"

"My mother became angrier and angrier at the neighbor. She saw me on the stairs and yelled at me to get upstairs." Chris paused to collect himself for a long moment. "The neighbor lady was trying to calm my mother down, but my mother was shouting at her to leave and mind her own business. Then, suddenly, there was silence. A strange silence. The next thing I knew, my mother raced upstairs, grabbed a suitcase, and started to throw things into it. She picked up the baby, told me to get in the car, and we left Stoney Ridge."

"Did you see the other woman leave the house?"

Chris shook his head. "No. We went out the back door of the kitchen to get to the car."

Sheriff Hoffman rubbed his chin. "What do you remember of this woman? Do you remember her name?"

Chris squinted his eyes, thinking hard. "No, I can't remember her name. Only that she was Amish." Out of the blue, a name popped out at him. "Mattie. No—Maggie." A cold chill ran through Chris. He had a feeling that he had just made things much, much worse by telling the truth. He should not have said anything at all. But he had to know. "Why? Did something happen to that woman? Did something happen that day?"

Sheriff Hoffman gave an infinitesimal nod of his head. "I was just a rookie that spring. I was told to make an arrest for accidental manslaughter. I did what I was told. I made the arrest. But something never added up to me. Something always bothered me about it."

"But . . . who did you arrest?"

Sheriff Hoffman's penetrating stare was unnerving. "Your grandfather. Colonel Mitchell."

Was it possible? How could this be? Amos followed Jenny Yoder's instructions to drive to her house. He felt a shiver up his spine when she pointed to a narrow drive that led to Colonel Mitchell's house. He hadn't been to this house in fourteen years, and he had never wanted to cross the threshold again. Not ever.

Fern and Jenny were debating bread dough and starters and yeast and he couldn't even make any sense of their conversation. All that he could do was to pray one prayer, over and over and over: Herr, hilf mich. *God, help me.* When Amos reached the house, he saw the water spewing out from the side yard pipe. He hopped out of the buggy and went straight to the pipe. He needed time to think and was grateful for something to do.

When he noticed Fern climb out of the buggy, he called out, "This won't take but a moment. You stay put."

She snapped her head up at the sharp tone in his voice and gave him a strange look. "Jenny is going to show me the house. It won't take long." She turned her attention to Jenny and helped her out of the buggy.

Fern didn't understand. But how could she, when he had never told her how Maggie had died? He had only told her it was an accident. That God had been merciful and Maggie hadn't suffered. He hadn't told her that she had been trying to help the English neighbor that bordered their farm, because there was no father, and the mother wasn't quite right. The woman had a little boy, a few years older than M.K., and a baby girl who cried a lot. And she lived with her father, Colonel Mitchell. A tough guy, he liked to call himself. A former Marine. And a former football player, in the days when helmets were flimsy, he would say.

His mind racing, Amos looked around until he found the main water pipe to the house and turned it off. Then he went to the broken spigot, wrenched off what remained of it, screwed on the new spigot, turned back on the main water. Checked to see if there was any leak, gathered his tools.

Why was Chris Yoder living here? *Why, why, why?*

And then it hit him—so hard he had to sit down. A melee of emotions—dread, anger, guilt—struck him all at once. He realized why he thought Chris looked vaguely familiar. Chris was the Colonel's grandson. Chris was that little boy Maggie was always worried about. Too serious, Maggie had said. Much too serious for a little boy. Always worried about his mother and his baby sister. It was as if he hadn't been allowed a childhood.

And Jenny—she was only a baby. A baby with colic, like his own son, Menno. Maggie had found goat's milk helped Menno's indigestion as a baby, so she wanted to take goat's milk over to the Colonel's house. He vividly remembered the day—it was the first warm day of spring after an exceptionally cold winter. The crocuses were blooming, and Maggie had been so excited to see her first robin that very morning. "Spring is finally here," she told Amos as she explained where she was headed. Julia and Sadie were in school. Menno and M.K. were in the barn with him, playing with some new kittens.

"Let them stay and play," he had told Maggie. "I'll watch them."

She had kissed him on the cheek and promised she wouldn't be long.

But she never returned.

Looking back, Amos viewed his life as if divided into two halves: before Maggie died, and after. He believed that God's hand was on Maggie's passing. He believed that her life was complete. He believed that God had a purpose. God had a plan. He believed that with his whole heart. He banked his eternal life on that belief. But the reality of living without Maggie was a harsh one. He likened it to how someone must have felt if he lost his sense of taste: a person might continue to eat, to provide sustenance and nourishment to his body, but life had lost all flavor. Grief-stricken was just the word: grief had literally reached out and struck him, and left a permanent mark.

"Amos, are you all right?"

Fern and Jenny appeared beside him, shocking him into the present. He picked up the wrench and the broken spigot. "Yes. Yes. I'm fine. I'm ready to go."

Fern looked at Jenny and dusted her hands together the way she always did when she was making up her mind. "I think we should organize a work frolic to help Chris with some repairs."

Jenny's face scrunched up. "I don't think Chris wants any help."

"Nonsense. It's our way," Fern said, being annoyingly practical. "Come back to the house and we can make plans." She started back to the buggy.

Jenny looked to Amos to intervene. "I don't think Chris is going to like that."

Amos had no idea how to respond. He still felt as if he was trying to process through a mountain of buried memories. "We can count on Fern to know what to do," he managed at last.

Back in the buggy, Amos flicked the reins over the horses' backs. Slowly the buggy started off again. His heart and mind, though, remained at Colonel Mitchell's house.

14

Early Monday morning, Teacher M.K. stood by the schoolhouse door, waiting for the scholars, smiling and talking with everyone in her mile-a-minute way. As hard as Jenny tried not to, she found herself growing increasingly intrigued by Teacher M.K.'s unique teaching style. And Teacher M.K. wouldn't let Jenny fade into the background like she usually did. She simply wouldn't allow it. She would call on Jenny in class even when she didn't raise her hand. She would read parts of her story out loud as if she thought they were any good. And they weren't. Jenny was sure they weren't. Anna Mae Glick told her so.

With Teacher M.K., the world got bigger and then it got smaller. Jenny was amazed. She was starting to notice things she had never noticed before.

First, Teacher M.K. taught them about the stars in the sky, and how the ancient mariners could find their way across the oceans by charting the stars. She brought in seashells and pieces of coral that she had found at a garage sale. She pointed out how a conch seashell looked like the inside of a person's ear, and that coral looked like veins and arteries.

Next, she brought in an old microscope she had bought for $5 at that same garage sale. She had the class look at things that were too small to see. She said there were much stronger microscopes that could see things even smaller than they could see with the garage sale microscope. A drop from the water pump became a regular sideshow of squirming cells. Jenny hadn't taken a sip of water from that pump since.

Today, Teacher M.K. had brought in fern leaves and put one on every single desk. "Tell me what you see," she said.

The room went very still as the scholars counted the leaves. Even the rowdy boys who usually whispered and snickered throughout the lesson sat as still as mannequins.

"The lines on the leaf are like blood vessels," Danny Riehl said. He adjusted his spectacles for a better look. Danny had this way of looking at things very carefully, even little things. He was always taking things apart and putting them back together. Anything he was curious about. Jenny was a little sorry that Danny was younger than she was, and even more sorry that Anna Mae had dibbs on him. Jenny thought he showed great promise. "And would that be the nervure?"

"He's always making up them big words," Eugene Miller sputtered. "He talks like he's playing Scrabble and is looking for points."

"*Nervure* is a word for the rib of a leaf," Teacher M.K. said. "It's just a more precise way of explaining something."

Danny looked at Teacher M.K. and smiled that smile of his, like when she told him about black holes in the sky and stuff like that. In a strange way, Jenny thought they understood each other.

Teacher M.K. said that there were all kinds of illustrations in nature that pointed to the Creator of the universe. God's handprint was on all of his work, just like when we sign our drawings. Just like that.

Gazing at the fern leaf, Jenny blurted out, "Count the little leaves! They come out just right! Look. On each row there's just one more leaf less, until it gets to the top."

Teacher M.K. looked pleased. "You, Jenny Yoder, just figured out today's arithmetic problem."

Imagine that, Jenny thought. *Me. Arithmetic.*

Mary Kate had been teaching for nearly ten weeks now. She had good days and she had bad days, but she wasn't thinking quite as often about running off to Borneo. Last week, she had a terrible, awful day and promptly sent off her passport application in the mail. Eugene Miller had gone too far, yet again, and put a snake in her pencil drawer. She hated snakes! Always had. She blamed Jimmy Fisher and a certain black racer snake.

Getting her picture taken for the passport made her feel as exposed as if she had run through Main Street in her underwear. She waited at the post office until she was sure no one was around whom she might recognize. Then she quickly had her picture taken by the postal clerk. As soon as it was ready, she signed the application, stuck the money order in the envelope with the application, and handed it to the clerk without allowing herself a second thought. It was a weak moment, one she wasn't proud of, but knowing it was a done deal gave her a feeling of satisfaction.

In the meantime, she had taken Erma Yutzy's advice to heart. She tried to find ways to connect to each pupil, to look for that golden moment. Teaching had become strangely satisfying, though winning the affection of the pupils was proving to be harder than she had expected. Not with the little ones, like Barbara Jean, or the bright ones, like Danny Riehl. But some of the older boys and girls were harder to convince, like there was Jenny Yoder. Jenny remained cool and distant. A bright spot occurred today when Jenny started to notice the patterns in the leaf and connected it to math patterns. That was good. Very good.

But later in the day, she had asked Jenny and Anna Mae Glick if they might like to stay after school and help her set up the art project for the next day. She had hoped that if Anna Mae could get to know Jenny, she might start including her with the other girls. But Anna Mae wrinkled her nose and scrunched up her face so tightly that M.K. thought she might suddenly be in pain. "Danny likes me to walk home with him from school." She swiftly made her escape without a word of farewell.

M.K. knew that wasn't true. Danny usually burst out of the schoolhouse as soon as she rang the dismissal bell and disappeared into the cornfield before Anna Mae had time to gather her things.

Jenny watched Anna Mae flounce out of the schoolhouse. And then she said, almost in a whisper, "She acts like I'm invisible."

"You're not, you know," M.K. pressed.

Jenny hesitated, her intense eyes searching M.K.'s face. "Not what?"

"Invisible."

Jenny looked at M.K., then looked away, but not before M.K. saw the way her eyes narrowed and two lines formed between her thin little eyebrows. "Fern is expecting me." She turned and hurried out the door.

M.K. could have kicked herself. Why did she always seem to say the wrong thing or do the wrong thing when she was around those Yoders? Just when they started to open up, she had to say something that scared them off. A turtle in its shell.

Wouldn't it be nice, Jenny thought as she walked to school, if you could shorten the bad days and save up the time to make a good day even longer? This morning, for example, she would like to swap out for two Christmas mornings.

She knew the entire day was headed in the wrong direction when she overcooked the scrambled eggs for breakfast. Fern had warned her to cook eggs slowly, but Chris was in a hurry, so Jenny turned up the flame on the stove. She burnt her finger on the hot pan handle and couldn't find a bandage. Then the eggs ended up looking like rubber cement. They tasted worse. Chris didn't complain, but Jenny was disappointed. Yesterday, Fern had given Jenny those brown eggs, still warm from Windmill Farm's henhouse, and Jenny had wasted them. Eggs were precious.

Chris hurried off to work and Jenny got ready for school. She heard a knock at the door and ran to get it, thinking it was Chris. But no! Rodney Gladstone, that overeager real estate agent who was always dropping by, stood at the door with that greasy smile on his face. He held out a handful of mail to Jenny. Her mail. On top was a thin gray envelope with her mother's familiar handwriting on it.

"I bumped into the mailman just a few minutes ago," Rodney said, still smiling. "Thought I'd save you a trip."

Jenny grabbed the mail from him and closed the door, but Rodney stuck the toe of his shoe in the threshold, leaving two inches of space to talk through. "I happened to be at the county clerk's office. Happened to discover that the legal owner of this house is a woman named Grace Mitchell. No one seems to know where she might be."

Jenny squeezed the door harder on his foot.

"I happened to notice the letter you just received is from a Grace Mitchell."

Rodney's voice rose a few notes from pain inflicted on his foot. "The return address says Marysville, Ohio."

Jenny leaned against the door and pushed as hard as she could, and Rodney finally yelped. He pulled his foot out of the threshold and Jenny closed the door tight.

"Any chance that Grace Mitchell is the daughter of Colonel Mitchell?" Rodney called through the closed door. "Any chance Grace Mitchell is your mother?"

Jenny locked the door behind him. She tore open her mother's letter:

Hi sugar! How ya doing? Listen, Jennygirl, I could sure use some extra cash right now. Would you believe they make us buy our own toothpaste here? I'll bet Chris has some moola tucked away. Check under his mattress—that's where he keeps it. SHHHHhhhhh! Just our secret, you and me. Thanks, babygirl! Never forget your mama loves you! XOXOXOXOXOXOXOXOXOXO

Jenny folded the letter and put it in her pocket as she heard Rodney Gladstone's car start up and drive down the driveway.

She had a very bad feeling about today. She often had bad feelings about days, especially Mondays, but this was different. This was worse.

M.K. had been certain Chris might drop by the schoolhouse or accept Fern's standing invitation to come to dinner. She thought she might bump into him somewhere. But she hadn't seen him in nearly two weeks. Their friendship had been progressing, and then, boom, it just ended. M.K. wasn't good at handling rejection. It had never happened to her.

It was a beautiful fall afternoon—slightly crisp, with the tangy smell of burning leaves in the air. Fern had planned to can garden-grown pumpkins all day, so M.K. was in no hurry to head home. No sir! Canning food in a steamy kitchen might be her least favorite activity. She took the long way and stopped at the cemetery where her mother and her brother, Menno, were buried. The tops of the trees swayed gently in the breeze. She walked up to her mother's grave and dropped down to clear away the dandelions and brush a bit of moss off the gravestone. Her mother had been gone for most of M.K.'s life, and she couldn't quite recall her like she wanted to. Sometimes, she thought she only remembered remembering her.

She closed her eyes, trying to think what life had been like before her mother died. The images were so mixed up they never made much sense. She remembered a time when her mother had lifted her into the air and laughed as they whirled breathlessly around the room. Her mother smelled like cookies. And she remembered her father coming into the room and wrapping his arms around the two of them. A sandwich hug, he called it, and his littlest girl was the filling.

That was it. That was about all she clearly remembered of her mother.

"Are you all right?"

M.K. lifted her face, and there stood Chris Yoder, his brow furrowed in concern.

"Are you all right?" he repeated.

She stumbled to her feet. "Where did you come from?"

"I was passing by and saw your red scooter by the fence, then I saw you drop like a stone—I thought maybe you'd . . . fainted or a crow was dive-bombing at you . . . something like that."

"I'm fine," she said, feeling oddly nervous, oddly pleased. Chris had been worried about her! She pointed to her mother's grave. "I was just pulling weeds."

Chris walked up to her and read the tombstone out loud. "Margaret Zook Lapp, beloved wife and mother." When he read the date, his eyebrows lifted. "You must have been young when she died."

She nodded. "Only five."

He half smiled. His smile was soft. He inclined his head as if he was weighing how much to say. "You must miss her."

Would she ever stop missing her mother? "I think about her every day. But you know what that's like. Don't you miss your folks?"

"Yeah, sure." But Chris looked away when he spoke, and M.K. could tell that he was lying. Too late, she recalled how Jenny had evaded the question about her parents, or where she was from, just like Chris was doing.

But then he smiled at her and his eyes crinkled at the corners. A funny sensation flitted through her. She felt that peculiar moment of connection weave between them, as if they shared something. Then the moment passed. He was gazing deeply into her eyes with his bright spring-water blue ones and he began to have a mesmerizing effect on her, the same way he had in the barn on that rainy day. She couldn't have moved away from him any more than the poles of two magnets could be pulled apart. "Are you coming from town?"

Chris nodded. "Your Uncle Hank needed a part for a buggy he's working on."

"You're working as much for Uncle Hank's buggy shop as you are for Dad's orchards."

"I don't mind. I need the work." Cayenne tossed her head and whinnied. Chris turned to look at her standing on the road, tied to a fence. "Your uncle is expecting me. I'd better get the part to him." He turned to leave, then stopped. "Do you need a ride home?" A slight smirk covered his face. "Unless, I suppose, your boyfriend is coming to get you?" He started to walk toward the buggy.

What? "Wait!" she called. "Who's my boyfriend?" She hurried to catch up with him.

Chris didn't answer. He helped M.K. into the buggy, tossed her scooter on the backseat, and climbed up beside her. He gave a quick "tch-tch" to the horse and a light touch on the reins and they were on their way home. He whooshed past a slow-moving car as if in a hurry to deliver M.K. as quickly as possible.

M.K. tried once again. "Why do you think I have a boyfriend? Because I don't. I don't know who told you otherwise, but I do not have a boyfriend."

"I see." He was trying not to grin, but she thought the news pleased him. She hoped so.

"Are you going to tell me who is spreading rumors about me?"

Chris remained quiet for a moment, then gave her a sideways glance.

Right, M.K. thought. The information flowed only one way.

Fern had left Jenny in the kitchen at Windmill Farm, waiting for the oven buzzer to go off and remind her that the last few pies were done, while she took one pie over to a sick neighbor. Jenny and Fern had made six pies this afternoon—three apple, three pumpkin—and the kitchen was filled with spicy cinnamon. Fern had showed her how to roll out dough and how to keep a bottom crust from getting soggy in the middle.

Jenny found a piece of paper and an envelope and sat at the kitchen table to write her mother a letter.

> Dear Mom,
>
> I met a nice lady who is teaching me how to bake. First she taught me to bake sourdough bread rolls. The first batch could have chipped a tooth, but by batch four, they were tasting pretty good. Now she's teaching me to make pies. Here's a secret: adding a teaspoon of vinegar into the crust helps to make it flaky. Did you know that?

Of course she didn't. Her mother had never baked a piecrust in her life.

Jenny didn't know what else to write. She didn't want to sound too happy, and she didn't want to seem as if Fern was replacing her role as a mother. Her mom could be touchy about that kind of thing. She had never wanted to hear about what Jenny had learned from Old Deborah either, and she always made fun of their Amish clothing. She used to whisper to Jenny, "As soon as I get out of here, I am giving you a makeover. The works!"

The first time that she could remember her mom getting released from jail, they moved from Old Deborah's into a halfway house. Her mom gave Jenny a short haircut and took her to a thrift shop for some new old clothes and plunked Chris and Jenny in a public school. Her mother stayed clean for a few months, but it didn't last long. She had found some work cleaning houses for rich ladies and might have helped herself to their credit cards.

That time, her mother was sent to jail for a longer time. Something about having priors—whatever that meant. Chris and Jenny settled back comfortably at Old Deborah's. They had made friends and quickly picked up the Pennsylvania Dutch language from Old Deborah and their friends. Three years later, when their mother was released, she yanked them away from Old Deborah and set up housekeeping in a grungy apartment with cockroaches. Chris and Jenny started yet another public school, but they hated it. They felt as if they were walking a tightrope between two worlds: Amish and English. Kids made fun of them for the way they talked or mocked them because they didn't know television shows or video games. Just as they had finally made a friend or two and life was beginning to be tolerable, their mother started using drugs again. She bought some meth from an undercover police officer.

Back Chris and Jenny went to Old Deborah's.

The third time Grace Mitchell was released from jail, Old Deborah convinced her to let the children stay at the farm and keep going to the Amish school. She offered to let Grace live with them too. Jenny's mom complained the entire time that her children had been brainwashed, but Chris noted that she didn't mind eating Old Deborah's food or sleeping in a clean bed. She stayed off drugs longer that time—six whole months, but it didn't last.

Jenny wanted her mom to get out of the rehab center, but she didn't want another makeover. It took years to grow her hair out again. She liked being Amish and she doubted her mother would let her remain in the church. Chris said not to worry too much about that because he didn't expect their mother to ever stay clean.

Jenny looked around the big kitchen at Windmill Farm. She loved being here. Everything was calm and predictable. Three meals were planned for, each day. Like right now she could open the cupboard and there would be cereal, and on the counter were some apples and pears, and there was milk in the fridge. It was the nicest family Jenny had ever known, and they were all so kind to her and Chris.

There were moments, like now, when she felt an overwhelming sadness. Why couldn't she have been born a Lapp? Why couldn't she have had a mother like Fern and a father like Amos? Not fair. It just wasn't fair.

The oven timer went off and Jenny peeked inside. She thought the pies needed just a little more time, so she set the buzzer for another five minutes. She noticed Fern's coffee can by the buzzer, the one where Fern kept cash. She peeked out the window to make sure no one was coming and opened the can. So much money! There must be hundreds of dollars in that can. What would it be like to have so much money that you could keep extra stored in a coffee can? For she and Chris, it seemed money was barely in their pockets, and it was gone. *Whoosh.*

Then she saw Fern's buggy turn into the driveway. She put the lid on the coffee can and tucked it behind the timer. She hurried to the table and picked up the pencil. It was always so hard to know exactly what to say to her mom. Finally she added:

Here is a little more money. Sorry it can't be more, but I have to be careful. Love you! Jenny

P.S. I've grown so tall you won't believe it!

She smoothed out two five-dollar bills and put them in an envelope addressed to her mom. Everybody had someone to depend on—but Jenny's mom only had Jenny. Even Chris didn't want anything to do with their mother. Taking care of her was up to Jenny.

It was one of those days that made you feel happy to be alive. On a chilly Saturday morning in mid-November, M.K. decided it was high time to winterize the beehives. The weather this fall had been unseasonably warm. Maybe not warm, but not freezing. Still, she knew winter would arrive, fast and furious. She had spent the morning in the honey cabin, bottling the last of the season's honey. Now she covered herself with netting and prepared the smoker. As she stapled fresh tarpaper on the outside of the hives, her mind wandered to the first time she had worked with her brother-in-law, Rome, to prepare the hives. It took months before he would let her come close to the hives—he said she had to learn how to be patient before she could be a beekeeper.

Had she learned to be patient?

In some areas. Wasn't she patient with Eugene Miller's fits-and-starts path to becoming a better reader? It was a slow, slow process, but just when she thought he would never make any progress, there was a breakthrough. Just this week, he had joined in recitations with the rest of his class. She hadn't asked him to, but she had given him the reading assignment a few days ahead so he could prepare if he wanted to. She had been doing that for weeks now and he had always refused. But this time, he read out loud in a clear, steady voice. Nearly flawless. Her heart swelled with pride for him. As Eugene's confidence grew, he was far less annoying to the other children. She couldn't wait to fill Erma Yutzy in on the changes in Eugene. She only hoped that he would have the skills he needed by late May, when he would graduate. Should graduate.

Such a thought amazed her. She was actually thinking about the end of the term. Wouldn't Rome be pleased? She was definitely becoming a woman of patience.

She stapled the last roll of tarpaper and stood back to examine her work. It had to be perfect. The cold weather would slow the bees' activity, but they could survive by keeping the hive at a comfortable temperature. These bees came from a strain of brown bees that Rome's mother had bequeathed to him, and he had bequeathed a hive to M.K.

A jolt shot through her—no one knew how to care for her bees like she did. When she thought about traveling to see a Maori village in New Zealand, she hadn't taken into consideration what would happen to her bees. How in the world could she ever leave her bees?

Jimmy Fisher finally located Hank Lapp in the weeds behind the barn. He had his hands held out in front of him, holding onto dowsing rods, gazing at the ground with intent concentration.

"Looking for water?" Jimmy asked.

Hank startled and dropped the rods. "I was," he groused.

"How do you know when you get close?"

"When I find it, the rods will move by themselves and cross in my hands."

"Let me save you some trouble," Jimmy said. He went over to the spigot and lifted the hose. "I'm pretty sure the water comes out of the faucets."

Hank scowled at him. "For your information, dowsing is a very lucrative skill."

"How so?"

"Let's say you're going to invest in a piece of land. Don't you want to know what's under the surface?"

"I'd probably hire a well company."

"But who's going to tell the well company where to dig, eh?" Hank picked up the dowsing rods, holding them lightly in his hands. In spite of the fact that the faucet and the pipes were just a few yards away, over by the barn, the rods did not jump in his hands or twitch or cross. Hank frowned.

"I just came to tell you that Bishop Elmo is over at the buggy shop. Mad as hops that his buggy isn't repaired yet."

Hank threw down the dowsing rods and pinned Jimmy with a look with his one good eye. "BOY, DON'T YOU HAVE SOMEPLACE YOU NEED TO BE?"

"I do, actually. I came over to look for M.K., but Fern said she's off visiting her scholars' homes." Jimmy mulled that over. "Why would she bother to waste a perfectly good Saturday afternoon on that?"

Hank wasn't listening. His good eye was peeled on an approaching figure. Bishop Elmo had spotted him from across the yard and was heading his way.

15

In the schoolhouse, the countdown to Christmas had begun. A secret gift exchange was planned, and parents were coming for a special program. A light dusting of snow one afternoon caused the scholars' pent-up enthusiasm to explode, like a shaken can of soda. The schoolhouse nearly vibrated with excitement.

M.K. handed out poems for some of the children who volunteered to recite. Anna Mae Glick chose the longest piece to recite. She was sure she had her part down pat. M.K. wasn't as sure.

Each day, the children rehearsed Christmas carols. Day after day, the strains of a miniature heavenly host singing "Joy to the World" wafted out of the schoolhouse. M.K. scanned the ranks—the sun glinted off Danny Riehl's spectacles. Barbara Jean's grown-up front teeth were about halfway in now. She didn't whistle and spit so much when she talked, but her little tongue kept sticking out. She'd grown accustomed to Jenny Yoder's earnest, birdlike look. A well of fondness rose within M.K. for these children. Imagine that! Fondness.

And here was another unexpected surprise in the schoolhouse this Christmas season: Eugene Miller. The boy had a beautiful tenor voice. M.K. started using him as a pitch pipe—to set everyone on the right note. He would roll his eyes whenever she asked him for a G or an E flat, but then he would sit up straight and open his mouth and the exact note would float out of his mouth, right on key. He tried hard not to look pleased, but M.K. could tell he was secretly delighted. The changes she had noticed in him lately were astonishing. There were good days and bad days, but Eugene Miller was becoming a different person.

She had known Eugene all his life, but for the first time she was catching glimpses of how vulnerable he really was. For all his outward swagger, he was a hurt little boy inside, hiding his pain behind pranks and laughter.

How had she not realized? Eugene Miller was starved for attention.

It was late in the day, and the day was late in the season. Winter was coming. The shadows were growing dusky. M.K. had just finished grading papers at the schoolhouse and had one more thing to do: she wanted to tape the scholars' new artwork up on the window as a surprise to them in the morning. She had pushed a desk up against the window and stood on top of it when she heard the door open and spun around to find Chris Yoder standing at the threshold.

He looked at her. "What are you doing up there?"

"Hanging pictures." Startled by his sudden appearance, she felt her face grow warm, so she reached over to smooth a piece of tape out against the window. "What are you doing here?"

"Jenny forgot a book she wanted to finish reading tonight. Which desk is hers?"

She pointed to the far desk in the back row.

Chris crossed the room, opened the desktop, and plucked a book out. "You shouldn't be teetering on a rickety desktop when you're alone in the schoolhouse. You could fall and hit your head and no one would know until morning."

She started to climb down because she had reached as far as she could on that desktop. "That's true. That's actually how my mother died."

Chris helped her down. "Then you should definitely know better." He was so tall he didn't need to stand on top of a desk. She handed him the pictures and he taped each one up, more precisely and evenly than she had been doing. He came to a picture of a snowy owl and stopped. "This should be hanging in a museum."

"I know. It was drawn by Eugene Miller. He's been my most difficult student and my most rewarding one. Both."

Chris looked at her. "Sounds like Samson as a foal. Stubborn and feisty. Every day was a challenge. But he's the one I've learned the most from." He taped Eugene's picture up on the wall. "I love that horse."

The way he said it touched M.K. She didn't know many men who would admit they loved an animal. They talked about the scholars' artwork as he continued to tape the pictures to the window. It struck her that she and Chris were actually having a conversation, getting to know each other, without any need for her to have to apologize for something stupid she had done to him. First time.

She made the mistake of looking up into his eyes, which were as blue as the sky on a clear autumn afternoon. She felt breathless, as if she were treading water and trying not to drown. *Think, think, think. Get my mind on something besides his beautiful blue eyes.* "Tell me about your family, Chris. Where did you grow up?"

A shadow passed over Chris's face. "Raised on a farm outside a town you probably never heard of."

Oh. That was it. It was as if someone had turned the lights off. She had frightened him off again. When would she ever get it right?

Silently, they worked through the last few pictures, then he handed her the tape dispenser. "Did you ever send away for a passport?"

She hesitated. He remembered that?

He read her mind. "The application you dropped that day I passed you on the road. That was *before* you turned me in to the sheriff."

Sheesh! What a memory. Would he ever let that go? "I did," she finally admitted. "It will take awhile before it arrives, though."

"Why did you want one? Are you planning a trip to Canada?"

He was gazing into her eyes, and suddenly, she lost her train of thought altogether. It took her a moment to remember the question. "Uh . . . yes. Canada. Maybe Mexico." She sighed. "Shanghai, Borneo, Istanbul, Paris. Those are just some of the places I want to go to someday. I want to see the whole world."

Chris gave a two-note whistle, one up, one down. "Why?"

Why? "Because . . ." Why? Why? "Because it's exciting. And interesting. And fascinating to see other places. Other people and other cultures." There. That was why.

No. That wasn't why. She had a restive search going on inside of her. She wanted to discover someplace that made her say, "This is it! This is what I've been looking for."

The sound was so faint she couldn't be sure, but she suddenly realized that she was saying these thoughts out loud. She wondered if she might be losing her mind. It was entirely possible. She blamed teaching. Too overwhelming. She hoped it was getting too dark in the schoolhouse for Chris to notice her flushed cheeks.

He smiled. A genuine one. He wasn't laughing at her. "My grandmother would have answered that in a hurry."

"What would she have said?"

He picked the book up from Jenny's desk. "She would have said there's nothing out there that isn't right under your nose." He started toward the door.

"What would you be, if you weren't born Amish?" she blurted, suddenly wanting him to stay.

"I'd be doing exactly what I'm doing right now."

"And what is that?"

"Fixing up a house. Planning to start a horse breeding farm on Samson's fine lineage. Hoping for a farm of my own one day." He stopped and glanced at her. "And if I weren't born Amish, I'd become Amish."

One thing about Chris Yoder—he was not one to linger. He started toward the door again, so she grabbed her sweater and keys to follow him out.

"So if things were different, if you weren't born Amish, and you could be anything in the world, what would you be?"

"I suppose . . ." Should she tell him? This was her deepest secret, after all. "I suppose I would be . . . a detective."

He groaned. "That should put fear in the hearts of all criminals."

"I would love to solve mysteries and help catch criminals. Though," she glanced at him, "I suppose there are some who think my reputation as a detective might not have gotten off to a very good start."

He guffawed. "Might not have?"

She gave him a playful punch on his arm and he ducked away, but it caused her to miss a step on the porch and she lost her balance. He reached out to steady her and somehow ended up with his hands around her waist. She put her hands up against his chest—her face was so close to his that she could even smell the pine soap he showered with—and before she thought twice, she closed her eyes and lifted her chin, expecting him to kiss her.

Nothing. Nothing happened.

When she blinked her eyes open, he was looking at her strangely, as if she might be a little sun touched. He released his hands from her waist as if she were a hot potato. He moved backward one step and held up Jenny's book.

"I got what I came for. So . . . uh . . . so long." He swiveled on his heels and walked away.

Oh. *Oh.* She felt a massive disappointment. Massive.

Jimmy Fisher had two serious things weighing on his mind, and that was unusual for him. First, he needed to find a way to convince Chris Yoder to loan Samson to him for a quick lap or two around Domino Joe's racetrack. Second, he needed to convince M.K. Lapp that she loved him.

First things first. He had done everything—dropped hints, offered to barter—everything but ask Chris outright for the use of Samson. He didn't know Yoder all that well, and he was one of those guys who kept his cards close to his vest. That was an expression Jimmy had picked up on the racetracks and liked to use. In the right company, of course. Never around his mother. But there was something about Chris's manner that made Jimmy hesitate to ask to borrow Samson. That, and he could probably beat Jimmy to a jelly if he took a notion to.

Today, he stopped by Chris's house with the intention of directing the conversation to the temporary loan of Samson. Somehow, he ended up helping Chris patch shingles on the roof before winter arrived. Chris was up on the roof, bareheaded and without a coat, though there was a bitter wind. He was muscled like a bull, tight as a tree. One after another, in a couple of mighty blows, Chris drove the nails into the shingles. Jimmy tried to keep up and finally just became Chris's assistant—handing him nails and shingles as he needed them.

Jimmy kept getting close to the topic of Samson, but Chris was preoccupied with how many more shingles he needed and didn't pay him any mind. That was the way it went with Chris. If he didn't want to answer your question, he'd just pretend you hadn't said anything.

Finally, Jimmy just came out with it. "Chris, I just need Samson one time. Just one little race. Half a day, and he'll be back in the barn. Or . . . garage. Whatever you call it."

Chris was on the other side of the roof peak, peering down at the front of the house.

"One time, Chris. That's all I'm asking for. I'm an expert horseman. You can have complete confidence in me." Still, Chris ignored him. Or maybe he couldn't hear him?

Jimmy climbed to the peak to see what Chris was staring at. M.K. Lapp had driven up in the buggy with Cayenne. Jenny climbed out of the buggy and M.K. leaned out the window to hand a pie basket to her. M.K. looked up at the roof and gave a small wave with her hand. "We brought some extra apple pies!" she shouted up to Chris and Jimmy after she climbed out of the buggy. "Come down and try a slice while it's still warm!"

M.K.'s timing couldn't have been worse. Jimmy needed to nail down borrowing Samson with Chris. Now. No distractions, even for Fern's apple pie and the girl who was destined to be his future missus. Time was running out. "So, what do you say?"

"Sure, whatever," Chris said absently, watching M.K. cross to the house, and the way she gathered her skirts. "I sure do like apple pie. I sure do."

That was a yes, Jimmy concluded.

M.K. rode better than a mile in silence. Her chin was set and she gripped the reins. For the last two weeks, she had taken Erma's advice and made a point to visit each of her pupils at their home. It was amazing what layers of understanding she had uncovered, even though she had known these families all her life.

Barbara Jean's mother seemed to be in very low spirits since this new baby had been born. She seemed frail and unhappy and overwhelmed. No wonder Barbara Jean constantly worried about her mother. M.K. was going to ask her sister Sadie to go fix her up with one of those teas or remedies she concocted. Sadie was good at helping new moms get over the blues.

Here was another thing that surprised M.K.: she had known that Anna Mae was an only child, but she never thought much about it. As she sat in the kitchen of the Glicks' home, she noticed that everything revolved around Anna Mae. M.K. was the youngest in the Lapp family, and nothing had ever revolved around her. Nothing. Not ever.

The Glicks had invited M.K. to stay for dinner, which she did, and ate a meal that was customized to suit Anna Mae's peculiar tastes. Everything was beige because Anna Mae didn't like to eat things with too much color or texture: meatloaf without onions, white bread, mashed potatoes. No vegetables or fruit because she didn't like them. Even the chocolate cookies didn't have walnuts, because Anna Mae thought walnuts tasted yucky.

On the way home from the Glicks', M.K. had two thoughts. One: what in the world would Fern have done with a child like Anna Mae? And two: Danny Riehl had better watch out—because Anne Mae Glick was a girl who got what she wanted. And she wanted Danny Riehl.

The last pupil to visit was Eugene Miller. She had held it off as long as possible. Dread swept her as she turned Cayenne into the long lane that led to the Millers'. She smelled the farm before it ever came into view: pigs. The smell watered her eyes. She had a fondness for most animals, but she took exception to pigs.

The house was in worse shape than the barn. M.K. turned Cayenne to the hitching post by the never-shoveled-out barn and climbed down out of the buggy. She made her way gingerly to the house—everyone knew you wanted to be careful where you stepped around the Miller farm. The only time it was mildly cleaned up was when it was the Millers' turn to host Sunday church, once a year. Deacon Abraham would ask for a work frolic for the Millers, two Sundays before they were due to host church, and there was always a quiet shuffling in the seats as people were loathe to volunteer. Finally, Amos would raise his hand and others would follow suit.

M.K. knocked on the door but no one answered. She turned around and shielded her eyes from the sun, and then she saw Eugene crossing over from the barn, a pitchfork in his hand.

"Why are you here?" he hissed as he approached her.

"I've been visiting everyone's home, Eugene. I just wanted—"

The door opened then and a large, grim-looking man appeared. Eugene's father. His dark mean eyes shifted from Eugene to M.K. and back to Eugene. "What do you want?"

"Good afternoon." M.K. tried to make her voice sound casual.

"Daddy, she's my teacher," Eugene said.

Could she have heard him right? Did M.K. hear the word "daddy" coming out of the usually sneering lips of Eugene Miller?

He pointed to Eugene. "Is he giving you any trouble?"

M.K. glanced at Eugene, who had lost all color in his face. He seemed to shrink the closer he got to his father. "No. No trouble at all." She turned back to Eugene's father and said, rather primly, as she smoothed the wrinkles of her dress, "I just wanted to stop by and say hello. To let you know that Eugene has been a real . . . pleasure . . . to have in the classroom."

Eugene's father looked suspicious. "He's not the sharpest tool in the shed."

M.K. looked at Eugene and felt a wave of pity for him. "I think he's one of the smartest eighth graders I've ever taught."

Eugene's father lifted a bushy eyebrow. "Ain't you new at teaching?"

She pulled out a manila folder. "I thought you might want this." She handed him the drawing of the snowy owl. "Eugene drew this. Isn't it wonderful?" She wasn't quite sure her voice carried a seasoned teacher-authority as she wanted it to, but she did the best she could under the circumstances.

Eugene's father squinted his eyes at the drawing. He grunted, gave Eugene the once-over, then, to M.K.'s horror, he wadded it up into a ball and tossed it on the ground. "That's how you'll give the boy a big head." He turned to go back into the house, stopping at the threshold to point at Eugene. "Get back out to the field with your brothers. Farms don't run themselves." He shut the door behind him, muttering something about "Just useless."

M.K. bent down to pick up the drawing and smooth it out.

Eugene clenched his jaw.

"I'm so sorry," she said. She saw a glassy sheen in his eyes.

He spat out an unrepeatable word before running out to the field.

Chris woke up one morning to a silent world. No birdsong, no wind rattling the windows. Groggily he lay there, wondering why he felt as if his ears were stuffed with cotton. The strange grayish light that filtered through the window slowly registered on him. The world outside was covered with a blanket of snow.

During breakfast, Jenny complained bitterly about the snow. "That schoolhouse is going to be freezing."

"There's a heater in there," Chris said. "A big thing. It should warm that room up quick."

"Teacher M.K. doesn't use it," Jenny said sourly. "She says it's good for our brains to be slightly chilled." She shivered. "My fingers are so cold in that room that I can't even hold a pencil."

Chris thought about that for a while as he ate his watery oatmeal. Jenny had been complaining about the chill in the schoolroom for a few weeks now, ever since the weather had turned brisk. Why wouldn't Mary Kate use the heater? Then it dawned on him. Of course! He bolted from his chair and grabbed his coat and hat from the wall peg. "I've got to go. I've already fed Samson. Turn him into the paddock before you leave for school."

As he hurried down the street to the schoolhouse, he found himself grinning. He loved the first real snowfall of the year, damp and clinging, like winter was trying to decide if it was ready to come yet. He picked up his pace when he saw a small black-bonneted figure down the road. He broke into a jog.

"You know, Jenny has been complaining about the temperature in the schoolhouse lately," he said when he caught up with Mary Kate. "But I told her just to wear an extra sweater or two. That her teacher must be feeling the need to save coal."

M.K.'s cheeks were red from the cold air and her brown eyes were snapping. "Absolutely. It's important for the children to learn to be frugal."

"Then she started wearing mittens all day, and scarves and ear muffs. Then she asked to borrow my coat. I told her that her teacher must have a pretty good reason to keep the schoolhouse well chilled."

"Well, the theory is that cold helps to keep them awake. Especially the big boys."

"Or maybe . . . the teacher doesn't know how to get the heater started."

Mary Kate stopped short, opened her mouth to say something. Snapped it shut. She looked up at him with those dark-fringed eyes. "Maybe I forgot to pay attention when Orin Stoltzfus was giving me his lengthy tutorial on the fussy heater." She cringed. "Oh Chris, I have tried to get it started every morning for two weeks now! I just can't make it work." She frowned. "The truth is, I think this heater has it in for me."

He laughed, and then she laughed. "Why didn't you just say something to someone?"

"I did ask Jimmy Fisher for help and he promised to stop by, but that hasn't happened yet."

"Why didn't you just ask your dad? Or your uncle Hank?"

She frowned. "Fern is forever telling me to solve my problems by myself. I nearly asked Uncle Hank, but he has a tendency to make problems worse. Yesterday I thought I had it figured out at last. Then it blew up and sputtered coal dust at me. Ruined my apron. And today, I wake up to find snow!"

They were at the schoolhouse now. Mary Kate unlocked the door and Chris went right to work. It was a temperamental old coal heater, he had to admit. But it wasn't too different a model from Old Deborah's old heater. Soon, he had a small fire started in the base of the heater, added coal, and it wasn't long before the chill in the air tapered off. Just in time too. He heard the sounds of children arriving.

Mary Kate was staring out the window, stunned. Chris came up behind her to gaze at the schoolhouse scene. Whoops and squeals, snowballs firing through the air, exploding on the back of one child or another, laughter as bright as sleigh bells. Excellent snowball fighting weather. He grinned, wondering how Mary Kate would adjust to the classroom climate today. The first snow substantially altered the environment. Boys would be chomping at the bit to stampede their way outside for recess. Remembering his own school years, it wasn't long before there was as much snow being flung through the air as was resting on the ground. An all-out free-for-all.

"Well," he said, "I could help you with the heater, but that, out there, is all yours." He grinned and turned to go.

He was practically to the door when she called out, "How did you know that I didn't have any idea how to work the heater?"

He shrugged. "Wasn't hard to figure out." He rolled that over in his mind as he walked down the lane to turn onto Windmill Farm's drive. It occurred to him that he was starting to understand the illogical logic of Mary Kate Lapp. The first few times he met her, he tried to follow her line of thinking and was often left pawing the air. Why was she starting to make sense to him?

Lately, thoughts of Mary Kate Lapp rose up time and again. He tried to kick her image aside the way he might scoot a cat out from underfoot, but back it came, silently slinking in. All he could think of were those eyes. Those deep, brown, lovely eyes.

Whenever his thoughts drifted toward Mary Kate, a sense of well-being sneaked up on Chris, which he normally only experienced after a hard day's work, when he was too tired to think straight.

Such a feeling worried him. And pleased him too. Both.

16

That first snowfall was just a tease of winter's coming, but Chris stopped by the schoolhouse every single morning to help M.K. start the heater. She thought she had a pretty good handle on it after watching him work that first morning, but she decided not to share that particular revelation with him. She liked having him there. Each morning, they would talk a little. He loved hearing stories about the scholars. A few times, he even laughed out loud.

Little by little, M.K. was discovering more about Chris Yoder. He fascinated her. Ever since that first predawn conference when he helped her start the coal heater, several days ago now, it seemed natural to be together. They met early on the way to the schoolhouse, talking as they walked, their breath puffs of fog. It intrigued her that as Chris went about the business of firing up the heater, his experiences seeped from him, episode by episode, as if they wanted out. But if she asked anything, he clammed up. Door shut. Conversation over.

So she *was* learning to be patient. Wouldn't Rome be proud of her? Wouldn't he be amazed? Mary Kate Lapp, starting to be patient. Learning to wait for a person to choose to share his past, in his time, rather than going after that information with reckless abandon, like she usually did. She was very pleased with herself. And those early morning moments with Chris were becoming her favorite of the day.

Late on Friday afternoon, she was wiping down the chalkboard. She heard her name. She turned and there he was. Chris, alone, standing by the door in front of the cloakroom. He had a smile that hitched up on one side. That smile of his, especially when it reached his eyes and made them crinkle in that way, it made her stomach do a flip-flop.

"Jenny left her lunch Igloo." He lifted it up. "Didn't want to leave it here over the weekend."

M.K. tossed the chalk rag on her desk and walked to him. "I was just finishing for the day." She grabbed her coat and bonnet off the wall peg in case he was in a hurry to leave, as he often was. But he wasn't. He held the door for her and stayed on the school porch, waiting for her to lock up. Something was on his mind. By now, she knew not to press him.

"I wondered if . . . maybe . . . next time there's a decent snowfall, maybe you'd like to go on a sled ride with Samson. I'd need to borrow your dad's sled, though." His cheeks flamed and he looked down at his feet, kicking a loose board with his boot top.

"Yes!" It burst out of her.

Chris's head snapped up. "Really? I mean, uh, good." His eyes crinkled into a smile.

Oh, there was that smile again. She thought for sure her knees were going to go right out from under her. A quiet spun out between them.

The most wonderful surprise happened next. *Don't breathe,* she thought. *Don't move.* Chris bent down to lightly graze her lips with his. Just a featherlight kiss. Her first.

Amos Lapp had gone to the schoolhouse phone shanty to see if there were any messages, and to place a call to his eldest daughter, Julia, who lived in Berlin, Ohio. Communication required patience—he would leave a message for her, and when she had time to check messages, she would return the call by leaving a message back for him. They were planning to head out to Ohio for Christmas to visit Julia and Rome and their four boys.

While they were there, they would take some time to visit little Joe-Jo, the child of his now-in-heaven son, Menno. Joe-Jo lived with his mother, Annie, in a Swartzentruber colony not too far from Berlin. Imagine that, Amos thought, pleased. Counting Sadie's two little ones, he had six grandsons and one granddaughter. Could a man ask for any greater gift? And he had a sneaking suspicion that it wouldn't be long before M.K. and Jimmy Fisher married. Seemed like that boy was at Windmill Farm on a daily basis. Perhaps Amos would have a dozen grandchildren before long. An even dozen!

Fern had a long list of things she had started for the trip and more than a few questions for Julia. He grinned—he never knew anyone who liked to make plans like his list-making wife. Except for Julia. She was like Fern in that way, wanting everything to be orderly.

He left Fern's questions for Julia on the message machine and closed the shanty door. It was getting dark—that gloaming hour of the day. As he turned the corner and came around the front of the schoolhouse, he stopped abruptly. There, on the school porch, was an Amish couple, kissing. He turned like a top and hurried back to the shanty to think things over.

He was uncertain of what he was supposed to do—he needed to pass in front of the schoolhouse to get home. He wished Fern were with him. What would she do? She would probably think it was appalling—to think of a young couple kissing out in public like that, though he had to admit he had done plenty of public kissing when he was a teenager.

But that was different. That was long before he had daughters. He had a different perspective on affection after he became a father of teenaged daughters. He knew what was on the mind of a boy. It occurred to him that he would be doing that girl's father a favor if he interrupted the couple right now. Better if he was the one to interrupt them than the bishop or ministers. Or imagine if Edith Fisher happened along! He was going to have to tap the boy on his shoulder and send him on his way.

Wait a moment. He suddenly realized something. The girl on that porch wasn't just any girl. He recognized that turquoise blue dress. Mary Kate had one just like it. She had worn it this very day. That girl *was* Mary Kate! A sick feeling came over Amos. That wasn't Jimmy Fisher she was kissing. This boy was too tall to be Jimmy Fisher. If he wasn't mistaken, that boy's thatch of blond hair belonged to . . . Chris Yoder.

Shocked and distressed, Amos had to sit down on the little stool. When had this romance begun? How could this have happened? This was terrible, terrible news. Of all the boys in Stoney Ridge, how could his little girl be involved with Chris Yoder? Should he fire Chris on the spot? Definitely. He definitely was going to fire him.

He took a deep breath, opened the shanty door, gathered every indignant bone in his body, and marched to the front of the schoolhouse to confront them.

But there was no one there.

HI JENNY GIRL!

Your momma is sure proud of you for getting so much money to me. You must be working really hard. What are you doing to get so much dough? Baking a lot of pies, huh? Ha!

I've got some AWESOME news! But, ssshhhh! baby, you got to keep this secret from Chris. I want to surprise him. They're letting me out of this crummy joint early cuz I'm clean! Clean as a whistle.

I want you to be here when I get out. You could take the bus, meet me, and we could surprise Chris together back in Stoney Ridge! It'll be the three of us, together again, for Christmas. This time it'll be different, Jenny. I promise. I'll stay clean. You know your momma is the only one you can depend on. Promise me you'll come, okay? Tuesday, December 23rd, 11:30 a.m. SHARP. DON'T LET ME DOWN! And remember: this is top secret! I'm counting on you!

For a long time, Jenny sat right there without moving, feeling a weird hollowness in her chest, like all her air had been sucked out. When she took a breath, it didn't go away. She didn't want to go to Marysville all by herself. She didn't think Chris would be at all happy to have his mother arrive in Stoney Ridge as a Christmas surprise. But how sad for her mother—to not have anyone waiting for her when she got out of rehab. To not have anywhere to go for Christmas.

Jenny's hands were shaking as she read through the note a second time. And then she began to make a plan.

M.K. heard someone call her name and looked up to locate the voice.

"Mary Kate!" Chris Yoder stood at a distance and waved to her. "I'm not coming any closer to those bees."

Her heart lifted like a balloon. She was repairing a loose piece of tarpaper that the wind in yesterday's storm had ripped off. The bees needed her, but this could wait. For Chris, they could wait. She put the staple gun down and set the smoker aimed at the beehives before she walked over to him. She hadn't seen Chris since that kiss at the schoolhouse last Friday and she felt giddy with anticipation. It was never far from her mind, that kiss. That sweet, tender, wonderful kiss.

She had woken in the night and relived it, over and over again. His lips had touched hers, as softly as a butterfly landing, and rested there for a moment before he moved closer and his mouth seemed to melt into hers. His arms slid around her waist and she felt the stubble of his chin as his face brushed against hers. The sensation was the most amazing, terrifying, wonderful, frightening one she had ever felt. All of it—the feel of his strong arms around her, his sturdy body next to hers, the way he breathed, the way he smelled. As his warm lips brushed against hers, she decided that a kiss was the most wonderful sensation in the world. It started where his tender lips joined hers and traveled slowly through her like a wave of warm water. That kiss was a moment in her memory that went on forever and ended too soon. M.K. finally understood why her friend Ruthie liked to kiss so much. Now M.K. got it.

She thought a lightning bolt had struck her, and she thought it was love.

She was glad she had the netting over her face as she walked toward Chris. M.K. was beaming. Beaming!

But something was wrong. Chris looked upset. "Do you know of any reason why your dad would fire me?"

"Fire you? What did he say?"

Chris looked past her to the hives. "He said there wasn't any more work to do at Windmill Farm for the winter." He looked back at her. "It wasn't long ago that he talked about all kinds of things he wanted me to do for him this winter. He even talked about expanding the Salad Stall with some winter crops—kale and cabbage. Did something happen? Could he be worried about paying me?"

"Not that I know of." Her father didn't share any financial problems with her. That never stopped M.K. from eavesdropping, but she hadn't overheard her dad and Fern talking about money lately. In fact, if anything, her father seemed awfully quiet lately. Quieter than usual.

Chris frowned. "You didn't say anything about . . . what happened between us at the schoolhouse, did you?"

"Of course not!" Did he think she was crazy?

He turned to leave, then turned back. He gave her a long, lingering look, like he was memorizing her face. "Look, about that. I apologize. It should never have happened. It won't happen again."

Why won't it happen again? M.K. thought, watching him stride down the hill. *Why not?*

Maybe getting fired was a blessing in disguise. Chris had been letting his guard down. He should stick to the plan—fix up the house, start looking for the right mares to breed with Samson. That's what brought him here—that was his grandfather's gift to him. A fresh beginning.

He would be twenty-one in six weeks. Then, he would feel safe. He would have kept his unspoken promise to his grandfather. He would have provided for his and Jenny's future.

It was the Lapp family that was starting to get to him—each one of them. Fern and Jenny were thick as thieves. Jenny was acting more and more like Fern. Baking bread, fussing over a clean kitchen, ironing his shirts with so much starch that they could stand up by themselves. It was preposterous.

And Amos? Over the months of working for Amos Lapp, Chris had developed a great admiration for the man. Amos had always been fair with him. He possessed a natural business sense that Chris respected. More than a few times, Chris had thought that Amos was the kind of father he wished he'd had. Caring, calm, kind, wise. There had been a subtle change in the way Amos treated Chris. He used to work beside Chris. For the last few weeks, he would start Chris on a task and leave him to complete it. Or he would send him off to work for Hank in the buggy shop. Chris thought Amos might not be feeling well, that maybe his heart was acting up. He didn't know much about Amos's heart problem, but he did see all those pills he took at meals.

At least, that was what Chris had assumed about Amos's cool treatment—up until thirty minutes ago, when he had been abruptly and inexplicably dismissed. For no apparent reason.

Chris felt like he'd had the wind kicked out of him. He racked his brain and couldn't think of anything he might have done wrong. He had no idea what had gotten into Amos. The only thing he could come up with was that kiss. Maybe Mary Kate had told him. But she looked stunned when he mentioned it, and she wore her thoughts on her face. If she were lying, he would have known.

Then there was Mary Kate. He had to get *that* girl off his mind. Kissing her like he did the other night—it shocked him. Where did that kiss come from? One minute they were talking, the next . . . he had leaned over to kiss her. He had always prided himself on his self-control with girls. He noticed women on occasion. What fellow didn't? But with discipline, he always guided his focus away. Something not as easily done with Mary Kate Lapp.

He wasn't like some of his friends from Ohio, who talked about girls constantly and, given the opportunity, could barely keep their hands off them. What was happening to him?

But he knew. He knew. He really was totally and hopelessly smitten with this girl. This had to stop. This wouldn't last. He had to keep remembering that. *This. Will. Not. Last.*

Maybe all this was a good reminder. Chris's only true family was with Jenny. That was the one person—the only person—he needed to take care of.

Chris passed by Hank's buggy shop to walk down the driveway. As soon as he realized Bishop Elmo was involved in a deep conversation with Hank over the state of his buggy, he veered away from the shop.

Normally a lighthearted, softspoken man, Elmo sounded exasperated. "You haven't made a lick of progress on fixing this buggy, Hank Lapp!"

Hank was shocked. "I've been utterly swamped!"

"Swamped, eh?" Elmo's hands were on his hips.

Chris tried to make himself invisible, but those yellow puppies spotted him and charged happily toward him, barking and yipping. Elmo turned to see what the commotion was all about.

Too late.

"Chris Yoder! Come over here."

Chris crossed over to the bishop, puppies tangled at his feet.

"Hank said you've been giving him a lot of help around here. Seems like Stoney Ridge could use another buggy shop. Hank is going to volunteer to teach you everything he knows about buggy repair."

"I am?" Hank asked.

"And when he's done sharing all of that vast knowledge, you are going to open up a buggy shop."

"I am?" Chris asked. He felt a shiver of dread run down his spine.

"You are." Bishop Elmo popped his black felt hat back on his bald head. He pointed to his buggy, up on blocks. "Starting with that one. I need that before Christmas. My wife's entire family is coming to visit." Then he marched across the driveway to his waiting horse and buggy. "Before Christmas!" he called out, as he slapped the reins on the horse and it lunged forward. "You have one week!"

Chris looked at Hank, shocked. "What in the world just happened?"

Hank was at an unusual loss for words. Hands hooked on his hips, he crinkled his wide forehead in confusion as he watched the bishop drive away. "There is one thing I have learned in my life. Don't waste your time arguing with a bishop." He tossed a wrench to Chris. "So, boy, let's get to work."

After supper, Amos went out to his favorite spot on a hill, overlooking the orchards, to watch the sun set. It was a habit he had when he needed reminding that God was sovereign, that he held the world in his hands. Amos stood watching, arms crossed against his chest, as the sun dipped below the horizon. How many times had he stood in this same spot when the sorrows of life overwhelmed him?

As his gaze shifted from the sun to the first sign of the North Star, he realized Fern had followed him and stood beside him. "That might have been the quietest meal we've ever had. Hank is bothered with Elmo for making Chris his apprentice. Mary Kate is bothered with you for letting Chris go. I'm bothered with all of you. Mind telling me why you told Chris you didn't need his help anymore?"

Amos glanced at her. His dilemma bounced back and forth across his brain like a volleyball in a match. *Tell her. Don't tell her. Tell her. Don't tell her.*

"Something's eating at you," she said. "It has been for a while now. Weeks."

He kept his eyes on the star.

"Is your heart giving you any trouble? Did the doctor tell you something at your last checkup that you didn't tell me—"

"No," he interrupted. "My heart's not the problem. Not in the way that you mean."

A long silence spun out between them. Finally, Fern sighed. "I can't read your mind, Amos."

He turned and gave her a sad smile. "Sometimes, I think you can."

17

Jenny jerked awake from a dreamless sleep and sat straight up, blinking, trying to gather information as fast as possible. Where was she? Was she late for school?

No. She was on a bus to Columbus, Ohio. Once there, she would catch another bus to get to Marysville, and then a city bus to meet her mother. She had sneaked out of the house before dawn and left a note for Chris:

```
Needed at the schoolhouse early. After school too.
Don't worry if I'm late. Lots to do.
```

It was tricky getting a bus ticket, since the woman behind the counter said she needed an adult to buy it for her. So Jenny lied. She *lied*. Her first lie ever—no, wait. It was her second one. She had lied to Chris in the note she left him. She wasn't proud of it. She told the ticket lady that she looked small but she was actually over eighteen. She said she had a genetic disease that kept her from growing like a normal person. She said it was a common ailment among the Amish and the ticket lady's eyes softened. Then she sold Jenny a ticket for forty-one dollars and told her to be extra careful.

As Jenny settled into the seat by the window, she felt like crying and didn't know why. The bus was quiet and a toddler in the back row with his mother fussed a little. It seemed like the loneliest place in the world. She wanted to be home, making soupy Cream of Wheat for her brother. She wanted to bake bread with Fern after school. She looked forward to being with Fern all day long, every day. Her stomach twisted in hunger as she thought of the smell of baking bread. Was there any better smell in the entire world?

Why did she do this? What was she thinking? Jenny felt that tangle of anxiety and sorrow and relief that always came up when she thought about her mother.

Get off the bus and go home, said a voice in her head. *Home.* Windmill Farm came to mind as she mulled over the word. That was how she felt when she was baking in the kitchen with Fern. She was thirteen years old and she felt she had found what she'd always wanted, even without knowing that she wanted it. She was home.

That was Jenny's state of mind as the bus rumbled along the freeway, passing on a rusty bridge over a winding river as it headed through West Virginia, then another bridge as it sped into Ohio. Every mile, pulling her farther and farther from Stoney Ridge. Tears choked her. She pressed her fist really hard against the bottom of her jaw to keep from crying.

But then she thought about her mom, who was counting on her to be there when she was released today. Her mom had been clean for a while now, so she would be in good shape. She wouldn't be a bundle of raw nerves. Maybe, at least for Christmas Day, her mother wouldn't say mean things to Chris. Jenny didn't know how her brother stood it—but Chris never fought back. He just quietly absorbed the awful things their mother said to him. That his birth had ruined her life. That Chris was stupid, just like his father, even though Grace often admitted she had hardly known the man. That Chris was a hypocrite—joining the Amish church was just his way to get back at her.

She didn't say such horrible things to Jenny. Only to Chris. She even talked about Jenny's absentee father in a nice way. "He works for the government, top secret stuff, so he can't let anyone know about us. But someday, he'll be back for us," she would tell Jenny. Or, if Jenny complained about her height, she would say, "Your dad isn't very tall, either. Good things come in small packages."

It didn't make any sense to Jenny. She had never known her father. Chris had never known his. Both men had gone missing long before their babies were born. She liked to hear those stories about her CIA father, but she knew they probably weren't true. Maybe, but probably not. She hated to hear how her mother talked about Chris's father. Her mother had a nickname for him: W.B. Why Bother.

Chris never defended himself, never said a word back to their mother. Somehow, his steadfast calm made her even more angry.

Sometimes, Jenny wished Chris would go ahead and argue back, tell their mom to stop. She had admitted as much to Old Deborah once. Old Deborah had cupped her liver-spotted hands around Jenny's small face. "Years ago, your brother read something from the Bible that spoke to him and settled deep. Something Jesus had said. From Matthew 10:16." Then she closed her eyes, as if she were reading the words in her head. "'Behold, I send you forth as sheep in the midst of wolves: be ye therefore wise as serpents, and harmless as doves.'" Old Deborah explained that Chris was wise enough to know that words were like tools. "Your mother uses her tools to tear down. Chris uses his tools to repair and fix up."

Her brother amazed her. Every single day, he amazed her. So kind, so faithful, so determined to live a better life, to be a better person, to build new memories.

Despite everything, despite how confused she felt, it was her mother whom Jenny couldn't stop thinking about. Her mother needed her. She should be there when her mother was released from rehab.

When the bus pulled into Marysville, Jenny hurried to the bathroom and washed her face. She was hungry but didn't want to miss the city bus that would travel to her mom's rehab center. She had brought all of the money she had earned by working for Fern—nearly one hundred dollars. She had visited her mom at this rehab center before, so she went to the right bus, paid the fare, climbed aboard, and sat down. Without Old Deborah beside her, the city felt especially lonely.

Why was she doing this? What was she thinking? Why didn't she tell Chris about this plan? He would know what to do. If Jenny had only talked to him about it, they could have figured out what to do together. Why did her mother want this to be such a big surprise? Suddenly, the bus came to a stop a block away from the rehab center and she jumped up. This was it. She was here. She had come this far. She might as well see it through. Jenny felt sick to her stomach. She knew this was the stupidest idea she ever had, but her mom needed her. She had to remember that.

At the rehab center, she sat for a long time in the dimly lit waiting room. Finally, the receptionist at the desk called her name. A door buzzed, then opened, and suddenly the room filled up with her mom.

"JENNY!" her mother yelled.

For a fleeting second, the sound reminded Jenny of the booming way Uncle Hank would enter a room and everyone would cringe.

But when Jenny saw how much healthier her mom appeared, her whole being came to rest and she was glad she had come. She jumped up to cross the room and hug her. "Mom!"

Her mother smelled like cigarettes and shampoo. Her arms were strong, and she had gained weight. Even her hair looked shiny.

"You've grown half a foot since I saw you last!" her mother said, pulling back to look at her.

"One-and-a-half inches," Jenny said, laughing. "Can you believe it?"

Grace stepped back to look Jenny up and down, holding on to her hands. "You look so beautiful! Even in that kooky get-up."

Jenny ignored that. "So do you, Mom." It was true. Her mom's face didn't have open sores anymore, and her shiny hair was pulled back into a tidy ponytail.

Grace looked at the clock on the wall. "Let's get out of here! Let's go to McDonald's and get us a Big Mac. I've had a craving for one for months and months."

They walked down the street to McDonald's. Jenny took her wallet out of her backpack and saw her mother's eyebrows lift in surprise when she pulled a twenty from it to pay the cashier. They went outside and sat on a bench in the sunshine. It was chilly, but the sun felt good.

Her mom wolfed down the Big Mac and then ate half of Jenny's. As she sipped on her giant soda, Jenny felt so happy to see her mom's healthy appetite. When her mom was doing drugs, she didn't care about eating. After her mom polished off the french fries, she took a cigarette out and lit it, blowing smoke away from Jenny. She smoked restlessly, her eyes constantly glancing at her wristwatch.

When she finished one cigarette, she lit a new one from the butt, then tossed the butt on the ground and stamped it out with her shoe. When she saw Jenny's frown, she said, "I'm cutting back. There's just not much else to do but smoke in there. Gotta do something with my hands." Her mother looked uneasy. "We need to catch that bus pretty soon."

"It's only 12:30. The bus to Columbus leaves at 1:00. We have just enough time. If everything goes according to plan, we'll be home by dinnertime. Chris will be worried if I'm not back before he gets home from work."

"Chris was born worrying." Grace flicked the ashes off her cigarette. "He thinks he does a better job raising you than I do. He thinks he's better than me." She took a long drag on her cigarette, blowing smoke away from Jenny but looking at her hard. "But he's not."

Jenny tensed, like she always did when her mother criticized Chris. Things had been going so well since her mom had left the center, a full twenty minutes without any digs about Chris. She desperately wanted this Christmas to be different. Her mom had promised. "He's been working really hard on the house, Mom. He works a full day job, then he comes home and fixes the house up till almost midnight. Starts all over again the next day. The house is looking great too. The yard is all cleaned up now and he patched the roof so it stopped leaking and he fixed broken windows so bats can't fly in."

Grace looked pleased. Very, very pleased. "Bet Rodney the Realtor is licking his chops."

Jenny's head snapped up. "How do you know about him?"

Grace kept her eyes fixed on a grease spot on the picnic bench. "You must have mentioned him in a letter."

Jenny couldn't remember mentioning Rodney Gladstone in any letter to her mother. Had she? Her mind skimmed through the different letters she wrote to her mother—

"We should get going if we want to catch that bus." Grace looked at her wristwatch again.

Jenny suddenly felt the effects of the giant soda she drank and needed to go to the bathroom. Really bad. "I'm just going to zip into McDonald's and go to the bathroom before we leave."

Her mother reached across the table and squeezed Jenny's hand. She smiled at her, her eyes softening with affection. "Take all the time you need, sweet girl."

Jenny smiled. She loved when her mom called her "sweet girl." That tense moment had passed and her mother was being kind again. Jenny was glad she had come. She had missed her mom. Everything was going to be all right. They were finally going to be a real family. Pretty normal. As close to normal as they could get. "I'll be right back."

In the bathroom, Jenny washed her hands and thought about Chris. By now, Chris might have figured out that she had left town. She hoped he wouldn't be too angry. She hoped he would see what she knew to be true—this time it would be different. Their mom was finally well. She took a paper towel to dry her hands, then carefully used it to open the door handle and avoid germs, the way Fern had taught her. When she stepped outside, she stopped in the bright glare of the winter sun, puzzled. Her breath snagged. A ripple of fear started in her toes and ended in her forehead.

Her mother was gone.

And so was Jenny's backpack.

Since Chris was no longer needed—or wanted—at Windmill Farm, he was back to finding odd jobs at the bulletin board at the hardware store. He had spent the day cleaning the garage of an English couple. He couldn't believe how much junk they had stored away, like chipmunks. He didn't tell them that, though. After work, he stopped by the hardware store again and was disappointed that there were no new jobs posted. The holidays, he figured. Everyone was busy with family. Everyone except those who had no family. He wasn't sure what he and Jenny would do for Christmas. Jimmy Fisher had invited them over for Christmas dinner, but Edith Fisher was a little terrifying. Erma Yutzy had invited them to her granddaughter's house. Maybe they would accept Erma's invitation.

It was Windmill Farm, though, where he and Jenny wanted to be for the day. Fat chance of that.

Chris stopped at the mailbox on his way to the house. He removed his black felt hat and hooked it on the peg by the door. In the kitchen, he tossed the pile of mail on the countertop and washed up at the kitchen sink. He thought Jenny would be home from the schoolhouse by now. He guessed the big project she was working on had something to do with the Christmas program planned for Thursday. Well, that was one good thing about not having any work. He could attend that program. He could hear Jenny's recitation. He could see Mary Kate. His spirits brightened considerably with that thought.

He glanced through the mail—all junk. As he tossed it into the waste-basket, he noticed a small postcard addressed to Jenny. His breathing slowed as he recognized his mother's handwriting. He felt a swirling undercurrent of fear from what might be coming.

> Hey Jenny girl! Can't wait to see you on Tuesday! Don't be late, sweet girl! We got lots of catching up to do.

The kitchen clock ticked loud in the silence.

With an overwhelming sense of worry, he ran out the front door and down to the barn, panting by the time he reached Samson's stall.

Help me find Jenny, he prayed. *Keep her safe until I do.*

M.K. looked out the kitchen window and saw a pitch-black horse galloping up the driveway—Samson, with Chris on his back. Something was wrong. She ran outside to meet him as he reached the top of the rise.

"Where's Jenny?" His face was tight with tension. "Was she at school? Has Fern seen her today?"

"No. I thought she was sick."

The kitchen door swung open. "What is it, Chris?" Fern asked, wiping her hands on a rag as she came down the porch steps.

Samson danced on his hooves as Chris held tightly to the reins. "Jenny's missing. She left a note that said Mary Kate needed her at the school early this morning and late tonight—but then I got this postcard in today's mail." He hopped off the horse and handed Fern the postcard.

Fern read it and pinned him with a look. "Chris, where exactly is your mother?"

Chris stared at Fern with a combination of surprise and humiliation. "In Marysville, Ohio. In a drug rehabilitation center."

That was the most M.K. had ever learned about Chris and Jenny's mother.

She was momentarily flustered. Even Fern seemed flustered. She couldn't remember a time when Fern was ever flustered. But it only lasted a moment.

Fern turned to M.K. with a decided look on her face. "Call Rome. He'll know what to do."

Thoughts burst in M.K.'s mind and ricocheted around like corn popping in a kettle. Something had happened and she couldn't tell what. "Rome? Why would he—"

"Do it," Fern ordered.

Flustered, M.K. picked up the scooter that was leaning against the porch and zoomed down to the phone shanty. Chris followed on Samson. A few minutes later, as she approached the shanty, she heard the phone ringing. M.K. jumped off the scooter and lunged for the receiver. "Hello?"

"M.K., is that you?" It was Rome! Rome's deep, bass voice.

"I was just going to call you, Rome. We've got a terrible dilemma and we need your help!"

"Is your terrible dilemma named Jenny?"

"Yes! How did you—"

"I've got your terrible dilemma right here. Jenny's here, M.K. She's safe."

M.K. poked her head out of the shanty and waved at Chris. "She's there! Jenny's with them." His face flooded with relief. She turned back to the phone, astounded. How did Chris and Jenny know Julia and Rome? More importantly, how did she miss that piece of information? Her detective skills were slipping. She blamed the teaching job. Too distracting.

"Ask him how she got there," Chris said.

M.K. repeated the question to Rome and held the phone out between them so Chris could hear Rome's answer. Despite the seriousness of the situation, she found herself extremely conscious of being so close to Chris, squeezed together in the small shanty. He was impossibly close now. She could hardly concentrate on what Rome was saying.

"Apparently," Rome said, "Jenny went to meet her mother just as Grace was getting released from the treatment center. Jenny went into McDonald's to go to the bathroom and Grace took off with her backpack. Jenny went back to the rehab center and someone there found a phone number for Old Deborah's. A neighbor picked up the message and called me. I just so happened to have an errand to do in Marysville, so I was able to pick Jenny up."

M.K. doubted that Rome had an errand in Marysville. He was just thoughtful that way. Always going out of his way for others and never making it seem like it was an inconvenience.

Chris closed his eyes and slumped. He let out a deep sigh of relief. "Can you put Jenny on?"

"Let me ask her." In the background, they heard Rome ask Jenny if she would come to the phone, then Rome covered the mouthpiece and they could only hear mumbling until he came back on. "She's not quite ready to talk to you, Chris. She's shook up. She feels pretty bad. But I'm hoping you'll come out to get her."

Fern suddenly appeared at the door of the phone shanty. "Tell Rome we'll all come. Tell Julia to expect four more for Christmas. Wait—make that eight if Sadie and Gid and the twins want to come."

"MAKE THAT NINE," thundered Uncle Hank, appearing behind Fern. "I AM NOT EATING CHRISTMAS DINNER ALONE!" Edith Fisher was still spurning Uncle Hank.

Fern rolled her eyes. "Nine, then. We'll tell the van driver to move it up a few days and be there tomorrow afternoon. Tell Julia I'll do the turkey because her turkey ends up as dry as the bottom of a canary cage. Oh . . . and no cranberry sauce from a can. Tell her you can always taste the tin. Tell her I've got most of it made already. Including the dressing for the turkey."

That was true enough. In the kitchen, wherever pies weren't, were big bowls of bread crumbs and bunches of sage, drying, waiting to be made into dressing.

M.K. turned her attention to report all of this to Rome, but he had overheard and was chuckling into the phone. "Tell Fern that I'm just going to inform Julia that Fern is planning to take over the entire Christmas meal. Then I plan to duck!"

Fern wasn't finished with her demands. "And tell Julia—"

M.K. handed the phone to Fern. "You tell him." She eased out of the phone shanty and walked over to Chris, who was untying Samson's reins from the tree branch. When she looked at him, she was overwhelmed by how little she knew him, really knew him. Who would have ever thought his mother was in a drug rehabilitation center? No wonder he didn't discuss his parents. How did it happen, getting to know someone? It took time. It took days spent together, weeks, months.

He glanced at her. "Your whole family doesn't need to go to Ohio."

"We were going, anyway." M.K. put a hand on his arm. "It's just a few days earlier than planned. Chris, you and Jenny . . . you're important to us. To all of us."

Their eyes met and held. Suddenly, Amos materialized out of nowhere, interrupting the moment. "What's going on?"

"AMOS!" Hank shouted from the phone shanty. "You won't believe the co-ink-a-dinky around here!" He patched together the story of Jenny-gone-missing-and-turning-up-at-Rome-and-Julia's for Amos, who took in the news with a stunned look. "So Fern's making plans for all of us to head out to Berlin a little early for Christmas to fetch Jenny."

Amos stood beside Chris and M.K., speechless.

"Amos, you don't have to go early," Chris said. "You don't have to change any plans. I can get there, fetch Jenny, and get back again by myself."

Fern stuck her head out of the phone shanty. "Nonsense! We were going anyway. What's a few days?" Then she popped back to resume her conversation with Rome before Uncle Hank could wrestle the phone from her.

"Really, Amos," Chris said. "There's no need—"

Amos raised an eyebrow. "You heard Fern." He looked at Fern in the phone shanty, chattering away with Rome. "Trying to shift my wife's plans is like trying to persuade a hurricane to change course."

Fern popped her head back out of the phone shanty. "M.K., skin on over to Jimmy Fisher's and tell him we need him to feed the stock for a few days. He needs to mist Chris's lettuce seedlings three times a day. Three times. Emphasize that for Jimmy. Write it down so he doesn't forget. He'll forget if you don't make it crystal clear. And then go to Sadie's and see if she wants to come along to Ohio. And then go sweet-talk Alice Smucker into substituting for you tomorrow and Thursday." She pointed to Chris. "You bring Samson over here by six in the morning. Jimmy can take care of him with the rest of the stock. The van will leave at six in the morning. Don't be late." She popped back into the shanty and picked right up with Rome where she left off. Never missed a beat.

"Well, you heard her." Amos stared at Chris awkwardly until Chris picked up the cue to leave.

Chris hopped on Samson's back. "Tomorrow at six. I'll be at Windmill Farm." He reined Samson around and trotted off.

What had just happened? M.K. was rarely astonished, but she was.

18

As Chris nudged Samson forward, a wave of exhaustion rolled over him. He wished he had been able to fend Fern off, to slip off and quietly fetch Jenny from Ohio. But there was both an urgency and a firmness in Fern's voice as she made plans, and against his better judgment, Chris found himself stepping back and letting her take charge. Worry and fear for Jenny weighed him down like a sack of rocks and it did feel good to share the load.

He felt grateful to Rome Troyer for being the one to rescue Jenny. But now the entire Lapp family knew about his mother. And how long would it be before the entire town of Stoney Ridge knew? He felt a deep shame—what must Mary Kate think of him?

The story of his mother was nothing he could ever share with someone as naïve and innocent as Mary Kate Lapp. He could hardly imagine the look on her face if he tried to describe the mean streak his mother had developed after she started to use drugs. She was a different person. He felt tainted—a feeling he had lived with his entire life. Stained by his mother's choices.

What kind of a woman would lure her thirteen-year-old daughter hundreds of miles away, only to steal her backpack and leave her stranded? And he couldn't blame that choice on drugs. His mother was clean, for now. He thought about that postcard—he knew she wanted him to see it. He had no doubt of that. It didn't surprise him that she had figured out where they were living. She was shrewd like that.

He was tired of carrying the burden of his unpredictable mother all alone. He was suddenly too sad for tears. His sadness took on a sharp, shining edge.

As M.K. rounded the bend toward Jimmy Fisher's house, she saw him heading to the hatchery with a bucket of feed and called to him. "Dad wants you to take care of the stock for a few days." She explained the need for the trip to Ohio, only lightly touching on the part about retrieving Jenny. She was still trying to process the news.

Jimmy howled like a lovesick basset hound. "I knew it. Chris Yoder steals my girl right out from under me."

As usual, Jimmy made little sense. "What? What are you talking about?"

Jimmy looked bothered. "Just what does Chris mean to you?"

M.K. blinked hard. "Have you been drinking again?"

"Does Chris Yoder make you laugh?" Jimmy asked.

"No," M.K. said honestly. "But you're not very funny right now, either."

"I can't believe you're doing this to me."

"I'm not doing anything to you. I'm going to Ohio with my family for a few days."

Jimmy shook his head. "The weasel. He's trying to snake his way into your family's hearts. And here I told him my intentions! I thought we were friends!"

"What intentions are you talking about?" M.K. shivered. She had grabbed her coat when she went out to meet Chris at Windmill Farm, but forgot mittens. "Look, the sun is starting to set and I need to get to Sadie's before it gets too dark."

He flashed her a brilliant smile. "The intention to make you my missus," he said softly, cupping her face with his hands. He leaned over and kissed her gently on the mouth. "That's my heartfelt intent. I've already spoken to your father."

Shocked, M.K. pushed him away. Jimmy Fisher was certifiably crazy. She didn't want to know any more right now. In a swift and sudden decision, she picked up the scooter and zoomed away.

"You just remember the thunder and lightning of that kiss while Chris Yoder is trying to woo you in Ohio!" Jimmy called after her.

M.K. was sure she had felt as astonished as a person could be back at the phone shanty. Now, she felt thoroughly flabbergasted. It was a very strange, new feeling.

Since Sadie thought they should stay home and keep Alice company for Christmas, Gid offered to fill in as a sub for M.K. Amos was a little disappointed—he had hoped that M.K. would have no option but to stay behind and teach, thus giving distance to Chris. He still hadn't gotten a handle on how churned up he felt after realizing who Chris's mother was and what she had done. Today's story only confirmed to him that this woman had a truly dark spirit.

Amos knew that he should be able to mentally separate Chris and Jenny from their mother. It wasn't their fault. He should be praying for God's mercy on that woman's soul. Yet all he could think about lately was how much he wanted Grace Mitchell to hurt like he had hurt. It shamed him. He had been taught to love his enemies for his entire life, and here, when it mattered most, he not only didn't love his enemy, he hated her and everything—everyone—connected with her. He would confess this hatred to God and ask for forgiveness. How could he ever expect God to forgive him for his many sins if he couldn't forgive someone else? Hadn't those words of Jesus been etched on his soul from the time of his childhood?

But there was one thing he wouldn't bend on. One thing he couldn't stomach: his darling youngest daughter must not, *must not,* get involved with *that* boy and his family.

Where was Jimmy Fisher and his charm when Amos needed him?

Jenny helped Julia finish setting the table for dinner and stared out the window, knowing her brother and the Lapps should be arriving any minute. She didn't know how she would face Chris after what she had done. Julia and Rome were so kind to her. Rome had hired a driver to take him to Marysville to fetch her and get home again—$35.00—and his only remark about it was that seeing her was worth every penny. Julia had drawn a hot bath for her to help her get warm. Jenny's jacket had been with her backpack too. Her jacket, her money, her book. How could her mother do such a thing? Where had she gone? Was she doing drugs? Probably. Jenny remembered the look in her mother's eyes when she had seen the cash in Jenny's wallet. It was a strange look, a hungry look.

Jenny still couldn't believe it. After all of those promises.

It was just like Chris had said: for their mother, drugs came first.

A sound caught her attention—it was the big van, turning up into the driveway. Julia's four boys flew outside to meet their grandparents. Rome came out of the barn and joined his sons.

Jenny looked to Julia. "My brother must be furious with me."

Julia put a reassuring hand on Jenny's shoulder. "We'll go out together."

Chris jumped out of the van before it came to a full stop. He bolted up to the house, taking the porch steps two at a time. The moment she saw him, Jenny was on her feet and running, out the door before Chris reached it. She launched herself into his arms, full body weight, and he caught her close to him, hugging her, and both of them were crying.

"I'm so sorry!" Jenny said through her tears. "I went to see Mom, and she stole all my stuff and left me at McDonald's, and I didn't know where to go or what to do. She stole everything from me. Everything! All of the money I made working for Fern."

"It doesn't matter," Chris said. "All that matters is that you're safe."

Chris spun her around and around until she started to laugh with relief. Everything was going to be okay.

In the morning, Fern shooed the men out of the house, saying she and the womenfolk were as busy as bird dogs trying to get ready for Christmas dinner tomorrow. Rome wanted to work on a project in the barn, but Hank talked Amos and those four little boys, like stair steps, into going fishing at Black Bottom Pond. Amos tried to insist that Chris come too, but Rome interrupted and said he was counting on his help with building a tree house for the boys for Christmas morning.

Chris was relieved to get a little space from Amos. He felt as if Amos was practically Velcro-ed to him—he sat next to him in the van, at the fast food restaurants on the road, at supper last night, and again at breakfast this morning. It was as if Amos was doing his best to keep Chris as far from Mary Kate as possible. Chris was pretty sure Amos was savvy to that kiss by the schoolhouse. Why else would he be acting so twitchy? It was as if Amos could read Chris's thoughts and knew Chris was trying hard not to think about kissing Mary Kate again. There wasn't much chance of that happening on this trip—he was never alone with her. He was never alone, period. This house was filled with people. Strangely enough, despite everything—the reason they were there—Chris loved every minute of it. He knew it wouldn't last.

He set up two sawhorses for Rome to place a two-by-four on top. The two worked side by side, talking now and then, but not about anything important. Until Rome looked up and said, "Chris, what is it you really want in life?"

Such a deep question startled the truth out of Chris and he blurted out, "I want a home of my own. Something no one can take away from me."

Rome sawed the lumber into two pieces, then picked up another two-by-four. "I can understand that. It's sort of like a homesickness for a place you haven't come to yet. Being with other families only makes that longing ache deeper."

Chris nodded. That was it exactly. As long as he could remember, he was well aware of a hollow place inside of him, like an air bubble caught in a pane of glass. It was always there hanging about, an ache. It wasn't until he went to live with Old Deborah that he was given a taste of the joys of a normal childhood. It was the main reason he chose to be baptized in the Amish church last summer. He felt as close to that feeling among the Amish as he ever could. But to his dismay—he had since found that the ache was still there, a longing for something that he couldn't seem to identify. "I don't think it's going to happen for me."

"Why not?"

"Let's face it. I've been raised differently. I'm not like all of you. Loving someone, being loved . . . it's too hard."

"You're wrong about love. Love isn't hard. *Life* is hard. But when two people love each other, they create a haven." Rome sawed the other board in half and set it against the wall. "That feeling of longing isn't going to go away when you marry and have children."

Chris looked at him sharply. "What do you mean? Why wouldn't it?"

"Because the problem is in here." He thumped his chest. "Because that feeling—wanting to belong, wanting to be valued—that can only get filled by God. You can't expect anyone to do that for you. That's God's work."

Chris was silent.

"I know you've had to face some hard things in your life. Ideally, you'll be able to bring everything together—and find God's purpose for your life in the process. He allows hard things like the one that involves your mother in order to shape us into better people. It's not his will that we suffer, but he can bring good from it if you'll let him."

Chris gave a little laugh that sounded more like a cough. "I can't see any good in having a mother who is a drug addict. Look at what just happened to Jenny. Hopes rise, our mother disappoints. Over and over again. It never ends. It never will end."

Rome picked up another piece of lumber and set it on the sawhorses. "Your mother's addiction brought you to Old Deborah. She brought you to church. Church brought you to us, and now to the Lapp family." He handed a saw to Chris to hold. "You're sweet on Mary Kate, aren't you?"

Chris looked away. Was it that obvious? "I didn't expect this," he said, finding his voice again. "I wasn't planning on this. But when I met her, she was the exact person I'd been waiting for. I'd thought I wasn't looking, but really I'd been just waiting for her without knowing that I was waiting, without knowing that I'd been missing her before we met."

Rome grinned and tossed him a pair of leather gloves to use. "Chris, all the loose ends start coming together when you trust God both with your past and your future. That's what I have found to be true in my life. I pray that you'll do the same."

Chris wished he could borrow some of Rome's confidence, some of his faith, the way he could borrow the leather gloves to keep his hands safe. If only he could be as sure as Rome. Sometimes, just being around Rome, he did feel more confidence, like Rome rubbed off on him. Made him a stronger man. But faith, Old Deborah had taught him, wasn't something you could borrow from anyone.

The kitchen smelled of cinnamon and coffee. Fern scattered a layer of fine white flour across the surface of the counter. She and Jenny worked side by side, elbow to elbow, kneading, turning, punching the dough. In that clairvoyant way she had, Fern sensed Jenny had something to work out. Julia slipped upstairs to lie down for a few moments while the house was quiet.

Last night, while Jenny and M.K. were getting ready for bed, M.K. had confided that Julia was in the family way and that she was having morning sickness all day long. Julia felt confident that this time she was going to have a girl. "Julia has thought she was having a girl four times now," M.K. had whispered. "Julia always thinks she knows everything, but Sadie and I don't put much stock in her sixth sense."

It almost made Jenny cry. Tears would actually have spilled if she hadn't swallowed fast. There was just something so . . . so sisterly about the whispered confidences. Somewhere along the way, despite her best efforts, Jenny had begun to grow fond of Teacher M.K.

She knew her brother was sweet on her teacher—she had known ever since that first dinner at Windmill Farm when she caught him watching her with that goofy look on his face. She knew there was a selfish part of her that didn't want to share Chris. For months, Jenny had felt suspicious about Teacher M.K., waiting to see if she started to treat her differently than the other scholars. Trying to gain Chris's favor through Jenny. It had happened in Ohio with other girls, more than a few times. But Teacher M.K. didn't seem to be changing in any way. She expected the best out of each scholar, even Eugene Miller. Jenny's wary caution was starting to ease up around Teacher M.K. Just a little.

Jenny bent over and inhaled the tangy scent of the yeast in the dough. Fern sprinkled another dusting of flour over the ball of dough. Their elbows bumped as they worked. It was like Fern carried a force field of quietness, and when she came close, it wrapped around Jenny. Tears prickled her eyes. Would she ever stop crying over her mother, ever stop feeling so fragile?

When the dough was finished, Fern put it in an oiled bowl, covered it with a damp dishrag, and set it on the windowsill to catch the winter rays of sun.

Then Fern took Jenny's hands in both of hers and gently squeezed. Jenny remembered when she had first noticed Fern's hands, months ago, and thought they were rough and worn and reddened from too much work. Today they looked beautiful to her.

"You know, Jenny, you live long enough in this world and you're going to get rained on. It's as simple as that."

Jenny took a deep heaving breath. "My mother is not ever going to be well, is she? God can't fix her."

"Just because God can heal her and that is what you want, it doesn't mean it will happen. Faith means we trust God will act in love."

"I hate her," Jenny sobbed. "But I love her."

Fern opened her arms and Jenny fell into them. "Remember, though, that sometimes you can love and forgive somebody, but you might still want to keep your distance."

There was something wonderful about that moment. She savored it and promised herself never to forget. Whenever she fell into Fern's arms—twice now—it was just like falling into the arms of a mother. A real mother. This terrible thing had sent her into the arms of something called Family.

Two kisses. In less than two weeks, M.K. had been kissed twice by two different men. Two entirely different men. She was surprised by how warm and soft Jimmy Fisher's lips felt against her skin. She was thoroughly confused by that kiss. Even more so by his professions of love and commitment. Where did such an outpouring of emotion come from? She never would have thought Jimmy had such deep feelings for her. For anyone! She always thought he was mostly in love with himself.

Nor would she have thought Jimmy Fisher could be such an accomplished kisser. But he was. She couldn't deny that his kiss was rather . . . noteworthy. Afterward, it had taken her a moment to regain her balance. But it was curiosity that she felt, not desire.

Now that she thought about it, Jimmy had been hanging around Windmill Farm more often than usual. And he hadn't even talked about Emily Esh since . . . hmmm . . . she couldn't even remember. How had she missed the signals? The obvious clues? She was completely losing her remarkable ability to sniff out news. She blamed teaching. Too consuming.

It was just this one time. That's what Jimmy Fisher told himself as he led Samson down to the horse track where Domino Joe waited for him. The amount of money he owed Domino Joe had grown into a staggering sum. Domino Joe had lost his friendly countenance toward Jimmy and was turning surly. Jimmy needed one big win to pay Domino Joe off, then he would quit pony racing—quit it cold turkey—and start courting M.K. He already mentioned his intentions to Amos last week, and Amos looked pleased. Jimmy would get serious about his future. It was time. He didn't want to end up like his brother Paul, who dallied through life.

When Jimmy had first seen Samson, he knew this was the horse that could get him out of debt, permanently, with Domino Joe. He drove Samson down to the track and put him in crossties to check him over again. Cleaned his hooves, brushed him down, talked to him about the racetrack. Jimmy thought it helped the horse to know what to expect. Or maybe it helped the rider.

Thirty minutes later, he walked Samson directly past Domino Joe to go to the starting gate. He might have slowed a little as he passed him. Domino Joe looked Samson up and down, appreciating the animal's fine form. He whistled. "Hey, Fisher—since it's the day before Christmas and I'm in a charitable mood, I'm willing to offer you a bonus. All or none."

Jimmy narrowed his eyes. "If I win, my debt is wiped out? All of it?"

"That's right," Domino Joe said. "And if I win, I get that horse. Deal?" He held out his hand.

Jimmy looked at Samson. He had tremendous confidence in this exceptional horse. Today's win would give him a fresh start, a clean slate. He stuck his hand out to shake Domino Joe's. "Deal."

Jimmy lined up Samson at the starting gate. He could feel Samson's tension build: his ears pinned flat against his head. His tail swished. The whites of his eyes were showing. The horse was practically prancing in the box, eager for the race of his life.

Perfect. The moment was perfect.

That afternoon, after the talk with Rome, Chris waited for Amos to return from fishing with his grandsons and cornered him in the barn as the little boys ran into the house with Uncle Hank.

"Amos," Chris said, boldly and firmly, though he didn't feel bold or firm, "there's a hardness between us. Have I done something to offend you?"

Amos's face tightened. "Something like, say, kissing my daughter in front of the schoolhouse? In broad daylight?"

Chris rubbed his face with the palms of his hands. "I thought that was maybe the reason you fired me. Maybe I should have talked to you first, to let you know I care about Mary Kate. I'm sorry about that. But I'm going to own my grandfather's house as soon as I turn twenty-one. Just four weeks from now. I've been fixing the house up so it's livable. I have plans. I want to buy some mares soon and start breeding Samson. I want to settle down in Stoney Ridge." He took a deep breath. "Amos, I'd like your blessing to court Mary Kate."

Amos's face was still tight. "You'll never have it. Never."

This wasn't going well at all. "Do you mind telling me why?"

Amos looked at him. "Your given name is Mitchell."

A feeling of dread rolled through Chris's stomach, but there was no turning back now. "How did you know?" He had been so careful.

"I knew your grandfather, Colonel Mitchell. So did my first wife, Maggie."

Chris tilted his head, confused. "But I thought your first wife's name was Margaret. I saw her grave at the cemetery." Chris felt the air whoosh out of his lungs. "Oh. *Oh.*" Maggie was a nickname for Margaret. He knew that. How had he not connected the dots? Chris had to sit down. The room started to spin and he thought he might get sick. He put his head in his hands. Maggie Lapp was the neighbor lady who came to help them. Maggie Lapp was the woman his mother had pushed down the porch stairs, the reason they fled Stoney Ridge. Maggie Lapp's death was the reason the Colonel went to jail.

Amos's hands tensed into fists. "I realize you were only a child. But I just can't let you court my daughter. I just . . . can't."

"I'm not good enough." Chris wasn't asking. He knew that was true. It always, always came back to that. He was tainted. He glanced up at Amos. He didn't blame him.

Amos's frown of worry eased from his forehead, but he didn't acknowledge Chris's comment. "M.K. doesn't know how her mother died. Neither does Sadie or Julia. They just think their mother tripped and fell and hit her head on a rock, that it was just an innocent accident. There's no need for them to know anything else. It's all too . . . complicated." He rubbed his face. "Jimmy Fisher spoke to me about courting Mary Kate last week, and I told him he has my blessing." He walked past Chris, stopping briefly. "If you truly care about M.K., you'll let her go."

M.K. said she was going to bed early, and that wasn't a lie. She did go upstairs and she did go to bed. But she kept one eye on the window, watching the barn. She knew Rome and Chris were in the barn, feeding the animals. Tomorrow morning, early, the van was coming to pick them up to return to Stoney Ridge. They had gone today to visit Annie and little Joe-Jo, who looked so much like her brother Menno as a little boy that everyone left Annie's home quiet and reflective, remembering Menno. Missing him. Annie was married now to a nice enough fellow, and they had two children of their own. Joe-Jo was happy, secure, growing up in a healthy family. What more could they want for him?

They had done everything they had come to do. Mary Kate didn't want the trip to be over, but in another way, she did. Chris was acting so distant that she couldn't stand another minute of being near him, yet so far from him. She had to do something. Now. Tonight.

Patience, schmatience. It was highly overrated.

She heard her father and Fern go up to their room, listened to the hum of their voices through the wall, and then there was quiet. Jenny, sleeping in the twin bed in M.K.'s room, was snoring a light whiffling sound. The coast was clear.

M.K. waited awhile, quietly dressed, tiptoed downstairs, grabbed her big sweater, tiptoed past Uncle Hank snoring so loudly in the rocking chair by the fire that it rattled the windows, and slipped out the back door without Julia or Sadie spotting her. She had always been particularly adept at sneaking past her sisters. It was one of her best skills.

M.K. hurried across the yard to the barn and pulled the door open. Rome and Chris were just about to leave and looked startled by her appearance. "Rome, would you mind if I had a few minutes alone to talk with Chris? Dad and Fern went to bed, and I got past Julia and Sadie without them seeing me."

Rome grinned. "I'm glad to see you've still got your sneaky side, M.K.

I surely am. You've been so quiet this visit that I've worried teaching has plumb worn you down."

"Oh, it definitely has," M.K. said. "But there's something I need to talk to Chris about. Without a crowd listening in."

"Like, a crowd that resembles Amos Lapp?" Rome walked past her and whispered, "I'll cover you for a while. But don't stay out too late. If Julia catches wind of my letting her little sister out in the barn, unchaperoned, with a young man, I'll be sleeping out here for the rest of the winter." He looked back at Chris and added, "Talking only, young man." He grinned, winked, slipped out the barn door, then shut it.

Chris's cheeks flamed. He looked at his feet. "Make it fast because I'm freezing."

M.K. blew out a puff of air. "Why are you acting like such a jerk?"

Chris snapped his head up. "How so?"

"Ever since you kissed me at the schoolhouse, you've treated me like I've got the bubonic plague."

Chris turned away, but M.K. pulled his arm, forcing him to turn back toward her. "Just tell me why you've turned so cold and distant. I deserve that much."

He looked right at her. "You do. You do deserve that. You deserve that and much more." He put his hands on her arms. "Mary Kate, you deserve better than me."

"Why can't I make that decision, Chris? Why does everyone think they know what—or who—is best for me?"

He dropped his arms and paced around the center aisle. She was so innocent, so naïve to the cruelty people were capable of. "You don't know me. You don't know anything about me or my crazy family. You don't know what I'm capable of."

"I might not know everything about you, but I do have a pretty good idea of the kind of man you are, Chris."

"No. You don't. You have no idea. My life's not worth . . . anything."

She straightened up as tall as she could and pointed at his chest with her finger. "Don't ever say that again," she told him, sounding like she was talking to one of her scholars. "Don't ever, ever say that again. Don't think it either. That's a lie you should never believe." She took a step closer and reached out for his hand. Her hand tightened around his fingers, and only then did he realize how much was at stake.

"Why me, Mary Kate? What could you possibly see in someone like me?"

"The thing about you, Chris Yoder, is . . . you make me want to be a better person." She reached out and touched his cheek. He turned his face so that he could kiss the palm of her hand. His lips brushed her hand, then again, and he took a half step closer to bring their bodies into light contact.

Then, abruptly, he stepped back, pressing her hands into a prayer, palm to palm. "I'm sorry, Mary Kate," Chris whispered. "I can't do this."

When Chris looked up, M.K.'s eyes brimmed with unshed tears. One finally fell and traced a path down her cheek. She backed up a step and crossed her arms over her chest. Then she turned and pulled the barn door open. She started to walk back to the house alone.

And he stood there and watched her go.

Was he going to let her walk out of his life?

No. No he wouldn't.

He ran to the barn door and whispered as loud as he dared, "Mary Kate!"

19

The van pulled into Stoney Ridge as the sun was starting to set. Amos directed the driver to drop Jenny and Chris off first. Naturally, M.K. thought, still exasperated with her father. As the van went down the long driveway, M.K. noticed someone's car parked out front, but no sign of anyone.

Chris groaned. "That's the realtor's car, Rodney Gladstone. He keeps after me to buy the house." He slid the van door open and let Jenny climb out. "Thank you for everything," Chris told Fern, before turning to Amos. "I'll get Samson in the morning, if that's all right." He gave M.K. a brief glance as he closed the van door.

The van turned around in the driveway as Chris tried to open the front door with his key. M.K. saw him look at Jenny with a puzzled face. "Hold up a moment, Ervin," she told the driver. "I think something's wrong." She unrolled the window.

A man in a business suit came around the side of the house. "Locks were changed, just this morning. Did you forget something?"

"What are you talking about?" Chris asked, coming down the porch steps. "Why would the locks be changed?"

Chris seemed to know this man, so M.K. guessed he was the realtor. She jumped out of the van, and Amos and Fern followed.

"That's what the new owners wanted done, first thing," the realtor said. "My brother-in-law is a locksmith."

"New owners?" Jenny asked.

Rodney Gladstone looked at Chris, baffled. "Didn't your mother tell you?" He scratched his head. "I hope I didn't spoil her surprise."

"Tell me what?" Chris said, his voice filled with alarm.

Jenny's eyes went wide.

"I contacted her a month or so ago to let her know I had a buyer for the house, to see if she might be interested in selling."

Chris fixed him with a hard stare. "How did you know where she lived?"

Rodney glanced at Jenny.

"He did it!" Jenny pointed at him, glaring. "He brought the mail to the house one morning and looked through it! He saw Mom's address on an envelope."

Chris looked at her as if she were speaking in Chinese. "What envelope?"

Jenny looked at him with wild eyes. "Mom and I . . . we've been writing back and forth, all fall. She figured out where we were living by the postmark."

Chris squeezed his eyes shut, opened them. He turned to Rodney Gladstone. "You had no right to meddle in our business. No right at all."

"But I did!" Rodney said. "I absolutely did. I was just doing my job. Grace Mitchell held the title to the house. She was the legal owner. It was all there, down in the title office. I had a buyer. It was the right thing to do. It was my duty to present an offer to the rightful owner. It's my job." His Adam's apple bobbed up and down. "Grace Mitchell called me right away. The same day she got my letter. She said she wanted to sell. I sent her the offer and she sent it back, accepted without contingencies. It went into escrow and she told me to get the paperwork ready for the notary public. She would be in Stoney Ridge to sign the papers on December 23rd."

"She was here?" Chris said. "My mother was here? In Stoney Ridge?"

Rodney nodded, paling. "December 23rd, just like she said she would be. Right before closing time. She said to keep the sale a secret from you and your sister—she wanted to surprise you and buy you a bigger spread. For your horse business."

"You sold our house?" Chris looked and sounded as if he couldn't get his head around this news. "You sold our house out from under us?"

Rodney started to sputter. "It was all legal! The title was in her name. She inherited the house from her father. It was all . . . legal. We had all the paperwork. I was just doing my job . . ."

"You gave her the money for the house?"

Rodney gulped. "A cashier's check." He licked his lips. "I figured she was doing you a favor. I mean, she's your mother."

"You figured wrong . . ." Chris's voice trailed off. He looked shaken, pale and dazed, as if he might pass out. "How could she have done this? How could she have masterminded this?"

Jenny started to sob and M.K. pulled her into her arms.

M.K. sucked in air, held it in her lungs. She wanted to shout, *That's terrible, terrible! . . . What kind of woman would lure her daughter and son to Ohio so that she could sneak back to Pennsylvania and sell their home out from under them? She's a monster.* Instead, she only murmured, "Everything will be all right."

Fern stepped up to Chris and put a hand on his shoulder. "It's late. We'll get this sorted out in the morning."

Rodney shook his head. "Not possible. The possession date was on closing. The new owners arrive with their moving truck at 8 a.m." He looked cautiously at Chris. "Your mother said she wants to buy you a bigger place. A better place."

M.K. couldn't tell if that was the wrong thing to say to Chris. Or the right thing. Whichever it was, it snapped him out of his shock. Chris's hands were clenching and unclenching rhythmically, his powerful chest shook. He gave Rodney a look as if he wanted to tear him apart. "My mother is halfway to somewhere else right now. She took that house money to feed her drug habit. She'll blow through that money within the month."

Rodney Gladstone's pale face went two shades paler. He looked horrified. "But she looked so normal, and seemed like a nice lady . . . and it was all . . . legal . . ." His voice drizzled off as he realized that he wasn't helping the situation, so he quietly got in the car and drove off.

M.K. watched Chris's arms fall to his sides, and something seemed to collapse inside of him. She couldn't bear him being hurt any more. She simply couldn't bear it. She looked to her father to say something, do something. But Amos Lapp did nothing. He seemed at a complete loss for words. So she turned to Fern, who seemed just as nonplussed. M.K. was going to have to take charge. "They should come to Windmill Farm."

Fern blinked a few times, then snapped into action. "Of course. Of course they should." She put an arm around Jenny, who was still crying. She led her into the van.

"Chris," M.K. said softly, "come to our house."

Chris didn't budge. He had a strange look, as if he were somewhere else. "Chris, you need to come with us," M.K. repeated. "You can't stay here. Jenny needs you."

With that, Chris seemed to jolt back to the present circumstances. Then his face opened for an instant: grief and loss. He nodded and followed M.K. meekly into the van.

They sat down to a silent dinner of cold turkey sandwiches from leftovers Julia had sent back with Fern. No one was very hungry, but Fern insisted everyone sit down and eat.

"Today, despite everything, is a gift," she said, right before they bowed their heads, "and we should return thanks."

And she was right. Remembering God put everything in its rightful place, even terrible things. Chris's face, Amos noticed, had lost that awful white color from when he heard the news of his mother's actions.

Amos felt disgusted by the treachery Grace Mitchell had pulled over her children. Even animals cared for their young better than that woman.

But there was a tiny glimmer of happiness inside of Amos. It shamed him to admit it, but he couldn't stop the thought from taking shape: Now, surely, Chris Yoder would leave Stoney Ridge. There was nothing to keep him here.

And then he silently upbraided himself for his selfishness.

A knock at the door interrupted his conflicted thoughts. He got up and opened the door to find Jimmy Fisher standing there.

"Come in, Jimmy." Amos pulled him in and closed the door. Ah, finally. Finally, Jimmy Fisher showed up when he was needed. Jimmy stood awkwardly in front of the family.

"Have you eaten?" Fern asked.

"Yes. No." Jimmy scratched his neck. "I have a couple of things to tell you." He looked at M.K. "First, Eugene Miller wanted me to give this to you." He handed her a note and waited while she read it aloud.

Deer Teecher M.K.

I am running off fer good. Don't worry about mee. I will bee fine. Yurs trooly, Eugene Miller

P.S. I am not leaving cuz of your teeching. Yur not half-bad.

M.K.'s dark brown eyes, so much like Amos's own, widened. "He's gone. Eugene Miller left home. He's run away." She passed the note to her father.

Amos's heart went out to his daughter. She had been encouraged by the progress Eugene had been making. He was just about to say something to comfort her when Jimmy blew out a big puff of air.

"There's something else." Jimmy moved from foot to foot, ill at ease. "Something I need to say, and I need to say it right away, while I still have the strength." He cast a furtive glance in Chris's direction.

"Did something happen to Samson? Is he hurt?" Chris jumped up from the table.

Jimmy looked at M.K., then took a deep breath. "He's not hurt. He's fine. More than fine. But . . . something has happened." Jimmy folded his arms against his chest. "I raced him. Over at the track."

"Domino Joe's gambling field, you mean," Fern uttered under her breath.

"Samson's not much of a racehorse, I discovered." Jimmy rubbed his hands together. "I underestimated his—" he glanced at Fern—"manliness."

Chris groaned. "His instincts would make him try to prove to the other colts that he's the boss. He's the keeper of the fillies."

Jimmy rubbed a hand through his hair. "Apparently." He cleared his throat. "But I was just so sure he would be a crackerjack racehorse." His eyes nervously took in the room. Quietly, he added, "So I bet on him." Jimmy carefully studied a crack in the ceiling. "And I lost."

There was a terrible silence that no words could fill. All eyes were on Jimmy.

Chris came around the table. "What exactly did you bet?"

"Samson," Jimmy said, barely a whisper. He cleared his throat. "I bet Samson. And I lost. I lost Samson to Domino Joe."

It took a moment for Jimmy's confession to sink in. A solitary feather would have knocked everyone down. It hit Chris first, full force. He opened his mouth as if forming an answer, then clenched his jaw and closed his eyes in despair. "The only thing that was mine . . . the *only* thing left . . . and you lost him in a pathetic pony race . . ." When he opened them again, he turned to M.K., then to Amos, with wounded eyes. He snatched up his hat and coat and left the house without a word, closing the door gently behind him.

Jimmy wrinkled his face in confusion. "What does that mean—the only thing left?"

M.K. looked at Jimmy with disgust. "Why don't you ever do what you're supposed to?"

He shrugged. "Because I can never figure out what that is."

Mary Kate leapt up to grab her coat off the wall peg.

"You're not going after him," Amos said.

She ignored him and put her coat on.

"Did you hear me?" Amos repeated. "There's more to the story than you know."

"What's the whole story?" Jimmy asked, eyes bouncing from Amos to M.K. and back to Amos.

M.K. glared at Jimmy, then turned to her father. "I know more than you think I do, Dad." M.K. pointed to Jimmy. "I know you'd rather I go out with him—a liar and a cheat and a gambler—"

"Hey," Jimmy said. "That's a little harsh."

"All true," M.K. snapped. "I know you're the one who has been dipping into everyone's coffee cans to pay off your gambling debt to Domino Joe."

Jimmy raised his eyebrows. "How would you . . ." He opened his mouth. Closed it. Opened it, closed it, as if he thought better than to deny it. "I'm not proud of that," he mumbled. "And I have plans to pay it all back."

"Out there is a man—not a *boy*—" she gave a glance in Jimmy's direction—"who keeps his word. Who is fiercely protective of his little sister. Who has plans and dreams for a future. And that future keeps getting ripped from him—through no fault of his own." She threw another dark glance in Jimmy's direction.

"This has nothing to do with Jimmy," Amos said. "This is about Chris. Chris and his mother."

"What about Chris and my mother?" Jenny asked. Everyone looked at her as if they had forgotten she was there.

A pained look crossed Amos's face.

"Dad, I know about Mom's fall. I know there's more to it than just an accident. Chris told me all about it in Ohio last night. He told me every detail." She walked up to Amos and took his large work-roughened hand in hers. "I realize this is complicated, but hasn't he paid enough?"

"I want to save you heartache, M.K. I want to stop you before it's too late. Before you think you're in love with him."

"With who?" Jimmy piped up.

Amos saw his daughter's face change before his eyes, from a young girl to a young woman. Before his very eyes. There was no mistaking. She wasn't his little girl anymore.

"Dad," she said gently. "It's already too late. You can't fall out of love with someone." She squeezed his hands one last time and went outside.

As she was closing the door, Jimmy pulled a chair out and said, "Think Chris is gonna finish that sandwich?"

"Immer dreizehn," Fern sighed. *Forever thirteen.*

Chris leaned his head against the door of Samson's empty stall. He had led Samson in there just a few mornings ago, gave him water and fresh hay, and told him he'd be back for him. Samson was gone. He couldn't believe it. He wondered if this was what Job of the Bible felt like, as messenger upon messenger brought him news of horrendous proportions. *Bam, bam, bam.* One blow after another. How much could a person bear?

Chris was rendered as motionless as stone, his brow furrowed. In his head, he heard Jimmy speaking about betting on Samson, he heard Rodney Gladstone talking about selling the house, but the sounds came to him as through a long tunnel, over the rush of a freight train roaring in his head. He fought to breathe, to maintain his footing. All he could picture was his mother.

How much would God give a person to bear? How many times had he asked God for guidance and help? To cure his mother of her addiction? To give him wisdom to take good care of Jenny? But apparently God didn't listen to prayers of that sort. Or maybe he just didn't listen to his.

"Where are you, God?" he shouted, pounding the rails of Samson's stall. "Old Deborah said we should trust you. She said to leave everything in God's hands. Now look at this mess! Where are you?!"

"Fern always says that when God seems most absent, he is most there."

Chris whirled around to face Mary Kate. He wiped his eyes with the back of his hand. "It just gets better and better, doesn't it?" He put his hands on his hips, gazing at the empty stall. His eyes were bleak. "You shouldn't be near me. Your father's right. My family is like poison."

She gave him a gentle smile. "I don't believe that."

"Of course not. How could you? You don't understand, Mary Kate. You couldn't possibly." His face contorted. "This is what it's like with my mother. This is what my life is like. Every time Jenny and I would get settled in somewhere, she'd swoop in and disrupt it all. Today is no different than the way my entire life has gone. This is what it will always be like. She will always find a way to take what doesn't belong to her." He snapped his fingers. "Everything gone in the amount of time it takes to fill your lungs with air one time. Gone." He snatched up an empty bucket and hurled it down the barn aisle. The sound of clinging and clanging down the cement path startled the horses so much that they shuffled in their stalls.

Mary Kate was unruffled. "She might. Or she might not. It doesn't matter. She can't take what's truly important."

The horses went back to their quiet munching of hay.

Could she be right?

Chris went very still, and for a long minute he frowned as he stared at Samson's empty stall, but little by little, tension drained from his shoulders.

He looked over at Mary Kate and he saw her tears through his own. And before Chris realized what was happening, she flung herself at him, clinging tightly to him, sobbing against his chest, telling him that she thought he was wonderful, crazy mother and all. He wrapped his arms around her, hugging her in return—the first embrace he had given or received for a very long time.

Right then, something happened inside his chest. Not a lightning bolt zinging him, but a soft and breathtaking peace that one day, someday, everything would be alright.

As Fern got Jenny settled into Sadie's old room for the night, Amos stood in front of the fireplace, watching the flames dance. He was hardly aware of the clinking and clanking of dishes as Fern cleared the table and put them in the sink to soak. Suddenly, he realized she was standing right next to him.

"Don't you think it's time you told me what's been eating at you?"

Amos put his face in his hands, then slowly dropped them. His voice shook with the effort of getting the words out. "I don't know how to tell you this. It's about Maggie."

Fern's look changed, softened. She reached up and brushed back the hair from his right temple. "Why don't you start at the beginning?"

They sat in front of the fire as Amos told her how Maggie had befriended Colonel Mitchell's daughter. He was able to keep his emotions at bay while he spoke, until he got to the part on that spring day when Maggie was long overdue from a quick visit to take goat's milk over to Grace Mitchell to help her colicky baby. Then, his voice choked up and he had trouble getting the words out.

Fern waited patiently as the scene of that afternoon played through his mind, as vividly as yesterday, and he tried to gather the words to tell her . . .

By the time Julia and Sadie had returned from school, Amos knew something was wrong. Maggie should have been home hours ago. He put Julia in charge of Sadie, Menno, and M.K., and crossed the field to go to the Colonel's house. As soon as he crested a hill, he saw the red flash of police car lights. He ran the rest of the way. There was an ambulance and three police cars. Amos knew something horrendous had happened. He charged through the backyard and was blocked by a policeman.

"My wife is there," Amos said, with a voice he didn't recognize as his own. He shoved the police officer away and went around the side of the house. And there he saw his Maggie, his darling, beautiful Maggie, motionless on the ground with a paramedic by her side. Colonel Mitchell sat in the back of a police car, his head hung low.

"She's gone," the paramedic had told Amos gently. "It looks like she was pushed down the porch steps. She hit her head on that rock and fractured her skull." He gave Amos a sympathetic look. "She must have died instantly. I doubt she ever knew what happened."

The police had pressed him with questions. Did he know why Maggie had gone over to Colonel Mitchell's house? Yes. Did Maggie have any kind of conflict or dispute with the inhabitant? Of course not! Did he know of any reason why Colonel Mitchell might have argued with her? No.

In the end, the coroner ruled the death as accidental manslaughter. The Colonel confessed that he was responsible for the accidental death of Margaret Zook Lapp, though he would not say anything else. Not how it happened. Not why.

It never made any sense to Amos. It never did. The Colonel was a hard man, but he was reasonable. And despite being a career military man, he was not violent.

It wasn't hard to figure out that the Colonel was protecting his daughter, Grace Mitchell. But the problem was that Amos knew who was truly responsible for Maggie's death. He knew, and he didn't do anything about it. Not a thing. It didn't even occur to the police to ask if the Colonel had someone else living at his house. Amos could have volunteered that information, but he didn't. If the Colonel didn't admit it, he wouldn't either.

There was a little part of Amos that felt justified. Vindicated. Someone should be held responsible. If not Grace, then the father who raised her. Weren't parents responsible, to some degree, for the moral outcome of their children?

And then swept in a wrestle with his conscience: who was he to make such an accusation against another child of God? God did not call him to judge another. He was given one soul to account for—his own.

But he knew. And he did nothing. The Colonel was sent to a minimum-security prison and died while serving his sentence, from some kind of swiftly moving cancer.

"So that's the whole story," Amos finally said, after relaying everything to Fern in fits and starts and sobs. "I just can't look at Chris without thinking of Maggie's death. Everything about it—the Colonel's look on his face while he was in the police car. The guilt I feel because I remained silent when I knew it was Grace Mitchell who had caused Maggie's death. I'm not saying she tried to kill Maggie. It might have been an accident, but she never owned up to her responsibility. As far as I know, she never came back to Stoney Ridge. Not even for her father's funeral. Maybe it's not fair or right or logical, but I can't get past it."

Fern didn't say anything for a long while. "Maybe you're not supposed to get past it."

He looked at her. "What does that mean?"

"God brought Chris and Jenny into our lives for a reason. They began here, then ended up with Old Deborah, giving them the opportunity to get to know Rome and Julia. Then back they come to Stoney Ridge. You told Bud at the Hardware Store that you needed someone to help you cut hay on the same day that Chris came in, looking for work. Who would have believed that Mary Kate would be teaching school this term? And that one of those pupils is Jenny. Coincidence after coincidence after coincidence. A sure sign of God's silent sovereignty. I don't think he wants you to get past this. I think he wants you to get *through* it."

"Fern, I don't know how."

"Every single day, you pray to God to help you forgive Chris and Jenny's mother. Pray for mercy for her soul."

Amos wiped his face with both of his hands. How long had he held on to this information, rolling it over and over in his mind? Always simmering, always in the back of his mind, like a wound that couldn't heal. He was exhausted. "I'm afraid I can't find the strength in myself to do that, Fern."

Fern leaned forward, smiling tenderly. "Good," she said. "Now we're getting somewhere."

But Fern wasn't done yet. "Amos, you need to reach out to Chris. To show him how to live with a problem that doesn't go away. Because something tells me we haven't heard the last of that mother of his." She rubbed her hands together like a little girl. "But I have just the idea to start redeeming this big mess."

Amos looked at his wife, amazed that she still loved him after what he had just confessed to her. "I don't deserve it." Grace, Amos meant. And mercy.

"None of us do," Fern answered, understanding.

On Monday afternoon, the pupils stayed late to finish up an art project. It was Uncle Hank's idea: he had a few way-past-their-prime rainbow trout in the freezer that Fern insisted he toss out, and M.K. had extra paint, so the pupils made fish prints. The schoolhouse smelled horrible but the pictures were wonderful. She thought about Eugene Miller, missing whatever his creative mind would have conjured up for a fish print. His empty desk grieved her today. It grieved everyone. Where was he? Was he going to be all right? She knew she would worry about him for the rest of her life. All she could do was to pray for him.

Mary Kate hung the last picture on the wall and stood back to look at the room. It was surprisingly cheerful. Everything about her life surprised her. Not only that she was a teacher, but that she liked it. In fact, there were moments, like today, when she was starting to love it.

She heard a knock at the door and Chris popped his head in. A big smile creased his handsome face. "Can you come outside for a minute?"

She hurried out to meet him. Chris stood beside a pitch-black stallion. "Samson!" She crossed the porch and put her hand out to Samson's velvet nose. "How in the world did you get him back?"

"I didn't," Chris said, grinning. "Your dad and Fern went to an auction this morning and bought him back from Domino Joe. Cost a pretty penny. I told your dad that I wanted to pay him back, but he said no, that it was a down payment."

"Down payment on what?" M.K. stroked his long neck.

"He said something odd—something like 'refreshing the sponge.' Fern explained that was bread baker's code for a fresh start." Samson dipped his big head up and down, making Chris take a step back. "I finished up minor repairs on the bishop's buggy today. The bishop was happy about that. He seems pretty determined that I should help your uncle in the buggy shop. But I don't want to step on your uncle's toes."

"Don't worry about that. Uncle Hank wants to retire from buggy repair. Just last night he said he's going full time into finding water. Much more lucrative, he thinks, especially after Edith Fisher corrected him about the puppies' mother. Turns out she isn't a poodle at all. She's a Portuguese water dog. So now he has a theory that he can train the puppies to find the water for him. All four."

Chris laughed.

"I knew he would never give those puppies up."

"Mary Kate, there's something else I want you to think about. Your father and Fern offered to have Jenny and me stay at the honey cabin." The air had gone quiet, falling into the purple hush of dusk as the winter sun slipped behind the trees. He glanced down at his shoes, suddenly shy. She understood that he was every bit as nervous as she was. "I wondered how you might feel about that, seeing as how it's your workplace for your bees."

But where would she keep her honey equipment? she thought, and then, Chris would stay in Stoney Ridge! Swirling in the back of her mind had been a nagging worry that he might return to Ohio since he no longer had a home to live in. Suddenly, she was filled with a wild sense of happiness. It seemed incredible. Miraculous, even. She wouldn't mind moving her honey equipment out of the honey cabin. Not one little bit! A smile uncurled. She didn't quite trust her voice. "I think it sounds just fine. Better than fine."

He watched her, a small smile turning up the corners of his lips. "We're alike, Hank and I."

"How's that?" M.K. said. She'd just noticed he had a large envelope behind his back and she craned her neck to see whose name was on the address label—better still, who had sent it—but he kept it away from her and slipped his other arm around her, pulling her close to him.

"Hank and I both know a good thing when we see it."

M.K. hid a smile.

He leaned closer to her. "And we won't let go of that good thing."

"Really?" The word came out as a soft gasp. "Not ever? Not even when your mother reappears and makes you feel like you're worthless? You won't believe her and retreat into your turtle shell?"

He looked at her as if he thought she had spoken in another language. Then his face slipped into a smile. "Not even then," he said, and just like that, she couldn't breathe.

Their eyes met—those familiar blue eyes that crinkled at the corners when he smiled. She stood without moving as he bent over to kiss her. Then she slipped her arms around his neck and he kissed her until she was too breathless to think straight.

He let her go and waved the large white envelope. "Fern wanted me to hand deliver this to you."

M.K. grabbed it from him and opened it up. In it was her passport. It had finally arrived in the mail. She looked up at Chris and smiled. She could go anywhere in the world.

But she didn't want to be anywhere else.

Acknowledgments

Last year, I read a short comment at the end of a scribe's letter in *The Budget*. It was written from an Amish woman who participated in an informal program with a women's prison. This woman fostered a prisoner's child and took her to visit her mother once a month. I started to do a little digging and found a similar program with the Mennonite Caregivers Program. This program's aim isn't to recruit children for the Mennonite Church or to be adopted. "And whoso shall receive one such little child in my name receiveth me" (Matt. 18:5) is the only motivation for these thirty Mennonite families who live in Southeast Pennsylvania. Studies have shown that incarcerated women who mother their babies have a lower recidivism rate. How remarkable! I felt so impressed by these quiet heroes, trying to strengthen family ties.

So that's how the story of Chris and Jenny Yoder began, with Old Deborah—another quiet hero. Remember, though, it is a work of fiction. Chris and Jenny's mother, Grace Mitchell, was caught in a cycle of drug addiction. It would have been nice and tidy to have Grace "see the light," but that just doesn't always happen in life.

There are many types of addiction—some that are obvious, like drugs, and some that are more sinister. Fern's comments to Jenny toward the end of the book had so much wisdom in them: "Remember, though, that sometimes you can love and forgive somebody, but you might still want to keep your distance." Sadly, some problems are just not going to be solved in this lifetime.

A special thank-you to my first draft readers, Lindsey Ciraulo and Wendrea How. You're the best!

A big shout-out to my insightful editor, Andrea Doering, named Editor of the Year at ACFW in 2011. And to my agent, Joyce Hart, who is always my Agent of the Year. Thank you to the support team at Revell: Michele Misiak, Janelle Mahlmann, Robin Barnett, Deonne Lindsey, Twila Bennett Brothers, Claudia Marsh, Donna Hausler, and so many others who help get my books from the warehouse to the shelves and into readers' hands.

As always, my gratitude goes to my dear family. And finally, I would like to give a heartfelt thank-you to the Lord who has been blessing this endeavor of mine. I hope I'm doing him proud.

Prologue

Surprises come in two shapes—good and bad. This one, though, felt indeterminate.

David Stoltzfus awoke in the middle of the night with a clear prompting in his heart: leave what was familiar and comfortable and go forth into the wilderness. He had developed a listening ear to God's promptings over the years and knew not to ignore them. God who had spoken, David believed with his whole heart, still speaks.

But where was this wilderness?

A week passed. David searched Scripture, prayed, spoke to a few trusted friends, and still the prompting remained. Grew stronger. A month passed. David's daily prayer was the same: *Where is the wilderness, Lord? Where will you send me?* Another month passed. Nothing.

And then David received a letter from a bishop—someone he had known over the years—in a little town in Lancaster County, inviting him to come alongside to serve the church. *Go*, came the prompting, loud and clear.

So David packed up his home, sold his bulk store business, and moved his family to the wilderness, which, for him, meant Stoney Ridge, Pennsylvania.

As the first few months passed, it seemed puzzling to David to think that God would consider Stoney Ridge as a wilderness, albeit metaphorically. The bishop, Elmo Beiler, had welcomed him in as an additional minister, had encouraged him to preach the word of God from his heart. It was a charming town and he had been warmly embraced. A wilderness? Hardly that. More like the Garden of Eden. When he casually remarked as much to Elmo, the old bishop gave him an unreadable look. "There is no such thing, David." Elmo didn't expand on the thought, and David chalked it up to a warning of pride.

No place was perfect, he knew that, but the new life of the Stoltzfus family was taking shape. His children were starting to settle in. They were a family still adapting to the loss of Anna, David's wife, but they weren't stuck, not like they had been. It was a fresh start, and everything was going about as well as David could expect.

Then, during a church service, Elmo suffered a major heart attack. In a dramatic fashion for a man who was not at all dramatic, Elmo grabbed David's shirt and whispered, "Beware, David. A snake is in the garden."

Later that evening, Elmo passed away.

The next week, Freeman Glick, the other minister who had served alongside David, drew the lot to become the new bishop, his brother Levi drew the lot to replace him as minister, and in the space of one month, the little Amish church of Stoney Ridge was an altogether different place.

Almost overnight, David sensed the wilderness had arrived.

Suzanne Woods Fisher is the author of the bestselling Lancaster County Secrets and Stoney Ridge Seasons series. *The Search* received a 2012 Carol Award, *The Waiting* was a finalist for the 2011 Christy Award, and *The Choice* was a finalist for the 2011 Carol Award. Suzanne's grandfather was raised in the Old Order German Baptist Brethren Church in Franklin County, Pennsylvania. Her interest in living a simple, faith-filled life began with her Dunkard cousins. Suzanne is also the author of the bestselling *Amish Peace: Simple Wisdom for a Complicated World* and *Amish Proverbs: Words of Wisdom from the Simple Life*, both finalists for the ECPA Book of the Year award, and *Amish Values for Your Family: What We Can Learn from the Simple Life*. She has an app, Amish Wisdom, to deliver a proverb a day to your iPhone, iPad, or Android. Visit her at www.suzannewoodsfisher.com to find out more.

Suzanne lives with her family in the San Francisco Bay Area.

Download the
Free ***Amish Wisdom*** App

DON'T MISS THE LANCASTER COUNTY *Secrets* SERIES!

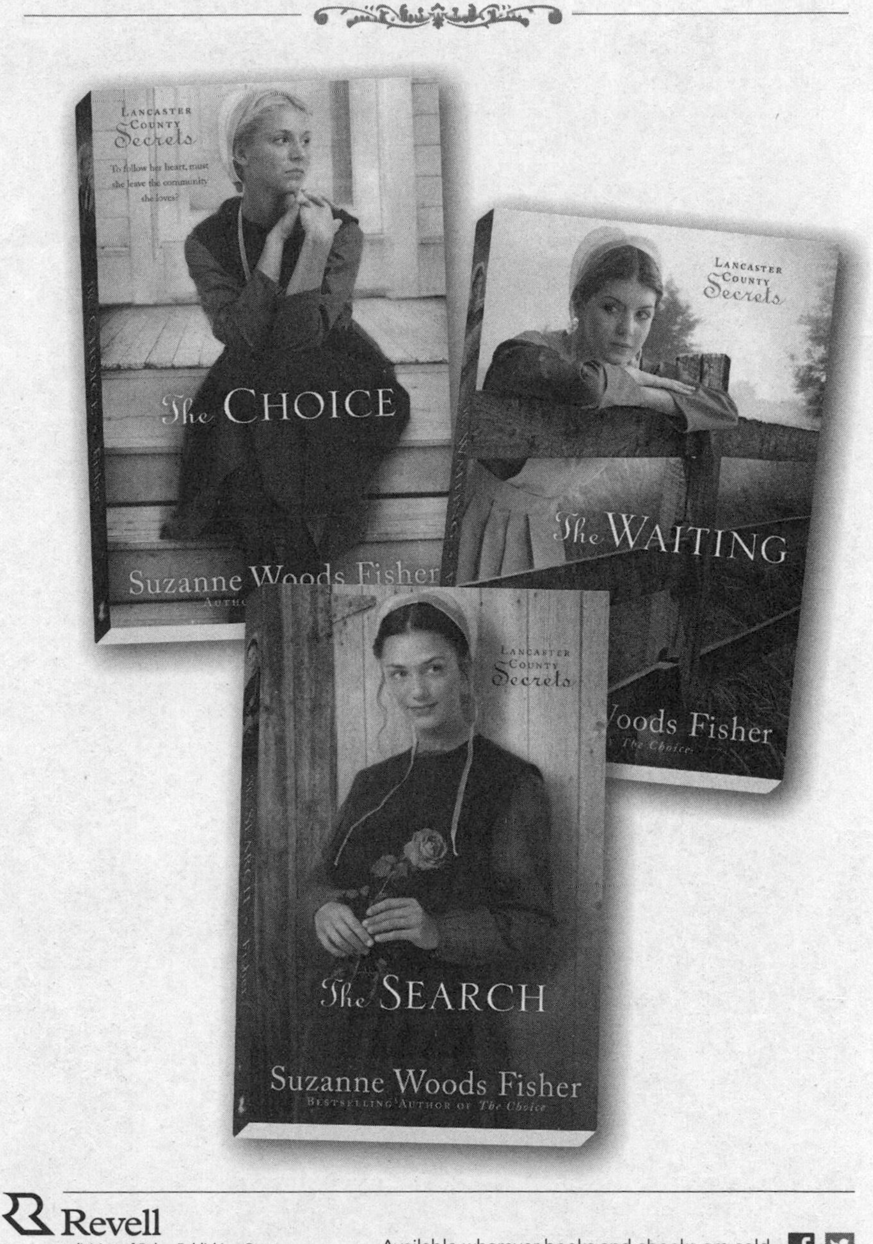